# Blood &
# Betrayals

*Avalon University*
*Book One*

ALEXIS RUNE

JEANETTE ROSE

Rose
& Star
PUBLISHING

Copyright © 2025 by Rose and Star Publishing
Cover by Opulent Design & Swag
Editing by Aisling MacKay Editorial
Realms Map by AaguirreArt
Campus Map by IllustratedBookDesign
Art by Megillustrates
Interior Chapter Design by Into the Forest Illustration
Rune Design by Eva Pink (Pinkerchu)

*For all the readers who watched their world burn to ash, and could do nothing but scream.*

# CONTENT ADVISORY

*Extreme Violence*
*Stalking*
*Gore*
*Explicit Sexual Content*
*Implied Sexual Assault [Historical]*
*Emotional Abuse [Historical]*
*Physical Abuse [Historical]*
*Torture*
*Alcohol & Drug Abuse*
*Death*
*Grief*
*Portrayals of Anxiety & Post Traumatic Stress Disorder*
*Portrayals of Undiagnosed Borderline Personality Disorder (Summer)* *

---

* *It should be noted that at no part in this series does Summer become diagnosed or come to this realization herself, nor should she be considered a completely accurate representation of those who experience this disorder. BPD affects 2 in 100 adults, mostly young women. People with BPD often have other mental health conditions, including anxiety disorders, eating disorders, and substance use disorders. You are not alone.*

The A

REALM OF ATLANTIS

REALM OF VALHALLA

REALM OF GAIA

UNIVERSITY

UNIVERSITY

REALM OF NHANG

REALM OF NIBIRU

# PROLOGUE

A fly crawls into her vacant eye socket. Its wings move back and forth rhythmically in the hypnotic dance of a scavenger. More move deeper into her flesh, nearly a hive of them filling the vacant cavity in her skull. Is it a hive if it's not bees? What's a group of flies called? A swarm? Maybe. I want to look it up on my phone, but my hands don't move. My eyes, either. I need to look away. I need to do something, anything, but I can't stop staring at that fly.

Its gossamer wings flutter back and forth, and it flits through the gore to the other eye socket. I stare, caught in her empty, pitiless gaze. Her head has dropped over the edge of the desk, her hair dark hair falling to the floor in a blood-matted mess. The fly struggles as it gets trapped in the dark rivulet of blood running down from her chin to her nose before dripping from her forehead.

At one time, this was a fae girl. Or I think she was fae. It is hard to tell with her staring back at me with those cavities packed with buzzing insects. It's as if they are seeking to replace her missing eyeballs. If I try hard enough, I can imagine them as they would have been in life, pale violet irises with a splash of dark magenta around the pupils. All fae have the same colored eyes, after all. I'd heard the more magenta a fae has in their eyes, the more powerful they are. That might just be a rumor, though.

I'm still pretty sure she's fae, even though whoever draped her over the instructor's desk in this classroom took her pointed ears. Or maybe it's just the angle. If I step forward, will I see them so similar to my own rounded ones? Will I see the graceful slopes ending in delicate points on either side of her head?

Her high cheekbones were left untouched, and her bow-shaped lips are still there.

The only thing that mars her face is the single streak of blood dripping down the middle and onto the floor. And her eyes. Oh, and her ears.

If I just focus on her face, I can call out for someone. I should do something, call for the deputy headmistress, anything but just stare. Hot coffee is spilling from the cups in my hands as I squeeze them, but I can't take my eyes off her. If I look at my hands, I'll have to come to terms with what I first saw when I followed that pool of blood leaking from under the door.

There were just too many things for my brain to process. Too many weapons impaled her naked form, pinning her to the desk at the front of the lecture hall. In that first look, I had identified spears, daggers, swords, broken chair legs, and sharpened pieces of metal. There are probably more, but I can't bear to look again. All I know is that there are too many, way too many, to not be fatal. Even with fae healing, there is no possibility that the girl could survive, even if I got those *things* out of her.

Her mouth is open wide, and the echo of her scream is loud in my head. How many of her screams came and went before the last one rattled out?

The coffee burns the back of my hands. They're shaking. The cups. Or maybe it's my hands. I can't pull my eyes away from the girl in front of me to check. There's the distant sound of some liquid splattering onto the floor of the classroom. It could be the coffee or the blood still dripping from her forehead, joining the lake of crimson beneath her.

I should move. Or scream.

The blood is creeping closer. It's about to hit my shoes.

Someone opens the door behind me and lets out a scream, snapping me out of my terror-induced trance.

# I

## SUMMER
### TWO MONTHS EARLIER

*Ber*

O bsession. *The temptation to feed into one's obsession is so obscenely delicious and relentless. How can something so perfectly decadent be so wrong? Once you've felt its claws sinking sharply into your very soul, there's no way to replicate the feeling, and there is no going back. The only way to combat it is to starve it, to take the object away and let the desire shrivel until you're nothing but a hollow husk. And that's exactly how it feels. The emptiness creates an aching void that nothing can ease.*

*Eagal. Teine. Furaidh. Chan eil fios gu leòr.*
   *Fear. Fire. Fury. To know is not enough.*
   The words are emblazoned on the wrought iron arch above the entrance to the campus. It marks the place where the protective barrier of the school begins. Even as the portal closes behind me, other students are eagerly approaching the campus from their home realms.
   *Fear.* I've felt it my whole life, and I've known it for as long as I can remember.
   There is no going back now, I suppose. Not that I have anywhere to go back to.
   *Fire.* Like the fire inside me, the only thing standing against the darkness permeating my every cell.
   The large iron gates herd students in, keeping some level of order to the chaotic surge of new blood into the university. They don't hesitate as they cross onto the

campus, calling out to old friends and looking around in eager anticipation. For them, this is a long-awaited day. For me, it's... something else.

*Fury.* The anger from never belonging.

For most, this has always been their plan.

*To know is not enough.* It never has been. The knowledge concealed behind these gates calls to me. It's a silent temptation that I find irresistible.

They pass by me, none looking twice in my direction. Most are in their late twenties or early thirties, and their plans have been neatly laid out for them. They spent their youth maturing their magic enough to meet the entry requirements, learning and building themselves up until they reached a point where they were found deserving of attending the prestigious Avalon University. I, on the other hand, shouldn't be here. This wasn't my plan, but things have changed. One stupid misstep, and I had no choice but to accept the offer of admission to the renowned university.

We funnel toward the center of the school, where staff are set up to welcome us. They provide our schedules and student IDs, everything neat and orderly, exactly what one would expect from the most elite and coveted Avalon University.

The quad bustles with students and families as they matriculate into the system. Multiple tables are set up to provide information and allow people to sign up for various social groups and activities. My eyes are drawn to one in particular, and my blood surges, rebelling at the oppressive sensation of the numerous fae gathered around the stall. Their presence surrounds my locked-down power and squeezes like a vise, causing my breath to explode from my lungs in a short burst.

Fuck.

I look around, seeking a hiding place, needing somewhere private to shelter myself and regain control. I shove into one of the bathrooms and pace the black and white tiled floor. Catching a glimpse of myself in the mirror, I walk toward it, taking in my flustered appearance. My light blue eyes glow eerily as they do every time I reach for my power. It wasn't intentional this time, just an instinctive response to the combined fae energy swamping me.

It had risen so eagerly to the perceived threat as if it were a starved beast sensing easy prey. I close my eyes and tighten my fingers on the sink, battling against my own power, determined to force it back into the abyss where I keep it. It has never been this difficult, but I've never been around so many of them at once before.

*Just do it, Summer. Show me what you can do.*

The voice echoes in my mind, sending a chill down my spine. I close my eyes, trying to shove the memory back into the abyss. My body trembles, and the porcelain groans beneath my hands, but the insistent press of my power finally eases. When I open my eyes and look at myself in the mirror, I am relieved to see a cooler reflection looking back at me.

Before coming here, I had considered colored contacts to hide the blue of my eyes.

I thought maybe I could hide in plain sight for a little while, but it would have been a complete waste of time. They can scent that I am fae, and the second they see my eyes, pale icy blue compared to their vibrant violet with the ring of magenta around the pupil, they'll know I'm *wrong*. I'd encountered enough of my kind growing up to know one thing. I needed to stay the fuck away from them.

I take a breath and reapply my lipstick. It still looks perfect, but the small, familiar action centers me a little more. The tension is still holding my shoulders, and I can see how fucking uncomfortable I am. No one else will be able to see though. My mask is as impenetrable as they come.

Unable to put it off any longer, I leave the bathroom, lifting my chin as I walk over the lush grass of the quad toward the induction tables.

"Welcome to AU!" an over-exuberant student exclaims at me, her hair in an alarmingly high ponytail. The rhythmic sway of it every time she moves is hypnotic.

"Thanks," I reply, trying to hold back my eye roll at the black and silver outfit with the words **AVALON CHEER** across her chest.

She smiles widely at me, her paper-white teeth gleaming in the sunshine. "Surname?"

"Tita—" I cut off, stopping myself from providing the fake surname I'd grown so used to. "Tuatha De Daanan," I correct, crossing my arms. The name rattled in my mouth, sitting sourly on the tongue.

The girl snickers. "Sorry, I should have noticed the ears. What is your first name?"

"Summer," I say. The tips of my pointed ears burn slightly from the attention, and I clench my fists against the need to cover them. We don't have real surnames. Instead, all fae claim *Tuatha De Daanan* as our last name. The acceptance letter had tacked it onto my name automatically, so I am stuck with it.

The cheerleader scrolls through something on her laptop and then searches through a bunch of packets.

"Summer?"

I can't help the glare that I shoot at her. She's entirely too cheery, and I'm immediately suspicious. "Yes."

She doesn't seem to notice, her smile never wavering. "You're in Kelpie 215! And there's the Fair Folk Club just over there." She points to the table at the other side of the quad, among the other club tables with first years lingering around them. "If you want to find out about their meetups. It's a popular club for your kind."

I blink at her. "The Fair Folk Club?" I ask, unsure why I'm surprised. Fae are as pack-like as shifters.

She nods, her eyes darting to the person in line behind me. "Well, you're fae, right?"

*Well, you're fae, right?* The question rattles around my skull. I snatch the packet from her. "Thanks for your help." I storm away in the opposite direction, seething. I'm going to have to get used to people reacting to me based on my species, but it's going to be difficult to overcome a lifetime of suppression.

The map directs me to the hall the cheerleader circled with a bright pink heart, charmed to flash and sparkle. This time, I don't hold back my eye roll as I continue toward my building, lugging my one bag of clothes. Around me, families and friends carry multiple bags into the dorms, helping their new students settle in, all chattering excitedly about the future.

The campus is extraordinarily green, more than any park I've ever seen. Trees line the pathways between the school buildings and the dormitories. The grass is spotted with small white daisies, making it look more welcoming than if it were perfectly manicured.

Even on this busy day, students use the space to study and play ball. It all looks so *normal*. That is until the ball soars high and an angel's wings appear from his back. He launches into the sky to catch it, his friends cheering.

The grounds are obviously well-loved and well-cared for, but there is a general feeling of ease with the fresh meat being inducted into the seemingly perfect harmony of the school.

Dodging through the emotional partings of families and excited reunions of old friends, I can't help but feel like everyone's eyes are on me like I'm some freak of nature that they've never seen before. Truthfully, I am used to that. I have always been out of place, an immortal in a sea of humans, and always a little too different than was comfortable. Every day, I braided my hair in the same way to hide my pointed ears. The icy blue of my eyes drew the gaze, too abnormal to pass for a mortal but not the violet of every other fae. I am too odd for mortals and too odd for fae.

I keep my eyes on the ground, not wanting to see their stares or answer their questions. How many times will I have to say *I have no fucking idea* before they realize it's the truth?

I run my fingers through my hair as I walk to my dorm, ignoring the way the multitude of different species go quiet but start to whisper as I walk past. No one is saying anything mean or derogatory, but they're curious. I don't look or smell exactly like a fae, but I'm different enough that they wonder what I am.

People are spilling out of Kelpie Hall, milling around the large sign out front that has MIXED SPECIES written on it in big letters. I assume some dorms are species-specific. That would make sense. How else would the fae be able to suck one another off if they weren't in close proximity at all times?

Logically, I know that not all fae are bad, but those I've had the misfortune of meeting and interacting with have all been arrogant, cruel, and devious.

*Show me what you can do, Summer.*

I shiver again. The hair stands up on the back of my neck, and I fight the urge to look over my shoulder.

Shifters tend to prefer to stick together as well, so they can remain in their archaic *might-makes-right* mentality throughout their whole lives. I'd researched some before coming here. What basic knowledge I could find was patchwork at best, mostly based on what had become legends in my old realm. I think that is what I am most looking forward to in coming here. Avalon University supposedly has one of the best libraries in all the realms.

I slide past more tearful goodbyes and embraces of excitement, making my way up the stairs to number 215. The door unlocks at the touch of my hand, and I step inside, surprised to find the space bigger and much nicer than I expected.

Someone is already standing in the middle of the room. The woman is shorter than me, and her hair is chopped in a messy bob. The tips are blonde, whereas the roots are a darker brown color. Her dark brown gaze is fixed on the mini refrigerator sitting within one of the counter spaces. She barely comes to my shoulder, yet anger radiates from her like a furnace, all directed at the miniature appliance.

"This is just pathetic," she grumbles, placing her hands on her hips.

My lips twitch. "Don't imagine you'd have much to put in there, anyway."

She jumps, her dark brown eyes swinging to me. "What the fuck! How did you sneak up on me?" she asks, placing her hand over her heart.

I tilt my head, dropping my bag on the floor. "An easily startled vampire? Interesting."

I had met a handful of vampires in my home realm, though they were all male. Were all the females so tiny? She gives me a droll look, crossing her arms over her chest. "Well, not normally. As you're some weird kind of fae, I'm going to pretend it was because of that and not because I was too busy considering the size of our ridiculous fridge." She holds out a hand to me. "Alice."

"Summer." I hesitate for a moment before shaking her hand. I had thought I'd slip into my room and drop my bag off, avoiding the person I would share my dorm with as much as possible over the next year. Friends aren't really something I've ever had. They ask too many questions and get hurt when I won't answer. It is easier not to have them, but something about this vamp is... familiar and comforting. Strange for someone whose main source of sustenance is blood.

Alice smiles, her long fangs sitting proudly among the rest of her teeth. Her eyes dart to my bag and then around, assessing me. "No family with you?"

Here they come. The questions I don't have any answers to.

I shake my head. "Looks like I'm not the only one," I say through clenched teeth, biting back the venom seeping into my voice.

Alice doesn't seem to notice the harshness of my words. "Oh yeah, Dad couldn't get rid of me fast enough. Surprised he didn't turn to ash with how fast he ran." Alice shrugs, her gaze going back to the fridge.

She says it so casually. *So yeah, me too, no worries.* A laugh bubbles in my chest, and

I blink as the sound fills the room. I look around, trying to find the source. Surprise fills me when I realize it came from me. When I look back at the vampire, she's watching me with a glimmer of humor in her eyes.

She was alone, like me, yet it didn't seem to bother her even a little bit. In some ways, she seems relieved her father had left as quickly as he had. Everyone else had family and friends surrounding them as they arrived here. I assumed I'd be isolated again like I was before. A loner like always, and maybe I will be, but it seems like maybe she will be, too. That thought makes me feel a little less alone.

Alice smiles, then shifts from foot to foot, glancing away. "I uh... don't know anyone here, so... Do you want to come with me to the first-year tour after you unpack?"

My stomach twists. Say no. Even if I have some strange sense of familiarity with my new roommate, I don't know how long I'll be able to stay here. It is better not to have any connections when I have to run.

"Sure," I answer. Wait, what? I was going to say no. Why did I agree to go with her? The word was out before I could stop it.

Alice looks up, her eyes flickering with something that looks like vulnerability before her smile morphs into an arrogant smirk. I can't take the words back now. Alice pulls out her phone and taps at the screen. Her smirk deepens. "The new fridge will be here in the next few days, thanks to Daddy dearest. I love some revenge spending."

# 2

## SUMMER

*Caer*

My bedroom is a basic empty shell. There's a bed sitting against the wall, a bedside table, and a desk. A faint smell of paint makes my nose burn slightly as I inhale. They must have redecorated before we newbies moved in, which was nice of them. I don't fancy sleeping in a room with peeling paint and the smell of pot laced into the walls. The only personal touch is the thick packet with my name expertly written on the front lying on the nightstand. I dump my bag on the floor and pick it up. The bed squeaks faintly as I sit down on it, and the sound of paper tearing fills the room as I open the envelope.

> *Welcome to Avalon,*
> *This is a time of upheaval and struggling to find your way in a completely new world.*
> *Many feel lost at first, adrift. I know I did when I was in your shoes many years ago.*
> *There is a mandatory assembly at three pm today so take some time to figure out the campus.*
> *Avalon can be a haven for the lost souls who have never felt like they belong.*
> *Headmaster Emrys*

Never felt like they belong, huh? From what I have seen of the student body, it doesn't seem that any of them feel out of place. I put the letter to the side and look through the rest of the contents. There is a pamphlet about the amenities on the grounds and some information about the neighboring town. They have included a printout of my class schedule and a calendar for upcoming events on campus. There are endless leaflets about the various groups, and my eyes are drawn to the one for the Fair Folk. My fingers clench on the paper, crushing it in my fist. I drop it onto the ground and glare at it, the words having melted into nothing. Fuck the Fair Folk Club. Fuck the fae.

"Ready?" Alice's soft voice pulls me from my staring contest with the crumpled ball of paper. I glance around at the room again, realizing I didn't get anything unpacked. Not that I really have anything to unpack.

I look at Alice, her pixie-like face pulled into a tentative look of hope. Is she hoping for a new friend in this unfamiliar place? Maybe we're not as alike as I thought because if a friend is what she's looking for, she has come to the wrong person.

Yet I can't help but feel at ease with this bloodsucker. It's disconcerting and altogether nauseating. However, it is there. I thought my walls were impenetrable, but somehow, this petite vampire is scaling them, digging her obsidian claws into the stone simply because her pained aloneness is familiar. I should be scrambling for any reason to keep her at a distance and excuse myself from going with her. But...

I stand up. "Ready."

The grounds are still bustling, but there is an obvious ease from the lack of parents now wandering around. The feel of the campus has shifted, the frenetic energy almost palpable. It practically reverberates through the ancient halls. I curl my shoulders in slightly, letting my hair fall forward to hide my pointed ears and freaky eyes.

Alice stays close as we navigate through the quad, trying to figure out the various buildings littering the perfect green space. She pushes a little more into my side as the crowd thickens and people get too close to her. Though it doesn't feel like it's from fear, it feels like she's seeking comfort.

"I swear, back home, these people would be dinner," Alice murmurs. She watches with barely contained distaste as a couple of cheerleaders cling to a pair of muscle-bound males dressed like members of a sports team. "They're so careless," she continues, and I can practically hear her roll her eyes.

Something in my chest tugs, loosening a little. She feels it, too. That everyone here is part of some understanding we're not. I thought she just started scaling the walls of my impenetrable fortress, but it seems she's also found a microscopic hole in the stone, allowing her to peer inside. Are Alice and I cut from similar cloths, full of torn pieces we desperately stitched together, hoping no one would notice how mismatched they are? I wonder how many tears and rips were in Alice's, probably nowhere near as many as mine. I'd lost count of mine. Maybe this place, this realm, will be different. Maybe I can be different.

"What?" Alice asks, glancing at me, a slight uneasiness in her eyes. Perhaps she thinks she's said too much.

My lips twitch. "You know, you're all right, vampire." Alice's eyes widen in surprise, but she leans a little into me, relaxing a little more. "What? It's true. I mean, we have blood rivers. Where do you think they come from?"

A girl smiles at Alice and walks toward us. Alice hisses at her, and the girl pales before hurrying in the other direction. My lips twitch, and my shoulders lose some of their tension. Something about this feral vampire resonates with me, and neither of us is comfortable being surrounded by people.

Alice points at a group of equally lost-looking first years. "I think that's our tour. Oh, Drac. Do not leave me with them."

"Please, you're the only interesting person I've met so far."

"Same. I think I scare people."

I laugh at the absurdity of the use of the word *think*. She'd just flashed her fangs at someone who smiled at her.

"All the best people do," I reply.

Alice chuckles as we join the group. A woman who appears to be in her early thirties looks over the group, her lips moving as she silently counts. She's dressed in a black polo and slacks with a proud silver *A* over her heart. That must be the Avalon insignia. I expected something more ornate from a school with such an ominous motto.

"Okay, that's everyone! I'm Fallon. I'm a senior here, and I'll be taking you on your tour of the campus." She walks backward down the hall, and we follow her like sheep. "Avalon was established in the year 303CE and was the first school in all of Annwn. It's why we call this realm Avalon instead of its true name, Annwn. It was originally only for the education of sorcerers until the current headmaster took control a little over a hundred years ago. Until then, other species were only allowed to attend Avalon, thanks to a very competitive exchange program. However, now we have members of almost every magical race!"

Alice rolls her eyes, and I sigh. There's being excited about a place and having a boner for it. This guide is already on the more over-the-top, annoying side, and the tour has just started.

"As you all might have noticed, we have a rather unusual motto." Fallon chuckles. "A fun historical fact is that Merlin originally put the first part of the motto, fear, fire, and fury, in place. When Avalon University was founded, persecution of sorcerers was at an all-time high. Merlin hoped the motto would serve as a warning to all who would come for the school. He wanted it known that anyone intent on such an attack should fear because it would be met with fire and fury."

Well, that explains it. I keep my expression of boredom in place, but I had wondered about the motto.

Our little group follows Fallon like ducklings as she continues the tour. "If you look to your left, you'll see the main building, Manananggal Hall. It is home to the main auditorium, a few classrooms, and the headmaster's office. This is also where you will find the administration offices. Oh, and the lockboxes."

*Lockboxes?*

I glance at the building. Emerald-green ivy almost completely covers the dark stone. It looks dangerous and a bit foreboding. The stone steps leading up to the large wooden door do not inspire thoughts of comfort or safety, yet I'm not afraid of the building or the power it contains. Knowledge, forbidden and ancient, awaits me within those walls, along with the dangers of knowing too much. It pulled at me, begging me to come, touch, taste, learn, and devour. I've always had a voracious appetite for learning, and the place where I grew up had very little to offer when it came to accurate information about the other realms. Most had been reduced to myth and legend, and it was hard to determine what was fact or fiction. It was partly why I accepted the offer of admission. It isn't the only reason, but it is a definite perk.

"As many of you already know, there are many esteemed, one-of-a-kind professors at Avalon. But the most elite is, of course, our headmaster." I don't miss the way Fallon's cheeks flush when she mentions him. They have done so every time she has brought him up. I guess everyone has their kinks, but an old sorcerer with a long white beard is not my type. "He has a bit of a cult following, and though he rarely teaches classes, they are always packed when he does. His only course offering this year is a fourth-year capstone with the most distinguished students."

Alice makes a gagging sound, and Fallon's gaze snaps to her, giving her a reproachful look. Fallon's face transforms slightly, her cheekbones becoming sharper and her skin turning slightly green and mossy. She is a dryad, a fae subspecies, one of many. I bristle at her aggressive response. Were fae or their subspecies always going to be underfoot here?

"Moving on..." Fallon contains her ire with visible effort and points out numerous other buildings, spouting rehearsed, boring facts about them. Elite training fields. State-of-the-art facilities. Elite faculty. The headmaster did this. The headmaster that.

"Want to bail? Cause I'm pretty sure if she uses the word *elite* one more time, I'm going to kill her." From the way Alice's eyes turn blood red, I know she is not joking.

"Fuck yes."

Alice grabs my hand and yanks, pulling me into a sprint and away from the group. Again, that pang of familiarity strikes me. What is it about Alice that is already making me comfortable? Normally, if someone acted this familiar with me, I'd be running in the opposite direction, not muffling a laugh of joy as I kept up with their mad race through the halls.

"Wait! Come back! The tour—" Fallon shouts, but her voice is lost as we round a large, gray stone building.

"You think she'll follow us here?" Alice asks, peering around the corner.

"And leave her group of frightened, little first years behind? I doubt it."

"They've gone the other way. She practically has steam coming from her ears."

I laugh, leaning against the wall. In just the few hours that I've known Alice, the sound has already become more familiar. Maybe this really can be a new chapter for me. *Careful Summer, hope is not something afforded to everyone.*

"Oh, this must be the library." Alice looks up at the building, pulling me from my thoughts. My head snaps back, and I notice the pointed turrets of the building. She glances at me and snorts. "Okay, the light in your eyes when I said *library* is concerning. Do you have a book fetish? If you try to summon a golem made of books to fuck, I'm bouncing."

I ignore her and walk toward the door, almost as if it is a compulsion. I am so desperate to smell the muskiness of knowledge. We walk through the door, and the scent surrounds me. Books have always been my solace, my haven, and there are so many here for me to choose from. I walk to the stacks, dragging my fingers over the spines of the tomes. I can practically hear them calling out to me, begging to be opened, to be read, to be learned. There is so much I don't know. The few books I managed to get my hands on before Avalon only scratched the surface. I need more. I crave more.

Alice snickers, watching me, and then tugs at my sweater. I glance at her, and she points to a large wrought-iron gate. It is held closed with a thick metal padlock below a plaque that reads, RESTRICTED SECTION. PLEASE ASK THE LIBRARIAN FOR A KEY. "Restricted section. Let's go!"

I can already tell that this friendship is going to get me in a lot of trouble, but the pull to enter the space is almost undeniable. In this realm, knowledge is power, and no one knows better than I the danger of being powerless.

I stop behind Alice and bounce on my toes impatiently, staring longingly at the books. She grips the lock in her hand and crushes it, her vampire strength decimating the heavy metal.

The restricted section is darker than the rest of the library, the books feel older and darker. I push the door open and slip through, walking into the shelves. Carefully, I graze one of the spines, the words glowing beneath my touch.

*The Dark Runes of Phineas.*

"I don't understand the idea of restricting books. I mean, aren't we supposed to be learning?" Alice ponders, carelessly sifting through a pile of books, barely reading the titles. She clearly doesn't share my reverence for books, but she probably hasn't been starved for knowledge most of her life, so I can't really blame her for that.

*Take me,* the book whispers to me. *Read me. Claim the secrets I hold. I have power you need.*

I start to pull the book from the stacks when the air shifts, and a dark voice fills the room. Power coils around me, and the air turns to lead in my lungs. The weight of my body triples as the gravity of the room turns oppressive. My knees buckle, and I grip the wooden shelf to keep myself from falling.

"You are far from where you belong." The voice is deep and laced with frigid ice, vibrating with annoyance.

# 3

# SUMMER

The command. The danger. *The power.*

I whirl to face the new dangerous presence. The oppressive gravity of his power levels off once I am facing him, but his silver eyes pin me in place. I can barely breathe under the weight of them, and any lightness that returned when he recalled his power vanishes beneath his gaze. He towers in the open doorway to the restricted section, swallowing the light from the rest of the library. It isn't just his size that has my instincts blaring in alarm and my nerves closing my throat. Every inch of this man screams lethal.

His dark golden brown skin is tight around his jaw, the muscles twitching under the dark stubble. An intricate rune slashes through his right brow, the white of it stark against the richness of his skin. *What species creates white runes?* His hair is swept back, but a rebellious wave in the raven black mars its perfection. Based on his clothing, he has to be staff. A three-piece black suit would be an odd choice for a student. Even dressed so urbanely, it is too easy to imagine him on a battlefield, his armor drenched in blood.

I open my mouth, trying to say something, but no sound comes out. My lungs burn, desperate for the oxygen I can't seem to take in. I take an involuntary step back from him, instinctively trying to escape his penetrating gaze. The books that had been so loud and persistent in their attempts to lure me in go silent as if also retreating from the man. I wish I could sink into the stacks, disappearing among the tomes to escape.

Unaware of the danger, Alice nonchalantly comes around the corner. His gaze snaps toward the movement, and a gasp of relief slips past my lips. Alice looks up and drops the solid gold book she is holding. The sound of it hitting the floor echoes loudly in the otherwise eerily silent space.

His gaze sharpens, and he looks at me again. His perusal is not as intense this time, but I can practically see the anger simmering in him. Whoever this guy is, we have not endeared ourselves to him. Maybe he's the librarian?

"Auditorium," he commands and turns to the side, waiting for us to leave. He obviously does not trust that we will go without his supervision.

I swallow and hurry past him. In my haste, I trip on a chair leg and fall into him. The ominous aura surrounding him folds around me, taking my breath again. He grabs my arm tightly, putting me back on my feet with a hard yank. I look up at him, intending to thank him, but his face is etched in annoyance. The words get stuck in my throat, and this close, I can see that it is not a white rune cutting through his brow. It's a scar in the shape of a rune.

"Breaking into the restricted section on your first day is a bold move," he grates out. His voice is a shiver of icy fury down my spine, and his grip on my arm is close to bruising. That rune turns even paler, his eyes a molten silver.

"It was my idea. I dragged her along," Alice fumbles out. She must sense the lethality oozing from this man. I suspect that for my new slightly homicidal vampire friend, being afraid is not something she is used to.

I force myself not to look away from his silver gaze, hating how my cheeks heat even as I lift my chin. "I apologize, sir. It won't happen again."

He releases my arm, disgust curling his lip. "Go. Now."

Alice grabs me and pulls me into a sprint, only slowing when we get to Manananggal Hall so we can safely ascend the steps, joining the stragglers filing into the auditorium.

"Why didn't you tell me he was there?" Alice whispers, her voice still shaking slightly.

"I..." *Fuck, use your fucking words, Sum.* The fear of that male's presence lingers on my skin, whispering of the danger coiled inside him. It felt like I had roused a sleeping dragon, and it had opened one silver eye to lock its gaze on me.

Whoever he is, I must stay away from him while I am here. I hate that out-of-control terror I felt, and I never want to feel it again, ever.

Alice pulls me through the doors of the building. "It's fine. I mean, I don't think we can get expelled on our first day. Right?"

I manage to shake off my stupor. "I'll take the fall," I say confidently. This isn't my world, not really, not yet. I can figure something out. Avalon is supposed to be the nexus of most realms. I am sure I can find a portal and fall into another.

Alice scoffs. "You wish. If someone is getting expelled on the first day and becoming a legend, it's me."

I roll my eyes, but inwardly, I smile as Alice and I find seats near the back of the auditorium. The room is comically big to accommodate all the students. The stage at the front is so grand it almost looks like a dais.

I look around, cataloging faces and species. Am I looking for other potential allies? Is that what I consider Alice? An ally? Maybe. My eyes sweep over the room, catching the markings of the various races. There was that dryad from earlier. A woman with silver hair and a shining shell necklace. I'm pretty sure she is a mere. The sorcerers are easy to spot. They wear their black runes on their skin with pride. Despite what the guide had said, they really do make up the majority of the student body. Great. I've never fit in anywhere, and I'm pretty confident Avalon will be no different.

A young sorceress sits next to me, talking to her friend. "Trust me. He's as scary as they say. And as hot."

Alice's ears twitch. "Who is?"

The sorceress shoots Alice a glare. "The headmaster, of course." Alice blinks blankly, and the sorceress sneers. "The son of Merlin. Wow, they really do let anyone in here nowadays."

I snarl, my hands curling around the arms of the chair. "Careful." I'm not sure where the outburst comes from, but hearing her talk about Alice that way felt like a personal attack.

The sorceress sniffs at me. "And what are you supposed to be?" she scoffs and rolls her eyes before turning back to her friend, giving Alice and me her back. The way she dragged the word *what* out reaffirmed what I already suspected. Sorcerers are elitist dicks.

"What a bitch," Alice murmurs.

A woman walks onto the stage. Her hair is swept back from her face, and the white streak at the front is stark against the shiny black. She narrows her dark eyes, tightening her already pointed and sharp features. The bright lights shimmer against the red silk fabric of her robe, glinting off the gold characters embroidered onto it. She claps once, the sound reverberating around the entire room, drawing everyone's attention to her, but there is still some hushed chatter.

"Hello, students. I would like to start by welcoming the new first years. We are thrilled to have you. Welcome back to our returning students. I trust you all had an enjoyable summer vacation. First, some introductions. I am Deputy Headmistress Locke. I specialize in advanced alchemy, specifically for use in combat, so I won't meet some of you for a few years yet." She gestures behind her. "This is Professor Draco, head of Shifter Studies."

There is a surge of whoops and hollers as Professor Draco steps forward, bowing his head in acknowledgment. I roll my eyes at the shifters' show of respect for their leader. I study Professor Draco's face, trying to work out what kind of shifter he could be. There's a slight shimmer to his skin when he moves a certain way, which looks almost like scales. That can't be right, though. They are extinct. He straightens a lock of black hair that had fallen across his forehead. His golden eyes tilt at the edges, and his smile is unnerving, too charming and handsome.

Deputy Headmistress Locke claps again, and the shifters' hoots and hollers die down. "Professor Harrison, head of General Species Studies. Professor Uxley, head of Occult Studies. Professor Reign, head of Realm Studies. Professor Buraeux, head of Combat Studies..."

She goes down the line, introducing all the heads of departments. By the end, my head is a mess of names and faces.

"Now, before I release you to no doubt celebrate the last night of summer, the headmaster has a few words of wisdom for the year." Deputy Headmistress Locke steps back, and the room goes completely silent for the first time since we entered the auditorium. I glance around in surprise. The quiet chatter and whispers had continued throughout the deputy headmistress's speech and the introductions, which only makes the silence that much more oppressive.

Everyone's eyes lock on the tall figure as he steps onto the stage. His power flares around him, swallowing the light and seeming to cast him in shadows. The same silver eyes that pinned me in the library make a searing sweep over the audience, taking in every student. That same terror locks me in place. I knew coming to Avalon would mean meeting all manner of beings, but the headmaster is... something else, something deadly. My primal instincts scream at me, begging me to run. I have no doubt there is no worse location to be than the center of this man's focus.

"Fuck," Alice mouths, slouching in her chair. I can't move enough to do even that, my muscles having locked in place.

"Welcome." His deep voice fills the room so there's not one crevice unaffected by it. The frigid cold that emanated from him in the library has failed to thaw. If anything, his voice reverberates with even more power, and I see people in the audience shiver with it. "Your time at Avalon can be the best and brightest of your life. It can be full of heartbreaks and parties, sorrows and studies, debaucheries and exploration."

He pauses, every student sitting transfixed and seeming to hold their breath, waiting for him to continue. My breath feels trapped in my lungs, and I flinch from the magnetic pull of him, something telling me to fight what feels like a compulsion.

"But I'm more interested in what you want these years to be. Who you want to be. Most of you have been told your entire life that you needed to be one thing, whether it was based on your species, your power, your family, or your realm. All of that is gone as of today. Wash yourself clean of those responsibilities and obligations. Within these halls, you have the freedom to figure out the one thing most of you have never gotten the chance even to consider. On your graduation day, you will cross the stage and shake my hand as you receive your Mark." He slips off a ring to show the Avalon seal on his finger, marking him a graduate of Avalon and a being at the height of knowledge and power. "When that time comes, I want you to be able to answer one question. Who do you want to be? For now, I charge you to work on your answer. Dismissed."

Everyone stands and gathers their things before heading out of the auditorium. Alice pulls me from the room as quickly as possible, shoving other students out of the way and snarling at them when they get upset. "Fuck, he's the headmaster?"

"It's fine. He's probably already forgotten about it." I try to make my voice sound as confident as possible, but my breath is still ragged. *What was that? Where did that ancient, forbidden power come from?*

"Forgotten about what, Miss Tuatha De Daanan?" His low voice makes my whole body tense. Alice crashes to a halt and lets out a squeak.

I turn and look up at him. He towers over me and the surrounding students. His size is just another thing about him that puts me on edge. I clear my throat. "E-Excellent speech, sir."

He glances at Alice, but his silver gaze quickly returns to me. He crosses his arms over his chest, and I try not to notice how his dark suit jacket strains a little over his muscles or how broad he is. Instead, I focus on the glint of obsidian rings on his fingers but become distracted by the runes covering his hands.

Okay, maybe I can see what that sorceress was talking about. He is hot and terrifying. The cult following makes sense now. This guy is the headmaster? He seems more like an evil warrior king plucked from the battlefields of old and slipped into a dark suit. The black runes that crawl up the side of his neck toward his jaw only seem out of place in an academic setting.

"I will consider today to be an aberration. Just two curious students who wandered too far from their tour. I will not make such an allowance again." Without another word, he spins on his heel and walks away. The dismissal is clearly from a male accustomed to wielding power and knowing the weight of his word. Air rushes back into my lungs so violently I nearly choke on it.

Son of Merlin. I don't know much about Merlin other than he founded the school and the Sorcerer's Guild. Well, there is also the King Arthur stuff, but I don't know how much of the Arthurian legends of my past world are accurate. They definitely never mentioned Merlin having a son. Or, if they did, they didn't mention how terrifying he is.

Alice lets out a breath of relief as we watch him walk away. Students part like the sea before him, and though several try to get his attention with heated looks, he never pauses.

"Fuck, that was close." Alice wipes imaginary sweat off her forehead, though the gesture is laden with genuine fear.

I smile at her, trying to cover my lingering unease. "Well, now that we're not being expelled, I should get back to unpack my things."

"We should stop on the way and get some tequila." Alice slips her arm through my elbow. I guess we are going together. After that encounter with the headmaster, I am grateful not to be traveling across campus alone.

We stop at the small shop to grab some tequila and limes. At least the university doesn't pretend we will not drink. Sometimes, it is the only thing that dulls my senses enough to come close to a semblance of normal. From past experiences in my old realm, some alcohol and recreational drugs take the edge off.

"You know, you're not like I thought fae would be," Alice says, juggling the limes on the walk home. I carried the bags with the tequila and other snacks she had picked up for me. She hadn't asked what I liked, just picked them out and paid for them. I don't know why I find it so endearing, but it is. Especially as a vampire, she has no idea what tastes good.

"Oh?"

Alice nudges my shoulder. "Yeah, but I mean, I don't know a lot. I wasn't allowed to leave Drăculea until Old Windbag finally died."

Old Windbag? Wait, does she mean Dracula? The ruler and creator of the vampiric home realm, Vlad Dracula, had just recently died under rather ominous circumstances, with no heir to the throne. Was that why I'd never seen a female vampire before? Were they not allowed to leave the Realm of Blood?

"Oh, right. I heard about that."

"He was the worst. You know I was betrothed at birth because of that asshole?" Alice shakes her head. "To a guy who is five thousand years old. Powdery motherfucker."

My lips twitch. "I take it you're not into age gap?"

Alice gives me a look. "I was a baby! I had squishy fangs!"

I laugh. "I'm messing with you."

"Well, all I know about fae is that you guys don't talk to anyone but... well, fae."

My laughter dies. Yeah, maybe other fae, but not me. I'm a blue-eyed enigma. I glance around, searching for a distraction. "Oh, look, that's the canteen. We should check it out."

Alice blinks at the change in subject but follows my gaze. It looks like they're hosting a student club fair. It seems the quad was only the start of the Hellscape that is group activities. What looks like hundreds of multicolored booths touting the various clubs clutter the enormous room. First-years mill around the tables while the clubs attempt to recruit them into their ranks.

"Hey, sexy, come sign up." The claws of an incubus' power rake down my back. It's a sensual lure, trying to find its way into my mind and manipulate my emotions. I don't even look in the direction of the beckoning voice. He could just back the fuck off. I'd spent my life ruthlessly aware of and suppressing my own powers. I could immediately sense the presence of someone else's, and I will never allow them through my shields.

"No," I state flatly.

"Why not? Scared? Our club is about realm politics." His voice is laden with suggestion. "At least, on paper."

I finally lift my gaze to give him the most bored look I can before moving past him with ease. The affronted look on his face as I bat off his magical wiles with the ease of swatting a fly is very satisfying.

Alice flips him off. "That fucker did not actually try to mesmerize us in the middle of the canteen."

"Really? I didn't notice," I add matter-of-factly.

As we move deeper into the room, more people call out to us, trying to get us to sign up to their various clubs. This school has a thing for group activities.

"Maybe you're immune to the incubus' lure. It might be because they are related to fae. Though, I guess, very distantly related," Alice says.

My power crawls along my skin, insidiously seeking a way out. My fight-or-flight instinct digs its claws in, and I don't have to look to know why. *Fae.* I'm sure the Fair Folk Club has a booth here. My body starts to hum, my magic about to rip from my skin. I shake my head and grip Alice's arm in a vise grip before turning around, hoping to get out of the canteen before I can no longer contain my power. I tug her toward the door, but a group of students steps in front of us, blocking our exit.

"You're strange," the female at the head of the group says, her voice tinkling like a chorus of silver bells. She slides her hand into mine. "And you shouldn't be hanging out with a vampire."

I keep my eyes away from the other fae and yank my hand out of her grip, holding tighter to Alice. I had hoped to avoid this, but... here we go. My eyes lock with hers, violet with a magenta ring around the pupil, just as I expected. Predictably, they widen in shock, and she takes a step back. Several of the other members of her club hurry to her side, each reacting with fear or surprise when I meet their gazes.

"The fuck?" Alice hisses, flashing her fangs. Several fae respond by showing their own, though they are far shorter and less lethal. Alice's are made for ripping out throats. Maybe that's why I'm drawn to her. She tugs her arm from my grip and steps in front of me, putting herself between me and the Fair Folk Club. Even my power goes silent as fissures form in the walls around my heart, and warmth seeps in. No one has ever fought for me, never protected me.

I take a step to stand right behind Alice. "If you want to keep those pointed ears on your head, I'd suggest going back to your little suck-off fest," I growl.

Two of the fae look at each other in confusion. One of the males steps forward, crowding Alice but ignoring her to talk to me over her head. "You're fae. You belong with us."

"I don't belong to fucking anyone, least of all you."

Alice shoves him back. "She said fuck off." She flashes her fangs at another when he growls aggressively, her eyes turning red with murderous intent. Alice oozes a killing aura. It swirls around her like a bloody mist, and as a group, the fae take a step back.

"What are you?" a small female asks, her violet eyes flickering between Alice and me, trying to figure it out.

"My name is Alice, but I also go by Mistress of Bloodshed, Lady of Carnage, that evil bitch, and please stop peeling my skin from my face," Alice says and flashes her fangs again. She flicks her fingers open, her nails darkening and lengthening into black claws. The fae backs up another step.

I put my hand on Alice's shoulder. "Alice. Let's go."

She turns to look at me, the red of her eyes fading to brown. "Yeah, let's," she says with a final snarl in the direction of the group of fae.

I grab Alice's hand again and barge forward, the group of fae parting to let us pass. We stalk toward the other side of the room, where food is still laid out. I can feel their eyes boring into my back, and my power coils tight, ready to explode from me.

Alice chooses a couple of bottles of blood, and I grab an apple before we head back to the dorm. Once I step into the fresh air, my roiling power draws back enough that I'm not worried about implosion anymore. We don't talk until we're almost home, and it's Alice who breaks the silence. "You want to go out tonight?"

Fuck yes. I need to let off some steam. "As long as those fuckers aren't there."

Alice smirks and unlocks the door to the dorm. "Yeah, what the fuck was that about? Just cause you're fae doesn't mean you belong to them. Like clearly, they're too late. I've already claimed you."

"Well, thank gods for that because I never want to belong to any fae assholes."

Alice smirks, flashing her fangs. "Good. Vampires are very territorial."

I take a bite of my apple, feigning nonchalance. "So, where are we going tonight?" I ask, changing the subject. I am still feeling rattled, but warmth continues to resonate in my chest. Alice stepped forward to protect me. Why? She had nothing to gain. Did she? None of this makes sense, including the defensiveness she provoked in me earlier.

Alice pulls her phone out of her pocket and scrolls through it. Alerts pop up, but she ignores them. "Looks like it's at some place called the Morningstar House."

"You drink, right?"

Alice snorts. "Yes, vampires do drink and not just blood. You didn't grow up around us, huh? I mean, like the beings of the maelstrom?"

How had she caught that already? I thought I was doing pretty well, considering my patchwork research. She is more observant than I realized. As comfortable as I already am around Alice, that could be a problem.

I hurry into my bedroom and come back through with two shot glasses. "I came prepared."

Alice makes grabby hands at the glasses. "Oh, I love you, Summer."

I laugh and open the bottle of tequila, pouring two shots. I lift my glass and clink it to Alice's. "To getting fucked up?"

"To getting fucked up!"

We down our shots, and Alice quickly pours two more, slamming hers. She's a partier. Good, so am I. Being trashed makes it easy to forget, at least for a little bit.

"I'm going to get ready before I'm too drunk to put eyeliner on," Alice says and takes another shot before heading to her room.

I take the bottle and wander into my room. Undressing, I pull on my one going-out dress. It's short, black, and silky, with a thigh slit that ends right below my hip. I slip on a pair of matching black heels. The outfit is the showstopper, so I decide on simple makeup and to leave my hair down, allowing the long, brown locks to lie in their natural waves over my shoulders.

"Too slutty?" Alice asks, twirling in my doorway. She is wearing jeans that look sprayed on and a lace bralette.

I shake my head. "You look hot."

I glance at myself in the mirror once more, tilting my head as I assess my outfit.

"You should wear this with it." Alice holds out a leather jacket that must have cost thousands. It is buttery smooth and supple, the color not rubbing off under my thumb.

"This thing must be worth everything I own and more." When I arrived at Avalon, my bank account was automatically converted to digital credits I could access from my phone. But since I'd barely had a balance, my credits were also low. It is a struggle I am pretty sure Alice does not share. I was lucky even to have a SIM card that allowed me to access the runic network before I got here.

Alice covers my mouth. "Shh, you're my roommate, and I've decided you're stuck with me, so I get to give you things. Deal with it."

I huff behind her hand, and she lowers it. She forces the jacket into my hands, and I pull the leather on and look in the mirror again. I shouldn't accept this.

"You look like such a sexy badass," Alice says, drinking some tequila straight from the bottle. Okay, she might be wealthy, but Alice is still definitely my kind of person.

We take two more shots of tequila each before stumbling out of the dorm, bringing the bottle of tequila with us, and heading in the general direction of the Morningstar House.

# 4

## SUMMER

*C*

*Hor*

I take another deep drink of tequila as we walk across campus, and I loosen up
with every mouthful. We pass multiple parties on the path from the dorms to
the separate houses for various student organizations, several of which are
homes to students, but Alice insists that the one at the Morningstar House is the one
to be at and that *anyone who is anyone is going there*. Whatever that means. Somehow,
she already has some kind of insider knowledge about the campus. It must be whatever app keeps alerting on her phone, but I don't recognize the symbol. It's a rune in
the shape of an **N**. Weird. It must be some special thing.

Students spill out of the ancient stone buildings. Some are snapping photos of
each other, several on loud calls to their parents, and even more to their friends. The
darker it gets, the more the giant dome that surrounds the campus becomes visible,
but only in flashes of light. The university is ancient, and the knowledge it contains
has the potential to create some of the most powerful beings across the realms and
the most deadly of villains. At every graduation, a student contributes to the magical
force field that protects the school, making up the arching shield.

It is one of the main reasons I accepted the offer to Avalon University. The protection it offers is the stuff of legends and too tempting to pass up.

By the time we make it across the campus, it becomes clear what Alice meant.
The music from the Morningstar House can be heard from half a mile away. It's not
even late, but all signs point to this party lasting all night. The front garden is littered
with people dancing and playing beer pong. The house is bathed in darkness, but
bright lights flash through the windows in time to the steady beat of the music. Alice
takes my hand and pulls me through the fray of people scattered on the front lawn

and into the heart of the party. The house is warm, and the place is a mess of wandering hands and tongues, writhing, sticky bodies plastered to each other. Discarded cups and beer bottles cover every available surface, and several groups of people sit around smoking out of some strange ball-shaped pipe that releases a pink smoke on inhale. From their relaxed postures and smiles, I figure it must be some kind of drug.

Holy fuck. It looks like immortals party infinitely harder than mortals. I don't catch all the arcane beings that are present, but thankfully, I can tell there are no fae. A little of the lingering tension slips from my shoulders.

"This is insane!" Alice shouts over the music, still pulling me through the crowd even as bodies slam and push into us. Alice doesn't stop, and soon, people are jumping out of her way. We finally make it to the makeshift bar in the dining room, and Alice grabs two red cups full of unidentified liquid and clinks hers to mine. "Here's to fucking shit up!"

"Let's fucking do this." I down the drink and slam the cup down.

Alice picks up an unlabeled bottle and sniffs it. "What is this?"

A blond man lounging against the wall smirks at Alice, even as the siren pressed against him nibbles at his ear. A stray flash of light catches on the gold band around his wrist, the halo marking him as an angel. I have never been this close to one of the Heavenly Host before, yet nothing about this guy seems angelic. From a quick glance around the party, it is easy to find the golden halos of his kind, and not a single one inspires any thought of purity. Almost all are drinking or doing drugs. Several are in intimate embraces, one entwined in a group of seven other bodies. I thought angels were the heralds of chastity and innocence.

"It's Eden Mist. Careful, it's strong," the angel says, his voice carrying over the music. The siren darts her tongue into his ear, making him shiver and his eyelids flutter closed.

Alice takes a deep drink and coughs. "Holy fuck!" she gasps out from a throat that sounds scalded.

The angel chuckles and focuses back on the siren, leaving Alice and me to hand the bottle back and forth. The first few swallows are tough, but eventually, we get used to the unique burn as it slides down our throats. It warms my chest and makes me feel almost weightless.

"That guy is staring at you, Summer," Alice says slyly into the lip of the bottle, using her eyes to direct me.

Following her gaze, I expect to see more of that morbid curiosity I'd experienced on campus as everyone tries to figure out what I am and what makes me different from other fae. Instead, my eyes collide with a pair of dark blue ones that sparkle with an entirely different kind of interest. Even if he wasn't wearing his halo, this guy screams *angelic*. His masculine beauty appeals to everything female in me. He towers over everyone here, and his form is filled out with easy muscle. With his tawny skin and wavy blond hair, his entire body practically glows.

This man is almost too perfect to look at, and I am not the only one to notice. He is surrounded by a throng of admirers trying to get his attention, but his eyes are on me. He tilts his head, obviously trying to put a name to the face.

*Good luck with that, angel boy.*

"Go get him." Alice nudges me, and I give her a wicked smile. Angel boy thinks all it will take is a single look, and I'll hurry over to him and beg for his attention? Not a chance.

"Absolutely not. Let's dance."

Alice laughs, her eyes sparkling. She pulls me back through to the living room, finding a space for us in the center of the mass of people. I let the music slide through me, and my body instinctively sways to the rhythm. The beat reverberates through my bones, the music flowing around me like the wind. Someone must have woven a spell into the speaker, but I don't care about that right now.

Alice spins me out, and I laugh as we dance. Maybe it is the alcohol, but I feel like I have known this little vampire forever. A shifter comes up behind her and wraps his arms around her waist, pulling her back against him. Her eyes darken, and I prepare to move away to give them some semblance of privacy. Strong hands grip my hips, fingers digging in only slightly, but enough that I know it's an intentional hold and not just one that creepy men do when they're trying to move past you. I glance over my shoulder at him and mask a smug smirk when I see my staring angel. A lock of his golden hair falls into his eyes, the wave in it making it look like a half curl.

He looks down at me, his lips pulled into a confident half-smile. "Why don't I know you?"

Oh, so he's cocky, too? I hate that I like that.

My voice lowers to a purr, and I coquettishly place my hands over his on my hips. "Because until tonight, you've been *extremely* unlucky."

"Connor," he says, trying to hide his quick glance at my lips, but I catch it and file it away.

"Nice to meet you, Connor." My lips curl into a flirty smile. This is a game I'm well versed in and one I enjoy. It's the only game I am willing to play.

He spins me so we're dancing face to face, his hands only leaving my waist for the briefest of moments. I slide my hands over his shoulders, digging my fingers into the wavy golden hair at the nape of his neck. "This is usually the part where you tell me your name."

I lock eyes with him. He's even taller up close. "You'll have to earn my name. Good luck with that."

Connor raises a brow, his thumbs skimming along the curve of my hips. "Oh, I'll definitely earn it. No luck needed."

"And what makes you think that?"

He dips me dramatically and looks down at me, his eyes sparkling with challenge. "Because I'm so charming."

My breath hitches, and my gaze wanders to his full lips. "Modest too..."

Okay, so maybe he's a little good at this game too. I can respect that.

"It's a gift," he adds. Connor lifts me back to my feet and pulls me close. He glances at my lips again before he leans down and brushes a kiss over them. It is gentle as if he is asking permission.

I pull back almost instinctively, and our gazes lock for a long moment. My lips tingle from the contact, my stomach twisting in such an intoxicating way. I push up onto my tiptoes and pull him down, kissing him again. It is deeper this time, my lips pressing against his a little more insistently. I slide my tongue along the seam of his lips. He opens for me, and his groan of pleasure vibrates through me. I almost moan in protest when he retreats.

"Want to get out of here?" he asks, his eyes dark and urgent.

"I should probably stay with my friend."

Connor's eyes dart over my shoulder, and I follow his gaze. Alice has cornered the shifter and is making out with him so hard it looks like she's eating his face off. I might try to rescue him, but the shifter looks to be *really* into it.

"Looks like your friend is occupied," Connor croons in my ear. I turn back to him and can't help but laugh at his cocky grin. This angel seems to think he has the upper hand.

I notice a group of angels keep glancing at him, smirking. "Your boys are missing you. I wouldn't want to take you away from them."

Connor rolls his eyes and chuckles. "Please, you'd be doing me a favor."

I step back and tip my head, looking him up and down. I glance at Alice once more to see she is still making out with her shifter and then back at Connor. "All right."

He smiles and slides his hand into mine, pulling me back toward the kitchen. There are calluses on his palm, maybe from holding a sword. The house has an open floor plan,  but there's a layering of runes on the floor between the kitchen and the living room. The second we cross over them, the sounds from the party dim.

"So, are you going to tell me your name?" Connor asks the moment we are away from the noise.

I walk to the counter and lean against it. "You still have to earn it, angel."

Connor stalks over to me, putting his hands on my hips and lifting me onto the counter. He spreads my knees and presses his powerful body between my thighs. He leans in and kisses me again, pulling back just enough to ask, "And how am I supposed to do that?"

I smile against his lips and brace my hands behind me on the countertop. "I'm going to leave you to work that out." I bite his lip and pull back, dragging it with me until it escapes my teeth.

His moan is low and guttural, but he steps back and opens the fridge. I blink in confusion and shiver, feeling the loss of his heat. What in the world is he doing? He stopped for a snack?

He rummages inside the refrigerator for a few moments before emerging and offering me a sandwich. "Eat."

I blink, staring blankly at the stacked bread in his hand. "Wait, what?"

He holds it closer to my lips, moving to stand between my legs again. "It will soak up the alcohol."

"And why would I want to do that?" I ask, tilting my head.

"So you will have a clear head when I kiss you again."

I blink and then burst out laughing. "Oh, no. You're one of those."

He raises a brow, some of his blond hair falling over his forehead. "One of those?"

I pull back, poorly imitating a bro voice. "I'm not like a regular guy. I'm a good guy."

Connor snorts. "Eat the sandwich."

"I'm not hungry."

He leans in and kisses me again. I pull him closer to deepen it and let out a soft moan, my tongue playing with his.

Connor pulls back slightly, panting a little. "How about now?"

I kiss him again. His lips are so velvety, and he tastes so fucking good. He needs to stop talking.

Connor accidentally brushes the tip of my ear as he plunges his fingers into my hair, and every pleasure center I have goes wild at the sensation. I wrap my arms around his neck, deepening the kiss even more, my tongue exploring his and my fingers tangling into his silky blond locks.

The angel from earlier falls through the ward wrapped around the kitchen in a loud burst of noise, pulling us from the moment. He looks between Connor and me, a slow grin curving his lips. "Con's with a *giiiiiiiiiirl*," he sing-songs.

Another angel follows him in. This one is darker. His features are similar to Connor's, but his hair is black and there is a broodiness to him that is absent in Connor.

"You're quite astute, Zach," the dark angel says, helping Zach up.

"And you're a sour one, Rafe."

"Get out!" Connor shouts, glaring at them.

Rafe, the one with dark hair, gives Connor a mocking salute before grabbing Zach and pulling him past the kitchen boundary.

"Brothers," Connor says with a sigh.

My lips twitch. I knew there was a resemblance.

"I should go."

Connor blinks. "What? Why?"

I lean in and kiss him again.

Connor tightens his fingers in my hair, holding me close. "Stay," he murmurs against my lips.

"Maybe for a little while..." I say, losing myself to the kiss, intoxicated and not by the alcohol.

Thankfully, Connor seems to have forgotten about the sandwich. He moans and moves closer, deepening the kiss. I lick at his tongue but pause when, through the haze of pleasure and soundproofing rune, I hear Alice shouting. I pull back and gently push at Connor before hopping off the counter.

"I have to go see what is happening with Alice," I say, heading toward the living room.

"Wait, tell me your name," he demands.

"Later, angel," I say, winking at him over my shoulder before hurrying into the living room.

Alice is being held around the waist by yet another angel. Fuck, how many fucking angels are here? This one looks scarily like Zach.

I push through the crowd to stand in front of her. "What happened?"

"She said I was being a whore," Alice snarls.

I look behind me at the object of Alice's fury and see a female wolf shifter smirking at her.

"You were being a whore, *leech*."

Alice squirms, trying to break free to lunge at her, but the angel tightens his hold on her and lifts her off her feet.

I walk toward the wolf shifter with a sweet smile on my face. As soon as I am within reach of her, I punch her in the face. The sound of her nose breaking echoes in the now quiet room. While everyone is too stunned to react, I turn back to Alice. "Ready to go?"

"Right, both of you out!" the angel holding Alice demands. He waits for me to proceed and just carries Alice to the door. Alice lets out a low oof when he sets her none too gently on her feet and goes back inside, slamming the door behind him. The music starts up again, and Alice and I burst out laughing. I swing my arm over her shoulders, and we head back home.

# 5

## SUMMER

*Hael*

Alice and I continue to chuckle and chatter as we head back toward Kelpie. I stop to take off my heels, carrying them in my hand. Alice wraps an arm around my waist as we stroll across campus. "How was the golden dude?"

"The golden dude tried to make me eat a sandwich mid-make-out." I wrap my arm around her shoulders. Even with her heeled boots, she barely reaches my shoulder.

Alice snorts. "Is that code for his dick?"

"What? No. He wanted me to eat an actual sandwich." I roll my eyes and let out a huff. What a way to ruin a perfectly good opportunity to fuck. Men. "To soak up the alcohol or whatever."

Alice frowns. "Why?"

"So that he could kiss me, knowing I wasn't intoxicated."

"Ugh."

I shrug, trying to shake off the lingering dissatisfaction. "Whatever. I didn't even give him my name."

"It's a big school. I doubt you'll see him again," Alice says. We walk arm-in-arm, supporting each other all the way to Kelpie Hall. I lean against the wall as she fishes in her pocket for the key to the dorm. While the rooms are accessed by our fingerprints, the main doors need a key, or entry is granted from within the dorms via intercom.

"Exactly," I agree.

"And that punch... Shit. It was perfect," Alice says, kissing her fingertips.

She stumbles into the building once she manages to get the door unlocked, and we practically crawl up the stairs. I laugh and follow her into the dorm, locking the door behind me with a wave of my hand.

"Well, we're a team, and she was being an asshole."

"Damn right." Alice holds out her pinky, and I link mine with hers. "If someone comes for one of us, they come for both of us." She shakes our hands before releasing me, the pact made.

Alice smiles sleepily, the alcohol obviously tugging at her sleep receptors. She yawns widely and salutes me before turning on her heel to shuffle to her room.

I grab a glass of water and peek in at Alice. She is already completely passed out on her bed, fully clothed. I pull her bedroom door closed before going to my room. I look at my still unpacked bag and the empty shell of my room. *Is this any more like home than the last place I dwelled in?*

I grab my still-mostly unpacked bag and pull out a small box. I open it and place it on my bedside table. Inside is a tiny sprig of wood with one single flower on it. A flower that's never wilted, living without water, sun, or even air, barely clinging to life for years. Just like me, barely living, barely breathing, barely existing.

It is the last piece of my home. My true home, and one I never knew.

I sigh, brushing my finger down the immortal sprig before curling up on my side and propping up the box so I can look at it. A single tear slides down my cheek. I only have a moment to think of my lost home before I fall into the abyss of sleep.

"Summer! We have to get ready!" Alice beats on the wall that separates our rooms, and my head pounds in response. The alcohol from last night churns in my stomach and regret crawls through me, dragging nausea in its wake. I groan, pressing my face into my pillow, trying to get control of my stomach before the contents of it end up on my floor. It must be that stupid Eden Mist. I've never been this hungover from regular alcohol.

Slowly, I open my eyes, and the room spins. Apparently, not only am I hungover, but simultaneously still drunk. Fucking perfect. I sit up and wait for my vision to stop kaleidoscoping the room before I risk stumbling through to the bathroom.

I press my back against the cold tile of the shower and allow myself to slide to the floor. Keeping my eyes closed is definitely the better option. Unfortunately, I didn't explore my ensuite last night and my impaired sight is needed to turn the shower on. The first spray of water is freezing, but my broken body barely jolts beneath it. I nearly sob in relief when it starts to get warmer.

The shower does wonders for my hangover, and I'm able to function enough to recall a rune to lessen the effects even more.

Runes have always come naturally to me. When I was a child living in the wrong realm, they used to get me into enormous trouble with my caretaker. She would admonish me for anything remotely to do with magic. Most, I was able to conceal, to hide within myself, accepting that it was somehow wrong. Yet, it's always been so potent in my life. They come into my mind when I need them most, and when they're so clear in my head, it's difficult to ignore the impulse to draw them. I used to have notebooks and diaries full of them littered around my caretaker's home, but without a key ingredient, runes are just symbols. They require magic to power them.

I grab a small blade from my toiletry bag and slice my finger. The sting is so familiar to me now that I barely feel it. Something within me always seems to wake at the small bite of pain. I wipe the mirror clear of condensation and then turn my back to it, slowly drawing the swooping rune of hydration onto my left shoulder. The long line curls at both ends and is tied with a sweeping slash across the middle. The rune is so clear to me that I don't have to watch as I draw it, though I do if only to appreciate how my fingers masterfully glide the blood over my skin.

The rune glows faintly before my skin absorbs the blood, leaving only the shimmer of its shape. I flex my shoulder, and the light catches on the iridescent mark. This is a temporary rune and only lasts a few hours. There are some runes on my body that are much longer lasting, but all of them are the same glittering iridescent shade.

The rune's effects are immediate, and I can brush my teeth without the fear of vomiting. I walk back to my bedroom and notice that the wardrobe doors have a note attached to them. I pull it off, reading it.

*Miss Tuatha De Daanan,*
*Avalon has a strict uniform policy, and we have provided all you need. Please wear as per*
*the school rules included in your information packet.*
*Regards,*
*Ms Dune, School Administrator*

I lift an eyebrow, dread filling me at what I might find behind the doors. Will the uniform be ugly? Shapeless? Oh fuck. What if it is brown?

Taking a deep breath, I open the door and am surprised to find it full of immaculate black clothing. Thank the gods. I sift through them, looking at the options, and I am impressed to note that they all seem perfectly tailored to me. It's probably an enchantment of some kind. I open the jacket, and as I suspected, find the runes embroidered along the hem with blood string. Someone drenched the thread in their blood and then used it to create the runes. Based on the black stitching, it must be a sorcerer.

Embroidered on the left breast of the jacket is the Avalon insignia. This isn't like the one the tour guide had on her shirt. This is much more akin to what I expected from such a prestigious university. The bordering circle proudly displays the school's motto, FEAR FIRE FURY. Within the circle is an intricate-looking *A* formed of hard lines and loopy swoops. Beneath is what looks like an unrolled scroll with the words *To KNOW IS NOT ENOUGH* written on it.

I pull out a pleated skirt and a black shirt. The black and silver tie I choose matches the stitches on the skirt and jacket. After I pull on my underwear, I slip the skirt on first and study my reflection in the mirror. It is short, very fucking short, but it's also the nicest skirt I've ever owned in both quality and design. I try the black shirt on and tuck it in, surprised again that it fits so perfectly. Instead of wearing the tie up at my throat, I decide to let it hang midway down my chest. The tailored jacket is cut tight to my form, the decorative silver stitching flickering along the edges.

Alice walks into my room, having opted for a pair of fitted black slacks and a black shirt. She's not wearing the jacket, but it is hanging over her arm. "I mean, I know why we have to wear them, but... uniforms are weird."

"Are there any rules about shoes?" I ask, glancing at her.

She shrugs and points to her black boots. "I'm just wearing these."

I decide to wear something similar for my first day. The skirt is enough, and I do not want to draw more attention to myself by wearing heels. I step in front of the mirror and tilt my head. Something isn't quite right. I roll the waistband of the skirt, making it even shorter, and then nod at my reflection before pulling on socks and my baseball boots.

"You're making it shorter?" Alice snorts.

"Why not?" My lips twitch.

As we leave the dorm, it's clear that news of our *fun* last night has flooded the campus. Several people stop to stare at us, whispering incoherently. People gawking at me is nothing new. At my last school, everyone knew there was something different about me, but it was my non-mortal nature that they suspected there.

"Coffee, please. Large," I order when we reach the coffee cart in the middle of the quad.

"Make that two," Alice adds, scrolling through her phone. "Oh, looks like somebody uploaded pictures of the fight last night."

She turns her phone so I can see a post from an account called *@TheOtherTwin*. The picture shows me punching the shifter bitch. The look of surprise on her face is incredible.

"Oh, my gods!" I gasp, grabbing her phone to look at it. "I looked so hot last night. You did not hype me up enough."

Alice snorts and pulls me closer, lifting her phone to take a selfie. I wink in the picture, pouting a little as Alice laughs. It occurs to me that I have arrived at a crossroads. I can hide away as I've always done or embrace this a little, leaning fully into it. If my time at Avalon is temporary, I may as well enjoy myself, right?

"What are you going to caption it?" I ask, glancing at her phone over her shoulder.

**@KillerLegosi.** *We survived, bitchesss*

I laugh and grab our coffees from the barista.

"What's your username? I'll tag you."

"Oh. I don't think I have that," I say, frowning at her phone. I've never heard of *Nexus* before. It looks kind of like the socials from my previous realm, but... more.

"Oh, my fucking gods! You've been deprived!" Alice shrieks. "We're making you one right now." She grabs my phone and downloads the app before making a profile for me. Her thumbs practically blur as she types out my bio.

She swaps my phone for her coffee, and I scroll through the profile she's made for me.

"Okay, I just need to tag *@RaysofSummer*."

The second Alice tags me in the post, my phone blows up with notifications as people follow me, obviously intrigued by the new weirdo who causes fights at the hottest party of the night.

"I can't believe I'm friends with someone who pouts in photos." Alice nudges me, rolling her eyes.

I look at the photo. "What? It's good!"

She mimics my artful pout. "Is this how you practice it?"

I roll my eyes, nudging her. "You're an asshole."

"You know, the other benefit to having *Nexus* is that you can access your class schedule on the app. The whole school uses it, and there's a portal for official school stuff only. Rumor is it started as a way to get school information to students fast, but eventually, it spiraled into a more social networking thing. And it's not just Avalon exclusive anymore. People from all over the realms use it."

I scroll through the app and pull up my schedule. My interest piques when I notice that my first class is Realms 100, and Alice is in it as well. The last book I read was on Realms, specifically this one. Alice is decidedly less enthused about the idea of going to class, and when we arrive, she tugs me to the back row of the classroom. I pull out my notebook, so ready to learn and excited to be in a place that reveres knowledge and hands it out.

A handsome sorcerer steps forward. Fuck, are they all this gorgeous? Though this one is far less intimidating than the headmaster. I am unsure if there is anyone who could top him on that.

"Welcome to Realms 100, first years. My name is Professor Ambrose, Sorcerer First Class. As part of this course, we will be analyzing each of the realms that no doubt many of you have either come from or visited. As part of your grade for this course, you will be asked to do a final project on a randomly assigned realm and its history."

The classroom door opens, and the angel from last night, the one who I made out with, the one who tried to force-feed me a *fucking* sandwich, walks into the room.

"Ah, Mr. Morningstar, thank you for joining us," Professor Ambrose greets him. "Mr. Morningstar will be assisting me today prior to his classes commencing tomorrow."

Morningstar? Why is that name so familiar? I realize why the second the door closes. Connor walks into the room and sits next to the professor. I slouch lower into my chair.

Alice looks at me, her eyes wide as she finally puts a face to the name. "Oh, shit," she whispers loudly, drawing everyone's attention in the otherwise quiet room.

Connor meets my gaze, and his lips pull into the most handsome, shit-eating grin I've ever seen.

*Fuck me.*

# 6

## SUMMER

*Jahl*

Professor Ambrose clears his throat and gives Alice a seething look for the interruption to his class. She mouths a silent apology. I glare at her, doing everything to avoid looking at the blond bombshell angel whose gaze is boring into me. His grin clings to me like plastic wrap around a burn. I have to be cursed. There's no other explanation. In a school as big as this one, how could I be *this* unlucky?

"As I was saying, your final project will be a paper on your assigned realm. I expect at least five thousand words on the subject, along with a critical analysis of the realm's leadership, the languages spoken, and information on the integral nexus points of the realm. As part of the project, you will also be asked to interview a native of the assigned realm. If you pull one of the Lost Realms, you will interview me or another faculty member."

I try to take notes, but I'm so on edge. Of course, I've had encounters with previous flings before, and the angel and I hadn't done anything more than a little kissing. So why do I want to crawl into a hole and never come out right now?

"As you are aware, there are thousands of realms, some so hostile that only those born there can dwell in them. However, within this course, we will mainly look into the realms closer to home, the ones most relevant to bright young persons such as yourselves. As you know, Avalon is surrounded by eleven main realms, and from there, they branch into many more. The second semester will focus on more hostile outer realms and delve into the beings that thrive in such conditions."

Fuck, I focused so much on learning about *this* realm. I don't know much about the others at all. I *hated* not knowing things.

"Can anyone name one of the Locked Realms?" Professor Ambrose asks.

Another angel at the front of the class raises his hand and says shyly, "Eden."

Professor Ambrose nods, smiling, "Ah, yes, Luke, another Morningstar in my class." Connor beams at what I can only assume is his younger brother. I don't recognize him from the party, but I was pretty drunk. "Let's hope you cause less trouble than the previous two. Now, Mr. Morningstar, can you tell the class what a Locked Realm is?"

Luke nods. "A Locked Realm is inaccessible unless you have been granted access or are brought by someone who has access."

Professor Ambrose nods. "Very good. This could be because a society has chosen to remain closed for security. Eden is closed due to their impressive military. The Legions are elite and consist of thousands of angels. Can anyone name another?"

I raise my hand, recalling one I'd read about recently.

"Yes?"

"Hell?"

Professor Ambrose nods, seeming impressed. "Ah yes, the more fiery of the Locked Realms. Does anyone know why Hell is a closed realm?"

"Cause demons are assholes," a shifter pipes up.

Professor Ambrose shoots him a dark look. "Incorrect, Mr. Henderson." He narrows his eyes at the dark-haired shifter, who wisely decides to shut his mouth. "Hell is closed as the demons require a solace where they can enjoy their depravity from time to time. Believe it or not, this is for the benefit of all. Many species here have similar realms to call home, often called a source realm. Any others?"

Alice raises her hand. "Drăculea."

"Correct, Ms. Legosi. Your own realm is a Locked Realm, and it has been for millennia. Only very recently, with the death of your progenitor, have beings like yourself been allowed to leave the realm."

Alice sighs and sits back in her seat. She hisses under her breath so only I can hear, "And by beings, you mean *women*."

"Mr. Morningstar?" Professor Ambrose hands Connor a hat with many small pieces of paper. "Will you hand these out?"

Connor stands and takes the hat from the professor, walking along the row of desks. Each student picks a sliver of paper. There are gasps of excitement and moans of despair as people react to the realms they have selected. As he makes his way to me, my hair stands on the back of my neck, my stomach knotting in dread. He leans down, his eyes level with mine, that maddening smirk pulling at his lips.

"Hello, mystery girl," he murmurs smugly.

I look up at him and select a slip of paper. I drag my gaze away from him, and suddenly, the apprehension about talking to Connor is completely eclipsed by the writing on the crisp piece of paper in my hand. It's one word, softly curling out, the six letters taunting me.

*Faerie.*

"Mr. Morningstar, have you handed them all out?"

Connor straightens and glances back at the professor. "Yes, professor," he replies, returning to the front of the room.

Alice nudges me, whispering, "What did you get?"

My gaze remains locked on the word. If I thought my stomach was in knots before, it's nothing compared to how it twists now.

"Summer?"

I glance at Alice, closing the slip of paper into my fist. "Oh, nowhere exciting."

The second class ends, I launch up and practically run to the front of the class.

"Professor Ambrose?" I ask, even as he directs the rest of the class.

"Everyone, please remember to collect the course syllabus from Mr. Morningstar as you leave!" He glances at me. "Yes, Ms..."

"Summer. I'm Summer."

"Ah yes, Ms. Tuatha De Daanan, I should have known. How can I help you?"

"I need to change my realm for the project, professor, you see—"

"Unfortunately, the picks are final, Ms. Tuatha De Daanan." Professor Ambrose holds out his hand to see which realm I chose.

I place the slip of paper in his hand. "But you see, professor, there are extenuating circumstances—"

"Ah, the great Lost Realm of Faerie! I understand why that would be difficult for you, Ms. Tuatha De Daanan, but you selected this subject for a reason, and therefore, it stands."

"But—"

"I understand you're hesitant to do your source realm, but given the fact you, like the other fae students, have never stepped foot in the realm, the previous rule does not apply. You will interview me, given that the only beings who have visited Faerie are those who are attendants of the king and other faculty."

*The king.* He means the King of Fae. Dread shoots down my spine.

I close my mouth and take the paper back from him, looking away as I shove it into my bag. "Thank you, sir."

I turn to leave the class and curse under my breath. Connor is still standing there, waiting for me. He has the course syllabus in his hand, and his lips are pulled into a bright smile.

Alice is waiting for me beside the door. Her eyes are darting around, and she is obviously planning for our great escape. Connor anticipates this and moves to block the door, handing a syllabus to Alice first and then one out to me as I approach. He holds on to the top of the paper as I reach for it.

"Thanks," I grumble, tugging on the paper and waiting for him to move.

Connor doesn't release the other half of the paper, so I slowly lift my gaze to meet his.

"What are the chances?" He grins, his eyes bright and joyful.

"Yeah. Later, angel boy." I brush past him and leave the room, Alice hustling behind me.

"See you later, mystery girl," Connor calls after me, amusement lacing his voice.

"Your luck is like... curse-worthy," Alice says, linking my arm through her.

"Whatever, we only made out like a little bit."

"Only a little." She snickers. "Are you going to make out again?"

"No," I growl, stalking toward our next class. For some reason, even the short make out session last night bordered on too intimate for comfort. I hurry into the classroom and sit down. Relief at being free of Connor washes over me, entwining with the excitement that my next class is Runes 100.

"Why not?" Alice asks, flopping into the seat next to me.

I pull out my phone, sifting through the thousands of notifications. "Because I don't date, and I don't backslide." I turn off the notifications. "Plus, he tried to feed me a sandwich."

Alice laughs. "You're really upset about that sandwich."

"I looked hot as fuck. I was sitting on a counter, we were making out, and his first thought was, *Oh, I should make her eat carbs.*"

Alice laughs again. "Here lies Summer Tuatha De Daanan, who never forgot the guy who tried to give her a sandwich mid-make-out."

I roll my eyes but am saved from the conversation by the professor's arrival. She is a short lady with bobbed red hair. "Hello, hello! My name is Professor Brooks, and I will be guiding you through your first semester of the intriguing world of Ancient Runes. Runes are vital to our magic. They are conduits that arcane beings have used since the beginning of time to channel the raw arcane ability that exists inside us. I understand we have different levels of knowledge within the class, but I'm sure that everyone has used at least rudimentary runes that make day-to-day life a little easier."

Professor Brooks waves her hand toward her desk. All the papers scattered across it flutter and arrange themselves into neat little piles of their own accord. The professor points to a rune on her neck that vanishes as she spends its energy for the small task.

I smile, taking notes. Runes, even the small rudimentary ones I've experimented with, have always felt natural to me, and I can't wait to learn more. I am nearly giddy with excitement. Here, I will learn to understand more words of power, words of knowledge, and words of magic. I need more power. I crave it.

"So the word rune, from the Latin *runa* and the Old Norse *rún*, is a group of ancient sublanguages used since time began. The first documented runic language was created by the fae Tiana. She created runes when they came to her in a dream, and she began speaking in a language so ancient the name is long lost. Their power was discovered purely by chance when Tiana was attacked within the deep forests of the lost realm of Faerie. Desperate to survive, she drew the rune on her arm in her blood. Legend says that her whole body glowed, shattering the gloom of twilight. The rune drawn upon her skin protected her from harm, obliterating her attacker. And most of the forest. The fae have always had a natural penchant for runic knowledge and creation. The skill has become almost hereditary among the fae, and throughout the centuries, almost every species has become adept. Beings of each realm have adjusted the concept to their own source language, but the term rune remains."

My fingers freeze mid-word. Is that why I am so attuned to runes and why they come to me so naturally? Just because I'm a fucking fae? My pen cracks in my hand, and I barely stop myself from breaking it.

"I should add that fae and sorcerers alike both have an advantage when using runes as they are not limited by their source language. In other words, if they know the rune, they are able to use the rune. This is different for other species, who are limited to the runes of their ancestral realm. Some runic languages are more proficient at certain tasks than others. If you want to cast a powerful elemental spell, it is best to use Ancient Greek or Archaic Latin. But if you want to cast powerful wards, Daoine Sith is your best bet."

Daoine Sith, the language of Faerie.

The professor continues, "I would like to start the lesson by having you copy out this literature on rune history and the structure of a rune, and then I will give out assignments for the end of the week. Before the end of the week, you'll need to pick your first school-approved implement." Professor Brooks lifts her glasses, drawing my attention to the sharp point on the very edge of the frames. "The implement is a very intimate choice to the rune caster, so pick with caution. Of course, shifters and beings with claws may use their natural advantage for this assignment. I want all of you to consider the reason for the implement. Without the pure arcane magic that flows through all of us, drawing a rune is no more than a symbol."

Professor Brooks slices the tip of her finger on the sharp corner of her glasses. Rolling up her sleeve, she draws a rune on the inside of her wrist. The blood darkens until it turns black, the spell now stored in her skin and ready to be summoned.

"And as you advance, you'll learn the difference between single runes and the far more complex runic circles." With a wave of her hand, her power fluctuates, and a glowing circle bursts into existence in front of her fingers. The runes it contains detail the more complex spell she'd stored somewhere on her skin. "Runes are only limited by the caster's knowledge of the language. In the world of the arcane, it is not might that will win every battle, but the one with the greatest knowledge of the runic languages. In future years, we will explore spell wheels and the best tactical ways to store and use them in battle, but that is far more advanced."

Alice groans at the assignment that's just popped up on our phones. "Fuck. I hate languages. Can't we make a new way to cast that doesn't require so much work?"

"They're really basic ones. I'm sure you'll do great," I assure her, but she throws me a skeptical look.

"So this angel..." Alice starts, not so subtly changing the subject.

It's my turn to groan and roll my eyes. "You know, you made out with someone at that party too, and I'm not giving you shit about it."

Alice looks at me innocently and holds up her hands. "Hey, I was just going to offer to kill him and make you a *divine-ly* good sandwich."

I groan again but can't hold back a laugh as I say, "I'll leave the consumption of human products to you. Thanks, though."

She snickers. "So cantina for lunch?"

"Yes, I'm starving."

The cafeteria is packed, and the noise of all the students chatting is almost deafening when we first enter the room. I pause just inside, trying to adjust as I look around for a table.

"Okay, we need to stake our claim. Where we sit for lunch means everything." Alice grabs my hand and tugs me toward a free table.

"Claim?"

"A table. This is now ours," she says, slapping her hand down against the solid wood. "For the whole time we're at Avalon, this is where we will sit."

"I don't know, Alice. That seems like a lot of commitment for the first day." I sit on the bench, plopping my bag next to me.

Alice laughs. "Oh, wow, you're even commitment-phobic when it comes to lunch arrangements. You've got it *bad*."

"You know what? This table is perfect. I can't wait to sit here every day at lunch, five days a week, for the next four years."

"That's the spirit," a tall brunette girl says as she approaches the table. She's about to sit down when Alice hisses at her. The girl jumps back and gives Alice a horrified glare before hurrying away.

"I may be a commitment-phobe, but you are a possessive queen," I say, standing up. "I'm going to get some food. You want blood?"

Alice looks up at me, and I see the flash of vulnerability mixed with surprise. "You'd... get me blood?"

"I mean, yeah. It's in the fridge right over there, and I'm going to walk right by it." Why is she looking at me like that? Is there some social taboo about getting a vampire blood?

Alice's cheeks reddened a little. "You don't think it's gross?"

I blink again. "No. I don't."

Alice's eyes gleam with relief. "Thanks. Can you get me some of the AB mortal stuff? I doubt the school offers the spiced stuff I love."

I nod, completely unfazed, and make my way across the room to get lunch for us.

# 7

## SUMMER

*Cai*

"Hello again, mystery girl."

My whole body groans at the sound of his voice. I thought this school was supposed to be big. How is it that I have run into this guy not once but *twice* in three hours? I glance at him dismissively before returning my attention to the salad bar. That look has shriveled men's egos in the past. This dude would be no different. I add some lettuce to my bowl and move down the bar to find the tomatoes. Angel boy follows me, relaxed, at ease, and undeterred.

"You're everywhere, huh?" I pile some chicken and croutons onto my salad and place it on the tray. Connor swoops in and picks up my tray, carrying it for me.

"I mean, I do go to school here."

I put a hand on my hip, quirking a sardonic brow. "Do you offer this service to all the freshmen? Or is it just the ones you make out with?"

His smile brightens, almost blinding me. I hate how handsome I find his stupid, cheerful face. "Nope, just you."

"I feel so honored." I try to grab the tray back, but Connor dodges me. He shifts it easily out of my reach and turns on his heel, walking away toward our table.

I growl and stalk after him, praying to every god that Alice hisses at him and scares him away. It's worked on everyone else. I blink in disbelief when Connor gives Alice a dazzling smile and sits down at the table. In response, she plucks the carton of blood from the tray. She glances at me and shrugs, and I don't even try to hold back my eye roll. I sit beside Alice, leaving as much space as possible between Connor and me.

"So, how's your first day going?" Connor smiles at me, and I want to slap him.

How can he be so immune to my fuck off face? It's sent men cowering before. Instead, he almost appears to enjoy it.

"Don't you have like... friends or whatever?" I wave my hand dismissively, spearing lettuce onto my fork a little too aggressively.

His smile only widens. "Yep, tons." Connor waves toward another table crowded with people. They are all watching us, and I recognize a few from the party, including his brothers. Several whistle at him, cheering him on, and I bristle. *I am not some prize to be won, dick.*

"Go get her, Con!" one of them hollers.

Connor turns back to look at me, his blond hair falling over his eyes. "Plus, being student body president doesn't hurt either."

I widen my eyes and gasp, clapping excitedly. "No way! Really? *You* are *the* student body president?"

Alice snorts beside me, sipping on her blood. Her eyes ping between us, watching the show.

Connor snickers. "Oh, yeah. My extra-curricular list would shock you."

"Oh my gosh, so popular and busy! Your friends look so cool, too." I drop my smile and narrow my eyes at him. "Go away."

"Yeah, we're not... *group* activity people," Alice says, the distaste clear in her tone. She takes another deep drink from the carton of blood before deliberately flashing her fangs and licking her lips, painting them red. What happened to my territorial vampire? Why isn't she hissing at this guy? She hissed at someone who had simply walked too close to me earlier.

Connor's smile only grows, his teeth blinding against his tawny skin. "Wow, someone's prickly." He scoots closer to me, pressing his thigh against mine and lowering his voice. "I didn't have anything to do with throwing you out. That was my brother."

I spear a crouton a little harder than I meant to, and it shatters beneath my fork.

He moves in closer, his breath brushing against my ear. "Are you going to tell me your name now?"

"No."

"Why?"

I keep my eyes on my salad, though I can hear the pout in his voice. I can even picture it on his stupid, perfect face if I try. I turn to face him. Irritation prickles beneath my skin, but it is mixed with something similar to admiration at his relentlessness. "Wow. You will just not take the hint."

He raises a brow, the picture of innocence. "Which hint would that be?"

I have to bite back my smile and train my face into an expression of irritation. "Go. Away."

"Tell me your name."

I stand up. "Bye." I nod at Alice before turning away from him and walking toward the exit.

"Tuatha De Daanan," he calls, his deep voice seeming to carry over the other conversations in the cafeteria. I freeze and turn to face him, narrowing my eyes. How had he figured out my name already? Who told him? His gaze remains locked on me as he stands up and strides toward me with unhurried grace. I'm not sure I've ever met anyone so sure of themselves. There's something extremely attractive about it.

Alice stands up and moves closer, watching us raptly, hungry for the drama.

"How did you figure out my name?" I ask, lifting an eyebrow and putting my hands on my hips.

He stops just a breath away, so close his cloud and citrus scent washes over me. I have to crane my neck to look up at him, and I hate that he's so much taller than me. Dick. It's just another absurdly attractive quality. I've always been extremely into big guys.

Connor slowly lifts his hand and pushes a lock of my hair behind my ear, his strong fingers lightly tracing the tip of my ear. "I didn't, but these tell me exactly what your last name is. Plus, Ambrose said it in class this morning. There's a game on Friday. Be my date to the after party?"

"No," I say. Batting his hand away, I lift my chin and narrow my eyes. I would rather die than let him know this might be working on me.

"Why not?" His lips quirk into that knowing grin. He expected that answer, even maybe hoped for it. He's enjoying the chase. No doubt it's normally easy for him with those panty-dropping dimples. Good luck cornering me, angel boy. I've been running from bigger and badder than you for a long time.

"Bye, angel," I say and turn away. Alice hurries to catch up, linking arms with me as we leave the cantina.

"Gods, you want to fuck him so *bad*."

"W-What? No, I don't!" I sputter.

"Please. Your eyes are practically black, and," Alice sniffs at me, "I can smell your pheromones."

"Stop. No, you can't." Fuck, can she?

Alice snorts. "So, you don't want to ride him into the sunset and wave at the passerbys?"

"That's exactly what I'm saying." I'm saved from defending my cooch's extremely tattered honor as we arrive at class and take our seats, though Alice keeps throwing me knowing looks and occasionally crude hand signals.

"Welcome to Intro to Species. I am Professor Draco, and I will be your instructor throughout the year." I am once again taken aback by how handsome he is. His face is angular and attractive, and you can tell he's honed his body over the years. "It's nice to see such a variety of species this year. I look forward to getting to know you all.

Next year, you will be given the option to specialize in a particular species if you so choose. For example, there are Celestial Studies for those wishing to study the Heavenly Host or Infernal Studies if you wish to study those they war with. My specialty is Shifter Studies, those like myself who can change into a different creature. I would love to welcome you into my advanced classes in the future."

I pull out my textbook on shifters and leaf through it, trying to identify the type of shifter Professor Draco is. There are so many possibilities. He could be a wolf shifter, but he doesn't have the same untamed energy I remembered from the few I'd met. Tiger? It could be. I've never met one of those. But he said *creature*, not an animal.

"Ah, we have an enthusiast in the class!" I snap my gaze up, noticing that everyone is looking at me. Professor Draco smiles at me.

"Oh, sorry, professor, I'm just fascinated with shifters and the different types."

"Please don't apologize for enjoying my subject, Ms..."

"Tuatha De Daanan."

He smiles kindly. "Right. I would like everyone to pair up and research the other species. Try to partner with someone of a different species, but I'm aware this particular class has a majority of sorcerers."

Much to her relief, I quickly grab Alice as my partner, and we spend the next hour researching various things about each other. At the end of the class, we hand in our findings. Professor Draco gives me a searching look, and our gazes lock, his golden eyes mesmerizing. It makes me feel like he's learning more about me than I want him to, and I almost take a step back. My instincts scream at me, but it's not what I sense when the headmaster is present. It's not dread or terror. It's *reverence*. After a long moment, he smiles and nods as if agreeing to something I said.

Alice nudges me, and I shake my head. She tugs me toward the door. Yet even as we leave the classroom, I can feel Professor Draco's gaze boring into my back, his golden eyes piercing through me like a blade.

# 8

## SUMMER

*Hahl*

After classes, I drag Alice to the library very much against her will. As soon as we are inside, she claims an empty table and pulls out her phone, adamantly refusing to explore the stacks with me.

The books call to me, and I scarcely know where to begin. I wander down the dimly lit aisles, brushing my fingers along the leather-bound spines of the books. Each conveys a slightly different feel based on how widely they have been read. As I turn the corner, I notice a tall figure browsing a book. He looks familiar, but only when I glimpse the halo on his wrist does recognition spark. My memories of the night before are a little hazy, but this is one of Connor's brothers. The tall, dark, broody one named Rafe.

I make my way along the aisle, not necessarily toward him, but continuing my perusal of the library's offerings. He doesn't seem to notice me as I pass behind him. Interested in what he is reading so intently, I sneak a look at the title of the book he is holding.

"Demonology?" I whisper, the question slipping from my lips.

He slams the book closed and flicks me an irritated look over his shoulder. While he is a darker version of his brothers, there is still a strong familial resemblance. The sparkle always present in Connor's blue eyes is absent in Rafe's, but they are just a shade darker and the same shape. He shares the same bronzed skin and strong jawline as his brothers.

"Do you mind?" he snaps at me.

I quirk a brow at him. "You're Connor's brother, right?"

He glares at me. "One of."

"And why is a Morningstar angel reading a book about demonology? Especially one written from a positive perspective. Aren't demons your natural enemies?"

"Don't you know the best way to defeat an enemy is to know them?" he says, his tone mocking. "And my name is Rafe. I will not just be known as *Connor's brother.*"

"I'd tell you my name, but I don't want your beloved brother to know, and I'm guessing you'd snitch," I say, leaning against the bookshelf beside him.

Rafe rolls his eyes. "Don't assume to know anything about me," he says, snapping the book closed and pushing past me.

I watch him round the end of the row and disappear. I shrug and continue to wander the stacks for a while before circling back around to meet Alice at the table. A male stands beside her, his hand on the back of one of the chairs. Alice hisses at him and shows him her fangs, her eyes tinged with red. I quirk a brow and hurry over, not wanting bloodshed in the library. It might get on the books.

"Everything all right?"

"This chode is trying to sit with us," Alice growls.

"Brett," he says, holding out a hand. "I was asking if I could sit since all the other tables are full. Your friend seems to hate that idea, though."

"Go die, shifter scum," Alice hisses.

Brett's eyes turn a predatory feline yellow. "I have no issue with your kind. Avalon is a safe haven. If you want to carry over millennia-long prejudices, that's on you."

I wiggle between them and sit down. "It's just a seat, Alice. You don't have to marry him."

Alice recoils and turns so she's facing away from him. Brett drops his hand. His cheeks flush in embarrassment from the spurned introduction, but he rounds the table and sits across from us. "So, you guys first years too?" he asks, trying to make conversation.

"Don't make me regret offering you the seat, Brett." I open the tome I found while exploring the stacks and flip through it.

Brett sinks back into his chair a little, and I can see he is starting to regret not just sitting on the floor. "Well, I'm first year," he says quietly.

Alice huffs loudly. "See? This is why you don't fucking feed the animals."

I glance at her, my lips twitching.

"I didn't know there were female vampires," he mutters, trying again despite Alice's vitriol.

I look at him over the top of my book. "You're taking your life in your hands here, but okay. Yes, we're first years. Yes, I'm a weird fae. And yes, she's a murderous vampire."

Brett blinks, regarding us both with newfound wariness. "Cool," he says simply and pulls out a stack of textbooks.

Despite not opening a book, Alice begs for a reprieve after several hours of studying. She had continued to make snarky comments and even occasionally hissed at Brett, but he still waves a friendly goodbye as we leave the library. There is something admirable about his persistent cheerfulness and the way he's still not taken the hint. Or maybe he's a moron. Either way, I kind of respect him more for surviving our study session. Alice and my similarities must end when it comes to the pursuit of knowledge. She hadn't been deprived of books like I had, so they aren't treasures to her.

Alice and I walk to the edge of the campus, heading for the pizza parlor in Camelot, the town just outside the gate of Avalon. From what I had read of this realm, Camelot is the city that connects the other schools of the realm. At one time, there was only Avalon University, but eventually, other colleges were established. There are now seven in total, with Avalon being the oldest and most prestigious.

"Apparently, the uniforms have built-in glamors. Once we're outside the wards, anything identifying us as Avalon students vanishes. Cool, huh?" Alice says as we reach the gate.

My brows furrow, watching as other students meet up and head off campus into Camelot. "Why would it matter if this is a realm full of magic wielders?"

Alice shrugs. "With all the other nearby schools, I'm guessing they just want us all to blend in. Maybe there are those bitter that they didn't get in, and they want to maintain the peace."

I nod thoughtfully. Just as Alice said, our uniforms change as we pass through the gate. My skirt remains a skirt, and Alice's pants remain pants, but any identifying school markings blend into nothing. The perfect pleats of my skirt smooth out, the simple black fabric now hugging my ass and thighs tightly.

Alice looks down as her slacks turn into a pair of dark denim jeans, twisting to look at herself in them. "Stop! Look at my ass! You could bounce a coin off it. How do I keep them?"

I laugh as we follow the signs to Camelot.

The path is like something out of a storybook. Trees line one side of it, and as the sun sets, bright sparks of magic flare to life, guiding us to Camelot. They hover, forming small spheres in midair, and I marvel at them as we walk.

Alice smiles, watching me. "I sometimes forget you didn't grow up around this stuff." I glance at her as she continues to chatter. "It's funny. I've never looked at twilight orbs with wonder until I saw you watching them."

I blanch. I need to get a better handle on my reactions.

"Tell me about Drăculea. Is it like this realm?"

Alice chuckles softly. "No. It's constantly overcast. Every single day. There is no sun ever. Most vampires are required to get a sun charm to enroll here. But it's not a perfect solution. It feels like wearing a second skin on top of your own. Poor fuckers."

I tilt my head. "You don't need one?"

Alice shakes her head. "I'm... an exception." Alice points ahead at a small pizzeria. "That's the place!"

"I can't imagine a place with no sun ever," I ponder, staring at the orange glow the sunset casts against the cobbles.

"I didn't really know any different. I also grew up in a palace surrounded by a moat of blood."

I blink, trying to keep the disgust from my face. "Huh." *A moat?* That can't be where they drank from, can it? That can't be sanitary.

Alice rolls her eyes. "Yeah, the flies that gather are the worst."

A bell jingles as we walk into Kingston Pie, and I'm immediately hit by the comforting smell of rich dough and herbs. The walls are covered in checkered white, green, and red wallpaper, hung with various prints and decorations. It reminds me of a place I once saw in Gaia. I'd pressed my face to the glass from the outside, imagining the taste and how it would feel to have a full stomach.

Alice inhales deeply, scenting those in the establishment as we wait in line to order at the tall counter.

"Heads up, your favorite angel is here." She nudges me, pulling my attention from the menu.

"Rafe is here?" I ask, the broody angel taking the top spot thanks to his unpleasant demeanor and general assholeness.

I look up and lock gazes with Connor. He's sitting in a booth with his brothers, his lips curled into a mocking smile. His head tilts, and he lifts his beer in silent cheers. Like a pack of vultures, the blue eyes of his companions lock on me.

I smile sweetly and wave at him coquettishly for a moment before turning my hand and lowering all but my middle finger, flipping him off. His surprised smile turns to a frown, and the two that have to be twins openly howl with laughter. I turn away to hide the way my lips tug into a genuinely charmed smile.

Alice snickers. I pull my phone out and start to scroll through the notifications from *Nexus*. A heavy arm drapes over my shoulder, and from the way Alice hisses, I imagine she has also been trapped by one.

"Hello, you two. No hard feelings about tossing you out of the party. Technically, it was my twin, my severely less good-looking twin."

I don't look up, continuing to scroll. "Fuck off."

Alice snarls, but then, like a switch, her voice turns seductive and mesmerizing. My eyes dart up in alarm. "No hard feelings at all. So long as you don't have *any hard feelings* about this..." A flash of silver slips from her sleeve into her hand. The only warning is the hardening of her smile before she slams a dagger into the angel's gut.

He lets out a strangled groan, and I nearly stumble as he leans heavily against me. I look around at the other patrons, knowing we'll be in massive trouble if we are caught causing violence in Camelot. The schools all have an agreement regarding students fighting in the small town we all share.

Connor is suddenly at our side. He shifts his big body to hide us with his bulk and shuffles his brother and me into a nearby booth, leaving Alice to order for us. "Luke, come here for a sec?" he calls, his voice still jovial.

*Luke.* He is the Morningstar from Realms class earlier. I watch as Luke hurries toward us. He has to be the youngest. His face is more innocent, but he has the same golden hair and kind eyes as Connor. As he crashes to a stop beside his brothers, the size difference between them is apparent. He's lankier, not as filled out, and barely six feet tall. He is a cherub surrounded by warriors.

"What's happened?" Luke asks, his eyes dark with concern.

"Mind healing the moron?" Connor asks Luke, his voice filled with affection. "Zach, I'm not going to say you deserved that, but you totally did." Against my will, warmth fills me at the obvious care and love he has for his brothers.

I glance up at Connor and find his eyes laser-focused on me. Still looking at me, he pulls the dagger from his brother's abdomen and hands it to me. There's something about the way his muscles flexed when he grabbed the blade and pulled it out that makes my body respond. Stupid, hot angel.

Luke nods and slides in next to Zach. He glances around and then at me, the tawny skin of his cheeks flushing pink. "Um... can you move closer to Con? My hand will glow a little, and it'll attract attention."

I step closer to Connor but leave as much space between us as I can. "You're a healer? That's very rare." No wonder his energy was so different from his brothers'.

Connor wraps his arm around my shoulder and pulls me tighter to his side, his scent surrounding me. How can a person smell so much like clouds? I take it back. Any softness I felt toward him at his brotherly affection is gone.

"He's the pride of the family." Connor beams at Luke.

I look at his hand on my shoulder and then up at him, fluttering my lashes while my voice turns venomous. "The last Morningstar that wrapped his arm around someone got stabbed in the stomach."

Luke chuckles but masks it with a cough. His hand glows white as he lays his palm over Zach's wound. Connor smiles down at me, not moving his arm. "If you want to stab me, feel free. I'm just trying not to piss off the headmaster."

Zach winces as his wound starts to mend. "The stab was a bit much."

Alice scoffs and looks at her nails. They have darkened and lengthened into deadly claws. "I don't like to be touched."

The glow from Luke's hand dulls as the healing finishes, and I move away from Connor when the server calls out our order number. "Well, this has been fun."

Connor glares at his brother. "Zach, apologize to them."

Zach pushes Luke out of the way and slides out of the booth, looking disgruntled.

"Sorry," he says and storms back to his table, dropping down beside a brooding Rafe and his smirking twin.

"Enjoy your dinner, ladies." Connor winks at me before heading back to his table.

"Maybe I'll see you at that party on Friday night." Why did I say that? I did not want to see more of this guy. It definitely had nothing to do with the sinking feeling I experienced when he turned his back on me.

Connor pauses and looks at me over his shoulder with a raised eyebrow. "Are you going to the game before?"

"You know my name yet, Morningstar?"

He smirks. "Not yet, but I'm enjoying the mystery."

A smile plays on my lips. And I'm enjoying being chased.

He winks again. "See you soon."

I grab our order, and Alice and I leave, my stomach still fluttering.

# 9

## SUMMER

### S

*Lae*

"Why won't you tell him your name again?" Her voice lilted in a gently teasing way. She knows the answer but seems to love making me say these things out loud. How do I know these things about her? And her about me? Is this what *friendship* is like?

My lips twitch slightly. My body warms at the thought of him, and I bite my lower lip. "It's more fun watching him work to earn it."

Alice snickers. "You want him so bad."

"I do not," I growl, but it's without venom.

Alice moves closer to me, sniffing loudly. "You so do."

I swat her away, chuckling. "Stop."

Alice skips gleefully beside me. "If it helps, he wants you, too. Like so bad."

I roll my eyes, trying to ignore how my core tingles a little. A girl likes to hear that she's wanted. Sometimes it's the little things.

As we walk back through the school's boundary, our uniforms return. Alice pouts, brushing her fingers over her slacks. I can tell she's already missing the jeans, and I do not doubt that the second we're home, she will embark on some serious detective work to find out where to buy an identical pair.

We walk into our dorm, and it hits me how much this space already feels more like home than anywhere else I've ever lived. It's safe, warm, and comfortable. I feel like I could be truly accepted in this space and with this vampire I have known for such a tiny portion of my life. She's already more like family than anyone in my past.

I sit on the couch, and Alice walks to the fridge, grumbling about how the new one still hasn't arrived. She grabs a bag of blood and rips the lid off, adding a sprinkling of some herbs she'd ordered from the pizzeria and a splash of what looks like hot sauce. She gives the bag a good shake and then takes a healthy drink before nodding in acceptance and joining me on the couch.

I open the pizza box, and the smell immediately permeates the apartment. I grab a slice and take a big bite.

"Can I ask you something?" Alice asks after taking another large gulp of her blood concoction.

Instinctively, I tense. Usually, when someone asks that, it means the question will not be easy to ask or answer. I take a napkin and wipe the grease from my mouth before nodding.

Alice watches me, tilting her head slightly. "I've noticed you don't like to talk about your past." I drop my gaze, picking at the cheese on my pizza, but she continues, "It's because it's bad, right?"

I remind myself that I am safe, but I feel myself start to shut down. I fight against the need to go into protection mode and build those adamantium barriers I've perfected after decades of constructing them.

*Show me what you can do, Summer.*

I think I trust Alice. And while I am grateful that she is offering me this space, opening up about my past causes more pain than it's worth. The words flow out of me almost instinctively, and I barely register them as they pass my lips. "I don't talk about it. And I won't."

The words are sharp, impaling, harsh, and unfair. I want to scream and burst free from my skin. Suddenly, the bite of pizza I've just swallowed sits as heavy as a rock in my stomach. I can't even look at her, unable to acknowledge the hurt I've caused.

"I'm not going to push." Her voice is soft, gentle, and understanding. I lift my eyes to look at her, and I'm surprised to see no hurt there, no anger or frustration. There is only care. "It's your business, but just know you can talk to me if you want." She pauses. "And don't think I'm a dick for only talking about myself."

The tension in my shoulders eases, and my lips quirk in a half smile. Before this conversation, similar ones have always ended in hostility and harsh words about lack of trust. I lean in against Alice, trying to show her that I appreciate her in the only way I can. The words won't come, and at this moment, it is the only way I have of telling her she had done the kindest thing for me.

Alice lays her head on my shoulder. "I shouldn't have stabbed him. Right? He just took me off guard."

I snort. "Next time, stab his brother."

Alice lifts her head, jabbing me in the side. "But you *looooooooooove* him." Her phone alerts, and she grabs it from the table and opens the notification. "Oh, look, a new follower." Her smile turns catlike. "Oh, I wonder who *ConnorMorningstar* is. Probably trying to find your name." Alice clicks on his profile and quickly blocks him. "Not through me, bird brain."

I burst out laughing at the pet name. "Well, that works."

Alice tracks the profiles of his brothers. "I better block his clan, too. By the way, can we talk about their poor mother? It looks like they're all enrolled here, so they must be like," Alice counts on her fingers, frowning up at the ceiling as she calculates. "Holy fuck, some of them must be less than a year apart." She blocks Luke, Rafe, and Zane but pauses when she gets to Zach's account. Instead of pressing the block button, she selects the option to send him a direct message.

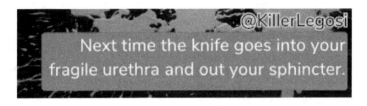

I chuckle at the message, and then Alice blocks him, too. "Yeah, their poor mom. She had five kids, five boys, five huge boys!"

Alice grimaces, squeezing her thighs together. "My box could never."

"Fuck, I know. Luke, the youngest one, seems sweet. He seems different from his brothers."

"Yeah, I've heard that healing is a super rare angelic ability."

"Well, Rafe is still my favorite."

Alice snickers. "Because he hates you?"

I shrug. "He's all angry and broody. Definitely my type."

Alice pouts, sticking out her lip. "But I'm your angry friend."

I laugh. "You are unhinged. Rafe is *I don't give a fuck* angry." I take another bite of my pizza, my stomach having finally settled. "You're coming to the game with me on Friday, right?"

"Well, duh." She smirks wickedly. "Want to piss off lover boy?"

I quirk a brow, intrigued. "What do you have in mind?"

Alice lets out the most malevolent cackle I've ever heard, and it only makes me appreciate her more. "I'm thinking we get some jerseys to support..." she pauses for obvious dramatic effect, "the opposite team."

I grin. "Abso-fucking-lutely."

Alice claps her hands together excitedly and grabs her phone. She starts researching the game and stores where we can buy custom jerseys.

"We should get them big and wear them as cocktail dresses."

Alice gives another maniacal laugh, typing away. "Connor is the captain of the Avalon team."

"Okay, I have so many ideas. We need the name of the captain of the opposing team. I'm going to write it on my cheeks."

"There are so many articles about the rivalry between the two schools. This is going to be so fucking delicious." Her thumbs are a blur as she types into her phone, her eyes darting over the screen. "We're playing Irachmoor Academy. Their team captain is Hector Montgomery."

I grimace at his name. "Is he at least hot?"

Alice pulls up a photo of him and turns the screen toward me. "Maybe in a hulking brute kind of way, I guess."

I tilt my head, considering. "I can work with that."

Alice smirks, ordering two of the jerseys in Irachmoor dark green, both with **MONTGOMERY** in large white letters on the back. "Oh, man, I can't wait to see his face."

"I doubt he'll want to go to the party with me after this." I chuckle, proud of us for thinking of such a petty and ridiculous way to get to the oldest Morningstar.

Alice holds out her hand. "I'll take that bet."

I narrow my eyes. "Five credits and... coffee for a week?"

"Done."

I shake her hand, and we both burst out laughing.

# 10

## SUMMER

*Dae*

Thanks to the absence of any hangover, getting ready for our second day is much smoother. Alice and I leave the dormitory looking much fresher than the day before. Both of us are wearing uniforms similar to what we wore the previous day, but I have opted for a white shirt instead of a black one, and rather than a tie, I've wrapped a small scarf in the school's colors around my neck. I forgo tights again today.

The sun is shining through the window, and my room is almost uncomfortably warm. I look at my selection of shoes and decide to go for a pair of heels this time. Sliding my feet into them, it's like I'm donning armor. When I face angel boy this time, I'll feel more than prepared. He may have grown up with a sword in his hand, but at the end of the day, a warrior has a moral code. A survivor has none.

Alice and I walk through the quad, and she lifts her face to the sky, closing her eyes. "This is glorious."

The sun is never something I've had to live without for long. In my old realm, the weather was cyclical, with certain times of the year colder than others. But usually, we wouldn't go more than seven days without seeing the sun. It's one of those things that can easily be taken for granted, but at the moment, I appreciate it as much as Alice.

We walk to Fenrir Hall, both of us deciding to skip the coffee before our first combat class. My stomach tightens and twists. I've never taken so much as a self-defense class, never mind partaking in actual combat. That combat is a general requirement for Avalon students is archaic. Why do I need to know how to throw a punch when I could just draw a rune?

When we step through the door, our clothes change again, this time into matching shorts and t-shirts. The clothes are easy to move in, but I frown when I notice I'm still wearing my heels. The gym is enormous and filled with various workout and sports equipment. A large male lifts heavy-looking mats, his muscles bulging under his dark amber skin. He drops them in the center of the room, keeping them pretty evenly spaced. The heavy mats slamming against the wooden floor echo in the cavernous room. A group of girls stand in the corner, watching him and giggling, and a few of the boys cross their arms over their chests, trying to flex their muscles. This is already unbearable, and it is made even worse by the fact that there are several fae in this class. I make a point not to look at them, but I can feel their eyes boring into me.

The tall man throws down the last mat and stands in front of our group. He gathers his long, midnight hair and secures it at his nape. "I'm Ike. I have taught combat at Avalon for ten years. Yes, I am trained to teach you. No, I am not a professor, so do not call me one." His nostrils flare a little as if he is scenting us. He moves his head to the side, and I see lightning flash in his dark eyes. *Thunderbird.* I thought they were a myth. "Two to a mat. Try to match up with people who are roughly the same size as yourself for this class."

I grab Alice and pull her to a mat on the other side of the room. When everyone has taken off their shoes and is standing on a mat with a partner, Ike walks through, looking at us all with a leveling stare.

"Combat has been taught at this academy since its founding, though as you can imagine, the lesson structure and techniques have changed drastically. Once, students would fight to the death in this very room."

I glance at Alice, who is smirking and nodding in approval.

"For this first year, we will be working primarily on defense and building from any knowledge you already have regarding restraint and deflection. We will use both magic and strength in these classes, but I am asking that for this first semester, while we settle into the year, none of you use your arcane powers. As you are aware, certain species have advantages in speed, stealth, strength, agility, and so on. These advantages are not to be used until after the end of term basics exams. While you are learning the basics, I want to utilize an even playing field."

Ike settles on his own mat at the front of the room. He conjures a moving mannequin and begins to go through a number of different defense moves. The mannequin attacks him, and my mind fires, analyzing the mock battle between our teacher and the mannequin.

Ike leans back as it swings, dodging its blow artfully. The mannequin's leg sweeps out to target his legs, but Ike jumps, lifting his feet toward his chest. Static zips around the room, making the hair on my neck rise. Ike launches both his feet into the dummy's chest, sending it flying into the wall with shattering force.

My eyes widen in awe. He used runes to enhance his own abilities. His kick was more powerful because he used a rune to focus his natural power.

"Right. Your turn," Ike says, the resonance of his voice pulling me from my thoughts. Nerves make my empty stomach clench, and the fascination dies inside me. "Whoever is on the left, use the moves I demonstrated to defend against the moves used by the dummy. Those on the right, watch and prepare for your turn." A dummy appears on each mat, and Alice moves out of the way.

Ike walks around the room, correcting people's stances. When he gets to me, he raises my right arm slightly and uses his foot to widen my stance. "Okay, good. Ready? Go."

The dummies all move in unison. I quickly duck to avoid the strike, but I overcompensate and lose my balance. I right myself but feel my cheeks burn. This is why I run.

Ike sighs and lowers his chin to his chest, his hands on his hips. "We have a lot of work to do. Switch."

Alice and I swap places. This time, when Ike calls for them to start, the dummies move, but fewer people fall over. Alice moves deftly, dodging the dummy's swing and countering with a blow of her own. She even manages to rip it with her claws.

"Switch," Ike calls again.

The class doesn't get much better for me, but by the end of it, I am able to remain on my feet for at least two out of the five defensive moves Ike showed us. Ike finally dismisses us, and our uniforms return. I say goodbye to Alice, my spirits lifting as I head to my next class. It's another rune class, thank the gods. This is the only class I'm doing that Alice won't be in. It's specifically for fae and sorcerers, and while I'm not overly excited about spending an hour with those two groups, the subject excites me. I found Ancient Runes to be so interesting yesterday. I cannot wait to see what the Elder Futhark runes have in store for me.

When I arrive, the class is already teeming with students, and I get some curious looks from some of the fae who are, unsurprisingly, standing in a pack. I swear, they are worse than the shifters. They drop their voices when I pass, but I keep my eyes forward and sit in a seat at the other end of the classroom.

A tall, slim woman walks into the classroom and claps her hands. Her bobbed, red hair barely moves as she walks down the middle of the classroom.

"Quiet! Quiet! I am Professor Henley. Welcome to Elder Futhark runes. Now, let's get started. We have a lot to cover today."

She walks to the blackboard and writes in an elegant script as she starts her lecture.

"Now, Elder Futhark runes, also known as Older Futhark or Old Futhark, is often described as the oldest runic language in existence. However, as I'm sure Professor Ambrose explained, we know this to be false. Though it is an old runic language, we now know the oldest and first to be that of Daoine Sith." She turns to face us again.

"For those of us able to use multiple runic languages, Elder Futhark is best utilized when attempting practical magic. For example, moving objects."

Professor Henley tilts her head, showing the Elder Futhark rune drawn on her skin just above her collar. It glows as she holds up her hand, sending her desk a foot away before pulling it back.

"This is push and pull. It can be accomplished with the more common Archaic Latin and Ancient Greek runic languages that Ambrose teaches you. But it is the utilization of each runic language combined with the being's most powerful intentions that makes the greatest of spell casters." She chuckles. "You'd never catch the headmaster using Archaic Latin or Infernal to move a desk, and that is the truth."

The class lets out a chuckle of understanding, but I barely hear. I take down every word she says, my hand flying across the page in my notebook. My brain feels alight with the prospect of learning about this language and the ways these runes differ from the ones I already know. My thirst for knowledge was something I'd never truly been able to entertain, especially in the realm I came from. In my world, the reality of the arcane world was relegated to myths and fairytales.

When I was young, my caretaker forced me to lock my power away. Later, after Torin, I repressed it myself, pushing it so deep that I could only hear the whispers of it beckoning me, a haunting echo from behind an impenetrable wall. Even so, I could never extinguish my love of runes and the magic they hold. Though, without the full use of my powers, they are never as strong or effective as they should be.

Professor Henley turns back to the blackboard and writes out the Elder Futhark alphabet along with each character's meaning in both the common tongue and a further translation into Latin.

"Once you have copied these down, I would like you to start on a 5,000-word paper on your current knowledge of runes. Include the implications of using them and the advantages of using them over base magic."

The second I finish copying the alphabet, I dive into the text she assigned for research and start taking notes. I am so engrossed that I don't notice the time, and class seems to end in a blink.

"Thank you, everyone! I am available for questions, but the papers are due by the end of class on Thursday. Until then!" Professor Henley says, dismissing us.

She waits a few moments but opens a portal when no one approaches her with questions. The rift glows brightly, the edges curling with yellow and green light. She steps into it, disappearing from view.

Alice is waiting outside my class, scrolling through her phone. She smiles when she sees me. "Ready for lunch?"

I nod. "How was your class?"

"Boring. My father insisted on me taking a class on the vampire monarchy. I think he's hoping to radicalize me, and this is his last-ditch effort to get me on his side. How was your other runes class?"

I frown, wondering what she means. There is something about her demeanor that has shifted, and I sense that she cannot say anymore about the subject without exploding into a furious rage.

"Oh! It was fascinating! We were learning about..." Alice's lips are pulled into a supportive smile, but her eyes are already glazed over with a look of soul-destroying boredom. I laugh. "Never mind."

I sigh when I notice that our table from yesterday is not empty. Connor fucking Morningstar is sitting in the exact seat I sat in yesterday, his eyes sparkling with mischief. Alice covers her mouth, and I can tell she's doing it to hide her smirk. Asshole.

We collect our food before walking to the table we've lovingly dubbed *ours*, even if Connor is sitting there. I sit at the other side of the table, intending to ignore him. Connor is immediately on his feet, rounding the table and sitting right beside me. His thigh brushes against mine as he turns his large body to face me.

Hundreds of phones start going off, the sound of the alerts filling the canteen. Alice frowns, and I look around, watching people read their screens intently. Even Connor pulls his phone from his pocket and checks it.

I open my yogurt. "Your brothers are lost without you. How can they possibly breathe without the golden brother watching over them?" I snark, eating a spoonful of peach-flavored yogurt.

Connor's deep laugh surrounds me like a blanket, and I can't help the shiver of pleasure.

"You think you got me pegged, huh?" he asks.

Connor's phone alerts again. "Shouldn't you be checking your phone to read the message from... whoever is in this thousand-person group chat you have going on?"

"Nah, it's just an alert," he replies with a shrug, not taking his eyes off me.

"Who knows? It might be one of your million friends or followers desperately needing your attention."

His lips curl into a half-smile. "The only person I want attention from is an evasive, beautiful fae."

Alice rolls her eyes so hard I can practically hear it.

"Evasive and beautiful? Who could you mean? I've heard that Landon is pretty hard to get to know. I could get you an in, though," I replied snidely.

Connor laughs again, and the sound is so full and infectious that I have to work to hold back my own. "So, are you going to be my date on Friday?"

"After I've put all this effort into setting you up with Landon? Ungrateful."

Alice cackles into her blood bag.

Connor hooks his finger under my chin and gently tilts my head up so I meet his gaze.

Oh, you smooth fucker.

"Be my date."

I find myself studying his mouth, enjoying how the bow curves. My lips tingle as if the memory of our last kiss still lingers there.

Alice slurps loudly from her blood bag, breaking me from his stupid angelic spell. I clear my throat and look away. "I'll be at the party. Maybe I'll see you there."

"I'll take that as a yes," Connor replies, confidence lacing his words.

I quirk a brow, looking up at him. "Take it as a maybe I'll bump into you and say hi before moving to talk to someone else."

Connor smiles and surprises me by stroking his fingers along my jaw before dropping his hand. "I'm taking it as a *I want to be your date, Connor. But I like being chased.*"

I roll my eyes. "Can you leave now?"

Connor winks. "Got to go. I have a meeting with the doom master."

"The doom master?" Alice asks.

Connor nods, grabbing his bag. "Headmaster Emrys."

My ears prick up a bit at the sound of his name. Once again, my stomach knots with the memory of the library and how I was almost expelled before I could even begin this journey. Unease wriggles through me, but I refuse to acknowledge the terrifying monster I sense in him, the one that calls to my own beast.

"I can see your thoughts."

I lift my gaze to Alice. "What am I thinking then, mystic Alice?"

She brings her fingers to her temples and rubs them dramatically. "Ommmmm, I see your thoughts, oh pretty little Summer. You are thinking... Ommmmm... What does angel dick taste like?"

I burst out laughing and swat at her.

Another surge of notifications fills the room, and I frown as Alice picks up her phone. "Okay, what the fuck is this alert all about?"

"It's *EverydayEmrys*," Rafe grunts as he walks past our table, heading toward the exit.

"What the fuck is *EverydayEmrys*?" Alice asks, but Rafe is already at the canteen door.

I pull my phone from my bag and search for it. Multiple results pop up, and I click on the first one. A picture of the headmaster walking through campus appears on my screen. He is holding a coffee and heading toward Ambrose Library. The accompanying post says:

*@EverydayEmrys. Spotted. Emrys heading for an afternoon reading sesh, I wonder what he's reading. What I'd do to be that coffee lid.*

Beneath the comment are hundreds of thirsty comments and some discussing plans for parties.

Alice shifts, taking the seat Connor just vacated. "I mean, they did say a cult following, but..."

"A stalker page?"

Alice nods. "I think it's also a way to avoid him if needed." She takes my phone and scrolls through the page. "Holy fuck. How far does this go back?" She hits the follow button from my account. I give her an annoyed look, but she just smiles innocently at me. "For research."

I grumble and snatch my phone back from her, stowing it in my bag.

# II

## SUMMER

*Han*

**W**ednesday and Thursday seem to pass in a blur of classes and assignments. Alice grumbled both nights about wanting to go out and did her best to pull me away from the many texts I had piled up. My thirst for knowledge is insatiable, and the books call to me, tempting me to devour the knowledge waiting inside. I hunger for the power found inside the pages of a book.

The only way to appease Alice is to remind her about the big party on Friday, and that I'll go all out with her for that. Instead of going to all the various parties alone, she lounges on my bed as I study. Instead of studying, she spends her time scrolling on her phone, making me watch videos posted on *Nexus*, and telling me all the gossip she uncovers as she explores the app.

Connor seems to have taken up permanent residence at our table. For the past two days, he has been sitting there, a wide smile on his face the second he sees me. Slowly, some of his friends and brothers have joined him. Today when Alice and I enter the cafeteria, all of his brothers are sitting with him. There really are far too many of them. Since it's game day, all but Luke are wearing school jerseys, no doubt to rile up the school pep.

Alice slides into the seat next to Rafe, throwing him a look of disappointment. "You too?"

Rafe, being an angel of few words, simply rolls his eyes and takes a bite of his burger. Alice has been trying to provoke him into a fight since Zach has taken to giving her a wide berth.

"Hey, gorgeous." Connor winks at me, that classic boyish smile pulling at his lips.

"You again?"

Zach tuts and pulls out his phone. His thumbs fly over the screen and the distinct sound of a transaction pings.

"Thanks for the credits." Zane smirks.

I lift an eyebrow at them, sitting in the only seat available which, of course, is next to Connor. "What was the bet?"

Zach grumbles, "I said you'd tell Connor to fuck off. Zane said you'd say you again?"

I shrug and smirk. "I like to change it up, you know?"

Luke chuckles, shooting Connor an apologetic look.

Connor playfully shoves his shoulder into Luke's and then turns his penetrating gaze back to me. "Have you picked out an outfit for the game? I brought an extra jersey."

Ah, the delusional hope that I'm going to just go along with this. I pop a berry into my mouth. "I'm good. I already have mine."

"Same," Alice agrees, slurping on her blood bag.

Rafe pauses in his eating and narrows his eyes, looking between Alice and me. Does the little brother sense my plans? Well, it's too late to stop them now, Rafey boy.

My lips twitch slightly, but I make sure to keep the facade of innocence around my demeanor. It's more fun if they don't suspect.

"So, Con, are you going to kill Monto-Monster today?" Zach smirks at his older brother before taking a big bite of his burger.

"No. Why do you always think I'm going to kill him?" Connor asks. There's a jingle of humor in his voice. Over the last few days, spending time with them all, it's become clear how much Connor adores his brothers, but it is certainly not softening me toward him. I'm not that weak.

"Because killing is fun!" Alice answers with a creepily cute smile on her face. There's a beat of silence around the table before everyone dismisses her comment. They've quickly adapted to her unhinged commentary.

"Don't kill him." I pick up another berry and plop it into my mouth, keeping the smirk off my face. "It would be a waste of such a hot body."

The guys go silent again, but this time their eyes lock on me one by one. I can feel the weight of their gazes resting heavily on my shoulders.

"What did you say?" Connor asks, his voice soft but with an edge of menace. Sexy. No, not sexy. Annoying.

I look at him. "The captain from Irachmoor? He's hot." I shrug, secretly pleased with myself that I've managed to get under his skin. He'd been so unfazed by me for this last week that I had started to think nothing would get him riled.

Rafe lets out a loud laugh that makes Alice jump, and the twins gape at him in surprise. Even I turn to look at him, surprised at the sound of joy coming from the most brooding Morningstar.

Connor's eyes narrow on me, and his smile remains, but turns sharp at the edges. Well, well, it looks like the golden boy act only goes so far. "You're talking about Hector Montgomery. Right?"

I nod. "Yep. Alice showed me his *Nexus* page. He's so muscly..." I trail off on the final word as if picturing the captain in my head.

Alice had taken the time to give me the basic rules regarding Infinity Slam, but I'm not sure how much of that I truly retained. Sports are not my thing.

Connor blinks, and Rafe covers his mouth, his shoulder shaking as he continues to laugh. The three other Morningstars are torn between looking at Rafe in astonishment and me in horror.

"I'm muscly." Connor crosses his arms, his muscles bulging beneath his shirt. I focus on his face, feigning an unimpressed look.

Alice bites her lip, struggling to keep a straight face.

I poke Connor's biceps and scrunch my nose. "He's definitely bigger than you."

Connor sputters, "I just...I wasn't flexing." He flexes again, his jersey straining over his impressive physique. I jab them again and shrug.

"I'm not sure that made much of a difference, shrimp."

Alice throws her head back, unleashing her cackle. Rafe stands, not looking at any of us as he leaves the cafeteria in absolute hysterics. Zach and Zane stare after him until he is out of sight before they turn back to watch Connor and me standing off.

"You're trying to make me mad," Connor says, glaring at me.

I place my hand on my chest and widen my eyes, sticking my lower lip out in an artful pout. "Me?"

Connor gently but firmly grasps my chin, tilting my head up. "Yes, you."

That hold does something to me, something I don't like. Somehow, it has made it impossible for me to look away from his lips.

"Manhandling me, Morningstar?"

Connor leans in slightly, his mouth a breath away from mine. From the corner of my eye, I see Zach and Zane grinning like lunatics. "You trying to make me angry, Tuatha De Daanan?"

I quirk an eyebrow. "Know my first name yet?"

"If I say yes, do I get a kiss?" Connor asks, and my stomach flutters.

I bite back a moan. Gods, have his lips always been so plump and perfect?

"I'll make you a deal, Morningstar."

He leans in closer, and his scent wraps around me. "Oh?"

"I will give you *one* kiss when you figure out my name, but you should choose your timing wisely."

His breath feathers over my lips. "And why is that, gorgeous?"

My lips curl into a half smile. "Do you really want to waste your *one* kiss in the school canteen?"

"Oh, I have no intention of wasting it," Connor says with a smirk, his voice having dropped an octave. He pulls away, and I fall a little toward him. I right myself quickly, my cheeks heating. "See you tonight." He chuckles, the sound full of masculine satisfaction. So annoying. He slings his bag over his shoulder before walking away. I don't watch his ass as he leaves, and I consider that a major win.

"So, you know he's known your name since like... Tuesday, right?" Zach asks.

I glance at him. "How?"

"Rafe hacked the records," Zach whispers conspiratorially.

Zane punches him hard in the arm. "Snitch."

I roll my eyes. "Rafe is definitely my favorite."

"Rafe is very special. I can see how the two of you would connect," Luke says, studying me. I struggle not to squirm under his gaze. He sees too much. Out of all the Morningstars, Luke feels different. He's kind and seems to put everyone around him at ease. I don't mean the others aren't kind, but there's something at Luke's core that makes him rare in more ways than one. He may never be a warrior like his brothers, but he is equally impressive.

"You are a very close second, Luke." I smile at him.

"And us?" Zane prompts.

"Tied for third, I guess."

"Con is last?" Zach snorts.

"Oh, absolutely."

"You are the only person who has ever put him last." Zach snickers. "Even our mom's list goes Luke, Connor, me, Rafe, and Zane."

"What did Zane do to get the bottom spot?" I ask with a chuckle.

"It's because he sucks," Zach answers for him.

Zane punches him hard in the arm again. "You're a dick, but he's right. Lukey is definitely Mom's number one." Zane clears his throat and sits up straighter, speaking in a falsetto. "Baby Luuuuuke!"

"My tiny baby, Luke!" Zach follows, using the same voice.

Luke blushes and looks down at his plate. "I am not. Stop."

"Where is my baby boy?" Zach continues, poorly imitating his mom.

Luke pushes at Zach's shoulder, forcing him against Zane, his cheeks scarlet. "Go away or the next time Alice stabs you, I won't heal you."

We all laugh, and Alice and I stand up. "Okay, I have to go think of more ways to antagonize your big brother."

Alice's phone alerts, and she grins when she reads it. "Those *things* are here, Summer."

I frown, trying to work out what she means.

"The *things* for the *thing*." She discreetly shows me her phone and the delivery confirmation for the jerseys we ordered. I smirk at her and the perfect timing of the message.

# 12

## SUMMER

*Deth*

A lice rips into the package, her eyes lighting up as she pulls out the first shirt. The forest green is not a color I would normally wear, but at least it's not a bright green. It's not that I don't like bright colors. I've just always been more into darker tones, but it will be so worth it to see the look on Morningstar's face will make it all worth it. He thinks he can make me want to kiss him like that and just walk away? Dick.

Alice throws the other jersey at me, and we disappear into our rooms to change. The sound of Alice chuckling away to herself carries through the wall, and I can't help but join in as I look at myself in the mirror. The dark green doesn't do much for my skin tone, but it'll do plenty to Connors. I can picture it already.

"You know, Rafe was crying with laughter earlier," Alice comments. There's a slight lilt of coyness in her voice.

I pause in the process of putting my mascara on and lift an eyebrow. "Alice?"

She pops her head around my door, her hair now in two low, spiky ponytails. "Yeah?"

I narrow my eyes at her. "Do you have the hots for the broody angel?"

"What?" Alice sputters. "No, I do not! We just…" she considers for a moment, "get along for some reason."

I cross my arms, giving her a knowing look. "Please. You want to hop on that angel dick so bad."

Alice rolls her eyes and inspects her nails. "Yeah, seems like you might be looking in a mirror there, Sum."

I flip her off and turn my attention back to my actual mirror, putting another layer of mascara on. Alice walks over and rifles through my makeup. She holds up a dark red lipstick. "Can I borrow this?"

I nod and pick up one of the eyeliner pencils from my floor. Carefully, I write **HAR** on one cheek and **OLD** over the other. I sigh at the sight. "I wish he had a hotter name..."

Alice chuckles, applying the lipstick.

"Boots or sneakers?" I ask, fixing my own lipstick.

"Sneakers. You want to be able to move fast when Connor sees you in that. Always have an escape plan," she advises, drawing on her cheeks. She writes **MONT** on one cheek and **DICK** on the other.

I laugh and pull my white sneakers from the closet. Carrying them and a pair of white ankle socks, I stop in front of the full-length mirror. The infinity slam jersey is massive, hitting me mid-thigh, and the subtle makeup just emphasizes the name on my cheeks. I sit back down and pull on my socks.

Alice turns to face me. Her lips quirked into a smirk. "Bird brain is going to lose it."

"Maybe I'll invite Harold to the party."

"I'm pretty sure his name is Hector. You should probably get his name down before you go and blindly support him to piss off the captain of our infinity slam team. Think the school will be pissed if we make Connor so angry that we lose?"

"Maybe. Who cares? It's just a game." I slide my feet into my sneakers and tie them up. My stomach tightens around the knot that has been growing since lunch. I'm not sure why I'm so eager to do this. Maybe it's in the hopes of pushing the devilishly handsome angel away, or maybe it's because of how he makes me feel and my desperate need to run away from him.

"Sum?" Alice pulls me from my thoughts, and I glance at her. "Ready?"

I nod and take one more look in the mirror, running my fingers through my hair before pushing to my feet.

Rae Field is just behind the health center and only around a ten-minute walk from Kelpie. Yet if looks could kill, Alice and I would have been incinerated not four feet from the dormitory doors. The sour looks and whispers continue as we walk toward the stadium.

The campus is awash in black and silver, with students of all years and species heading to the field to support our team. Other than us, there is not one speck of dark green in the sea of excited people. Talk about a home court advantage. Everyone is eager for the first game of the year. Many girls are sporting **MORNINGSTAR** across their cheeks or bare stomachs, and many students are carrying banners and signs.

"Connor, the star of my morning," Alice reads out loud. "These people are thirsty."

My lips twitch. "We should have brought one for Harold. We did not come prepared."

"I think our outfits will make enough of a statement." Alice laughs. "And his name is Hector."

When we arrive, the bleachers are already filling up. I hear someone calling my name, his voice just barely audible over the roar of the crowd and the music blasting from the speakers. I grab Alice's hand and wave at Luke before pushing and darting through the throngs of people, making our way to the front where the youngest Morningstar sits.

Luke smiles warmly and leans in when we make it to his side. "Con asked me to save you guys two seats at the front." He notices what we are wearing, and he pales, his smile slipping. "Oh, no..."

I throw my arm over his shoulders. "It's fine, Luke!" I use my hand to cup my mouth, trying to amplify my voice over the others. "Go, Harold!"

Alice nudges me. "Hector, moron."

"I mean, Hector!" I shout into the void of noise. Alice clutches her stomach as she cackles.

"Not good. Not good," Luke mutters, grimacing. He pales more when the announcer's voice rises above the rest.

"Are you ready, Avalon?" The announcer's voice rises above the rest, echoing around the field. Luke pales even more as everyone erupts into a cheer that almost ruptures my eardrums. "I said, Are. You. Ready. Avalon?!" The crowd gets even louder, screaming and chanting. "Please, welcome to the field, your team, the Avalon Knights!"

Connor leads his team onto the field. His muscular body looks even bigger thanks to the various guards used to protect his body from serious injuries during the game. The black jersey looks like it's been melted to his skin. The silver Avalon logo on the front flickers in the light, appearing like molten metal as he moves. He is carrying his helmet under his arm and has what looks like war paint on his cheeks.

"You're practically drooling," Alice says, nudging me again.

"I am not." I give her a black look, though I have to make a conscious effort to keep my face neutral.

The rest of the team filters out behind him, and I notice that many players have halos on their wrists, not just the Morningstar brothers. Other species are playing, but angels are by far the majority. The cheerleaders spread out in the center of the pitch and start shaking their pom poms.

"They are the knights! They are the knights! Come to destroy and show their might!" I glance at Alice, about to roll my eyes, but see that hers are already nearly embedded in the back of her head.

"They are the knights! They dominate! Winning isn't luck! It's their fate!" The cheerleaders jump and dance, doing handstands and backflips. Sure, it's impressive, but they're just so... peppy. I can't stand it.

The team starts their warmups, running around the field and stretching out.

"And here comes the competition. Please give a big Avalon welcome to... the Irachmoor Ravens!" the announcer yells, and the Avalon cheerleaders move to the side, glaring at the other team and their cheerleaders.

Harold leads the other team out, and the vibe in the stadium changes. People all around boo and hiss, and that angry attention extends to Alice and me.

The Ravens cheer squad starts their routine but they can barely be heard over the roaring crowd. The noise level dies down as both teams head for the middle of the field. Zach, his helmet marked with wings on either side of his face like the rest of his team, looks toward us. I can see his teeth flash in a snarl. He nudges Rafe, who's lined up next to him on the field. Rafe holds back a frown as he nudges Connor. Rafe nods toward us when Connor looks back at him. Connor's eyes lock with mine, but his bright smile fades the moment he realizes what I'm wearing. His entire body tenses when I blow him a kiss and wink at him.

Connor looks away just as the ball is launched into the air. He grabs Rafe and tosses him after it. Midair, Rafe shoves a member of the other team out of the way and grabs the ball. He nods at Zane, who charges down the field. Rafe throws it to him, but Zane is tackled by one of the Ravens. Luckily, Zach is right on his tail and catches it. Zane hits the ground so hard it trembles. Players from both sides collide, all trying to get the ball. Zach passes it, and Connor almost misses catching it because he's glaring at me. The moment it hits his hands, a huge opponent slams into Connor, taking him to the ground.

"Get your head in the game, Morningstar!" the coach calls. The teams reset, and I can tell that Connor is trying to shake it off and focus on the game. The Ravens score a point, and Zach curses loudly enough that it's heard across the stadium. Harold winks at me, noticing my jersey. I give him a little wave right before Connor slams into him. They both fall to the ground, and the referee blows his whistle, pointing a little yellow card at Connor. Rafe jogs to Connor, assumingly to calm him down, but Connor shakes his head and beckons the coach over.

The coach holds his hands up in the shape of a T, and a time-out is called. I'm no expert, but I'm pretty sure this is an odd time to call a time-out. Connor takes off his helmet and locks eyes with me, walking toward the edge of the field with Rafe at his side.

Oh, shit. They are heading for the bleachers, and their target is clear.

"Oops, time to run!" Alice laughs and yanks me to my feet, pulling me past the people in the seats next to us, scrambling for the stairs.

Connor jumps over the barrier. The stadium is eerily quiet as everyone trains their hungry eyes on us. Rafe darts under the bleachers and up the other set of stairs, blocking out escape when Alice and I try to change directions.

"You can run, but I'll catch you," Connor warns in such a way that I stop in my tracks and turn to face him. I wanted to make him mad, and based on his thunderous expression, I've more than succeeded. The crowd moves to make way for the irate angel, leaving me nowhere to go.

Even though he has stopped a few steps below me, he's still taller than me by at least a head. I quirk an eyebrow at him, trying to maintain my nonchalant expression.

"Hello, *Summer*." He doesn't waste another moment before pulling me against him and slamming his lips to mine, kissing me hard. I'm vaguely aware of the whoops and cheers from the crowd around us, but it all seems to blur away as he tunnels his fingers in my hair. His lips are just as pillowy as I remember, and I lose myself in them way too easily.

Connor pulls back after a moment, and I blush when I instinctively lean forward, wanting more. Connor glances at Rafe and gives him a curt nod before bending and heaving me over his shoulder. He carries me down the stairs and onto the field, heading back toward the locker room. I can hear Alice's protests and assume Rafe is following with her.

"Put me down, Morningstar!" I squeal in outrage.

Connor ignores me. The noise of the crowd grows muffled when we pass into the tunnel and enter the locker room. Connor gently puts me down and turns to rummage through his locker. Rafe places Alice down beside me, and Connor throws a clean jersey to her. I expect him to throw one at me, too. Instead, he smirks at me, and with a devilish glint in his eyes he pulls off his jersey and hands it to me.

"You know, even if I put this on, I still have his name on my cheeks," I say defiantly when he turns to pull a new jersey out for himself.

Connor turns and pulls his new jersey over his head, tugging it into place before reaching for me again. He grips my chin between his thumb and forefinger, holding me in place. His lips slant over mine as he brings a towel to my cheeks, wiping away Harold's name. I growl and pull back, slapping at his hand. "I said one kiss, dickbag."

"And you wore my rival's jersey to provoke me. Looks like we both had different plans."

Zach bursts into the locker room, his cheeks pink from exertion. "Coach is pissed. You both need to get out there. Now."

Connor leans in, brushing his tongue along the seam of my lips. I moan and open for him, but he pulls away before I can sink into the kiss. "I'll be back after the game," Connor says, brushing his fingers along my cheek. He winks, and he and his brothers leave the locker room.

Alice and I look at each other for a long moment before we burst out laughing. We change into our new jerseys, accepting that we lost. My lips tingle from the lingering memory of his lips on mine, and the promise of more makes my core thrum in anticipation.

"Well, I guess he knows your name now."

I laugh again, filled with a giddy lightness that is equal parts terrifying and wonderful. "Let's go watch the game."

Alice spots a mirror in the corner. "Wait."

She pulls me closer and poses us so our backs are to the mirror. **MORNINGSTAR** is emblazoned in huge letters across our backs. We both look over our shoulders and pout. The moment Alice snaps the photo, I take her phone and post it to *@KillerLegosi*. Immediately, her phone begins to blow up with alerts.

"I guess I can unblock them all now," Alice says as we walk back to the bleachers.

# 13

## SUMMER

*Heth*

Luke grins when he sees us, immediately noticing our outfit change. I lift the jersey to my nose, inhaling Connor's scent of clouds and citrus and savoring his lingering warmth on the fabric. The Knights pick up their game through to the second half and beyond. Every so often, Connor looks at me in the bleachers, and I can't help but smile back at him. The energy in the stadium is so infectious that it's difficult not to cheer along with everyone else when the Knights score and to commiserate when the Ravens sneak a point.

Game time is running out, and the Knights are ahead by eight points. Connor is running down the field, chased by two hulking Ravens. The power he exudes and the flex of his thighs as he runs are wildly distracting, but I try to keep my mind on watching the game and not how much I want him to continue the punish—

"What the fuck!" Alice springs from her seat, watching as Harold comes seemingly out of nowhere and tackles Connor hard. They fly through the air before slamming into the unforgiving ground, Connor taking the brunt of the fall. The whistle blows and time is up, the game over. Connor sits up, clenching his side, his face twisted in pain.

The Knights rush toward Connor, crowding around him. Luke launches over the bar of the bleachers and runs onto the field, his hands already glowing. My heart swells as he pushes through the throng of chaos, shoving aside the much larger players in his haste to reach his big brother. It seems none of the Morningstars will hesitate to protect their family, no matter the risks.

Harold smirks as he walks away, covered in mud from head to toe but otherwise unharmed. The way he struts is horribly smug, especially considering the Ravens just lost the match. The slam was completely uncalled for, nothing more than a punishment.

A roar comes from within the huddle around Connor, and Rafe emerges, fury clear on his face. He storms toward Harold, fists clenched, and once again, I see the true difference between Rafe and his brothers. Wild anger spills off him as he closes the distance to the other team's captain. One of the Ravens nudges Harold, gesturing to Rafe's approach.

Harold lifts an eyebrow and turns to face him but is met with Rafe's fist. The power of the hit shudders through Rafe, and for a second, the charmed Avalon emblem on his uniform glows brightly. The emblems are supposed to hold back the most dangerous portions of the player's abilities, making the playing field safer and slightly more even. Rafe's emblem almost looks like it is shattering. Instead of the bright white light fading as it is absorbed by the charm, it is growing brighter. Black cracks are forming, revealing dark flames lurking within the fissures. Harold stumbles but quickly recovers. He pulls his arm back to defend himself, but Rafe is on him, punching him mercilessly. Every blow makes the Avalon emblem on his chest glow. Each strike weakens the charm, breaking the power seal more and more. If Rafe keeps at this, he will completely unleash his fury. Veins bulge beneath Harold's skin and his eyes glow emerald green. His body grows in size, the berserker struggling to break through his own emblem.

Connor pushes through the swarm and runs to them, yanking Rafe off a bloody and beaten Harold. Rafe struggles against Connor's hold, his fury still pinned on Harold. Connor spins him around and roughly grabs his face. His words are inaudible over the sounds from the stadium, but his gaze is locked on his brother. Rafe's nostrils flare as he finally seems to see Connor. Connor doesn't release Rafe's face, his features pulled into a look of anger and concern. In spite of that, Rafe's shoulders do relax a little, and his bloody fists unclench. Rafe nods curtly and yanks his head from Connor's hold before storming off the field. Connor's shoulders slump as he watches him leave. He runs a tired hand over his face before walking toward the locker room with his teammates.

I glance at Alice. She looks excited and maybe even a little turned on by the display of violence. "Woah, that was—"

"Crazy hot. I know. It's too bad his brother has claimed you."

I blink. "Absolutely not what I was going to say. And Connor hasn't claimed me."

"Please. If he were a shifter, he'd have peed all over you the second he sniffed you out."

I roll my eyes, amusement playing on my lips. "Should we wait for them so we can all go to the party together?"

Alice thinks for a moment. "Nah, they might be reigning in Rafe for a while. We'll meet them there."

I nod, though I keep glancing toward the tunnel where Connor disappeared as we leave.

Alice and I follow the masses to the wolf shifter pack dorm, where the party is already in full swing. Everyone is high on the Knight's win, and the dorm is packed with students. We push our way through the crowd to the makeshift bar. Alice pours herself a drink, but remembering the great sandwich debacle, I grab a bottle of water. Unable to hear each other over the music and yelling, I tug Alice toward the wall where we have a view of the door. We spend the next thirty minutes fending off advances from over-excited shifters, Alice taking every opportunity to hiss and spew insults at them.

My heart jumps when I see a tall, blond guy walk through the door. Zach spots us the second he steps into the house and makes a beeline for us. "Well, well, well, look who it is."

I shoot him a scathing look. "Which one are you again?"

Zach pulls me against his side and ruffles my hair. I bat him away, and he chuckles. "You know, Con is going to be piiiiiiiiiissed when he gets here."

Alice rolls her eyes. "I'm going to go get another drink before I stab you again, asshole."

I look at Zach, crossing my arms across my chest. "And why should I care about that?"

He just snickers and glances over my shoulder, his smirk widening. "I guess we'll see."

I'm about to turn to follow his line of sight when two large hands squeeze my shoulders. I tense at the contact, but the scent of clouds surrounds me, leaving my concern no room to grow. My captor spins me to face him, and I look up into Connor's beautiful eyes. The anger and disappointment I'd seen him display on the field has melted away. He looks perfectly at ease again, but the tension I can feel radiating from him tells me it is not gone, at least not completely.

I rest my hands against his chest, allowing myself a moment to take in every dip and curve of his face. "Congratulations on your win, captain."

Connor cups my cheek, tilting my head back a bit more and gently holding it there. "Thanks, but I really don't care about that right now." He glances at my lips. "Have you had anything to drink?"

I shake my head. "Nothing but water."

"Good." Connor bends and cups his massive hands behind my thighs. He lifts me and presses me back against the wall. I wrap myself around him, and he seals his lips over mine. Eagerly, I deepen the kiss, and when his tongue brushes against mine, I can't stop the low moan of need.

There is a loud yell and someone slams into Connor. He braces himself so as not to crush me, but I pull back, remembering that we're in a packed room and that there are probably hundreds of eyes on us. "What are you doing, Morningstar?" I whisper against his lips.

Connor ignores the question and pushes away from the wall. He kisses me again and shoulders his way into the writhing mass of students. His arms tighten around me, but the crowd parts easily for us. Feeling safe in his arms, I sink into the kiss, barely aware of him ascending the stairs. He knocks on the first door we come to. A deep groan comes from within, so he moves to the next, which appears to be empty. Connor doesn't break the kiss, not for a moment. Not as he opens the door, not as he closes it and flips the lock, not as he walks across the room, and not as he lays me down on the bed.

His large body pins mine to the mattress, and he moans against my lips. "You are insanely sexy. You know that, right?"

I slide my tongue along his bottom lip. "We're missing the party..."

Connor groans, panting into my mouth as his fingers trail down my body, searching blindly for the edge of my jersey. "Fuck the party."

He finds the hem and slowly pulls it up my body. I lift my hips to help him. I have no idea if what we're about to do is a good idea or not. All I know is that my body is desperate to be touched and pleasured, and I want it to be him who does it. This type of intimacy is familiar to me and easier than all the complicated emotional stuff. This is all I know and all I want to know.

"Seeing you wearing someone else's jersey... Oh, you made me so..." He doesn't name the emotion, and at the moment, I'm not sure he even knows what he was feeling.

Connor pulls the jersey up, and I arch, helping him get it over my head. He tosses it aside, and I collapse back onto the bed with a moan as he dips his head to brush his lips against my skin. My eyes roll in pleasure as he licks along my bra line. His eyes are nearly black when he looks up at me, and the desire in his expression completely undoes me. "You did it to get a response, and you got it."

I slide my tongue along my lower lip, my voice breathy and low. "And it was so much fun..."

Connor narrows his eyes at me. "Every game. You wear my jersey." He slides up my body and kisses me again, pulling back to nip gently at my lower lip. "No one else's."

A shiver runs down my spine. It must be how Connor's breath teases over my skin. It can't be his words. I know I can't trust the words shared during intimacy or the feelings they invoke. They don't hold the same value. They're clouded and confused by hormones.

I push the thoughts from my mind and claim his mouth, deepening the kiss and arching against him. Connor hooks his thumbs into the lace of my panties and slides them down my legs, throwing them to the side. He kisses down my body, every touch of his lips like a mini electric shock, shooting straight to my core. My chest heaves, and

I force my eyes to remain open, watching him move lower. He settles between my thighs, and I lift my knees, opening to him.

I tilt my head, watching him. Surely, he's not going to do this right now. This has never been my experience. Usually, it's straight to penetration and then a 3:00 AM sneak-out. But Connor proves me wrong when he leans in and slowly slides his tongue through my core. Heat pools low in my belly, and I swear I see stars. I'm not sure what noise I make in response, but whatever it is, I can tell he likes it from the way he immediately takes another taste. A low guttural sound leaves his throat as he licks me again, and I lift my hips, needing more.

"Fuck..." I moan, digging my fingers into the sheets as he swirls his tongue over my clit before sucking on it. My hands move to his head, and I tunnel my fingers into his hair, holding him close when he hits the most perfect fucking spot I've ever felt. "Gods..." I gasp and cry out again.

Connor slowly pushes a finger inside me, and my hips buck again. He slowly presses another finger in, and I writhe against his hand. The pressure builds with the burning stretch and the throb of my clit beneath his tongue. My pussy clenches around him, liquid heat bathing his hand and my arousal spilling out of me as he plunges his fingers in over and over. His lips wrap around my clit, and he sucks.

Connor looks up at me, meeting my gaze. The second his dark blue eyes meet mine, I am completely lost to my orgasm. I cry out, his broad shoulders holding my thighs wide when they reflexively try to close. My release explodes within me, and I throw my head back as pleasure rips through me. I pant and go boneless as he kisses his way back up my body. Through the aftershocks of my release, I find the strength to push myself up and slam my lips to his. The sweet taste of my pussy lingers on his tongue, and I've never tasted anything more erotic.

Connor slides his hands between us, unbuckling his belt and opening his pants. He kicks them off and somehow manages to never break the kiss.

He pulls back, panting and looking down at me. He holds up a condom. "Are you sure about this?"

I simply kiss him back and take the small foil package from him. Connor sits back on his heels, and I rip the condom open, reverently sliding it over his length as he pulls his shirt off. He tosses it aside and eases me back onto the bed, his heavy body covering mine as he settles back over me. His hips shift so his cock is pressing against my opening, and I drag my nails down his back, rocking my hips to welcome him in. He groans, his biceps flexing as he braces above me and sinks deeper, stretching my pussy around his girth. I bring my knees higher on his hips, opening myself up for him.

He continues to push inside me and moans against my lips, "Fuck. Tight."

I lift my hips, greedy for more. My pussy throbs in need, desperate to be filled. I nip and suck at his lower lip, urging him for more, silently begging him to take me hard and pound deep.

Connor groans again, and the sound makes my skin break out in goosebumps. "Fuck. You feel so good."

I drag my nails down his back and dig them into his ass, pulling him fully into me, and I moan at the fullness, my cunt wrapping painfully tight around him. His shout of pleasure turns my core molten, and he thrusts, slow and gentle. I can't tell if he's testing the waters or teasing me but now is not the time. Wrapping my legs around his waist, I arch beneath him, trying to spur him on. I want more. I want harder.

"Harder," I beg.

"I... I don't want to hurt you," Connor whispers into my lips.

Hurt me? Fucking fuck me! Growling, I wrap my arms and legs around him and roll us over. It only works because I take him by surprise, but I end up on top, straddling him. Without giving him a moment to react, I lift until just the head of his cock remains inside of me and then slam down again. Connor bucks beneath me, his hands grabbing my hips. "Fuck!" He digs his fingers into me, his hold gentle enough that I won't bruise but hard enough that he's taken a small portion of the control. He looks up at me, and there's something in his eyes that I don't want to identify. Not now.

I brace my hands against the heavy muscles of his chest and sit up on him, riding him hard. My stomach muscles clench as I slam my pussy down on him over and over, taking him as hard as I need to. Connor sits up and buries his fingers in my hair, pulling my lips to meet his and kissing me breathless as I fuck him.

"Summer. Fuck. You're so... good."

I bite his lip and move faster on him, desperate pleasure coursing through me.

"You're... Fuuuck. You're going to make me cum." Connor groans, and his body tenses beneath mine, his cock thickening a little as he nears his release.

I move faster on him, knowing my release isn't as close as his. "Not yet."

Connor growls breathlessly. "Can't really control it."

"Not. Yet." I moan. "Fuck..."

"All right. Fuck, you just feel so fucking good," Connor grunts, releasing a hiss through his clenched teeth. He grips my hip in one hand and pulls me down, his cock pulsing deep inside me as he grinds against my clit.

I dig my nails into his shoulders, reaching for the delicious familiar burn of my orgasm, the tight coil in my core. It is so close.

"Connor... now!" I cry out, hurtling into pleasure. My pussy clenches around him, the tight, wet heat quivering around his cock. Connor shouts, his fingers fisting in my hair as my orgasm shoves him into his own release.

Connor pants and presses kisses along my neck, breathing curses against my skin like filthy promises. We fall back onto the bed, both of us out of breath and sated. I roll off him, looking at the ceiling as aftershocks of pleasure ripple through me.

# 14

## SUMMER

The party continues downstairs, but our labored breathing is the only sound in the room. Our shoulders brush as we both try to catch our breath and calm our bodies.

"You know," Connor pulls me against him, kissing along my jaw, "I was planning something romantic for when I kissed you again."

I quirk a brow and nuzzle against him. "Romantic?"

He nods. "Yeah. I was planning to have the entire team do a dance, and then I was going to ask you to be my girlfriend. It was a whole thing."

I blink. "Girlfriend? Absolutely not."

Connor brushes his lips over mine, completely unfazed, as if he expected that exact reply. "Why not?"

I pull back, needing a little distance. "Because I don't do that."

"Do what?" he asks, brushing his fingers over my cheek.

"Relationships," I reply plainly, leaving absolutely no room for misunderstanding.

He glides his thumb along my bottom lip. "Fine. How about we date?"

I laugh and shift a little, putting a bit more space between us. "I don't think so."

Connor pulls me back and rolls on top of me. "Hey."

I look up at him, unsmiling.

"I get it. I like you." He keeps that penetrating gaze on me, and while I can tell he's trying to read me, I can also see that he's not getting anywhere. "Do you like me?"

"No," I reply, but there's no bite in my words. Connor's lips curl into a smirk, and there's a slight twinkle in his eyes.

He leans down, biting my lower lip. "Do you want to know a little angelic trade secret?"

Connor nuzzles my jaw, and I tilt my head when he presses his lips to my ear. "We can taste lies."

He trails his lips along my cheek, kissing me deeply when he reaches my mouth. I gently bite his tongue, pulling a pleasing groan from him.

Connor pulls back, rubbing his nose against mine. "So... dating? We can go super slow."

"So slow that I don't see you again for months?" I quip.

He smirks. "As in we date—"

"Summer!" Alice's shout comes right before she bangs on the door. "We have to go!"

I frown, glancing at the door. I want to tell Alice I'll be down in twenty minutes or so. Morningstar and I can go another round before I shut this thing down for good, but something in her voice tugs at me. I push Connor off me and climb out of the bed. "Just a sec, Alice," I call, pulling on the discarded jersey.

She bangs on the door again, and I am not mistaking the urgency in it this time.

Connor sighs and rolls out of bed to pull on his jeans. "What does she want?"

"Summer!" Alice shouts and bangs on the door again, making it rattle dangerously on its hinges.

"I'm coming!" I yell and open the door. Alice looks furious, and she throws a death glare at Connor over my shoulder. What am I missing?

She pulls out her phone and turns the screen toward me. Zach's *Nexus* page is already loaded up, and a video is playing. It is focused on a door very similar to the one I'm standing beside. My stomach drops when I hear the moaning that's coming from within the room beyond. Embarrassment shrouds my skin like a heavy cloak, and my cheeks heat with humiliation as the video continues to play.

Not again. Not again. How could I have been so fucking stupid to let my guard down so quickly?

"Connor is going for the species cup!" someone says off-screen. It sounds vaguely like one of the twins, but between the chaos of the party and the moaning, it's difficult to decipher voices. I feel Connor come up behind me as I click on the comments. There are hundreds of comments already, and most seem to add to the not-so-secret tally being kept.

Connor tenses against my back, but if he's about to say something, I don't give him the chance. I look at Alice. "Let's go. Now."

I brush past her, not looking back.

"Summer! Wai—" Connor's groan of pain replaces his words, and then Alice is at my side, sliding her hand into mine. Every pair of eyes is on me as I do some fucking, messed up walk of shame out of the house. All conversation has died, and the only sound is the booming bass coming from the stereo.

"Summer! Just wait!" Connor calls, running after us. I don't stop, not even looking back. My stomach twists with anger and something else I've never felt before. I'd actually allowed myself to start to *like* that feather-brained prick. This is why you have your rules, Summer. This is why you don't allow feelings to get involved. You know better!

Connor grabs my arm, and I whirl on him. Alice snarls. She doesn't interfere but stays close, ready to step in if needed. Blood is trickling from Connor's nose, no doubt thanks to my vampiric roommate.

"I didn't know." Connor searches my eyes. His expression is soft, apologetic, and beseeching.

The anger builds inside me, the video playing on a loop in my head along with the words about his own personal species cup. I yank my arm free. "Leave me alone. You got your fae. Congratulations, asshole," I snarl at him.

Connor shakes his head and steps forward. I step back, maintaining the distance between us. "No! That's not... I didn't want that. I didn't even know about that," he says beseechingly.

"Whatever," I snarl at him before turning and walking away. Alice is hot on my heels, but I can also hear Connor following. I throw a basic shield up, a skill I learned in my latest combat class.

"Fuck off!" Alice sneers at him over her shoulder.

I barely register the walk home. Not even the lights lining the path can pull my attention from the betrayal of a guy who owed me nothing. What does it even matter? He deserves no more trust than any other stranger. When we get back to the dorm, I go straight to my room and slam my door. I climb into bed, desperately wanting to cry, but there are no tears. There are so rarely tears anymore. I once believed I'd used up all my tears as a child, that I drained my ducts dry, and now they are as barren as the barest of desert plains. It used to be a relief, yet at this moment, I wish I could cry. Maybe it would release some of the fury within me.

Alice keeps her distance for almost an hour but comes to my room when someone, presumably Connor, starts slamming on the dormitory door. She wordlessly climbs into bed with me and just lays there.

I throw up another shield, making the room soundproof and drowning out the noise of Connor's useless apologies.

"Sum?" Alice eventually says into the darkness of my room.

"Hm?"

"Sorry," she whispers, then surprises me by cuddling into my side.

"I don't want to talk about it."

Alice nods and throws her arm over me, holding me tight and offering comfort in the only way she knows how.

The anger curdles in my stomach, pain threatening to overwhelm me. I stare up at the ceiling, hoping for sleep to take me.

# 15

## SUMMER

*Loth*

The sun creeps up on the darkness, eating the shadows of the night. My body is tired, yet my mind is so painfully awake. I hate this feeling. I hate that I feel hurt and used. Alice sleeps soundly next to me. She's weirdly warm for a vampire. I thought they were meant to be cold, but she's like a small heater. I climb out of the bed, trying not to wake her. Though it seems that while she may be warmer than I expect a vampire to be, she sleeps like the dead.

I grab a pair of yoga pants and a sports bra before going into my bathroom to change. Running will make me feel better. It always does. The wind in my hair and the burn in my lungs is oddly soothing.

The spandex hugs my curves, and I turn, looking at myself in the mirror. I don't know why I'm checking myself out. I'm hideous today, like a worn-out shoe. Yet, while the pants are navy and as bleak as my mood, my ass looks amazing in them. The matching sports bra is my most comfortable and gives great support. At least physically, I don't think anything is going to bolster me emotionally today.

I pull my hair into a high ponytail and return to the bedroom to slide on my running shoes. My lips twitch as I look at my roommate. Alice hasn't moved, still out like a light with her mouth open a little and her chest barely rising as she sleeps. What a little weirdo.

Grabbing my dark gray hoodie, I pull it on and zip it up as I leave my room. I fling open the door, desperate to get downstairs for that first draw of fresh morning air, but I step back in surprise when a large mass of muscle falls into the entryway. Connor Morningstar blinks up on me. His eyes are red and the bags under them are just as purple as mine are. Did he sleep at the door?

"Summer..." he sputters and sits up. I sigh heavily and step over the heap of him slumped on the floor. He's surprisingly nimble and quick even with all those muscles, so I take off down the stairs and burst from the building, kicking into a run the second I step over the threshold. I'm not a sprinter, but I can definitely get a good pace going. I've barely made it to the coffee cart in the middle of the quad before his large hand wraps around my wrist.

"Summer." His voice is sad, but it does nothing but inflate my fury. How dare he be sad when I'm the one that's been used? *Humiliated. Used.*

The growl that rips from my throat surprises him enough that he loosens his grip, and I yank my arm away from him. "Leave me alone, Connor."

Connor grabs my arm again and pulls me around to face him, his other hand wrapping around my biceps. "I didn't know, Summer. I wasn't..." He hesitates, but I don't even look at him. I can't look at him. "This was all news to me!"

I'm about to reply, to tear into him with words sharper than any dagger when an icy cold voice beats me to it. "Mister Morningstar."

I tense at the sound of that voice, at the roiling presence behind me. He wasn't there a moment ago, but now his intimidating aura permeates the air. How had I not felt his power until now? Can he conceal that menacing energy *that* effectively? What a terrifying thought.

Connor's body goes rigid, and he raises his gaze to the looming being at my back. "This is a personal matter, headmaster."

The headmaster walks around to my side, glancing at me before returning that icy, malevolent stare to Connor. "It is happening on school property. Therefore, it is my business."

I realize he's not wearing his usual formal wear. Instead, he has on a long-sleeve, black t-shirt that pulls tight over his muscles and a pair of black sweatpants. He's obviously been running, yet he looks completely perfect. He doesn't have a hair out of place, the midnight black a beautiful contrast to the rich golden brown of his skin. My eyes catch on the black runes inscribed along his neck, several in languages I don't recognize. Most sorcerers cover their runes. They intentionally hide the spells they are armed with, making them unknown weapons waiting to be launched, but not the headmaster. Is it arrogance or confidence?

I look up at the headmaster to see he has fixed his gaze on me again.

"Miss Tuatha De Daanan?"

I swallow. While his stare feels like a weight on my shoulders, perversely, it also feels like a feather's caress against my skin. Oh fuck, this has already been an awful twenty-four hours. I can't handle any more emotions to deny or sort through, and I definitely don't need a lecture from the doom master right now.

"I'm all right, sir. Thank you."

Without another word, he pushes his headphones back into his ears and continues on his run. I can't help but stare after him as he sets off.

"Summer—"

"Goodbye, Connor. Enjoy whatever species is next on your creepy-ass list."

"Summer, you are the only person I want on my list," he says, shaking his head. I finally meet his gaze to find his eyes pleading harder than his words.

I roll my eyes and turn away from him, intending to resume my run. Connor grabs me again. "Nothing has changed for me. I still want to date you. I want you to be my girlfriend."

I rip my hand away. "Leave me alone," I snarl and stalk away, fully intending to get as far from him as possible. He catches me easily and pulls me against him, kissing me hard. It's so difficult not to get lost in the kiss. Luckily, I have an eternal pit of hatefire inside me, and I tap into that, forcing myself to pull away. I push against his chest, even more furious now that his lips aren't clouding my better judgment. It would help if he weren't such a good kisser. Fuck.

Connor keeps his hold on me, his gaze locked on mine. "Last night was the best night of my life." He brushes his thumbs along my arms. "My brothers are morons, especially when they're drunk."

I narrow my eyes on him. Connor carefully lifts his hand and cups my cheek as if he is afraid I will hit him. "I'm absolutely not making excuses for them. I just... really fucking like you."

The rage within me dies a little, not completely, but enough that I don't want to push him off a cliff. "Fine. I forgive you. Will you go away now?"

Connor smiles sadly. "I can taste lies, remember?"

I glare at him, unrelenting. "I'm not lying, but I'm also not dating you."

"Why? If you have actually forgiven me."

Men are so stupid, I swear.

"Because I don't want to," I reply simply. "What I want to do is finish my run. Alone."

Connor looks so defeated that it extinguishes my remaining anger, but the hurt is still there, heavy and oily against my skin. He slowly drops his hands and pushes them into his pockets, his eyes dull. "I'm sorry."

"See you."

Connor turns on his heel and wanders sadly in the other direction. I take one last look at him before I start to run again. Something in my stomach is off, a feeling I've never felt before, not like this, anyway. I frown as I continue on my run, trying to figure out what I am feeling. Could it be guilt? No, it can't be. I have done nothing wrong. Fuck.

My phone pings in my pocket, and I stop on the path to read the message. Alice's name pops up, followed by a photo of Zach and Zane walking around campus wearing large signs with the word **SHAME** spelled out in bright red letters. My lips twitch at the image. My phone pings again with another text from Alice.

ALICE

Brunch?

SUMMER

Student Union in 20?

ALICE

Sounds good.

I check my running app and am pleased to see I've met a new personal best, probably thanks to my anger at stupid Connor Morningstar. I have no doubt it was Connor who forced his brothers into humiliating themselves as punishment for humiliating me. Connor Morningstar is probably telling the truth about not having anything to do with what they did.

I run to the student union and grab a table outside in the sun. The summer days are still so lovely here, but I know it won't be long until fall is upon us, and sitting outside won't be nearly as pleasant.

"So... how was your run?" Alice asks, dropping into the seat across from me around five minutes later.

I glance at her. "It was fine."

"Did you chat with... you know who?"

I roll my eyes. "You can say his name, Al. I will not burst into flames or curse you for eternity."

Alice chuckles softly and lifts the menu, using it as a fan. "Well?"

I nod.

Alice blinks, waiting for more details, but when it becomes clear I'm not going to provide more without prompting, she asks, "And? How'd it go?"

"I believe he had nothing to do with it." My stomach twists again, and this time, there is no doubt it's guilt. Connor Morningstar's stupid, sad face keeps flashing in my head. There is probably no feeling in the world I hate more than guilt, especially when I have done nothing wrong.

Alice stops fanning herself and looks at me expectantly. "Uh huh, and...?"

I pick up another menu and read through it. "And what?"

"I wasn't sure if I should show you this, but..." Alice picks up her phone and taps on the screen a couple of times before turning it toward me.

RAFE

Connor is acting like a war widow waiting for her husband to come back from sea. What did Summer say to him?

I glance at Alice, one eyebrow raised. "You've been texting Rafe?" I roll my eyes. "Fine. Send Rafe my number to give to Connor. He did look like a kicked puppy when I told him to leave."

"Why?" Alice asks, tilting her head.

"Why what?"

"Why give him your number when you asked him to leave?" Alice asks, her eyes assessing.

"I don't know, okay? Stop asking difficult questions, or maybe I'll have some difficult questions like why do you have broody, dark angel boy's number?"

Alice tenses and rolls her eyes. "Okay, well, his brothers notwithstanding, how was it?"

My lips curl into a half smile. "It was... pretty good."

She leans forward and lowers her voice. "Only *pretty* good."

"Maybe a little more than pretty good."

Alice smirks. "Well, he carried you up the stairs like a caveman."

My cheeks heat a little, but I push away the memory. It is quickly replaced by the one that started when Alice banged on the door. "Whatever. It's not happening again."

Alice's phone alerts, and she grimaces when she looks at it before showing me. It's a photo of Connor sitting on the window ledge and staring out of what I assume is his bedroom window. Rafe wasn't lying. Beneath the photo is another message from Rafe.

RAFE

I'm going to have to build him a Summer watch instead of a widow's watch.

I sigh again, but my stomach knots a bit more as I look at the photo. "Send him my number to give to Connor."

"You know, I'm not sure that's the best course of action here, Sum."

I frown and hand her back her phone, her use of the nickname surprising me once more. "What do you mean?"

"I think you need to give it to him yourself," she says, shoving her phone back into her pocket. "Listen, I know you got your stuff, but I think Connor is," Alice scrunches up her nose like she's smelled the most vile thing, "a good guy." The effort it takes for her to grate out the end of her sentence is almost painful, and I grimace along with her.

"Gross." The idea of a guy being anything other than a bastard is probably the most unbelievable thing I've ever heard. That is saying something, considering I was a fae living in a mortal realm before coming to a magical university that I didn't even apply for.

"I know." She shudders. "It's the worst, but I think you should give him a chance."

I think about his eyes, his smile, and the gentleness of his touch. I think of the ease I feel around him, which is something I've never experienced. What happened last night was shitty, and I'm still deeply hurt by it, but can I blame him for the actions of his moronic brothers?

"Well, fuck," I curse and stand up. "I'll be back in twenty. Order me chocolate chip pancakes?"

# 16

## SUMMER

My stomach flutters the entire walk to the Morningstar House, and I take deep breaths to calm my nerves. I'm not good at apologizing. It's not something I do very often, or ever, because I've rarely had anyone in my life important enough to apologize to. But the closer I get to his house, the more I realize I'm partially at fault here. Yes, I was running on emotions, and honestly, if I were in the same situation again, I'm not certain I'd change my actions. I needed to have those emotions. I have always been like this, unable to just push feelings away. Only once I've felt and processed them can I then return to some level of rational thinking and move forward with a clear head.

The Morningstar House looks very different in the light of day without dozens of students littering the front lawn. It's a pretty idyllic house, to be honest. The light blue paneling with the white porch makes it look homey and inviting. The garden is beautifully landscaped, and the house is obviously well-cared for. A lot of thought has gone into making this house a home for these boys.

I pause at the gate and take a steadying breath. I truly hate admitting that I was wrong. *Just do it, Sum.* I exhale and walk up the path, not allowing myself any more moments of hesitation before I knock on the door.

Rafe, in all his broody glory, opens it. When he sees me, something lightens in his eyes, but his face remains blank. "Summer."

"Is Connor in?" I ask.

Rafe narrows his eyes, but that sparkle is still there. He opens the door a bit wider but shifts, blocking my entry. "That depends. Are you here just to tell him to fuck off?" He's obviously glad I came, but he is also extremely protective of his brother.

I roll my eyes and push past him. He moves easily, which I imagine wouldn't be possible if he were truly trying to keep me out. Like his brother, Rafe is built like a brick fucking wall.

Zane groans on the couch, his face buried in a pillow. "He's upstairs. Can you just... not be so loud?"

I flip him off and head up the stairs. The banisters are painted white, and the wall-paper is a lovely sky-blue color with the faintest pattern of clouds. The decor I can see is plush, comfortable, and completely stunning.

The stairs open up on a wide landing. There are two bedrooms to the right with silver *Z*'s hanging on the door. Almost directly in front of the stairs is Luke's room. His door has a lovely cross-stitched sign with his name on it. To the left of the landing, there are two more rooms. Rafe's has an *R* similar to the one the twins have, but his is black with red reflective flecks throughout. Connor's room is to the right of Rafe's. His door doesn't have a letter or a stitched sign. Instead, **CONNOR** has been etched into the door. It is not a skilled carving. The letters are shaky and extremely poorly executed. I knock softly on the door.

"Go away, Rafe." Connor's voice is barely audible, but the sadness is clear.

I open the door. Connor is no longer looking out the window, but he's staring at the wall, which seems even more depressing, to be honest.

"I'm much hotter than Rafe," I say, stepping into his room.

He tenses but doesn't look at me. "I thought you wanted me to leave you alone."

I take another step into his room, watching him. All I want is to erase his sadness and then punch his brothers hard in the balls.

"I came to give you something."

Connor turns his head to look at me, his eyes guarded. "Give me something?"

I nod. "Let me see your phone?"

Connor's brows furrow a little, but he stands up and pulls out his phone. He unlocks it and hands it to me. I take it and key my number into it before snapping a quick selfie to set as the contact photo. I toss it back to him, and Connor catches it easily. He looks at the new entry in his phone and then back at me, confusion clear on his face.

"Why?"

I take the steps separating us and lift to my tiptoes, kissing the corner of his lips. "I'll see you later, Morningstar."

I'm about to pull away when his big hand wraps around my upper arm, keeping me close. "Why, Summer? You pretty much wanted me to die earlier."

I give him an exasperated look. "Okay, that's dramatic. I was pissed off and being very slightly unreasonable."

Connor strokes his thumb along my biceps. "I really like you, Summer. I like that you're weirdly obsessed with school and that you smile every time you get near the library. I like how your eyes light up when you open your runes textbook. I like that you and Alice have bonded, though literally no one can understand why you guys are friends. But..."

His *but* makes my stomach sink, but there's something about hearing all the ways he seems to have gotten to know me simply by being observant. He can only have seen those things while he assisted in that one class or maybe glimpses at lunch. How could he have seen so much in such a short time?

"I don't think you like me that way. And I guess I'm going to have to get used to that," he continues. His words don't inspire truth in me. They once again prompt emotions that are completely foreign to me. I think I *want* him to get to know me, and that is fucking terrifying.

Connor brushes his thumb along the inside of my arm again, and I know that he's about to pull away from me. I reach up and grasp his shirt, fisting it in my hand and pushing to my tiptoes. I slam my lips to his, kissing him hard. Connor hesitates for just a breath before he kisses me back. He snakes his arms around my waist and fits my body against his, deepening the kiss. I can taste his desperate need, but he pulls back, leaving me breathless and wanting more. He really needs to stop doing that.

"This is," Connor pants, "very confusing to me."

It's confusing to me too, so fucking confusing. This is so much more than I've ever done for anyone. Well, almost anyone...

*Show me what you can do, Summer.*

The memory tugs at me, and the echo of his voice makes me want to run and hide. Everything in me demands that I throw those walls back up and never speak to anyone ever again. Yet, when I look up at Connor and his sad eyes meet mine, the panic constricting my chest seems to ease.

"One date," I say, watching the darkness ease from his eyes. The words make me uneasy, but something is pushing me to do this. Maybe I'm longing to prove something to myself.

He blinks in surprise, gaping a little. "W-when?" he finally stutters out.

"I suppose you'll have to text me to set it up."

Connor wraps me in his massive arms, bending to kiss along my jaw. My eyes droop in pleasure. "I meant what I said. Last night was the best night of my life until... until it turned into the worst," he says, squeezing me to him.

I moan softly as he moves his lips closer to my ear. "The best?"

Connor nods. "Easily. I've never had a girl wear my jersey, either."

"Unwillingly," I add, a smile tugging at my lips.

"You knew what you were doing when you wore his jersey."

"What was I doing?" I ask, quirking a brow.

"Provoking me." He growls softly, and it's the most feral sound I've heard him make. It sends a wave of heat directly to my core.

"And why did that provoke you, Morningstar?"

Connor nuzzles against my neck, his stubble a delicious rasp against my skin. "Two reasons."

I reach up, tunneling my fingers in his hair. "I'm listening."

He presses a kiss to my cheek. "First, Hector is a bad guy." He kisses my other cheek. "Second, you're my girlfriend."

That word is like a bucket of ice water, bringing my fucking pussy back under control. I pull back and glare at him. "I am not your girlfriend."

"Well, I was planning to ask you that night."

I boop him on the nose. "Okay, listen up, Morningstar. This one date thing is under the proviso that you know we are, in fact, not boyfriend/girlfriend."

Connor pouts a little, and it's so fucking endearing that I have to bite the inside of my cheek to keep from smiling. What is he doing to me? This behavior would normally irritate the fuck out of me.

"Fine, but we're also not dating anyone else."

Oh, here we go with the macho man bullshit.

"I didn't agree to that."

He narrows his eyes, and there's a flicker of... jealousy? "Why not?"

"Because we're not together," I say plainly.

"So, you want to date other people?" he asks, his voice a disgruntled rumble.

"I didn't say that."

"Okay, I'm back to being confused." Connor blinks. "So you don't want to date anyone else, but you don't want to be exclusive?"

I groan internally. I understand he doesn't get how difficult this is for me, but...

"Connor, I'm trying, okay?" It's all I can offer him at the moment. Maybe it's all I will ever be able to offer anyone. This is completely unfamiliar territory for me. I can't tell if I'm being unfair or not, but the idea of commitment makes me wish the ground would swallow me whole and burn my skin off in a fiery inferno.

"All right." He cups my cheeks, looking down at me. Any despair or sadness has melted from his expression, and that familiar Morningstar sparkle is back in his eyes. I wonder if he inherited it from his mother or father because all the boys have it, even Rafe.

Connor bends, brushing his lips over mine. "Tonight. I'll pick you up at seven."

I nod and deepen the kiss a little, and I can feel his lips pull into a smile as he kisses me back, his fingers tunneling into my hair.

He tastes so good, feels so good, but I pull back when I remember Alice is still waiting for me. "Tonight at seven."

Connor just stares at me, his eyes roaming over my face. There is a hunger there, but it's the gentlest hunger I've ever seen. It's caring and adoring, "You're so beautiful."

I smirk up at him. "Don't make me cancel on you."

He laughs that deep, delicious laugh and my smile broadens at the sound. "So, no compliments?" he asks, and the question is so earnest that I can't help but reach up and kiss him again, moaning into his lips.

"Gods, you're so mushy."

Connor bites my lips. "The mushiest."

I pull back reluctantly. "I have to go."

"But... kisses." Connor pouts.

I laugh, trying to pull away, though I put in very little effort. "No, I left Alice at the union."

Connor holds me with ease and leans in again to kiss me deeply. "Well, she's a big vampire."

My hands are on his arms, and I am supposed to be pushing him away. Instead, I end up holding him tighter. I moan into the kiss, letting him taste my need. Connor backs me toward the bed, his lips never leaving mine. My legs hit the edge of the mattress. He breaks the kiss and gently eases me onto the bed. I look up at him and lick my lips, my chest heaving.

He pulls his shirt off over his head, and I sit back to appreciate his abs, his scent surrounding me. "Still have to leave?"

Fuck... I can't tear my eyes away from his stupidly hot body.

"Yes." I pant. "Fuck." I push at him and try to wiggle off the bed but get distracted by the heat of his skin beneath my palms. Connor laughs and bends, kissing me again. I practically lay back on instinct, desperate to feel his weight on top of me.

"I'm serious, Summer. Do you want to go?" he asks, kneeling between my legs.

*Say yes, say yes, say yes.* I've finally found a friend. I need to be a good friend. Maybe we can be quick, though?

I grab his shoulders and pull him down on top of me. His mouth slams over mine, our tongues tangling. I slide my fingers into his thick hair and fist my hands, yanking hard. Connor groans into my mouth, and I answer with a needy moan.

Without breaking the kiss, Connor unfastens my sports bra and slides it down my arms. He chucks it to the side and cups my breasts, teasing the nipples before trailing his fingers over my stomach. He hooks his thumbs into the waistband of my leggings and panties, pulling them off in one go.

I lift my hips to help him. The gesture is almost futile, given the strength he puts into pulling them down. My panties are barely off before he's plunging two fingers inside me. My core is soaked, my body ready for him. He groans at the feel of the tight, wet heat and crooks his fingers. My eyes roll back, and I gasp. I spread my thighs and reach for him, eager to get him out of his pants. My phone rings loudly, the shrill ringtone cutting through the moan-laced air.

"Ignore it," Connor moans into my mouth. He pulls his fingers almost completely out before pushing them back in. I arch to meet the slow thrust. My phone continues to ring, and I find enough strength to push his hand away, needing some space to find some clarity. Connor curses, low and filthy, rolling onto his back as I fumble for my phone and blindly answer it. "Hello?" I gasp out, my body quivering with unmet need.

"I thought you were dead!" Alice's voice sounds anything but concerned. She actually sounds smug. Asshole.

"No, I'm... just coming." I try to hide my labored breathing. My pussy is so horribly empty and greedy for release that it throbs uncomfortably. I reach for my bra and start to pull it on.

"You sure? I can just meet you at—"

"Babe..." Connor groans, his big hand grasping his rigid cock through his pants.

I cover his mouth, balancing the phone between my shoulder and ear as I fasten my sports bra. "No, I'll be there in five." Connor grumbles beneath my hand, and I end the call.

I pull on my panties and pants before sitting back on my heels and looking down at him. His eyes are dark, his pupils blown wide with desire. Thanks to the extremely noticeable bulge in his jeans, I can see how affected he is. I lift his hand and bring the fingers he had buried inside of me to my mouth. Connor's eyes get even darker, and he moans when I close my lips around his fingers and suck on them. The sweet taste of my arousal explodes against my taste buds. I slide my tongue up and down the long, thick fingers, pulling them deeper into my mouth. Connor whimpers, his cock straining the front of his jeans. I hollow my cheeks, sucking hard before I release them with a wet pop.

I climb out of bed and wink at him, checking my hair in the mirror.

"Wait... come back." Connor whines as he sits up, reaching for me.

I apply some more lip balm and blow him a kiss. "See you at seven, Morningstar."

He groans, falling back on the bed. "Do you stay awake at night thinking of ways to torture me?"

I wink at him before leaving his bedroom and heading toward the front door of the Morningstar House. Rafe catches me before I leave, pinning me with his gaze as he leans in the kitchen doorway.

"He's a good guy, Summer."

I glance at him. "I'm starting to believe that," I say, saluting him before leaving the house, feeling much lighter than I did when I arrived.

# 17

## SUMMER

I make my way back to the student union, and while I may be painfully horny, I can't get rid of the huge smile on my face. Alice slurps on a bag of blood, watching me smugly as I approach. Her aura practically radiates knowing arrogance.

"I ordered you an iced coffee, but all the ice has melted. I'm not sure why. You were only away for, like," she checks her watch, "an hour."

Fuck, had it really been an hour? I guess it was optimistic, thinking I would only be gone for twenty minutes. I slice into my finger and draw a quick rune of reparation with a twist to make it specific to food. My chocolate chip pancakes start to steam, and my coffee once again has formed ice cubes.

"Sorry. I didn't realize I was gone for so long."

"I'm surprised you came back. I thought you'd fallen and impaled yourself on his dick, never to be separated." Alice makes a sign across her heart, like a stake through it. I discovered it was the vampire version of throwing salt over one's shoulder.

I level a flat glare at her and sip my coffee.

"So," she smirks into her blood bag, "how did it go?"

I cut into my pancakes, trying to keep that annoying, weird smile at bay. "We're going out tonight."

Alice's eyebrows lift until they're almost popping off her forehead, her smile wide and cat-like. "Look at you."

"Don't make a big deal about it. It's one date."

Alice chews on her straw a little. "I can picture it now. Summer Morningstar…"

"Right, I'm canceling." I pull my phone out. I may not have his number yet, but Alice doesn't know that.

"No!" she practically shouts, lunging to snatch my phone.

I shove my phone into my bra and quirk an eyebrow at her. Alice flops back into her seat and glares playfully at me. It's my turn to grin smugly at her. I take a bite of the fluffy, chocolaty pancakes and moan. They definitely use alchemy to cook here. The mix is too good.

"It was weird, though. Rafe wasn't as broody, and he seemed to… approve of me being there. As protective as they all are of each other, I thought he would be furious with me."

"It's possible Rafe and I have been in cahoots," Alice confesses a little bashfully, fluttering her lashes coyly at me.

"But you're the one who suggested the jerseys!"

Alice shrugs, smiling unrepentantly. "I'm still chaotic, okay?"

I roll my eyes. "Well, you've been as subtle as an atomic bomb today."

"We just… think you'd be good together. It was a meeting of the minds."

"Rafe hardly knows me. What makes him think I'd be a good fit for his brother?" I tilt my head, taking another bite of my pancakes.

Alice thinks for a moment, "You two just have a… spark? I can't explain it." She shrugs. "I just think you deserve a guy who will worship you."

I sip my coffee and look away, unsure how to respond to such unfiltered kindness.

Alice covers my hand and waits for me to look at her again. "Sum? I just…" She pauses, trying to formulate her sentence correctly. "You should see your face when he's around. Even when he's annoying you."

My brows draw. "My face?"

She nods. "You just… Look, I know you're guarded. Clearly, I am, too. Which is probably why we are the way we are. You just look a little less… mistrustful when Connor is there."

I roll my eyes but regret it immediately, realizing how fucking rude it is. She's just trying to be kind, and I am pretty sure that acts of kindness do not come easily to Alice. I can endure this for her sake, begrudgingly and under extreme duress.

"I suppose," she scrunches her nose, "very selfishly, if I can see you be happy, maybe I can be too. Someday."

"We're going on one date, Al. Not binding our souls for eternity."

Alice flips me off. "Shut up and let me dream."

I laugh and take another bite of my pancakes.

"So, what are you going to wear?" she asks, ordering herself an iced coffee. She's been eyeing mine since I sat down.

I shrug. "I'm not sure what we're doing yet."

Alice brightens. "So, we need to go shopping?"

# BLOOD & BETRAYALS

I nod. "I guess, but I'll need to wait for Connor to text me so I can ask him."

"Wait, you don't even have his number? You're such a bitch. So you were screwing with me earlier—"

My phone alerts, cutting her off. I pull it out of my bra and put it on the table where we can both read it.

> CONNOR
>
> You know, it's really not fair you left me for Alice.

"Yeah, well, better get used to it, bird brain. I will always be her number one," Alice grumbles.

My lips twitch, and I pick up my phone. I quickly add him to my contacts before responding.

> SUMMER
>
> I thought you would be using the time to plan our ONE date tonight.

The text bubble immediately starts to jump up and down as he types out his response. Eager angel.

> CONNOR
>
> Oh, I already have a plan.

I give Alice a knowing look, and her chair screeches as she moves it closer to read over my shoulder.

> SUMMER
>
> Can I know the plan?

> CONNOR
>
> Dinner.
>
> And then something else.

"Oooh, cryptic, I love it. Maybe he'll take you to a virginal shifter sacrificial ritual." Alice pats my arm excitedly.

"You know, for someone who is supposed to hate shifters, you sure were sucking the face off one of them the other night."

Alice gives me an affronted look. "You dream of angel dick. I sometimes make out with shifter scum. We all have our flaws."

> SUMMER
>
> Just tell me what I should wear.

> CONNOR
>
> Um... Nice clothes. Warm.

There is absolutely no way I will cover myself up on a beautiful summer day like today. If he's planning to realm hop with me so we can fuck against an iceberg or some shit, I'll simply refuse.

"Nice clothes, but warm? Why are guys so thick? That could mean anything," Alice protests.

SUMMER

Okay, see you at seven. I'll be the one in a snowsuit.

Alice chuckles at my reply and then tugs at my arm. "Eat faster. I want to shop."

I laugh and finish up my pancakes. Alice holds up her hand when I go to pull up my card on my phone. "I got this." She reaches into her pocket and pulls out a small solid gold rectangle. **HRH ELVIRA ALICE LEGOSI** is engraved on the front in small letters. The waiter swipes the card, and I barely manage to snatch up my phone before Alice grabs my hand and pulls me out of my seat.

"Alice?" I ask as she drags me across the quad.

"Hm?"

"Your card... HRH?" I didn't even know there were cards you could use across realms, but apparently, Alice has one.

She glances at me, nodding. "Her Royal Highness." She rolls her eyes. "Pain in my ass."

I'm about to ask more, but from her body language, I can tell she doesn't want to tell me anymore about it. Considering she has been so supportive of my hang-ups and not delving into my past, she deserves her boundaries to be respected as well. There is more to Alice than meets the eye.

# 18

## SUMMER

*Lyr*

Alice and I shop for hours, and by the end of the day, I swear there isn't a single bralette or crop top I haven't tried on in all of Camelot. Alice put everything we bought on her gold card, even though I protested heavily every time she brought it out. Unfortunately for her bank account and me, she seemed to come down with temporary deafness when we reached the checkouts. At first, I thought it might be pity that made her so eager to pay for my things, but every time she used the card, a malicious gleam sparked in her eyes. She definitely had other motives for pulling out the card, which hadn't been present when she used her phone credits earlier in the week.

When we arrive home, it doesn't stop there. Alice makes me try on everything at least twice before we settle on the white co-ord, with the long-sleeved cropped top, matching miniskirt, and black chunky heels. It's not exactly the warmest option, but it's got sleeves. I stare at my reflection in the mirror, unease churning in my stomach. It's not because I'm not looking forward to the date. I've just never done something so... *formal.*

Alice claps from where she is sitting on my bed. "You look perfect. That outfit was an excellent find!"

I glance at her over my shoulder. She's the picture of calm, laying in my bed wearing a gray onesie. The graphic on it makes it look like it's covered in blood splatter. When she picked it up at the store earlier, she insisted she needed it so that when it's actually drenched in blood, no one will notice. She rolls out of bed and stands next to me. I smile at our reflections in the mirror as she snaps a photo of us.

I look at the photo and laugh. "That's honestly the perfect picture."

Alice opens the Nexus app and posts the picture.

*@KillerLegosi.* Baddies go out, Bigger Baddies stay home

Alice looks me over in the mirror again. "Damn. You know, if I weren't cursed with heterosexuality, I'd snatch you up."

I snicker, nudging her shoulder.

Connor knocks on the door at precisely seven, and I answer, my stomach doing somersaults.

"Woah." The word escapes him on a whoosh of air as he takes in my outfit, and I take a moment to appreciate the effort he has made. His black jeans fit him perfectly, and the white button-up shirt must be tailored to him. He's clean-shaven, and his eyes are glowing slightly.

"You don't look so bad yourself."

Connor blinks, still staring at me. "Woah."

"Hello?" I wave my hand in front of his face. "Are you still in there?"

Connor blinks and slowly shakes his head. He clears his throat. "Sorry, just... damn." He clears his throat again and holds out his elbow. "Shall we?"

I roll my eyes, but a smile teases at my lips as I slide my hand through his arm.

"Have her home by midnight, Morningstar!" Alice shouts from inside, having made a nest on the couch.

"Will do."

"And use protec—"

I close the door before she can finish her sentence and sigh. "Sorry, she's—"

"She's Alice. Yeah."

I laugh and shake my head as we leave Kelpie Hall. I can almost feel Connor's gaze on my face, just taking me in.

"I'm trying to get my brain going again, but it's taking a minute," Connor admits, clearing his throat again. I sigh and stop walking. Connor turns and looks down at me, concern creasing his brow. "Summer? Are you—"

Grabbing his face, I pull him down and kiss him deeply. Connor groans and backs me against the wall of Ammit Hall, crushing me between it and his body. Suddenly, the wall behind me vanishes, and I fall back. Connor's arm wraps around me, keeping me from landing on my ass. I glance over my shoulder to find a student standing there, blinking at me. I blush when I realize Connor hasn't backed me into a wall but up against a door to the building.

Connor grins at the guy. "Sorry, couldn't help myself."

I bite the inside of my cheek to stop my laugh and grab his hand, pulling him away from the dorm. The laugh bubbles up my throat, and I can't hold it back anymore.

"You're laughing at me?" Connor squeezes my hand, his mouth pulled into a broad smile.

"With you, big guy. I'm laughing with you." The pet name seems so familiar, and it leaves me almost instinctively. It fits him so well, and my chest warms a little when I use it.

Connor smiles bigger and drapes his arm along the back of my shoulders while still holding my hand as if he has to have me as close as possible. That does not make some of the knots in my stomach ease. It does *not*.

"Where are we going for dinner?" I ask as we wander toward the gate. The sun is only just starting to set, and the orange light stretches over the grounds, casting everything in a warm, romantic glow. The mist that normally lingers at the edge of campus is absent.

"I thought we'd go to Magnolia Bistro. There's a not-so-secret space in the back that is quiet and intimate." He brushes his lips over the top of my head. "Let's hope we don't run into the doom master again, or he might invite himself on our date."

My lips twitch, hearing the fear lacing his voice. The headmaster seems to terrify other people, too, not just me. Thank gods.

"I have to say, I was a little shocked you came over."

I glance at him, unsurprised to find him already looking at me. "Me too."

It is unlike me to seek someone out and risk rejection or even give someone the chance I've given Connor.

"I hope you know," he twirls a lock of my hair around his pinky, "I beat the heaven out of Zach and Zane."

The memories of last night threaten to overwhelm me. How it had felt to believe that he had used me, betrayed me for his own gain. I can't go through that again and repress the thought, shoving away the emotions that so eagerly seek to strip the joy from tonight. Super healthy of me, I know, but I refuse to return to that place of weakness.

"Please tell me you filmed it. I'd pay to see that."

Connor snorts. "Not this time, but don't worry, knowing them, it won't be the last time I have to do it."

We walk through the wards and into Camelot. It is the most perfect summer evening. Flowers bloom in large pots along the sidewalk, and the air is still and calm. A bit like Connor, or maybe that's just the way I feel when I am around him. There is an ease that comes with being with someone who seems to... see me or at least one version of me.

We arrive at the bustling restaurant, and Connor waves at the hostess. She is a student from Avalon and chats animatedly with him as she leads us through the main restaurant and past a curtain to our table. There are fewer booths back here, and soft music wraps around us. Lit candles on each table create a lovely ambiance, casting an air of romance throughout the room completely different from the one next door.

We slide into the booth, and I smile at Connor as she hands us our menus. Connor holds out his hand, waiting for me to take it across the table. I raise an eyebrow and stare at his hand, unused to romance. Some would say I'm allergic to it.

"I won't bite. Unless you want me to." He winks at me.

I exhale and place my hand in his with a glare, though there's no anger in it. Connor absentmindedly runs his thumb over my knuckles as he watches me. "You've never done this, have you?"

I tilt my head. "Eaten at a restaurant?"

Connor laughs. "Dated. With the plan of more."

"More?"

"Of being... committed. Sometime in the future," Connor says, holding my gaze.

"That's not the plan."

He smirks. "Oh, it so is."

I roll my eyes and try to pull my hand from his, but he catches it and interlocks our fingers. "Nice try."

I narrow my eyes at him, giving him my most intimidating glare, but he simply lifts my hand to his lips and presses a soft kiss to my knuckles. "We're going to take it slow. Super slow. Just a kiss after the first date."

I blink. "Wait, what?"

Connor looks down at the menu. "I'm starved."

I snatch the menu out of his hand. "What was that about taking it slow? We're still going to fuck, right?"

Connor blinks, releasing a small, strangled sound. "I thought you wanted to take it slow?"

I do want to take it slow. In fact, I don't want it to be any more than what it currently is. But withholding sex isn't taking it slow. I tug my hand from his. "You were knuckle deep in me like seven hours ago."

The waiter clears his throat as he approaches. Connor blushes deeply as the server fills our wine glasses, but I just watch him, waiting for an answer, undeterred by the intrusion.

When the waiter leaves, a slow smile creeps across Connor's face. "So you don't want to take it slow?"

I sit back in my chair. "We're not taking it anything. We're on a date and we fuck." I tilt my head, my smirk filled with challenge. "Are you up for it, big guy?"

His stupidly handsome smile just keeps growing, and he shifts around the booth, pulling me in closer to him.

Connor grasps my chin gently and leans in, his lips a breath away from mine. "You want to fuck, we fuck," he says, his voice husky and low. Those damned butterflies surge in my stomach, but I don't pull my gaze from him. "But I have one condition." I quirk a brow, waiting. Connor brushes his lips over mine. "While we are. I am the *only* one fucking you. And you are the *only* one fucking me."

I shiver at the small show of possession, at the desire in his voice. Fuck, why does that make me turn to fucking putty? There is something seriously wrong with me.

"Fine," I agree. It's not like I've encountered anyone else that I want to fuck, anyway.

Connor kisses me again, the touch of his lips whisper-soft. I scoot closer, wanting more, but he releases me and pulls back a little. "Good, because I think about last night and that... thing you did. Constantly."

I glance at his lips. "What thing?"

Connor's cheeks flush. "You know, when you," he swallows hard, "grabbed me."

I purse my lips, thinking. I know he's talking about when I pulled him into me, that moment when I took control, but it's more fun to play with him. "Hmm..." I lean in, biting his ear and whispering, low and filthy, "Maybe you should follow me into the bathroom and show me."

I pull back, appreciating how his pupils have almost completely swallowed up the blue of his irises. Sliding out of the booth, I glance at him one more time before turning and heading toward the restroom.

# 19

## SUMMER

I step into the bathroom and check the few stalls. Once I ensure they're all empty, I stand in front of the mirror and touch up my lipstick as I wait for Connor. The door slowly creaks open, and I meet his dark eyes in the mirror.

"Hey, big guy," I purr. "Fancy meeting you here."

Connor steps inside and closes the door. I hear the lock click, and then he slowly walks toward me. He stands behind me, his hands sinfully gliding down my sides to my hips. His fingers close into fists, bunching the material of my skirt and slowly sliding the hem up my thighs. He keeps his eyes locked on mine in the mirror, the blue nothing more than a thin ring around the darkening center.

"I've never done anything like this before." His normally unshakeable voice wavers with nerves, but the press of his cock against my ass tells me just how badly he wants this. My big angel likes this. Something about the forbidden appeals to him, and I wonder if the golden boy has ever toed the line of darkness.

"No?" I ask, my voice even.

His gaze strays lower in the mirror, and he groans at the sight of my bunched-up white wool skirt and the white lace panties beneath.

"Have you?" he asks, captivated. He slides his hand over my stomach and into my panties. The lace is already completely saturated from my arousal. "Fuck." The curse slips from him, low and filthy, as he slides a finger through my core.

I moan. "Maybe…"

Connor presses his thick finger inside me, stirring it slowly, stretching me. I widen my stance, opening to him. He rubs his erection against me and slowly starts to push another finger inside me. I grab his wrist, and he pauses, his gaze linking with mine again.

"Rule one of sex in a risky place, big guy. We don't have a lot of time." I pull his hand free of my panties and spin around, slamming my lips to his in a desperate kiss. Connor groans and lifts me onto the counter. My hand flies to his belt, and I practically rip it open before shoving his pants down. Connor already has a condom ready, and he rolls it on while I shift and wiggle, pushing my panties off. He grabs my thighs and pulls me to the edge of the counter, plunging his thick cock deep. I gasp and wrap my legs around him, savoring the burn mixed with the pleasure. Desperation hums through us, infecting our bodies, and I kiss him again, using his mouth to muffle my moans as he settles into a steady rhythm.

I bite his lip and move my hands to his ass. I sink my nails into the heavy muscles and yank him against me. At the same time, I arch against him, taking him so deep I ache with it. Connor's shout vibrates through me, and he thrusts faster, his pace turning frenzied as he responds to my silent demand for more. Harder. Brutal. Frenzied.

*I need to be punished.*

"Love that. Tell me what you want," he pants into my lips.

I slide my lips over his jaw and to his neck, biting him hard. No doubt, it will leave a bruise, and I can't wait to see it. I dig my nails in deep, pulling him harder against me. He stumbles forward, his cock pounding deep into my wet pussy. Connor curses into my ear, and I suck on his neck. The pleasure and ache are so overwhelming, and my need is so intense that my orgasm comes quickly and unexpectedly. I try to muffle my cry into his neck, but I'm not entirely convinced I'm successful. My pussy clenches around him, pulsing and demanding his release. Connor slams deep, and his body goes rigid, his shout of pleasure echoing mine.

Connor pants against my shoulder, clinging to me as his hips slow. "Hell of a way to start a date," he says with a breathless laugh.

I smirk and bite his neck again before pulling back and unwrapping my legs from around his hips. Connor slowly pulls out of me, and we both hiss. A shiver goes through me at the loss of his heat, and I take a few deep breaths. Connor steps back, his massive chest still heaving and his eyes glazed. I jump down from the counter, hoping my shaky legs will hold me. I push down my skirt and glance in the mirror, blushing at my appearance. My lipstick is messy, and my lips are bruised and swollen. His hands have made a mess of my hair, and my eyes are overly bright from my orgasm. I quickly freshen my makeup and run my fingers through my hair, trying to make myself look less like I've just been fucked in the restroom.

Connor leans against the wall, watching me in the mirror. He fixes his pants and steps up behind me. Pressing a kiss to my shoulder, he whispers, "I'll see you back at the table." His hand lingers on my hip for a moment, and he squeezes as if loathe to let me go before leaving the bathroom.

I take a few more minutes to put myself back together, barely recognizing the woman staring back at me. Her smile is too genuine to be mine, and the flicker of hope in her eyes does not belong to me. The walk back through the restaurant is almost empowering. Maybe people know what we were doing, maybe they don't, but I know what we were doing. I felt it, experienced it.

Connor is perusing the menu when I slide into the booth. He clears his throat, his cheeks still pink. "Well, that was…" He clears his throat again, his blush deepening.

I lift an eyebrow, waiting for the end of his sentence.

"Well, you wonder why I want to make you my girlfriend." He chuckles.

I open my menu, lifting it so that I can hide the delicate little smile that's lighting up my face, unsure if I'm ready to share it yet.

The rest of the meal goes by with lots of talk and laughter. Connor really is very charming and handsome. It's a dangerous combination, and I know it, but an ease quickly develops between us. Too fast.

Connor takes my hand in his as we leave the restaurant. We start back toward campus, and the next part of our date, which he still refuses to tell me anything about. The air is laden with the comforting scents of food and coffee. The sounds of laughter, conversation, and music fill the late summer night. We walk through warm pools of light cast by streetlights, and the windows we pass glow with welcome.

"You know, I've never had a girlfriend before." His statement cuts into the otherwise amicable stroll through Camelot.

I glance up at him. "That cannot be true."

Connor looks at me, lifting an eyebrow. "Why not?"

"You're the hot-as-fuck golden boy."

He blushes again, another infernally endearing quality of his. "Well, I haven't really been interested." He smiles, looking ahead again. "In relationships, I mean."

"Why?"

Connor shrugs. "Well, I'm busy. Not just with school but also with my brothers. It's not easy being the oldest." He's not wrong. I'm sure his brothers are a handful, especially the terrible twins, and Rafe clearly has his own set of problems.

"So why now?"

Connor lifts my hand to his lips, kissing my knuckles. "Well, I saw this girl at this party, and all I could think was *Her. She is the reason I didn't date before.*"

I look down at the ground, that annoying smile pulling at my lips again.

"Alice gave me a tip for our date," Connor says. "You know, for only having met like a week ago, you two are already like sisters."

"What tip?"

He shrugs. "She said that your past is off-limits."

I look away again, something like shame twisting in my stomach, but there is also a deep gratitude.

"She also said that she'd have fun finding out what my insides look like if I hurt you."

I look up at him, happy to see a glimmer of humor in his eyes. "You like her? Alice?"

Connor nods. "Don't get me wrong, she's batshit, but I would love to call her a friend one day." I squeeze his hand. It's the only way I know how to thank him for understanding someone important to me and someone who has had trouble being understood in the past.

"You know, and I don't particularly want to quote him, but the doom master always says that Avalon is a place to be different from who you were and decide who you want to be. And I just..." He pauses, his brow furrowing a little. "I don't want you ever to feel uncomfortable around me."

As we are about to cross through the boundary of the school, Connor stops and turns me toward him. "Are you ready for the surprise?" he asks with a grin.

I nod, a little apprehensive but even more concerned with how much I trust the angel already. I don't trust anyone. Ever. What is it about this place?

Connor brushes a kiss over my forehead, and we start walking again. He takes my hand and squeezes it as we cross the boundary. "You're not scared of heights, are you?" he asks, glancing at me with a broad, boyish smile filled with excitement.

"No," I reply warily. "Why?"

Connor just smirks at me and leads me along the path and into the forest behind the dorms. It's almost completely pitch black amongst the trees. "Con? Are you planning to murder me out here? Cause that would severely reduce your chances of a second date."

Connor laughs, leading me deeper into the forest. After twenty minutes of walking, the trees thin out, and I can see the sky's midnight blue with silver stars winking down at us. All of his brothers are waiting near a cliff at the edge of a clearing. An ominous black box sits between the twins. Rafe approaches us, unsmiling as usual.

"For your ears," Rafe says, dropping a pair of small foam cylinders into my hand. He hands a set to Connor, and Connor pats him on the back in thanks.

I frown at Connor, but he just smiles at me as he puts the earplugs in his ears. I follow suit and wait. Connor backs away and stretches out his shoulders, and I can't help but gasp as a pair of feathered wings burst from his back. I've seen angel wings before on campus, but these are... bigger and brighter.

"How...is your shirt still intact?" I ask, my brows furrowed. Rafe gestures for Connor to turn around, and I see that there are two slits in the back meant to accommodate his wings. I nod and step forward, eager to touch the beauty of those wings, but Connor turns back around, grinning at me.

Connor swoops me up into his arms, holding me bridal style. He winks at me before running toward the cliff edge and leaping off it. The scream catches in my throat. I cling to him tighter as we fall. Connor tucks his wings tight against his back, and we fall into the abyss. He keeps his eyes on my face the whole time, not a care in the world. Unexpectedly, he snaps his wings out, and with a powerful downward flap, we start to rise. He takes us higher, and we shoot past the cliff edge and his brothers. We fly until we're hovering at the tree line, and Connor asks, "You okay?"

His voice is very muffled by the earplugs, but I can see his delicious lips shape the words. I don't loosen my hold on him but nod, trying desperately to resist the stupid urge to look down.

Connor smiles and looks at his brothers, giving them a nod. Less than a minute later, something whistles through the air, shooting toward us. A loud boom shakes the air, and a flurry of light erupts all around us. The inky blue of the sky explodes into a kaleidoscope of cyan, fuchsia, white, and silver.

*Fireworks.* Connor's brothers are launching fireworks around us as we fly, giving me the fantastical, up-close view only angels get. His wings beat steadily, and he spins slowly in the air, grinning at me, his face illuminated with the colors exploding all around us. He shifts me in his arms so the front of my body is pressed against his. The fear ebbs out of me as I look at him, his eyes sparkling as he watches me. I slide my fingers into his blond hair and lean in, kissing him deeply.

Heat pushes against my skin, and Connor pulls back, spinning us in the air and dropping, narrowly dodging the explosion. "Fuck! Careful, Rafe!"

Rafe holds up his hands in apology, and Connor looks back at me. "You okay?" he mouths, and I nod, kissing him again. The fireworks freeze in place, and Connor tenses, pulling back. His muscles tighten around me, and I see his lips form a soft curse when he looks at his brothers. I follow his gaze and see the headmaster standing between them, his arms crossed. Even from this distance, I can see the anger in his gaze. He towers over all the Morningstar boys by several inches as if he weren't intimidating enough. I pull my earplugs out as we fly back down to the cliff edge, and Connor sets me on my feet. His face is flushed, but I can't tell if it is from anger or embarrassment.

"Headmaster—"

I place my hand on Connor's arm, stopping him. "It was my fault. I told them how much I love fireworks, and they were kind enough to—"

The headmaster's steely, silver gaze slides from me to Zane. Connor's younger brother is practically vibrating, his face pale and contorted into a look of disgust. "You haven't spent much time around angels, have you, Miss Tuatha De Daanan?" the headmaster asks, his heavy stare focusing back on me.

"No, sir." My cheeks heat.

"Zane Morningstar has a more enhanced truth ability than most angels. Say a lie around him, and he can't help but react."

Zane seems to shrink more into himself, and Zach hits him on the back of his head. The headmaster looks back at Connor. "This will not happen again."

"I was—" Connor begins.

The headmaster interrupts him, his gaze hardening. "I understand you wanted to impress a pretty girl. However, this was not the way to do so, and not on my campus."

My stomach flutters from the small compliment from the headmaster, and I am disgusted with myself. That reaction is so fucking ridiculous. He was simply making a point. He doesn't actually think it. Plus, the last thing I need is the attention of a being of his power.

Connor nods. "I know. My apologies, headmaster."

Headmaster Emrys gives a short nod and looks at all of us. "My office on Monday morning. Bright and early, Morningstars." He turns his attention back to me, and my stomach knots. "This is the second time I've found you at the center of trouble. Not a good start, Miss Tuatha De Daanan."

I drop my gaze to the ground, cursing the blush that heats my cheeks. "Sorry, sir."

"A third time, and you'll be suspended," he continues, his voice ice cold and his anger cutting through me. "Clean this up."

There is a faint whooshing sound as a portal opens behind him. He steps through, disappearing into the swirling light. We release a collective breath of relief when it closes behind him with a soft thump.

"Sorry." Connor places his hand on my arm, squeezing gently.

I look up at him through my lashes. "You're taking me back to your place, right? Say yes."

He nods. "Fuck yes."

I lean against him, kissing him deeply. Connor lifts me into his arms and starts walking back into the forest. His brothers shout out in protest, and I wink at them over Connor's shoulder. "Thanks, boys."

Connor and I lay on his bed, both practically naked. He looks over at me, his chest heaving and covered in a light sheen of sweat from our carnal activities. He rolls onto his side and pulls me into him, holding me against his chest.

I tense, looking at him. "What are you doing?"

"Cuddling you," he replies, burying his face into my neck.

"Uh... why?"

"Night, Summer." Connor's voice is groggy, already falling toward sleep. I lay there, uncomfortable and unsure of what to do. This can't happen. I don't do sleep-overs. I never have. There is something too intimate about sharing someone's bed for anything other than sex. I glance at Connor's sleeping face, looking so calm and peaceful. Even that riddles me with anxiety. Falling asleep next to someone is a huge vulnerability. He trusts that I will not slit his throat. I'm not ready for this. I can't stay here.

I carefully shift out of bed, trying not to wake him. He barely even stirs as I climb over him and silently pull on my skirt and top. I open his door and leave his room, carrying my heels as I leave the house so as not to wake anyone else. It's fairly comical how walk-of-shame-chic I look at the moment. Lucky for me, it's the middle of the night. It's interesting how safe I feel on campus already. Usually, walking alone in the middle of the night is not something I would risk, but here, I know that the thing I am afraid of cannot get to me. I refuse to consider that knowing the headmaster is nearby is also a factor.

I decide to forgo my heels and wander back to my dorm barefoot. I pull my phone out of my purse and scroll through my feed, clicking through the stories I've posted over the past twenty-four hours. As I'm tapping through them, I notice an icon in the bottom left-hand corner of the screen. I frown, looking down at it. There is a collection of small circles with the profile photos of people who have viewed my story, but one isn't a photo. It's a small gray icon with a generic faceless shape. I frown and open up the list.

The school's *Nexus* network has a policy that you can't view anyone else's account unless you have a verified photo on your profile. I scroll down the list until I find the profile. It's not a name, simply four numbers: *1015*. I tap on the name and open the account but find it completely blank. I back out of the page, clicking through the rest of my stories. The *1015* account has viewed every one of them. They don't seem to be following me, though. Maybe it's just an error or a bug? Could it be... No. It can't be. I shake my head and push *1015* from my mind, but unease gnaws at my gut. I put my phone away in my purse again, deciding to focus on enjoying the still summer night.

# 20

## SUMMER

*C*
*Mahl*

"What are you doing home?" Alice asks, appearing in her doorway. Her cheeks are flushed, and while she's still wearing that blood-splattered onesie, it's buttoned up wrong. I give her a look, and she leans on the doorframe, trying to fake nonchalance.

I tilt my head and drop my purse on the sofa. "I live here..."

"Yeah, right. I mean, why are you not with angel boy?" Alice frowns and glances behind her, waving frantically.

"I was," I respond simply, pulling at my fingers as guilt surges inside me. I don't feel good about not staying with Connor and leaving in the middle of the night. But I'd rather die than face that crazy, intimate moment in the morning when our eyes meet, and there are no barriers.

Alice searches my face, her eyes slowly softening. "Ah, okay. Just give me one second."

She disappears back into her room, and there are a few hushed whispers before Alice re-emerges, pulling a naked incubus behind her. She pushes him out rather forcefully and tosses his clothes after him before slamming the door in the poor guy's face.

"Okay, tell me everything." She comes over and drops down next to me on the couch. Her shoulder-length hair is mussed, no doubt from the incubus' fingers.

I sigh and sit back, resting my feet on the edge of the coffee table. "We had a really good time."

"Okay..." Alice waits for more, but I'm unsure how to articulate the thoughts in my head, knowing how neurotic they sound. "So dinner was good?" she prompts, trying to get more information from me.

I nod.

"What was the secret plan?"

"He took me flying." I smile at the memory. "His brothers set off fireworks."

Alice rolls her eyes, but her lips are pulled into a genuine smile. "He's such a mush."

"Then we got caught by the headmaster, who was furious."

Alice grimaces. "Fuck. What did he say?"

I shrug. "Something hot," I reply without thinking. Now that I try to recall his exact words, I just remember how he made my cheeks flush and my stomach flutter and knot simultaneously. I really dislike how much I agree with everyone about how gorgeous he is.

Alice bursts out laughing. "Oh, no! You have the hots for the headmaster."

I roll my eyes. "Please, Alice. Even you can see that he's annoyingly attractive. Even if you don't think he's physically attractive, his attitude is hot, in a terrifying and intimidating kind of way."

"So, what did he actually say?"

I frown as I try to remember, and his voice shoots through my skull like a threatening caress. "This is the second time I've found you at the center of something," I begin, poorly imitating his voice. "This is a poor start, Miss Tuatha De Daanan."

"Okay, so all that command and strength might be a little hot, but you better not get expelled, Sum." Alice laughs. "So then, what happened?"

"Then we went back to his place."

"And... then you came home?"

I nod. "Well, he went to sleep." My stomach churns, and I desperately want to stop talking about this. I want to push it from my mind so I can rid myself of the horrible, unfamiliar clawing of guilt down my spine.

Alice watches me for a minute before standing and walking into the kitchen, pulling out a bottle of tequila. "Drink?"

I nod. "Absolutely."

Alice hands me the bottle and then slumps down next to me again. I take a deep drink before handing it back to her. We pass the bottle back and forth, and I remain silent until I've had my third deep swig of tequila. Then I exhale heavily and blurt out, "We fucked in the restaurant."

Alice chokes on her drink and lurches forward, coughing. I hit her on the back, trying to help clear her airway. "Like in the middle of it?" she gasps out.

I grimace. "In the bathroom, before the appetizer."

Alice snorts. "Man, you got it bad."

"I do not," I grumble, snatching the liquor bottle from her. I know I didn't want to talk about this, but there is something inside me that needs to. Alice and I haven't known each other long, but I know she won't judge me for my insanity.

"You absolutely do, and he's definitely got it bad for you." She thinks for a moment. "Plus, he's hot in that angelic, weirdo way."

"Okay, chill. He's fine."

"You think he's super dreamy." Alice flutters her eyelashes. "You liiiiiiiiiiiike him."

I roll my eyes, handing her the bottle back. "Whatever, I'm going to bed."

"Summer and Connor sitting in a tree, K-I-S-S-I-N–"

I swat at her. "You're an asshole," I say and snatch the bottle back, not making any move to get up from the couch. Our laughter dies, and I take another deep drink of the tequila.

Alice looks at me, and I feel the weight of her gaze on me, tension sitting heavy between us. "I've never had a friend before," she says finally. I lean my head back against the sofa and turn it to look at her, waiting for her to continue. She pulls the bottle from my hand and takes a drink. "I've never been wanted, and I've never fit in with my people. It's nice... having someone to talk to. Even though I know you'll probably never understand, it makes me feel less alone." Alice's eyes are sad, and I can tell this isn't something she ever talks about or admits out loud, "My father has tried to kill me twice. He is terrified by the mere thought of being usurped." Her laugh is humorless. "If he spent even twenty seconds with me, he'd realize that's the farthest thing from what I want."

I look ahead, an internal war raging within me, but I feel the resolve as it settles. The truth starts to travel through my body toward my mouth. I take the bottle and another deep swallow, trying to use the liquor to push it back down, but all it seems to do is strengthen my resolve. The silent seconds drag on until I can't fight it anymore.

"I killed someone." I have never uttered the words, and the truth tastes worse than any of the lies I've spouted.

Alice's gaze swings to me, yet there is no sense of fear coming from her. Vampires are known for violence, so it wouldn't surprise me if she had a mixture of blood on her hands, but that is their nature. It's as integral to them as the runic languages are to fae.

"I didn't mean to," I continue, the words barely a whisper. "I was young and stupid, and I thought I was..." I close my eyes, steadying myself. "I thought I was in love, but I was wrong about so much. So desperate to *belong* to someone."

His face flashes against the darkness created by my closed eyelids. I inhale sharply and open my eyes, hoping to banish his image.

"I could blame it on manipulation or naivete, but it was me. Whether it was an accident or not, I did it." The phantom tears that will never fall burn at the back of my eyes. "I was abandoned when I was a baby and brought up by a mortal. She rarely showed me kindness, but she was there and saw to my basic needs. When she died, I sought... something, anything to oust the loneliness. That's when I met Torin. He was the second fae I'd ever met, and he was... so interested in my... strangeness." The truth spills easily from my lips, like it was desperate to be spoken, to be heard.

Alice slides her hand into mine, listening intently.

"I'd spent my whole life suppressing my powers. If I slipped, I was punished. Severely. So severely that soon, the roar of my suppressed powers became nothing but a hum. Torin knew what I was immediately. He wasn't fooled by the way I braided my hair over my ears to hide the points. I don't know how he was able to scent me, but he did. He told me it was because we had a bond, a fae bond. Looking back on it now, I think he was trying to convince me that we were mated, and truly, I was so ignorant back then that if he'd have come out and said it, I would have believed him."

Alice's eyes go wide, and her hand tightens on mine.

"We're not," I assure her, and she nods, relaxing. "He tried to coax my powers out of me. He was desperate to see what power I held, but I'd buried it so deep. When I couldn't perform, he punished me too. Then he would spend hours telling me he loved me, and it wouldn't happen again. He would always follow that up by telling me I just needed to show him I was powerful enough to be his. I was desperate. I thought I loved him, but I was so stupid. One night, we were in the woods, and a group of his friends were there. I had never met them before, and it was a little weird and awkward."

*Show me what you can do, Summer.*

I squeeze Alice's hand tight and take a few deep breaths, willing the words away.

"He stood me in front of them and demanded that I show them what I could do, but I couldn't even summon a flicker of light. They all laughed, and Torin joined in their mocking of me. They said... such horrible things. I begged Torin to take me home, but he refused. Torin told me they were all going into the forest to perform a special fae ritual, but I was to stay behind since I obviously wasn't a true fae. I was nothing more than a defective fae with no powers. So I did. I always did exactly what I was told."

The words stick in my throat, and I swallow hard. I am so angry with that young girl. She was so weak. I feel so disgusted and filled with shame when I think about her. The pressure behind my eyes builds, and I wish I could cry. Alice doesn't press me, and she doesn't offer advice or platitudes. She just sits in the darkness with me and holds my hand, not expecting more, but letting me know she's here if I have more to say. Her steady support gives me the courage to keep going. I lift the bottle and take a few long gulps of the tequila before continuing.

"They all left, disappearing into the woods, leaving me alone in the dark. Except they didn't all leave. One of his friends stayed behind, and he tried to..." I close my eyes and shake my head. "That was the moment my powers burst free, and I blasted a hole right through his chest. I remember the feeling of his weight on top of me, and how he got so much heavier when his soul left his body."

Alice grabs the bottle from me. Startled, I look over at her. Her irises are ringed with red, and I realize she is growling. Without letting go of my hand, she takes a long pull from the bottle, and I wait until she waves me on before continuing.

"I was nearly hysterical, but I finally managed to shove his body off me. When I sat up, Torin was watching me from the tree line. To this day, I'm not sure if he saw the whole thing or not. I thought he would punish me or maybe just kill me. Instead, he just gave me a wicked smile and said, 'Oh, Summer. You've been withholding from me.' I knew I had to get out of there, so I ran, and he chased me. He is still chasing me to this day."

Alice shifts to face me. "Wait. What?"

"I've been dodging that male for years. It's one of the reasons I agreed to come here. He can't get to me here."

"Well, fuck," Alice says.

I nod and grab the bottle, taking another drink. Exhaustion tugs at me, emotionally and mentally drained from telling the story and having to relive the memories. I am sure the tequila and my sexcapades with Connor have also sapped my strength, but I can barely keep my head up.

"When did you last see him?" Alice asks.

"Last year. I caught a glimpse of him in the town where I had settled, so I left." I look at her. "Alice, you can't tell."

Alice nods. "I'll take it to the grave."

I sigh heavily. "Thank you."

Alice and I finish off the bottle. The conversation is much lighter, and our friendship is stronger. When neither of us can keep our eyes open any longer, we get up and stumble to our rooms. I collapse into my own bed and pull the covers up around me. I glance at the closed box on the bedside table but decide that tonight is not the night for sinking into that loneliness. Tonight, I chose to be lonely, but something good came from it. At least, I hope it's good. The vulnerability feels like oil against my skin, but the burden of my past feels a little lighter.

I roll onto my back and look up at the ceiling, letting my mind wander. I wonder again about that strange account that had watched all of my stories. Uneasiness settles on my shoulders. Could it be Torin? I grab my phone, tapping through my stories again. The account is still there and active. I thought it might have been flagged and taken down, but it is still there, even with the gray amorphous blob profile picture and the simple 1015 username. I shove my phone under my pillow and drift off, thinking about my mysterious watcher. But it's not thoughts of Torin that haunt me tonight. Instead, it's my stranger, and I don't feel fear but excitement.

# 21

## THA

She's been busy. I slide my finger across my phone, glancing at the pictures she just posted. One was with her roommate, the two flipping off the camera with shots in their hands. My jaw ticks when the next is a blurry image of her and the boy. The following two are of her, the boy, and his brothers.

I click on the small icon and watch her stories, studying each one, learning and absorbing more. The first several are *Outfit of the Day* variations of her uniform, tiny accessories changing as I watch them. In the last, she'd left her hair unbraided, wearing it back in a ponytail for the first time. She must be getting comfortable.

Once I knew of her existence, I made a point to find out all I could about her. I know she had to conceal her heritage when she was growing up, and when others did find out, she was persecuted for it. I am surprised she has let her guard down so readily.

The following story is of her roommate and her with some sort of filter that gave them dog ears. The two are indeed an odd pair, but they have gotten close in the short time they've known each other. I study her face as she laughs with Alice. Very few haven't heard the rumors of Elvira Alice Legosi. They call her Elvira the Impure and many other less charitable names. She is reviled by her people and more than a little murderous. Yet, she seems incredibly protective of her roommate.

I swipe through to the next story. Someone was filming her as she studied, slowly zooming in on her face. It took a while before she caught on and chased the person around to get her phone.

I wonder how well she did on her recent exam. She is very bright and has an affinity for runic languages that surpasses her peers.

She's in the library now. That's the third time today. She only does that when she's feeling anxious. Does she sense there's something wrong? That she's living her days in idyllic comfort, but there's something *more* she's missing?

The man tied to the chair whimpers and slouches forward. With my free hand, I yank the dagger out of his throat and lift his chin with the flat of the blade. His eyes lock on mine as the last lingering remnants of life leave his body. I want my face to be the last he sees.

I flick through her page again. *Hmm.*

An alert pops up on my phone. I frown and swipe it to check the spell, my fingertips leaving a smear of blood across the screen. I wait impatiently for the surveillance spell to appear. The runic network is a bit slower this far from Avalon, but eventually, a video feed appears, hovering over my phone, suspended in mid-air.

My eyes narrow when I see her pull that boy into the stacks. My screen cracks a little in my grip as I watch him lift her. Red clouds the edges of my vision when she wraps her legs around his waist, and he begins to fuck her. The only thing stopping me from completely shattering the phone is her eyes. They're not filled with pleasure but frustration.

She's not getting what she needs from the boy. But then, how could she? She is still only an echo, a partial silhouette of a person who is slowly coming to realize who she is. How can she fully surrender when she's not even fully herself?

I close the security spell and grab the dead male's shoulder. Shooting my power into him, he comes back from the beyond with a gasp of air. His blood stains his neck and the skin over his heart from all the other times I'd killed him over the last three days.

His eyes fill with tears.

I wave my knife at him, the blade dark with his blood. "Now, now. It's no fun if you die on me so easily, is it? This time, we'll make it last."

His scream was heard for miles.

# 22

## SUMMER

*Rae*

I burst through the cantina doors at a near run toward Kelpie. Fear tightens my stomach, squeezing until I feel nauseous. A week. It's only been a week of Connor and I settling into casually seeing each other. Though the only firm rule of our *relationship* is that we don't fuck anyone else, I have my own set of rules, all of which I have broken.

Walls that I had spent years building crumble like clay every time he gives me that flirtatious smile or makes me laugh. I had spent years building those barriers, and I thought they were made of steel. Today, when I pulled him from whatever he was doing to fuck him in the library stacks like some horny teenager, for whatever reason, my stomach twisted into knots. The worst part is that I don't know why. It just felt like something was missing. Maybe it's because I wished he'd be rougher with me? A part of me wants him to dig his fingers in enough to leave bruises, to grab me, mark me, claim—

No. I'm not going there. It's fine. I'm enjoying being with him. It's not complicated, and that is what I wanted. When we started this, I set some personal boundaries to help me cope with the commitment. Even the thought is laughable. It's barely a commitment, but I want to claw off my skin whenever I think about tying myself to someone, even with something as simple as a verbal agreement to be true to one another. I've never been able to rely on anyone enough to promise them anything, but this is different. He's the perfect golden boy. He's patient, funny, smart, and loyal.

*And too good for me. Fuck.*

Okay, let's go through it again. I was out for a run. Connor popped into my head, and I texted him. A booty call in the dusty old stacks of the library does not a relationship make, but sending him the message prior still feels like too much advanced planning. My original boundary was that we would not arrange hookups. Doing so leads to expectations and then disappointment if plans are canceled. To avoid all that, we would simply fuck spur of the moment. At least, that had been the plan.

My second rule was to limit dates to the evenings and no more than once a week. Today, after having sex in the library, we went for lunch. Halfway through my Caesar salad, I realized what we were doing. I'd lurched to my feet, whacking my knee on the table in my hurry and babbling an excuse about forgetting plans with Alice. Connor took it in stride as he did everything. He simply stood and cupped my chin, kissing me so softly and with so much familiarity that my chest ached. He's too good, patient, understanding, and willing to put up with me. That pleasant ache quickly turned to a sharp stabbing pain as the panic set in.

My third and final rule is one that I have had for years. I established it when I became sexually active, and I haven't thought twice about it since. But with Connor, it causes guilt to claw down my spine like a wolf shifter on the hunt under the full moon. This past week, I have fucked Connor four times, and every single time I managed to convince him that we should go to his house instead of my dorm. At this point, he probably thinks my room is a filthy mess or that we're housing some kind of demonic beast. Or worse, he's waiting for me to open up to him. No matter the lameness of the excuse, he would simply lead me back to his place.

Once back at Morningstar House, we would race to his room, both of us undressing manically and falling sloppily onto his bed before getting down and dirty. Every night, after we each had an orgasm or two, I would wait for Connor to fall asleep, and then I would sneak out, just like I did that first night. Every time I do it, the guilt eats away at me a little more. For some reason, it feels like a solid stone of betrayal inside me, but I don't know how to let these rules go. I put them in place to protect myself and to keep from repeating past mistakes.

Three mornings Connor asked me where I was when he woke up, and three mornings, I gave him some bullshit excuse about why I had to leave his house at 5:00 AM. Sex is a carnal need. It's passion and fire, but sleeping in someone's bed and waking up with them in the morning is so intimate. There is an intense vulnerability in facing someone the moment you open your eyes. Your walls lowered enough for them to climb through.

Kelpie Hall has never looked more inviting. I sprint inside and upstairs to our floor, practically wrenching our door open. Anxiety is buzzing under my skin, making my chest tight. I slam the door behind me and start pacing the empty living room, trying to calm myself. My breath is shallow and frantic. There is such a conflict of emotions inside me, emotions I have such little experience with. On the one hand, I am dealing with the guilt and betrayal that persists every time I sneak out of Connor's bed after he dozes off. On the other hand, there is the deep-seated terror at the idea of committing even more to Connor, allowing him to see more of me.

Alice comes out of her room, and her gaze turns wary when she sees me. "You okay?"

I glance at her, grateful to see her face. I had worried that things would be weird after I opened up to her, but honestly, it only made us closer.

Why couldn't Connor just be like Alice? I know instinctively that no matter how close Alice and I get or how long we are friends, she will never ask me to open up and be vulnerable. We are too similar in that way. We were both made this way by pasts we'd rather die than revisit. The only difference between us is that Alice's past was written in blood and mine in stone.

I just pace, my brain racing a million miles a minute, her words getting lost in the fray. Something soft and squidgy hits me on the side of the head. I stop. Shock makes everything inside my head go completely silent. I blink at Alice and then down at the half-empty blood bag on the ground at my feet.

"Oh, good. I thought I was going to have to commit you. What's going on?" Alice says, moving around the couch.

"I went for a run, and then..." I pause, the words not coming to me easily thanks to the adrenaline still coursing through my system. "Well, I wanted to have sex, so I texted Connor."

Alice nods. "Against your rules, but fair."

She is the only person I'd explained my personal boundaries to. It seemed more important she know them than Connor because they have nothing to do with him. They have nothing to do with Alice either, but honestly, in just the two weeks I've been here, she's become the best friend I've ever had. She'd just nodded as if they all made perfect sense, making me feel slightly less crazy.

Alice waits for me to continue, and eventually, I start pacing again, but slower. "He was at the library, so we did it there. Then we went for lunch."

Alice blinks at me, and I give her an incredulous look. "For *lunch*, Alice!"

Alice's lip curls. "How very... coupley of you."

I scoff derisively. "Fucking tell me about it!" I stop pacing and yank the tie out of my hair, running my fingers through the long strands. "I fucking hate it, and now I'm freaking out. Alice, I've only known him for like... two weeks. Two fucking weeks and suddenly we're going for lunch."

"So, I know why I hate it because... gross, but why do you hate it?" Alice asks, watching me owlishly.

"I didn't hate it! That's the problem! We were actually having a..." I have to hold back another panicked breath, "nice time."

Alice shudders. "Oh, fuck. You're in deeper than you thought."

I start pacing again. "You know what? It's fine. I just need to establish my boundaries again. We're fucking. That's it."

Alice picks up the blood bag from the ground and opens it again, taking a loud slurp as she grabs a magazine from the coffee table and flops onto the couch. "You think it'll be that easy?"

"Fuck, you're right. I'm ending it."

Alice rolls her eyes and sits up, tossing the magazine back onto the table. "Summer. Connor does it for you, right? Like he *does* it for you."

I frown. "What are you talking about?"

Alice groans and looks up at the ceiling, obviously seeking some higher power to give her strength. "Do you like having sex with angel boy?"

"I mean, yeah, but you know about my past, and Connor is just... too perfect."

Alice speaks very slowly like I'm a moron that's not getting her point. "Why complicate it? He knows you're not together, right?"

I sink onto the couch, slouching next to her, my exhausted body humming. "It already feels complicated."

Alice nudges me. "Okay, answer me this. What would you do if you saw Connor kissing someone else?"

I glance at her, truly stumped. "I don't know."

"You'd at least be conflicted, right?"

I shrug. "I guess. I don't know. But, Alice, he wants more. He wants a... relationship."

"He's obviously happy with the situation at the moment. Enjoy it for now and deal with the rest of it later." I sigh, and Alice chuckles. "Want me to run interference with him until you figure it out?"

"Interference?"

"You know, do you want me to come up with some reasons why you can't see him? It might take the pressure off."

I nod. "Thank you."

Alice holds her pinky finger up in the air between us. "Here is to Summer figuring out which is more powerful, her commitment issues or her libido!"

I roll my eyes but link my pinky with hers and laugh, finally relaxing. "Okay, whatever. Are we going out tonight?"

Alice pretends to think as she pulls out her phone. I don't miss that the first thing on her screen is the invite to the shifter house party tonight. She quickly closes it and scrolls through her phone. "Sorcerers mixer, no. Incubus *study session*? Gods, no. Huh..." She scrolls back to the shifter invite. "There's a party at the shifter house. It'll be lame, but it's better than the other options."

I give her a knowing look. "You want to go party with the shifters?"

"Ew, no. But they usually have a ton of booze, and it'll be packed with loads of guys." Alice tries to hide her blush with her hair. I roll my eyes.

"Shifter house it is. Can't wait for archaic rules and female oppression." That was one of the consistent things I'd read when studying Nhang, the realm of therianthropes. Even with its ever-changing landscape, climates, and varying factions, one ideology resonated through each shifter group, no matter how much they differed from each other. *Might makes right.*

"Oh, they're not that bad anymore..." Her words trail off when she meets my gaze. "What?"

"I am once again going to remind you that vampires and shifters are natural enemies," I tease, trying to get under her skin. It is a common thing to see vampires and shifters facing off, both in classes and outside of them. Alice is the only one who doesn't seem to care.

"Please. I loathe them," Alice asserts, dragging out the word. I don't need to be an angel to know she is lying.

"I'm sure you do," I say and stand up, heading toward my room. My smirk widens when I hear her frustrated growl. I stop short, noticing a man's hoodie on the floor. Glancing back at her, I bend and pick it up. On the back, there are the signs for alpha, beta, and omega. Alpha and omega are white, and the beta symbol is blue. I slowly turn to face her.

"Alice?"

Alice watches me in horror, her mouth opening and closing.

"You're fucking a shifter, aren't you?"

Alice bristles, standing up and clenching her fists. "Okay, first of all..." She walks around the couch and snatches the hoodie from me. "Maybe. And second of all, maybe I'm fucking more than one of them."

I burst out laughing. "Never change."

Alice blinks and then starts to laugh, too.

# 23

## SUMMER

*Tae*

I read through my assignment for ancient runes and start tracing them on my pad. Ignis. I pick up my small dagger and prick my finger, carefully writing the archaic Latin on my skin. As my blood dries, the rune turns iridescent. Holding out my hand, I focus on the rune drawn onto my arm and snap my fingers. A small flame flickers above my thumb, and my lips twitch as I open my hand. I let the tiny flame dance through my fingers, controlling it with my mind. Too quickly, the rune fades and the flame dies.

My nose scrunches in disappointment. Professor Brooks said there was a balance with runes, and their temporary nature is one. Once a rune is activated, the timer starts, and depending on the caster, it can last a matter of seconds or days.

Flipping to a later chapter, I copy down another rune, Ancient Greek this time. I trace over the character again and again, learning the feel of the swooped lines as they curl into a sharp edge. The rune is meant to open a lock made of steel. I tilt my head, studying it.

The rune seems to glow in my mind's eye, and then it starts to change. The curved line at the top inverts, scoring through a newly formed crescent-shaped line. I watch in amazement as things continue to shift. Another line angles to the left, and the rune bends slightly, making the entire thing something I've never seen before. I quickly flip the page of my notebook and start sketching out the new rune I can see so clearly in my mind.

"You're still studying?" Alice asks, barging into my room. The rune dims a little and then completely disappears into the recesses of my mind as I complete the drawing. I stare at the pad, frowning at the new rune, trying to make sense of it. What language is this?

"Summer?"

Her voice snaps me back to the present. "Sorry, I'll be fifteen minutes."

Alice nods and leans toward the mirror, focused on correcting her eyeliner and barely paying attention to me. She is wearing a microscopic dress, and she is definitely trying to impress someone tonight. I stand up and stretch. My muscles are stiff from sitting for so long while lost to the fascinating world of ancient runes. Where had that rune come from? I must have seen it somewhere and remembered it, but where?

The questions continue circulating through my mind as I sort through the new clothes Alice bought me. I've never had a wardrobe this extensive, and new things continue to appear in my closet. When I ask Alice where they came from, she just shrugs. She is such a little weirdo.

I pull out a racy, royal blue number just as short as Alice's postage stamp of a dress. The silk whispers against my skin as I pull it on, and the straps are so thin that braless is the only option for the evening. The cowl neckline plunges low enough that I'm showing a good amount of cleavage, but I am in no danger of spilling out of the top. I've always thought the tits and ass gods had blessed me. I appreciate and don't mind showing off those parts of my body, and this dress definitely highlights them.

I slide my feet into a pair of silver stilettos before leaving my closet. Alice is still checking herself out in the mirror, and I can't help but roll my eyes at her vanity. But then I'm the biggest hypocrite in all the realms because I start to primp beside her. I gently push her out of the way and apply my lipstick, bending slightly to get closer to my reflection. I finish my makeup and put my hair half up, holding it in place with a sparkling bow clip.

"Damn, we look hot," Alice says, grabbing my phone and snapping a photo of us in the mirror before immediately posting it.

For someone who never used to record their life, I certainly enjoy doing so here. I post multiple times a day, and my page is full of photos of me and my friends. *My friends.* I never thought I'd have even one friend. Now, I have multiple people who want to know me. At least as much as I'll let them, at least the side I am willing to share. I may not know who I am becoming here, but she is someone who has friends and posts on *Nexus* regularly. I always have at least ten stories up a day, each showing a different aspect of my life, and I'm weirdly enjoying it.

Alice wraps her arm around my waist as we leave the dorm. "Thanks for coming with me. You sure you wouldn't prefer a meal of angel dick instead?"

I snicker. "Shut up."

The house is just coming into view when I feel my muscles start to tighten with awareness. My blood surges, my power rising from the depths when I sense the fae. I have no idea why my power roils when they are near, but I'm going to have to work on controlling it. They crawl all over campus. How are there so many of them, yet not a single one has eyes like mine? Alice squeezes my hand when I slow.

"You okay?"

I nod and resume walking. *Control it, Summer.* "Yeah, I just need a drink."

None of the other fae react like this when I am nearby, at least not visibly. They are uneasy with the difference in my eyes, but they mostly seem curious. However, the more time I spend near them, surrounded by them, the more my visceral reaction to them grows. It coils and brews, itching under my skin until the need to lash out is nearly unbearable. Sometimes, it is impossible to resist. It wants violence. In class, if there are enough of them, my notes turn—

I shake my head. I need to stay focused here in the present so I can get this under control.

Like that night at the Morningstar House, the party has spilled out onto the front lawn and the chaos from inside is bleeding into the night. Music booms, and the techno rhythm rattles my bones even out here. Alice and I enter the house, and as we make our way through the mass of bodies, I try not to look around for Connor. I'm not sure if I want to see him here or not.

Brett, the snow leopard shifter from the library, catches sight of us and waves. We make our way toward him, bobbing and weaving through groups and couples dancing and swaying to the beat.

Brett leans in to speak into my ear. "Hi! Good to see you!"

I smile at him, looking around the room. Alice is already making eyes at a wolf shifter who is throwing suggestive looks her way. I wonder if he's the owner of the hoodie or just another from her roster. I grab Alice, and we wander into the kitchen.

Brett is pulled into a serious-looking conversation with a guy who looks like an older, angrier version of himself. They both have dark auburn hair and a smattering of freckles across their noses, but the older one has darker eyes and a sinister air about him. Alice watches shamelessly as she pours an amber liquid into a bright red plastic cup.

"It looks like Brett is related to the alpha," Alice remarks, taking a deep drink from her cup before heavy-handedly topping it up.

"Okay?" I down a shot of tequila and shiver slightly before pouring another.

Alice leans against the counter behind her, nursing her drink and watching the two shifters. "His name is Fergus. I've heard he's a massive prick."

I glance at them and see how Brett shrinks under his brother's glare. Fergus snaps one last thing and then storms away. He is none too gentle as he forces his way through the crowd, obviously looking for someone. Brett stays rooted to the spot until Fergus returns, pulling a woman behind him. She keeps her eyes on the ground as Fergus bares his teeth at Brett, snarling loud enough that his words surge over the music.

"Man up and get it over with, little brother," he growls. Brett looks at the woman, a slight glimmer of apology in his eyes, but she keeps her gaze on the ground.

Before I know what I'm doing, I'm across the room and stepping between Brett and Fergus. I'm unsure why, but my instincts are surging, telling me to intercede.

"Who the fuck are you?" Fergus sneers at me, and Alice hisses at him from my side, rage radiating from her.

"I'm someone you don't want to piss off." I lift my chin, looking down my nose at him even though he is taller than me.

"This is pack business, little pointed-ear freak."

My lips curl into a smile.

"Back the fuck up," Fergus snarls at me.

"Ferg—"

"You shut up, too. You're already enough of an embarrassment to the pack," Fergus interrupts Brett, turning his furious gaze on him.

Fergus's body shakes as he struggles to contain his rage. I don't move, and he shoves me. The second he does, the entire room moves, trying to get away from him. Alice calls for me, but she's washed away in the sea of people.

I shove him back. "You're a fucking asshole bully, throwing your size around to intimidate your pack."

One minute, I'm looking up at him, and the next, pain explodes across my face, my ears ringing with the force of his backhand. The power I've repressed most of my life stretches awake at the threat. I realize now that I have just been pretending to have it leashed. It has grown stronger and more unruly each time I've encountered another fae. The wall holds, but just barely, my power eagerly pushing through the fissures created by the force of my anger. It is raw, untamed, and vicious. Light sears my eyes, and the sound pierces into my ears painfully.

No. Not again. How could I have done this again?

*Show me what you can do, Summer.*

I blink away the light, a deep exhaustion permeating my body. Chaos reigns around me, assaulting my senses. Fergus is in a heap on the floor, and the room is a mess. People are screaming and scrambling for the doors. Someone obviously managed to erect some sort of force field to limit the harm to the other partygoers, but the furniture was not so lucky.

Blood trickles down my cheek, but I don't care. The room quickly clears except for Brett. Fergus narrows his eyes at me, his body vibrating and his rage palpable. His form explodes, shreds of his clothes and skin fluttering to the floor. In his place is a massive snow leopard with bright yellow eyes filled with malice. Brett shoves me out of the way, and I see that his eyes have gone completely feline, the same luminous yellow as his brother's.

"Run." A roar laces his voice as he starts to shift.

I shake my head. Fuck that. I have been running my entire life. This time, I am going to fight. Besides, I've already burned through decades of repressed power. Why not finish this? Swiping my cheek to gather the blood there, I try to recall some of the runes we've been learning and push away the frustration that I'm not further on in my studies. I draw the runes on my arms and push, casting circles illuminating before my palms. The power throbs, writhing within my hold, eager to get free. How can it still be throbbing like this after being unleashed so ferociously? I look down at the general runic circles that I have managed to create. They are not great, but I grit my teeth and focus on fueling them. Carefully, I draw only what I need, trying not to consider the depth of my power.

"Come on, kitty cat. You can't bully me," I purr.

Fergus's maw pulls back in a snarl, revealing his large canines. The light of battle flashes in his eyes, and I know he relishes the approaching fight.

The scrap of power I've sunk into the circles tempts me, pushing for release, urging me to let it out to play and destroy. If I unleash it without direction, I could hurt people. Again. The wall is now imperfect, and my power is barely contained, even with the runic circles and the runes to help me. The wall is now imperfect. Many of the runes I've been storing on my skin now fill the circle, ready to be used, and I am thankful I've been practicing.

Fergus leaps for me, and I throw one of the spells at him. I lean into my power, and my reflexes become sharper, everything clearer.

*Power. Make them pay. Stain the realms with blood.* The words whisper through me, teasing at the edges of my mind, the darkness in me peering out from the abyss.

Fergus snarls when the magic hits him in the shoulder. I ready myself to throw another spell at him, but he lunges again, pain exploding through my thigh as his claws slash deep into my flesh. My leg gives out, and I crumple to the floor, struggling to hold on to the casting circles. The light of victory flares in Fergus's yellow eyes, but he only manages one step in my direction before a blur collides with him, pinning his huge feline body to the wall.

"His throat, Sum. Aim for his throat," Alice growls. Her fangs are larger than I've ever seen them, but she is still struggling to keep him pinned. Even a vampire's natural strength will have trouble against a fully transformed and super pissed-off shifter.

I delve a little deeper into my power, fighting through the pain and anxiety to summon another spell. I throw it at him, watching in satisfaction as it hits the center of his neck.

*More. Revenge. Kill. Destroy. Obliterate.*

The chant is oddly familiar, comforting, and irresistible.

*No. Only maim,* I command, refusing to cede control.

Fergus slumps and Alice releases him, letting him fall to the ground in a clumsy heap. I stare at him, fear coiling through me until I see his chest rising and falling with life.

I struggle to my feet, every muscle in my body groaning as I move. Awkwardly, I kick a broken piece of a coffee table out of my way with my good leg. "I just want to go to one fucking party without getting into a fight with some dickhead," I groan.

Alice is right behind me as I limp out of the house and walk directly into a hard body. I bounce back and look up, surprised to see Professor Draco's handsome face glaring down at me. His eyes flash gold, his pupils narrowing to eerie slits.

I take another step back and cross my arms over my chest, preparing to be in trouble for the third time in two weeks. I want to care, but my body feels so broken, even as my magic simmers wildly.

Professor Draco looks at me and then at Alice. "Jim said to look out for you two."

I try not to shrink beneath his golden stare. It is almost as bad as the headmaster's. "Who's Jim?" I ask.

Professor Draco looks at my bleeding leg and cheek, then at Alice, cradling her arm close to her torso. I'm not sure when she got hurt in the madness, but it was probably when she tackled a giant snow leopard into the wall. "The headmaster will not be happy about this."

I look away and sigh. Another strike and another lecture from the headmaster would be a delight. Not a good start, *Miss Tuatha De Daanan*. His words from the cliff ring in my head, and it's not like I can disagree.

"But since he is on sabbatical," Professor Draco adds, "He has left me in charge of all school matters, including punishments."

My gaze snaps up. Professor flicks his hand, and a blast of scorching heat blows my hair back and makes me flinch. When I open my eyes, I see the open portal beside him.

"Go," he commands.

Alice and I peer through the portal, and I can see the infirmary on the other side.

"Now," he insists, growing impatient.

We step through, and the portal closes behind us with another blast of heat. Flame portals? But shifters can't summon portals like that. It is a high-level sorcerer ability.

The nurse lifts her head when the portal closes. She expertly finishes making the bed, but her gaze is on us. Her brows knit as her eyes find our injuries, and she assesses them. She stands up and straightens her gleaming white dress and hat. She walks toward us, her hand slightly outstretched and her palm glowing.

"I am Matron Dolly. Please lie down on the gurneys. Your wounds are not serious, but you both require some mending."

I glance at Alice before lying on top of one of the beds. The starched cotton is rough against my skin, and there is a strong smell of disinfectant in the room. My leg throbs painfully, but nothing can distract me from the way my power is rioting within me. I turn inward, struggling to repair the walls around it.

Matron Dolly disappears into a side room and emerges with several bottles and dressings. Her hair is in a severe bun, pulled so tight her face looks pinched, and my head throbs in sympathy at the sight. She sets her supplies down on the table beside me before hovering her hand over my leg. It glows brightly, and her eyes go somewhat vacant, turning from solid purple to molten violet.

"A shifter?" Her voice is monotone, completely different from when she addressed us before.

I nod, but she doesn't respond, still staring out into the distance. "Yes," I confirm after another moment of weird silence. Alice is watching from the other bed, looking a little anxious about her upcoming examination. My leg tingles beneath her hand, the muscle and skin slowly knitting back together. She blinks, coming out of her trance, and smiles down at me, looking much more human.

"Shifter wounds can be tricky. Luckily, this one wasn't poisonous. Much easier to heal." She looks at the table and selects a bottle filled with neon green liquid. The narrow top has a label that reads: **Do Not Ingest**. She turns the bottle upside down several times, not quite shaking it, but disturbing the shimmering liquid. The pop that sounds as she pulls the stopper from the top is much lower than I expected. Carefully, she measures three drops into her small mortar before selecting a tub of seeds. She adds one small scoop into the bowl and then three spoonfuls of paste.

"This wouldn't be something you could fully heal on your own at your level, though you have potential. You could be a great healer."

Yeah, I don't think so. Healers are sympathetic and kind. They don't have the swirling darkness of the abyss within.

I look down at my wound. It is no longer gaping, but there are three angry red lines, the skin on either side still jagged and gruesome looking. Matron Dolly uses her pestle to mash up the concoction she made. I watch her closely, counting exactly how many times she mashes and twirls the pestle. I am always learning and preparing.

Matron Dolly then picks up a large white piece of cotton and smears the newly made paste on it before placing it on my leg. She waves her hand over my thigh, and a bandage wraps around it, covering the dressing. She decants the rest of the paste into a small tub and hands it to me.

"Apply the paste three times a day for four days, and it'll be good as new."

"Thank you."

She nods and goes to Alice to tend the bite wound on her arm. She also gets a paste to take home, but hers is gray and nastier looking than mine. Apparently, it's not one paste fits all.

Alice and I are saying goodbye to Matron Dolly when Professor Draco strides in. He nods to Matron Dolly, and she smiles before making herself scarce. He regards us both, crossing his arms over his chest. If his goal is to be as intimidating as Headmaster Emrys, he's failing. That doesn't mean he's not scary in his own right, just in a different way. A different, sexy way.

"Well? Who would like to go first?" he asks. His voice is soft, though woven with anger.

"He's a complete dick. And a bully." I bristle, instantly furious.

"And who used magic first, Miss Tuatha De Daanan? You or him?"

"Me," I say truthfully, refusing to back down.

Professor Draco purses his lips, no doubt considering my punishment. I wonder if he's been talking to Headmaster Emrys about it. No doubt if he had, the decision would be expulsion, thanks to my previous faux pas.

"You are aware, Miss Tuatha De Daanan, that using magic against other students outside of class is forbidden?"

"He assaulted her first!" Alice chimes in, coming to my defense. "And he's a huge, hulking brute! What would you have had her do? Try to punch him?"

"It's fine, Al. This is strike three," I say, smiling gratefully at Alice.

Professor Draco's phone alerts, and he pulls it out of his pocket, reading the message. He doesn't look up as he addresses us. "You are both on a two-week restriction. No leaving campus. You go to your dorm and to class. Nowhere else."

"And Fergus?" Alice hisses. "No consequences, I'm guessing."

I roll my eyes, but honestly, I'm so relieved that I've not been expelled that I don't much care what happens to Fergus.

Professor Draco finally looks up from his phone, his eyebrows drawn. "It is a pack affair. The council will see to it."

"Unbelievable," Alice growls.

"Come on, Al," I say, grabbing her hand.

Professor Draco's eyes flash as we pass him. "Be grateful it is me handling your punishment and not Emrys. He would not have been as lenient," he says, his voice low and angry.

I stop in my tracks and meet his gaze, practically able to feel the fury stoking in my gaze. "And you should be grateful, *professor*, that I saved a young shifter from his asshole alpha who was forcing him into something he didn't want to do."

He scowls, and Alice yanks me out of the room before I get us into more trouble. We walk back to the dorm, our phones blowing up with notifications the entire way. I grimace at the sound of each one. No doubt some idiot recorded the whole thing at the shifter house, and now it is all over *Nexus*. I'm really going to get a reputation around here for fighting. Ironically, the only time I seem to be able to throw a punch is outside of combat class.

When we arrive back in the sanctity of our dorm, I finally face my phone. As expected, there are at least a hundred notifications from *Nexus*. I sigh. Exhaustion has settled into my bones. All I want to do is go to bed and sleep for an eternity, but I open my texts. My eyes go to the one at the top from Connor, and I open the chain, sighing at the number of messages.

CONNOR

Why did I just hear about your getting into a fight at the pack dorms?

Are you all right?

Summer?

What happened?

I send a quick reply to him.

SUMMER

I'm fine. I'll tell you all about it tomorrow.

Done with my phone, I chuck it on the couch and walk to the fridge to grab a bottle of water.

"Fucking pack affairs. He'll get a slap on the wrist at most," I grumble mostly to myself, but Alice nods in agreement. She continues to scroll through her phone, unconcerned with our growing reputation and all the attention.

"I just want to go to bed and forget about today. I'll see you in the morning."

Alice nods again, and just as she stands from the couch to head to bed, someone knocks on the door. She looks at me, and I shrug. She opens the door to a panting Connor.

His gaze immediately locks on me. "You're okay."

# 24

## SUMMER

*Mai*

"You're okay," Connor says again, looking me over. His gaze snags on the bandage around my thigh. "Shit."

I exhale wearily. "What are you doing here?"

Connor gently shifts Alice out of the doorway and walks into the dorm. He closes and locks the door before swooping me into his arms. "I'm taking care of two insane freshmen. Go to bed, Alice," he says.

He carries me into my room and lays me on my bed before looking around. His brows furrow a little, and I can practically hear him questioning why we never come here.

"We didn't start it," Alice grumbles from the living room. I can hear the pout in her voice and then the soft click as she pushes her door shut.

"Connor, I'm okay, as I said in the text. You should go home," I say, pushing at his shoulder.

"Shhh. I'm here to take care of you."

I sigh, feeling my muscles tighten. "Con…" He glides his fingertips just beneath the bandage. "You should leave," I say. The guilt is already sinking its claws into me, deeper than Fergus ever could.

"No," he replies simply.

I cross my arms, glaring at him.

"You're already healing or I would wake up Luke," he continues, unaffected by my anger. He tilts my leg slightly and when I don't react, he looks up at me. He finally seems to notice my ire.

"You're being stubborn. Why?"

"Why are you here, Connor?" I know I'm being an asshole. He just cares about me, but I am already very overwhelmed, and him being here and trying to take care of me is intensifying everything. I'm not ready for this.

Connor blinks, hurt lining his eyes. "Because I heard you were hurt?" The question in his voice makes my heart squeeze, but I don't reach out to comfort him. His uncertainty is a vulnerability that I can use, and it's better this way.

"Why? You're not my boyfriend." The words are like acid on my tongue, and I force myself to swallow down the emotion that's threatening to crack my voice. Just leave me now, Con.

A flash of hurt crosses his face, but then his features relax into a serene smile. I can tell it's not a coverup. Something has just happened in his mind that has justified this, and that's honestly more terrifying than his hurt because it makes me wonder if he might actually know a little more about me than I'd like him to.

"Ah, I see. All right. Then, of course, I'll head out."

I blink at him, confused. This is exactly what I wanted, isn't it? Why do I feel so disappointed?

"Whatever. Later." I tug at a stray thread on the bandage.

Connor leans down and kisses me softly. "Bye." He stands and winks at me, a broad smirk on his face. I frown, watching him leave the room.

A few minutes after the front door closes, Alice calls through the wall, "Did you kick him out?"

"Yes," I admit, the same heavy disappointment settling over me.

"Good," Alice replies, her voice muffled. "Night, Sum."

"Night, Al."

With another deep sigh, I grab my phone off the bedside table and open my messages with Connor. I start typing out a message but delete it. My fingers fly over the keypad, composing another message. This one is much angrier, but I stop and delete it all again. I growl, the cursor taunting me as it winks at me from the screen.

I whisper a curse and open the *Nexus* app, mindlessly scrolling through posts and trying to avoid all the videos and photos of my fight with Fergus. Instead, I focus on catching up on what everyone else was up to while I was standing up for a baby shifter. A notification flashes at the top of the screen.

*1015 liked your post.*

Tapping on the notification, I frown when it pulls up a photo of me from a few days ago that Alice took when I was in the library, searching through the stacks. The post has over 500 likes, but only one intrigues me. I open the option to see the likes and there is the username 1015 right at the top. I go through my other posts to see if 1015 has liked any of them, and then I go through Alice's profile to see if they have interacted with any of her posts. This single image is the only one that 1015 has reacted to. I scroll through my stories, checking who has viewed them. 1015 has watched every single one of them.

I click on the icon for the blank profile, hoping there will be more answers this time, but the account is still just as blank. Puzzled, I lock my phone and place it back on the bedside table. Who is this person and why are they watching my stories? How do they have a blank profile when it shouldn't be possible?

Staring up at the ceiling, I inhale deeply and then exhale heavily, hoping my mind will eventually quiet enough that I can drift off.

Alice and I enter the canteen at lunch, chatting about our previous class. She scrolls through her phone, moaning about how boring runes are and how she'll never understand them anyway, so what is the point? I have long since given up on trying to convince her that while runes are complicated, they are wildly interesting. Every time I brought it up, she usually replied with some insult about being a teacher's pet.

We walk to our usual table, and I'm unsurprised to see Connor and his brothers already there, chatting away. It's the seating arrangement that makes me pause. For the past week and a half, Connor made sure there was a spare seat next to him for me to sit in when I arrived. However, today, he is sitting between Zach and Zane. Nothing else is different. He still gives me the same bright smile that fills my chest with warmth. He still winks at me in that devilish way, making my belly clench with need.

Alice glances at me and then takes a seat between Luke and Rafe. I sit down on the other side of Rafe, and Alice tips her head, looking at Connor. She obviously expects him to move to the vacant seat next to me, but he just continues to chat and laugh with Zach, who is talking animatedly about some video game that's just come out. Alice and I share a look.

When Zach finishes his story, Connor looks at Alice, directing his attention to her.

"Heard you're on suspension," he says. I know that if he's heard about Alice's suspension, he's heard about mine too, but he doesn't even glance my way.

Alice wrinkles her nose, violently stabbing the straw into her blood bag. "Yeah, no fun stuff for the next two weeks." Alice glances at me. "Summer is also on suspension."

Connor nods, still not turning to look at me. "I also heard that Draco personally handed down your punishment. Rough."

I bristle at being ignored by him, though I'm not sure why.

Alice narrows her eyes at him, leaning back in her chair. "For both of us, yeah."

Connor smiles at her and then goes back to speaking to Zach and Zane about video games, and I roll my eyes, stabbing my fork into my salad a little too forcefully. The table shakes a little, and I swear I can see Connor's lips quirk ever so slightly from the corner of my eye. I try to start a conversation with Rafe, but he just broods down at his burger, curling his lip slightly. I sigh and turn back to my salad, getting more and more irate at the stupid fucking angel sitting across from me. One second, he's smothering me, and the next he's ignoring me? The fucking gall. Pick a lane.

There are still ten minutes until the end of lunch when I decide I've had enough of being ignored. The chair scrapes noisily against the floor as I lunge to my feet and storm away from the table. I've barely made it halfway across the cavernous room when Connor's large, warm hand wraps around mine, stopping me in my tracks. I turn to look at him, fury radiating off me. Connor just smiles down at me and leans in, brushing his lips over my cheek.

"Got to run," he whispers and starts to pull back.

I tighten my hold on his hand, my brows drawing tight. "What are you doing?"

Connor tilts his head and gives me a boyish grin. He looks so endearing that my chest squeezes a little, but I don't miss the mischievous twinkle in his eye. "What do you mean?"

I lift my chin, searching his eyes, trying to read his thoughts and motives, but I have no fucking idea how to read people. So I push to my toes and brush my lips over his, the barest of whispers against his lips. "Bye."

He melts a little from that small, intimate action, and his arm snakes around my waist, pulling me close. He brushes his nose against mine, and I hold his gaze.

"I'll text you," he says, his voice low and smooth like honey.

I nod and lean in to kiss him again. I'm not sure what's come over me. Kissing him in public like this? Kissing him completely sober and in the middle of the cafeteria? But at this moment, I need these tiny reassurances. I'm not entirely sure what he's reassuring me about. I just know I like it.

Connor's big hand cups the back of my head, his lips still moving on mine and his arm holding me tight. I press closer, savoring the heat from his body and searching for more. What is he doing to me?

"I have to go to class," he groans into my mouth.

I deepen the kiss a little, and I know we're drawing attention, but at this moment, I don't care.

Connor tightens his arms around me. "You have class too…"

I bite his lip, pulling a deep groan from him. "You better get going, student body president."

Connor smiles, and I can taste it on my lips. "I'm also on the honor roll."

Something about that drives me wild, and I move onto my tiptoes to deepen the kiss more, wrapping my arms around his neck. Connor moans but pulls back reluctantly.

"Okay, I really have to go."

I pull back as Connor loosens his hold on me. "See you later, big guy." Connor smirks, looking down at me, visibly thrilled at the endearment.

I watch him leave, waiting for the undeniable urge to push him away, but the panic that usually surges inside me when I am near him is nothing more than a trickle of unrest. What is happening to me here?

Alice appears at my side, linking arms with me. "Well, that was quite the show," she quips.

"Please, it was just a kiss." I roll my eyes, my lips still tingling from the feel of his.

"It was borderline indecent." Alice laughs as we head to our next class. As I sit down, my phone buzzes in my bag. I discreetly pull it out and glance at it as the professor walks in and begins class.

CONNOR

You're going to be bad for my reputation.

My lips quirk and I quickly type out a reply.

SUMMER

Why is that?

CONNOR

I was late to class and someone asked if I was too busy making out with one of the disaster duo.

"As I mentioned last week," Professor Draco begins, "sprites are tricksy creatures, but since the fall of Faerie, they have become somewhat of a rarity. It is believed that a small population of them live in the wetlands of Notoria, and during the wet seasons, they are known to realm jump. From your reading, can anyone give me a characteristic of a sprite or a sprite colony?"

SUMMER

I wonder if they thought that because you turned up to class hard as a rock.

"Miss Tuatha De Daanan?" Professor Draco's eyes are on me, his ire from the night before still clear. Fuck. I think back to my reading about sprites, trying to remember literally anything about them.

"They prefer to live near water areas. They can breathe easier in water and absorb energy from the river beds."

Professor Draco lifts his chin, obviously displeased that I was able to answer his question when he believed me not to be listening. He nods once. "Correct."

My phone buzzes again, but I tuck it away, deciding it's best not to provoke Professor Draco any further.

The class on sprites ends up being fascinating. I learn a lot about their history in Faerie. Many subspecies of fae had to migrate from their source realm, spreading to others before the Fall. It was the only reason they had survived the event. All fae that still live, even our subclasses, are a part of a lost realm. My chest aches for a home I'd never know, yet yearn for. It's comforting that its history continues even when it does not.

As soon as class ends, the emblems on our uniforms glow faintly, reminding us and everyone around us that we are suspended and need to return to our dorm immediately. Everyone stares at us, and I know that I should feel embarrassed. It's as if we have the word **SHAME** tattooed on our foreheads. Yet, I don't. The darkness swirls inside of me, a delicious reminder of how it felt to fight, to push back, to be punished, to succumb to the deep, depraved instinct.

And I crave more.

# 25

## SUMMER

*6*

*Rin*

Connor is sitting between the twins again. I frown as I sit down. Did I imagine what happened yesterday? Did I imagine we made out in the middle of the cafeteria for all to see? No, because *Nexus* is filled with visual proof. Multiple people had posted snapshots of the event, and I am tagged in every one of them. The captions vary greatly from *Looks like the disaster duo is corrupting the captain* to *Getting down and dirty in the cafeteria* to *Connor, you can do better.*

Normally, those comments would slide off me. Do better? Please. But with Connor putting distance between us, doubts are creeping in. Once those start, they spiral, and it is almost impossible to stop them from festering.

I sink down in the seat next to Rafe, who is glaring at his burger again. Rage radiates from him all the time, even when he seems to be in a pleasant mood. Well, a pleasant mood for Rafe, anyway.

Connor once again turns all of his attention to Alice, directing his questions regarding our classes and our evening to her. Alice does her best to sidle the conversation back to me by including me in discussions regarding our classes and assignments, but Connor barely registers me. I dig my nails into the table and try to keep my mind from heading down the path of self-doubt.

"So, Alice, how is Runes going? I know you *love* that subject." Connor smiles at her, and I can't stand it. One second, he can't get enough, and then I'm beneath his notice. This angel will not reduce me to a quivering mess of insecurity. I refuse. I will never succumb to that kind of manipulation again. The moment I stand from my seat and storm away, Connor is at my heels, following me through the canteen.

"Where are you going?" he asks, doing an annoyingly charming slow run alongside me.

I don't stop, and the doors wobble as I shove them out of my way. "Well, clearly, you don't want to talk to me, so I'm going to the library."

Connor wraps his arm around my middle and spins me to face him. I glare up at him, trying to make my stare as venomous as possible. He cups my cheek, his dimples showing as he grins down at me.

"Do you miss my attention?"

I narrow my eyes at him, absolutely refusing to add to his enjoyment of my obvious ire.

Connor leans in, his breath tickling my lips. "I miss giving it to you."

I can't help the way my gaze flitters down to his lips, hating how inviting they look.

"I miss sitting next to you," he whispers, brushing his thumb over my cheek.

I drag my gaze away from his mouth to meet his gaze. "Then why aren't you?"

Wait. Do I... miss him? Oh, fuck.

Connor smiles down at me, his expression calm and unconcerned. "Because I've done my chasing."

My whole body tenses. What the fuck does that mean? He doesn't want to be with me anymore? He's not going to try to be more with me? Why does that bother me so much? My stomach knots at the thought of him giving up on me, and I struggle to justify my uncertainty.

Connor brushes his lips over mine. "I scared you by going too fast. So, now, I'm..." Connor pauses as if he's choosing his words carefully so as not to spook me. "Giving you space to come to terms."

"Come to terms with what?" Connor looks as if he's about to explain when annoyance surges through me, and I cut him off. "Never mind, don't answer that. Bye."

I push out of his arms and move away again, but Connor wraps his large hand around my wrist, tugging me to a stop. He waits until I look up at him and tilts his head when our eyes meet, his smile kind and soothing. "Come to terms with the fact that I'm not going anywhere." He leans down and kisses me softly, his lips barely brushing mine but lingering. "See you tomorrow."

He winks at me, and while I'm still stuck in that stupid cloud of confusing desire, he turns and goes back into the canteen. I've barely made it into the library when my phone pings in my bag. I pull it free and glance at the message, fighting to maintain my annoyance.

CONNOR

You're very prickly when I don't give you enough attention.

I give in and smile down at my phone like an idiot. There is no one here to judge my capitulation. Well, no one but myself.

Go away.

You'd miss me terribly.

I roll my eyes and shove my phone away, relaxing into the dusty peace of the library. Strolling through the stacks, I let my mind wander. Thoughts flow through me as I brush my fingers over the soft leather of the books. My gaze trails over them, taking in every title as I walk. As I move deeper into the library, everything seems to get darker, the shadows taking up more space than the light. The wood of the shelves is richer, and the area smells of old books and pine.

*"Come to us."*

It's a soft croon, brushing against my ear, but there is nothing frightening about it.

The lights are few and far between here, and any sunlight dwindled about seven rows ago.

*"Power hides here, find it, use it,"* the voice continues.

I walk deeper into the seemingly never-ending room, willing myself to get lost. I long to be forgotten like the ancient tomes that line these walls. It is so quiet here, and it feels like I've entered another realm.

*"Don't you want to be strong? Dangerous? Deadly?"*

It's like a secret world, protected from light and noise. The only sound is my breathing and the echo of my heels against the wood floors.

*"You have so much to learn. There is so much you don't yet know."*

I slow as I come to a particularly dark shelf. Shadows cling to it differently than any other, and it intrigues me. Slowly, I reach for one of the barely visible books. My fingers anticipate the feel of the old, worn leather, but I pause. The hair stands on the back of my neck, and my muscles ache with tension. Whatever lured me to this part of the library has gone silent. The beckoning voice that whispered of forbidden power is gone. My breath fogs in front of my face, and my fingers ice over where they are resting on the shelf, locking me to the wood.

My heart pounds in my chest, but not because my fingers are stuck. Someone is watching me. I can feel the eyes on me from somewhere in the shadows. The need to turn and face the stare is perfectly counterbalanced by fear, so I remain perfectly still.

The gaze isn't kind. It isn't intrigued. It's *hateful*. A tremor goes down my spine, and goosebumps form over my skin. It doesn't feel like the gaze of my hunter. It feels worse. I swallow and slowly turn my head. The morbid curiosity wins out, and I peer into the darkened shelves behind me. Nothing. There is only the yawning abyss of the dark stacks, hoping to swallow me whole. I slowly drop my hand, surprised to find the ice gone. My fingers burn slightly from the cold, the only indication that it ever existed. I twist my shoulders, searching deeper into the shadows.

"Hello?" My voice is shocking, and my heart is pounding so hard in my chest that I can barely hear the oppressive silence.

There is no reply, yet those eyes are glued to me. The malice is palpable, waiting to sink its teeth into my spine. I tilt my head, trying to pierce the solid darkness with my eyes.

"There you are."

Connor's deep voice shatters the silence, and my head snaps around. I exhale in relief when his smiling face appears at the end of the row. He strolls over to me, cupping my cheek.

"Hi," I manage to grate out, my relief audible.

Connor tilts my chin up and brushes his lips over mine. "I missed you, so I came to find you."

The fear and the adrenaline course through me, and suddenly, they morph into something else. I place my hands on his waist and lean into him, deepening the kiss a little. Connor backs me up until I'm pressed against the wood of the shelves. He smiles and whispers against my lips, "This is becoming our thing." He pulls back, looking around. "Though, a much spookier area than last time."

My lips twitch, and I reach up, tunneling my fingers into his hair and pulling his head down so his lips meet mine again. Adrenaline still courses through me, and I need to get rid of this lingering unease. I need Connor. He groans, and I expect him to cup my ass and lift me so that I can wrap my legs around him, but he doesn't. Instead, he pulls back and drops to his knees. His eyes are so dark, the blue almost completely swallowed by his arousal.

He slowly glides his hands up my thighs and over my hips. Slipping his fingers into the waistband of my panties, he tugs them down my legs and helps me step out of them. I pant, watching him as he hooks one of my knees over his shoulder, opening my core to him.

Connor leans in and brushes his lips over my pussy, his tongue caressing lightly over my clit. The surge of pleasure washes away my fear and unease, and I lean my head back against the shelf. Connor's hot breath teases at my wet core, and I grip his dirty blond hair, seeking an anchor. He digs his fingers into my thigh and licks from my opening to my clit. I arch toward him, using the shelf behind me as leverage.

"Don't stop..." I moan, rocking my hips. Connor flicks his tongue against my clit and slowly pushes a finger inside me. I grip harder at his hair, angling his head until his tongue hits that fucking perfect spot.

"Gods. Right there..."

Connor moans but is careful not to change the rhythm, giving me exactly what I need.

Adrenaline floods my system again and unease filters past the wall of sensations. All my senses go on alert, and I open my eyes. It's back, but it feels different now. It seems less angry and more... interested. The hair on the back of my neck stands on end, but I see nothing. My eyes remain transfixed on the shadows, even as Connor pushes a second finger inside me. My body clenches against the stretch. At the same time, I finally connect with the gaze of whatever is watching me. The sensations overwhelm me, and I bite my lip hard to hold back my cry as I come. Connor lets me ride out my orgasm against his tongue, gradually slowing his licks and gentling the pressure. He sits back on his heels and eases his fingers from me. Still, I stare into the darkness, my chest heaving.

Connor grips my hip in one large hand and carefully lowers my leg, holding on to me until he is sure I am steady. I drag my gaze from the shadows to look at him. He has a satisfied smile on his face, and my core throbs as he licks his lips, enjoying every last drop of me. As if it is a compulsion, my gaze flicks to the darkness between the stacks. I just imagined it, right? Connor stands up and kisses me hard, the taste of him and my release mingling on my tongue in such a heady and erotic way. He breaks the kiss and smiles down at me.

"I'll see you tonight," he says confidently.

"I'm practically under house arrest, remember?"

Connor's smile only brightens. "I remember. I'll bring pizza."

I quirk a brow. "And condoms."

The happiness that infuses his grin at my acceptance of evening plans with him is borderline painful. "It's a date." He kisses me quickly and hurries away.

I consider chasing after him to protest, but my gaze is drawn again to the end of the stacks. I take a step toward the presence, wanting to reach out, but the malevolence has returned, and it is stifling. My stomach twists, and my instincts scream at me to run. Run. Run. Run! This time, I listen.

# 26

## SUMMER

I emerge from my room in search of water, wearing Connor's discarded shirt. It swallows me, the hem sitting at mid-thigh. He was reluctant to release me, but I convinced him by promising to bring him back some dessert. The guy is a bottomless pit. How does his mom cope with five of them?

I open the newly installed large double door fridge and pull out two bottles of water. I grab the pastry I got from the bakery yesterday that I forgot to eat and bump the door closed with my hip. Strong arms wrap around me, and Connor presses his soft lips to the sensitive spot beneath my ear. I inhale deeply and relax against him, reveling in the smell of clouds.

"Summer?" His voice is still a little hoarse. I did put him through quite the workout.

"Hm?" I ask, tilting my head as he trails the softest kisses down my neck, teasing me.

"Sometimes it scares me, too." His voice is so soft I almost miss his words.

"What does?"

He nuzzles my neck, his nose brushing against my pulse. "Us."

I frown at the way I instinctively lean back into him, seeking the comfort of his powerful body wrapped around me. "Us?"

Connor nods against my neck, his stubble brushing against my jaw a maddening distraction. "How much I like you. How fast it's going."

Defensiveness writhes through me, and I fight my body's instinct to tense. If Connor notices, he doesn't let on. He simply kisses my neck again, and I can feel my traitorous heart jump in response.

"I'll try to... not go so fast."

Something inside me melts at his words, and I turn to face him, looking up at his handsome face. His lips are curved in an easy smile, but his gaze is shadowed, betraying his anxiety. The sea blue of his eyes washes over me, soothing and calm. There is something both comforting and maddening in how he is always trying to read and understand me. Normally, I hate it because the knowledge has always been used to manipulate and use me, but Connor does it for no other reason than to know me better. He cares about me and wants to know who I am. He wants to understand the intricacies of *me*. I have never allowed anyone this close.

In the past, if anyone looked at me like Connor is right now, I'd bolt in the other direction, cut all ties, and never look back. I would not spare them one further thought. Not one tear. Not one regret. Yet, the longer Connor and I stand like this, the more I realize things are different with him. Unsure what to say, I stand on my tiptoes and brush my lips against his. The kiss is so soft, so filled with emotion, that if he knew me better, he'd know it was both an admission and a thank you. Then again, with the way his eyes are sparkling, maybe he does know.

"Food, then more sex?"

He grins and swings me into his arms. "Don't need to ask me twice!" He carries me into my room and positions us on my bed before grabbing his laptop.

I frown at him. "What are you doing?"

He tilts his laptop away from me while he types in his password suspiciously fast.

"Worried I'm going to hack you, Morningstar?"

He blushes a little before turning the laptop around again so I can see the screen. "You never know," he says, typing something into the browser.

I blink, watching him. "What are you doing?" I ask again.

"Putting on a movie while we eat."

"Oh..."

Connor grins at me. "Unless you were planning to eat while having sex. Though I think there's a rule against that."

I roll my eyes. "Pretty sure that's swimming. Put a movie on, dick."

Connor tucks me tighter against his side, the laptop between us. He's chosen an action movie with lots of guns and explosions. I barely pay attention, my mind drifting to the library and the sensation of eyes on me. The weight of the gaze felt both sinister and... possessive. There was something about it that was almost preda-tory. Angry. Jealous. Lethal. How could it have felt like two separate entities watching me? Why did I let Connor do what he did if I knew someone was watching? What if it was a student recording us? I had to have imagined it, but my reaction was so visceral.

Stupid, Summer. Stupid and reckless.

Connor shifts, arranging the laptop on my bedside table and pulling me down with him. He spoons behind me, forcing thoughts of the library and the mysterious lurker from my mind.

"Oh, no. Not cuddling again," I groan, but wiggle back against him.

Connor nuzzles into my hair. "What do you mean? We cuddle whenever you stay over."

I go very still. "Right."

Connor lifts himself on his elbow, and I can feel his frown as he looks down at me. I chew on my lower lip, trying to remember how to lie, something I've never struggled with in the past. I've never been allowed to be anything but a liar. My survival insisted upon it. The truth has never been a luxury I could afford, yet with his eyes pinning me in place, I seem to have forgotten the skill.

"Summer."

"Hm?"

"You do stay, don't you?" Connor asks, his face more severe than I've ever seen it.

"Well, I—"

Connor curses and rolls onto his back. I cringe at the loss of his warmth, both emotional and physical. He rubs his hand over his face. "Summer."

I roll over to face him, preparing myself for the words of anger and insults about to be thrown at me. Finally, here is the proof that this angel is not the angelic guy he seems to be. I take a deep breath, relaxing into the idea that this will be it, even as something within me breaks. Connor turns his head to look at me, and I'm surprised to see no anger there. There is only... concern?

"You sneak out when I'm sleeping?"

I nod and look down, plucking at the blanket as shame buzzes around me.

"Fuck, Summer. You walk across campus alone in the middle of the night?"

I blink, my gaze snapping back to his. I open my mouth to speak, but no words come out, surprise silencing me. He doesn't know this is the safest place I have ever lived. Avalon is a haven compared to what I am used to.

"You should have woken me. I would have walked you home."

"Well—"

"We can take this at your pace, and if us having a curfew makes this easier for you, we can do that. But no sneaking out in the middle of the night. Okay?"

I scoot closer to kiss him. He kisses me back, and everything he puts into the kiss feels sincere.

"Are the sleepovers too much?" he asks, cupping my cheek.

I nod. "I don't do sleepovers. I'm sor—"

He interrupts me with a kiss and then pulls back. "I'll leave every night at ten. Or I'll walk you home. Deal?"

"Eleven."

Connor laughs, the booming joyful sound irresistible. He pulls me close and effortlessly flips me over, arranging us into a spooning position again. I groan, but my lips twitch.

"You're really into this cuddling thing, huh?"

He kisses my head. "I am. I'm the worst. Though it's your fault."

I glance at him over my shoulder. "How is it my fault?"

"Because you're so cute and cuddly."

I blink, genuinely confused. "I'm not cute." No one has ever called me cute before, not even when I was a kid.

Connor rolls me onto my back and starts smothering me in kisses. "You are so cute!"

I push him off me and climb on top of him, straddling him and pinning his wrists by his head. "I am not cute." Connor's eyes flood with black, and my lips twitch. The angel boy likes to be pinned down, huh? I bend down and bite his ear, growling, "Say it. Say, I'm not cute." I rock my hips, my bare pussy rubbing against his erection.

Connor groans and bucks his hips. "So... cute."

I bite his neck hard, and he cries out in a mix of pain and pleasure. "Try again, Morningstar."

He whimpers, but there's a clear heat in it. I rock my hips again, slicking his cock with my arousal. I reach over and grab a condom off the nightstand. "I think this is the last one..." I purr into his neck before pulling back and ripping the packet open with my teeth.

Connor watches me, completely enraptured by the sight. His groan is low and desperate as I lean over and lick the bead of precum from the tip of his cock. Slowly, I glide the condom over the head and roll it down the thick shaft, squeezing when I reach the base. Connor moans, his eyes not leaving mine until I shift.

I crawl back up in body until I am straddling him again, and his gaze flashes down to where we are about to join. I drag the tip of his cock through my slick folds until he's pressing against my opening. Connor's eyes darken even further as I lower my hips, slowly sheathing his cock inside me. He grips my hips, his fingers digging deep. Again, not enough to bruise me, but enough that I feel the slight bite of his nails.

I moan and take more of him, my pussy stretching so perfectly for him. My inner muscles protest a little, burning as I take him to the hilt, the bite of pain bringing its own sort of pleasure. I roll my hips, savoring the feel of him fully inside me.

At some point, Connor shifted his gaze back up to me. He is watching me now with such awe that my chest tightens a little. I swallow, unsure what to do with the feeling or even what it means. It is true that I see him as more than just a generic fuck buddy who I can use and discard, but there is something in the way he is looking at me. It makes me think that he's feeling something that goes even deeper. I lift my hips and slam them down again. My pussy tightens in protest, begging for a break from being hammered into, but I lean into the pain, into the pleasure. I throw my head back, losing myself to it, desperate to escape the turmoil of all the unfamiliar emotions.

Connor comes after another few bucks of his hips, and I follow him, allowing myself to descend into the chaos of my orgasm. I collapse forward, my chest heaving against his. Connor pants, brushing a kiss against my damp forehead and stroking a hand over my hair. I start to roll off him, but he snakes his arm around me, holding me there.

"I'm crushing you," I protest, but don't make any further attempt to move.

He tightens his arm around me, his voice soft and sated. "Stay right there." He brushes his lips over the top of my head, practically humming with contentment. "Summer?"

"Hm?"

"Will you tell me if I'm moving too fast?"

I sigh. "Yes."

"Thank you." He pauses for a moment. "What else can I do to make you more comfortable? Other than the sleepover thing."

I lean up on my forearms, looking down at him. "Sit next to me at lunch, weirdo," I say and press my lips to his.

# 27

## SUMMER

*Mar*

Alice emerges from her room as Connor and I enter the living room. She cautiously pulls off her headphones and eyes us warily. "Is the decathlon over?"

Connor grins and kisses me. "I'll see you tomorrow."

I nod and wave, waiting for the front door to close behind him before wandering into the kitchen. I open the fridge and grab a bottle of water, taking a deep drink.

"So..." Alice begins, shifting from foot to foot. I pause mid-drink and look at her, one eyebrow raised. I may not have known Alice for very long, but I know her well enough. She's about to tell me something very bad, probably chaotic or dangerous, but more than likely both. "I did something in my room during your sex sprint. You know how we're basically trapped in our dorm room? Well, I thought maybe I should redecorate." Alice's eyes brighten a little as they always do when she's planning something mischievous. "But then I needed more space. So, I... tried to create some."

I try not to choke on my water. She didn't... "Alice, please tell me you didn't use a rune..."

Alice blinks and then points a slim finger at me. "Listen, shush, you."

She stalks to her door and pushes it open. I cautiously take a few steps closer, my mouth dropping open. "So... a rune then," I say, turning in a small circle to take in the massive hall she created inside her room.

"Listen, I'm a fly-by-the-seat-of-my-pants kind of vampire."

I shake my head. "Not with runes, you're not. They're very dangerous if you don't know what you're doing." My mind starts working on how to undo this, but I'm not sure which rune she used, so countering it will be challenging. Before I can undo the spatial rune, I'll need to make a rune to give the room a limit. She's created a limitless space and could easily get lost in here forever.

I sigh. "I'll fix it."

"Or..." she draws out the word, "we could throw a party without breaking suspension."

My lips twitch, and I consider for a moment. The rune to limit the area forms perfectly in my mind, sparks flicking off it. "Fuck, yeah."

I cut my thumb with my dagger and draw the rune onto the door, the room beyond creaking and rattling. After a series of loud clunks, walls slam into place, and the endless room ceases. The rune on the door glows brightly before turning a shimmering iridescent. My brow furrows, and I trace the curving loops of the spell. What language is that?

"Yours," that voice whispers in my head. I yank my hand back, my lip curling, tempted to rub the rune away. Fuck Daoine Sith, and fuck the fae.

"Let's do it. That prick Fergus is blacklisted."

Alice nods. "How are we going to get the word out?"

Alice taps her chin, thinking for a moment. "If only we knew the most popular guy in school..." She gives me a pointed look. I roll my eyes but pull my phone out.

> SUMMER
>
> So I need a favor and in return you'll get to attend the biggest rager this school has ever seen.

The three dots immediately start jumping on the screen as he types his reply.

> CONNOR
>
> That's a tall order. What's the favor?

> SUMMER
>
> I need you to (discreetly) get the word out that we're having a party in our dorm on Friday night.

"I'd better start conjuring things! We're so behind!" Alice says, throwing her hands up and starting to pace.

"Maybe leave the conjuring to me. Otherwise, we'll end up with a forty-foot stone lion, a pair of wooden clogs, and a toilet seat."

Alice hisses at me, obviously not in the mood for my teasing. "Maybe that's the vibe I'm going for. You never know."

> CONNOR
>
> In your dorm? Isn't it a little small?

"I'll conjure stuff. Or better yet, I'll tutor you!" I say. Alice grimaces, and I look back at my phone, texting Connor back.

SUMMER

Don't ask. Alice was playing with space manipulation runes, and she's an opportunist.

CONNOR

Almighty, is she insane?

SUMMER

Absolutely.

Alice wanders into her room, typing out a list of what she wants us to conjure for the party.

CONNOR

I'm going to ask for something in return.

I quirk a brow, watching the three little dots jump.

CONNOR

I want you in my jersey for the game in two weeks. And my name on your cheeks.

My lips twitch.

SUMMER

Deal.

CONNOR

Good. I've let Zach and Zane know. They'll sort it.

SUMMER

Perhaps I should wear their jerseys. One of my cheeks could say Zach"the other Zane.

CONNOR

Hilarious. Goodnight succubus.

SUMMER

Goodnight, big guy.

# 28

## SUMMER

"Summer!" Alice calls from the living room, and I lurch into a sitting position. My dream melts away, leaving only the shroud of an unsettling foreboding against my skin. Rubbing my eyes, I climb out of bed and stumble out of my room. Alice sits on the couch, obviously having slept there. She is wrapped in the blanket from her bed, her hair sticking out at all angles.

She scrunches her nose, looking adorably grumpy. "We need a new couch."

I blink, my eyes barely open. "Why are you on the couch?"

She groans and flops her head back. "There was something in my hall last night. I tried to catch it, but it kept running."

"Something?" I ask, glancing at her unassuming door.

Alice stretches, yawning. "Like a clawing sound. I don't know."

I sigh. "Another thing we'll have to deal with before the party."

"I'll catch it after class." She shrugs, fighting another yawn.

As Alice and I prepare for the day, we discuss plans for the party, but the conversation drifts as we leave Kelpie.

"So, what are you going to do about Connor?" Alice asks.

I flick a quick glance at her. "What do you mean?"

"Are you considering him for more than just fun?" Alice gives me a knowing look that I return with a look of derision. She knows the answer to this. Or does she? Do I? I can't deny that the lines are blurring. No. They only blur if I let them. I just need to... redraw them. In permanent marker.

Alice stops at the coffee cart halfway between the dorm and Manananggal Hall.

She orders two large coffees, smiling at the barista as if she hasn't unraveled every-thing within me with one stupid fucking question.

"Summer?" She glances at me expectantly.

"I'm fucking him exclusively. Isn't that enough?" I blurt out. Alice blinks at me, and so does the barista, who looks increasingly uncomfortable.

"Uh... So, do you want your Danish?" Alice asks again, pointing to the bag the barista is holding out.

"Oh. Yeah, sure," I mumble, my cheeks heating a little. I grab my coffee and pastry with an apologetic smile at the barista before hurrying away.

Alice hurries to catch up with me. "Do I detect tension? Is that why you just bit my head off about a Danish?"

"I'm sorry," I say, sighing heavily.

"What is it?" Alice asks, nudging me.

"I'm bad at this stuff," I say, sipping my coffee.

Alice nods. "I'm bad at it too," she says, holding open the door of Manananggal Hall for me.

We sit down in our usual seats in Intro to Realms, and Professor Ambrose walks in a few moments later. His steps are sure and direct, his ego filling the room in a stifling wave. It's the same with all sorcerers. I'd judge them more harshly, but it's the same with fae.

"I hope everyone is preparing for their upcoming interviews. Ms. Tuatha De Daanan has the pleasure of interviewing me, and I am excited to hear the questions she has come up with about her realm."

I groan internally, thinking about the paper I have to write about Faerie. What's the point in learning about a realm that is lost? I slide the list of questions out of my notebook, brushing my fingers over the tear stain on the paper. I'd completed it over a week ago, writing them down while looking at the tiny sprig of Faerie. Do I even want the answers to these questions? It won't change anything, especially my past.

Professor Ambrose continues, and I turn to a new page in my notebook. My pen glides over the crisp white paper, but my mind drifts to palaces made of trees, spin-ning silver in the leaves, and a hidden door with scrolling vines— The bell rings, snap-ping me from my stupor. At some point, my perfect notes have become what looks like a mixture of strange-looking runes and possibly a map? I slam the book shut.

"What were you doodling?" Alice asks, shoving her notebook carelessly into her bag.

"Nothing. I was in a whole other world."

Alice nods and links arms with me as we head to our next class. Luckily, I'm more focused on this one. If anything can get me to focus, it's an hour of ancient runes. By the end of class, my mood has lifted, and I am much more grounded, the odd runes and map nearly forgotten.

When we arrive at lunch, our table is occupied by the Morningstar clan as usual, but today, there is an empty seat beside Connor. I try to ignore how my stomach flutters and sit next to him. He gives me a huge, contagious smile that infects me like a plague.

"Hi."

My lips twitch. "Hi, big guy."

He slides his arm around my waist and pulls me in closer, nuzzling my cheek. "The twins have some questions about the... happy accident."

I turn my head and brush my lips over his. For some reason, a kiss seems less intimate than him nuzzling into me, and it is habit to keep that barrier between us in place. Connor doesn't seem to notice. He just pulls me in closer and smiles against my lips.

Zach loudly clears his throat. "Anyway." He drags out the word, conveying his frustration at not being the center of attention. I pull back from Connor and give Zach a flat look. "Spatial magic? That's batshit!"

Alice scowls. "I had a vision. It needed space."

Connor laughs into my hair and kisses the top of my head, his thumb gently stroking my side in a comforting rhythm.

Rolling my eyes, I pop a grape into my mouth. "I've already lectured her, and I'm going to tutor her in runes." I shake my head. "She was sloppy."

"Maybe I was just distracted by the marathon sex you two were having."

I quirk a brow. "You were thinking about the sex I was having?"

Zane gasps in mock outrage and covers Luke's ears. "Summer! Alice! Please, there is a child present."

"He's the same age as Alice and I!" I retort as Luke elbows Zane, nearly pushing him out of his chair.

"He is and will always be baby Luke, even when he's in his thousands." Zach takes a chip from Zane's plate, earning himself a scathing look from his brother.

Alice ignores them and says to me, "It was the volume with which you were having it."

"You were wearing noise-canceling headphones!" Connor says, pressing his smile against my head.

"And they were not canceling enough." Alice crosses her arms.

"Enough about Connor's and Summer's sex life! Back to the party!" Zach shouts, drawing attention back to him.

I brush my thumb over Connor's thigh. When did I rest my hand here? Why is this so simple? Connor places his hand over mine and squeezes, a warm smile on his face.

"So, part of the Council's mission is to have a party in every building on campus," Zane says,

"Council?" I ask, glancing between the twins.

Zach nods and leans in, dropping his voice. "The Council of Epic Parties."

Wow, that is an awful name. "Okay..."

"Why?" Alice asks, narrowing her eyes at them.

Zane puts his hand to his chest, looking affronted. "Because this is an art."

Connor chuckles, and I can feel the vibration of it against my side.

"Well, the point is, we've never held one in Kelpie because the dorms are so small," Zach answers.

"I hope you know my willingness to wear Connor's jersey to the next game rests solely on your ability to make this party happen. Some would say your brother's happiness rests on your shoulders." I squeeze Connor's thigh in commiseration.

Connor hooks his finger under my chin and tilts my head up, so I meet his gaze. His eyes are sparkling with humor and dark with lust from watching me go head-to-head with his brothers and come out victorious. "Is that right?"

"You forgot about our deal already, big guy?" I purr at him.

Connor smirks. "I believe the favor was for me to get the word out, which I have."

My lips tug up. "I'm changing the terms."

Rafe drops his bag heavily onto the table, startling everyone. He sets his lunch down and sits, tension and restlessness radiating off him. Everyone stares at him, focused on the black and purple bruise under his right eye.

"What happened to you?" I ask when everyone else remains quiet.

Rafe picks up his sandwich and takes a bite. "Nothing."

I glance at Connor. His gaze is locked on his younger brother, his eyes shimmering with concern. Luke shifts in his seat, turning toward Rafe, his hand already glowing with his healing magic.

"Just because the headmaster isn't here doesn't mean you won't get in trouble, Rafe." Connor's voice is low. All signs of the relaxed happiness he was feeling moments ago are gone. This is the older brother, the protective angel.

Like he's approaching a skittish animal, Luke slowly lifts his hand to Rafe's face. I can tell this isn't the first time this has happened. All the Morningstar brothers look tense, but none more so than Connor, who keeps his eyes locked on Rafe.

"You're not my father," Rafe snarls with such viciousness that Luke winces. Even the twins pale.

Connor stiffens beside me, a muscle in his jaw clenching. "I never said I was."

I squeeze Connor's thigh in a silent show of support. There's a battle being fought with words in front of my eyes, and they are doing far more damage than swords ever could.

The glow from Luke's hand dims, and he carefully pulls back. As the bruise fades, Rafe stands and storms away.

I look at Connor, and he squeezes my hand. His eyes locked on Rafe's retreating back. "He's fighting again," he says after a moment.

"He's not done that in a while," Zane adds, all humor gone from his voice.

"Who's he fighting?" Alice asks.

Connor shrugs. "There's some kind of fight ring he's a part of. We don't know how he gets there or when he goes."

The bell rings, and all the Morningstars gather their things and stand up. He kisses my cheek and smiles sadly at me before heading to class.

Alice nudges me when I don't move. "Coming, Sum?"

"I'll meet you there."

# 29

## SUMMER

*Tel*

I search for Rafe all over campus. Classes are over by the time I admit defeat and head home. The next day, Connor and his brothers aren't at lunch. They are no doubt still out looking for Rafe or trying to help him. I don't see or hear from him all day and refuse to admit how much I miss him. My phone rings just as I am climbing into bed, a photo of Connor's face filling the screen. I answer the video chat and shift around in bed to get comfortable. Connor's lips are pulled into a smile, but I can see how tired and worried he is. It is in the lines etched into his brow and the darkness shadowing the sky blue of his eyes.

"Hi, big guy," I say, smiling at him.

"Hi, gorgeous."

"How are you? How is Rafe?" I curl into my pillow, still holding my phone up.

Connor sighs and rubs his hand over his face, looking completely worn out. It's strange to see him like this. He's always the sunshine, and I'm always the rain. "I'm a terrible brother."

I frown. How can he possibly think that? He is devoted to his family. Even when he's rolling his eyes at their antics, he wouldn't hesitate to lay down his life for them.

"Yesterday is a day that I... I usually spend the day with Rafe. Every single year. But this year, I forgot." Connor's face is drawn, his eyes sad, and my chest aches. He's always so adaptable and positive. Seeing this warrior angel so defeated carves a few more inches from my walls.

"Connor..."

"I forgot," he repeats, sighing heavily. His shoulders are hunched under the weight of the responsibilities he normally carries with such selfless ease.

"Con?" The nickname slips from my lips. It's another sign of the growing familiarity between us. The warmth of him is melting the walls of my icy fortress. Maybe this place really can become my home.

He smiles, but it is sad and doesn't reach his eyes. "Yeah, babe?"

"You're a good brother. You're a good person." My chest grows warm, tasting the truth in my words. *I'm not. I'm not a good person.* The sinister thought whispers through my mind, reminding me why I am not worthy of him, love, or friendship.

Connor exhales again, but this time it sounds less strained. His eyes sparkle, the shadows not quite as dark or deep. "I missed you."

I look away, mumbling incoherently. My cheeks heat, but I will go to my grave before admitting it.

"Hm?" Connor tilts his head, cupping a hand behind one ear.

"Missed you... too," I grumble, my lips barely moving as I murmur the words.

Connor sits up and puts a finger in his ear, wiggling it around. "Sorry, I didn't hear you."

I growl and narrow my eyes at the smirking angel. "Don't push it."

Connor's smile lights up the screen. I wait for the inevitable icy fist to squeeze my heart, but nothing happens. For some reason, I'm comfortable saying these heavy words to him, admitting that I might want him around, and I think of him when he's gone. It is a weakness, and I usually cut those out of my life the second I think one might form. But the idea of walking away from Connor makes my stomach turn.

"Summer?" The way he says my name, with an intensity that borders on reverence, adds another flicker of warmth to a heart I encased in ice.

"Thanks for being okay with me having to hang out with Rafe."

I frown. "Of course. Why wouldn't I be?"

He shrugs. "I don't know. Maybe you had plans for us."

"We're not joined at the hip, big guy." I chuckle. "Go to sleep. I'll see you tomorrow."

"I love spending time with you." Connor yawns.

"Night, Con."

"Night, Sum."

I stare up at the ceiling in the silence after the call. Reality creeps in, the familiar chill edging out the precious bubble of sunshine and warmth that wraps around me when Connor is near. Something inside me is still so broken. Why can't I be normal? Why can't I move on from my past? I want to be able to have a conversation with the man I am seeing and not be crushed under the weight of my own uncertainty in the aftermath. When I'm around him, I'm so much more at ease, more comfortable with the things that once terrified me. I trust him as much as I am capable of, and I do think he's genuine. Would being open with him be the worst thing in the world? Maybe, but he's not Torin.

My phone pings with a notification from *Nexus*. I open it up and reply to the direct message from one of my classmates before mindlessly scrolling through my feed. Alice posted a photo of us from earlier, and I frown when I notice that the first notification is from that strange account 1015. I click through my stories, and sure enough, whoever this is has viewed all of them.

I did some more research since I first noticed the account, confirming that blank accounts are supposed to be more than impossible. It is actually built into the creator's first code, not that I could find anything about the creator.

The window rattles, and I startle at the sudden noise. Sitting up, I stare at the window as another gust of wind batters against it. My ears twitch. That is not the sound of branches against glass.

The clouds obscuring the moon shift, letting the bright light flood my room. I slip out of bed, intending to close the curtains, but stop when I reach the window. While the leaves rustle, they aren't blowing nearly enough to explain the gale that made the window shudder. But that's not what has me frozen in place.

A shadowy figure shifts impatiently beneath the trees, nearly lost in the night gloom. Like at the library, my skin prickles with awareness. I can feel their eyes searing me, scalding my skin like a burn. There is nothing kind in the way the gaze lingers on me. The hair stands on the back of my neck, but I refuse to look away. I can feel the menace and malevolence rolling from the being in waves, yet I am still drawn to the figure. Slowly, I lift my hand and press my fingertips to the cool glass.

I gasp and pull back as something slams against the glass, an unknown force from outside. My chest heaves, and I yelp when a second blow makes the window shake. Suddenly, the wind stops, and everything goes eerily silent.

# 30

## CUID DE CHEISTEAN

I watch my little fae retreat to her room, but it doesn't matter. I know she can still hear the song.

My lips curl into a cruel smirk. I wonder how much longer she's going to pretend that she's someone who can live in the light. How long will she deny that the call of the dark hums through her veins?

The boy has given her hope that she can. For that, he gets to live another day, but I'm adding another mark to the debt she owes me. Every time I have to practice truly divine restraint, I place another tally. One day soon, I'll force her to pay up with interest. For now, shackles of obsidian stay my hands, keeping me from taking what belongs to me. My efforts tonight released me in part, but there is still much to be done. Closing my eyes, I can hear the echo of the dark symphony that accompanies the breaking of another chain.

*The Shifter Council let out early, the heads of the various shifter races filing out. The meeting must not have gone well. Many wore grim and dour expressions. I know what they'd deliberated over. It is the same thing they always deliberated over—the future of their kind.*

*Their ineffectual little council of elders will always hold Nhang back from being a realm of any particular note. It is why their spawn will never experience any true form of power.*

*They still think that might is only defined by physical strength. Deviation from their core philosophy of might makes right is brutally culled. It's a callback to a time before the Grand Arcane and the artificial realm that is the Sorcerer's Guild. It worked before the gates that connected all the realms, a time many realms left behind in favor of technology and modern advancements.*

*Nhang's single bastion connection to the Runic Network only proves how antiquated the realm has become. If anyone in Nhang wants to contact the rest of the realms, they have to travel to the capital of Sevan. It is a very long commute for some because they refuse to invest in the technology needed for modern travel.*

*Fools.*

*My gaze focuses on the hulking brute I am here for, and I follow as he struts out of the council room. No doubt, his oppressive strength served him well within. That is the thing about those who rely on their physical power. They build their own demise with their arrogance. Every being has a weakness, even the strong.*

*I follow the worn path, stalking the elder along the dirt road. He pauses to scent the air every few steps, sensing the looming threat. He is used to being the predator, and he is in most walks of life. People avoid drawing his gaze, afraid to invoke his ire. I've known people like him since I was a child. Some children are allowed to be innocent, at least for a while, but I was never one of them. How could I be? My hands were stained with the blood of many by the time others learned to read. I've never been a child or innocent.*

*I was born a force, and the older I got, the more powerful I became. Magic is not about talent, not at all. Magic is about pain and the ability to turn it into power. No one knows that better than I.*

*Lowering my shield, I allow the elder to sense me. Just as I expected he would, he spins on his heel. His yellow glowing eyes turn to predatory slits, and his body trembles, close to changing. Another person, any other person, might have retreated. At the very least, they would have hesitated, but I feel nothing.*

*"You are not welcome here," the elder snarled. "There is an accord."*

*I stalk closer, my steps unhurried. The elder's eyes become more feline, and I can almost see the massive snow leopard lurking beneath his skin.*

*"Are you stupid?" he hisses, taking a hesitant step back as I continue moving closer. "You are going against the Grand Arcane."*

*He retreats a few more steps before stopping and snarling at me. Snowy fur erupts from his neck and his face contorts, his teeth shifting and lengthening into those of his leopard. In his burning golden eyes, I can read his thoughts. He's thinking that he's the apex predator here. Oh, how wrong he is.*

*He lets out a mighty roar, the sound stuttering into a gargled gasp when I press my palm to his chest. The white runes on my hand glow, and the shifter freezes.*

*His heart arrests under my hand. Blood vessels struggle all over his body, bursting in his eyes under the pressure of trying to circulate his blood without the use of his heart. His regeneration is trying to heal the damage, but it can't, even as an elder, because I won't let it.*

*"The sins of the son are paid by the father," I whisper, the great Elder of Snow Leopards crumpling into a heap at my feet. One by one, I close my fingers into a fist. The white runes on my forearm glow, the corpse turning to dust beneath my power.*

*Everyone has a weakness. Even me.*

# 31

## SUMMER

*Neth*

I tentatively open the curtains and peer outside. The trees sway gently in the breeze, and there is no evidence of the heavy winds from the previous night. That shadowy figure followed me into my dreams, stalking me and always watching. Within my dreams, it doesn't feel threatening, but out in the light of the day, I am wrapped in a cape of unease. Even as it lies heavy on my shoulders, a side of me feels like *performing* for the dark being. That side of me wants to please it.

I, of all people, am aware of the danger, but last night when I was searching the darkness, I was hyper aware of the difference between this feeling and when Torin is chasing me. This is different. I'm almost one hundred percent sure it's not him lurking in the shadows. It just isn't his MO. He doesn't have this kind of patience.

Alice's eyes are heavy-lidded as she walks into the living room, barely awake and yawning wide. There is a large, angry scratch down her arm. It must have been bad if she is still healing. I grab my bag as I walk to her, giving her an inquisitive look.

"I found what was living in my hall," she explains dismissively, brushing out of the dorm. Alice doesn't speak the whole walk to the coffee cart. After her fight with the unidentified creature last night, her black mood practically oozes from her. I hold my phone out to pay for our coffees, but strong arms wrap around me, and another phone taps the payment square. Connor orders his coffee and then nuzzles into my neck, inhaling me. I sigh and lean back against him, not even trying to fight it. Alice grunts a thank you at him before stomping away.

"Hi." He smiles against my neck, inhaling me again. His cloudy scent has become a source of comfort to me. I know that should scare me, and I should run. I would have been sprinting away from this a couple of months ago. Instead, here I am, leaning into him.

"Hi, big guy." I take my coffee. "Thanks for the coffee."

He nips at my neck. "I require payment in the form of affection."

I roll my eyes and pull him around the corner before turning in his arms and wrapping his tie around my fist. Tugging him down, I kiss him softly, catching his surprised gasp in my mouth. I let my lips linger against his but don't deepen it.

"I like it when you do that with my tie," he groans against my lips.

I deepen the kiss, backing us up until I'm pressed against the stone wall, feeling it dig into my back. Connor braces one of his hands beside my head and presses his body against mine. "Succubus needs feeding? Did she starve last night?"

I suck on his bottom lip, the taste of vanilla lingering on my tongue. "We need to get to class."

Connor moans into my mouth, fitting his hard body to mine. "Yeah, we do," he says, making no move to pull away from me. "Tonight, I'm going to steal you for a bit. Need to keep you fed."

I wrap my arms around his neck and tangle my fingers in his hair, only vaguely aware of the people staring as they pass us. "Is that so?"

"You don't think I'd neglect you?"

"You want it as much as me, big guy," I whisper, shifting so he knows I can feel his hardness against my stomach.

Connor groans, and my fingers tighten at the sound. "Oh, you have me trained, babe. All I have to hear is *big guy*, and I'm ready to go." He pulls back and looks around to make sure we're not being watched before pressing my hand discreetly over his bulge. "Try."

I drop my voice, my words coming out low and husky. "Big guy."

His cock twitches under my hand, and I squeeze his length. I pull him down and claim his mouth again, the kiss deep, hot, wet, and oh so carnal. My core tightens, and I whimper against his lips before pulling back to gasp for breath. "I want to suck on you..."

Connor moans, moving his lips to my jaw and trailing sinfully hot kisses toward my ear. "I'll be over after practice." He reluctantly pulls back, and I bite my lip, watching him. He takes another step back, his dark eyes roaming hungrily over my body. "I'll see you later?"

I nod, and Connor winks and turns, discreetly fixing himself in his pants.

"Con?"

He stops and looks at me over his shoulder. "Yeah?"

"Rafe?"

Connor sighs. "Gone for now. He does this sometimes. He'll be back."

The way his eyes go from happy to defeated tugs at my heart. I close the distance between us and cup his face, trying to offer him some comfort. It's something I've never truly known, but I'm learning.

"Rafe isn't like the rest of us. He has... demons."

"He's lucky to have you, Con," I say, stroking his cheek.

Connor leans his head into my hand, his eyes shimmering. "And I am lucky to have you."

I press against him and push up on my tiptoes. This time, there is no heat in the kiss, just genuine comfort and care. Connor's big hands rest on my hips, and he relaxes against me. When we separate, his shoulders are a little less burdened.

# 32

## SUMMER

*Sai*

I brush my fingers over my slinky silk dress, the black stark against my pale skin. Connor stands from the bed, and I lock eyes with him in the mirror as he walks up behind me. He kisses my shoulder and gives me a satisfied grin before disappearing into the bathroom.

There's a loud bang through the wall from Alice's room, and I sigh, shooting a glare at it. Connor emerges a few minutes later and pulls some clothes from his backpack. He slips into his pants but leaves them unbuttoned as he pulls on his shirt. I lick my lips and walk over to him, sliding my fingers over his stomach before working the buttons closed on his jeans. Thanks to my heels, the top of my head comes to his nose, but he still smirks when I have to lift my chin to lock eyes with him.

"Still a big guy." I brush my lips against his jaw.

He wraps his arms around my back. "There are only a few people at this school taller than me. Mostly professors."

I bite his jaw. I've always been into big, muscular guys, but there is something magnetic about Connor that drives me wild. It's an energy he permeates, a golden wave of kindness, loyalty, protectiveness, and confidence. He is the complete opposite of Torin.

That kind of soul-deep goodness is something I will never possess. He is something I can never be.

"My dad is taller, though," Connor continues, brushing his fingers down my back. His touch easily mutes the voice in my mind that whispers such harsh truths. He is the only one who can do that. I don't know why, but he is able to quiet and calm the unceasing noise of anxieties and doubts that echo in my head. Since the moment I stepped through the gates of Avalon, I have struggled to free myself from the chrysalis I hadn't realized I had wrapped around myself. I'd buried myself so deeply in it that I barely remember who I was before. With every day that passes, I am pulling myself from the hardened casing of trauma and pain, and the feeling of vulnerability is terrifying.

"Summer!" Zane shouts, pounding on the door. "We need your conjuring abilities!"

Connor's lips pull into a smile as he calls back, "What's wrong with yours?"

There's no reply for a moment, and then he slams his fist against my bedroom door again. "Summer!"

I laugh and kiss Connor once more before leaving my room to face whatever carnage is going on next door.

It turns out they only needed some cups and couches, and although I hate to admit it, given how horribly it could have gone, the room looks pretty good. Party-goers flood into the space, filling the hall to the brim. Music, alcohol, and recreational drugs are out in force. The dorm looks normal until you pass through Alice's door, and then chaos reigns.

"Want a drink, babe?" Connor asks, cupping my elbow. His breath tickles my ear as he leans in to be heard. It is blaringly loud in here, but I know there is no danger of it being heard outside the room. The silencing runes I decorated the walls with continue to throb in time with the rhythm of the music, containing the sound and adding to the ambiance..

I nod and smile up at him before softly pressing my lips to his. I watch him walk away, my stomach twisting. It was such a familiar and easy kiss. It was the kiss of a couple comfortable within their relationship, with a solid foundation to stand on, not one plagued with insecurities and doubts.

When Connor returns, he is followed by a group of his friends. He hands me my drink and kisses me again before going back to his conversation with a vampire senior I kind of recognize.

"So you're the infamous Summer?" a small woman asks.

Her black hair looks like liquid silk, and her bright green eyes are jewel-bright. As she tilts her head to look up at me, I catch a flash of spattering embers licking along her lips. The effect is dangerously mesmerizing, and I realize what she is.

This woman is one of the Calamities. She can become a giant black dog and breathe fire from her mouth. Unlike shifters, it isn't an animal spirit possessing them, but rather a powerful creature pretending to be mortal. The human form is nothing more than a mimicry. They are beings capable of great and devastating destruction, yet no one seems to treat them any differently here.

I keep a kind smile on my face, feeling like a politician's wife schmoozing the crowd. If I stay with Connor, will this be my future?

"Infamous?"

"Our president hasn't shut up about you for weeks." She laughs, the sound like the burble of water over smooth stone. "My name is Yvette, and this is Josie," she says, motioning to the woman beside her. I'm surprised I didn't notice her sooner. With her ghostly pale skin and shock of white hair, she should be difficult to overlook. Josie smiles at me, and I notice the thick black stitches marring the perfection of her lips. Miniscule ghostly runes glow on the thread, keeping her mouth sewn shut. The haunting intensity of her eyes captures my gaze, and I feel as if she is peering into my soul.

Connor brushes his lips over my temple, distracting me. "They talking your ear off?" he asks, smiling at the three of us.

I glance up at him as Yvette and Josie step away, pulled into another conversation. "Just telling me how obsessed with me you are."

"Well, you already knew that." He chuckles, pulling me against his side.

I glance back at the ghostly girl. She looks even more haunted now as she listens intently to a gorgeous brunette talking animatedly about something. Is she haunted or... forlorn?

"What's her deal?" I ask Connor, nodding toward Josie.

He follows my gaze. "Oh, she's a banshee. If she speaks, she foretells death and wails. It's supposed to be horrifying." He frowns slightly. "Apparently, their parents sew their mouths shut like that when they are babies."

I look back at her, but she seems more at ease now, standing with other friends and nodding along with the conversation. Foretell death? And I thought I was cursed.

Alice and the twins suddenly appear with more shots, interrupting our conversation. We each down a few to toast the success of our first dorm party before Connor pulls me onto the dance floor.

"Hi, my big guy," I say, the alcohol simmering in my veins, lowering my inhibitions. The room seems to spin and sway, but in a pleasant way, making me feel like I am floating. Connor's large body keeps me steady as we dance to the pounding music, his strong arms keeping me safe. "You're so sexy..."

"Not as sexy as you," Connor groans against my lips, his hands cupping my ass.

"I like you." The admission slips out of me, but my tequila-addled brain likes how the words sound. They don't scare me as much as they should, and the way Connor's face lights up makes them worth it. It is so easy to make him happy.

"I like you too. Very much."

The room melts away, and my eyes trace his features, memorizing him. "You've given so much attention to others tonight. Are you trying to make me jealc

"My eyes never left you." Connor bends a little and locks his arms under my ass, picking me up. When he stands, I am above him, looking down at his upturned face. I brace my hands on his shoulders and he smiles up at me. "You want to stay or go?"

I look around, but the room spins. Chaos is happening all around us, and I think I see the twins riding something that vaguely looks like a dinosaur. Surely that can't be. I have probably just had too much to drink, and it is proof we should go. I smile down at him again. "Let's go."

Connor carries me to my room and falls back onto my bed, so I'm straddling him. I smother his face in kisses and nuzzle his nose with mine. He's just so *Connor*. Ugh. His stupid face, his stupid Connor face.

"I love this." Connor grins, glowing.

"What?"

"The affection."

"Don't get used to this, big guy," I say firmly but lean down again, nipping lightly at his lips. I sit up, resting my butt at the top of his thighs, and demand, "Show me your wings."

Connor chuckles but lifts his shoulders and upper back off the bed. I get distracted for a moment by the strong flex of his abs, but only until his wings burst from his back. I gasp and plunge my fingers into them, desperate to touch such beauty. The downy, soft feathers beneath the strong outer layer caress my fingertips, and I drape myself over his chest, curling into him. His body is the hardest pillow, but this is the most comfortable I've ever been. Suddenly, exhaustion hits me. I suck on his neck, pulling a groan from him.

"My big guy."

"My succubus."

I nuzzle into his neck and everything goes black.

Sunlight streams through my window, and I frown at how hard my mattress is. I poke the pillow, trying to make it softer, but I am hit with the scent of clouds. I slowly open my eyes. My head pounds, the light piercing and the hangover sitting heavily on me. My body rises rhythmically with Connor's soft, deep breaths. Normally, I would find it soothing, but my stomach is not a fan at the moment. Carefully I climb out of bed, trying not to jostle him, but he continues to sleep like the dead. I stand beside the bed and stare at him. There's something almost comical about this over-the-top masculine figure sprawled out on top of my pink floral sheets. Then it hits me.

There is a man in my bed. A man I *slept* with. Oh, gods... What have I done?

I shove off my dress from last night, quickly pulling on yoga pants and a sports bra. I'm yanking my hair into a high ponytail as I step over people passed out on the floor of our dorm, and I am out of Kelpie within moments.

The second I'm outside and running, I start to feel better. The familiar burn in my lungs is the most comforting feeling in the world. It even eases the lingering symptoms of my hangover, though seeing Connor in my bed has more than sobered me up. I push the image from my mind and run, barely considering my route. Usually, I go between the campus and the forest, taking different paths depending on my mood. Today, I'm concentrating less on the direction and more on the toll on my body. I push myself, allowing the discomfort to distract me.

Music blasts in my ears, drowning out my gasps for breath when I finally drop into a quick walk to take a break. I wasn't aware that I had entered the forest, so intent on outrunning my thoughts that I didn't bother to notice.

It's a foggy day, the thick mist between the trees gray and oppressive. Now that I am focused outside myself, I can sense those malevolent eyes on me again. I slow my pace and pull my earbuds out. I peer into the shadows, trying to find the source and instinctively knowing that is where it will be. The gaze is angrier this time, more dangerous, and I don't know how long it has been on me. I want to run, but my legs are like lead, and my body is nearly vibrating as adrenaline floods my system.

A powerful wind slams into me, making me stumble. A phantom foot kicks me in the chest, and my lungs seize as all the air is forced from them. The invisible attack is all I need to make the decision between fight and flight. My body bursts into motion, and I take off in the other direction. I pant as I sprint toward the mouth of the forest. I refuse to look back, but I can feel the eyes on me. The presence is not retreating but following me, maintaining the same speed and distance behind me. It's toying with me.

Behind me, I hear a twig snap and leaves rustle. When the fog thins at the forest's edge, I finally risk a look behind me. Nothing. There is nothing there, but I don't stop running until I slam into a wall of muscle. Large hands wrap around my arms, steadying me, and I look up to see Rafe's usually angry expression set into one of concern.

"Summer?" He shakes me a little. "Are you okay? What's wrong?"

With his hands on me, I'm aware of how violently I'm shaking. My lungs burn as I try to pull in oxygen, but I can't seem to get enough. Terror courses through me, and I just stare up at him.

Rafe's eyes flick over my shoulder, and a fresh wave of panic washes over me. I wait for his expression to turn to terror, readying myself to run, but he simply narrows his eyes and swings me into his arms. His wings spread from his back. They're not white like Connor's. They have a gray hue that looks almost dirty. He meets my gaze and nods once before launching into the air with me.

Rafe carries me away from the forest. I wrap my arms around his neck, looking back at the trees over his shoulder. I see a group of unicorns flee from the area where I stopped, and even with the growing distance, I can hear their frantic breaths and beating hooves. The slowest is yanked back into the forest, and I turn my face into Rafe's neck as the animal screams. The cry cuts off mid-note, and the sudden silence is even worse. I don't raise my head, but I can still feel the malevolent stare. It sits on my shoulders like the weight of the realm.

A few moments later, Rafe lands on the roof of Kelpie Hall. He sets me down with a gentleness I didn't know he was capable of.

I swallow, my throat dry. "D-Don't t-tell C-Con," I stammer out, slowly releasing the death grip I have on his neck.

Rafe nods and steps back, his features set in hard lines. "What happened?" he asks, crossing his arms over his chest. He is willing to let me keep it from Connor, but clearly, he is expecting an explanation.

I shake my head, looking away from him. "Nothing."

It probably was nothing. I was imagining things. Absently, I rub my stomach, remembering the brutality of that kick. The intent behind it was nothing less than pure hatred, filled with vitriol I thought I only felt toward myself.

"Summer," Rafe says, his voice gruff, like he hasn't spoken in a few days. "You were shaking."

"It's fine. I should get back inside. I wasn't even supposed to be out for a run..."

He scoffs. "Okay, you're right. Let's just go get Connor and let him know what happened, shall we?" he says and starts toward the door.

I grab his arm. "No."

Rafe turns back to look at me expectantly.

"Nothing happened, I promise. I overreacted."

Rafe gives me a bored look. He obviously knows I am lying, and he's waiting for a different answer.

"I have never pushed you to talk about things. I'm hoping that we can come to an agreement. We both know Connor is the best of us, but you and I have a different perception of the world. Sometimes things suck, and sometimes we seek to avoid burdening others with the suckage of our lives. So how about you and I agree to bail the other out from time to time and then never speak of it again? Sound good?"

Rafe narrows his eyes at me.

"So let's just forget this happened. Okay?"

"Was someone following you?" he asks, his eyes flashing with determination, flecks of black glittering in the blue.

"No." The truth? A lie? Who the fuck knows?

Rafe snarls, and his jaw tenses, and I know he can taste the borderline lie. "Why were you scared?"

"Where did you go?" I throw back.

"Fine," Rafe growls.

I watch him and soften a little at his obvious frustration that I won't allow him to help me. I walk to him and gently squeeze his arm. He flinches and pulls his arm free of my touch.

"Your brothers missed you," I say softly before leaving him on the roof.

# 33

## SUMMER

### Val

My heart is still slamming in my chest, remnants of fear still surging through me when I slide into my bedroom. Connor is still passed out in my bed, and while that brings about another wave of anxiety, it's nothing compared to the spikes of adrenaline piercing me. I press my back to the door, squeezing my eyes closed as I grapple for control. In the quiet, Connor's easy breaths become a guide, leading me into calmness. I inhale for five and exhale for ten, syncing my breathing with Connor's.

The sweat on my skin lingers like slime, the essence of that predatory gaze still on me. I push away from the door and nearly run to the bathroom, shoving at my clothes, needing them off, needing to be under the water. I turn the shower on, adjusting it until steam billows around me. The scalding water pours over me, and I welcome the burn. I scrub at my skin until it's pink and raw, but I can still feel it there, clinging like poison. The worst part is that it isn't unfamiliar.

A hand glides along my lower back and wraps around my waist. My body goes rigid, but the scream lodges in my throat when the scent of clouds fills the shower. I relax a little and lean back into Connor.

"Holy shit, babe. It's hot!" He reaches out and turns the temperature to a much less punishing one. He bends his head and kisses my shoulder, his voice still slightly hazed with sleep. "Morning."

"Morning, big guy," I reply, my voice shaking slightly.

"Did I scare you?"

I turn in his arms slowly, my confident mask fully in place again. "Did you enjoy your first and *only* sleepover?"

"I loved spending time with my very affectionate pre-girlfriend most of all." He cups my cheek, his eyes shining brightly with sincerity. "I didn't mean to stay."

I roll my eyes, trying to push some distance into the moment between us. "I woke up on top of you. It's not like you had a whole lot of choice."

He nuzzles my nose, and the distance I'd managed to put between us disappears. The icy walls I've put so much effort into melt in the presence of his warmth. He is able to do what the scalding water couldn't manage.

"Just making sure. My pre-girlfriend's boundaries are important to me."

I reach up, twining my fingers into the golden hair at his neck. "I don't remember agreeing to that label."

"Soon, you'll be begging to be my girlfriend. I'm just so damn charming," Connor continues as if I hadn't spoken.

I laugh and pull back. "Fine. Pre-girlfriend."

I'm not sure why I agreed to it, but I realize I don't want to deny his claim.

When Connor and I finally leave the shower, we dry off and go back into the bedroom. Connor collapses on the bed, leaning against the headboard to watch me dress. He's always watching me. *Sap.*

"Do you want me to go home?" he asks, tucking a pillow behind his back, his abs rippling with the movement. "Am I smothering you?"

That's another thing Connor does. He is constantly checking on where I am emotionally with him. I tilt my head and watch him, trying to process my emotions to answer him truthfully. Am I overwhelmed? Maybe. Am I uneasy that we actually slept in the same bed? Perhaps. I shake my head. "I'm not ready for regular sleepovers, but I don't want you to go."

Happiness radiates from him, his smile nearly blinding. Unable to resist the pull of his desire just to be with me, I walk to the bed and straddle him, kissing him deeply.

He grips my hips lightly and gently breaks the kiss. "Are you sure?"

I quirk a brow. "Unless you want to leave?"

He pulls me close, kissing up my neck and along my jaw. Connor's phone rings and he sighs against my throat. He reaches out, blindly grabbing for his phone off the bedside table as he continues kissing over my cheek.

"Hello?" His voice is low, his desire clear.

"Hi, baby boy!" A bright, kind voice comes through the phone. Connor's eyes go wide, and he bolts upright, sending me flying back onto the bed.

"Hi, Mom!" His cheeks flush brighter than I've ever seen.

I bite my lip to keep from laughing. I grab the shirt he wore last night from the end of the bed and pull it on, but keep some distance between us. There is something oddly indecent about being nearly naked in bed with him while he is on the phone with his mom.

"How's one of my six favorite boys in the whole world?" Her voice is muffled, but thanks to my fae hearing, the phone may as well be pressed to my ear instead of his.

"I'm great, Mom. It's weird you call Dad a boy, though." Connor laughs. Any trace of embarrassment has vanished from his face.

"He's my first boy! You know he's a big kid, especially when it comes to rough-housing with our babies!"

There's something so endearing about hearing this conversation between them. It is so filled with familial love that I can't help but be drawn in, and I shift closer to him. Connor wraps his arm around me and pulls me closer.

"So, uh... speaking of roughhousing." Connor pauses, and I feel tension fill his body. "I need to tell you something."

"Rafe's missing,"

Connor's mom says, and a pang of guilt spears through me. I should tell him I've seen Rafe and that he's fine, but I can't. I need to keep the agreement Rafe and I made this morning.

"Luke called me this morning," his mom continues. "Do you need us to come to Avalon?"

"No, I can handle it." Connor tightens his arm around me as if absorbing strength from me. "He's fighting again."

"I figured." She sighs, and I can hear the burden entwined with the concern in her voice. "That sweet, perfect boy." My brows draw at that. How can she think of him like that, knowing what he's doing? He's inflicting pain not only on those he fights but his family, as well. Is that what a mother's love is supposed to be?

"Your father and I are planning a visit soon anyway since none of my perfect boys have visited us in weeks!" Again, I hear nothing but love in her voice, no lingering disappointment or hurt, only the desire to see them.

I wave, pulling Connor's attention and mouth to him, *"Do you want me to go?"*

He shakes his head and pulls me closer. "Not too soon, Mom. I have to be official with Summer first."

His mom squeals. "How are you both? You promised me a photograph of her for the binder! Is she beautiful? I bet she is absolutely stunning. And so kind. Just perfection. The best for my Conbear."

My lips twitch at the adorable pet name, but discomfort squirms in my stomach at the rest of her words. How could I ever live up to such steep expectations? I am nothing more than an outsider, an interloper.

Connor looks at me, his blue eyes searching mine. "She's gorgeous. But you don't get a photo until she is officially my girlfriend."

"Is she not wanting to be exclusive with you? I could talk to her! A lot of girls are just traumatized by men, Con."

You have no idea, Mrs. Morningstar...

Connor laughs. "No, Mom, we are exclusive. She's just a little shy."

"She's shy? How unexpected!"

Connor kisses my temple. "Not shy in that way, Mom. She's just shy about committing. You know I'm a patient guy."

"You are. My perfect, Connor. Fine. Your father and I will stop pushing about visiting, but remember, parent's weekend is coming up! Please send me a photo. I want to know who my baby boy is so besotted with!"

"Farrah, my love, he will send it when they are ready," a male voice gently interrupts. The affection and love in his voice make my heart ache.

"All right. But you'll keep updating me on your brothers' romantic escapades?"

Connor shifts and lays down, pulling me with him. "Well, Zach is definitely dating someone, and he thinks no one knows, but he's so embarrassingly obvious about it."

I can hear his mom shifting, probably settling in to listen. "Tell me everything."

Connor runs his fingers through my hair. "Well, the last couple of days, he's been coming home in the morning wearing the same shirt as the night before. He's also been sneaking out of the house but in the loudest way possible."

"Uriel!" his mom exclaims. "Zach is dating! We need another binder!"

His dad's laugh is so similar to Connor's that I can't help but smile. "Is it serious? I told you we only make them for serious relationships now."

"He's not telling people about her, Uriel! Of course, it's serious."

"I'm the only one who's in a serious relationship, Mom."

I pull back, lifting an eyebrow at him.

"But we're taking it slow, aren't we, babe?" Connor continues.

"She's there?! Uriel! She's there!" Farrah is practically shouting in excitement.

"You'll just scare her, Mom. She's a little nervous about how perfect I am."

I can't stop the laugh that escapes, and his mom gasps at the sound.

"Oh! Such a pretty laugh! I wish I could put that in the binder. Uriel, can you believe Connor thinks we'll scare her off?"

His dad chuckles. "Ridiculous. We're so charming!"

Connor smiles contentedly and continues to stroke my hair. "For the rest of us, no one of interest is showing up."

"Hmm," Farrah hums softly. "Okay, go spend time with my future daughter-in-law. If you need help with Rafe, we'll be there."

"I can handle Rafe. Don't worry, Mom."

"I love you, my Con. I miss you terribly."

Connor pauses for a second, his hand stilling in my hair. "Mom?"

"Yes, my darling?"

"One of my feathers... turned."

"Already?" Her voice is a little more tentative now. "Uriel, did you hear that?"

"You're so young," Uriel says, sounding strained.

"This is... wonderful news!" his mom begins, and I glance up at Connor. His face is more serious than I've ever seen it. "It doesn't change anything, Con. It just means that, well," her voice breaks, "you're so, so special. Even more incredible than we already thought!"

"Farrah." Uriel says her name with such tenderness, and I realize I have heard the same in Connor's voice when he says mine. "Connor, I'll talk to Uncle Michael. Maybe the Almighty has spoken to him about this."

"We love you, Connor."

"Give our love to your brothers," Uriel says, ending the call for Farrah.

I look up at Connor. "Your family is pretty close, huh?"

"We are."

I smile and take his phone. Tapping on the camera app, I switch it to the front camera and hold it high, focusing it on our face. "Smile, big guy."

Instead of smiling, Connor turns his head and presses a kiss to my temple. I smile up at the camera and snap the photo. I turn my head and kiss him, blindly taking another photo before pulling back and handing him his phone.

"Send the first one to your mom."

His brows shoot up. "Babe, you need to understand. My mom is obsessed with—"

I cover his mouth with my fingers. "Send it. It'll make her happy. If we break up, she can burn it in anger."

Connor nips at my fingertips. "We're not breaking up." He sends the first photo to his mom and sets the second as his wallpaper. Almost immediately, his phone pings with multiple messages. He glances at the screen, smiling at the messages from his mom. "And so it begins..."

"I'm glad she likes the photo, *Conbear*," I quip.

Connor gives me a look.

"Oh, don't like that nickname?" I laugh and curl closer against his side.

"Only my mom calls me that."

"You're such a momma's boy."

# 34

## SUMMER

T he days of our restriction pass quickly, and I fill the time with catching up on schoolwork and getting a head start on other coursework. Most of my evenings are spent with Connor, and it's becoming easier to relax into him. I enjoy my time with him, and on the plus side, he's not a bad lay. Falling into Connor is easier than falling asleep. His warmth lures me in, making me believe that maybe I could be the right person. A person good enough to be a fit match for an angel. Maybe I could exist in a perfect world of light, family, comfort, and ease.

"You're really that nervous?" Alice asks, pulling me from my thoughts. She lounges on my bed, sprawled out and scrolling through her phone.

I tug at the hem of my rust-colored corduroy mini-skirt and then pick a piece of lint off my cream cashmere sweater. I tip my head, assessing the brown knee-high boots and the black tights covering the rest of my legs.

"Does this look okay?"

"Maybe you should do your hair half up, half down," Alice suggests.

I gather the hair on either side of my face and pull it back, both of us studying my reflection.

"Nah, it looked better down." Alice narrows her eyes, tilting her head. "Have you ever considered bangs?"

I exhale heavily and unclip my hair, running my fingers through my long locks.

"Sum, it's going to be fine."

I tug at the sweater. "I've just never done this before."

Alice comes up behind me and wraps her arms around me. With my heels and her bare feet, I'm significantly taller than her. "You're going to do great," she reassures me again.

"We're not even officially boyfriend and girlfriend yet. Should I even be meeting them?" It is simply poor timing that Avalon's Parent Weekend lands on this weekend. While I have been warming to the idea, a prickly feeling still runs down my spine when I consider making things more official. My commitment issues are so deep-seated that I can't even find the true root of them anymore.

Alice snorts. "You're the only one who thinks you're not a couple."

I lean into the mirror, touching up my makeup. "What if they don't like me, Al?"

Alice peers around my arm, meeting my eyes in the mirror. Smiling savagely, she flashes those lethal fangs of hers. "Then I'll kill them."

The nerves tear at my stomach, ripping through me. "I'm not good enough for him." The words slip out. My walls don't matter with Alice. The little vampire has taken up residence and lives inside them with me.

She snaps her teeth. "You are perfect, the best of the best, and angel or not, he's fucking lucky to have you."

"How can you think that? Knowing what you know?"

Alice rubs her cheek on my arm, looking at our reflections. "The only thing that story told me was that you are so fucking strong, Summer. You survived, and you are not your past. It is simply a part of you, and you get to decide how large that part is."

I take a deep breath and silently count to thirteen. I am allowing myself this time with Alice to have this mini breakdown and wallow in these insecurities. I will fix the mask and get it back in place when I am done. It is brittle after all these decades, but it will hold.

"Okay. I need to go."

Alice pinches me hard. "Hey. I mean it. None of that *not good enough* shit. You are a badass."

I nod and straighten my shoulders. "Right, I'm a badass." If Alice knew the extent of my twistedness, would she still think I deserve those words?

"You got Connor fucking Morningstar to settle down with a single look. You know more runes than most fourth years. You are Summer Tuatha De Daanan."

I nod again. "I got this."

Maybe I can convince myself of this lie, too. What is another in a lifetime of them?

"You want my lucky skull?" Alice asks sincerely.

"No. You should keep that."

Alice nods gravely, a glimmer of relief on her face that I didn't expect. It means the world to me that she would have parted with it for me. I look back at the reflection of us. We are two jagged shards honed by the injuries dealt to our souls.

The whole way to the Morningstar House, I work through various scenarios in my head about how this initial meeting will go. All of them end with his parents telling me I'm realmless trash and casting me out of the house.

Good gods, I need to stop this. I have this. It's going to be fine.

The house seems bigger somehow, the door almost daunting as I walk up the path. It's a path I've walked fifty times, and logically, I know there is nothing to fear. I reach out and politely knock on the door, my heart hammering in my chest. I can see the slight tremor in my hand, and I drop it to conceal the shaking.

The door opens and a slightly taller, more rugged version of Connor grins down at me. "Summer!" he exclaims and wraps his massive arms around me, picking me up into a large bear hug.

I gasp, unsure what to do. "M-Mr. Morningstar!"

He puts me down, his smile as bright as it is broad. I notice how similar he is to Connor. They share the same handsome features, but Connors are less burdened.

"Call me Uriel!"

"Lovely to meet you, Uriel." I smile politely.

Uriel steps back, and I am barely in the house before I'm pulled into another hug. This one is just as warm and loving, but this time, the hugger is shorter, maybe a little shorter than me, and she smells like freshly baked cookies and daisies.

"There she is!" Farrah says, her voice familiar. The affection in her hold is almost intoxicating, and unlike anything I've ever felt before.

"Hi, babe!" I glance toward the stairs. Connor is stomping down the steps, his face glowing with happiness. His mother finally pulls back to cup my cheeks. I'm taken with how beautiful she is, and it's now obvious where Connor gets his more bronze tones. Her skin is flawless and a deep tan. Her dark eyes search mine, and while I know she's trying to read me, an aura of calmness suffuses me.

"It's a pleasure to finally meet you, Summer. Please call me Farrah."

Uriel walks over and kisses his wife on the temple. "She's prettier than you said, Son."

Farrah drops her hands from my face and leans into Uriel, turning her whole body toward him. I look past them at Connor. "Darling!" I blurt out. Connor frowns and glances over his shoulder to see who I am talking to. I keep the faux smile on my face, trying to keep it polite and endearing. Where did that endearment come from? I am such an idiot.

"Hi, babe." Connor wraps his arms around me, and I feel like I can breathe for the first time in hours.

I kiss him softly on the cheek. "Hello."

"Don't I get a proper kiss?"

I glance at his parents, who are looking at us with affection. Uriel has shifted to stand behind Farrah, his arms wrapped around her middle. They don't even try to conceal the way they are watching us.

I look back at Connor, unsure what to do, my brain short-circuiting. Do I kiss him and show them I can be warm? Or do I act proper and professional? Fuck, this isn't a business meeting.

Connor swoops down and steals a kiss, whispering against my lips. "I see you met my parents."

I pull back just a little from the kiss but relax into his embrace. "I did, and I—"

"Summer?" Farrah says, smiling at me. "Rest assured. Your aura is pure and mingling wonderfully with our Conbear's. We want to get to know you."

My aura?

Connor sighs, but amusement sparkles in his eyes. "Mom, you promised you wouldn't do that."

"I'm sorry!" Farrah holds her hands up. "But she's glowing!"

Uriel chuckles against the top of her head, squeezing his wife. Their bond is so pure and so clear. It is one of the most beautiful things I have ever seen.

"Meddlesome," he teases.

The twins come charging down the stairs, sounding like a herd of hyenas. "Is it time to eat?" Zane whines. "I'm starved."

Rafe comes down next, but much more sedately. "You just ate a whole pizza. I saw you." Rafe is looking a little better than the last time I saw him. His bruises are yellow, so he hasn't fought in at least two days. That explains why Connor had been a little more relaxed.

Farrah kisses Uriel's jaw and says, "Dinner will be ready in twenty minutes, boys."

Zach collapses dramatically on the couch. "That's forever, Mom!"

Rafe rolls his eyes. Farrah walks over to Rafe and cups his cheek. "I have hungry babies."

Rafe's gaze hardens, and he pulls away, walking past her and going to the kitchen. Luke winces as he sits on the couch, and I glance at Farrah just in time to see the flash of sadness and pain crossing her face.

Connor walks over to his mom and wraps an arm around her shoulders. My heart warms at the small gesture, at their bond. He does it in such an easy way, in such a *Connor* way. His mother instantly brightens.

"So, Mom, I know you've been snooping, but did you know Summer is already at the top of her class?"

"Of course she is! Perfect in every way!"

"You know," Uriel pats Connor's shoulder, "men in this family love smart women."

Zane groans. "Dad, please."

Farrah beckons for Uriel to come closer, and he complies without hesitation. It is clear that her wish is his command. She grabs the front of his shirt and pulls him down to kiss him. He bends, and she pushes to her tiptoes. The move is so smooth that you know they have done it thousands of times.

This time it's Luke's turn to groan. "Guys..."

Zach throws a throw cushion at them which Uriel catches easily. He doesn't bother to open his eyes, and his lips never leave Farrah's.

"We've had to deal with Connor and Summer making out constantly for the last two months. Enough."

Connor flips him off and returns to me, pulling me close. "We're not that bad."

Rafe comes back into the room, silently handing me a drink as he passes me before sitting on the couch beside Luke.

"Dad, let's go out and practice! We have a game tomorrow!" Zane calls out, obviously trying to distract Uriel.

Uriel pulls back, but his eyes stay on his wife.

"Yes, outside! Fighting!" Zach jumps up excitedly, desperate to escape.

Uriel finally drags his gaze away from his wife to look at his twins. "You boys ready to be thrashed by your old man?"

"Summer can come out and cheer for our team. Give me some extra motivation." Connor laughs.

"Summer a cheerleader?" Zach bursts out laughing.

I give him my best hard look. He doesn't notice, still laughing his ass off, tears forming in his eyes.

"You know, if Summer decides to try out for the team, she will follow," Rafe says, nudging Zach.

Connor shrugs. "How bad could that be?"

Rafe snorts.

I look between them. "She?"

"Your vampiric bestie," Rafe says. "The Mistress of Bloodshed."

"Wait. I'd pay to see Alice Legosi on the cheer team." Zach bursts out laughing again.

"Maybe she'd cheer for the dismemberment of both teams." Zane snickers.

I pinch Connor's side. "You just want to see me in the cheer uniform."

"Not just that, they practice with us."

Rafe rolls his eyes. "You don't spend enough time together?"

I look up at Connor. He's watching me warily, obviously waiting for me to freak out, but I'm surprisingly calm. I reach up and press a kiss to his jaw and he glows with happiness.

I wrap my arms around Connor's waist and he whispers into my ear. "Still nervous?"

I nod. "But less."

Connor smiles and kisses my temple.

# 35

## SUMMER

*Wyn*

"**B**oys! Dinner is ready!" Farrah calls as I put the bread on the table. They all stumble in, laughing and joking. Even Rafe looks mildly amused after practicing with his brothers. Connor makes a beeline for me and kisses me deeply. He pulls out a chair at the table and waits for me to sit down before settling into the seat beside me and slinging his arm over the back of my chair.

"So, Summer, have you picked a major yet?" Uriel asks, settling into the head seat at the table. His sons push and shove as they grab their places around the table.

I shake my head. "No, not yet."

"If you're proficient with runes, it's too bad old Jimmy isn't here to teach you," Uriel continues. Farrah rolls her eyes and goes back to the kitchen to get the plates.

Connor leans in. "Dad and the headmaster don't get along."

I lift my eyebrows. "Oh?"

Uriel smirks. "Well, before Jimmy took over and opened Avalon to all species, there was a very limited exchange program with the University of Eden."

All the boys groan, obviously having heard the story multiple times.

"And I happened," Uriel continues, "to be attending Avalon as an exchange student at the same time as Jimmy."

Farrah comes back, holding a heaped plate. The smell of roast chicken fills the room, and my stomach rumbles in anticipation. "Oh, Uriel. It was one date."

"I hadn't got there yet, my love."

Connor chuckles. "Two hundred years ago, Mom went on a date with the headmaster before Dad could muster up the courage to ask her out."

"Mom was the first non-archangel in the program. It was a big deal at the time,"

Rafe adds. Everyone looks at him, a little surprised he decided to contribute to the discussion.

"He's also mad because the headmaster so easily beat him at everything," Connor says, pulling the attention from Rafe.

Uriel points at Connor. "Not true." He looks at Farrah, holding his hand out for her. "And anyway, I got the most coveted prize."

"Can we eat?" Zach groans.

Farrah puts a bowl filled with creamy mashed potatoes down, and Zach and Zane practically lunge for them.

"Mom is a fantastic cook, as you can tell by the feral twins," Connor says, stroking my shoulder with his thumb.

Farrah swats at Zach's hand. "My darling, manners." She lays out more plates full of food and pours wine into everyone's glasses as we help ourselves. Connor spoons various dishes onto my plate, explaining what the delicacies from Eden are.

I take a bite of chicken. The flavor explodes in my mouth, and I moan. It is perfectly cooked and seasoned, with a slight heat to it.

"This is delicious, Mrs. Morningstar."

"Please, call me Farrah. Or Mom!" She smiles at me and then watches her boys lovingly.

Connor flushes a little. "Mom..."

"What? I didn't mention the binder!"

He groans. "We're not official yet."

Uriel smiles, pulling Farrah's chair closer to his. "Your mom just wants you both to be happy."

I slide my hand under the table and squeeze Connor's thigh. I can tell he's working hard to make sure I'm comfortable, to make sure I'm not about to freak out and bolt, but I'm just so fucking endeared by him and his family.

Connor covers my hand with his. "I want to take it slow because she matters."

Everyone goes silent, all attention on Connor. Zach breaks the quiet with a retching sound. "Do you practice these lines?"

Connor smiles at Zach, looking perfectly at ease. "So, Mom. Has Zach told you about his sneaky link?"

Zach narrows his eyes. "Dick."

Farrah throws a stern look at Zach. "Zachariah."

He blushes in response. "Mom, not the full name."

Farrah narrows her eyes. "Apologize. Now."

Zach mumbles a barely coherent apology.

"Zach."

"Sorry," Zach grumbles.

Farrah smiles, reaching over and pinching his cheek. "There's my darling boy."

Uriel lifts his glass. "To family, both old and new." We all lift our glasses and clink them together before sipping our wine. I smile up at Connor, and he smiles back.

"So, Uriel." I look at the archangel and catch him watching Rafe with more than a little concern in his eyes. He quickly turns his attention to me. "Tell me about being the most badass archangel."

Zach snorts. "You'd have to ask Uncle Michael that question."

Uriel gives him a look. "It's good working with my brothers. Though, being the youngest, I had to work even harder to be recognized."

I nod. "The whole military construct of the archangels fascinates me. I read *The Archangel's Arc* a few weeks back and loved it."

Uriel's brows shoot up, and I can feel Connor's surprised stare against the side of my face.

"Yes, well, the Almighty prepares us for the war between brothers." His lips twitch sadly. "Archangels are a part of the Heavenly Host, but we're different from other angels and set apart by our wings."

"It's so devastatingly stunning and heartbreaking at the same time. I've been reading about the war between Heaven and Hell since I was a child. It's ingrained into Gaian lore."

The reading material on all things immortal had been scarce throughout my upbringing, but the legends surrounding *God* and *his angels* are held in high regard, so the stories are very well known. Since coming here and having more accurate texts available to me, I have discovered that some of the stories are very much based on fact.

Uriel tilts his head, watching me. "It's not dissimilar to the war of the fae, I don't suppose."

Connor tenses beside me. "She doesn't talk about her people."

I squeeze his hand comfortingly. "I've made it a mission of mine not to involve myself with the fae or their various troubles." Uriel nods, softening a little. I smile but change the subject. "Can I ask, why did you take the name Morningstar?"

Farrah squeezes Uriel's arm in a silent show of support. "Because I love all of my brothers. So I may fight for Heaven, but," Uriel pauses for a moment, "a part of me belongs to Hell."

"Yeah, and Morningstar is way better than going by Taxiarch," Zane says.

Silence follows Zane's comment, weighted with all that needs to be said.

"All our boys are on track to become archangels, except our baby. Lukey is our healer," Farrah says. Her tone, more than her words, lays a soothing balm over the table, and everyone relaxes.

"Connor has even begun the transition." Uriel beams at his oldest son proudly.

"We don't know that for sure." Connor blanches.

"The gold feathers? That's what it means?" I ask Connor.

Connor nods, his expression bleak. Uriel shifts in his chair, and his wings appear behind him. He spreads them wide, every single one of his feathers beautifully gilded.

I gasp at the sight, the beauty of his wings, and I don't miss the way Farrah's eyes darken at the display.

"Once the transition starts, an angel's feathers will turn. It is a process, and it can take a while for them all to change," Uriel explains.

"When did yours begin to turn?" I ask, unable to look away.

"It was different for me because I am a direct descendant of the Almighty. I didn't tap into my full potential until I met Farrah, the other half of my soul."

Zach snorts. "Was that before or after the headmaster took her on a date?"

"Before." Uriel glares at his son, snapping his wings back in.

I glance at Connor and frown slightly, unable to miss the worry in his eyes.

The second we finish eating, everyone gets up and charges outside for more practice. Farrah declares that she will pick teams, and I smile at the thought of her going up against her huge boys. I'm about to join them when Connor tugs on my arm, pulling me back. I reach up and wrap my arms around his neck.

"Not too bad?" he asks, his arms snaking around my back.

"I like them a lot." I smile up at him.

"They like you, too."

"Why are you apprehensive about becoming an archangel?" I ask, watching him.

Connor exhales, pulling me in closer. "I've always known it would likely be my destiny. It's not something I have any say in, and I am not sure it is something I would choose for myself."

I tilt my head, watching him.

"I have a lot to live up to. My dad's Legion is the largest. I'm not always sure I have it in me."

"Well, I know you do."

Connor's gaze locks on mine, a little of my apprehension melting away. He brushes his lips over mine. I smile up at Connor, and something within me snaps into place. It's a decision I wasn't sure I would ever make.

"Con?"

"Hm?"

I push up on my tiptoes and lean against him so I can brush my lips over his. "You can drop the pre," I say. I pull back and wink at him before turning and heading outside. Connor recovers quickly and catches up to me, sliding his hand into mine.

"Mom!" he calls, and I laugh, nearly running to keep up with him.

Farrah looks up, clutching the ball. "Yes, my perfect, sweet baby boy?"

Connor smiles brightly. "You can talk about the binders now."

Farrah squeals, not even noticing as Zane takes the ball from her. "Uriel!"

Uriel hurries over to her from the other side of the garden. "Yes, my love?"

"They're official! Where is the binder?"

Uriel blinks. "It's in Eden, my love. I don't travel with it."

"Poor planning, my love!" Farrah chastises, and Connor and I can't help but burst out laughing.

"They'll have to come visit, I suppose!" Uriel says, grabbing her around the waist and picking her up.

"Uri!" she protests, but her eyes darken even as she wiggles to get down. "Not in front of the children."

He kisses her deeply and slowly slides her down his body. The moment her feet touch the ground, she rushes over to me, her hair coming loose from her braid. "Oh, Summer, I need all of your measurements and flower preferences."

Rafe claps from the middle of the field. "Can we get back to the game? They've been official since the moment they locked eyes."

I laugh, and Connor reluctantly releases me, heading to join the game.

"Hey, Morningstar?" I call after him.

Connor glances back at me.

"You'd better win this, or I'll break up with you."

Connor scoffs. "Please, your ass is mine, Tuatha De Daanan."

"Okay, team A is Uriel, Connor, and Zach. Team B is Rafe, Zane, and Lukey!" Farrah claps. "Let's hustle up boys!"

The game is dirtier than I imagined it would be, but in the end, Connor's team wins by one hard-fought point. The boys are all covered in mud and sweat, but they're all beaming. Even Rafe looks more at ease than I've ever seen him.

"Okay, I've got to walk my *girlfriend* home. I'll be back in a while," Connor says, sliding his hand into mine.

Farrah pulls me into a hug. "You'll come to Eden soon? Please?"

I nod. "I'd love to."

Uriel pulls me from Farrah's arms, engulfing me in another bear hug. His eyes glow with the joy of being with his family. There is still a sense of awkwardness within me, but I know it's my own trauma. I've never felt accepted or loved by a family, and I wonder if this is what it's supposed to feel like.

"I'll see you guys later."

I wave as we leave, reaching for Connor's hand as he walks me across campus.

# 36

## SUMMER

### Bath

"**S**o? What did you think?" Connor asks, his eyes searching my profile as we walk through the campus. The weather is still mild, though there's a nip to the evenings that suggests the beginning of fall.

I look at him, smiling. "Your parents are incredible, Con."

He lifts our joined hands and loops his arm over my head, resting it along my shoulders. Mine drapes over my chest, our fingers remaining interlaced near my shoulder.

"They're pretty special. They like you a lot." He smiles down at me with the same awe that's always in his eyes when he looks at me, but something has shifted. The burning desire to run has completely dissipated, and instead, my stomach coils with something else as we approach my dorm. I don't want him to leave. Not yet, anyway.

I linger when we arrive at my front door, reaching up to nuzzle my nose along his jaw. "So, boyfriend..."

He snakes his arms around my waist, pulling me against his chest. "Girlfriend..."

I laugh. "You're enjoying this far too much."

"Oh, I'm going to be unbearable." He smirks. "I'm already considering changing my jersey to say *Summer's Boyfriend*."

"Stop."

Connor grins and pulls out his phone. I watch as he goes into drafts, pulling up a post he has all ready to go. The photo is from last week, during the clean-up after the party. I'm on Connor's back, pressing kisses along his neck. His lips are pulled into a bright smile, his head turned as he kisses my temple. The photo is so sickeningly sweet, and I can't believe I was ever a part of something so... mushy. The longer I look at the photo, the more I realize what Alice was talking about. We've been acting like a couple for weeks. The only one I've been fooling is myself.

Connor is about to press *Post* when I stop him to read the caption.

**@ConnorMorningstar.** *She was elusive but she's finally accepted me as her boyfriend.*

"Absolutely not," I say, rolling my eyes and grabbing his phone. I delete the caption and start typing.

**@ConnorMorningstar.** *We official, bitches.*

Connor cringes and takes his phone back, deleting the caption and retyping it again. He turns the phone to show me with a mischievous grin.

**@ConnorMorningstar.** *I go by Summer's boyfriend now.*

I laugh and press *Post*.

Connor shoves his phone into the back pocket of his jeans, and then his lips are on mine. He kisses me hard, desperate, and I deepen it. He presses my back against our door but then pulls back reluctantly. "I wish I could come inside."

I stretch, brushing my lips over his teasingly. "Why can't you?"

"My parents are waiting..."

"You can't even stay for a few minutes?" I moan against his lips.

He groans. "It's never a few minutes with us. But I'll come by tomorrow with breakfast. My parents are leaving early tomorrow morning."

I bite his lip. "But I'd make it worth it..."

"I know you would." Connor groans again. "Fuck."

I drag my nails down his chest, nipping and kissing along his jaw.

"Maybe just a few minutes..." Connor leans into my nails and moans low when I cup his cock through his jeans, squeezing gently.

He curses and grabs my hand, yanking me into my dorm and straight to my bedroom. "We have to be quick."

The second my bedroom door closes, he's on me. His lips against mine, his hands fucking everywhere as he pushes and tugs at my clothes, trying to get them off as quickly as he can. I pull his shirt over his head, only breaking the kiss long enough to get rid of the barriers between us. I yank his jeans open and shove them down. He kicks them the rest of the way off, and we fall onto the bed. Connor takes the brunt of the fall, and I shift to straddle him. I sit up and look down at him, sliding my wet pussy against his cock. My clit throbs as I grind it against his rigid length, and I moan.

Connor's eyes are dark, his massive hands gliding up my thighs as he lifts beneath me, sliding his cock through my slick folds. "Please, Summer?" he moans, nearly writhing beneath me.

A tickle of dissatisfaction plays against my desire. *I want to be the one begging...* Fuck. I push that thought away and lift my hips. Connor's cock springs up, the tip pressing against my sensitive opening. I brace my hands against his thick chest and slowly lower myself onto him. Connor looks down at where he's pushing into me as I impale myself fully. I hiss and rock against him, the burn of the stretch now familiar and welcome. His eyes go wide.

"Wait, shit. We forgot a condom." He pulls me off him and grabs his pants, fishing in the pocket for one. "Fuck..." He fumbles with the small foil packet, obviously in a desire-filled haze.

I take the condom from him and open it before slowly sliding it down his length. Moving back over him, I slam my hips back down. I cry out at the feeling of being full and take his hands, putting them on my hips.

"Dig your fingers into me... please." I press his fingers into my hips, showing him what I want. He moans as he rocks his hips beneath me and tightens his grip a little.

"More... Please?" I beg, needing that thrill of pain.

Again, he increases the pressure, but it's still not enough. I lift and drop down hard onto him. Connor cries out and thrusts beneath me, his nails digging deep.

"Shit, did I hurt you?" Connor asks, easing his grip and pulling back a little.

"Do it again. Fuck. Please?" I slam my hips down harder, getting wetter for him. When he digs his nails in again, I throw my head back, pleasure radiating through my body. I drag my nails down his chest, riding him harder and faster. I crave that bite of pain with my pleasure, but he is giving me just quick tastes that keep my orgasm just out of reach.

"Gods, Connor... More!"

"Summer. Fuck..." He digs his finger in hard and pulls me down as he thrusts up, slamming his length deep into my belly. My orgasm teeters on the edge and then surges through me, my whole body bowing from the pleasure. Connor roars, the tight clench of my body sending him into his own release.

I circle my hips, pulling every last bit of pleasure from both of us before slumping forward, my sweat-slicked body pressing against his.

Connor runs his finger through my hair, panting as we both come down from our orgasms. "Fuck..." He moans as he presses his lips to my forehead.

I laugh softly. "Did I make it worth it?"

"You have no fucking idea, babe."

I laugh and then roll off him, allowing him to get up. I cover myself with my sheet as he stands on shaky legs, pulling on his pants.

"Con?"

"Hm?" He glances at me, his lips pulled into a satisfied smile.

"Why did you freak out so much when you realized about the condom?" I look away, feeling my cheeks heat. "I mean, we're not sleeping with anyone else."

Connor sits on the edge of the bed, brushing a lock of my hair away from my face. "Well, we've never spoken about it, and I didn't want to just jump to it without discussing it with you."

I nod. "Okay, well, give your parents my love."

"Babe." He waits for me to look at him, "Feeling you without a condom was... fuck. I want more." I search his eyes. "Do you not want to use condoms anymore?"

I tilt my head, watching him. "Well, we're exclusive. Plus, I have the contraceptive rune. So—"

Connor leans in, kissing me hard. "Then we won't use them anymore."

I pull back, cupping his cheek. "Were you going to talk to me about it?"

Connor thinks for a moment. "I've never done it without one before."

"Me neither, but I've also never been a girlfriend before."

"I like being your first," Connor says with a wide smile.

"You should get back to your parents." I laugh and kiss him again.

Connor pouts a little. "But I'll miss you."

I trace the strong line of his jaw with my lips.

"Thank you for coming to dinner. I know it wasn't easy for you, but I'm happy you came."

"Me too, big guy."

Connor stands up. "I wish I could stay longer."

"Breakfast tomorrow, though, right, boyfriend?"

He bends down and starts smothering my face in kisses. "Just try to stop me." He gives me one last deep kiss before tearing himself away.

I stretch out on the bed, savoring the slight ache between my thighs, before sighing happily. I pull on pajamas before going to Alice's room and climbing into bed with her. She's in almost complete darkness. The only light is coming from the television. She's watching that shitty vampire drama show again. The characters are speaking in some vampiric language, but Alice doesn't even ask before turning on the subtitles, so I know what the fuck is going on.

"Okay, so Demetri is fucking Hectore, but Sylivia has just found out she is having a baby that was conceived the night they all were part of this major orgy. Sylivia is married to Demetri but is in love with Toma. Oh, and Hectore and Toma are brothers."

I blink at the screen. An extremely pale lady is sitting on a throne, holding what looks like a still-beating heart.

"Oh, that's her pet heart. It's called Ruiz."

I look at Alice. "How do you watch this shit?"

"Excuse me? *I Got the V from His D* is the best thing on television."

I laugh and grab my phone to scroll through *Nexus*. The post from Connor is at the top of my notifications. I accept it, and it pops up on my page. I wonder if 1015 will see the post. The ever-present grey blob is a constant watcher of my stories.

"Did you see Connor's post?" I ask, shoving my phone away and glancing at Alice.

"I did. What made you take the plunge?"

I smile, looking up at the ceiling. "I mean, how could I not?"

"He's annoying like that. I've tried so hard not to like him." Alice shrugs.

My phone starts vibrating like mad, and I glance at it, seeing the likes coming through for the post. "Fuck, this post has hundreds of likes already."

"Well," Alice smirks, "you are dating the most popular guy at Avalon."

I sigh, a little more uneasy than I was a moment before. "I'm not sure that I want to be in the spotlight."

"Summer, I hate to tell you this, but I think regardless of whether you decided to become official with Connor, you were never going to be a wallflower."

"I didn't..." I glance at her. "Make a mistake, did I?"

Alice tilts her head. "Does it feel like a mistake?"

I turn inward, trying to focus on my gut instinct. Since the first night I escaped, I have listened to it, and it has never steered me wrong. But this is completely uncharted territory. I wish someone would give me a fucking map.

"No," I answer honestly.

"Then that's it, but if you want, we can still kill them all," Alice adds, returning her attention to the television.

"Oh, by the way, we're going to try out for the cheerleading team."

"What? Why?" Alice blinks at me.

"Because I want to, and you're my best friend."

"I respect the guilt trip." She sighs heavily. "Fine."

I climb out of bed. "I'm going to bed. Con is coming round for breakfast in the morning."

"Night, Sum."

"Night, Al."

# 37

## SUMMER

O

*Sha*

I'm already dressed when Connor knocks on the door. I expected him around thirty minutes ago, but he hasn't replied to my texts. How dare he make me rely on his presence and not text me back? I've obviously become accustomed to him instantly responding and being at my beck and call. I open the door, and any frustration I feel melts away at the sight of him. His face is pale, his eyes haunted, and he's visibly shaken. The sight of his distress puts me on immediate alert.

"Con?" I whisper, touching his cheek.

"N-no classes today. A-a student has been killed." Connor's voice is quiet, uneasy, and trembling.

Connor barges past me, bolting into my room, and I hear him retching into the toilet. I run after him, kneeling next to him and rubbing his back. "Connor?"

He pants into the toilet, his hands clinging to the porcelain. "Fuck. Her eyes are full of flies…"

I grab a towel, running it under the cold water before pressing it to his forehead. He's dripping with cold sweat. My stomach rolls as his words finally sink in. A student has been killed.

Connor sits back, looking down at his hands. Horror lines his face as if he can see the victim's blood clinging to his skin. I know that look. There was a time I sat in the same exact place and stared at my fingers in the exact same way. Though I actually had blood coating my skin. I glance at Alice, who nods and goes to the kitchen to get him a glass of water.

"Fuck." Connor's whole body is shaking. "I got… I got the deputy headmistress. She-she said she would bring the headmaster."

I nod, cupping his cheek and pressing the cool, damp cloth to his face. "You did well, big guy. You did well."

His eyes fill with tears, and the sight nearly breaks my heart. "She was…" He closes his eyes, squeezing them tight. A look of agony flashes across his face before he opens them again. "They fucking *broke* her. There was barely anything left."

I've never seen him like this. He's sunshine. He's happy. Now, something's shattered in him. And his eyes… Oh gods, I know those eyes. I see the same haunted shadows in mine when I look in the mirror, the same grief and devastation of spirit. My chest aches. Something pure was lost today, and it is a tragedy. Connor should have remained unspoiled his whole life. There needs to be some true good left in the realms.

I shift so I'm kneeling between his legs and cup his cheek, gently lifting his head. "Con. Look at me."

He whimpers, and his haunted gaze meets mine. "I was such a coward." A tear slowly trails down his cheek, and another pang echoes through my chest. He is a warrior angel, raised to fight in the Heavenly Host, but theory and reality are very different.

"She was dead when you found her, big guy." I move closer and press my forehead to his.

There is another loud knock on the front door. "I'm here to speak to Mr. Morningstar." The headmaster's voice rumbles through the dorm, carrying into the bathroom even though there are two doors separating us. Within a few moments, his tall build fills the doorway. I wipe the tears from Connor's face but look up at the headmaster, surprised to see him in something other than his tailored suit. He's wearing well-fitted dark jeans and a sweater that hugs every muscle.

"Mr. Morningstar. Miss Tuatha De Daanan." Even his voice is different. It's less icy, though there is still no warmth in it.

I stand and offer Connor my hand to help him up.

"We have some things to discuss," the headmaster continues, gesturing for us to leave the bathroom. The headmaster leads the way back into the living room, and I make sure to keep myself between him and Connor. Alice offers Connor a glass of water.

I sit on the couch next to Connor, and the headmaster picks up one of the dining room chairs, placing it across the coffee table from us. I forgot how suffocating his presence is in a normal-sized room. His silver eyes slide over me before settling on Connor. Every nerve in my body lights up with that single look, and I know he has seen more than any of us wants.

Connor swallows, placing his hand on my thigh, and I link my arm around his, holding onto his wrist.

"Did you see—"

"I did." The headmaster nods solemnly. His face gives nothing away, but his eyes whirl, the silver alive. "Her family has been notified, and we will release a notification to the school once they collect her."

I shift against Connor, and the headmaster immediately turns his attention to me as if he is hyper aware of my every breath. "Who was she?"

He lifts his chin, his gaze locked on mine, caging me there. "She was a third-year fae. Gia Tuatha De Daanan."

Connor closes his eyes, and I look at him, placing my other hand on his arm. I scoot even closer, pressing against his side as if I can protect him from the horrors he witnessed. If I could, I would soak them from his skin and into me. What's a few more in a lifetime of them?

"What were you doing on campus so early, Mr. Morningstar?" the headmaster asks, and my eyes flash back to him.

"He was coming to have breakfast with me," I reply for him. The headmaster's gaze flits back to me. There is something within it I can't identify. "Before class," I add, lowering my gaze.

Connor nods. "My parents left this morning, and the plan was to have breakfast early before heading into class, but I..." He swallows, squeezing my thigh, his fingers digging in for mooring. "I saw blood leaking from the—"

The headmaster holds his hand up, stopping Connor. "I believe you may have seen more than you realize. I would like to look through your memories. With your consent, of course."

I muffle a gasp of surprise. Memory walking? That is supposed to be some borderline impossible magic. Erasing memories is easier than walking through them without shattering the person's mind. How powerful is the headmaster exactly?

Connor swallows audibly. "All right."

The headmaster stands and looks at me once again, that impenetrable stare pinning me to the couch. "May we use your bedroom, Miss Tuatha De Daanan?"

I nod. "Of course."

Connor stands and walks to my bedroom. I move to follow, but the headmaster steps in front of me, stopping me in my tracks.

"This is not something you should see, Miss Tuatha De Daanan."

"But—" I hear Connor protest from behind him.

"No," the headmaster replies, his face hardening into a mask of stone. His eyes lock on me. Does he sense that I'm the one who's more likely to protest?

"But, sir—"

His lips tighten even more. "This is not a request."

"Yes, sir," I say, lowering my gaze again, instinctively knowing not to push anymore.

The headmaster turns on his heel and disappears into my room.

"I'll be right out here, big guy," I whisper. Connor smiles wanly at me as he closes the door.

Alice paces the living room, mumbling half in English and half in some vampiric tongue. "Fuck. A murder? And it wasn't me?" She continues to mutter, wearing a path back and forth as she tries to connect the information she's already gathered about the murder. She's way too nosey for her own good. Normally, I'd be riling her up, encouraging her research and tangents, but now all my thoughts are on Connor.

My head snaps toward the closed door when I hear Connor whimper. I wince at the pain he must be going through in having to relive something so traumatic. I hurry to the door and lean against it in a show of support. Touching my fingers to the wood, I close my eyes, mentally reaching out to him. After ages of listening to Connor's pain, his whimpers taper off, and the door swings open. I practically fall into the headmaster. He grips my arm reflexively to steady me. He still wears that blank expression, his face locked into a mask of hardened *nothing*. Does he feel anything?

"Miss Tuatha De Daanan. Were my orders unclear?" he says coldly.

My cheeks heat slightly. "You told me I couldn't come into the room, and I didn't."

He narrows his eyes and then locks his gaze on Alice. "Not a word to anyone."

Alice nods, and then he looks at me, waiting until I also acknowledge his command with a nod. Not waiting for him to say anything else, I skirt around him and into the bedroom, careful not to touch him. Connor is lying on my bed and seems to be lingering somewhere between consciousness and unconsciousness. Memory walking is incredibly draining to the subject.

"Thank you for your assistance, Mr. Morningstar," the headmaster says.

I sit on the edge of the bed and glance at him over my shoulder. "Is there anything I can do to help, sir?"

He shakes his head. "I will take care of it. No one harms my students. *No one.*"

With that declaration, resolute knowledge wraps around me. No one crosses the headmaster and lives long. I almost pity the person who becomes the focus of his fury. I look at Connor. Almost.

My brows furrow when the headmaster clears his throat, drawing my attention back to him. He lifts his chin again. "Not a word," he commands before spinning on his heel. One step, he's in casual clothes, but by the time he passes the doorway, he's dressed in his normal suit. His magic is effortless and completely undetectable. There isn't even a residual hum in the air.

"He's acting like he just heard a weather report," Alice grumbles, stomping into my room and flopping down on my desk chair.

"He said..." Connor whispers, his voice a little shakily. "He said I saw them or... saw something."

I brush a lock of his hair back from his forehead and then slip fully onto the bed, curling around Connor. He buries his face into my neck and quickly falls asleep.

# 38

## SUMMER

*Tha*

"Is he going to be okay?" Alice asks, watching me run my fingers through his hair, trying to comfort him even in sleep. Connor's out cold, his big body heavy in my arms.

I nod and shift slightly, getting comfortable with him lying partially on top of me. "Yes. Will you text Rafe to let him know Connor is safe and that he's here? I can't reach my phone." I wasn't moving an inch while Connor needed me.

Alice pulls her phone out of her pocket, and her thumbs fly over the screen as she types out the message. A reply comes almost immediately, and Alice's lips twitch. "He said, big surprise. I guess no one knows about the murder yet."

Connor whimpers, and his body tenses. I stretch for the small dagger on my bedside table and slice the tip of my finger before blindly drawing an overly familiar rune on the back of Connor's neck.

"What's that for?"

Connor immediately relaxes on top of me. His breathing evens out, and I kiss the top of his head. "It's for dreamless sleep. It's not perfect. Sometimes, the darkness of nothing can be just as terrifying as anything the mind can conjure up, but I think he needs it now."

Nothing is always a comfort to me. The yawning abyss of darkness feels closer to a cradle, shielding me from the horrors of my history.

Alice looks at Connor, something like concern flashing over her face before her attention diverts to an alert on her phone. "Fuck, socials are already suspicious. *EverydayEmrys* caught him in casual clothes." She scrolls through the comments. "They're wondering what brought him back." Alice looks up at me. "Sum?"

I glance at her over Connor's shoulder. "Hm?"

"Memory walking is some heavy shit." She gestures gravely at Connor, the concern back in her eyes. Until now, Alice only acted as if she tolerated Connor's presence for my sake, but she's openly revealing that she actually cares for him.

"My dad tried to learn it once. It got us in a lot of shit with the Sorcerer's Guild when he kept ripping open vamp's heads with his attempts." Alice grimaces a little. "Though, I did warn him that gouging the eyes from the guild representative's head was a bit much." She stands from the chair and walks over to the bed, carefully climbing in behind me. "I'll order breakfast."

"Delicious, an eye-gouging story followed by waffles." My lips twitch and Alice lets out a loud laugh before grimacing again and whispering an apology to Connor, but he doesn't even stir.

Alice only leaves our side long enough to collect our food from the door, and she dutifully hand-feeds me with a care that surprises me. I'm half surprised she didn't just launch pieces of waffle into my mouth from the end of the bed.

I finish eating and am sliding my fingers through Connor's hair again, but I can sense Alice's gaze on me. I know she would never hurt me, but she is a predator, and my neck still tingles with the primal acceptance of that knowledge. Her body is tense, and she is worrying her lower lip with her fangs. "What is it, Alice?"

"I wasn't sure whether to mention this, Sum, but when the headmaster was here, I looked up Gia on *Nexus*."

I tilt my head, shifting slightly beneath Connor. "Okay?"

Alice taps on her phone and then turns it to show me the screen. The photo is of a fae female. She's paler than I am, but her hair is almost the same length and shade of brown as mine. I frown at the photo, noticing how similar she looks to me. Her nose may be a little wider and her jaw more curved, but there is a definite passing resemblance. It could just be a coincidence, though, right? There are a lot of brunette fae on campus.

"She—"

"She's like the poor man's version of you. Weird, right?" Alice turns her phone back to look at the photo.

I shake my head. It is paranoid and self-centered to think this is about me. We're not that similar. It's ridiculous. "I mean, we both have brown hair and faces."

Alice squints at the screen and tilts her head a little. "Hm, maybe. Maybe I'm just being paranoid."

I nod and go back to stroking Connor's hair, but as the hours trail past, I can't keep from thinking about Gia and our physical similarities. Was it that *thing* that was chasing me in the woods? Had it thought I was her? But then my mind supplies an even more terrifying thought. Maybe whoever killed Gia was looking for me.

I'm confident this has nothing to do with Torin. This isn't his style, not even a little. I've been running from him long enough to know how he operates. But why would anyone else be after me? I'm nobody. Just some random female who was cast out and lost when I was an infant, a fae freak with pale eyes.

"Babe?" Connor's groggy voice pulls me from my thoughts, and I look down at him, brushing a lock of hair from his forehead. "Hi, big guy."

Alice nods at me and quietly leaves the room, giving us time.

"Do you think I'm a coward?" Connor whispers, pain in his eyes. The question spears me through the chest. Connor is an angel. He is a protector at his core, and now he believes he has failed.

I hold his gaze, tunneling my fingers in his hair. "Absolutely fucking not. You did what needed to be done, and then you came to me. Just as you should have."

He buries his face into my neck, mumbling against my skin. "I'm supposed to be a warrior."

"A noble warrior does not look into the face of death with indifference."

Connor's voice drops to barely a whisper, and if it weren't for my elevated hearing, I would have missed it. "I–I have killed before," Connor begins. No part of me feels any less safe with him. If it did, I would be a hypocrite. I ache to tell him my truth so he feels less alone, but I can't.

I feel like I know Connor, and I know he wouldn't have done something so drastic without a proper reason, unlike me. Plus, my best friend has definitely killed multiple people, likely somewhere close to legions.

"It was a demon, but I ended it quick, painless. But what was done to Gia... They obviously tortured her. Even in death, she looked..." His jaw clenches, and he rubs at his eyes. "Agonized."

I stroke his back, my eyes stinging with tears. "Shhh, big guy. I'm here."

The memory of that fae male's body slumping on me fills my head, and I have to work to force it away.

Connor pulls back, his eyes completely wrecked. "I know we have rules about sleepovers, but can I stay here tonight?"

I nod, not even hesitating. If he hadn't asked, I would have insisted on it, anyway. I had to know that he was okay. Is this growth? Connor exhales in relief and buries his face back against my neck, but his stomach growls loudly.

My lips twitch. "I ordered pizza. It'll be here in five minutes." Alice had handed me my phone after we'd eaten breakfast, and I had anticipated that Connor would wake up hungry.

Connor squeezes me and inhales deeply. "Thank you."

The silence echoes between us. Each pass of my fingers through his hair is as loud as a scream. Every breath is a metronome, keeping a rhythm. I just hold him until someone knocks at the dorm door. "That's the pizza, big guy."

Connor squeezes me harder and nuzzles my neck.

"I'll be right back. I promise."

He reluctantly releases me, and I climb over him and out of bed. Alice is passed out on the couch, and after I've grabbed the pizza, I turn the television off and cover her with a blanket before returning to the bedroom. I close the door. "Con?"

"In here," Connor replies, stepping out of the bathroom. He looks a little fresher, though his eyes are still haunted.

I hold up the pizza box. "Meat lovers with extra bacon. Your favorite."

Connor's lips tilt into a small smile. "Thanks, you're the best." He walks to me and kisses me softly before taking the pizza box and sitting on the bed. His head falls back against the wall as if he is too tired to keep it up. "Fuck."

I sit beside him, watching him from beneath my lashes, trying not to hover. Being *there* for someone else is new territory for me.

"I feel weak. If I saw them, I could have—"

"Connor, no," I interrupt, taking his hand.

He glances at me, his eyes sad. "I'm supposed to be an archangel. A great warrior."

I shake my head, cupping his cheek. "No. Con. You're a university student."

Great destinies are not for the present. They are for the distant future.

Connor sighs and takes a bite of pizza. I shift to sit beside him, and he relaxes into me. We sit in silence while Connor eats three full slices of pizza. When he's done, I pick up the pizza box and put it to the side. "You should take your pants off. You'll be more comfortable."

He gets up to slip them off before lying back on the bed again. I pull on the sweater he was wearing earlier and curl up beside him. I watch him as he stares at the ceiling.

"Con?"

He glances at me and then turns to face me, wrapping his arm around me and pulling me in close. I rest my hands against his chest and nuzzle his nose with mine, sharing his breath. His lips twitch, but he closes his eyes and drifts off to sleep. The rune on the back of his neck should still be active, but I brush my fingers over it, testing the power in it. I exhale and relax when I feel the pull of the rune, knowing it'll last all night.

Not ready to sleep yet, I grab my phone and start to scroll through *Nexus*. I click on the 1015 account to look at their blank profile again. They continue to watch all my stories and have a strong presence on my account. Whoever they are, they are always watching.

My phone pings.

**1015 WANTS TO SEND YOU A MESSAGE.**

I swallow, my thumb hovering over the notification. I tap it, and my stomach knots when the message appears on the screen.

My breath catches in my throat as I read the words repeatedly, my heart pounding in my chest.

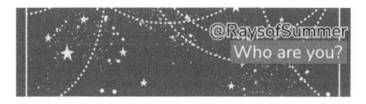

A response comes immediately as if they were waiting for that very question.

I quickly block the account, but then I go back to the messages, reading them over and over. Anxiety coils and writhes inside of me, growing worse every time I read the messages. Their threatening tone sets my teeth on edge, and fear makes me sick to my stomach. Thanks to my shaking hands, it takes a few attempts to lock my phone. I toss it aside and bury my face against Connor's chest as he sleeps in blissful ignorance, letting his scent comfort me. His arms tighten around me, holding me close even in his sleep. Surrounded by his strength, my sense of security slowly returns, and I eventually fall asleep.

*Run. Run. Run.*

*I pant, the whispered chant continuing in my head. The voice is unfamiliar but familiar at the same time. My lungs burn as I fly through the forest. The impact of the forest floor beneath my feet sends jarring reverberations through my whole body.*

*A twig snaps behind me. It's gaining on me. It's going to get me.*

*Run. Run. Run.*

*The words are more urgent this time, getting louder.*

*I take the chance to look over my shoulder and immediately trip on a branch, hitting the ground hard.*

*Run! Run! Run, Summer!*

*The voice screams so loud that a sharp pain spears through my mind. I gulp down air, about to get to my feet, when something cold wraps around my ankle and yanks me back. I cling to the ground, my nails dragging through the mud and moss.*

*I struggle as I'm yanked back so hard my ankle snaps. Unbearable burning pain radiates up my leg and down into my foot. I try to scream, but there is no sound.*

*Suddenly, my ankle is released. The only sound is my loud, terrified breathing and the pounding of my heart. A loud snarl triggers terror deep in my primal brain, and the urge to run is nearly overwhelming. Despite my broken ankle, I get to my hands and knees and crawl. I'm wrenched from the ground by my hair and slammed into a tree. My mouth opens wide, gasping for air that won't come. As I lay on the ground, unable to move, a face appears in front of me. It's one that I've seen before. I saw it for the first time yesterday. A face so similar to my own.*

*The voice that comes from her mouth is anything but human. It sounds like scorched earth and brimstone. "Summer... they're coming for you." Her smile is cat-like, and dirt and maggots fall from her mouth as she starts laughing. She slams a dagger into my stomach and twists it.*

I wake with a start, the phantom pain of the blade in my belly and my broken ankle slowly dwindling. My alarm is blaring, and I grab my phone and turn it off, noticing a school-wide notification about an assembly this morning. The memory of the dream and her lifeless eyes still plague me.

It's not the first time I've dreamed of being chased, but it is the first time something other than Torin was chasing me. Gia's face, her broken, lifeless face lingers in my mind. I exhale and shake my head.

Connor is still sleeping peacefully, and I nuzzle his cheek. "Big guy?"

He groans sleepily. "Yeah?"

"We have an assembly."

Connor opens his eyes, and his gaze locks with mine, his eyes still holding the memories from the day before. "All right."

"Shower with me?" I ask, needing to do anything I can to get back that glimmer of sunny joy that has been there since I met him.

He nods and climbs out of the bed, holding his hand out for me. I slide my hand into his and let him tug me to my feet before leading him through to the bathroom. I turn the shower on, setting it nice and warm for us, and then pull off his sweater and my panties before stepping in. Connor follows me in, and I wrap my arms around his neck, pressing my naked body to his.

"Thank you," Connor whispers, pressing his forehead to mine.

I place my hands on his chest and close my eyes, enjoying the safety of being in his arms. The remnants of the nightmare slip off me with the hot water.

I pull back, looking up at him. "Hi."

"You put a rune on my neck," he says, his voice thick with affection.

I nod. "I wanted you to sleep without nightmares."

"You're incredible."

I smile up at him and then press a kiss to his shoulder before grabbing my bottle of shampoo. Connor ghosts his fingers down my side, tracing the curve of my hip and the dip of my waist as I wash his hair. "Your shampoo is very," he pauses for a moment, "scented."

I laugh softly. "Do you not like it?"

"No, I do! Just not used to smelling as good as you."

Smooth fucker.

"Just relax, big guy. Let me pamper you."

"People will gossip if I smell like a giant strawberry." He is playing with me, but his words are still edged with sharpness, the trauma still lingering. I wish I knew how to lessen his pain, but I don't even know how to deal with my own.

"I promise I'll buy some of your shampoo to keep here, okay?"

Connor's eyes shoot open, and then he grimaces when soap cascades into them.

"Con!" I yelp, directing him under the spray.

Connor winces as he rinses the shampoo from his eyes. As soon as they are clear, he looks at me, his eyes bloodshot but still wide. "You're not just offering that because of what happened, right?"

My brows furrow, and I brush the lingering shampoo from his forehead. "What?"

He blushes, and my heart softens even more. "About the shampoo."

I lift an eyebrow, waiting for an explanation.

"W-Well, you've never suggested I leave stuff here before," he stammers clumsily, rinsing the lingering shampoo from his hair.

"You've never slept over before." I shrug. "It just makes sense if it happens again."

Connor's breath leaves him in a whoosh. "Babe," he cups my cheeks in his large hands, "I want to, but I don't want you to offer because I'm a wreck."

I frown a little. "That's not why."

He searches my eyes. "It's not?"

I shake my head.

Connor tips his head. "So you want me to sleep over again?"

I shrug noncommittally. "Maybe."

A smile brightens Connor's face, and this one reaches his eyes. He brushes his thumbs over my cheeks. "Really?"

"Maybe occasionally."

Connor presses his lips to mine, and the taste of his smile prompts my own. "I love you," he says, licking at my lower lip.

My body goes rigid, the words making every joint lock. My skin crawls with discomfort and then grows so tight that I want to rip it off.

Connor pulls back, looking down at me, his eyes wide. "Fuck. I didn't say that." He looks around, dropping his hands from my cheeks. "Forget that, okay?"

I blink and stare up at him. My lips move silently as I try to force myself to say something, to say anything, but my mind is blank.

Connor turns the shower off. "Fuck. Summer, that didn't happen."

I just blink again, not even sure if I'm fucking breathing. Connor practically falls out of the shower in his haste to escape. I stand there, the tiled stall getting cooler without the constant stream of hot water. My eyes are fixed blindly on the wall where Connor's face was a few minutes ago. My hand is still slightly extended in the same position it was in when I was brushing my fingers over his abs.

I'm only vaguely aware of Alice popping her head around the shower door. There's no embarrassment in her seeing me naked, not in this state of paralysis.

"What did you do to Connor? He just ran out of here half naked."

I try to answer, to tell her what happened, but the words are lodged in my throat, choking me.

Alice steps in front of me, waving a dainty hand in my face. "Hello?"

"I... Uh..." I manage to choke some sounds out, though I'm unsure if they are actual words.

Alice studies me for a moment with a frown and then slaps me across the face. My cheek stings from the hit, the pain snapping me back into my body.

"Fuck," I croak out, looking at Alice. "Ouch."

"You were freaking me out!" Alice replies unapologetically. I am grateful that she got me out of the stupor, even if her method was violence.

I pull my towel from the holder and wrap it around my body. Alice is hot on my heels as I go to my room, my breath growing a little ragged. He didn't say that. He didn't mean it. Right? No way. It was just a joke. Maybe it's not a joke but a trauma response. He's vulnerable and sad.

"What happened?"

"Nothing. We need to get to the assembly. Did you see the alert?"

Alice gives me a flat look. "I'm ready to go. You, however, are rocking the towel chic look, and I'm pretty sure that's against our uniform rules."

His words circle my mind as I dress and push my feet into my heels on autopilot. I grab my pack, not noticing that Alice is glancing at me every few seconds until we are outside.

"What?" I snap.

"Well, Connor isn't here. He left like his tail was on fire, and you were standing in the shower catatonic, so—"

"We're going to be late." I walk faster, trying to avoid her questions.

The hall is over half full by the time we arrive, and my gaze locks with Connor's almost immediately. He blushes deeply and waves. I've never known Connor to be shy or embarrassed, but now, he looks both. He regrets it. Maybe he didn't mean it. He's been through a lot, and we shared a bed, so maybe it was just a slip of the tongue.

Alice and I settle into the seats he's saved for us. He smiles at me politely, with none of the confident charm I've grown so used to. "Hi."

Alice looks between us, narrowing her eyes. "Okay, what the fuck is going—"

Stillness and silence settle heavily over the room just before the headmaster's powerful presence precedes him onto the stage. He sweeps his gaze over the crowd, taking in every student, reading them. My stomach twists when it's my turn for that impenetrable gaze to lock with mine, and he holds it for what feels like an eternity before moving on to his next victim.

There's an audible intake of breath from the assembly, preparing for his words. Even without his power vibrating through the auditorium, he's commanded us to complete silence with only his presence.

"No doubt you're wondering why I've summoned you all here, and why I cut my sabbatical short. I'm sure some of you have heard the rumors circulating around campus." He glances at a man in a black suit and sunglasses standing just offstage, barely visible. His face is set into flat lines, giving absolutely nothing away. The headmaster sweeps his gaze over the hall again. "I have been advised not to tell you anything, to keep you in the dark. But I am going to ignore that advice. This is *my* school, and one of my students was murdered yesterday."

Gasps fill the room, and Connor's hands clench into fists. He knew what was coming, but obviously, it had a bigger impact than he expected. I shift a little closer to him, trying to offer comfort but unsure how to after this morning's revelation. Rafe is sitting in the row in front of us, and I watch as his back goes straight and his shoulders tighten. He slowly turns in his seat, his eyes narrowed. Connor sinks lower in his chair, slumping under his younger brother's stare. Rafe has clearly figured out what the text Alice sent last night was all about.

"Her family has taken her to lay her in her final resting place," the headmaster continues. "But that's not why I have summoned you all here." His eyes meet mine

again, the silver even more molten than usual. "I have always placed high expectations on you. Some think they are impossible to achieve, and now, I'm going to expect
even more. Someone here knows something. Has seen something. Heard something. I
will make time for everyone today. No detail is too small. You may notice there are a
couple of strangers present." He gestures to the male at the side of the stage. "They are
members of the Arcane Intelligence Bureau, dispatched from the Grand Arcane. They
are here to look into the murder, and they advised me to keep this from you." The man
in the suit shifts slightly under the direct call out by the headmaster. "You are the best
the realms have to offer. The strongest. The smartest. The most powerful. Use it. Be
the students I know you are. The ones who will shatter the realms when you leave
these halls."

He lifts his chin, and for the first time, the icy facade he utilizes, like a mask, drops
from his face. My breath catches, seeing the rage sparking in his eyes. The fear that
always skirts up my spine in his presence comes roaring to the surface, and now I
understand why. *This* is what I sensed. This is the son of Merlin, one of the strongest
beings *ever*.

"Now, lastly, I'd like to send a message." His voice lowers, and the gravity in the
room intensifies. The air becomes oppressive and uncomfortable, the lights flickering.
"To whoever harmed my student, I will find you. And when I do," he casts his eyes
over the room once more, "you'll wish I had simply turned you over." The lights stop
flickering the second he stops talking, and the air becomes lighter again. "Dismissed."

# 39

## BU CHÒIR SIN

t's a message, a simple one. Yet it echoes like a scream in the quiet classroom. *You're next.* Each move is so deliberate, almost a caress along the skin. It will seem chaotic to those who don't know what to look for, an act of nonsensical gore. They are the ones who don't understand the language of violence and blood and pain. They don't see how each strike, each moment of prolonging the pain, adds to the song that can only be heard by those with the same darkness.

My hand curls around the shaft of one of the sharpened spears. It once hung on a stone wall of this classroom, but now it pierces the fae girl sprawled over the desktop, its tip embedded deep into the wood beneath her. I doubt I could yank it out unless I exerted some true strength, and it would be noisy, bringing people to the scene. Forty-nine weapons are buried into this single body, another deliberate choice. Like the strokes of an artist's paintbrush, every part of this is intentional.

Violence is a song, a painting, and a dance for those who know the steps. For us, it is more. They will look upon this display and think it is overkill, senseless and need-less. I know better. They're a bell reverberating through the realms. A challenge. A message.

This is more than a message to my little fae. It is a message to the powers that dared to provide her shelter at this university. They proved that no matter the wards, the abilities of the faculty, and the reputation of their revered headmaster, they could not protect the object of their desire.

I look at the wall above her, my fingers hovering over the letters, tracing the message drawn in blood.

**SHE BEARS THE MARK OF NIMUE. SHE WILL BE OURS.**

Nimue was one of the last handmaids lost during the Fall and one of the great enemies of the leader of the guild. She'd been gone for centuries. It's a game, lives being weighed and discarded as chess pieces, all in pursuit of the final objective.

The capture of the white queen.

# 40

## SUMMER

*Thu*

After the assembly, Connor goes to speak to his brothers. Rafe's furious stare nearly burned a hole through Cons's forehead while the headmaster spoke. He'd wasted no time in cluing in the rest of his brothers about Connor being the one to discover the body. I stare at Rafe with a scowl. He has some nerve being pissed at Connor for keeping him in the dark when he's been putting Con through the ringer for the last two weeks.

Alice turns to me the second they are out of earshot, her eyes surprisingly serious. "You should tell him."

"Tell him what?" I know the answer, but telling him and vocalizing my concerns will just make them more real. Ignorance is a silly little blanket I can wrap around myself and hide in.

"About Gia. That she kind of looks like you. He said nothing is too small."

I finally pull my gaze away from Connor, who looks like he's getting the verbal ass-kicking of the century led by a very angry Rafe.

"It's probably just a coincidence. We have no proof that it's more than that."

I've been running for so long, Alice. Let me stay wrapped in my blanket of delusion. It shields me from the glare of reality. The messages from the blank account warning me. The fact that Gia looked like me. The way my acceptance to Avalon showed up right when I needed it. So many threads of truth are wrapping around me, and I want them to be coincidences. I need them to be.

Alice nods slowly, her eyes narrowing on me. "So, you're going to stay and tell me why you and Connor are weird? Cool."

My stomach rolls, and without saying anything else, I stand and start for the headmaster's office. I hate that I'm so fucked up that I'd rather face the fear of someone potentially wanting to torture and kill me than face up to the words my boyfriend said to me in the shower. But here we are, and this is my reality.

Every step through the long corridors is heavier than the last, and my stomach drops when the headmaster's office door comes into view. He'll think I'm an idiot and a narcissist for making everything about me. But you know, maybe I can live with that and even find comfort in it because if someone as smart as the headmaster can't see any merit in the idea, then I must just be paranoid. I can go back to my blanket. There is no evidence that the person chasing me actually mistook me for Gia. I wasn't even being chased. The eyes on me were simply a figment of my imagination.

I stop in front of his door, the dark wood looming in front of me. A faint buzz of power emanates from it. No doubt it's covered with so many runes that the wood is struggling to conduct them all. Or, maybe the headmaster's power is so vast it can't be contained by something as mundane as an office.

I lift my hand and knock twice. The sound echoes, followed by an eerie silence before his low voice seeps through the crack beneath the door.

"Enter."

One word, it's so simple, yet it's dripping with power, strength, and fury. Clearly, the veil he'd dropped during the assembly is still down. At least now I understand why he doesn't cover his runes up like other sorcerers. It's a threat and a promise. They could know all the magic he could throw at them, every spell, every secret, and they would still be unable to defend against him.

I swallow, taking an extra beat to steel myself before I open the door.

The room is not at all as I expected. It is a large circle lined with bookcases filled with the most ornate books. The floor is composed of dark stones perfectly aligned and laid in a pleasing pattern, a large, luxurious midnight blue rug covering over half of it. The desk is in the center of the room, expertly littered with books and papers. It's perfectly organized but also chaotic to the untrained eye. I can't help but think there is a purpose to this. Sorcerers are known to conceal their abilities. Knowledge is power, and it is often best to be underestimated.

There is what looks like a skylight just above the desk, but instead of a view of Avalon's sky, an orb of light blue light ebbs and flows in the space, lighting the room. Occasionally, sparks of bright light spark away from the sphere and fly through the room. A small model of the campus sits at the corner of his desk, small lights moving through the intricate map. A spelled crystal hovers above it, projecting a surveillance feed into the air.

"Miss Tuatha De Daanan," the headmaster says, a note of impatience in his voice.

I step further into the office, finally pulling my gaze from the splendor of the room. His penetrating silver gaze pierces the astral projection. The closer I get to the desk, the more I notice. The small-scale campus surveillance feed switches from place to place. He waves his hand, and it disappears before I can make sense of it. Sorcerers and their secrets.

I stop in front of his desk. "Headmaster Emrys."

He lifts his chin, his silver eyes stormier than I've ever seen them. "What is it you wanted to speak to me about?"

I nervously play with the pleats of my skirt, averting my gaze, looking anywhere but at him. Fuck, this is so stupid. I focus over his shoulder, staring at a particularly ornate book. "Gia. Well, not directly about her, I don't suppose, but—"

He slams his hand down on his desk, making me jump in surprise. "Miss Tuatha De Daanan, when you speak to me, you look at me. Otherwise, this is not a conversation I need to be here for."

My cheeks heat as I meet his gaze. There is something very intriguing about the way my body reacts when he speaks to me like that. His fury is palpable, but despite his harsh words, I can tell it's not directed at me. Even with that knowledge, it doesn't make it any easier to bear.

The question I came to ask disintegrates into nothing, the ludicrosity of it too much to handle. "I was just wondering if," I take a breath, trying to keep my voice even, "there is a potential motive yet, or if it is all just random."

The irritation in his eyes melts a little, and he gazes steadily at me for a moment, thinking. He waves his hand again, and the door closes behind me. He reaches into his desk drawer and pulls out a small box. I tilt my head, watching as he opens it and pulls out a small pendant of raw black tourmaline. The shape is rough, with a rim of gold around it, but what makes the gem so captivating is the eight-pointed star of obsidian at the center. It is so polished and perfectly cut compared to the rough beauty of the tourmaline that they shouldn't work together, but they fit.

The headmaster holds up the necklace by the chain. "You will wear this, tell no one, and never take it off."

I frown, looking at the necklace. "Why?"

He quirks a brow at me, looking unimpressed. "It was not a request."

"Will everyone be receiving one?" I ask.

His jaw twitches in annoyance. "No. You asked about a motive. There is one. You will wear this." He waves his hand again, and an image appears in front of me. I can't see the body, but I can already tell this is the scene of the crime. The gore is clear even from this angle, but that's not what he's showing me. On the wall behind her, written in blood, is a message.

**SHE BEARS THE MARK OF NIMUE. SHE WILL BE OURS.**

The blood trickling down from the letters turns my stomach, and a sense of foreboding slams into me, rattling my bones. A moment later, the screen is gone and the headmaster hands me a file. I look down at it, dread filling me.

"Open it," he commands.

I try to swallow down my fear, but it lodges in my throat. Reluctantly, I open the folder. Inside is my completed application for the school. The handwriting is sloping, delicate, cramped, and flurried. It's nothing like mine. The headmaster stands from his chair and rounds his desk, pointing to a seal in the top corner. The red wax curves into a half circle at the bottom, and above it is what looks like a woman standing in a lake. Her arms are at her sides, slightly outstretched, and her head is turned slightly to the left. It's the most intricate seal I've ever seen.

"The mark of Nimue. Whoever applied for you has marked every single page with it." He looks at me again and then lifts the necklace. "Now, are you going to continue to be stubborn?"

Maybe my original question wasn't so ridiculous after all.

I shake my head, brushing my fingers over the mark. "No, sir. I just... I don't understand. This is very overwhelming."

The headmaster stands in front of me and sits on the edge of his desk. He gently pries the file from my hands, and it disappears into thin air. "I understand, but you're not a person who will buckle under the strain, are you?"

My spine straightens at the challenge, and I meet his gaze. "No, sir."

He nods once and then pushes off the desk. Standing behind me, he puts the necklace around my neck, and I twist my hair up to help him. "You tell no one." I shiver when the pendant touches my chest. When I look up, the headmaster is standing in front of me again. "The authorities do not know about the connection to you, and I would like to keep it that way. Unfortunately," his jaw ticks, "they know about Mr. Morningstar. I could not prevent it."

I swallow, touching the pendant. The power sparks under my fingers, but it immediately warms to me, licking curiously at my skin. "She... She looked like me. Do you think they thought—"

"It's a possibility," he replies without letting me finish my thought. Obviously, he had noticed. "Do not blame yourself for the actions of a killer," he says as if reading my thoughts.

I look away, the guilt sinking deeper into me.

The headmaster tsks. "You are stronger than this, Miss Tuatha De Daanan."

Why does he keep saying that? And why is it working on me? Why do I want his words to be true? Why do I want to be stronger?

I look back at him, nodding. "Yes, sir."

"There are those who die in the fire and those who thrive in it." He walks back around his desk and sits down in his chair. "We'll speak soon."

I nod and turn, walking toward the door, but I pause before leaving his office, my hand on the handle. I glance over my shoulder at him. "I'm glad you're back, sir."

He looks at me, those silver eyes seeing way too much, but he simply nods and picks up another file from his desk.

Connor is leaning against the wall when I leave Headmaster Emrys's office. He smiles sheepishly when he sees me. "Hi, babe."

"Con? You're going to see Headmaster Emrys?"

He shakes his head. "Alice told me you were here."

I lift my eyebrows, making a mental note to discuss with Alice how much of this situation we should tell Connor. If any of it.

He pushes off the wall and reaches for me. "Can we just... forget what I said?"

"Con..."

He clears his throat and pulls a dagger from the sheath strapped to his thigh, the silver hand ornate and polished. Obviously, he wants to move past this conversation as quickly as possible. "Will you keep this on you?"

"Why?"

"Just... please?"

I exhale but nod. I should probably tell Connor I'm more of a danger to myself with that thing than anyone else, but I'll do anything to take that look of pure helplessness off his face. Connor kneels in front of me and pulls a smaller sheath from his bag. He attaches it to my thigh and stows the dagger inside, pressing a soft kiss to the sensitive skin just above. My skirt barely conceals the leather, and I tug on it as he gets to his feet. The awkwardness returns immediately, and I can't stand it. I close the distance between us and brush my lips over his.

"Let's talk later?"

Connor smiles against my lips, and I feel the tension leave his body. "Okay, babe. I should get to class."

I nod. "See you later?"

Connor kisses me again. "Be safe, okay?"

I pull back and look up at him, looping my fingers into the waistband of his pants to keep him from leaving. "Tell me I'll see you later."

Connor's smile is easy. "I'll see you later."

"And I'll be safe."

Connor hesitates for a moment before he wraps his arms around me, pulling me into a hug. He inhales my hair, and I wrap my arms around his waist, holding him tight. Connor gives me one last hard kiss before we both head to class.

# 41

## SUMMER

*Sho*

I sit down next to Alice in class, and she immediately pounces on me with questions.

"So? What did he say?"

I'm about to answer when Professor Ambrose enters the room, clearing his throat to get our attention.

"In light of yesterday's events, I will be postponing the pop quiz until a week past Friday at the request of Headmaster Emrys. Today we will continue to study the effects of different atmospheres on different species. If you would turn to page two hundred and fifty-nine of your textbooks, we will begin."

As everyone flips through the text, Professor Ambrose writes on the board. "We are going to discuss the Grand Arcane today." My brows shoot up a little, surprised by the change in the course. "Who knows about this realm?"

A few mumble responses, but no one answers.

"The Grand Arcane is one of the thirteen closest realms to Avalon. It is the artificial realm, created by the Unification of the Realms that came after the Fall," Professor Ambrose's mentee supplies, when it's clear we're too rattled by the assembly and news to respond. Like most sorcerers, the fourth-year is covered in runes. His hands nearly glow with them, and several extend past his collar to his neck. He's never been in class before, but I've noticed that Professor Ambrose often has different seniors assisting in his classes, probably to earn extra credit.

"The Fall?" Another student asks, earning a harsh look from Ambrose.

"Yes, the Fall of Faerie." My hand tightens at the mention of the fae home realm.

I'd purposely been avoiding that assignment. "Prior to the Fall, it was thought impossible for a realm to experience such a world-ending event."

"But what about Draconis?" A shifter asks. This time, Ambrose doesn't censor him with a harsh look. Instead, he leans back against his desk and actually seems to be *enjoying* teaching. I didn't think that was possible.

"Draconis did experience a similar event. However, it was an extermination event of the shifters who lived there, not the realm itself. The ruins of Draconis still exist and can be visited, even if the dracanae have all but died out. Faerie no longer exists on any plane. If you were to open a portal to its former location, you'd find nothing but empty space. But I don't want to delve too deeply into the Fall or the Culling, as I believe both Faerie and Draconis are assigned to some of you for your final project." He smirks. "Can't be doing all the work for you, can I?"

Ambrose continues on about the Grand Arcane, and I want to focus on the topic, but my mind is a mess. Gia's face keeps flashing in front of my eyes, the pendant warming ever so slightly each time.

Exhausted after fighting with myself to stay focused all morning, it is a relief when it is finally time for lunch. Connor and his brothers are already sitting at our usual table when Alice and I walk into the cafeteria, our lunch waiting for us. Connor smiles up at me, and I kiss him softly as I sit in the seat next to him.

"So... it's later," he says, watching me.

"Not here," I say, taking a bite of my food.

Connor taps his foot. "Okay, where?" I can feel the anxiety radiating off him.

"Somewhere private."

Connor is about to reply when a pretty blonde girl sits in an empty seat next to Zach. He shifts uncomfortably, keeping his eyes on his food. The girl beams, showing me her perfect white teeth. She's wearing a cheer uniform with the school's colors, the silver flashing in the sun streaming through the windows.

"Hi! I'm Ashley!"

I can practically feel Alice's eye roll, but I give her a faint smile. I'm not really in the mood to speak to a cheerleader, even though there's a layer of sincerity to her peppiness.

"You're Summer, right? I saw on the sign-up sheet that you're trying out?" She beams at me, her attention pinned on me. Trying out? I barely remember adding my name to the list. She's thinking about tryouts after what happened yesterday and the assembly this morning?

"Oh, I was thinking about it, yeah."

Connor casually wraps an arm around my back. His touch and show of affection are calming, even with the sliver of awkwardness lingering between us.

"Well, you definitely should. You'd fit right into the squad! Plus, you're dating the captain. We delayed tryouts because of what happened, but we'll update you soon."

"What am I, chopped liver?" Alice grumbles beside me. Ashley glances at her, her smile wavering only slightly. She is definitely aware of Alice's reputation. Usually, this is the fun part for me, where people wonder if the rumors about Alice are true. Then they bounce to whether they can hold their own against her, and Alice educates them. But right now, I am finding it hard to find the fun in anything. I keep seeing Gia's face, so much like mine.

"Ah, Elvira, right?"

I wince. Well, that isn't a good start. If I know anything about Alice, it's that her given name is not one she enjoys or appreciates.

"Alice," she growls.

Ashley nods. "Well, I'm sure you'd be a great... asset to the team." She looks at Connor and then the other Morningstars, but carefully avoids looking at Zach. "I'll see you all at practice?"

They all nod, and Connor smiles at her. She walks away but looks back over her shoulder, and I don't miss the sharp glare she throws at Zach. I glance at Zach, about to ask him about it, but his face is thundery. Woah. That's new.

Connor leans in, dropping his voice. "Want to cut and go to my place?"

I nod and let Alice know I won't be in class before we leave the canteen, heading to the Morningstar House. Connor glances at me as we walk, his fingers interlocked with mine.

"What?" I ask, looking at him.

"Just nervous."

I squeeze his hand, trying to comfort him, but I'm not sure our conversation will go well, given I know that I'm not ready to say what he has. The truth is, I am not sure I will ever be able to say it.

We've barely stepped into the house when Connor turns to me. "So privacy."

I nod and sit on the couch. Connor sits next to me, watching me carefully. He keeps his hands to himself, not touching me as we sit. His fingers lock together on his lap, but his thumbs twitch, betraying his anxiety.

"Why did you run?" I ask. I doubt it would have been better if he had stayed, considering I went completely catatonic and had to be slapped out of it, but he doesn't need to know that.

An adorable blush creeps up his cheeks. "Because I..." His cheeks redden more. "I didn't mean to... I–I got flustered and embarrassed."

I search his eyes, trying to read him, to see what's really going on in his mind. "So you didn't mean it?"

He shakes his head immediately. "I meant it. I just didn't mean to... say it."

"Con."

Connor rubs the back of his neck, looking away. "I just... It kind of slipped out, and I don't expect you to say it back or anything. I don't want you to feel pressure—"

I lean in, cutting him off with a kiss. He tenses at the contact before he relaxes into it, deepening it. His fingers tangle in my hair, and he angles my head to fit his mouth better to mine, consuming me with his kiss.

He moans and pulls back after a minute, searching my face before his gaze lingers on my lips. "So you're not upset with me?"

"For loving me?"

Connor blinks, his brows furrowing a little. "Well... yeah."

My lips twitch, and I brush my lips over him again. "No, Connor. I'm not upset with you."

"Did I freak you out?"

Do I take the scary route and be honest? Or the comfortable one and lie?

"I freaked out a little initially. But I trust you, and I want to be with you." I lean in, kissing him again. "And I've... No one's ever said that to me before. I've never felt loved before." While I thought I was in love before, Torin never said those words to me. That's not who I was to him. He only saw the potential of my power, a pawn in a greater plan. "But now..."

Connor pulls me into his lap so I'm straddling him. "You feel loved?"

I nod, tunneling my fingers into his silky blond locks.

"I love you," he says again. The words are still tentative, but much less so.

I roll my eyes, swatting at him. "Ugh, stop. I may be possessed by the mush demon when we're together, but I'll never be as mushy and embarrassing as you."

Connor leans in, biting my cheek. "You are so mushy now."

I grab his face, squeezing his cheeks slightly and then kissing him hard. Connor groans into my mouth, his flirty smile melting as he deepens the kiss. He's been hard since he pulled me into his lap, but I can feel his cock throb beneath me as I kiss him, his body sensing the intent.

I growl into his lips. "Don't tell anyone that I'm mushy. I have a reputation to uphold."

Connor lifts me and lays me back on the couch, his large body hovering over mine. He kisses down my neck, and I reach between us to open his pants. I pull his cock free as he pushes my panties down my legs. He flips my skirt up, and I tug at his shirt, needing to feel the endless hard muscle above me. His cock nudges my opening, and a guttural groan leaves his lips as he slowly presses his bare cock into me. My core aches in response, my pussy clenching, needing more. I drag my nails down his back and dig them into his ass. I thrust my hips up at the same time I jerk him toward me, gasping when he slams into me to the hilt. Connor shouts in pleasure, and I arch beneath him, grinding my clit against him.

"Bruise me, big guy," I beg as Connor slides his hand down my side.

"What?" he groans, nuzzling against my neck.

"Dig your fingers into me."

He presses them in a little, but not enough, and I slide my hand down his arm and push his fingers in more. The bite of pain makes me cry out and buck against him, needing him to move. Connor cups the back of my thigh, hitching my leg higher on his hip. He presses his fingers into the flesh, and the pleasure is almost exquisite.

"Fuck, Con. Don't stop." He pulls back until only the tip of his cock remains inside of me and then slams in deep again. Our moans of pleasure mingle in the silence of the empty house. Connor tugs my shirt open and pulls my bra down. Dipping his head, he takes my nipple into his mouth, sucking it deep. He grazes his teeth teasingly over the sensitive bud, and I tighten my fingers in his hair, yanking hard in a silent plea. He moans but doesn't make any move to follow my nonverbal instructions.

I hiss, rocking my hips to take him deeper, and he lifts his head, his body shuddering. His thrusts become more ragged and desperate, and I know he is getting close to his release.

He looks down at me, his eyes dark with lust and a soft, tender emotion I am just beginning to recognize. "I love you," he gasps out and kisses me deeply, swallowing my cries of pleasure.

"Harder, big guy. I'm so close." I moan, my orgasm just out of reach. A tingle goes down my spine at the intoxicating bliss of it.

Connor thrusts harder, bracing his hand against the arm of the couch, giving him more leverage.

"Bite me," I moan. Connor slams deep and sinks his teeth into the curve of my shoulder. My pussy spasms, and I scream. My release rips through me, pushing Connor into his own orgasm. His shout of pleasure makes my core clench, and his release spills into me for the first time.

Connor collapses on top of me, panting into my neck. I smile and lightly glide my fingers down his back.

"I don't even know why they were talking..." Zach's voice trails off. I tense and then hear someone yell.

Connor grabs the blanket off the back of the couch and pulls it over us, glancing over his shoulder.

"Your ass is like a searchlight! Do you ever tan?" Zach asks, his voice filled with disgust.

"You have a bedroom! This is a communal space, asshole." I look around Connor's arm and see Zach and Zane standing at the door, both of them with a hand over Luke's eyes.

Connor grabs a pillow and throws it at them, hitting Zane in the face. "Get out!"

"It's our house, too!" Zach complains.

My lips twitch. "Okay, fair point. Can you just leave for a second so your brother can unpenetrate?"

"*Unpenetrate* makes me want to die," Zach groans, but they all turn around.

Connor pulls out of me, and I quickly pull on my panties while Connor buttons his pants. I check the time and curse.

"Shit, I have to go."

Connor blinks. "Where?"

"I said I'd study with Alice and Brett at the library after school. Well, Brett and I will study. Alice will fuck around on her phone."

"Aren't all the quizzes and deadlines being extended?" Zane asks, turning around.

"Yes, but that means it's a perfect time to get ahead."

Zane grimaces. "Almighty, Con. Your girlfriend is a nerd."

Connor laughs and kisses the top of my head. "I'll walk you there."

I nod. "My protector."

Connor's smile becomes forced, but he relaxes again when I slide my hand into his. It breaks my heart to know that he thinks he failed Gia even though she was already dead when he found her. He is still beating himself up about not being the warrior he thinks he's meant to be. The one he's trained his whole life to be.

"Shall we, babe?" Connor asks, offering me his back. I jump on, and he reaches back to catch my thighs, both of us laughing as he starts toward the library.

# 42

## SUMMER

*Thae*

When we get to the library, I playfully bite Connor's neck before sliding off his back. His goodbye kiss is hot and deep, leaving me panting and needing. He grins and winks before jogging down the steps, heading toward Manananggal Hall for a student council meeting.

I watch until he is out of sight and then hurry inside. Alice is already there, and I slide into the chair next to her.

"Where's Brett?" I ask.

"He's running late." Her intense stare burns into me, and I sigh, turning to face her. "I don't even know where to start. The headmaster or Connor," she says, tapping her chin in thought.

I wait for her to decide, unsure if I want to part with any of the overwhelming information that's been thrown at me today. Neither topic is one I want to delve into. Even after the conversation with Connor, I'm still on edge.

"Okay, the headmaster. What did he say?"

"Before we discuss this, I'm not sure how much of it I want Connor to know, so can we keep it between us?" I whisper, not wanting to be overheard.

Alice nods and scoots her chair closer. I search her eyes, deciding how much I should tell her. Would it be smart to tell her everything? Should I put that burden on her? Perhaps it's best to keep it to myself and tell her only a sliver of the truth until I know more.

"He said he had noticed the similarities between Gia and me, and he is going to investigate further." The words taste like acid. Something inside me longs to tell her the whole truth, to have a true confidant. But then I'd have to tell her about the messages from 1015. Why didn't I tell the headmaster about them? Fuck, why am I like this?

Alice watches me, and I can see she knows that I am not telling her everything. Her gaze fastens on the pendant around my neck. She sniffs at it and then eyes me suspiciously. "Where did you get that?"

I close my fingers around the stone, trying to guard it from view. "Oh, it's just an old necklace."

Alice's eyes flash with hurt. She knows I lied. Her gaze turns hard and determined between one blink and the next. I brace myself. This is it. She is going to walk away.

"Will it protect you?" she asks.

I flinch, having expected her to yell at me, completely unprepared for that question. I nod once and open my mouth to apologize to her, but no words come out.

Alice slides her hand into mine and smiles. "Then that's all I need to know."

I swallow the thick emotion clogging my throat and squeeze her hand. She leans in again, all trace of lingering hurt gone.

"Okay. What happened with Con? You guys looked cozy."

"Hi, guys!" Brett drops into the chair across from us, and Alice rolls her eyes.

"Later, then," Alice grumbles, grabbing her phone and scrolling through it, making no effort to hide her dislike of the shifter who has become somewhat of a study buddy for me.

I smile at him. "Hey, Brett."

He looks at my lack of textbooks and raises his eyebrows. "Are you studying wood grains?"

My lips twitch. "I came from Connor's, so I don't have any of my books. I'm going to go search for one right now, smartass."

"Oh, right. I saw the announcement on *Nexus*. Congrats," he says, though his voice isn't as vibrant as usual. The news of Gia has put a damper on everyone's mood.

Pushing back my chair, I smile at Brett and gently tug on a lock of Alice's hair as I head into the stacks. I slide my fingers over the spines of the books, unconsciously seeking the comfort they bring me as I think through my study schedule. I should delve into some combat theory, but ugh, combat. It's so stupid when magic exists. There is realms, and I still have that essay it would be good to get started on.

*She bears the mark of Nimue.*

*Nimue.* The name niggles something at the back of my mind, a memory not quite given form.

"Can I help you find something, dear?" Mrs. Brunswick, the librarian, asks me, stopping her cart just behind me. Her glasses sit low on her nose, and her hair is pulled back in a bun, aging her immortal form. She waves her hand, and three books fly back to their shelves, nestling between the two on either side.

"I was wondering if there are any books on Nimue? Specifically, the mark of Nimue?"

Mrs. Brunswick frowns, her eyes darting over the stacks. "The mark of Nimue hasn't been seen or used in centuries. It may as well be a myth at this point, but I believe there are a handful of books on the Lady of the Lake."

She walks past me, and I follow as she expertly navigates the stacks. No one knows how long she has worked here, but it's long enough that she has started to resemble the books that line the shelves, a little dusty and faded. The gray tinge to her skin betrays a lack of sunlight, and it wouldn't surprise me if she hasn't left the library in decades. She leads me deeper into the library, stopping at a less visited section. The books here look newer due to how little they are handled and read. She stops midway down the aisle and pulls out a red leather-bound book. The title is embellished in gold, and the edges are similarly gilded. She hands me the book.

*The Great Loves of Merlin.*

I wrinkle my nose in distaste. In Gaia, the realm where I grew up, Merlin is depicted as an elderly sorcerer with a long white beard and a pointy hat. The thought of him with a *great love* and all it entails is a little gross. Though his son is... something else, and Merlin must have been young at some point. It is interesting that I haven't come across any images of the great sorcerer in my exploration of the school.

Mrs. Brunswick reaches up and pulls two more books off the shelf, seemingly at random. "So, I think this is all we have for now. We don't keep very many for obvious reasons."

I frown. "Of course."

"Happy reading," Mrs. Brunswick says, patting the top book. She shuffles away, leaving me alone in the stacks. I look around at the surrounding books, noting how stunningly beautiful they are. Why are these never chosen to be read? There is a treasure trove of information here, from alternate rune techniques to potion recipes to the history of pixies.

A shiver runs down my spine, and I look around. I don't feel those increasingly familiar eyes on me. Their absence is so undiluted that it almost feels false, like a ruse and another way to set me on edge.

I clutch the books to my chest and wander back to our table. Brett glances up and gives me a quick smile before focusing back on his essay. Alice barely acknowledges my existence, her nose practically buried in her phone. I open the book on the top of the pile and start leafing through it.

Though the book is named *The Great Loves of Merlin*, it seems to focus more on Merlin's achievements in the bedroom than the people he had actual relationships with. I flip through the pages until I find the description I am looking for.

*Nimue, or The Lady of the Lake, is renowned as a goddess of water and nature and has held her place as such for centuries. Many mortal congregations worship Nimue, though it is known that she was, in fact, fae. She was born in Faerie not long after its conception, and when she was of age, she left to spread her elemental gifts elsewhere, dissatisfied with paradise.*

*On her travels through the realms, she acquired many followers and worshippers. These were devoted people who followed her every order. Her power and vibrance drew people in, captivating and encapsulating. As she grew in popularity, she began to rank certain members of her following. For an honored select few, she bestowed the mark of Nimue.*

There's no depiction of the mark or description of her connection to Merlin. I turn the page to continue reading, but blink in surprise. The next page picks up in the middle of detailing someone named Sebile. I flip the page back and forth in disbelief, knowing that I didn't make a mistake but compelled to try to fix it. Of course, it doesn't, and I have to accept that a piece of the book is missing. Someone didn't just tear the pages out. It looks like they cut a section out and then pushed the other pages together to cover up the lack. Why? Why remove pages from a book barely read and nearly forgotten? Why bother trying to eradicate such an obscure piece of knowledge?

I glare at the page. Can I fix this with a rune?

One starts to form in my mind, and I slice my finger with the small dagger in my purse. I press down on the broken page with one hand and slowly craft the small rune in the corner. The curves swoop before joining at three points. The pages begin to materialize, and I smile widely. It feels so good to use my magic, even in this small way. I watch the pages fill in, waiting impatiently to continue reading. The book starts to shake, making the entire table vibrate. Alice glances up, looking between me and the book.

"Sum? What's going on?"

The book vibrates harder, rattling violently against the table before bursting into flames. The thick, heavy paper and beautiful cover turn to cinders. Alice, Brett, and I lunge away from the table, our chairs scraping loudly against the floor. The fire rages for a few seconds and then is ousted by... nothing. Once the flames clear, the book is completely gone, with no evidence of it ever existing. I swallow and brush my fingers over the table. Not even a scorch mark remains. I look up, my mouth hanging open in shock. Brett and Alice are watching me wide-eyed, but no one else seems to have noticed.

"I'm going to head home," I say abruptly.

Alice nods. "Me too. Studying has taken it out of me." We leave the library and Alice links her arm through mine. "That was some crazy shit. What was the book about?"

"The Lady of the Lake," I say, still slightly freaked out.

Alice curses under her breath. "Is this another assignment I've forgotten about?"

225

I shake my head, distracted by thoughts of the book.

Alice nudges me. "Summer?"

I glance at her, blinking. "No, no assignment. I was just reading."

Alice rolls her eyes. "Reading nonfiction for fun is truly the most depressing thing." She nudges me again. "So what happened with Connor?"

"Connor said he... loves me," I manage to grate out, and I can feel Alice gaping at me. "We're good, though. We talked it through, and he feels how he feels. He has no expectations of me getting there anytime soon."

"And how are you feeling about it all?" she probes, probably shocked that I haven't fled the realm already.

"Better than I thought I would." Rather than the usual inky feeling that coats my skin when I'm uncomfortable, I am surprisingly at peace. Connor's love is warm, comforting, and completely undeniable. There's something almost concerning about how undeniable it is.

Over the following week, things on campus slowly get back to normal as people return to their lives. The ground outside of the room where Connor found Gia is still covered in flowers, crystals, and stuffed animals. People have tacked photos and poems of her to the wall and door. Sadness still hangs over the campus like a heavy miasma, but some of the fear has died down. Everyone seems a little more at ease, everyone but me.

Connor is pretending to be more all right than he is, so I conspired with his brothers to arrange a weekend in Eden. I know how tight-knit his family is and how much they ground him. Connor and I are advancing with our relationship, and it doesn't seem too big a step to spend a couple of nights at his parents' house. Connor is still in the dark about this plan, and I'm excited to see his reaction when he hears I'll be joining. Or at least that's what I'm telling myself, but I know he won't go without me.

I set down my overnight bag and frown at Alice. She is sitting on my bed, wearing that blood-stained onesie again, pouting and tugging at my plush cow's ear somewhat violently.

"Hey. Don't take it out on Mabel." I snatch the stuffy from Alice's grasp and carry her to the safety of the desk.

"I can't believe you're leaving me." She crosses her arms.

I unzip my bag and rearrange the contents for the thirtieth time. "It's only for two nights, and I can be back in thirty minutes if you need me." I look at her, a pang of concern trickling down my spine. "Promise me you'll be safe." My worry grows more intense. An image of Gia from my dream fills my mind, but this version has Alice's pixie-like face. "Fuck. Never mind. I'm not going." I pull a sweater out of my bag and turn to put it away, but Alice grabs my arm, turning me to face her.

"Summer, I'm joking." Alice pries the sweater from my hand and shoves it carelessly back into the bag. "You know what my nickname is back home?"

I shake my head, fear making even my fingers tingle.

"Mistress of Bloodshed," Alice says, rolling her eyes. "Among others."

I exhale heavily, taking her hand. "You'll be okay? You'll text me all the time?"

Alice snorts and throws her arms around my neck, pulling me into a tight hug. "Yes, you little psycho." I hug her back, the affection feeling almost familiar. "You should be more worried about the killer running into me than the other way around." Alice tries to pull back, but I don't release her, clinging to her tightly.

"I can just go to Eden for the day and come back tonight."

Alice struggles in my arms and manages to wriggle out of my hold. She cups my cheeks. "I will be fine. Connor needs this. And Sum?" She looks at me, concern lining her features. "I think you do, too. I can see the toll this is taking. You're not sleeping."

I sigh and look away. As if reminded by her words, my body aches from exhaustion. Every night since Gia's death, I've had the same nightmare. She haunts me, and even the rune I used on Connor doesn't stop it.

"You like his parents. It wouldn't be the worst thing to go and spend a weekend being... hugged or whatever parents are supposed to do." Alice's voice is soft, but she grimaces as the words leave her lips, the very idea repulsive to her. I nod and rub my hand over my face, exhaling on a soft laugh.

"Text me every hour."

Alice rolls her eyes. "That'll really ruin the mood during my forty-two-hour orgy marathon."

I pause, quirking a brow. Though I've not known Alice that long, I'm almost eighty percent sure she's joking, but I can't say for certain.

"No fucking in my room. And please vacuum after. Shifters leave fur everywhere."

Alice tips her head. "How does one use the vacuum?" The question is more to herself than to me. I laugh and pull her into another hug, kissing the top of her head.

"Use protection," I say, pulling out the sweater Alice stuffed into my bag and refolding it. I zip the bag closed and sling it over my shoulder.

Luke is waiting at the gate when I arrive at the Morningstar House. It's still early, the sun rising lazily in the east. Luke waves at me, his smile warm. "Hi, Summer! Connor is still sleeping. We thought you'd like to be the one to wake him."

I grin at him and step into the house. All the Morningstars are in the living room. Zach and Zane are quietly arguing about something. I could probably figure out what they are up to if I tuned into the conversation, but I do not want to get involved in any of their schemes. Rafe lifts his chin in a quick nod as he sips his coffee, and I quietly sneak upstairs.

Connor is sleeping peacefully in his bed, and I wince when the door creaks a little. He barely stirs at the sound, and I close the door as I creep into his room. I climb into bed with him and kiss his forehead.

"Big guy?"

Connor stirs a little, burying his face into my chest and inhaling me. He's done this both mornings that we've slept together. True to his word, he's never pushed me or pressured me into staying over, and the two times it has happened, I've initiated it. Connor nuzzles against me, humming softly. He suddenly lurches up, his hands gripping my arms to keep me from flying off the bed. His eyes are wide with panic as he searches my face.

"Babe? Are you okay?" He cups my cheeks, looking me over, checking for any visible injury.

I cover his hand on my cheek. "Con, I'm fine."

He looks around his room, clearly disorientated. "What's—"

I smile at him. "I have a surprise."

He yawns and stretches, relaxing as he realizes I'm all right. "What time is it?"

"A little after six."

He blinks. "And you're awake? What's happened?"

I chuckle lightly. "Nothing! I have a surprise."

He frowns, searching my face.

"We're going to Eden for the weekend."

Connor blinks and then blinks again. "We?"

I nod. "All of us."

"You're coming too?" Connor asks, the hope in his voice nearly painful. I nod, and his face breaks out into the most dazzling smile. He lovingly cups my face and kisses me deeply.

I moan, longing to sink into the kiss, and then let him sink into me. But we have somewhere we have to be. "As much as I like that plan, and as fun as it would be, I'm not sure how long we have before—"

Zach and Zane burst into the room with super soakers, shooting freezing cold water at Connor and me.

"Get up!" Zane yells.

"Mom's making waffles!" Zach screeches.

I squeal, trying to avoid the icy water and climb out of bed. Connor grabs me around the waist and holds me close. "Blame Summer! She's being too sexy!"

I laugh. "Connor! Let me go!"

The boys keep shooting at us, and we laugh, rolling in the bed until we both fall on the floor. Connor groans as I land on top of him, pushing all the air out of his lungs.

"You have three minutes," Zach warns.

"We'll be back," Zane finishes.

I giggle and roll off Connor, both of us soaked. He lies on his back, his laugh free and easy. Even the idea of going home for the weekend seems to be healing for him. I push to my feet and offer him my hand to help him up. Connor grins at me and takes my hand, careful not to pull me over as he stands. He kisses me deeply and playfully slaps my ass before tossing me a towel to dry off while he gets dressed.

We pound down the steps exactly two minutes and fifty-eight seconds later. The twins are waiting at the bottom of the staircase, their super soakers primed and ready. They deflate a little when they see us, knowing they can't attack again, but perk up when Connor flexes his shoulders and his wings spring free. His brothers eagerly follow his lead, their wings exploding from their backs. There are a few more gold feathers in Connor's stark white wings, and they sparkle in the dawn light. Zach's and Zane's are a warm ivory and nearly identical. Luke has the whitest, most pristine-looking wings. I glance at Rafe expectantly, but he has made no move to ready himself. For the first time, I notice he doesn't have a bag, and my smile falls.

Connor looks at him. "Ready, Rafe?"

Rafe looks down into his mug. "I'm not coming."

"Why?" Connor drops my hand and walks over to him.

"I have stuff to do here," Rafe replies, his words clipped.

"It would mean a lot to Mom..." Connor says, dropping his voice.

"I said I'm not coming," Rafe growls, pushing away from the breakfast bar and going upstairs to his room. The door slams, and Connor deflates. He catches my eyes and forces a smile, though the worried sadness lingers.

Connor looks at each of his brothers. He squares his shoulders and grabs our bags before stalking out the door, Zach, Zane, and Luke following. The moment I am within arm's reach, Connor scoops me into his arms and launches into the air. I wrap my arms around him, burying my face in his neck to keep it out of the wind.

When we get above cloud cover, the wind dies down, and Connor whispers into my ear, "Babe? Ready to see my home?"

I lift my head, and Connor presses a kiss to my temple as I look around at the clouds. They are fluffy and white except for the one right in front of us. It's more pearlescent than the others and seems to have more substance. Zane flies ahead, tapping something on his halo, and the cloud becomes transparent, rippling like a drop in a lake. We soar through the portal, and while the sky looks similar, it also looks completely different. A beautiful city lies below, but thousands of clouds are scattered through the sky. They look more pillowy than the ones in other realms I've been to, and each supports a city of its own.

Between the clouds, the air is a stunning mix of blush pink and baby blue swirls. Zach expertly glides through the sky, his brothers close behind. He dives, and Connor tucks his wings. I tighten my hold on Connor, feeling like I've left my stomach behind as we drop. With practiced ease, Luke swerves past a flower shop and grabs a bouquet. Zane is right behind him and drops money into a box labeled FLY THROUGH.

Connor pulls up and flares his wings wide, cupping the air to slow our descent. He lands on a cloud beside Zach, Luke and Zane touching down beside him. Connor puts me on my feet, bracing his hands on my hips to steady me. They chat happily as they walk to the single door at the center of the cloud. Zane presses a button on the pad to the left of the door, and I look up at Connor, wide-eyed and a little overwhelmed.

He smiles down at me. "I promise I'll show you everything," he says, brushing his lips over mine.

There is a small ding, and the door opens.

"Are you coming or what? I'm hungry," Zane groans.

Connor softly kisses me again and slides his hand into mine before leading me into what looks like an elevator. Once we're all in, Connor presses his halo to a scanner, and the lift starts to move.

"Do you guys live in an apartment?" I ask. I'm unsure where the apartment could be, considering the only thing that seemed to be above the elevator door was more cloud.

Zach rolls his eyes, and Connor's lips twitch. "Not quite."

A few moments later, the elevator pings again, and the door slowly opens. My jaw drops. An expanse of the greenest, most lush grass stretches out into the clouds. Round stones create a path through the velvety perfection of the lawn, leading to the most welcoming house I've ever seen. It's similar to the Morningstar House, though it is bigger, and I can already tell it's homier.

Zach and Zane break into a run. "Mom!" they shout as they head toward the house, Luke following behind them.

Connor squeezes my hand, and we walk up the path. A feeling of comfort and warmth envelopes me the moment we step onto the porch. We pass through the open door, and I'm hit with the smell of waffles, maple syrup, and strawberries.

Uriel smiles brightly and pulls Connor and me into a bear hug. "Hello."

I pat him on the back and silently curse myself for my awkwardness. I'm still not used to all of this affection, except with Alice and Connor. Uriel pulls back, and Farrah walks into the room, holding Luke's hand.

"Ah! There's my other boy!" She beams at Connor, her love for them so clear and tangible. She hugs Connor first, kissing him on the cheek. "And my girl!" Farrah pulls me into a hug, and I try to return the embrace a little less awkwardly.

"How do you like the Silver City, Summer?" Uriel asks as Farrah leans into his side, wrapping her arm around his waist.

"It's beautiful!"

Connor kisses my head. "I'm going to show her more of it this weekend."

Something in the kitchen smashes, and Farrah sighs, but the content smile remains on her face. "Excuse me for a second. Zach! Zane! You better not have started eating!" She disappears into the kitchen, and Uriel nods, slinging his arm around Luke's shoulders. "You'll need to show her the Godiva Pond."

Connor nods. "Absolutely."

Farrah returns, holding a vase filled with the flowers Luke picked up on the way in. She places the vase on the table and then looks at Connor, her skin practically glowing with her joy.

"No Rafe?" she asks, and I can hear the hope in her voice that maybe he'll be coming in later.

Connor shakes his head and squeezes my hand. "He has a project due Monday," he lies, and I can feel the toll it takes on him to do it. As an angel, his mom knows the truth, and he knows it, but it's easier to taste the lie than to hear the truth.

Deep sorrow flashes across her face. The longing for her son dims her light, but she covers it quickly. Only her eyes let her down, still dark with hurt. Uriel walks over to her and rubs her back in silent support. He doesn't have the same hurt as Farrah. It's obvious he didn't expect Rafe to attend. "We're glad you came. We were worried when Jimmy called us."

I frown. "He called?"

Uriel nods. "He wanted to tell us before the authorities did."

Connor pulls me tighter against his side. "It's not been easy."

I wrap my arms around his waist, hugging him. A flash of pride warms me at how far I've come. I was beating myself up about how awkward I was with Uriel and Farrah, but with Connor, the need to comfort him when he needs it is almost instinctual.

Uriel tucks Farrah against his side. "I'm happy you both made time to come home for a few days."

I smile and relax into Connor, his body more at ease now than it has been since before it happened. "Me, too. It's so good to see you both."

Farrah perks up a little and reaches out to cup my cheeks. "Me, too. We have lots to do!"

I glance at Connor and then back at Farrah. "We do?"

She nods and tugs me away from Connor, leading me through the house to the back door. "We have a binder to look at."

"Mom, we just got here. Don't scare her away already," Connor groans.

Farrah looks a little affronted, but then Zach and Zane burst out of the kitchen. "Mooooooooooom," Zach whines, dragging out the word like a kid would. "Can we please eat now?"

Farrah chuckles and nods. "Fine. Breakfast, then binder."

# 43

## SUMMER

Marthae
WINDOW

Breakfast is as incredible as the dinner Farrah made when she visited Avalon. I am completely awestruck at the way she seems to maneuver effortlessly among her sons and husband, a smile never far from her lips. Warmth radiates from her, yet every so often, I catch her glancing at the door and then at the full plate of lemon bars still sitting on the table. A flash of grief would shadow her eyes, and every single time, Uriel would tighten his arm around her or kiss her on the head in a silent act of support. Not a glance went unnoticed, and finally, he deliberately picked up a lemon bar and ate it.

When we're all finished eating, Connor stands and takes my hand, leading me to the front door.

"Where do you think you're going?" Farrah asks, her tone more serious than I've ever heard it. I freeze on instinct.

Connor sighs, his shoulders slumping in defeat. He turns back to face her. "I was going to show Summer around Silver City."

Farrah crosses her arms. "I promised Summer I would show her the binder."

"But, Mom…" Connor groans.

Uriel laughs and pats Connor on the shoulder. "Come on, Son. Let them be. You knew this was going to happen when you came. She's barely slept since she heard you were coming."

Connor glances at me, and I nod, reassuring him I'm not going to get freaked out and flee the realm. Farrah holds out her hand, and when I take it, she leads me through the house back to the garden. Off in the distance, I can see where the cloud drops off, their level ending. Even Eden has limits, I guess.

She pulls me to where she has the binder open and two glasses of iced tea set out. A white wooden pergola shades three loveseats, circling a small white table made from the same wood as the structure. Like everything else here, they look plush and comfortable. The blush pink and cream cushions are expertly scattered across the small sofas, and dusky rose-colored teddy bear blankets are draped over the back.

Farrah curls up on the loveseat and pats the space beside her, smiling expectantly at me. I sit down and take a minute to view the garden from this angle. When we first left the house, it seemed perfect and pristine, but there are so many signs that this was home to five rambunctious boys. There are multiple flower beds, all well-preened and cared for. The closest of which is sprouting the most incredible peonies I've ever seen. But the more you look, the easier it is to see that this is just a small part of the grounds. To the back, nestled in a tree, I can see a treehouse. Nailed to the trunk is a sign that says, *No Girls Allowed*. Beneath that one is another sign that says, *Except Mommy*. My lips twitch. The way the *s* has been written the wrong way is absolutely adorable.

Deeper into the garden is a large area that seems to be a vegetable patch. It is neatly sectioned, each of the boys having their own little plot. Their names are written on little signs in their messy script, and they have all chosen something different to grow. Farrah must be seeing to them while the boys are at Avalon. But it's easy to imagine her there, teaching her sons to tend to their patch and nurture life.

"So," Farrah says, pulling my attention as she reaches for the binder, "this is the binder."

It sits heavily in her lap, the edges bursting and tabs of every color bristling along the sides.

"I understand you and Connor are very new, and if you don't want to look through this, I completely understand." She taps her fingers against the cover. "My boys are my whole life, Summer, and I want them to be happy." She hesitates for a second. "Connor has never... spoken of any girl he has dated." Her lips twitch and she looks up as the guys burst from the house, roughhousing and yelling playful insults at each other. Uriel throws a ball to Zane and Connor runs out onto what I assume will become a makeshift field. "He called me the morning after you met." She laughs softly. "He said, Mom, I've met the one. I started your binder after that call."

I watch as Connor tackles Zane to the ground, his booming laugh carrying over the garden.

"He's a special guy." I smile. "You did a really good job." My stomach curdles at the truth in my words. Surrounded by such a happy and close-knit family, I worry I will never be enough.

Farrah smiles widely, looking at her boys. "Thank you." She looks at me, holding my gaze. "He did well in choosing you."

I look away.

"I know you don't know me very well, and I know you don't trust easily, but I know what it's like to feel as if you're not enough. All I'm going to say to you is..." She waits until I meet her eyes again. "You do not get to decide your worth to someone else. Only they do."

The words strike true, spearing me through the chest, but there is no pain. Instead, I am filled with a warm, fuzzy comfort that I imagine is what a mother's love feels like, and I don't know what to do with any of that.

If Farrah senses my confusion, she doesn't show it. She taps the book again with her nails. "Okay, are we ready to dive in? Again, these are just preliminary thoughts. We can change whatever you want."

I nod, and Farrah opens the binder. The front page has *Summer & Connor* in the most intricate calligraphy I've ever seen. She's about to flip the page when Connor jogs over and sits on the arm of the loveseat, kissing my head.

"Time's up, Mom. I'm going to show Summer around."

Farrah closes the book. "But we've barely started!"

Uriel walks over and kisses Farrah's head. "My love, there will be all the time in the world for binders."

She sighs. "All right then, later," she says, looking up at her husband with such tenderness. This has to be why she's obsessed with marriage. She hopes for her children to have something similar.

Connor stands up, pulling me with him. "I know, Mom. It's torture."

We're about to walk back into the house when I turn back to Farrah, hesitating for a moment before saying to her, "The binder looks wonderful. I look forward to working on it with you." I force a smile, trying to hide my unease at even that small admission of belonging.

Farrah's eyes go wide, and she beams. Uriel chuckles, sitting down in my space and pulling his wife into his side.

Connor squeezes my hand. "Want to see my room?"

I nod and follow him up the stairs. Connor smiles at me. "You know, that comment will probably make her cry later."

My lips twitch, and I look at the photos lining the wall. The entire family is perfectly represented. The house has a similar layout to the Morningstar House on campus but is less frat boy and infinitely more homey. Connor's room is in the same place in this house as the one on campus, and he leads me down the hallway to it. I smile when I notice his door is missing the poorly etched *CONNOR*, and in its place is a blue and white placard with his name expertly engraved.

"Mom and Dad wanted us to feel at home in Avalon, so they had the Morningstar House built for us," Connor explains as he notices me looking around. He opens his bedroom door, and I smile when I'm greeted with his scent. Though the room is somewhat familiar, there are differences. The room reads like a visual history of him. There is a large light blue toy box with CONBEAR painted on the front. He has little metal cars, a slew of action hero figures, karate equipment, a wall of archangel posters, and framed articles about his dad. Then there's a full wall of Avalon memorabilia.

Connor walks over to his window and holds his hand out to me. I walk over to him, sliding my fingers over his palm. The view outside steals my breath with its beauty. Silver City sparkles in the sunlight. Silver and gold skyscrapers stretch into the sky. Their bases are rooted firmly in the various clouds, but they drift slightly, rising and falling through the pastel-hued air. The sun here emits a light so pure that the feel of it against my skin is almost soothing. The beams catch on the tops of the buildings, sending a spattering of rainbows through the room.

"Woah." I gasp the word and take a moment just to feel the space and bask in the wonder of it. Connor wraps his arm around my back, pulling me close to kiss the top of my head. We stand in comfortable silence, and I savor the calm. I didn't realize until now that Connor has been everything but calm since Gia's murder.

"So, what will the sleeping arrangement be while we're here?" I ask after a moment.

"What do you mean?"

"Well, am I staying in a spare room or...?"

I look up at him when he doesn't reply immediately. He is staring down at me, his golden brows drawn in confusion. "You think there's a spare room around here?"

"Rafe's room, then?"

Connor grimaces a little. "No."

"So, your parents will be cool with us... sharing a bed?" I look around and drop my voice. "In *sin*?"

Connor bursts out laughing. "What?"

I cross my arms, glaring up at him.

Connor manages to control his laughter just enough to reply to me. "We've been dating for months and you think I've been *sinning*?"

"Well, I don't know. You're an angel."

Connor laughs so hard that he snorts. "Oh, babe, I guess you don't know the big secret. That book that mortals are so obsessed with? It was written with separate agendas. They muddled the Almighty's message. Greatly." He pulls me in closer to him, still chuckling. "I mean, the fact they think the Almighty is a *man* is a big hint about the liberties they took."

"Con, are your parents cool with you sharing a bed or not?"

"Yes, they are."

I nod, only the barest hint of anxiety lingering. "Okay, then let's continue the tour."

"Babe," Connor pulls me closer, "do you want to sleep in bed with me?"

I shrug. "Whatever."

Connor's grin is filled with male satisfaction. "You want to," he says, brushing his lips over mine. I growl, but he just kisses me again. "And that's really perfect because I want you to." He smothers my face in kisses, and I can't help but smile at being showered with such pure, playful affection. It is just one more way he shows me how much he cares about me.

I gently push him away. "Stop," I groan, but I'm not really forcing him away, or even really wanting him to stop.

"But I love you," he says, pressing a kiss to my nose and each of my cheeks.

I giggle and lift my face, softening against him. He's turning me into such a mush. I have spent years pushing people away. I am very good at it. How did this angel figure out how to care for me in a way I would accept?

"And I'm excited to wake up with you tomorrow morning."

I grab his face and kiss him deeply before pulling back. "The tour."

Connor smiles brightly. "To Silver City!"

# 44

## SUMMER

Berthae
NORTH

"Just let me get changed quickly?"

Connor nods and moves in closer. He bends his head slightly, kissing down my throat.

I moan softly. "How am I supposed to get ready like this?"

He playfully bites my neck. "Well... half of getting ready is getting undressed, and I happen to enjoy undressing you very, very much."

I shiver, my fingers grasping his shirt. He slowly tugs my shirt up over my stomach, his lips leaving a trail of heat wherever he touches. He pulls back to slide my shirt off and throws it to the side, but then his mouth is on mine, and he is kissing me deeply. His tongue slides along the seam of my lips, begging for entry.

I open for him and tug at his shirt.

"Connor!" Farrah calls from downstairs.

He groans against my lips. "I'll be right back, okay?" I nod and lick my lips as he pulls back. He groans again, his gaze locked on the flick of my tongue. "Seriously, Summer. Don't move. I will be right back."

I grin up at him. "I will be right here."

Connor leaves the room at a near run, eager to get back. I sigh and look around. There is a stack of old notebooks on his desk. I smile and wander over, picking one up off the top and sitting on his bed, flipping it open. His handwriting is disjointed and young, filled with such innocence. I turn to the first page and start reading. It's a personal profile with a small photograph of a mini Connor attached to the corner of the page, the familiar kindness in his blue eyes unmistakable. His features are boyish and soft, but the potential of what he will become is still there. His short blonde hair is windswept, and he smiles brightly at the camera, his wide grin revealing a missing front tooth.

*Name: Connor Azrael Morningstar*
*Age: 8.5*
*Favorite color: I like the blue on the dress capes for the Legion!*
*Favorite food: My mom's triple chocolate cake is the yummiest!*
*Best friend: My little brother Rafe and my dad*
*What do you want to be when you grow up? I want to be an archangel and I want to have a beautiful wife, just like my mom, who has the brightest wings!*

My phone rings, and I glance at the screen, immediately answering when I see Alice's face.

"Are you okay?" I ask in place of a greeting.

"Yeah, I'm good. Just thought I should check in," Alice replies, and my whole body relaxes. "How's it going with his family? Are you freaking out yet?"

My lips twitch as I look back at the profile. "Not yet," I say, but uncertainty wiggles through me as I read it again. These are the words of a child, but at some point, he dreamed of being with an angel with bright wings. He wanted an affectionate, loving, and open woman, someone like his mom. None of those things are me.

"Al?"

"Yeah?"

"Nothing. I need to get ready to go out." My lips curve in a smile, but I can feel myself shutting down. I try to stop it. The newly awakened part of me that craves connection and warmth screams to remain free. But the more dominant side of me has trained for decades to build walls the moment there is even the slightest risk of getting hurt, and it is already hard at work.

"Summer?" Alice asks, obviously having heard a shift in my tone.

"I'll talk to you later." I end the call, feeling like a dick, knowing that I shouldn't have cut her off like that. Looking back down at the journal, the shroud of my impostor syndrome drapes over me, heavy and oppressive. This isn't right. Something isn't right. I don't belong here. I'm a spore of negativity ready to latch onto the slightest ray of joy, to feed from it, and there is so much of it here, so much I could destroy.

I need to get out of here. I close the journal and quickly change before leaving Connor's room and heading for the front door.

Connor catches me around the waist before I can escape, and I tense in his arms. "I was just about to come back up, babe. My mom just needed help with something."

"So, where are we going?" I ask, carefully trying to shift out of his hold, desperate to get out of the house.

"Oh, you're going to have the best time!" Farrah says, coming through from the kitchen. "If you're scouting for future houses, make sure to look near to here! I want to be close to my grandbabies!"

My stomach twists, and I swallow, the reality of this weekend crashing down on me. I'm being unreasonable, but I can't stop it. The panic has sunk its sharp claws into me, and I can't escape.

"Mom, you're going to freak her out," Connor says, tightening his arms around me and kissing my head.

"Oh, I'm sorry," Farrah says, her face falling a little. The sight is so upsetting that my panic subsides a little.

"It's okay. Honestly." My words surprise even me, and the way my voice betrays none of my inner panic is borderline impressive.

"We're just going to the edge of Heaven, and then we'll be back," Connor says, kissing my head again.

*The edge of Heaven.* The words prompt a visceral reaction. Eden is only a small part of the larger realm. It is home to the Heavenly Host, those who prepare for the inevitable war against Hell, but there is much more to the vast realm.

Uriel walks up behind Farrah, wrapping his arms around her.

"Oh, Uriel. Remember the first time you took me there?" she says, leaning back against him.

Uriel cups her chin in his big hand and tips her head back, feathering a kiss over her lips. "Yes. And I remember Michael catching us when we were—"

Connor releases me to cover his ears. "Okay, we're leaving!" he exclaims before lowering one of his hands to grab my wrist and yank me out of the house. I wave at Uriel and Farrah, but they are gazing lovingly into each other's eyes, and I don't think they notice.

The perfect moment between them amps up my panic again. That is what Connor wants, and it is what he deserves. That isn't something I will ever be able to give him.

When we get into the elevator, Connor pulls me close, kissing my cheek and nuzzling my throat. I don't move or even react, too lost in my own mind to feel it. With every brush of his lips over my skin, I retreat more. Fuck. I hate this. Why am I like this?

If Connor notices, he doesn't mention it. When the door opens, he leads me to the edge of the cloud and scoops me up in his arms, cradling me against his chest. He grins down at me, his eyes alight with mischief, and then he falls. The wind rushes at us, and I clutch at him, feeling his chest vibrate with a chuckle. His wings explode from his back, turning our descent into a long, arching swoop. My scream turns to laughter as he weaves through the clouds toward the massive city, and I am grateful for the distraction.

Connor lands on a wide, flat clearing on the edge of the city that looks like it was designed for exactly that. As we walk along the pristine streets, angels bow their heads to Connor and he smiles back at them. The quaint stores have lovely window displays, and large planters overflow with color, vibrant flowers spilling over the sides.

"I'm never going to get used to that," Connor whispers into my ear. I tip my head questioningly. "The bowing," he clarifies.

I smile, though I can tell it doesn't reach my eyes. "I'm sure you will in time."

It's his future. Connor is one of the leaders of the Heavenly Host. He is meant to serve under the Seven, Michael, Gabriel, Rafael, Azrael, Jophiel, Zadkiel, and Uriel, his father and uncles. Gods, he is royalty. He is meant to have a wife with perfect white wings.

"I doubt it." He scrunches his nose and then squeezes my hand. "How's Alice?"

I frown, looking up at him. "Alice?"

"I'm assuming you called her when I went to help my mom."

My heart clenches painfully with the proof that he already knows me so well. He is always watching and listening, always so focused on me and my needs. He has made it his goal to truly know me, and he has committed himself to the endeavor.

"Oh. Well, she called me. I didn't call her, but she's fine."

Connor stops walking so suddenly that someone bumps into him. At first, the angel looks affronted, but when he realizes who he's walked into, he apologizes profusely. Connor doesn't acknowledge him, his eyes boring into me. I turn to face him.

"All right, I'm picking up on some signals. Something's wrong," he says, crossing his arms over his chest.

I look away, unsure how to react. This isn't something I've ever had to deal with. I suppose that's because I've never allowed someone to get to know me before. Oh, look, if it isn't the consequences of my own actions. I am such a fucking idiot.

"Nothing's wrong," I lie.

"You know, I'm not as good at it as Zane, but I can still taste lies." He narrows his eyes at me. "And yours taste like acid rain."

I sigh. "Con, let's just go."

"No."

There is something about the determination in that word, about the *surety* of it, that makes me want to push back. I want to test the limits and see what will happen if I do. I lift my chin, staring him down for a long moment.

Connor doesn't move. He just keeps staring at me. It's actually more of a glare, and I'm borderline impressed. I had no idea his perfect, happy-go-lucky face could look so angry. At this moment, I realize how similar he looks to his dad.

My stubborn side takes over, and I turn on my heel and walk away, deciding to explore myself.

# 45

## SUMMER

Caerthae
ROYAL
MONARCH

"I can do this all day, Summer," Connor calls, still standing in the same place. His words spur me on, and I plunge into the crowd of angels moving along the street. I round a corner and am delighted to find a charming market. White tents line the cobbled streets, and this area is quainter than the rest of the city. It is so different in feel and looks that it could be a separate realm. A sense of joy seems to permeate the air here. Angels bustle around, purchasing flowers and produce. There are stacks of colorful spices and bright cloth, intricate carpets, and perfumes spilling from various stalls.

I wander down the street, quietly observing and enjoying the feeling of pushing back against Connor, but my impostor syndrome is still plaguing me. I know that this is just a distraction. Pushing Connor away gives me some semblance of control, and I am desperately holding on to it.

I bob and weave through the other patrons, enjoying the feeling of the sun against my skin. The air feels purer here, and for a realm known for its military, I see a lot of beauty within it. I pick up the reddest apple I've ever seen and tap my phone against the reader to pay for it before continuing my stroll. The apple is as crisp and delicious as it looks, maybe the sweetest apple I've ever tasted.

As I weave through the market, I feel eyes land on me, tracking my progress along the street. There is nothing angry or hateful in this stare, and is nothing like what I felt in Avalon. Instead, there is a deep sense of *knowing* that I can't quite define. I look up and meet the piercing, dark gaze of a stunning woman with ebony skin. Her full lips are unsmiling, but her eyes are gentle. Her hair is shaved close to her head, but what she does have is bright white, the color stark against her brown skin.

An unheard beckoning emanates from her, and I answer its call, not pausing to consider the dangers. She smiles at me as I approach.

"Are you all right?" she asks, her low lyrical voice wrapping around me like a melody. Power surrounds her, almost a physical mist of omnipotence, but there is nothing sinister about it. It's pure, true, and *good.*

"Yes, thank you," I reply quickly, realizing I had let the silence stretch. "I am just ignoring my stubborn boyfriend." I don't know why I say it. The words left my lips before I knew what I planned to say. Was she watching me because she knows I don't belong here? Because she recognizes that I'm some weird fae-like creature wandering aimlessly around Eden?

She laughs, and the sound surprises me. It's like wind chimes jingling in the breeze.

"Ah, well, the males can definitely be stubborn. Especially Connor."

I blink in surprise. How the fuck did she know I was talking about Connor? Is our relationship as newsworthy up here as it seems to be in Avalon?

"How did you—"

"You are not what I expected." She interrupts me with a smile, and shame creeps over me. Even this complete stranger is disappointed in Connor's choice. "But I can see why," she continues. Some of her words are more accented than others. She looks at me so intensely that my hair stands up on the back of my neck. "Such a great destiny," she whispers, her eyes faintly glowing as she continues to analyze me. She hums thoughtfully, and then she sighs. Her eyes stop glowing, and her stare becomes soft again. "Tell my grandson he will get nowhere acting as such."

I blink again. "Grandson?"

She smiles kindly and links our arms, leading me back through the market toward Connor, our steps slow. "My name is Yahweh. But most call me the Almighty these days."

My eyes go wide. I've read about the Almighty. Connor has spoken of the Almighty. Surely not. Surely...

"I know I'm probably not what you expected, either." We stopped walking, and she turned to face me, smiling. All I can do to blink, completely speechless.

"I know he's a male, but he is a good one. And I know you lack trust. If you let him in, he will be kind about your past. He will be kind about the hidden side of you," she says.

My brows draw.

The Almighty nods. "The part you hide even from yourself."

I look away, the unease returning, but there is a sprig of relief knowing that someone sees that part of me. It's no longer a secret to be held by only myself. While telling Alice of my past eased that burden, what I showed her barely scratched the surface. I may have told her what I did, but I have not told her about the deep, penetrating darkness that inhabits my soul. While at first there is a sense of relief, having someone else acknowledge the darker side of me only intensifies it. I can feel it roiling inside me. It feels like the first deep inhalation after too long underwater, a mix of relief and agony.

She cups my cheek, guiding my eyes back to hers. "Summer, your destiny is great. Greater than you can even comprehend. You will not be able to hide this part of you forever."

I swallow, fear clutching my heart.

"I grant you one question. One truth. Ask, and I shall tell you." The Almighty says, watching me.

My eyes sting from phantom tears, my vulnerability stripped and laid bare. I have so many questions and so many truths to uncover, but there is only one screaming in my mind, bouncing around and desperately trying to get out. It's the one question I have screamed into the lonely nights. My soul begs for the answer, desperate for the truth, but I am completely terrified to voice it. Already, I feel the sorrow of possibly having all my fears realized, but I take a deep breath and steel myself.

"Will I ever find peace?" I force the words out through that barrier of fear, the desire to know greater. I have to know. It is the one thing I have craved more than anything else in the nearly thirty miserable years of my life.

The Almighty's eyes flicker, and the warmth filling her smile transcends joy. She seems to relax, and I can tell she wasn't expecting that question, or maybe it's not one she's ever been asked. She strokes my cheek with her thumb. "You will find more than peace, my child. You will find happiness. Joy. Belonging."

I watch her, looking for any shred of deception, but there is none. The words are so difficult to believe. To ask for peace is one thing, but I wouldn't dare even hope to find joy or belonging. Those things are so far out of my reach that they were not even on my list of possibilities. I would settle for peace. I only asked about peace, so why did she offer more?

For someone who doesn't trust easily, her words seep into me and melt, merging with and warming every cell of my body. A spark of hope ignites inside my soul, a single light in the penetrating darkness, refusing to be swallowed. Perhaps this is the reason for all the pain and suffering. My path has been treacherous, but it led me here, and maybe this is where I am exactly supposed to be. The Almighty wipes the tear from my cheek and then links arms with me again. We continue to walk toward Connor, who is still standing where I left him and frowning at us. There's a glimmer of lingering frustration on his face, but there is also a note of concern. No doubt, he was approximately three seconds from coming to retrieve me.

"He does not know it is me. All he can see is an angel walking beside you. You can tell him about speaking with me. Or not. The choice is yours." She smiles proudly at Connor. "Go back to my grandson."

I take a step toward him but look back at her. "Thank you."

She nods once, and then she disappears. In her place is the angel Connor sees, a pretty brunette woman smiling and waving to me.

Connor strides toward me, closing the distance between us as if he can't stand it any longer. He frowns after the angel walking back toward the market. "Who is that?"

I look up at him, sliding my hand into his. "Take me to the edge of Heaven."

He looks down at me, searching my eyes. I can tell he's deciding whether to probe for more information. "Okay." Connor's wings spring out, and he picks me up. With a powerful downbeat, he launches us into the sky. "Where did you go?" he asks once we are airborne.

"You were being stubborn," I reply as he soars across the city, his golden feathers catching the light.

Connor gives me a hard look. "Look who's talking."

"I went for a walk," I reply, clinging to the words of the Almighty, trying to accept them.

Since I started at Avalon, I have experienced genuine kindness for the first time. Yet, the Almighty confirming that things will work out in my future might be the kindest thing anyone has ever done for me.

Connor sighs heavily and slows. I can tell he doesn't want to arrive at Heaven until we've talked. "I don't like it when you're being aloof with me," he says, looking straight ahead. Something in his voice makes any irritation I still feel disappear. "It makes me uneasy. I hate it." He sighs again. "I know I'm being unfair."

"Con." Connor meets my gaze. "Kiss me."

He leans in and brushes his lips over mine. I open to him, and Connor deepens the kiss. It is sweet, loving, and perfect, but I can feel his anxiety.

"I love you," he whispers. Sighing softly, I bury my face in his neck, letting my worries melt away. I had barely managed to erect new walls, and here he is, demolishing them without even knowing it. Connor is worth the risk, and so I let myself trust him. I need to strive for peace, and I think this might be the first step.

"Want to just go home?" Connor asks into my hair.

I pull back, looking up at him. "Why?"

"So I can just hold you."

"Can you hold me where we're going?"

Connor nods. He picks up his pace again, and I bury my face back into the curve of his neck, shielding myself from the wind. I take the opportunity to inhale his scent and cling to him, showing him how I feel about him in the only way I know how. His arms tighten on me, holding me closer as we soar through the clouds.

Connor lands softly and closes his wings in a soft susurration of sound. He slowly lowers me to my feet, his gaze still a little guarded.

"Welcome to the gates of Heaven, Summer." He smiles and places his hands on my hips, turning me around slowly.

I gasp. The most beautiful garden stretches in front of me. The grass is plush with wildflowers strewn through the meadow. Trees line a pathway that leads to the edge of the cloud and garden. In the distance, there is a large, ornate gate. It's at least fifty feet tall and surrounded by pillowy clouds.

"This is the Garden of Eden. It's why the realm is named what it is. It was built around this gateway," Connor explains, walking deeper into the meadow. "The path to Heaven is serene for the pure souls and treacherous for those with something to prove," he recites as he looks at the gates. "This is merely a show. No one knows what the true entrance looks like. No one on this side of life, anyway. It's purely symbolic now." I hurry to catch up with him and slide my hand into his, looking up at him and then back at the gates. "Even the highest of angels don't know what Heaven is. Not really. Only the Almighty does."

I sit on the soft grass and tug on Connor's hand until he looks down at me. "You wanted to hold me."

Connor sits down next to me. He wraps me in his arms and lays us both back, pulling me against his side. I shift onto my side and rest my head on his shoulder, my hand sliding across his chest. The grass is just as plush as it looks, and I sigh in contentment.

"It's hard when you shut me out." He idly traces shapes down my back, caressing me.

I sigh heavily. "I was snooping."

Connor stops drawing on my back for a moment but then resumes. "Snooping?"

I nod, feeling embarrassed.

"Snooping where?"

I sigh again. "In your bedroom."

"And what did you find that upset you?"

"Your notebook from elementary school." The new clarity makes me hear how fucking ridiculous I'm being, but I need to hear the words from him. I need to hear him say I'm what he wants, even though I'm broken and messy.

Connor's hand slows again. "You didn't like how I wrote my *A*'s?"

I glare up at him. "No, I saw..."

Connor's gaze bores into mine as he waits for me to continue.

"It was a student profile, and you... you said you wanted to marry an angel with the whitest wings. Someone just like your mom."

Connor shakes his head. "Summer."

I bury my face against his chest, my words practically a jumble. "IknowI'msostupiditsridiculousandI'mawful."

Connor's laugh rumbles through his chest, and he shifts, cupping my chin and tilting my head up. "Summer. I must have been like nine when I did that profile."

I look away. "Eight and a half," I grumble, correcting him. "I know it's silly, but it's clearly something you wanted, and it is the complete opposite of me."

"Summer, I am in love with you, not some angel with the whitest wings. And honestly, the fact that I said I want someone like my mother makes me feel like I need some intensive therapy." He brushes his lips over mine. "You are what I want, Summer."

I search his bright eyes and the only thing I see is sincerity. "Yeah?"

"Yeah." Connor leans in, kissing me again. His desire is unbridled this time, and I can taste his need. I deepen the kiss, moaning softly into his mouth, but pull back before I get lost in him.

"I'm sorry."

Connor tilts his head and brushes a lock of hair off my face. "For what?"

"Shutting you out."

"It's okay, babe. I know today was overwhelming for you. I love you," he whispers and kisses me again. There is no sense of dread at hearing those words. They almost sound familiar now. They feel easy.

I deepen the kiss, tangling my tongue with his and throwing one leg over his thigh. Connor's hand slips under my shirt, his hot palm cupping my breast.

"You are just like your father. I swear." The amused voice comes from above, and I practically jump out of my skin from the surprise.

"Uncle Gabe!" Connor smiles and gently disentangles us before standing and helping me up off the ground. The archangel smiles, his teeth dazzling against his dark skin.

"Hello, Connor. Is this the famous Summer I've been hearing so much about?"

I nod, my cheeks heating. "That's me. Hi." I smile, brushing some grass off my pants.

Connor nods. "Do me a favor? Don't tell Dad you caught us here."

Gabriel laughs. "He wouldn't have a leg to stand on."

"Believe me, I've heard," Connor groans.

"How are you enjoying Eden, Summer?" Gabrial asks.

"It's stunning," I admit. "This garden, in particular, is simply... spectacular."

Gabriel beams with obvious pride in his home. "You better hurry home. It's getting late, and you know your mother will have dinner ready soon." His eyes sparkle with that something special that all the Morningstar males seem to possess, though Gabriel's is slightly more wicked than the others. "It was nice to meet you, Summer."

I nod. "Nice to meet you, too."

Connor smiles and leads me past his uncle, back through the meadow. "Thank the Almighty, it was Uncle Gabe. Uncle Michael would have been a dick."

I laugh as Connor scoops me up and launches into the air again.

# 46

## SUMMER

Daersha
L II

"Well, you've had a productive first day in Eden. You got caught making out with me in the Garden of Eden. You went for a stroll through the market with..." He glances at me as we step into the elevator, waiting for me to fill in the blanks. He must suspect there was more to my walk and sudden change in attitude. Smart guy.

"Nice try." That moment with the Almighty is just mine for now. Her words continue to burn in me like a small light in a sea of darkness.

Connor sighs and presses his halo to the pad on the wall. The door closes, and we immediately start to ascend. "Can't blame a guy for trying."

I laugh and squeeze his biceps. The elevator pings and opens, revealing the family house sitting serenely atop the cloud. It is the perfect picture of domestic bliss.

Uriel walks out onto the porch, smiling at us. "Just in time for dinner!"

Connor and I walk to the house, hand in hand, and when we step inside, the smell of food hits me hard, my stomach immediately rumbling with hunger. This house always smells like food. It smells like love and care. I've never had a home that smelled like this. Now that I have experienced this, I know I've never really had a home. However, Avalon is quickly becoming a place I would like to call home.

Connor chuckles and nuzzles into my hair as we walk into the dining room. He pulls out my chair, and I sit down, smiling up at him. He brushes his lips over mine and sits next to me. Zane and Zach are already at the table, practically vibrating in anticipation of the food.

"Are you two ever not hungry?" I ask, amused.

"No. It's a gift," Zach says, flipping me off.

"We're actually doing Dad a favor. Whatever we eat, we're stopping him from eating," Zane says. Luke sits down next to him, chuckling quietly.

Farrah comes through, carrying multiple plates. Somehow making it look effortless, she places them all on the table and then goes to the kitchen to get more. After another two trips, the table is full of food, the wood practically groaning under the weight.

Uriel pulls out her chair, and I smile, remembering how Connor did the same for me. It is obvious where he learned how to love. Farrah sits down, gazing adoringly at Uriel.

Zach and Zane almost lunge for the plates, but Farrah pins them with a stern look. "The guest is served first. Your father and I taught you better than that."

Zach groans. "She's barely a guest."

Connor smirks and rests his hand on my leg. I wonder if he is keeping me close so I don't run.

"Even when she shares our last name, she is a guest, so she is served first." Farrah lifts her chin, her voice clipped and stern.

I blush a little at the suggestion that I might be a Morningstar one day.

Connor chuckles and reaches forward to grab a spoon. He scoops up some vegetables and puts them on my plate. "Summer Morningstar has a nice ring to it."

Farrah beams at him. "My wonderful boy."

Connor smiles. "I know. I'm almost the favorite."

Farrah clicks her tongue. "All of my boys are in joint first place." She keeps smiling at Connor, but her eyes flash a little. "However, that will change if you don't remove your hand from that plate, Zane Morningstar."

Zane pulls his hand back like he's been scorched. "But, Mom," he whines, "she has food on her plate!"

Farrah gives him a reproachful look, and then she finally nods, giving them permission to serve themselves. The twins ravage the plates like they have never seen food before.

Farrah gives Uriel an exasperated look, but he simply smiles softly. "You wanted them to visit more, my love."

She chuckles as we all begin to eat, the joy and love in her eyes never wavering.

"So," Uriel begins, giving Connor a knowing smirk, "Gabe caught you in the garden, hm?"

Connor sighs. "He said he wouldn't tell!"

Zach snorts, biting into a chicken wing. "And you believed him? Uncle Gabe is the biggest gossip."

Zane nods. "Horn of the Almighty, my ass."

"Zane!" Farrah scolds.

"Sorry, Mom." Zane sighs.

"Has he caught you up to no good, Zane?" I ask.

"Not yet. But he tries." Zane snorts.

Zach shrugs. "As long as it's not Uncle Michael or the Almighty."

Connor snickers. "You think the Almighty just walks around? Like she doesn't have better things to do?"

I glance at Connor, thinking about the Almighty. There are so many questions. Why did she seek me out? Did she seek me out? Or was it just a coincidence that I was in the same place she was at the same time? I doubt that anything she does is a *coincidence.*

The rest of dinner is filled with more laughter and teasing. The food is delicious, and we all happily stuff ourselves. I relax into the feeling of safety and warmth. It is the perfect family dinner.

"Okay, who wants dessert?" Farrah asks, pushing her chair back. I stand to help her clear the table, but she shakes her head. "Absolutely not, Summer. I have five boys here to help me." Luke is already collecting plates, and Farrah looks at her twin boys expectantly.

"You already have hel–"

"Boys. Now," Uriel commands. He doesn't raise his voice, but it does deepen, his tone making it clear that he will take absolutely no bullshit from his sons. Zach and Zane reluctantly spring into action, collecting the plates and taking them into the kitchen.

Farrah is looking at her husband, her eyes dark. Uriel winks at her, slowly sipping his wine.

I look away, feeling like I'm intruding on an extremely private and intimate moment between them.

"Hello, my love," I hear Uriel croon as he pulls Farrah onto his lap.

Luke comes through with the dessert and rolls his eyes when he sees them. "Guys..."

Zach wraps his arms around Luke's shoulders. "This is how you were created, baby Luke!"

Luke groans, his face contorting into a look of horror. "By them making out at the dinner table? If that were true, Summer would be *very* pregnant by now."

Connor chokes on a mouthful of water. I blush deeply, glancing at Uriel and Farrah to gauge their reaction, but their attention is still fully locked on one another.

"Want to go work on another kid, my love?"

Farrah smiles and nips at his lips. "An inspired idea."

Uriel pulls back and looks at his sons. "Enjoy dessert and clean up afterward." He stands with Farrah in his arms and carries her out of the room. I can hear them whispering as they disappear upstairs.

Zach rolls his eyes, taking a big bite of apple pie. "Every family dinner."

Farrah's laughter fills the house before their bedroom door slams shut.

"So your parents are... really in love, huh?"

Connor slings his arm across the back of my chair, taking a bite of his dessert. "They've always been like that."

Zane nods. "Since we were kids.

I smile, looking at Connor. "It's nice."

Zach snorts. "Not the word I'd use."

"No?" I ask Zach.

Luke blushes but chuckles into his dessert.

"They were like that even when we had friends over as kids. Imagine having to explain to your friends that they should just ignore your parents, who act like horny teenagers in love whenever they are in the same room. Got me a weird rep at Eden Academy."

"They're in love! It's sweet!" I protest. They have no idea how amazing it is that they grew up surrounded by this kind of love.

Connor chuckles and scoops me up into his arms. I yelp in surprise, and he looks down at me. "Off we go, my love! To make another baby!" He mimics Uriel's voice so well that I can't help but burst out laughing as he whisks me off upstairs.

"Wait, you dick!" Zach shouts. "You're leaving us to clean up again!"

Connor hums loudly to drown them out as he carries me upstairs to his bedroom.

# 47

## SUMMER

*Deth'thu*
RING, BAND, LOOP

C onnor falls into bed with me, nearly glowing. "Thank you for planning this whole thing and coming with me, babe."

"You're welcome," I say, smiling up at him.

Connor leans down, brushing his lips over mine. The kiss is soft, but I'm tugging at his shirt, trying to pull it off, needing to touch his skin. Connor sits up on his knees and rips his shirt off, tossing it aside. I slide my hands over his thighs, and his eyes dilate with lust. He tugs at my clothes with the same urgency I feel. I moan and shift beneath him, sliding my fingers over the growing bulge beneath his jeans. A loud bang comes from downstairs, and we both freeze. Connor looks over his shoulder at the door.

"It's probably nothing." He looks back at me. "The walls are pretty thin."

I moan. "Right, so maybe we should... wait until we're back on campus?"

Connor glances at my lips. "But—"

I kiss him again, cutting off his protest. He groans and slides his hand beneath my shirt. His fingers glide over the dip of my waist, and I can't hold back my moan when he cups my breast and gently squeezes. I open the button on his pants and am working on lowering his zipper when there is another loud bang from downstairs, followed by someone running up the steps.

"Zach, you're a moron!" Zane chides as he chases Zach.

I sigh heavily and drop my hand from his throbbing length. My core pulses with need, but a theoretical bucket of ice water has been tossed onto my libido.

Connor groans and rolls off me. "Movie?"

I nod and turn my head to look at him. Connor looks at me, and we burst out laughing at the absolute absurdity of the situation. Once we get ourselves back under control, we both get up to put on our pajamas. As I remove my clothes, I try not to watch as Connor strips down and pulls on a pair of gray sweatpants. Inhaling deeply, I steal one of the t-shirts from his bag and slip it on.

We snuggle back into bed, and Connor turns to look at me, his expression soft. "I couldn't have... felt normal without you here," he admits, watching me.

I curl my pinky finger around his, linking our hands.

"It's hard to act..." He pauses for a beat. "To *feel* normal after—"

I roll to face him, cupping his cheek. "My big guy."

"You ground me," Connor says, closing his eyes and relaxing into my touch.

I lean in, brushing my lips over his again. There is no intent behind it this time, only care and affection. I lie back down, and Connor opens his eyes, looking at me.

"My parents love you."

"Yeah?"

Connor nods.

"I have no idea what being loved by a parent feels like." The words slip from my lips, resonating heavily the moment they hit the air between us. My smile slowly falls, and I blink as the grief of them sits heavily on my shoulders.

Connor brushes the back of his fingers along my cheek. "My parents are more than happy to show you."

I try to smile, attempting to accept the comfort he is offering me with his words. I hope I can at least make him think I've found it, but I can tell I've been unsuccessful when he pulls me close.

"Babe."

I brush my fingertips along his cheek. "What movie do you want to watch?"

Connor watches me for another moment before he sits up, grabs his bag, and pulls out his laptop. He lies back down and chooses a movie at random. I barely pay attention, unable to ignore the grief from the lack. I didn't even understand what I was missing until I saw what a family is supposed to look like.

"I'll be your family. If you want me to be," Connor whispers into my hair, not turning his attention away from the movie, allowing me the space if I need it. Affection bubbles up inside of me, and I can't help but grab his face, kissing him hard. Connor groans and opens eagerly. I climb on top of him, straddling his hips. His hands grip my waist, digging his fingers in to hold me to him. The desperation came out of nowhere, my body responding to his words with overwhelming need.

"You're going to have to be quiet, big guy."

Connor groans. "Fuck, okay."

I lift myself onto my knees and push down his sweatpants before shifting my panties to the side, the soaked lace slick against my fingers. I roll my hips until the tip of his cock lines up with my entrance. Bracing my hands on his chest, I meet his eyes and press down, slowly taking him inside my pussy. Connor's groan is guttural and so filled with need that it takes my breath away.

I lean down and claim his mouth hungrily, muffling our sounds of pleasure and tasting his need. Slowly, his cock fills me, my body sinking onto him until I have taken him to the hilt. My inner walls tighten and pulse around his length, adjusting to the delicious stretch. Connor moans loudly, and I pull back, covering his mouth with my hand and stilling my hips. I pant as I look down at him. "You need to be quiet. Okay?" I whisper.

Connor nods, but I don't move my hand from his mouth as I start to move on him. I lift my hips and slowly drop them down again. His eyes roll back in pleasure, and I bite my lip to mute my moan as I move faster on him. Connor grabs my waist and digs his fingers into me. His grip is just about hard enough to bring me pleasure, but not quite. I drop my hips down harder, the sound of my labored breathing and our skin slapping together the only thing that fills the room. It is erotic and filthy in its own way, made more so by the occasional muffled groan.

I look down at him, recognizing the way his eyes have darkened. He's close, too. I add my free hand to the one covering his mouth to muffle his shout and bite my lip hard enough to make it bleed as I come. My orgasm surges through me, and I throw my head back in ecstasy. Connor's shout is still loud even beneath both of my hands, but I am too lost in orgasmic bliss to care. His shout could have blown the house down, and I wouldn't have given a fuck.

I roll off him, panting. Connor lays next to me, completely spent. He links his fingers through mine.

"Babe?" he asks breathlessly.

"Hm?" I roll, curling into his side.

"Does it bother you when I tell you I love you?"

I frown. "What?"

Connor looks at me. "Does it make you uncomfortable?"

"No, I... I like it," I answer honestly. I like the way it makes me feel. I like the way the truth of it surrounds me like a fuzzy blanket.

Connor nuzzles his nose against mine. "Good. I like saying it. I just wanted to make sure."

I tense a little. "Does it bother you that I—"

"No." Connor stops me, his eyes locked on mine. "Because you show me."

I cup his cheek, staring up at him. "Con?"

"Yeah, babe?"

"That angel earlier." I brush my thumb along his cheek, desperate to give him a truth. This truth. "It was," I drop my voice to a whisper, "the Almighty."

Connor blinks, taking a moment to process. "Shit, it was? What did she say?"

My lips twitch. "That you're a good guy. But I've to tell you that you won't get anywhere by being an ass."

Connor quirks a brow. "I'm calling bullshit. No way she'd say the word ass."

I laugh. "It was something to that effect."

Connor laughs with me and nuzzles my nose. "I knew you were special."

I briefly consider telling him about the question she granted me and the answer I so desperately needed, but a part of me wants to keep it for myself. It's a slim beam of hope amongst the ruin that is my soul.

*"You will find more than peace, my child. You will find happiness. Joy. Belonging."*

Connor pulls me against his chest, wrapping me in his warmth and scent. Safe and warm and loved, I fall into a deep sleep.

The bed shifts as Connor climbs out, and I bury my face into his pillow, inhaling deeply. I brush my fingers against the sheets, still warm from his body, and I groan at the lack of hard muscle beneath my fingers. Barely awake, I stumble out of bed and through to his bathroom. I strip off on the way and then climb in beside him. The warm spray of the water is soothing and comforting against my skin. Connor pulls me into him, wrapping his strong arms around me. I nuzzle against his chest, pressing kisses along his collarbone and neck.

"Good morning, beautiful."

I mumble sleepily in response and brush my lips back and forth over the stubble on his jaw.

"You know, I like waking up to you, but I love how you followed me into the shower, still mostly asleep."

I smile and lean heavily against him, my breasts crushed against his chest. "Oh yeah? Why is that?" I ask, my voice still thick from sleep.

Connor cups my cheeks and tilts my head back. I finally blink my eyes open.

"Because you were barely awake, but you came to find me."

"I needed my big guy," I say, kissing him deeply.

Connor groans, and I can feel him smile. "Fuck, I love when you call me that."

"Big guy?"

Connor nods. "Yeah, it makes me smile."

"Why?"

"You only call me that when you're happy."

"You make me happy." I glide my hands over his biceps. "And you're so big and strong..."

Connor flexes his muscles beneath my touch. "Oh?"

I nod, moaning softly as I dig my nails into his bulging muscles.

Connor smirks. "Maybe I should get some training in with my dad before we head back to Avalon."

I lean in, kissing his neck. "Can I watch?"

"You want to watch me train?"

I bite his neck. "Watch my big guy in action? Fuck, yes. And then I want you to fuck me against something."

Connor groans, snaking his hands around my back. "You are just... You have so much control over me..."

"Control?" The word sparks a flicker of heat in my core,

"Kids! Breakfast in thirty minutes!" Farrah chirps, knocking on the door.

Connor jumps. "Coming!" he yelps, blushing.

"Surely she won't come in here."

Connor gives me a look. "She absolutely will, and when we protest, she'll hit us with a, it's nothing I haven't seen before."

I chuckle, but Connor and I quickly finish in the shower and get dressed for breakfast.

# 48

## SUMMER

*Haelsho*
DARK, SHADOW

"Nice shower?" Farrah asks, giving us a knowing smile as we sit down at the table for breakfast. I blush and look away, silently cursing myself for not taking the time to dry my hair before we came down.

Connor smiles brightly at his mom and shakes his head, splashing her with water from his wet hair. "Yup!"

Farrah yelps, swatting at him. "Crazy boy."

Uriel laughs, coming up behind his wife and wrapping his arms around her waist. "Don't let your mother fool you. We haven't taken a separate bath or shower in almost two hundred years."

Connor grimaces, and I smile, enjoying how in love they are.

Luke blushes. "Dad, please."

Farrah walks to Luke and kisses the top of his head. "Showering with your lover is good for the soul, Lukey! It makes it glow!"

Luke groans, looking like he wants to die. "Mom, please."

"You'd all be complaining if we were like Matthew's parents. They hate each other."

Zach comes downstairs, kissing his mom's cheek as he passes. "That's because they had an arranged marriage." Zach sits down and serves himself eggs and bacon from the plates on the table.

I smile at Farrah. "I think it's nice that you're both so in love after all this time. And five kids."

Farrah looks at Uriel lovingly, and he immediately moves toward her, like one magnet attracted to another. "Do you want to know the secret?"

I nod.

Farrah slips into Uriel's arms, looking up at him. "We choose each other every single day."

Uriel nuzzles his cheek against hers. "No matter what, good or bad."

"And it doesn't hurt that he's easy on the eyes," Farrah quips, smiling up at him.

Uriel laughs. "I snatched you with my rugged good looks, and you captivated me with your incredible beauty."

I smile at them and lean against Connor. He, like the rest of his brothers, is engrossed in eating and completely ignoring his sappy parents. Farrah kisses Uriel, and he dips her over his arm.

"Please, can we have one meal without the public display of grossness? I'm begging you." Zach groans.

Farrah pulls back from Uriel and walks over to Zach. She grabs his ears and smothers his face in kisses.

I laugh and lightly elbow Connor. "Ah, so this is where you get it?"

Zach's expression is mutinous, but his eyes sparkle, revealing his enjoyment as his mom showers him with affection.

Connor puts down his fork and shifts in his chair. He grabs my head in his massive hands and starts kissing all over my face. I squeal and swat at him, not trying very hard to push him away. He laughs and pulls me onto his lap before going back to eating.

Farrah pulls Zach into a hug. "Trouble number one."

I glance at Uriel. He is staring at his wife with nothing short of awe. "Con mentioned he wanted to train with you a bit today if you have the time."

Uriel raises a brow, glancing at Connor before looking at me. He has the same blue eyes as his sons, but they're sharp with wisdom. "Would you like to train with me? I noticed a holy dagger on your thigh."

I touch the dagger Connor had insisted I wear everywhere I go, even here, and the small bubble of denial about the events that drove us to Eden pops.

"It's for protection, Dad," Connor says, covering my hand with his.

Uriel nods. "Well, she should know how to use it then."

"I'd be very out of my depth with an archangel." Who am I kidding? I am still very out of my depth in combat class. It is the one class I do not excel in.

Uriel shrugs. "Unless you know how to wield it, that weapon won't offer much protection." He looks at Connor, his eyes harder than I have ever seen them. Here is the archangel. "You haven't told her what that is, have you?"

Connor looks away, sipping his coffee.

Uriel sighs and holds out his hand. "May I see the dagger, Summer?"

I pull the dagger from the sheath, offering it to Uriel hilt first. He wraps his hand around it and lifts the knife from my palm. The second it leaves my skin, bright white flames surround the blade.

"Holy daggers are not manufactured, Summer. They are not created as you would expect. They appear to an angel in times of need. As we grow older and stronger, more holy weapons will appear to us." Uriel tilts the blade, studying it, and the flames slowly die. "It is a part of an angel's essence. This is a part of Connor, and it is one of the few weapons that can actually cause us harm."

My gaze snaps to Connor, who is sheepishly watching me. Fear swamps me, but it quickly morphs into anger. Why did he give me this? It is not just a weapon capable of devastating damage, but it is meant to protect him, and he gave it to me. I don't even know what to do with it.

Uriel flips the blade expertly, holding the hilt out toward me. "It became yours the second he gave it to you. However, you won't be able to summon holy flames without some practice. Holy flames are lethal to most species, but you will require training for this weapon to provide the most protection."

I nod. "Do you have time to train me?"

Uriel nods and grabs a piece of bacon and a pancake from the table. He tenderly kisses Farrah's lips and says, "Let's go, boys."

I slip off Connor's lap and say goodbye to Farrah and Luke before walking toward the door. Zach and Zane jump up, chatting excitedly as they follow me. They burst past me and into the morning sunlight. Connor catches up to me, and I see the wariness in his eyes as he tries to figure out how pissed I am with him. I follow Uriel out, ignoring Connor. When we enter the elevator, I navigate through the big men, ensuring I am as far as I can get from Connor.

Connor shoves Zach and Zane out of his way and crowds me against the wall. "Why are you mad?"

"Even I know the answer to that." Zane snorts.

I don't look at Connor.

"Would you have taken it if you knew?" he asks.

I cross my arms, ignoring him.

Connor shifts so he's in my line of sight. "Would you have?"

I just growl.

He sighs. "I want to protect you."

I duck around him and move to the other side of the elevator, leaning against the wall. The other Morningstars are doing their best to ignore Connor and me. Of course, it is impossible. The space is not small, but it's definitely not big enough for a fight or any sort of privacy. Connor follows me and places his hands on either side of my head, caging me in.

"Look at me."

I meet his gaze with a glare so seething it would have destroyed a lesser man.

Connor doesn't shrink from it. He leans down, kissing me hard, and I silently curse myself when I kiss him back. My body always wants him. It doesn't care if I am mad. It is as easy as breathing. "I needed to give you the best chance of coming back to me." He presses his forehead to mine. "All right?"

"You tell me next time," I growl softly.

"We're here," Uriel says a moment before the elevator pings and the door opens. Connor kisses me again before stepping back and leading me onto the field. As we step onto the grass, their clothes change to golden armor. The armor is truly striking, and each piece is perfectly tailored to the wearer. The breastplates are covered in intricate, swirling designs with a stylized sun at the center. My eyes linger on Connor, and my core heats with the way the metal molds to his large muscles. Everything about the armor screams strength, respect, and safety.

Uriel nods to several angels already training on the field, and they either nod or salute.

We stop in a marked patch of ground. "Zane, since you need the most practice, why don't you show Summer how to wield?"

"Did you have to call me out like that?" Zane grumbles.

I shake out my limbs, trying to loosen them like they do in the movies. "Okay, Zane. Show me what to do."

Uriel crosses his arms, ready to observe. "Summer, the dagger," he reminds me to arm myself.

"Oh, yeah." I nod and pull the dagger from its sheath strapped to my thigh. Zane smirks, and with a wave of his hand, he summons his holy sword. It's huge, with an iridescent blade and a silver handle.

My mouth drops open, my eyes pinging between the two weapons. What the fuck? This small dagger against that huge ass sword?

Zane laughs, the sound reminding me why we are here. I focus as Uriel walks around the marked circle, analyzing us.

"What are the advantages of having a dagger over a sword?" Uriel asks.

"Lighter?" I reply uncertainly.

Uriel nods. "Also faster and easier to conceal. Can you think of any disadvantages?"

"You need to be closer to your enemy to strike," I say, more confident after getting the last answer right.

"That's right. Good. Zane, take a typical stance. Summer, I want you to show me how you would get close enough to use that dagger."

Zane widens his stance, winking at me. "Bring it on."

I simply step forward, and Zane shifts, blocking me easily. "With a shorter weapon, you need to move faster and think smarter," Uriel says, watching.

I frown and step back. Zane moves quickly, shifting on his feet and lunging toward me. I feel a slight twinge from deep within, some dormant part of me stirring, but I stumble and fall to the ground, cursing.

"What the fuck, Zane?" Connor yells.

Zane quirks a brow and smiles at me cockily. "At least stand your ground."

Uriel hits Zane across the back of the head. "What did that prove?"

"That I was not built to be a warrior." I stand, dusting myself off.

"Let me show her, Dad," Connor says.

He walks into the ring, and I adjust my grip on the dagger, thinking he is going to take up a stance across from me. Instead, Connor kisses my forehead and gently ushers me out of the ring. Disappointment and shame writhe through me. I know he only wants to protect me, but he truly doesn't believe I can learn how to fight. I feel breakable and weak, but maybe he is right. Connor's obvious lack of confidence in me adds a layer of vulnerability when I already feel so exposed.

With my eyes on the ground, I find a spot out of the way and sit down. When I came here, I knew I had no chance. I knew I would be useless, but I don't like the feeling of defencelessness, and I like Connor taking over for me even less. I force my gaze up, determined to at least pick up anything I can by watching.

Zane smirks at Connor and takes up his fighting stance again. Connor summons his own holy sword, which is much more impressive and intricate than Zane's. I watch the way they square up, assessing each other. Zane swings, but Connor moves at the last possible second, and Zane's sword misses him by a breath. Connor brings the hilt of his sword up and hits Zane in the chin. Zane drops to the ground. Uriel snaps his fingers, and Zach jumps in to take Zane's place, facing off with Connor. Zach feigns a swing toward Connor's neck but drops his strike, slicing at his legs. Connor is forced off balance, and Zach takes advantage. Connor anticipates Zach's rush, and the second Zach commits to his course, Connor sweeps his legs out from under him, using the momentum to push him down. Zach hits the ground hard, and Connor lays his holy sword against his neck.

Zach and Zane switch out another few times, but neither of them can take down Connor, even with Uriel calling out instructions.

"Enough," Uriel commands after a few rounds.

Connor releases his brother, winking at him.

Uriel looks between the three of them, nodding. "You have combat classes. Make sure to take them seriously. Summer, I expect you to keep training with that dagger. Go home and say goodbye to your mother before heading back to Avalon."

We all say goodbye to Uriel since he plans to stay and do additional training with his Legion. I slide my hand into Connor's as we step back into the elevator, and I once again consider my weakness. Perhaps it's time to try harder in combat classes.

# 49

## SUMMER

*Hansha*
LESS, FEW

T he elevator opens to the lush lawn once again. Farrah is sitting on the porch, looking through a large binder, a fluffy cream blanket wrapped around her shoulders. She looks up when we leave the elevator, smiling brightly at us.

"Mom, we have to head back to school," Connor says as we approach the porch. Her smile falls, and there is a clear longing in her eyes for her children to be close to her.

"Already? But you just got here!" She closes the binder and sits forward.

"I know. The weekend was short." Connor takes her hand.

Farrah nods as she stands up and pulls him into a hug. Luke comes out of the house, looking around for someone. His brows draw when he doesn't find who he's looking for.

Farrah whispers something into Connor's ear, and he groans, his ears flushing a little in embarrassment.

"Mom... stop." He makes a strangled sound, pulling back from her. Farrah cups his cheeks and kisses his face. Connors' shoulders visibly relax, and he chuckles as his mom loves on him. Farrah then moves her attention to the twins, giving them equal amounts of affection.

"Now. You two, don't get into too much trouble." She cups one of Zach's cheeks and one of Zane's, her gaze a blend of desperate love and grave seriousness. "And, Zach, I want to hear all about this mystery girl."

"There's no girl." Zach sighs, rolling his eyes.

Zane coughs loudly as if trying to clear his throat. Farrah looks at him, then back at Zach. "You know, Zach, my darling, feigning ignorance is a lie, and you just made your brother choke on it."

Zane bursts out laughing, his face still slightly pink from his coughing fit.

Farrah shakes her head and then cuddles Luke. He engulfs her in his arms, holding her tenderly, the love flowing between them one of the most beautiful and pure things I have ever seen. She pulls back and kisses Luke on the cheek before turning to me and pulling me into a hug.

"I am so grateful for you, Summer," she whispers into my ear as she squeezes me affectionately. I let her aura seep into my bones, warming them. She kisses my cheek and then lifts a wicker basket from the table, handing it to Connor. "Will you give this to Rafe? It's all of his favorite home-cooked meals and snacks. I've runed them to keep the twins out."

"Hey!" Zach and Zane protest in harmony.

"Of course, Mom." Connor smiles.

"And will you.." She pauses, trying to center herself. "Will you tell him I love him? So very dearly." Her voice cracks on the last word and the sound nearly splits my heart.

"Of course, Mom. And you know he loves you too, right?" Connor says, his voice gentle. Farrah steps back, looking at all of us. Her lips are tilted in a smile, but her eyes shine with the sadness of saying goodbye to her boys, her pride, her heart.

"Goodbye, my darlings."

Connor kisses her head, and Luke hugs her tightly again before we all step into the waiting elevator. Farrah watches us, and Luke's anxiety practically radiates off him. Farrah raises her hand in a final goodbye, and the doors slowly close.

"I hate leaving when Dad isn't here. She looks so lonely," Luke says, his eyes boring into the metal like he can still see her. From the feeling in the elevator, I can tell that I'm not the only one who didn't buy the mask of happiness she pulled on to convince us all that she was okay.

Connor nods. "I hate seeing her look so sad."

Luke turns to face his brothers. "Why didn't dad come back with you?" His voice is harsh and cutting. The sharpness is so foreign in his usually gentle inflection. "He knows how sad she gets when we all leave." His shoulders are tense as he stares at them.

Zach shrugs, but he seems a little surprised by Luke's outburst. "He was training with some of his Legion."

Zane puts his hand on Luke's shoulder, trying to calm him down. "Hey, he knows her. I'm sure he appeared the second we left."

Luke shrugs out of Zane's touch and starts pacing angrily, though I can also feel the underlying sadness and maybe a shred of guilt. Luke is the youngest, and I don't imagine it was easy for him to leave this year, knowing how important family is to Farrah and Uriel.

Zach rolls his eyes. "Baby Luke—"

"Stop it, Zach." Luke is nearly yelling, and he doesn't stop pacing. "She was sad! And we just left her alone."

I watch as Luke gets angrier, and I wish I knew how to help him. I wish I knew what to say to take his pain away, but truthfully, none of these feelings are ones I understand. Sure, I understand anger, upset, and guilt at their core, but not for the reasons Luke feels them. There is something about his empathy that claws at me. It is another blatant difference that casts me aside from the Morningstars.

"She's not some helpless woman, and you reacting like this discredits her strength," Zach growls.

"She misses us!" Luke raises his voice more, his whole body tensing. "In the last five years, we have all left. One after the other. And Dad wasn't there when she needed him. I'm going back."

I glance at Connor, who is watching his brothers spar. I can tell that he's gotten very good at playing the middleman and peacekeeper over the years. Out of all of his brothers, he's the one with the best temperament to do it. I understand that to take on that role, he has to be able to hear both sides and then consider the best course of action, but this fight needs mediating now. I gently nudge him. Connor glances at me and nods once before reaching out and catching Luke's arms, stilling him.

"Luke." Connor waits until Luke meets his gaze. "You know how much mom loves us. We all do. But do you know why Mom and Dad live in Eden and not Avalon?"

Luke considers for a moment, his shoulders relaxing a little beneath Connor's steady calm. "Because of the Legion?"

Connor shakes his head. "Because they decided years ago that when we started at Avalon, we would go and find who we are, find our independence. Just like she and Dad did after they got married."

All the anger melts from Luke's face, and all that's left is a gut-wrenching sadness. "But—"

Connor nods. "I know it's hard. But we have to let her find her independence again, too."

Luke drops his gaze to the floor, his voice soft. "I hate that Rafe didn't come."

Ah, potentially the crux of the anguish. I try not to intrude or invade this space that I'm imposing on, but what used to feel like a spacious elevator now feels tight and uncomfortable, the emotion taking up all the air.

Connor nods. "Me too. But he... Rafe has trouble with being happy. He has his demons, Luke."

Luke just nods sadly, and Connor pulls him into a tight hug. "Thank you for loving Mom enough for all of us."

Luke wraps his arms around Connor and leans into his big brother, releasing a shaky exhale.

Connor drops his voice, but his words are still loud in the enclosed space. "I know you have big, wonderful feelings, Luke, but just because they're expressed differently by the rest of us doesn't mean they're not there. Okay?"

Luke nods and turns his head, looking at Zach. "I'm sorry for snapping, Zach."

Zach shrugs and punches Luke lightly on the shoulder. "Just give Mom more credit. She went hundreds of years without us. Plus, she can be a dragon when pissed off." He thinks for a moment. "Hm, I suppose you've never seen that side of her, goody-two-shoes Lukey."

"I've seen her get angry at you and Zane plenty, though," Luke admits, a small smile tugging at his lips.

My eyes sting as I watch them. Not only because I am, once again, witnessing this incredible family bond. But also because, while I may be watching this from the side-lines through an incredibly clear window, this will never be something I can be a part of. Not really. Their bond is the purest of water and the sweetest of wine. They are the most pristine of gardens, and I am nightshade growing within.

"I know it's been hard being away from her, Luke. I cried like a baby when I first got to Avalon."

Luke's eyes go wide, and he gapes at Connor. "You did?"

Connor nods. "I was all alone. I didn't have you guys. It was my first time away from Mom and Dad for an extended period."

Luke thinks for a moment. "At least I have you guys. And Summer and Alice."

"And Rafe," Connor adds. "I know he doesn't act like it, but he loves us too."

Luke shakes his head. "Not me. I'm not a fighter like you guys."

Connor blinks, taken aback by the statement. "No, you're not a fighter. You're way more special than that, Luke."

"Okay, wow," Zach grumbles, leaning against the elevator wall.

Luke sighs heavily. "You should see how Rafe looks at me when he sees my wings."

Connor winces. "That isn't about you, Luke. Like I said, Rafe has some demons. It's not you. It's never you."

Luke runs a hand through his hair, stepping back to stand tall on his own.

We arrived at our floor a while ago, but no one had even looked up when the doors opened. They were focused on Luke and making sure he was a little more healed than he was when we stepped into it. His eyes are clearer now, more unburdened, and Connor smiles at him. "Ready?"

Luke nods, and we leave the elevator together. Connor scoops me into his arms, and we launch into the sky. Connor holds back, his brothers racing each other as they weave through the clouds.

"What is it?" I ask, watching him. Some of the burden I saw on Luke's face now shrouds Connor's.

He sighs, watching Luke in the distance. "Luke and Rafe are more alike than either of them knows."

I search his face, my heart aching for him. I pinch his chin and tilt his head toward me before brushing my lips over his.

Connor hovers in midair. "What was that for?"

"You're just a really good guy, Con." I press a kiss to his cheek. "You're strong." I kiss the other cheek. "Kind." I kiss the corner of his lips. "Handsome." I kiss the other corner of his lips. "Mushy and wonderful." I hover my lips over his. "And you have the biggest heart."

Connor smiles. "I thought you hated my mushiness," he teases.

My lips twitch, and I brush my lips over his. "You make it hard to hate."

He smirks. "Well, you're going to have to endure more of it now because I was holding back before."

I groan. "Oh, no."

Connor laughs and spins us in the sky before rapidly descending toward the portal to Avalon.

# 50

## SUMMER

Heth'thae
SUPPRESS,
DAMPEN

We land back at the Morningstar house, tension still radiating from Luke. It escalates when Rafe steps onto the porch. Deciding that I can't handle another confrontation between the brothers, I excuse myself and head home. I barely make it back onto the quad before I'm tackled by a small, solid body. She takes me to the ground, clinging to me.

"I missed you!" she shrieks, nuzzling against me. I groan, trying to shift off the large stone, digging painfully into my back.

"Hi, Alice." I smile. She disentangles from me and stands up, pulling me with her. There is pure joy on her face, and I'm not sure I've ever seen her look so elated. It seems the supposedly murderous, loner vampire missed her psychotic, broken best friend.

"I missed you, too," I say with a sincere smile, hugging her tight.

"You owe me. This place is painfully boring without you," Alice whines, her voice conveying her utter despair at having to endure Avalon without her partner in crime. Oh, man, I hope she didn't actually commit any crimes...

"If you want, we can watch that trashy show you love so much tonight?" I suggest.

Alice immediately brightens, but her face pulls into a look of reproach. "That *trashy* show has won not only the hearts of over forty million viewers, and it has an array of awards!"

I quirk a brow, glancing at her as we walk back to our dorm. "Alice, the last episode we watched together revolved around a female mortal trying to become a vampire. So she signed a contract with the Emperor, who promised to turn her if she signed her soul over to him for eternity."

"Okay, woah. Do not diminish Demetrius's and Carolina's love like that. It's called an arranged marriage trope. Look it up." Alice crosses her arms over her chest, pouting.

"Oh, my apologies," I say, unconvincingly.

Alice glares at me. "How was it anyway?"

I sigh, my lips tugging up at the corners. "It was good, actually."

"Good?" Alice asks.

I nod. "His parents are kind of incredible."

"And did you and Connor work things out?"

"We did. It turns out what nine-year-old Connor and what thirty-year-old Connor wants are two completely different things."

Alice laughs. "Who knew?" She nudges me. "So... did you reach the Heaven High Club?"

I blink, glancing at her. "What?"

"Did you and Connor..." She pauses for a moment, looking around in a show of secrecy, but I can tell it's simply dramatics. "Sex in a stratus? Cunnilingus in a cumulus? Cock in a cirrus? Anal in—"

"Alice!" I interrupt.

Alice nudges me again. "Well?"

I give her a look and then sigh heavily. "Yes, we had sex in Eden. Okay? Happy?"

"Ew, no, that would be weird. Did his parents walk in on you?"

"What an odd question," I say, wrinkling my nose.

"Well, I know his brothers already caught you on the couch."

I gaped. "How did you know about that?"

Alice shrugs. "Zane."

"I'm going to staple that boy's mouth shut."

Alice snorts. "He'd learn sign language just to spite you."

"I need to find out about this secret girl Zach is seeing. If I blackmail dumb, the dumber will also fall into line."

"Oh, that's easy." Alice snorts. "He's fucking Ashley."

"Ashley?" I frown.

Alice nods. "Ashley Troy. You met her the other day."

I look down, trying to place her, and then it clicks. "The cheerleader?"

"Cheer *captain*. You'd better get it right if you're serious about wanting to join the squad." Alice opens the main door to Kelpie, and we climb the stairs plotting against the twins.

When we open the door to our dorm, every instinct I have goes on alert. There is something wrong. Alice, too wrapped up in chatting about Zach and Ashley, doesn't notice and just walks through to her room, continuing to talk. Her voice fades into a faint hum as I zero my senses onto the strange energy in the dorm. Slowly, I walk toward my bedroom door. It is sitting ajar, and a pang of fear sinks into me as I brush my fingers down the wood, following the grain. The hinges squeak as I cautiously push it open, my heart racing in my chest. As my room comes into view, my stomach sinks. It is completely destroyed. Drawers have been dumped, my wardrobe has been emptied, and my clothes are strewn across the floor. Pictures have been ripped from my walls, some of them torn to pieces. I step into the room and pick up one of my shirts. There is a huge slice along the back of it.

"So I was thinking about cheerlea..." Alice's words trail off as she rounds the corner into my room. "What the fuck?" She inhales deeply like I have seen her do when trying to get a scent. "Nothing. Fuck, Sum. What do we do? Call the authorities?"

My hands start to shake, and I drop the ruined shirt. "I think we should notify the headmaster first." I grab my phone and open my school email account.

To: J.emrys@avalon.edu
From: S.tuathadedanaan@avalon.edu
*Sorry to bother you, sir. Someone has ransacked my dorm room. Should I contact the authorities about this, or is it a school matter?*
*-Summer.*

The second I hit the send button, regret churns in my gut. "Fuck, he already hates me, Alice. Now, I am emailing him on a Sunday. He is going to expel me for sure."

I've barely finished my thought when someone knocks on the door. It's a familiar knock, sure and strong. I already know who it is before Alice opens the door for him. The headmaster steps into the dorm wearing a casual version of his usual professional attire. His steely eyes rake the living room, taking in every detail.

"Miss Tuatha De Daanan, Miss Legosi," he says. His voice is clipped, but there is no unkindness in it.

"Headmaster Emrys, thank you for coming."

He nods once. "Your room was ransacked?"

I nod, leading him into my bedroom. He steps just inside the door, looking around at the mess. "Was anything taken?"

"I'm not sure, sir."

He steps deeper into the room, taking care not to trample any of the destroyed clothes that litter the floor. I appreciate the gesture but also don't understand the point of the courtesy.

"Did you touch anything after finding your room like this? Move anything?" He asks, scanning the room.

"Just that shirt," I reply honestly, pointing to the one I had picked up. The head-master glances over his shoulder, noting the shirt. He nods once and slides his forefinger along the inside of his ring, slicing the skin. Turning on his heel, he walks to the door and presses his bloody fingertip to it. He drags the pad over the painted wood, leaving a precise line in its wake. I notice he is careful not to lift his finger as he loops the line in a series of curves. To finish, he presses two dots in the center. It's not a rune I'm familiar with, but from the way it's rounded, I think it's supposed to show motion.

The rune glows softly and pulses three times before a ghostly figure appears in the room. A ghostly figure moves through the room, carelessly tearing through my belongings. The projection isn't perfect, and obviously, the being took precautions to avoid being identified. It flickers in and out, sometimes showing them yanking items of clothes out of my wardrobe, sometimes throwing papers around.

My throat tightens, and I wrap my arms around my torso, surprised at the sense of violation. Unable to watch anymore, I instinctively turn toward the headmaster. He is watching the scene, trying to get as much information as possible from the grainy, incomplete projection. I glance back at the scene just in time to watch the being lift something.

"Sir! There! Stop!"

The illusion pauses immediately, and he moves closer. "A notebook?"

Even from the poor quality of the projection, I can tell what it is. It's a book with a small daisy on the front and a soft pink background. "It's my journal. Though, I never use it."

The headmaster rubs his hand along his jaw, and I notice his stubble is a little heavier than usual. "They must have known you were away for the weekend." He turns his piercing gaze on Alice. "And you didn't hear anything, Miss Legosi?"

Alice blushes a little. "I uh... I wasn't here last night."

I blink at her.

The headmaster just nods, turning his formidable attention back to the scene. "They knew the dorm was empty."

"Do you think they've been watching?" I ask, my mind flashing back to the feeling of someone watching me through the window, the way the unnatural wind pounded against the glass.

I feel the headmaster's icy stare settle on me. "Yes, which makes little sense. If they knew who you are, why Gia?" he ponders, though I'm not convinced the question is for Alice or me.

Alice gasps, drawing our attention. "Miss Legosi?" he asks.

"Gia looked like you, Sum!" She smacks her palm against her forehead. "I just remembered. When I was young, there was this rogue vampire who went around killing the same person over and over." She pauses at my confused expression. "Well, not the same person, but people who looked very similar, but he never targeted the object of their obsession. The OG lookalike."

I stare at her blankly, trying to put it all together.

Alice rolls her eyes in exasperation. "Maybe this person killed Gia because she looks like you, and they are obsessed with you."

My brows draw, and I continue to stare at her, a little dumbfounded.

The headmaster hums thoughtfully, rubbing his chin.

"That's ridiculous. No one is obsessed with me." I wrap my arms tighter around myself. Well, except for the obvious, but Torin is not so much obsessed with me as he is obsessed with controlling me. Or, more specifically, he wants to control my power. I consider whether I should mention Torin to the headmaster now, but it seems pointless, and I'd rather no one else know about my murky past.

"We should not be quick to discount Miss Legosi's theory." The headmaster frowns and then waves his hand. I watch in amazement as my bedroom puts itself back together. "No one should know about the break-in. Not yet," he says, the command in his voice stealing my will. "Understand?"

We nod, and it feels like the air has thickened, making it difficult to breathe.

"The AIB have been less than collaborative with this whole situation."

I stare at him, overwhelmed with the information, the danger, the unknown.

"I will find them, Miss Tuatha De Daanan," the headmaster says, watching me.

"Yes, sir," I reply, though I can hear the fear in my voice.

"Be careful. Both of you." The headmaster summons a portal and steps in. It snaps shut behind him, but I continue to stare at the spot where he disappeared. Without his powerful presence, my fear turns to terror, the metallic taste of it coating my tongue.

I sit down on the bed, and Alice sits next to me. She looks around and whistles softly. "That male can *clean*."

My lips twitch, and I look down at the floor, thinking. "We can't tell Con," I say, already feeling the unease and seeds of guilt from keeping this from him.

"Sum?"

"Yeah?"

"This could still be a coincidence. Or a prank," Alice says, hopefully.

"It could be."

Alice wraps her arms around me. "They won't get you. They don't realize you've got a murderous vampire wife, and I will remove their spine through their asshole if they hurt you."

My lips twitch again, and I lay my head on top of hers.

"I'm glad you have that necklace," Alice whispers.

I close my fingers around the pendant, feeling it warm under my hand.

"Sleep in my room tonight?" she asks.

I nod. "I'm going to take a shower first."

"I'll make popcorn!" Alice announces.

"You don't eat."

Alice shrugs. "I like the smell, don't hate. Plus, you eat, and I need to feed my wife."

I laugh softly and squeeze her before going to the bathroom to shower. I set the water temperature to scalding, trying to rid myself of the violation I've felt since I realized someone had been in my room, rifling through my things. It feels like an oily patina over my skin. It isn't an unfamiliar sensation, just another layer. I am so tired of constantly looking over my shoulder, feeling as if I am being watched and hunted. After all these years, I should be used to it by now, but this feels like a whole other level. I scrub my skin until it's bright pink and sore and desperately try to push the feelings away, containing them deep in the recesses of my mind.

# 51

## SUMMER

*Jahltha*
TOSS, THROW

My alarm goes off, early morning light streaming in through the window. Beside me, Alice growls softly and tugs the blankets up. I snatch my phone up and turn it off before I become a vampire's breakfast. I slept fitfully, and for the few moments I was able to drift off, I was back in the forest, the feeling of being watched making my skin crawl. Gia's lifeless corpse lay on the forest floor, her head turned so she was looking at me, the fear in her eyes present even in death.

I climb out of her bed and pad through the living room to my room. It doesn't feel like mine anymore. Whoever had done this had meant to take from me, and they had succeeded. Some malevolent being had been in here yesterday. They had touched my things and destroyed some of them, but worse, they had taken what sense of home and security I had managed to carve out for myself here.

I push through the unease and walk through the room, going straight to the closet. As quickly as possible, I change into my running clothes and then hurry from my room. I burst through the door and nearly sprint down the stairs, shoving my earbuds in place. The first song of my running playlist blasts in my ears, and I already feel more relaxed. As soon as I shove through the dorm door, I push into a run, somehow feeling safer outside in the open than in my own home.

The air is cooler now. The afternoons warm up a little, but the crisp nip of the fall is creeping in. My cheeks and nose go a little numb, my lungs burning slightly from the cold air invading them as I push myself on the run.

An image from my nightmare flashes in front of me, and I shake my head, trying to clear it, but they are persistent. Another one flashes across my mind's eye, and this one is worse. Instead of Gia's dead body just lying on the ground, she has me pinned against a tree and is choking me. I clench my fists, trying to lose myself to the music, to the beat of my feet against the ground. I am so caught up in my thoughts, in trying to push myself to distraction, that I completely miss a large body moving into my path until I collide with hard muscle.

"You should not be here."

I blink, looking up and meeting the steely eyes of the headmaster. His hands are braced on my upper arms, steadying me after the collision. I frown and pull my earphones out.

"You should not be here, Miss Tuatha De Daanan," he repeats, his gaze hard and angry as it so often is in my presence. He releases me and crosses his arms over his chest.

I stare up at him, but I am having trouble focusing on him. Now that I am paying attention, something is pulling at me, my instincts telling me to look past him. Something is calling to me, chanting my name over and over. I crane my neck, trying to look over his shoulder, but he moves with me, his enormous frame easily blocking my view.

Whatever it is behind him, it wants me to see, and it pulls at me again. When I move this time, something in me rises to help. The magic behind him calls to my own, and the compulsion to know what is there overshadows my fear of my powers. I take the headmaster by surprise and use my fae speed, blurring as I duck around him. I freeze, my breath catching in my throat. A message is messily drawn onto a large boulder in red, gooey liquid. It's thick and dark, and the early morning sun shines off it in a grim way. It is unmistakably blood.

**YOU CAN ONLY PROTECT HER FOR SO LONG, SON OF MERLIN.**

The headmaster growls and shoves in front of me, blocking my view again. I look up at him, my eyes wide. "Sir..."

He lifts his chin, holding my gaze steadily. "The message is for me. They are aware I am protecting you."

I try to swallow the lump of fear clogging my throat. "Why are they doing this?"

He regards me with his usual coldness. "They want you scared."

"Why?" I ask uselessly. My power coils in on itself inside of me, that taste surging into a deep desire to use it, to dive into it and never resurface, to hide there.

"They seem to enjoy playing with you. They want your fear. The question is, are you going to give it to them?"

I lose myself in his gaze for a moment, grateful for the chill in it, the icy unfeelingness. I straighten my spine. "No, sir," I reply, my words strong and sure, not reflecting the fact that my organs have turned to mulch inside me.

He nods once. "I would suggest using the school gym from now on." Without waiting for my response, the headmaster turns back around and resumes studying the message on the boulder.

I have obviously been dismissed, and I turn, sprinting home, running on pure adrenaline. Who is this person? Why do they hate me? What have I ever done to deserve this?

Could it possibly be Torin? No. There's no way. He's not clever enough to pose any sort of challenge to the headmaster. Not patient enough to toy with me.

Alice steps out of her room, wrapped in a blood-red towel. She frowns at me. "You're back early."

I don't even pause on my way to my room. "Wasn't feeling it," I lie. The truth is not even a consideration at the moment. What the fuck even is the truth?

"The real question is how you ever feel like running," Alice quips, returning to her room to change. In a daze, I shower and dress in my uniform. Alice is waiting for me in the kitchen and looks at me expectantly when I come out of my room.

"Let's go. I need coffee."

"Absolutely," Alice agrees. We leave the dorm, walking toward the coffee cart. I am sure it is just a phantom pull, but I can't keep from looking in the direction of the boulder. I can't stop thinking about how it called to my magic so potently. No doubt the headmaster has already had it removed. It would create a massive spectacle on campus, plus the Arcane Intelligence Bureau would no doubt want to analyze it and interview every single person on campus.

"Good morning, babe," Connor says as we approach the coffee cart. He's holding two large coffees in his hands.

I smile up at him, some of my tension fading away. "Good morning, big guy."

Alice snatches the coffee from him. "Thank you, bird brain," she grumbles into her cup as she takes a long sip.

I laugh softly and brush my lips over Connor's. He smiles and wraps his arm around my waist, and another fleck of tension breaks off.

"How was your night with your brothers?" I ask, pulling back.

Connor smiles down at me. "It would have been better if you'd have been there." He squeezes me to him. "I missed you."

Alice slurps her coffee loudly and impatiently, obviously done with watching our mushiness.

"You're going to be late," Connor groans as I kiss his jaw, both of us ignoring Alice.

I lift my face for him, waiting for a kiss. "Don't care."

Connor brushes his lips over mine. "Okay, well, I'm going to be late."

I ignore him, deepening the kiss, my tongue dancing with his. Connor moans but pulls back. "Okay, now I really have to go."

"Fine," I pout.

Connor nuzzles his nose against mine. "I'll see you later," he says before turning and setting off at an easy jog.

Alice and I are some of the last to enter the classroom, and when we sit down, my mind immediately begins to wander. Though I'm sitting in a class about runes, and normally I would be completely captivated, I find myself doodling in my notebook. They are not the usual doodles of boredom. Instead, I'm recreating the message from earlier, down to the way the blood trickled down the stone. As I draw the final *N* in the message, the page glows faintly. I sit up and stare down at it, watching in horrified amazement as a message appears. It looks like someone else is writing on the paper. The script is elegant, precise, and neat, the words curving along the lined page.

*It is a warning.*

I frown down at my notebook and then flip my gaze up, looking around. Alice is busy with something on her phone, and no one else seems to be paying me any attention. I look back at the page in front of me and grip my pen harder, pressing it to the paper before writing out a reply.

*From you?*

*No.*

The reply comes almost instantly.

*Who are you?*

I write back while trying to sort through my feelings about this situation. I try to lean into my instincts, but they are eerily silent. It's like I have gone numb, just one thing too many, and I can't process all the potential dangers lurking around every corner.

*A stranger.*

They write back, the words sending a shiver down my spine. It's such an obvious answer, but it's truth, and the ambiguity behind it is chilling. This feels strangely familiar to me, but I'm not sure why. It's nothing like my situation from before.

*Do you want to hurt me?*

I ask. The question hangs in the air like an oppressive cloud.

There is a beat this time, almost a hesitation before the reply comes.

*An odd question. Why would you ask that, little fae?*

I shiver at the term and how it makes me feel like prey. Like I am being stalked by the most fearsome of predators. So then, why does it make my stomach flutter?

*Leave me alone.*

I'm not sure why I didn't say it sooner, why I'm replying to a haunted-ass notebook.

*No.*

The reply, once again, comes immediately.

I slam the notebook closed and shove it roughly into my bag. I stand up, and the entire class turns their attention to me as the chair drags over the stone floor.

I swallow and quickly excuse myself from class. My heart pounds painfully hard, and my lungs struggle to expand, the air feeling light and thin. I walk through the corridors, trying to find somewhere to go where I'll be able to breathe. Everything is spinning, and I stop to lean against the wall, concentrating on breathing. A soft touch slides over my shoulder, and I whip around. I reach back, seeing if something is crawling on me because there is nothing and no one behind me. The touch was faint, but it was definitely there.

"Hello?" I ask into the void. There is no answer, and I'm about to turn away again when something moves in front of me. It's barely visible, but I can see the slight shift in the air around it when it moves. I take a deep breath and take a small step forward. Very slowly, I lift my trembling hand, reaching out to touch. A hard mass of muscle meets my fingertips. My throat closes, killing my scream, leaving nothing but quiet whimpers between shallow breaths. I want to pull my hand away, but I am frozen in place, feeling the warmth of the... something beneath my fingers. My hair is brushed behind my ear. It's a gentle gesture, but I still flinch.

"I will not hurt you." A soft voice carries to me, surrounding me like the gentlest of winds. It is a deep male voice, and I can tell it is warped from the power humming faintly against my skin.

I frown, watching and waiting for its next move. Hearing him speak eases some of my terror. It almost humanizes the apparition, and it helps that there is no anger in the voice. The feeling of malice I had when I was being watched earlier is completely absent now.

The being slowly moves his hand and brushes his fingertips along the back of my wrist. I tilt my head, trying to see more of him. All I can make out is that he is taller than even Uriel and broader than him, too, muscle packed onto a powerful frame. I brush my fingers along his chest, trying to understand it. An elemental avatar like this is not something many can achieve, and having enough control over it so that they are able to talk via the embodiment is very impressive. Why don't I feel the overwhelming urge to run? Why am I lost to curiosity?

My phone chimes in my bag, and I jump slightly. The form, which appears to be made of wind, disappears, leaving only the echo of a breeze in its wake.

I look around and then hurry into the women's bathroom, locking the door behind me. I close my eyes and press my head against the door, taking deep breaths.

"Fuck."

Less than five minutes later, there is a soft knock at the door. "Babe?" Connor's voice is muffled through the door. "Alice texted me."

"I'm okay, Con. Just not feeling well." I pause for a long moment. "I'll see you later?"

Connor pauses for a second, trying to sort through the heavy meaning between my words. "I'll just wait here."

I sigh heavily, realizing that he's not going to leave. I quickly splash water on my face before opening the door. Connor is leaning against the door frame, his concerned eyes sliding over me.

I walk into him and bury my face against his chest. Connor wraps his arms around me, holding me close. "I got you, babe."

After a long moment, I tip my head back and look up at him. "I'm okay."

"It's okay not to be," Connor whispers, cupping my cheeks.

I smile and kiss him softly, delving deep within myself to find some truth in the words I'm about to say to my angel boyfriend so that he can't taste my lie.

"I'm okay, promise."

Connor exhales in relief, and I take a moment to enjoy the small achievement. The fucked up achievement of successfully lying to my boyfriend. Nice.

"Do you want to cut and go to my house?" he asks, stroking my cheek with his thumb.

I shake my head, knowing the anxiety he will feel cutting a class. "You need to go to class."

Connor presses his forehead to mine. "I need to be where my girlfriend needs me."

My heart flutters at the care he's giving me, the love he never fails to show me. My thoughts scramble, trying to figure out how I can reciprocate and take care of him. He needs to go to class.

"Con—"

"Okay, well, come with me," he interrupts, obviously knowing I'm about to object again to him skipping school.

"You want me to come with you to your senior class?" I ask, quirking a brow.

Connor shrugs. "Why not? You'll probably outperform us all."

"Con, I'm okay. Go to class, and I'll see you later. Honestly—"

"Summer. Everything in me is telling me to stay by your side right now." He looks into my eyes, the sky blue shining with sincerity, with concern. My poor, haunted big guy.

I sigh. "Okay. Let's go to your class."

Connor relaxes immediately and closes his eyes, kissing my forehead. "Thank you."

# 52

## SUMMER

*Laethae*
SLOW,
DECELERATE

Connor slides his hand into mine and gently tugs me against his side as we walk to his next class. I look over my shoulder as we go, my eyes searching for the mysterious being I had the strange encounter with. It should have been terrifying, especially because an unknown entity is hunting me. Well, an unknown entity and a psychotic fae male. I was scared in the beginning, but then... I wasn't. While dangerous and filled with power, the energy coming off him didn't feel directed at me but in defense of me. No part of me wants to run and hide. Instead, I am intrigued.

As we round the corner, the corridor out of view, Connor brings my hand to his lips and presses a soft kiss to my knuckles. I look at him, letting the kindness and love in his eyes wash over me. The sky blue encapsulates me in a sea of calm. Connor smiles at me before he opens the door to his classroom. Everyone is already seated, and Headmaster Emrys's words trail off when he sees us.

"Miss Tuatha De Daanan. I don't recall inviting you to join my senior capstone class."

I blush, about to reply, when Connor answers for me. "Apologies, headmaster. This will be a one-time thing if you allow it, of course." He gives the headmaster a pointed look, and I get the sense he's not going to let him not allow it. My sexy big guy.

Headmaster Emrys lifts an eyebrow, regarding us both with those steely gray eyes. After a long, tense moment, he nods once and walks around his desk, perching on the edge of it. Connor squeezes my hand, and we sit down near the back of the classroom.

"Combat runes," the headmaster continues. He unbuttons his left cuff and rolls the sleeves up his arm, unveiling some of the most intricate runes I've ever seen. Unlike fae, with our iridescent runes, sorcerers' runes are black, the kind of black that swallows light. The headmaster's runes are drawn expertly, and while they're usually concealed by a shirt, it's fascinating to see how they connect to the always visible ones on his hand. And also incredibly sexy.

The headmaster does the same with his other sleeve, and I take time to study the runes on that arm as best I can. There are some that adorn both, but there are a couple that differ between arms. Some battle runes can be drawn onto the skin in one place, affecting the whole body, while others must be applied to each arm or leg. Placement is very rune dependent..

"At the end of our previous lesson, we had just started to delve into the different advanced combat runes, and I had asked for you all to research a subset of the combat runes from your species." The headmaster turns back around and begins to draw various runes on the whiteboard. His work is effortless, and I briefly wonder how much knowledge he contains in his brain. He labels them one to eight and then turns back to the class.

"Mister Morningstar, which is the angel advanced combat rune?" His steely gaze locks on Connor, pinning him there. I feel uneasy on his behalf, but Connor's effortless confidence remains a welcome presence beside me.

"Number three, headmaster," Connor answers easily.

Headmaster Emrys nods once and then draws the symbol of the angels beneath the third rune. "Specific archetypes?" he asks, still looking up at the rune.

"Along with the base advancements in combat, the angelic advanced combat rune also affects our wings. The feathers toughen, becoming shield-like while also turning even lighter, allowing for a faster and more silent glide," Connor recites as if he's memorized a passage on this very subject. I look at him, smiling proudly at my angel and feeling a little turned on by him. Overall, this is just a very erotically charged class.

The headmaster nods and casts his gaze over the classroom, landing on another student. "Miss Denya."

The girl pales, disappointed that her plan to avoid eye contact with the headmaster has failed.

"The vampire combat rune?" the headmaster probes, and Miss Denya turns a sickly shade of green as her eyes nervously dart between the different runes and the headmaster.

"Number four?" she squeaks out.

The headmaster's cool gaze is locked on her, waiting. "Is that your answer or a question, Miss Denya?"

She swallows loudly. "The answer?"

The headmaster continues to stare her down, and she squirms under the attention. Connor slings his arm along the back of my chair, enjoying this takedown. There is obviously some ill will between him and the quivering vampire.

"Wrong." The headmaster's steely voice cuts through the tension in the room like the sharpest of blades, and he looks over the room, taking in every single student.

"Can one of those who have actually done the reading tell me which species the fourth one is for?" Everyone in the room stares blankly at the whiteboard.

From the moment he started drawing the rune, I knew it was a fae rune. There is something about the way it curves and bends. As much as I hate to admit it, there is a finesse to it that was first perfected by the fae folk. Their rune work is some of the most intricate. Even if I hadn't recognized it by the design, I would have known for sure once he completed it. It looks as if It is hovering above the whiteboard, calling to me.

"No one?" the headmaster asks, a slight growl to his voice.

"It's fae." I tense and press my lips tightly together, the words having slipped out. The sound is so soft that it's not reaching to hope that he didn't hear it, but the second my answer hits the air, his eyes snap to me.

"That is correct, Miss Tuatha De Daanan." He looks at his students. "Disappointing." Done with trying to get answers from his class, he points to the first rune. "Shifter, non-winged." He points to the second one. "Shifter, winged." He points to the third one. "Angel." He points to the fourth. "Fae. Berserker. Valkyrie. Vampire and siren." He points to them one after the other. "This demonstration is anything but exhaustive. These are just the ones relevant to the class." He leans against the wall. "Now we know the runes, and we have the ability. What stands in our way of simply drawing them and utilizing their abilities?"

"Emotions," a siren boy in the second row answers.

"Elaborate," the headmaster replies cooly.

"Combat runes are volatile by their very nature. More so if the creator's emotions are also volatile."

The headmaster pushes off the wall and walks back to the board. "As you know, runes draw on emotions. Combat runes are no different, though the consequences are. For example, if you were to draw a rune for hay fever while angry, the worst that would happen is that the rune would be ineffective. Perhaps it would cause a headache. Drawing one of these runes while allowing emotion to rule you could result in self-destruction, madness, blackouts, elevated homicidal tendencies, or uncontrollable rage." The headmaster writes notes on the board as he speaks. "While you want to control your emotions, these particular runes require a very delicate balance. Someone completely at ease, for example, will not have enough will to power the rune sufficiently. Can anyone tell me the three M's of drawing these runes?"

I tell myself to remain silent, but when no one else speaks up, I whisper, "Malice.

Murder. Malevolence." The headmaster turns around and looks at me. Does he look impressed?

"Correct. And what do they mean?" he asks.

"The runes are defensive and are primarily to be used in combat. However, holding any of the three Ms in your soul as you draw the runes changes the rune to be offensive, which is not the nature of them."

The headmaster nods. "These runes, while meant for battle, can be lethal if used in conjunction with feelings of malice, murder, or malevolence. These runes are incredibly powerful, and they become uncontrollable when fed with these emotions. Say the rune is activated on the battlefield after you have just witnessed a loved one being killed, and the core emotion is malice. Yes, the rune would assist with the surface goal of revenge, but then it would feed off that malice and crack. When it does, it won't just warp your abilities but your mind as well. Every single person on the battlefield becomes a target. Friend and foe no longer matter. There is only malice. There is only *more*." The room is completely silent, the lesson settling over us like a suffocating quilt. "Miss Tuatha De Daanan, since you seem to know more than my advanced class, congratulations, you have just volunteered to demonstrate."

I blink at him, his words slowly sinking in. The headmaster just watches me, his gaze becoming a little more impatient, clearly annoyed that I haven't jumped to my feet. He obviously isn't used to having to say things more than once or having to wait.

Taking a deep breath, I slowly get to my feet. I smooth out my skirt as I walk to the front of the class, nerves tingling down my spine.

"Are you feeling particularly malevolent this morning, Miss Tuatha De Daanan?" the headmaster quips, and while it sounds like he's being sarcastic, I swear I see a twinkle of humor in his eyes.

"I'd say my malevolence is probably sitting at a solid three out of ten," I reply, using humor to deflect from my nerves. The idea that he is in real danger from me is ludicrous. Not only is my mood fairly placid, but I'm only a first year. My powers are still growing. Plus, they are still deeply repressed, and to power a defensive rune like this fully, I'd need to put in years of practice.

"Draw the rune and use it against me."

I take a breath and hold out my hand, summoning my small rune dagger. I slice my finger and draw the rune on my forearm without even looking at the board. The memory of the rune is so clear in my mind. It's like I've always known it. Even before he drew it on the board, the rune was building itself in my mind as he was drawing the previous ones. Mine ended up looking only slightly different from the actual rune, and I'm pretty sure mine would have worked in the same way, but it would have allowed for slightly more control over the power channeled into it.

The dark red blood is stark against my skin, and it starts to glow even before I've completed it, my body anticipating the power I will need. The second the rune is complete, I feel all of my joints tighten, but my bones become more pliable and flexible. My hearing sharpens, making the ticking clock almost painful, but I also have more control over it, able to tune myself into the sounds. I hear the heartbeat of everyone in the room, and with little effort, I have sorted through them and identified Connor's. His heart is beating a little faster than normal. I turn my hearing, searching for the headmaster's heartbeat. It takes a little longer, but I eventually find the slow, even thud within his chest.

I sense the headmaster moving toward me, his attack imminent. Not giving him the chance, I send a charged ball of purple power right at him. He blocks it easily and nods, never removing his hands from his pockets.

"Very good, Miss Tuatha De Daanan," he says, and I feel my confidence grow beneath his praise. "Do you know how to counteract the rune?"

I concentrate, and the counter rune forms in my mind. I slice my finger again and draw over the defensive rune. The effects dim almost immediately.

"Very good," he says before turning his attention to his class, who are all gaping at me. "Next," he says, waiting for the next person to come up and do the same thing.

By the end of the class, I was the only one able to draw and channel the rune successfully. As the students leave, there is a mixture of reactions as they walk past me. Some smile at me, seeming impressed. Others glare at the temerity of a first-year daring to show them up.

Connor slides his hand into mine. "You made that look easy."

I shrug, but I feel a smile tug at the corner of my lips.

"Lunch?" Connor asks.

I nod and we walk to the cafeteria, discussing the different techniques for rune drawing. When we arrive at our table, Zach, Zane, Luke, and Alice are digging into their lunch.

"Summer just showed up a room full of seniors," Connor announces to the table with a wide, proud grin.

"Hardly." I roll my eyes as I sit down, but that annoying warmth fills my chest, and a smile plays on my lips again.

Connor raises an eyebrow. "You were the only one the headmaster had to use his shield for."

I shrug. "Whatever, it's just a rune." The second the words leave my mouth, I regret them, not only because they are not true, runes are complex and fascinating, but also because of how Connor's face drops.

"Oh," he says, sounding a little defeated.

I turn to face him. "Con, the only reason I'm good at runes is cause I'm fae. They're really hard, and that one today was super complex. You almost had it."

Connor looks at me, his brows furrowed. "I've had classes with fae for years, Summer. They aren't like you."

What does that mean? Do I even want to know?

I flutter my eyelashes and move in closer, doing my best to act cute. "Are you proud of me?" I ask, deliberately making my voice a little higher.

Connor wraps an arm around me. "I'm always proud of you, babe. But I want *you* to be proud of you."

I melt at his words but then cringe at the impossibility of what he's asking. There have been very few reasons for me to feel pride in myself. Shame and I are much better acquaintances. I sigh softly. "I'll try. Okay, big guy?"

Connor smiles, brushing his lips over mine in one of the most tender kisses I've ever received. "That's good enough for me."

Alice nudges me and drops her voice so the others can't overhear. "Everything okay?"

I nod, still leaning into Connor's side. "I'm good."

Rafe slams his tray down on the table, making me jump in surprise. "Fuck Emrys," he growls.

"What happened?" Connor asks, squeezing me a little, the tension already building in him.

"He's making me take on an extra class to make up for missed work," Rafe growls.

I glance at Rafe, his face set into a furious expression. "Maybe I can help?" I offer.

"Can you attend my class for me?" Rafe asks, his words dripping with ungrateful sarcasm.

I shrug. "Okay, my bad."

"Rafe, she was being nice," Connor scolds.

Rafe looks at Connor, his eyes flashing. "I don't need your girlfriend's fucking pity offer."

"Rafael," Connor warns.

"Fuck this, I'm out of here." Rafe stands from the table and storms off.

Connor sighs, kissing my temple. "Sorry about that, babe. He didn't mean it."

My heart warms at the way he is sticking up for his little brother, even though I can tell he's struggling to justify his actions internally. I turn my head to face him and kiss the corner of his lips, comforting him.

"My offer stands. I'm happy to help Rafe if he'll accept it. I know he's a junior, and I'm just a freshman, but I'm also a nerd."

"Ain't that the truth," Alice scoffs into her blood bag.

Connor looks over my face and exhales. "I don't deserve you."

I stare up at him, my stomach clenching. Connor is right. He doesn't deserve me. He deserves so much more.

# 53

## SUMMER

Lahsha

COVER, SHROUD

Connor leans against the stacks, bracing his arm against the wood of the shelves. He pants, his breath hot against my cheek. "Fuck, babe." After the showdown with Rafe and my offer to tutor him, Connor pulled me to the library and to the stacks that are slowly becoming *our* place. He barely managed to shove my panties down before he was thrusting inside me.

"Did that feel good, big guy?" I purr into his ear.

Connor brushes his lips along my cheek, shakily searching for mine. "So fucking good," he moans as our lips meet, and I kiss him deeply.

"What are you doing later?" Connor asks into my mouth, still pressing me against the stacks.

"Well, I have cheer tryouts today. Then I thought maybe you could come over, we could order dinner, and perhaps my dessert can be a mouthful of you..."

Connor groans, his cock throbbing inside of me. "Is that right?"

"Are you up for it, Morningstar?"

"Fuck, absolutely I am."

"Perfect." Connor reluctantly pulls out of me and then lowers me to the ground. He zips up his pants, and I look around for my panties, frowning when I don't see them. The bright pink lace should be stark against the dark stone of the library floor, yet they are decidedly absent. I get onto my hands and knees to search under the stacks, hoping that maybe they just got kicked under there in the frantic, heated moment, but all I see are shadows.

"Con, do you know where my panties are?"

Connor finishes tucking his shirt into his pants and turns to face me. "They were on the ground."

"Well, they're not anymore."

Connor helps me look, but it quickly becomes clear that they may be lost, destined to be found by some poor, unsuspecting, studious person.

"Commando, it is then, I guess."

Connor cups my cheek. "My place or yours for tonight?"

"Mine," I reply, considering the fact that while I have Alice sharing the dorm with me, he shares the house with his four brothers. I lean in, brushing my lips over his. "I'll see you later, big guy."

"See you later, succubus."

"Do we *have* to?" Alice groans, repeating the same questions for at least the twentieth time since we left our last class.

I give her an exasperated look. "*You* don't have to, but I do. I'm doing this for Connor."

"Stupid bird brain jock," Alice grumbles, crossing her arms over her chest. "You know, to be a cheerleader, you have to be actually *cheer-y*. As in, you need to have cheer in order to lead."

I glare at her.

"What? I'm just saying. You have that dark and mysterious, angry, don't-talk-to-me vibe." Alice glances at my face and continues quickly, "Which you know I love. But say you're successful today, just don't get all—"

"Summer! Alice!" Ashley hurries over, holding a black and silver pom pom in each hand. Her smile is overly bright, though it wouldn't surprise me if this is simply the way her face is stuck, thanks to what looks to be a painfully tight ponytail. "I am so glad you decided to try out! You're going to do great. Just remember to relax and smile!" Ashley's smile grows if that is at all possible, and Alice glances at me, giving me the most scathing look I've ever received from her.

"Like that," Alice continues, her gaze wandering to Ashley and the rest of the squad. If looks could kill, this would be the biggest massacre Avalon has ever seen.

Alice and I join the group of nervous, prospective cheerleaders, and we start to warm up. Well, I do. Alice is more invested in sussing out the cheerleaders, and I've no sooner bent down to touch my toes when she abandons me to interrogate one of them. I can only see the back of her head, but I know she's conspiring to get all the gossip. She'll no doubt lock it away in the recesses of her mind, only to use it at the moment it will cause the greatest chaos.

Damn, my best friend is cool.

Ashley claps, drawing our attention as the guys flood onto the other side of the field to start their own practice.

"I'm so excited to see such an incredible turnout! So, as you know, there are three spots on the team, and there are thirty of you trying out, so you'd better bring your A-game!" Ashley grins and pulls out her phone, tapping at the screen. "Okay, everyone spread out. The first round is to see who can keep up with us." Ashley taps again, and suddenly, there is a blast of music. The cheerleaders fall into formation and start their routine. The moves are basic and repeated to the rhythm of the beat. Alice throws me a mutinous look, and I grin at her as I copy their steps. Others follow, and a few cheerleaders seamlessly extract themselves from the dance to walk through the group. Ashley's eyes scan us all as she dances, not missing a step.

One of the cheerleaders stops in front of me. Her mousey hair is pulled back in a single braid, and I can't help but notice the challenge in her stare as she eyes me. Never one to back down, it is nearly instinct to hold her gaze. She narrows her eyes at me before slowly moving on. Every so often, when someone messes up, the wandering cheerleaders tap them on the shoulder, the dreaded signal that they have not made the squad. By the end of the routine, only ten of us are left. Ashley grins at us all.

"Congrats on making it this far. Next, we'll test your speed, agility, and flexibility."

My gaze wanders across the field and invariably lands on Connor. I'm immediately captivated by the way his muscles flex as he catches the ball and throws it to one of his teammates. As if his gaze were a magnet drawn to mine, he lifts his head and throws me a wide, easy smile.

"So, everyone ready?" Ashley asks, and I grimace, looking at Alice. Fuck, I really should have been listening. Fuck, fuck, fuck.

"Georgie, you first," Ashley says, and a brunette shifter girl steps forward, smiling sheepishly. "High kick," Ashley demands, clicking her pen, preparing to take down notes. Georgie does a high kick, and Ashley purses her lips, her pen flying across the clipboard. "Back handspring." Again, Georgie immediately attempts a backflip, but her landing is wobbly. I grimace for her. "Okay, and handstand." Georgie inverts into a handstand, her legs anything but straight. Ashley smiles at her. "Thank you, Georgie. Isabella will time you running the field now, and we'll get back to you." Georgie trots off, following a pink-haired cheerleader.

"Summer, you're up!" Ashley grins at me, and we go through all the same drills. Ashley nods, making notes on her clipboard. "Okay, perfect. If you want to foll—"

"I'll time her, Ash," the cheerleader with the mousy hair offers sweetly, though I can feel the dislike in her gaze.

"Okay, Tarran. Thanks!" Ashley says. "Alice! You're up next."

"Sorry!" I mouth to Alice as I follow behind the angry cheerleader.

"Okay, *Summer*, let's see how fast you are." She starts the timer without giving me any warning. I roll my eyes but immediately push into a run, setting a quick but even stride. My instincts call on me to lean into my powers, but I push them away, unwilling to utilize my natural abilities. Keeping them contained and dormant has become second nature, but what used to be a dull ache has become a dangerous, dark tempest desperate to be free.

I glance at Connor because not looking at him when he is in my vicinity is an impossibility. Irritation stabs at me when I see that the cheerleader who is supposed to be timing me is standing next to him with her hand on his arm. She throws her head back and laughs, the sound harsh, annoying, and overly loud even on the busy field. I change course and run over to them.

"Hi, babe!" Connor says, brushing her hand away and wrapping his arms around me.

"Hi, big guy." I smile up at him.

"You're supposed to be running," the cheerleader grumbles.

I look at her. "And you're supposed to be timing me."

She tamps down her fury and turns her gaze back to Connor, fluttering her eyelashes unashamedly. "Anyway, Connor. I had a really good time with you at Finch's party. We should hang out again soon."

Connor blinks at her, seeming genuinely confused. "Oh, sorry, Tarrow. I'm not on the market." He squeezes me and playfully bites my cheek.

"It's Tarren," she mumbles under her breath.

I laugh and swat at him. "My big guy looks sexy on the field. No one can resist him," I say, wrapping my arms around Connor's neck.

Tarren clenches her fists and stomps off, her braid swinging furiously against her back.

"You know, I'm probably not going to make the team now," I quip, running my fingers through his blond locks.

Connor frowns. "Why?"

"Because Tarot hates me. And because you fucked up my times by being so irresistible that you attracted sour cheerleaders."

Connor laughs, the sound full and joyous. "It'll be fine, babe. Ashley is very fair when it comes to her girls!"

Connor leans in to kiss me, but Zach throws the ball, hitting Connor in the back.

"Hurry up, dickwad," Zach yells.

I laugh softly and press a soft kiss to Connor's lips before pulling back.

"Summer!" Ashley calls.

I sigh and try to hold back my eye roll. I press one last kiss to Connor's lips before jogging back to the group.

Ashley claps her hands, grinning widely. "What a great effort! We'll review all the data and announce our picks at the end of the week!"

Before Ashley even finishes talking, Alice grabs my arm and pulls me toward the exit. I try to get her to wait so I can say goodbye to Connor, but she just growls at me and walks faster. I wave at him as we pass, and he winks at me.

Alice slows down once we are outside the stadium. "Well, I hated every second of that," Alice grumbles.

"I know, but I appreciate you doing it with me, Al."

Alice mumbles something that sounds like, "You're welcome," and I can see the smile playing on her lips. I wonder if anyone has ever shown her gratitude before.

We stop at the cafe on the way home, and I order a very berry smoothie for myself and a tropical spiced blood smoothie for Alice. I pull out my phone, about to pay when a large shifter approaches. His dark eyes are fixed on Alice as he taps his card against the machine.

"Actually, we got it," Alice growls.

The machine beeps once, and he smiles wolfishly. "Already done, sweet cheeks." He winks at her and then swaggers away. Alice stares after him and then glances at me when she's managed to fix her face into a look of ire.

I smirk at her, one eyebrow raised.

"Damn it," she says, stomping over to the other end of the counter.

"What?" I ask, following her.

"Pretty sure I'm going to hate-bang him later."

The barista puts our smoothies on the counter. I pick mine up and take a long sip before saying, "You should. He's hot."

Alice pulls out her phone and taps at the screen.

"What are you doing?"

Alice starts scrolling. "I'm ordering a new ball gag. He seems like a talker."

"And cuddler..." I feign a shudder as we leave the cafe. I'm a total fraud, given that I enjoy a little dirty talk, and with Connor, I'm not entirely opposed to a cuddle.

Ugh. The smoothie curdles in my stomach at even the silent admission. Connor is ruining me. I don't even recognize myself anymore.

"Gross," Alice hisses, taking a drink of her smoothie.

"Well, at least he bought our smoothies."

Alice gives me a withering look as we approach the dorm. "Holy fuck. The bar for men is subterranean."

I laugh, shrugging. "I don't know. Mine is pretty all right."

Alice rolls her eyes. "Please. Connor doesn't count. Even I like him."

Connor knocks on the door an hour and a half later, and Alice lets him in. She's dressed for going out, wearing tiny leather shorts and a top that looks like it is made of fishnet, her black bra visible beneath it.

"Big date?" Connor asks.

"Gross, no." Alice rolls her eyes, closing the door behind him.

"She's going to fuck a shifter," I clarify, greeting him with a kiss. "He bought her a smoothie, and she's going to thank him with her snatch."

Alice sputters. "I am not! I'm going to tie him up naked in the woods and leave him there."

Connor thinks for a moment. "What kind of smoothie?"

I laugh, kissing his jaw. "Sure you are, Al. See that, Con? All you needed to do was buy me a smoothie."

"Maybe I'll take his cock and mount it on the wall as a trophy of torture," Alice growls.

"Not the direction I would have gone with the decor, but..." I ponder for a moment.

"Who's the shifter?" Connor asks.

Alice looks indignant, almost offended. "I don't know his name. That is not information I need."

"Right, right. Sorry." Connor holds one of his hands up, the other squeezing my hip. "What does he look like?"

Alice shudders. "He looks like a talker. Luckily, my ball gag just arrived." Alice holds it up, the black leather strap gleaming dully in the light.

Connor presses a kiss to my neck. "What's wrong with a talker?"

"He looked like he'd want to cuddle." I grimace.

"What's wrong with a cuddle?" he asks, wrapping his other arm around me.

I roll my eyes at how much of a sap he is. He and I are so different, yet we both bend to accommodate the other. We strive to ensure we're both comfortable and satisfied, emotionally and physically. It is a dance where we give space and come together when needed.

"With a one-night stand? What's right with it?" I counter and turn to wrap my arms around his neck, enjoying being enveloped in his strength.

"I was supposed to be a one-night stand, remember?"

I reach up on my tiptoes, kissing him tenderly. "You were supposed to be a tipsy hookup until you stopped mid-make-out to feed me a sandwich."

Connor laughs. "You were trashed, and I wanted to not be a one-night stand. I knew that first night I wanted to be more to you."

"Ugh, you guys are gross. Later," Alice says, leaving the dorm.

"She's right. You're so grossly mushy," I say, tunneling my fingers into his hair.

"You're one to talk," Connor groans and grips my hips.

"So, dinner will be here in thirty minutes, and I believe we had some... interesting plans for the evening that we should probably get started on."

Connor slides his hands down to cup my ass. "Well then, Tuatha De Daanan, better get to it." He picks me up, and I wrap my legs around him, giggling as he carries me to my bed.

# 54

## SUMMER

Loth'thu
ROOM

"So, Carmelina is sleeping with Joylee and Henderson?" Connor asks, his gaze firmly glued to the laptop screen.

I may end up regretting this. After Connor and I feasted on one another, enjoying our dessert first, we curled up in bed to eat dinner. I just pulled up the show that Alice likes for some background noise, but Connor took to it like duck to water and is already completely invested.

"I think so, but Carmelina is also sleeping with her stepsister, Hilly."

Connor blinks. "How does she have the time?"

I scoff. "Please, I know all about your player history, Connor Morningstar, *so-called* angel."

Connor sputters, finally dragging his attention away from the screen. "Excuse me. I was not a player. I just enjoyed…"

My lips twitch as I wait for him to continue, enjoying watching him struggle to justify his slutty, slutty past. I burst out laughing as I watch him scramble. "Chill out, Con. I'm joking."

Connor narrows his eyes at me, pouting his lips in that insanely adorable way he does. I'm still laughing as I climb out of bed and pull on my silk robe. I collect the takeout containers and take them into the kitchen. Noticing that the trash can is full, I decide to take it out now instead of putting off the grim job until morning when it'll smell worse, and I'll be even less inclined to do it.

I tighten the ties of my robe, grab the trash bag, and slip quietly out of the dorm. The quad is eerily beautiful at night. The street lamps cast white, almost magical puddles on the path, but I find the shadows thriving between the pools of light infinitely more interesting. I start down the small sidewalk, heading for the communal trash cans around the back of Kelpie. There is the slightest hint of a breeze, but apart from that, the night is calm and cool, making it all the more startling when something brushes a lock of my hair from my forehead. Startled, I yelp and jump, throwing the garbage bag into the air and scattering trash everywhere.

There is a slight shift in the air, something as casual as the brush of a stranger's hand as you pass by. Slowly, the trash disappears from view, disintegrating to nothing before my eyes.

*I am not alone. I am not alone. I am not alone.*

I feel the start of a shiver trickling down my spine. I slowly lift my hand, reaching forward as I did in the school corridor. My breath catches in my throat when my fingers meet hard muscles, and I can feel a faint, steady thud of a beating heart.

I tilt my head, and the being becomes a little less translucent, a solid piece of the shadows detaching from the night. He is still barely visible, but I can definitely see an outline. It's definitely a male. His shoulders are broad, and even in this form, I can tell how muscular he is. As my eyes roam his silhouette, I feel his heart beat a little faster. My gaze flicks up, locating the outline of his head and focusing on where I imagine his eyes would be. I'm once again surprised at how at ease I feel, especially given the circumstances.

"You're back," I say, my voice soft. He lifts his arm slowly, as if trying not to spook me, and carefully wraps his hand around my wrist. His touch feels like a cool breeze against my skin, but I can faintly feel the calluses on his palm and fingers. He lifts my hand and gently presses my palm to his cheek. He nods, finding a way to communicate with me even in this form. Can he not always talk? It does take a tremendous amount of power to do so, but he could do it the other day.

I slowly lower my hand, my fingers brushing against his mostly translucent form. "H-hi," I stutter out, looking up at him.

I should be running. Why am I not running?

He tilts his head, watching me. I can't see his eyes, but I can feel them fixed on me. Occasionally, his form flickers in the shadows, integrating with them. There is something so familiar about the feel of his gaze but also so foreign, and I stare at him as I try to sort through my thoughts. My gut instinct tells me I don't need to run, which makes no sense. There is a murderer on the loose who seems desperate to hack me to pieces and a fae hunter from my past, desperate to find and weaponize me. Yet here I am, standing with the fucking blustery Bigfoot. Okay, that's a bit harsh. He seems to be a good deal less hairy than Bigfoot.

So, while my instincts aren't screaming at me to run, I can't put my finger on why, and that is infinitely scarier. Could this be a ruse? A trick? A spell? I sort through the possibilities, trying to think of any runes that might have the power to grant the wearer the ability to twist another's thoughts, feelings, and worries, but I keep coming up empty. All I can think of are runes to make myself more fearless, which I *certainly* have not used on myself. I make enough bad decisions without adding faux recklessness into the mix.

I back up a step, wanting to see what he will do, but he just continues to watch me. At least, I think he's watching. I can feel those eyes on me, but there is something unnerving about not being able to see them. While my face heats under the alleged scrutiny of the stranger, I can't tell where he's focusing his attention. I back up again, still not feeling that fight-or-flight response, but simply forced survival instincts. While I don't feel like I'm in danger, there is no disputing that I'm in a vulnerable position. If anything, my lack of reaction is causing me more concern than the actual shadow male standing four feet away from me.

I take another step back, and another until my back hits the door of my dorm, and I hurry inside. Once within the safety of Kelpie Hall, the instincts I was waiting for finally kick-in, and my heart pounds in my chest. I pant and lean against the door.

Fuck.

I turn, peeking through the peephole, but see nothing there. Even the breeze seems to have stilled. I press my back against the door and close my eyes, taking a moment to consider what the fuck just happened.

# 55

## SUMMER

Marsha
DOOR

Once I've collected myself, I go back up to my room. Connor is where I left him, completely immersed in the show.

I walk past him, going straight to the window and peering out into the black of the forest. There is nothing to see, nothing to feel. The only thing staring back at me is my reflection in the glass, my eyes a little glazed with fear.

"You okay, babe?" Connor asks. The laptop goes quiet as Connor pauses the show and focuses on me. I keep looking out the window, unsure what I think I'll see, uncertain what I'm afraid to see.

"Babe?" Connor prompts. The mattress springs groan a little as he shifts on the bed.

"Yeah. I'm okay," I finally reply, closing the curtains. I turn to face Connor. His eyes are shadowed with concern, but his lips are curved in a small smile. He shifts, sitting on the edge of the bed and holding his hand out to me. I walk to him, sliding my hand into his. Connor pulls me between his legs and wraps his arms around me, looking up at me. I tunnel my fingers into his soft blond locks and look down at him.

"Hi, big guy."

"I missed you." Connor tightens his arms around me.

I giggle softly, any unease melting away. "While I was out at the trash can?"

Connor presses his face into my stomach, inhaling me. "Almighty, you're sexy."

I tighten my fingers in his hair, smiling.

He looks up at me. "Can I sleep over?"

"Yes, big guy."

While I'm still not fully comfortable with the idea of sleepovers, I'm trying. Plus, with the odd things happening on campus, I'd rather he didn't walk home alone tonight. I nod and tug his hair, tilting his head back a bit more to brush my lips over his.

"Good, because I'm still feeling boneless after you rode me into another realm."

I laugh, and Connor pulls me down onto the bed. Connor tugs me close, and I curl into his side. I wave my hand, and the covers move up and over us. The lamp switches off, leaving us in complete darkness save for the soft glow emanating from Connor's halo.

Connor yawns and buries his face in my hair. He inhales deeply, and soon his breathing evens out as he falls into a deep sleep. I kiss his chest, about to drift off myself, when my phone vibrates on the nightstand. I carefully reach over Connor to grab it and open the message.

I frown when I see the new message is from 1015. How? I blocked that account. My thumb hovers over the notification. How could they be messaging me again? I've been keeping an eye on my *Nexus* page, and they hadn't viewed my stories when I checked earlier today. It should be impossible, yet there is the message, sitting mockingly at the top of my inbox with the large blue dot in front of the username, indicating a new message. I take a deep breath and then tap on the box. The previously empty thread now has one message sitting at the bottom, and my stomach clenches as my eyes skim over the words.

@1015

You are reckless.

I worry my lower lip, reading the message over and over. Now I wish I had taken a screenshot of the last messages 1015 sent before I deleted them and blocked the account. It would be proof of them and a reminder of how threatened I felt. Similar to how I feel now. There is something so domineering about the words.

*You are reckless.*

Reckless. That is hilarious.

The last time I was reckless was with Torin, and I have never been again. I have never had the freedom to be. In order to keep myself out of Torin's hands, every single one of my moves had to be planned carefully. Yet this person has reduced me to nothing more than a careless, silly girl, diminishing me within a three-word sentence. I feel like a child being admonished by an angry parent. Not that I know what that feels like.

Three little dots appear in the corner of the thread. They're typing. My stomach knots as I watch the circles bob up and down as they type their next threat.

Yes.

I type out the message before I've considered my actions. Maybe I am becoming reckless. Perhaps this new sense of comfort is turning me careless.

I frown, reading the message. Does this person think they are being forthcoming while I'm being the difficult one? That they didn't threaten me last time we spoke?

I try to remember what they said before. It was something about watching my back. It definitely sounded like a threat.

Warnings?

Oh, I don't know. Maybe it's the fact you told me to "watch my back" and the predatory "little fae" tagged onto the end that makes me feel like I'm being stalked by an unidentified predator like I am prey.

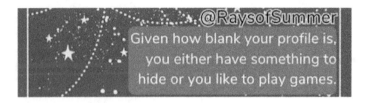

There is a pause before the three little dots appear again, and they bounce for a while before the message is sent.

I read the message once, twice, three times. The knots in my stomach seem to fray a little. When have I ever enjoyed the chase? I am so fucking tired of running, but I'd be lying if I said this stranger did not intrigue me. 1015 rouses something inside of me, something I want to oust as soon as possible.

I read the message over and over, and he continues when I don't reply. I realize that I've started to think of 1015 as male, and I'm unsure why. There is just a sureness in the tone of the messages that can only come with the arrogance of a male.

I snap when he mentions Connor.

I can practically hear the cruel smirk in his message.

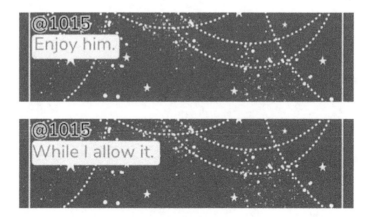

I stare at my phone. My stomach clenches with fear, but there is that flicker of something I don't want to identify.

I swallow the lump in my throat, and it feels like sandpaper as I choke it down. My hand shakes a little as I tap on the little gray blob of a profile photo and hit the large red block button.

There is no sense of relief as I do it.

Because deep down, I know this is far from over.

# 56

## SUMMER

Noesha

PUSH, LAUNCH, SHOVE

Connor's large, muscular body is warm. It's like a furnace, actually, and I wake up sweating. At some point during the night, he's shifted in the bed, and now he's resting his head on my chest, using me like a pillow. His even, peaceful breaths tease my skin, and I smile down at him. I kiss the top of his head, his blond hair ruffled in sleep.

I try to ease from beneath him, but he tightens his arms and pulls me in closer. His semi-hard cock brushes against me, and desire floods my core, eliciting a deep groan. I shift, and my gaze lands on my phone. I remember the conversation with 1015 and the threatening and dominating nature of the messages. Adrenaline floods through me, beating back the desire.

My dream is long forgotten, but my body is tight as if every muscle has been flexed all night. I know I need to go for a run this morning. I ache to chase the elusive clarity that only exercise brings me, but then I remember the many dangers vying for my attention. Perhaps today is the day to try the gym.

After much gentle coaxing, I manage to scoot myself from beneath Connor. He doesn't wake, but he grabs my pillow and buries his face into it, inhaling deeply. Some powerful, warm emotion fills me. What a mush.

I pull on hot pink shorts and a matching sports bra before shoving my feet into my white sneakers. I grab my black hoodie as I leave the dorm and pull it on when the bite of the early autumn air nips at my skin. Combat class is held on the training field or in a designated classroom, so I've never been to the gym, but I have a rough idea of where it is. I push myself into a run, headed in that general direction.

All the lights are on in the building, and I can see various equipment and weights through the glass doors. I push inside, and a wall of air-conditioned air hits me. My skin breaks out in goosebumps, and I feel my nipples tighten uncomfortably in my sports bra. I tug the zip of my hoodie up higher and walk deeper into the gym.

I look around, appreciating the clean aesthetic of the place. Exercise machines and weights are neatly organized into different zones. There are open areas for cardio, strength training, and yoga or floor exercises. At the back is a large empty room separated from the rest of the gym by a glass wall. Its floor is covered with mats, and there are multiple racks and shelves filled with various weapons. The gym is empty, except for a few trainers chatting or completing their own workouts before the gym fills up.

I look around, feeling a little overwhelmed and missing my simple run-of-the-mill outdoor daily run. This space may be beautiful, but it's not as beautiful as running through the forest or in a park. I sigh and pull my hair into a high ponytail before walking to one of the treadmills. It's the farthest one from the rest of the gym, and it has a sense of safety to it.

I climb onto the treadmill and tap the start button. The belt moves, and I start with a leisurely walk. It only takes moments before I'm bored, and I gradually increase the speed until I'm at a pace similar to my outdoor runs. It takes a little longer than usual, but my anxieties and fears do finally melt away. I'm able to relax into the solace of the burn in my lungs and the way my legs move in perfect rhythm as I settle in.

A tall, muscled male appears beside me. "You're new."

My peace disturbed, I look at him, forcing as much venom into my glare as possible. He's even bigger than I appreciated in my peripheries. His face is not conventionally handsome like Connor's, but there is an attractive, rugged charm to it. His dark hair is sheared close to his scalp, somehow making him look even more intimidating.

His lips pull into a cocky smile, and he crosses his arms across his chest, making his unreasonable biceps look even larger. I look away, but I can still feel his annoying smirk as he waits for my reply.

I continue running, my gait still even and unshakeable. "Oh, this must be the warm welcome from the resident gym rat."

He snorts and walks around to the front of the treadmill. He braces his arms on the console, making his pleasing but irritating face much harder to avoid looking at. "And that must be the response from the resident prickly female."

I smirk. "Prickly *and* poisonous, better watch yourself."

He snickers. "Lucky for you, that's my type." He winks at me. "I'm Max."

Oh, no fucking way. Is he hitting on me right now? When I'm working out and clearly have *Fuck Off* stamped across my forehead?

I roll my eyes. "Taken."

Max tilts his head. "Your name is Taken? Woah, that's different."

My lips twitch, and the ludicrousness of the conversation is weirdly comforting to me. It somehow makes me warm to him a little. "Summer," I reply, still running.

Max's smirk deepens, his eyes sparkling. "Do you fight, Taken Summer?"

I burst out laughing. "Fight? Absolutely not." I bristle as I feel Max's eyes trail over me.

"Yeah, you do seem like the *damsel in distress* type."

I slam my hand down on the stop button. "Excuse me?"

Max lifts a dark eyebrow, watching me, and there is a flicker of enjoyment in his brown eyes. He is obviously getting his kicks from my anger. "Oh, did that hit a nerve?"

I narrow my eyes at him, trying to devise the perfect scathing comeback. His eyes sparkle again, and instead, I decide on the simpler and infinitely more juvenile route of flipping him the bird. His remark sits under my skin, annoyingly scraping at my flesh. I think he said it just to get a reaction from me, but why? Maybe it's a weird asshole way of flirting. Or maybe he wants to add a fae to his roster of clients. I don't imagine that fae come here very often. They prefer to train together and in private. Fucking weirdos. So, I must be somewhat of a novelty.

Max isn't the first guy I've had to put in his place, and I know that engaging will just keep him interested. I step off the treadmill and look around at the other scary-looking machines. I am unsure what most of them do or how to work them, but I notice one resembling stairs. Making a beeline for it, I step up onto it and press the start button.

I've barely climbed a flight when Max saddles up beside me again, that same infuriating look on his face. "Switching machines? Definitely not a damsel move. If you want to prove your not-damsel status, class starts in ten minutes."

"Class?"

"Today we're working on defense," he croons, his words sounding weirdly dirty.

"Why would I join your fighting class when I have combat twice a week?" I hiss.

He takes a few steps back. His grin is so cocky it sets my teeth on edge. "Because you clearly need the extra help." His gaze flicks to the dagger sheathed on my thigh, and he shakes his head, chuckling softly under his breath. Does he know that I have no fucking idea how to use it?

I growl under my breath as he turns and swaggers away, but I can't keep from glancing at the room in the back a few times. I consider what he said and the implications of being a damsel in distress, the vulnerability I've been feeling. Slapping my hand down on the control panel, I end my workout on the stair machine. I casually walk past the room, taking a long drink from my water bottle so it doesn't seem like I'm creeping on the class.

Max is at the front of the class, demonstrating various moves. He meets my gaze and quirks his brow, silently asking if I'm going to join. My jaw sets, and I glare at him before slipping out of the hoodie and returning to the treadmill. Forty-five minutes later, the class ends, and everyone leaves the room, dripping in sweat but chattering excitedly. Max's gaze zeros in on me the moment he enters the gym, and he struts toward me.

"Checking me out?" he croons.

"Gross. Absolutely not. I was just drinking my water." I press the button to up the speed, trying to work through my frustration even though the cause of it is still standing on my left.

"Treadmill. How... damsely."

"Will you fuck off?" I growl, glaring at him.

Max moves back in front of the treadmill, leaning against it. "Why does it bother you? Being called a damsel."

"Cause it means weak. Defenseless," I reply honestly. I could have come up with a nasty retort or even some lie to shove him away, but the truth pushes its way out. Since the night I... While I've been running from Torin, I've also been running from feeling weak and vulnerable, feelings that have only intensified since I embarrassed myself while training with the Morningstars.

"Are you?"

I stop the treadmill, my breathing only a little labored. Am I defenseless? I felt weak and afraid when I was in the woods. I feel it whenever I feel that dark gaze on me. I feel it when I am not protected by Avalon.

"Let's fight," Max says, lifting his chin slightly. "You know, the stronger you are physically, the more powerful your magic is."

Does he not see me exercising right now?

"No, I don't want to fight you."

Max shrugs. "Hm. Too bad. Always wanted to train a fae."

Fucking knew it. Asshole.

I step off the treadmill and pull on my hoodie again. I walk toward the exit and am halfway across the gym when I hear Max's stupid voice. He only says one word. One stupid word, but it's the only word he could have said that would make me pause here.

"Coward."

I feel my spine lock up, but I force myself not to engage, knowing he's goading me. He is trying to push me into fighting him, a stupid manipulation to add a fucking notch to his training mitts or whatever the fuck fighters use. I take a deep breath and keep walking.

Connor is just waking up when I get to my room, and I bend, planting a sweaty kiss on his lips.

"Gym?" Connor moans softly against my lips.

BLOOD & BETRAYALS

I nod and straighten, starting to undress for the shower. "I met this complete dick-head gym guy."

Connor frowns and sits up in bed. He leans back against the headboard, the sheet pooling low on his hips. "Short buzz cut and stubble? Huge muscles?"

I nod.

"Maximillian Romulus. I hate that guy. He's a dick."

Surprised, I stop and look at him. "You do?" That someone would have such a reaction to Max is not what shocks me. What surprises me is that it's Connor who is reacting this way. I've never seen Con display anything less than mild disinterest.

"He's always acted like my existence insults him. He's a dick to all of us, even Luke."

I lift my eyebrows as I pull off my sports bra. "Luke? How can anyone be nasty to Luke? Maybe I should have taken him up on his offer," I ponder as I walk through to the shower. I hear Connor scramble out of bed.

"What offer?" Connor asks, following me.

"To fight him." I turn on the shower and push off my panties before stepping in. The warm water makes my muscles groan in ecstasy. Connor joins me, looking down at me with an intensity I am not used to from him.

"Why would he offer that?"

I shrug, tilting my head back to wet my hair. "He wants to train a fae."

"Sum, he's a berserker. If you tried to fight him... it wouldn't be pretty."

My lips twitch. "Well, I flipped him off instead."

Connor chuckles and relaxes a little. "That's my girl."

I look up at him and trail my hands up his chest. Wrapping my arms around his neck, I press my naked body to his. "No more talk of gym rats."

Connor laughs, his hands already roaming over my curves.

I pull him down and kiss him deeply. His tongue flicks mine, my belly clenching at his groan of pleasure. He cups his hand at the back of my thighs and hoists me against him, wrapping my legs around his waist. He slides his fingers through my folds, checking to see if I am ready for him. Finding me hot and slick, Connor thrusts inside of me. He buries his cock to the hilt, supporting my full weight with his arms.

"Fuck. This is my favorite workout," I moan against his lips.

Connor laughs, but it trails into a deep moan as he rolls his hips and thrusts, fucking me deeper. He takes a step, and I arch as my back finally meets the cold tile of the shower wall, but it somehow only adds to the pleasure. Connor uses the slick tiles to move me faster on him, and I tunnel my fingers into his hair, yanking hard.

"Fuck, Sum..." Connor hisses into my mouth, his cock pulsing inside me. He thrusts and circles his hips again, grinding against my clit. "I'm close. Are you close?"

I nod, biting the tip of his tongue.

I rock my hips, taking him deeper with each thrust, and I cry out as I find my

307

release. Connor's groan is guttural and primal as he follows me into pleasure, his thrusts becoming more disjointed as he pushes his release into me as deep as he can.

"We're going to be late..." I moan, kissing Connor again.

"I just want to stay here with you," he whispers.

"You're so weirdly obsessed with me," I say with a smile. "It's gross."

Connor laughs and eases me off his cock. He sets me back on my feet but keeps hold of me until I am steady enough that we can quickly finish our shower.

# 57

## SUMMER

Raesha

FIRST, FORMER,
BEFORE

Connor and I hurry through getting dressed. We do a quick search of the dorm, but it looks like Alice must have stayed at her shifter's place after her dirty little rendezvous. As we leave the building, our phones ping with a notification. Connor pulls his out and lets out a bark of surprised laughter when he reads the message.

"What?" I ask, unable to find my phone in my full bag.

"So you know how Alice mentioned chaining him to a tree in the woods when she was done with him?" Connor asks, and when I nod, he hands me his phone. The alert was a post on Nexus. It's a photo of the shifter from yesterday, naked and chained to a large tree. There is a sign stuck to his stomach, fortuitously hiding his dick. The message scrawled across the paper says, Captain of the Little Bitch Club.

"Apparently, she wasn't joking."

I sigh. "This is not even a little surprising to me."

Connor laughs, wrapping his arm around my waist and pulling me closer as we walk across the quad.

"I like getting up with you like this," he says, kissing my temple.

"Maybe next time we'll be ready in enough time to have breakfast together."

Alice is waiting at the coffee cart and has already ordered for all of us. She hands me mine first, and I take a long sip.

"Oh, hey, did you get me a muff—" Alice cuts me off by holding up a brown bag with a blueberry muffin in it. She then hands Connor his cup, and he grins at her.

"So," I begin as we walk toward the building, "you destroyed him, huh?"

Alice takes a loud sip of her coffee. "Hm? Who?" she asks, feigning ignorance.

I give her a look and then reach out to her, wiping a drop of blood from the corner of her mouth. "And you say I'm obvious."

Alice smirks, flashing her fangs. "I'm not the one having sex in the very public stacks."

I glance at Connor, looking outraged. "The stacks? What could she be talking about?"

Connor coughs, dropping his voice. "How does she know these things?"

"Because you may be the boyfriend, but I am the best friend. So I know everything."

Connor tenses, and I laugh, pressing a reassuring kiss to his shoulder.

Alice dry heaves at my small show of affection. "You two are too much."

When we arrive at the end of the corridor, I lean up on my tiptoes and kiss Connor deeply. "I'll see you at lunch?"

Connor nods but deepens the kiss.

Alice yanks at my arm, pulling me away from him and to class.

I decide to skip lunch and go to the library to study. I invite Alice to join me, but as expected, she laughs in my face at the suggestion and trots off to the canteen to terrorize Connor and his brothers unchecked by me.

The library is mostly empty, and I savor the quiet. I sit at one of the tables at the back and dig through my bag. As usual, I want to study runes but I'm already weeks ahead of my class in both my runes courses, so I pull out my realms textbook and open my notebook to a blank page. I'm about to start taking notes when words start forming on the paper, the elegant script scrawling along the faint red lines.

*Actually studying?*

I frown down at my notebook. Who is doing this? Could this be my invisible watcher finding another way to communicate with me?

I take my pen and draw a line through the message. A surge of rage fills me at the defensiveness I feel, and I score out the message over and over. When the words are nearly lost to the angry black pen marks, I tear out the page and throw it in the trash can. In the time it takes me to discard the paper, another word appears on the blank page.

*Prickly.*

I stare at the word, unsure why it seems to stick out to me. Then I remember my unfortunate encounter with Max yesterday. I slam the notebook closed and grab the crumpled piece of paper from the trash can before storming out of the library, leaving all my belongings on the table.

I barge into the gym and storm straight up to Max. He is spotting one of the infinity slam players at the weight bench.

He raises an eyebrow at me. "Look who's back."

"Where is it?" I snarl, looking around.

Max blinks, looking at me like I belong in an asylum. "Uh... Where is what?" he asks, helping to rack the bar and stepping away from the student.

"The magic pen or notebook or whatever the fuck you're using."

Max snorts. "I'm sorry?" I cross my arms over my chest and glare at him. Max shakes his head and frowns at me, putting his hands on his hips. "I'm lost. Are you going to invite me onto the crazy train?" he says, obviously wildly confused about what I'm talking about.

"You didn't..." I hold out the piece of paper. If Max has been in here training, it couldn't have been him sending me messages. Even if he is the best liar in all the realms, I'm not sure he could have pulled off looking that confused as quickly as he did.

I growl in frustration and turn on my heel, stalking toward the door. Max catches up easily and grabs my arm. I turn to face him, but my gaze locks on the hand he has gripping my arm.

"You seem tense," he says. "Want to fight? It'll help with... whatever it is you're going through. Plus, you'll get to punch me."

I roll my eyes and yank my arm free. I storm from the gym and head straight back to the library, muttering curses under my breath. People scatter before me, but I barely notice. My anger simmers, and I welcome it, thankful it is rage and not fear fueling me. Sinking into my chair, I open the notebook. The word is still there, taunting me.

*Prickly.*

I grab my pen and reply to the message, so tired of all this.

*Who are you?*

I write.

The words sit uselessly on the page, and I'm about to rip the paper from the pad when a reply appears on the line beneath my message.

*A stranger.*

It is simple and direct, yet it doesn't answer my question in the least.

*What do you want?*

I try to keep my script legible even though my hands shake.

*Nothing.*

The elegant handwriting continues along the page.

*For now.*

My stomach knots at the addition, and I look around the library. I'm not sure what I think I'm going to find. I look down at the paper, the words humming threateningly against the page.

*But later?*

*Yes, little fae. Later.*

I swallow, my breaths coming out shallow and labored. 1015 calls me little fae. Could this be the same person? Or is this just a massive coincidence? Another person who sees me as weak. Is this fear I'm feeling? Yes, but it feels different.

*Are you watching me?*

The pen glides across the paper, and I look down at what I wrote. I quietly curse myself for asking the question. My hair is standing up on the back of my neck, and I can feel eyes on me from every direction.

*Yes.*

The answer comes after a single beat, a fraction longer than it took last time. Was there a note of hesitation? My head snaps up, and I look around, still finding nothing out of the ordinary. But there is still that feeling of nails raking down my spine.

*You won't find me, little fae. But don't worry. I'm not a threat.*

The words appear beneath his latest message, and they're almost comical. Nothing about this situation feels non-threatening.

My heart thunders in my chest as I press the tip of the pen to the crisp white paper.

*Are you a liar?*

It is a useless question. What liar admits to lying?

*Not to you.*

And for some weird, sick, twisted reason, I believe the words I'm reading.

*Tell me who you are.*

*A stranger.*

*That isn't an answer.*

*It is the only one I can give you.*

I feel a wave of rage, and I turn the page, the paper tearing a little. I open my textbook to a chapter on the realm of Gytera and begin taking copious notes, trying to distract myself. My pen stutters on the page as a new message forms on the next line, stopping me from continuing.

*You're getting very used to getting your way.*

I growl and angrily score out the message so hard that the paper tears under my pen.

*Brat.*

The word shocks me into pausing, and I grip the pen so tight it creaks in my hand. Constantly needing to get your own way.

I slam the notebook shut and lunge to my feet, shoving the textbook into my bag. I draw a rune on the cover and throw the notebook into the trash can on my way out of the library. It immediately bursts into flames, a contained inferno that reduces the notebook to ash and cinders. By the time I've calmed down enough to notice that the sun is setting, I'm almost home. Irritation ignites in me again. My rage with a faceless weirdo has kept me away from both studying and enjoying this beautiful evening.

Alice is lounging on the couch, cradling a bottle of red wine. She has her legs tucked up, leaving just enough room for me to collapse next to her on the couch. Alice holds the bottle out to me, not saying anything, not even moving her gaze from the television. Sighing, I take it and gulp down a few deep mouthfuls, grimacing at the bitter taste.

"You know, for vampire royalty, you have shit taste in wine."

Alice finally drags her gaze away from the television to look at me. "It's not my fault your palate is as refined as a haystack."

I flip her off, but my lips twitch. I take another deep drink, settling into the burn of the alcohol as it travels down my throat and sits comfortably in my stomach.

"Connor came round," Alice says, having turned her attention back to the television.

"Oh?" I pull my phone from my bag and start scrolling through my messages.

"I told him we need a girls night."

I nod, tapping on the messages from Con.

CONNOR

Home safe, babe?

I smile at the message and the care woven into those three words.

SUMMER

Just got home.

The three impatient dots immediately appear. He was obviously worried about me and waiting for my reply. He sent that first message around thirty minutes ago. No doubt if I'd delayed replying any longer, he'd have enlisted his brothers and become the most chaotic of search parties.

CONNOR

I miss you.

SUMMER

Miss you too, big guy.

"Right, enough of bird brain!" Alice exclaims as she jumps up and walks to the kitchen. She grabs six shot glasses and pours tequila into all of them.

"Girls night! Just you, me, and a bottle of tequila."

Alice lifts a shot glass, waving it a little, beckoning me over. I'm impressed that she doesn't spill a drop, even though the glass is filled to the brim with the golden liquid.

I push off the couch and take the glass from her, slamming the shot. The burn from the tequila is more pleasant than that of the heinous wine, deeper and darker. I slam another shot before I notice Alice watching me, guilt etched on her face. I freeze, my eyes narrowing on her. It's the kind of look that tells me I'll either be trying to get her out of something or exacting revenge on someone.

"What?" I ask her, knowing that she's avoiding telling me. It's funny how much Alice and I know each other. It's like we have a lifetime of knowledge about one another, even though we've known each other for mere months.

"I, uh..." She smiles sheepishly, but there is a gleam in her eyes. Whatever she's done, she's proud of herself. "I might have stolen some of those funky mushrooms from the forest greenhouse."

Well, this is a bad fucking idea, but I am going through so much at the moment. Someone was murdered on campus, someone who looks enough like me to be suspicious. Along with that, I am being hunted by a psycho male, potentially a murderer, and who the fuck knows what's going on with the magic notebook and the invisible man? My life feels more chaotic and dramatic than Alice's show. Escaping all of this for a short time is so very tempting. I know it won't change anything, but I am so tired of feeling scared and weak, and we're in the safety of our own dorm. I purse my lips and hold my hand out.

"Fuck it."

Alice smirks as she drops one into my hand. Fuck, this looks like the least appetizing thing I've ever seen. It's murky brown, and there's a weird, sickly sheen to its wrinkled surface.

Alice pops hers into her mouth and chews thoughtfully. "Hm, not as bad as it looks. It's just very earthy."

I take a deep breath and count to three before placing the mushroom on my tongue. Grimacing, I hold my breath and start to chew the monstrosity. I guess the taste isn't too bad, but the texture is truly disgusting.

Alice holds up another full shot glass. "Wash it down with this." I take the shot, the tequila burning away the taste of the weird little mushroom. Alice flops down on the couch, pouting a little. "I don't feel anything. Must have been a bad batch."

I grab the tequila bottle and two shot glasses before curling up on the couch next to her. I pour us another two shots and hand one to her. Alice and I clink our glasses and down the drink. Four shots later, I blink and look around the room.

"Al?" I slowly turn my head to look at her. She's rocking slightly and staring down at her hands with wide eyes. The room spins, and I shake my head, trying to clear the sensation, but that just makes it spin faster. The colors start to play with each other right in front of my eyes, doing unspeakable things with each other and birthing new colors.

"Hmm?" Alice finally replies, shifting her bleary, unfocused eyes to me. I tilt my head as I look at them. Her pupils seem to be changing shape. First, they're oval, then square, then heart-shaped, then they start to look like lightning bolts. I burst out laughing, fumbling for my phone. I need to close one of my eyes to keep the phone from moving too much to operate. It takes me a few tries, but I finally get it unlocked and manage to get onto the music app. I choose the first suggestion, which is some rock song, and the music blasts out of the speakers we installed throughout the dorm.

"Fuck, yes! I love this song!" Alice shouts and jumps to her feet. She loses her balance and collapses onto the floor, bursting out laughing.

I get up to help her but immediately forget what I am supposed to be doing, distracted as the song gets to the bridge, which I love. I climb onto the table and start dancing.

"Yes, Sum! Work it!" Alice squeals. Still on the floor, she lifts her hands and starts making motions like she would if she were showering a dancer with paper credits.

I drop low on the table, wobbling slightly thanks to the swaying and spinning of the room.

"Damn! Should have been a stripper. Do it again for the fans." Alice pulls out her phone, and I drop low again. It all seems hilarious, and I laugh hard as I dance. Alice cackles as she finally manages to get off the floor. I offer her my hand and successfully pull her onto the table on the second try. We sway together, and the next time I drop, I grab the tequila and take a deep drink. I pass the bottle to Alice, and she guzzles it like water.

"Momma didn't raise no bitch." She stills, swaying on the spot. "Well, actually, she didn't raise me at all."

I watch her, sobering up only a fraction at the expression of pain on her face. It takes me a couple of attempts, but I finally grip her arm and squeeze. She looks at me, trying to focus on me. "I never had one."

Alice shrugs, the pain melting from her expression. "It's not like I remember her. And my dad went from secretly hoping I died to plotting my murder."

"I never had one of those either," I say, nudging her and grabbing my phone. "We don't need any of them, Al. Just each other."

"Damn right, wifey."

I nod and start taking selfies of us on my phone, posting some of them immediately.

After hours of laughing, dancing, and drinking, Alice passes out on the couch. I listen to her snore and stare toward the window, my mind comfortably fuzzy. The silver moonlight streaming into the room beckons to me, promising the peace of the night. I push off the couch, stumbling a little as I pull on my boots and leave the dorm. Just because I wasn't able to enjoy my walk earlier because of some stalker asshole doesn't mean I can't enjoy it now.

The alcohol warms my blood, but my skin still reacts to the nip of the cool night air. The campus is so peaceful at this time of night. Everything is peaceful, calm, and safe. Is it safe? There is still a killer out there, and they are more than likely after me.

But thanks to the liquid courage I've been drowning myself in all evening, I can't bring myself to care right now.

The night is so still that it surprises me when a soft breeze brushes against my hand. I stumble and look down at my hand, confused. The whisper of air caresses up my arm, and the higher it trails, the more it feels like an actual touch. I gasp as it becomes firmer and stumble again. The breeze catches me, stopping me from falling. I look up and can finally see him again, shadows curling at his edges. He takes my hand and places it on his chest. I feel the steady heartbeat, the one I'm growing familiar with. He lifts my other hand, brushing my fingers against something prickly and along what feels like a very chiseled jaw.

"So you are a man," I whisper, mostly to myself.

His chest shakes a little with a laugh, and I can feel him nod.

"Who are you?" I whisper again.

He turns his head. I feel the stubble brush over my fingers and then the gentle press of something soft and pillowy against my palm. A kiss?

"Are you scared?" The sound makes me gasp, and I swallow hard. His voice is soft, almost inaudible, yet it brushes past my ear like a caress. It doesn't make any sense because I can still feel his lips pressed against my palm.

"Yes," I reply honestly. The fear is creeping back in as the alcohol burns off.

"Why?" He turns his head again, and though I can't see his facial features, I can feel his gaze on me. "I'm not going to hurt you."

I tilt my head, watching him, and it all comes together. "Have you been communicating with me?" I pause. "In other ways?"

I feel his nod.

My stomach drops. "My notebook?"

Another nod.

My heart starts to race. "My DMs?"

There is a thoughtful pause and then another nod.

I stumble again, proving I am still nowhere near sober because I am standing still. He catches me again, this time his hand gripping my waist. My breaths are shallow, yet my chest is heaving. Fear holds me hostage in this space, and I stare up at the projection in front of me.

Is this it? Is this the moment I die?

I feel his other hand moving, and I wait for the pain to come. Run, Summer, do fucking anything. But I'm frozen in place. Defenseless. A damsel. Fuck. I close my eyes, ready to accept my fate, but no pain comes. Instead, he gently brushes a lock of hair behind my ear and then cups my cheek. My eyes snap open, and I lurch away from him.

"This is... I... I have a boyfriend." I shake my head and turn, walking away from him. This is all too confusing, and I don't know what to think or believe. My instincts have been useless where this *stranger* is concerned.

"Go home, little fae." His voice is louder this time and right at my ear. It is commanding, arrogant, and laced with irritation.

His command makes me bristle, but I keep walking in the other direction. A gentle breeze pushes at me, redirecting me back toward my dorm. My jaw clenches, and I push back, walking the way I want to, trying to hold on to a scrap of my dignity and decision-making. I know I'm headed in a random direction, but if he's not going to kill me, he's also not going to tell me what to fucking do.

"Where are you going?" His voice is angrier now.

"Away from you," I snarl back.

"Your dorm *is* away from me."

I whirl on him. The outline of his form is still in the same place, watching me. "You are not the boss of me, *Stranger*."

In the blink of an eye, his form is right in front of me, and then I am hoisted over his shoulder.

"Put. Me. Down," I snarl, struggling against his hold.

"Brat," he growls, his voice even clearer now. He carries me easily, despite my wiggling and complaining, and it is just moments before we're back at Kelpie Hall. He opens the dorm without a key or a pass and puts me down before slamming the door, leaving him on the other side of it. I try the handle, but I know it's useless. A second later, a bright glow shines from beneath the door, and I know he's sealed it shut with a rune. I feel the power of it pulse softly. Bastard.

I climb the stairs louder than necessary, still furious. Alice is still sound asleep on the couch, a blanket thrown over her. I go to my room and collapse into my bed. I'm about to drift off when my phone lights up with a message. Against my better judgment, I check it.

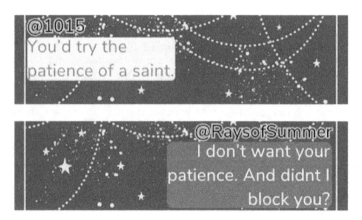

@1015
You'd try the patience of a saint.

@RaysofSummer
I don't want your patience. And didnt I block you?

I growl. If blocking him doesn't work, surely there's something I can do? Perhaps I should ask one of the tech guys tomorrow.

I block him again. I know it is useless, but there's something enjoyable about knowing it'll piss him off. My phone alerts again, and I smile when I see Connor's name pop up instead of that weirdo stalker.

CONNOR

I miss you. Also, your ass is on Nexus.

I frown at the message, confused by it, but pass out before I can investigate further.

# 58

## SUMMER

Ruesho
RUNE

My head throbs, and the light burns despite my eyes still being closed. Blindly, I reach out, and even that slight movement makes me want to hurl. I grab one of my pillows and cover my face, nearly weeping at the sweet darkness it brings.

Alice groans from the living room. "Fuckkkkkkkkk. Not to alarm you, Summer, but I think I might be dead."

"Aren't you already dead?" My words are heavily muffled by the pillow, but Alice hears them clearly.

"Okay, re-dead."

My stomach rolls suddenly. I bolt from the bed and run to the toilet, just barely making it before I hurl the entire contents of my stomach up. After vomiting another three times, I feel well enough to crawl into the shower and turn it on. The hot water hurts as it taps against my already banging head, but the warmth is also comforting. Slowly, I remove my clothes and throw them out onto the stone floor, where they land with a wet thud. My whole body trembles from the hangover, but I feel slightly more alive once I get clean.

Stepping out of the shower, I wrap a towel around myself and manage to brush my teeth without throwing up before going in search of water or coffee. Alice is lying on the cool kitchen floor, and I nearly trip over her. It looks like she made it that far but then couldn't stand up.

"Kill me? If you love me, you'll have mercy and kill me."

I grab a bottle of water and take a sip, bending to rest my forehead against the cool counter. "Those mushrooms were lethal. Tequila would never do this to me."

Alice nods. There is a loud knock at the door, the sound piercing my brain like a hot poker.

"Whoever that is will be dead soon," Alice growls.

I drag myself to the door and open it, nearly weeping when I see Connor holding a tray of coffee.

"Hey, babe, figured you'd need this."

I groan, taking one of the cups and burying my face against his chest.

Connor wraps his arms around me, and the hug calms the hangover shakes. He lifts me and sits on the couch, cradling me on his lap. I sip my coffee and moan in pleasure. It tastes like the nectar of the gods.

Alice crawls over pathetically and takes one of the cups.

Connor presses a sweet kiss to my head. "Is there any alcohol left in the realm, or did you two drink it all?"

I nuzzle into his neck, needing more cuddles and kisses, more affection. If I were myself, my neediness would make me feel ill, but I can't help it right now. Fuck it. It feels good to need someone and to know I'm not setting myself up for disappointment.

Connor, understanding the assignment, tightens his arms around me and kisses the top of my head again, giving me what I need.

It takes until I'm mostly done with my coffee before I start to feel better.

"My poor girl." Connor smiles into my hair. He's clearly loving this, and at the moment, I can't even muster the energy to give him a hard time for it.

"At least we were just in the house. So no *hangover fear*."

"Hmm," Connor says, and I pull back, looking at his face.

"I was at home, so I didn't publicly embarrass myself. Right?"

Connor laughs softly. "No, Alice did it for you."

Alice props herself up, looking at us. "Huh?"

Connor pulls his phone out and loads up Alice's *Nexus* story. There, the first fucking story, is me dancing on the table. What's that at the end? Oh, that's my bare ass, barely covered by my thong.

I grab his phone, replaying it. "Fuck."

Alice grimaces from the floor, watching it on her own phone. She takes a sip of her coffee, and I can't help but wonder how she is doing that while lying down.

"What are the chances no one has seen it yet?"

"Uh, extremely low." Alice grimaces again and turns her phone to show that the video has thousands of reactions and comments.

I nod. "Well. The whole school has seen my bare ass then, I guess," I say matter-of-factly. What am I going to do now? Run around trying to pull the memory from everyone at school?

"It's a hot ass," Connor says, and I bury my face in his neck. Connor laughs. "Babe, it's fine. Everyone will forget about it when the next drama happens. Probably next time Alice gets into a fight. So sometime today."

Alice flips him off.

I just nuzzle into Connor again, inhaling his cloud scent.

"I like it when you are all cuddly," he says, and I can hear the easy smile in his voice.

I press a soft kiss to his neck.

"So I take it you're both cutting today?"

I shake my head. "I'm going in."

Alice lays back down and lifts one of her arms, her hand the only thing visible. She shoots a finger gun at Connor and says, "I'm staying home and dying."

Reluctantly, I slip from Connor's lap and pad into my room. I change into my uniform and grab my phone from the charging pad. Checking my alerts, I see an email from the headmaster. With a frown, I open it.

To: s.tuathadedaanan@avalon.edu
From: j.emrys@avalon.edu

*Ms. Tuatha De Daanan,*
*I wish to discuss a matter with you. Please come to my office prior to your first class.*
*Headmaster Emrys*

With a sigh, I lock my phone before pulling on my uniform and accessorizing with a large pair of black sunglasses to shield my eyes from the devilish sun. Connor wanders into my room and laughs when he sees me. "You look adorable."

Grumbling a thank you, I continue to plait my hair into two French braids, making sure they aren't too tight but will keep my hair out of my face. Connor comes up behind me and wraps his arms around my waist. "I know. I'm the worst."

I turn in his arms and wrap my arms around his neck. I gaze up at him and ask for something I have never asked for before. It's something I never in my life thought I would ask for. I tunnel my fingers into his hair and say, "Tell me you love me." There is something about this moment. Something about the vulnerability I feel that makes me need to hear the words from him. Connor and Alice are the only people I ever need to hear it from.

Connor smiles, something like pride shining in his eyes. It's not because he's feeling arrogant that he's tamed the beast that is me, but because he knows I genuinely need to hear it. Somehow, he knows I *believe* him when he says it. "I love you." The words are so sweet and sincere that I can't help but brush my lips over his. At this moment, it finally clicks. Connor is my peace. When I asked the Almighty if I would ever find peace, she told me I would, and here it is right in front of me.

Connor pulls back after a moment and turns, crouching to offer me his back.

I pat his shoulder as I walk past him. "Not today, big guy. Motion sickness."

Connor laughs and catches up to me, sliding his hand into mine.

Connor walks with me all the way to the door of my first class. I've not told him about my meeting with the headmaster because I know he'll ask about it, and I don't want to lie to him. I'm pretty sure it's about the murders, and I'm still committed to Connor not knowing anything more about it, not until I know more. He's only just lost that haunted look.

Connor kisses me and then heads to his own class. When he turns the corner, I hurry to the headmaster's office. I stand and stare at the door for a long moment before knocking, the same nervous energy filling me. I always feel like a kid about to get a telling-off when I'm preparing to speak to the headmaster.

"Enter," he calls, his deep voice rumbling through the door.

I step into his office, and he looks up at me over his glasses, the scent of allspice and oak surrounding me. I'm not sure I've ever seen him wear glasses before. Somehow, it makes him look even more intelligent and maybe a little more approachable.

"Miss Tuatha De Daanan, thank you for taking the time to see me."

I nod, stepping further into his office. I look away. "How can I—"

He tsks. "What did I say last time, Miss Tuatha De Daanan? About when you speak to me?"

I clear my throat and lift my eyes to meet his silver ones.

"I have something to give you," he says. He waves his hand, and a heavy-looking book lands on his desk.

Intrigued, I move closer. "It looks like a grimoire," I whisper, mostly to myself. The cover is intricate, well-loved, and perfectly worn, yet still ornate. From this close, you can tell it's a powerful book, but it wards off inquisitive eyes from a distance. I'd read a little about them, but they're not something there is much literature on.

"That's because it is. It is my personal grimoire."

I try not to gape in surprise. Usually, sorcerers don't even admit to having grimoires. They are that precious. That he is planning to lend this to me—

"You are wondering why I am letting you borrow it," he says. It's not a question. It's as if he's plucked my thoughts straight from my mind. I nod in confirmation.

"Please, sit."

I hesitate before sitting on the very edge of one of the two chairs opposite him. He removes his glasses, placing them on top of the book he was reviewing.

"Grimoires are a source of information, but they are also a source of power. Now, I'm guessing from the look on your face when I told you that the grimoire belongs to me, that you understand their importance to my kind."

I nod.

"This was my very first grimoire. It has notes about Nimue, things I jotted down from the information I was able to extract from my father and other fae that he knew. It's not much, but the mark is mentioned. Maybe you can make more sense of it than I can." He lays his hand over the book. "It is also full of runes, runic circles, and dangerous magic. It is not something to be handed off without thought." His eyes lock on mine. "I sense whatever dared to breach my school and harm my student is far from done. You'll need to prepare yourself, Miss Tuatha De Daanan. I am not a being that one crosses unless the goal is worth the cost. You must be worth a cost that even the devil hesitates to pay."

He sits back in his chair and puts his glasses back on, returning his attention to the book he was reading when I came in. Not only had he just given me a wealth of knowledge beyond imagining, but he is potentially the most powerful sorcerer in existence. That was widely suspected, but now I had confirmation. The information contained within the grimoire is not simply what is written in the pages, but the words are imbued with his power, ready to be unlocked.

Carefully, I stand up and pick up the tome. My hands tremble, reacting to the power radiating from the book. It feels odd to stow it in my bag, but I know I can't just carry it around for all to see, so I carefully tuck it in amongst my other books.

I glance at the headmaster, who is deep in concentration, and see myself out.

# 59

## SUMMER

Soltha
WEST

I am still dealing with the effects of my hangover when I get to lunch, though it's slightly improved. The rune I would usually use isn't effective when there are other substances in the system. Because I don't know much about the mushroom I had, I'm unable to form a rune to counteract it. I sit down next to Connor and lay my head on his shoulder.

"Hi, babe. How are you feeling?" Connor asks, wrapping an arm around my back and pulling me closer to him. Gods, I'm so disgustingly needy today.

"Shit," I reply, grumbling as I close my eyes behind my sunglasses.

"How's your head?" Connor asks, kissing my forehead.

"Sore."

Connor's lips twitch, and he nuzzles against the top of my head. The cafeteria is loud as usual, but the noise pierces my skull today.

"Have you eaten yet?"

I grimace, even the idea of food turning my stomach, and I shake my head.

Connor holds his sandwich to my lips, and I groan, trying to move away from the smell of the bread. Why is he always trying to feed me fucking sandwiches?

"Just a little bite, babe. You need to eat."

"Con, you've offered me a sandwich twice in the time you've known me. It didn't end well the first time, and unless you want me to vomit on you, it will not end well this time."

"You and that first sandwich," Connor says with a laugh.

Pulling back, I push my sunglasses to the top of my head so he can see the look I'm giving him. I immediately regret it when the light tries to boil my eyes, but I push through the pain and turn to Zach. "Zach, you're making out with a girl, right? Like really making out. She's on the counter with her legs wrapped around you."

Zach blinks and then nods. "Woah. Okay."

"Do you A. Keep making out with the hot girl who is DTF or B. Stop making out with her and offer her a PB&J?"

"She's extremely trashed, FYI," Connor adds, squeezing me tight, humor filling his voice.

"Mildly tipsy."

Zach looks between us.

"You were way more than tipsy," Connor scoffs.

"I was not." I look back at Zach. "Well?"

Zach looks between us and shrugs. "I wouldn't sleep with her, even if she was only slightly tipsy."

I put my sunglasses back over my eyes and cross my arms over my chest. "Fucking angels."

Luke chuckles from the other side of the table. "Would you make her a sandwich, though, Zach?"

"Nice ass, Summer," a shifter purrs as he walks past the table. I cover my face, sinking into Connor. Not only do I feel like death warmed up, but the whole fucking school has seen my bare ass.

"It is nice," Connor replies, sliding his hand down my back and squeezing my ass. "And all mine."

Connor's reply gives me a boost, and I growl, "And unless you want my foot firmly lodged up yours, you'll keep walking."

The shifter grumbles and walks away. Luke nudges Zach to prompt an answer. I glance at Zach, but he is no longer paying attention. I follow his gaze and see Ashley giggling and chatting to one of the senior sorcerers. His lips are pulled into a devilish, charming smile, and her cheeks are tinted blush pink.

Zach's expression darkens, and he looks away. "Whatever, I shouldn't be put in between foster Mom and Dad."

My head throbs again, and I rest it back against Connor's shoulder. "Zach, if you were my foster kid, I'd return you."

Zach's expression changes from fury to one of reproach. "Rude. Why?"

"You take this one, big guy," I say, nudging Connor.

Connor chuckles and shrugs. "I've always wanted to return him."

I nod. "Okay, it's settled. We're only keeping Rafe and Luke. Z squared can go to Alice. She's always wanted a pet."

Zane's brows furrow, obviously deep in thought. "I think I'd probably make myself a sandwich."

We all turn our attention to Zane and burst out laughing.

I gulp the rest of my coffee. "Okay, I'm going to the gym to try to work off the rest of this hangover."

Connor lifts an eyebrow. "On an empty stomach?"

I roll my eyes and take a bite of his sandwich. My stomach protests, but I feel confident I'll be able to keep it down. At least until I get to the gym, and I can hurl it up over that dick trainer. That thought makes me smile.

"I'll come round later?"

Connor nods. "Please."

I lean in and kiss him deeply. Connor slides his fingers into my hair, and his brothers groan at our public display.

I bite his lip. "Later, big guy. It's been too long."

"It's Mom and Dad 2.0," Luke groans, and my lips twitch.

"Look who's back." Max zeroes in on me the second I step into the gym. He is spotting someone in the weights section again, but his stupid voice carries through the busy space.

I ignore him and keep walking, going to the locker room to change into my shorts and sports bra. Unfortunately, Max is waiting for me when I come out, an eyebrow raised as if in question. I walk right past him, happy that the treadmill I used last time is free.

"Still not wanting to fight?" he asks, falling into step next to me.

I sigh and step onto the treadmill. I try to push away the feeling of defencelessness from last night. My memories are hazy, but I remember the feeling of the adrenaline coursing through me. I remember the hopeless feeling. I remember accepting that I was going to die. Should I learn to fight? Probably. But should Max the Ass be the one to teach me? Fuck no.

I turn on the treadmill, and the second it starts, I can feel the effects of last night in how my limbs are sluggish and my head pounds. Even my lungs feel bruised.

"You should join the class. I'll go easy on you since I heard you had a wild night." Max smirks, leaning against the treadmill next to me.

I glare and increase the speed. "Gods. Do you harass everyone who enters the gym or just me?"

Max snickers. "Just you. Feel special?"

I flip him off, pushing myself harder, and fuck, this is kicking my ass. Max laughs again and struts away to start his class. Listening to my body, I slam my hand down on the stop button and head to the mats for some easy stretches. I sit down and glance into the sparring room, watching for a few moments as Max demonstrates a few defensive movements. Max meets my gaze, his arrogance making my blood boil. I flip him off and start my stretches.

Trying to find my center, I take deep breaths and stretch out my aching limbs. My peace is disrupted when booming music blasts from the sparring room, and my head throbs in pain. I straighten and look through the window. Fucking Max is smirking at me. He knows exactly what he's doing. Fucking asshole.

I stand up and grab my bag and water bottle. On my way out, I spot the electric box. A wicked smile curves my lips as I slice my finger with my rune dagger and start to draw on my palm. The dark red blood is stark against my skin until the rune takes shape. As I near the end, it becomes iridescent and glows faintly. I press my runed palm to the door of the electric box. There is a loud pop, and then the power cuts. The music stops, and the gym is plunged into blissful darkness. There are yelps of surprise and then grumbles of annoyance as everyone's workouts are interrupted. I glance over my shoulder at Max, who glares at me with narrowed eyes. I wink at him and smile sweetly before walking out the door.

# 60

## SUMMER

Multha
DEAD

"So, that's four cheeseburgers, four hamburgers, three triples, eight doubles, and sixteen fries?" the server recites back to me.

I confirm I got everything on the list Connor texted me when I told him I'd bring in dinner. "Oh, and five chocolate shakes."

The server nods and hurries away with the order.

Alice snorts beside me. "Fuck, how does their mother manage?"

"Farrah is a saint, I swear. She cooked all of their favorites when they were home and made a selection of Rafe's favorites for Connor to bring back to him."

Alice whistles, half distracted by texting. I pull out my phone while we wait and scroll through the Nexus app. I click through my stories, checking to see if they've been viewed by 1015. Of course, they have, and I click on his profile. It's the same bare bones of a profile, with no posts and no information. Just that username that I have been dreading seeing.

My phone vibrates.

I look around, trying to find him, but everyone is on their fucking phone in this place.

I glare at my phone. He has a point. The stories are out there for public consumption, but surely, that point is negated by the fact that he refuses to stay blocked. Somehow.

They call my name, and I shove my phone into my pocket, nudging Alice to pull her from the social media hole.

"Come on, let's go feed our men."

The Morningstar's ability to eat is borderline impressive, and an hour later, the only things left from dinner are the cartons. Connor nuzzles into my neck, and I smile, curling into him.

"Stay with me tonight?"

I run my fingers through his hair. "I can't. Alice is here too, remember?"

I feel Connor pout against my neck.

"And I somehow don't think she'll want to top and tail with Zane."

Connor laughs, pulling back. "She'd kill him."

Alice saunters in from the kitchen, where she'd been playing cards with the guys. "If you want to sleep over, I can stay in Zach's room. He snuck out an hour ago."

"He did?" I ask, sitting up.

Connor pulls out his phone. "Oh, Ashley seems to be on a date."

I grab his phone, and Alice moves so quickly she seems to just appear beside me. She presses against my side as I enlarge the photo on *Nexus*.

"That's the sorcerer from earlier. They looked really flirty," I say, tipping the phone so she can see it better.

I look at Connor. "You know him?"

Con nods. "He's in one of my classes. He's a senior. One of Emrys's apprentices. He's constantly trying to get the doom master to notice him."

"Huh." I ponder, looking through his posts.

"I mean, he's hot in that arrogant, *I'm better than you* kind of way," Alice says, looking over my shoulder. "He and Ashley would look good together."

I close out of the app, and my heart squeezes when I see Connor set his phone background as a photo of us. Not only because it's a really cheesy photo where I'm kissing him, but also because it's blurry. It was obviously taken by someone who'd had a little too much to drink. Connor blushes a little, and I hand him his phone, brushing my lips over his.

"Oh! Ashley just posted!" Alice shows me her phone and a photo of Ashley with the sorcerer is on the screen. "Gods, she is so transparent. That photo looks fake as fuck."

"You think Zach's not wanting to commit, or do you think it's her?" I look at Connor. "Is Zach a commitment-phobe?"

Connor frowns. "I don't think so, but now that you mention it, he is kind of a serial dater."

"I have an idea!" Alice exclaims, crawling over me and wiggling in between Connor and me. She laughs maniacally and then shows us her phone after she's posted. It is a photo of her and Zach, obviously very edited, with the caption,

*@KillerLegosi.* *Just Me and MY guy.*

No sooner has she posted it than she receives a DM from Ashley.

I shift closer to Alice, and Connor pouts at the distance Alice put between us. "Is she joking? The photo looks so fake!"
Alice laughs. "She's unraveling."

I chuckle and nudge her. "She's got it bad. Look at all of those exclamation marks."

Alice gets another DM. This one is from Zach.

I grab Alice's phone and type out a message for her.

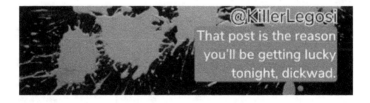

@KillerLegosi
I'd suggest approaching you
dirty little secret within the
next few minutes and dont
fuck it up.

"We'll see how happy he is when he gets home." Connor laughs, pulling me back against his side.

"He'll be staying at Ashley's. Now that we have sorted the sleeping arrangements, I think it's time for bed, big guy. What do you think?"

Connor's eyes darken and he springs up, grabbing my hand and pulling me up the stairs.

"Night then," Alice calls after us, laughter in her voice.

I lay awake in Connor's bed, staring up at the ceiling. He fell asleep a little over an hour ago, and he is snoring softly. I grab my phone and open *Nexus*. Doom scrolling through socials isn't quite as relaxing as it used to be before my stalker. A wave of anger washes over me when I notice I have an unread message from 1015.

@1015
You need to be brought
to heel. Too used to
getting your own way.

I narrow my eyes at the message, at the suggestion in it. He's crossing boundaries, and I'm going to nip it in the bud.

@RaysofSummer
You know I have a
boyfriend, right? That I'm
in a committed
relationship.

The reply comes almost instantly. He was obviously watching for my message.

I stare at my phone, reading the message over and over.

Tame? Something about the word sparks a heat low in my stomach, and I block him again before I reply with something stupid. There is no doubt he is powerful and dangerous. I don't need to truly anger him.

Moments later, another message comes through.

**@1015**
What's the matter, little fae?
Did that make you think
about me turning that brat
ass of yours red?

**@RaysofSummer**
The thought of your
hands on me turns my
stomach. Leave me alone.
You don't know me.

**@1015**
Oh? So you don't want to be
strapped down and controlled?
Taken to the edge over and over
until you cry with frustration?

**@RaysofSummer**
Leave me the fuck alone.

**@1015**
Let me make something clear,
little fae. You are with someone
else because I am allowing it.
But my benevolence will only go
so far.

I throw my phone aside, my breathing shallow. The fear is paralyzing me, but there is something else, too. Something deep and that I don't dare name.

Could that be... something I want? Something I crave? Is that what's missing? Is that why I'm... wrong?

# 61

## SUMMER

Taethu
AVOID,
CIRCUMVENT

The sun is still deep in slumber when I finally decide to stop trying to sleep. My brain is too active, and my body feels too restless. I climb out of bed and quietly creep out of the Morningstar House. The cool early morning air nips at my skin, and I pull the zip of my cropped hoodie up a little. As I push into a run, my frustration bubbles up, and I replay the conversation with the stranger. How I should have replied differently, how I need to find a way to keep him away permanently. By the time I get to the gym, I'm in a foul mood, which turns even more sour when Max's stupid face is the first thing I see when I step into the establishment.

He smirks when he sees me. "I thought you'd have given up by now."

"Leave me be, berserker." I walk straight past him to the punching bag. The first hit sends a shock wave of pain along my forearm, but I do it again. The bag bobs a little from the force, but not enough that I feel like I've gotten a good hit. I try to punch it harder, but my strikes seem weak and ineffective.

Max walks over and stands behind the bag, holding it steady. "Come on, let's fight," he wheedles.

"Fuck off," I growl, swinging my leg around to kick the bag. Max grabs my ankle in midair, my foot never meeting the bag.

"Come on, this is embarrassing."

I snarl and hop in place, trying to free myself while also trying not to fall on my ass.

"I promise I'll go easy on you," Max says, finally releasing my ankle. I stumble a little but manage to stay on my feet.

I narrow my eyes at him. "Then you'll leave me alone?"

He shrugs, that maddening smile tugging on his lips.

I turn on my heel, storming into the sparring room. "Hurry up."

Max chuckles and follows me in, grabbing a set of boxing gloves from the wall and chucking them at me. I catch them easily and pull them on, wanting to get this over with.

Max grabs another set of gloves off a shelf with his name on it. They're more worn than the others, obviously well-loved and used. He puts them on the bench at the back of the room before walking over to me, rolling his shoulders.

"Give me your best hit," he says.

His cockiness makes me grind my teeth, and without hesitating, I slam my gloved fist into his chest. Max doesn't move. In fact, the only reaction from him is his chest shaking with laughter.

"You can't be serious," he says mockingly.

I growl and hit him again, putting more weight into it.

He just continues to chuckle. "Aren't fae supposed to be strong?"

I recoil, his words slicing into me. This is why I didn't want to do this. I turn away from him and throw the boxing gloves on the floor before grabbing my stuff and leaving the room. My whole body feels wrong. His question was meant to strike a nerve, to spur me on, but it hit the wrong pressure point. He wanted to incite anger and fire. Instead, he touched on something vulnerable and raw. It is so deeply buried that I didn't even know it was there.

"Coward!" I hear him call out to me, but I just keep walking. My fight-or-flight response has taken over, and I have chosen flight.

The wind chill makes me shiver, and I up my pace a little, feeling eyes on me again, feeling him there. There's a soft growl in my ear, and I stop walking.

"What do you want from me?" My voice shakes a little, and I curse his ability always to find me at my lowest point.

His shadowy projection steps in front of me, and I'm once again taken by how large he is. He softly brushes a lock of hair behind my ear.

"So gentle now?" I whisper.

"When it suits me." I can hear his smirk, and his voice sounds a little louder than before as it brushes past my ears.

"You want to hurt me," I state.

He circles me, his presence brushing against me and making me shiver. "You think you have me all figured out?"

"I don't know anything about you," I say, and even I can hear the hopelessness in my voice. "And you know nothing about me. So, please," I swallow, "leave me alone. Please."

His laugh is dangerous, terrifying, and intriguing.

"Please. Please leave me alone," I beg, and I hate the sound of it. I long to be strong, but I've been hunted for years. While this feels completely different, it exhumes feelings and desires I am desperate not to examine.

"Why?" The question is short and simple.

I look up at his form, shadows curling around him, and try to muster up an ounce of the inner strength I used to pride myself on having. I needed it when I was alone, but I am not alone anymore, and it might be making me weak.

"Because I want you to," I say lamely.

He snickers cruelly. "Do you always get what you want?"

I look away. My eyes burn like they do before those rare, precious tears leak down my cheek, but as usual, none come. "Hardly ever," I whisper.

"Soon, little fae."

"Leave me alone. I am with Connor."

He shrugs. "It won't matter."

Confusion furrows my brow. That sense of danger amping up inside me again.

He cups my jaw, dragging his thumb along my bottom lip. "Better run home, little fae. The monsters are still out."

I back up a step, and I can feel his gaze on me, his head cocked predatorily.

"Run." The word brushes against my ear and down my spine like a lover's touch. I take another step back before turning and sprinting toward the Morningstar House. My heart races in my chest, pounding in my ears.

I slip through the front door, panting. I press my back against the solid wood and close my eyes, trying to calm my breathing.

"It happened again." My eyes fly open at the voice, and I meet Rafe's gaze. "Didn't it?"

"What?" I ask wearily, closing my hands into fists to keep them from shaking.

Rafe rolls his eyes and heads upstairs to his room. The second I'm back in control of my breathing, I hurry back up to Connor. He's barely moved. I strip out of my clothes and crawl into bed with him, trying to settle into his warmth.

Less than an hour later, Connor's alarm goes off, and he kisses me tenderly. I groan softly, trying to deepen the kiss, but he chuckles and gets out of bed.

"Where are you going?"

"I have early practice this morning, babe. You have another hour. Go back to sleep." He kisses me again, but I'm already drifting off again.

When Alice comes into the room an hour later, I'm grumpy and ready to kill everyone. Maybe this is the way to prevent my vulnerability, keep me sleepy, horny, and cranky.

"Come on, Sum. I need coffee."

I grumble under my breath about also being in dire need of coffee and hurriedly get dressed. I grab my bag, push my feet into my heels, and follow Alice downstairs. It's not until I am halfway through my coffee and we are walking down the corridor to class that I feel alive and start listening to what Alice is saying.

"He came back this morning, and he was furious about something or other. I swear, he's like in love with her, Summer."

"You think they fought?" I ask.

Alice shrugs. "Probably, but he also smelled like sex, so who knows?" She pauses, and her nose twitches a little. Her normally animated face has gone stony cold, and I am suddenly looking at the legendary killer. Her gaze is fastened on one of the doors off the long hall, her eyes burning crimson.

"Al?" I squeeze her arm. The pendant pressed against my chest pulses. It's barely noticeable, and I doubt I would have realized if it weren't for Alice's reaction.

"Summer." She turns to look at me, her red irises glowing. "Get the headmaster. Someone else has been killed."

# 62

## SUMMER

Teltha
TOUCH, INTERACT,
CONTACT

I feel the color drain from my face, my entire body going cold as those words fully sink in.

"What?" I ask, hoping that I've heard her wrong.

She hisses, looking back at the door. "Get the headmaster. Now."

I turn on shaky legs and run to the headmaster's office. I barge in without knocking, not even caring if he yells at me. My blood rushes in my ears, and my head spins as my eyes lock on him. He takes his glasses off, dropping them on the desk.

"Miss Tuatha De Daanan. What's wrong?"

My whole body is numb, but as I stare at him, my mind clears a little, and I can think again. "Sir, someone else has been—"

He is out of his seat and standing beside me in a flash. "Show me."

My heart is pounding, and my lungs burn as I try to gulp down oxygen, but I nod and lead him back to where I left Alice.

She is standing in front of the door like a diminutive guard dog, looking more intimidating than I have ever seen her. If anyone approaches, they're immediately dissuaded by a glare and a snarl. I stop about ten feet away from her, but the headmaster breezes past me straight to Alice.

"I know the scent. It's too much blood to be living." Alice glances at me, fear flashing in her eyes before she looks back at the headmaster. "Definitely fae," she says. Her voice is low, but I can still hear her as clearly as if she were standing right next to me in an empty room.

The headmaster nods once. "No one in, Miss Legosi."

My gaze remains fixed on the door, imagining all the horrors it conceals.

The headmaster slips into the room, and for a few minutes, I remain frozen, staring at the door. But then my feet are moving of their own accord, taking me closer. Alice blocks my way, and I stop. I don't say anything, but I hold her gaze, silently asking her to move aside, telling her with my eyes that I need to see what is behind the door. I need to know one way or the other if this is something I need to be afraid of or if it is just random.

Alice stares at me assessingly, and I wait patiently for her to decide. Finally, she nods and moves just enough to let me through. The room is exactly how I imagined it. There is blood everywhere. Gods, how can there be so much blood? Now that I'm in the room, the coppery smell mixed with the fear of the victim is overwhelming. She is in the middle of the room, propped up on the desk, left like some broken, discarded doll.

The headmaster spins and closes the distance between us in two strides, his large body blocking my view. "Out," he growls.

I try to look around him, needing to see more and work out if there are similarities here, too.

He grabs my arms, holding me still and keeping me in front of him. "You should not be here."

I look up at him, shocked to feel the unfamiliar warmth of a tear sliding down my cheek. "She looks like me. Doesn't she?"

He holds my gaze with his mercurial eyes, and after a long moment, he nods.

I close my eyes, feeling another tear escape. "This is my fault," I whisper.

"This is the fault of a murderer," he growls.

I try to move again to see her, needing to give her this sign of respect. It is only fitting that I am forced to feel an ounce of the pain that was inflicted on her. It's a decision I regret immediately.

"I asked you before if you were strong. Has your answer changed? Because it looks as if it has," he asks harshly.

I look up at him, feeling more tears fall. My cheeks burn with the unfamiliar sensation, but they don't stop. While I have always hated my inability to cry, I hate more how vulnerable it makes me look now. It makes me look weak, and I am so tired of being weak.

"This is senseless savagery. In the face of horror is when true strength appears," he says. "Leave. Now."

I brush my tears away and leave the room, but her face is burned into my mind. I walk past Alice without stopping, wrapping the numbness around myself like armor. Alice calls after me, but it's like she's on the other side of the realm. I walk through campus, dazed and in shock. My body feels like it's shutting down. The only thing I can see is her with her pallid skin, the dark holes where her eyes used to be, and her hair matted with blood. Blood. So much blood.

I'm deep in the forest before I feel him. His hands grab my arms, and he shakes me, his voice loud in my ears. "Little fae."

I struggle to get away from him, but he pulls me against his chest, and I stop fighting, all my energy draining from me. My breaths are painful and labored, making my chest seize. For the first time in decades, I feel tears pouring from my eyes and hysterical sobs wracking my body.

The stranger holds me, and I should be scared. I am scared, but fear surrounds me so thoroughly that I'm frozen in this terror. It takes minutes, hours, days, who the fuck knows before I manage to push myself away from him. My eyes are sore, not used to the salty tears.

"What happened?" he asks, not attempting to touch me again.

"Was it you?" I ask, my voice cold as ice, hoarse from the sobs.

He tilts his head.

"Don't play dumb. Was it you?" I watch him, frustrated by his blurred form. "Did you kill her?" My voice shakes only a little as the question hangs between us.

"No."

"You had nothing to do with it?"

He shakes his head and slowly reaches for my hand, pressing my palm to his chest. "I had nothing to do with it." There is no flutter as he says it, no whisper of a lie, but maybe he's just a very good liar. I'm a good liar, or at least I used to be, so I know it can be done.

I can tell he can sense my disbelief. "Why would I lie?"

"I don't know why you do any of the things you do."

"Did you know her?" he asks.

I pull my hand away and take a step back. "No."

"Then why are you crying?" he asks.

I look away, shaking my head. "Just go away."

"You're scared," he says. "Why? You could find them. Kill them if you want with barely a thought."

I tense, the shock of his words shaking me from my stupor. "What?"

I feel him move closer to me, my body hyper aware of his presence. "You could kill them, this person. These people."

I don't move, staring up at his wavering form. Can he feel the same dark power in me that Torin could? It drove Torin wild with desire. He saw it as something to harness, something to control.

He crouches and starts drawing something on the ground. I narrow my eyes at him before looking down at the rune that's taking shape in the mud between us. It's not one I recognize, but I know it's powerful.

When he's done, he stands and brushes his hand against mine. "To reveal hidden things." I look at him. Maybe today has just been too much because I do not understand what he is saying. "I can show you more. Teach you," he says.

"Teach me?" I repeat.

It only makes sense to decline, to scream at him to leave me alone, but something stops me. This feels different. Torin never wanted to teach me to wield my powers responsibly. He wanted them wild and untamed because if I had control over them, then he didn't.

I know I would benefit from his teaching. It is quickly becoming apparent that I cannot hide from my reality and the danger I am in, but there must be a price, something he wants, and I don't know if I can pay it. Perhaps if I set some boundaries, I can turn this in my favor, ensuring the safety of not only myself but my relationship with Connor.

The darkness that rises and fills me with delicious hunger when the stranger is around must be tamped down. I can do that as long as he does not brush against the thinning membrane containing it.

"I have a couple of conditions," I say, studying his featureless face, trying to read him.

"Which are?" I can hear the interest in his voice.

"You stop harassing me. Stop saying inappropriate things to me." I pause briefly. "And we only discuss business," I finish laying out my boundaries.

Surely, they will keep me safe, not only from him but also from the sick thrill I feel whenever I am with him, talking to him... thinking about him. Maybe putting some distance between us will protect me from the desires of the coiled darkness within me. I've been repressing it my whole life, but now it roils and stretches impatiently within me.

"Harassing you?" he asks, tipping his head.

I glare at him. "Yes, and you respect my relationship with Connor." I tack on that last bit, given his penchant for diminishing it.

He crosses his arms over his chest. "I fail to see any benefit to me in this."

"I'll willingly hang out with you while you're teaching me. You clearly want to be around me."

"I want to protect you. It's not the same thing," he hisses, the vitriol clear.

"Well, if we eliminate the threat, you protect me. There's your benefit," I snap back, just as viciously.

"You're using my..." I hear his jaw clench. "My focus on you."

I narrow my eyes on him, trying to pretend my stomach doesn't flutter at his words, but I also consider the word he chose and the hesitation before using it. It was as if he had stopped himself from saying something else, and I really wanted to know what that was.

"You want to die. Is that it?"

"Is that a threat, Stranger?" I snarl.

"Why won't you just accept my help?" he growls back.

"Because you won't accept my boundaries," I hiss.

"Between you and me, there are none," he growls, his voice raised.

"You and me? There is no fucking you and me. I don't even know who you fucking are!" I shout back.

He grabs my face roughly, his fingers digging into my jaw. He's not hurting me, but I feel how easily he could. "You will," he says, his face inches from mine.

My breath hitches, and then he's gone.

I fall to my knees, and without my anger fuelling my adrenaline, without the distraction of the stranger, the trauma hits me like a ton of bricks. It slams down on top of me, crushing me beneath its weight. I fall to my side, and everything goes black.

# 63

## SUMMER

Wylthe

SPREAD, WAVE

She's there, right in front of me. Her head is artfully tilted to the side, blood-soaked dark brown hair matted to her scalp. Her face is pale, and her eyes are gone, leaving dark pits in her face. The corners of her mouth have been pulled up, gruesomely stitched into an eternal smile. It's the smile of death. The smile of pain. The smile of torture.

I reach for her, hoping to help her, but when I lift my arm, I see my own blood. It's warm and thick against my cool skin. The pain explodes within me the second I see the wounds. Someone has carved the mark of Nimue into both my arms.

Movement from the desk catches my attention, but I can barely see. My eyes are blurred with tears? Blood? Who knows?

"You're next," a child's voice whispers in my ear, followed by the most bone-chilling laugh I've ever heard.

I blink my eyes open. My body still feels numb and useless, nothing but a void. The mud beneath me is still cold. That girl will feel this forever, nothing but the cold, hard earth pressing down on her.

The sun has disappeared behind gray clouds, and a low fog hovers around me. The necklace pulses again, a little stronger than before, and I shiver as the fog becomes thicker, higher, and more menacing, creating a shroud where horrors can hide. I sit up a little and reach forward, moving my hand through it. I expect the mist to part for me and break beneath my hand, but it doesn't. Instead, it clings to my skin and slithers past my wrist, curling up my arm like a serpent.

I yank my hand back and look down at my arm. There is a slight red mark where the fog held me, but I barely felt it. I shift, intending to stand and get the hell out of the forest, but the fog has wrapped around my ankles. I try to pull away, but this time it feels more solid. It still looks like fog, but it feels like something more tangible. The pendant pulses deeper, alerting me to the danger, but there is nothing I can do.

The fog snakes up my calves like ghostly tentacles, and I scream, struggling against its hold. When it gets to my hips, I twist, reaching for a tree, hoping to pull myself from its grip, but its grip on me is relentless.

Fuck. Fuck, what do I do?

I scream again, clawing at the ground when it starts to pull me deeper into the forest. Mud flies everywhere, and I try to struggle, but I can't move my legs. I feel paralyzed from the waist down. The fog moves up my stomach and slithers around my chest, squeezing so hard it forces all the air from my lungs. It continues up my body until I can't see or hear anything, and there is only darkness.

Suddenly, a bright light penetrates the fog, and an instant later, I am freed from its grasp. I look up at the trees, gulping down air. A violet-eyed fae pops her head into my line of sight, her chest also heaving.

"Are you all right?" she asks, tilting her head.

I press my hand over my pounding heart, trying to calm my panic. The fae stares down at me with wide purple eyes, waiting for a response. She tilts her head the other way and brushes her hand over her shaved platinum hair.

I sit up, looking around. "Fuck."

"You good?" she asks, crouching in front of me.

I nod and slowly stand up. My muscles ache, and I can feel hundreds of deep wounds all over my body. I look down, assessing the damage. My uniform is covered in mud and holes. My skin is bloody, muddy, and bruised, but all in all, I'm in one piece.

"Thank you." I force a smile for the fae woman. She rose with me, but now she is just standing there staring at me. My power objects to her proximity, but my reactions seem to lessen the more I'm around them. It's now more of an awareness.

"You know, they frown on students wandering this deep into the woods," she says, moving in a little closer, trying to brush some of the dirt off my arms.

"I'll keep that in mind," I say, stepping back, her touch making my stomach turn. My powers may not be objecting as much, but I am still uncomfortable being this close to another fae.

She smiles at me a little too brightly. "I'm Aqua."

I nod. "Well, Aqua, we should get out of here. Talk to the headmaster."

Aqua nods. "Absolutely. Wild magic is not a good omen." She moves in closer and looks around dramatically before dropping her voice. "It's a sign of the return of Darias, you know."

I clear my throat, resisting the urge to take another step back. "Right." I'd read a little about this. There is a cult of immortals who believe in a higher power figure called Darias. Supposedly, wild magic is a sign of his existence, but this didn't feel like wild magic. This felt like... something else. Besides, there are bigger monsters out there.

We trudge through the forest, the thickets and bushes brushing painfully over my ruined skin. For some reason, I am barely healing. We don't talk while we walk, which I'm thankful for, though Aqua hums an odd song.

The building is empty. It looks like the headmaster canceled classes due to the... event earlier. I don't even glance at Aqua as I knock on the headmaster's door.

"Enter."

I step into his office for the second time today, again with bad news, and I'm aware of how fucking awful I look. My wounds still haven't started to heal, probably thanks to whatever magic imbued that fog, and every one of them is burning and throbbing.

The headmaster is up and around his desk the second he sees me. "What happened?"

"I was... attacked," I say, glancing at Aqua.

She nods, stepping forward. "Wild magic, headmaster. In the form of carnivorous fog." She shrugs animatedly. "I heard her scream."

"You're dismissed," the headmaster says abruptly. "Well done for your quick thinking," he adds. I wouldn't say there is warmth in his voice, but there is definitely a tone of relief that he didn't lose two of his students in one day.

Aqua nods, and I feel her look at me before she leaves his office. I turn to follow, unsure what else I can add, given I was being consumed by the carnivorous fog and unable to see or hear when it was happening.

"Not you, Miss Tuatha De Daanan." He clears his throat. "I apologize."

Confusion furrows my brow. "Sir?"

"I was unfair earlier. I have looked in the face of death many times, and I have learned to compartmentalize. It is a skill that needs to be honed."

I blink, stunned at his apology.

"I should have sealed the door so you could not follow this morning. I know you have a penchant for being where you are not supposed to be." He gestures to one of his chairs and waits for me to sit down before looking over my wounds. "Wild magic?"

"Apparently, sir. But I'm not convinced."

He nods, his expression tight as he waves his hand over a particularly deep wound on my leg. "Why were you so deep in the forest?"

I push away the memories and swallow down the lump of emotion. "I needed space."

His eyes turn hard. "You are aware someone is toying with you?"

"Yes, sir," I say, looking away.

"Why do you do that?" He waits until I lock my gaze with his. "Pretend to be meek. Is it because that's what you believe others expect?"

"I'm never what people expect." Or what they want.

"Hm." He looks back at my wounds. "Wild magic will take longer to heal. I have a salve, but it will only help with the pain."

"So you think it was wild magic, sir?"

"I think that wild magic has the potential to be controlled. So, yes, I do believe it was wild magic. However, I don't believe it was a random attack." I nod. "Did the necklace alert you to the danger?" he asks.

I nod. "Yes, but too late, sir."

"Hmm," he says but doesn't pursue it. "Shall I summon Miss Legosi or Mister Morningstar?"

"My phone. I must have dropped it." I look around as if it will suddenly appear.

The headmaster holds out his hand, and my phone appears on his palm. It's cracked and a little worse for wear, but it's still working. I unlock it and see all the missed calls and texts.

I'm about to call Connor when I look at the headmaster. "Does everyone know? About—"

"Lucia," he finishes. "No. Only Miss Legosi, myself, you, and the authorities. Though I assume the students have guessed something is going on." He looks at my many cuts. "While you won't be able to hide these, I would appreciate your discretion."

I nod.

"The authorities are going to want to speak with you. They very well might wipe your mind after. I have been very strict about them speaking to students without my presence, but with a second murder, I will lose some control over the situation."

I frown. "Surely, the news of her murder will need to be circulated. I need to remember, sir."

"You are underestimating their authority. They are not bound by mortal laws. If they want something to be secret, they will do whatever it takes to ensure that happens." He tilts his head. "Why would you want to remember what you saw?"

"She deserves to be remembered. Plus, I need to know what's coming if they are after me. No detail is too small, right, sir?"

He nods. "Study the book I gave you, Miss Tuatha De Daanan."

My phone rings again, and I glance at it, seeing Connor's face on the screen.

"Thank you again, sir."

He nods and walks around his desk. He sits down behind it and continues with his work. I leave his office before answering the phone.

# 64

## SUMMER

Bathsha
U.P, LIFT

"Con?"

"Babe?" He sounds frantic, and I can hear the panic in his voice. "Are you okay? Where are you?"

Leaning against the wall, I close my eyes. "I'm fine, big guy. I lost my phone."

"Where are you? Alice and I are coming."

"I'll meet you at my dorm."

Connor exhales. "Babe? You're... all right?"

It takes work to keep my voice even. "I'm okay, Con." I don't know how much longer I can keep this from him, and I don't know how I'm going to explain why I'm covered in cuts and bruises. Would it be kinder to lie to him rather than put him through the worry he'll feel knowing the truth?

"She's okay?" I hear Alice ask him.

"She's okay. She's going to meet us at the dorm. We're almost there, babe."

My muscles groan as I push off the wall. "I'll be there soon, big guy." I end the call and start the hike across campus.

The gray sky is heavy with clouds. It's as if the weather is reflecting the grimness of the day. I round the corner of Kelpie Hall and slam into a solid wall of muscle. Connor's scent surrounds me at the same time as his arms enfold me in warmth. I inhale deeply and melt against him, dismissing the discomfort of the cuts and bruises as he squeezes me.

"Fuck, you scared me," he whispers into my ear. He cups my thighs and lifts me against him. I wrap myself around him and bury my face into his neck, plunging my fingers into his golden hair.

"I'm okay, big guy."

He nuzzles his face into my hair and inhales. "Where were you?"

"It's a long story."

Connor carries me up to the dorm, and Alice is on me the second he steps through the door. She wraps her arms around me from behind. "Fuck, Summer."

I untangle myself from Connor and turn in his arms, pulling Alice into a proper hug. Connor keeps his arms around me as if scared to let me go.

"Where did you go, Summer? And why are you covered in blood?" Alice asks, obviously still very anxious.

Connor pulls back and really looks me over. "Fuck, Summer. What happened?"

I pull away from them, feeling selfish but also needing a little space. I try to cover myself, but my uniform is so ruined it doesn't do much.

Connor follows me, refusing to let me put distance between us. Alice and Connor share a grave look before she nods once. Her eyes soften when they meet mine, and I can feel her love and concern permeate me. She holds my gaze a moment longer, before turning and disappearing into her room. Connor brushes my hands away and crouches to look closer at my wounds. "Babe."

"Con, it's fine."

He tenses, feeling my withdrawal, but he continues to look over the thousands of cuts and gashes that decorate my skin. "What happened?" he asks.

"It was wild magic. It'll be fine in a week or so."

Connor stands up, staying close but allowing me a little bit of space. "Where did you see wild magic?"

"I was in the forest," I reply honestly.

As if he can't help it, he moves in closer, cupping my cheek. "Alone? Why?"

"I–I needed some air."

Connor presses his forehead to mine. "You call me next time."

I nod. "I'm sorry." The words are a barely audible whisper.

He slips his arms around me. "Alice said there was another murder, and then we couldn't find you, and I—"

I brush my lips over his, stopping him.

He pulls back, his eyes full of tears. "I couldn't... If something had happened to you—"

I cover his lips with my fingers. "I know. I'm sorry. I'm here, and I'm fine."

"It could have been you." A tear slides down his cheek.

Connor scoops me up and carries me through to my room. He closes the door, needing some privacy with me. He sits on the bed, and I wrap my arms around him, kissing all over his face. I brush the tears away, trying to reassure him I'm still here and I'm okay.

Connor's breaths are shaky, and he's clearly still panicked. I gently grab his face, making him look into my eyes. He focuses on me. His eyes are still a little glassy, and in them, I can practically see what he sees. He is imagining Gia's body, but it's me instead.

I lean in, kissing him softly at first but allowing it to build. He doesn't kiss me back immediately, but as he relaxes, he deepens the kiss. I flick his tongue with mine, letting him taste me, grounding and keeping him with me in this reality where things aren't perfect, but they're better than they are in the one he's imagining. We spend long moments just kissing and touching each other, healing each other.

Connor brushes his nose against mine. "You scared me so bad."

I close my eyes, pressing my forehead to his. "I know. I'm sorry."

"We should get you bandaged up."

I shake my head. "Not now. I just want to be like this with you for a while." The cuts sting and throb, but I can't bear to remove the pain right now. It feels like I deserve it.

"Headmaster Emrys needs to know," Connor says, squeezing me.

"I've seen him already. I went there straight after it happened. That's why I was delayed."

Connor exhales in relief, and then his stomach rumbles loudly.

I pull back, my lips twitching. "Hungry, big guy?"

Connor blushes. "I missed lunch because I was freaking out."

I nuzzle my cheek against his. "Let's order dinner."

Connor grabs his phone and starts scrolling through the options. "What do you fancy?"

The thought of any food right now turns my stomach, but Connor needs to eat. "Anything, big guy."

# 65

## SUMMER

Wynthn
BONE

The forest is dark, the moonlight barely shining through the canopy. A stick snaps in the distance, and my head whips toward the sound.

"You're next." The whisper comes from behind me, beside me, above me. "You're next," the voice chants.

Another snapped twig comes from behind me, this one louder and closer. I spin around, but there is only darkness.

"You're next. You're next. You're next." The voice pauses. "You're next, little fae."

I gasp, stumbling back. My foot gets caught on a root, and I fall back. There is no ground beneath me, and I keep falling. Falling. Falling.

I land hard in a classroom. Lucia sits there on the desk, posed as she was before, her lifeless face staring at me maliciously.

Slowly, her head straightens, black blood leaking from her empty eye sockets. She groans, trying to talk, but her lips are stitched shut. She slowly lifts her bloody hand and starts to pull at the stitches, tearing them out. The blood trickles down her chin, and I can do nothing but stare, my body frozen. I watch in horror as her jaw hangs limp, and then she lets out the most blood-curdling scream I've ever heard.

Behind her, a bony hand appears on the desk, and then another, the nails pressing into the wood until it splinters. The light dims behind her, and Lucia starts to laugh. The sound is maniacal and horrible, her jaw still limp. Blood seeps from her eyes, her mouth, her nose, and her ears, but all she does is laugh.

The room goes pitch black, and all I can see is a pair of bright red eyes just behind where Lucia was.

"You're next," the voice snarls.

I lurch awake, my heart slamming against my ribcage. The image of her is still there, that voice still ringing in my ears. I look at Connor sleeping peacefully next to me, and I exhale, closing my eyes and trying to ground myself in this reality. It was just a nightmare. I rub my hand over my face and climb out of bed to grab a bottle of water from the kitchen.

The wounds tingle and throb a little, but I can definitely feel an improvement from yesterday. After he fed me last night, Connor lovingly tended to my injuries while offering to get Luke approximately a million times. Each time, I stubbornly stated that I was fine and reminded him that the headmaster had said these couldn't be healed magically, anyway. The pain was grounding me, and it lessened the guilt enough that I was able to function.

*"You're next, little fae."*

A warning from my gut? Fear playing tricks on my mind?

I grab my phone, intending to clean it, trying to keep my hands busy and my mind distracted. But it lights up the moment I touch it, showing me my messages, and of course, there is one there from 1015.

The tone is accusatory like I am to blame for what happened. No doubt he knows what has happened. He probably caused it. Right?

I reply somewhat unfairly, but I don't care. I'll say anything to get the fucker to leave me alone at this point.

I feel my rage boil beneath my skin.

He starts to type, and then the bubbles disappear. The bubbles bounce again, then disappear. This happens a couple more times before they stop altogether. I delete the conversation and block his account for good measure. Locking my phone, I chuck it down on the couch before returning to bed. I climb in beside Connor, my thoughts in turmoil and my emotions out of control. As if he's aware of it, he turns toward me and pulls me against his chest, wrapping his entire body around me. His hold is suffocating, but I bury my face against his chest and wiggle until I am nearly beneath him.

I consider drawing the rune to ward against nightmares, but something stops me. Not only do I feel like I deserve to experience these nightmares, but something inside me whispers these dreams are important, and they may hold some vital information I need.

This time, when I drift off, I embrace the fear.

I wake early, still tucked tightly against Connor. He is dead to the world, which is the only reason he doesn't wake when I disentangle myself and climb out of bed. I leave a note instead of waking him to tell him I'm just going to the gym. The tortured terror I saw in his eyes every time he thought about me lying dead somewhere was devastating, and I never want to see it again.

*C.*
*Gone to the gym. Will bring back breakfast.*
*-S*

Carefully, I pull on shorts, a sports bra, and my black cropped hoodie, trying to avoid the bandages as much as possible. My run to the gym is a little slower than usual, but I am ready to face stupid Max head-on. When I arrive, he is engrossed in his own workout. His eyes glow a faint green, no doubt the berserker fuelling him. I take a steadying breath before walking over to him. I must look like a cross between a mummy and a professional fighter, thanks to the cuts and bruises covering my body.

It takes a long moment before Max notices me. "What happened to you?" he asks, pausing his workout.

"I don't want to be a damsel," I reply, lifting my chin and trying to appear confident.

Max drops the heavy weight he is holding and quirks a brow. "Yeah? What do you want to be?"

"A threat," I reply.

A slow smile tugs at Max's lips, and he nods. "Good. Let's get started then."

I turn without any further comment and go straight to the sparring room. I walk to the wall, grab a random pair of boxing gloves, and pull them on.

Max follows behind me. "All right, let's start slow." Max shakes his muscles out. "Show me your stance."

I quickly stretch, my muscles groaning, and then I get into the only stance I know, the one I've seen on television. I awkwardly angle my body sideways and put my fists up.

Max grimaces and tips his head. "What are you doing?"

"You said... you said to get into a stance, so..."

Max sighs and steps behind me. He puts his hands on my hips and adjusts my body. "Fae are fast, so you must make yourself a small target." He pushes a foot between mine, widening my feet. "Speed can take down even the biggest of targets. Even a Goliath can fall from a thousand tiny cuts."

My brows furrow. "And if I'm not... fast?" I ask cautiously, knowing how devastating my powers can be and unwilling to rely on them.

Max moves around me, lifting one of my elbows slightly. "What do you mean?"

"I mean what I said," I say, a little more harshly than I mean to.

Max steps back, studying me, but not in a way I've ever been studied before. This isn't him looking to get to know me. He is watching me like an opponent would. "You don't have to use your powers. The only problem is, your opponent probably won't have the same consideration."

"I understand. I know I need to be smart, and I need to know what I'm doing. You know what to do, and I'm smart. Together, I shouldn't have any need for fae anything."

Max shrugs. "I can teach you to fight. If you want to leave your best weapon behind, that's between you and the mirror." He checks over my stance again and nods. "All right, show me a punch."

I thrust my arm forward into the air between us and am pleasantly surprised at how well the stance holds up. I feel balanced and still fairly strong.

But any joy I feel from the small achievement is instantly ousted by Max's look of disappointment. "You'll throw your shoulder out if you keep doing that. Punch from the hip, and you're going to feel the power start from here." He touches my right hip. "It will travel all the way up to your shoulder, down your arm, and then into your fist. Try again."

I bristle a little. I don't enjoy not being good at things, especially when my teacher is such an arrogant jerk. I reset, and Max has to correct my stance again. Concentrating on how it feels, I focus on following his instructions. This time, I push through my right hip, and the punch feels more controlled and stronger.

"Better," he says.

"Can you just show me? I'm a visual learner."

Max smirks and summons a fighting dummy. I'd say the pasty, faceless, floating torso is the creepiest thing I've ever seen, but after the last few months, that would be a lie.

Max settles into his stance as if it is second nature, and I circle him, trying to see from all angles so I can replicate it. He twists, pushing the weight through his hip. When his fist connects with the dummy, it flies across the room, hitting the wall with a loud crash.

I feel a surge of determination when he smirks at me again, and I get into position. Max summons the dummy again and corrects my stance only slightly this time.

"Though the hip," he reminds me, and I nod.

I throw a punch at the dummy, following Max's movements almost exactly. The dummy rocks back a little but doesn't move, and my hand throbs a little in pain. This thing is fucking heavy.

Max laughs. "Better. Okay, again."

I nod, and I soon settle into the flow of punching the dummy. Max watches and only occasionally has to make slight corrections to my stance or technique.

"Right, now kicking."

Max demonstrates the kick, then readjusts my stance, shifting my center of gravity. I kick out at the dummy, and Max grabs my ankle in midair.

"Hold it there. I'm going to try to make you lose balance."

He slowly releases my ankle, and I wobble a bit but manage to keep my leg in the air. I feel the bandage on my thigh start to unravel as the muscles flex.

Max shoves my foot down and then to the side, trying to make my planted foot falter. I sway a little, feeling a bite of pain in my thigh. I feel the rumble of power inside me, my instincts trying to kick in to stop me from falling, but I quickly oust them and fall to the mat.

Max looks down at me, an eyebrow raised. "You're not a hundred percent hopeless. You definitely held on longer than I expected." I bristle at his comments, but he continues, "Ice when you get home, and I'll see you tomorrow."

Painfully, I push from the floor. The bandage on my thigh completely unravels and falls to the mat.

Max winces at the particularly gnarly wound on my thigh. "Come on," he says and turns, not waiting for me to follow.

I grab the bandage. "It's fine. Bye!"

He blocks my path and grabs my arm with a surprising amount of gentleness, pulling me with him to the trainer's room. It is large, the walls white like an asylum, and it smells pleasantly clean. Max pushes me into a chair and walks to the other side of the room, returning with what looks like a first aid kit.

"This is a wild magic wound," Max says, tucking his hands under my knees and pulling me to the edge of the chair. I ignore him as he starts to wrap my wound. "Let me guess, little damsel went into the forest alone and went too deep."

I glare at him.

"Carnivorous fog is a cunt," Max says.

My lips twitch at his unexpected comment. "Oh?"

Max nods, looking up at me. "Yup."

I burst out laughing, and Max snorts, looking back at the wound. He finishes quickly and stands up, gathering the first aid supplies.

"Thanks," I say, wondering how often he has done this to be so competent.

Max nods and gives me a quick smile.

"So, tomorrow?" I ask, gingerly getting to my feet.

"Bright and early," he replies.

I leave the gym feeling a little less defenseless than I was when I entered.

# 66

## SUMMER

Wylsha

ORBIT, SURROUND

Walking through the campus, I have more of a spring in my step than ever. For the first time, I feel like I have made a positive step toward protecting myself and my loved ones. I'm far from being able to say that I can take on whoever or whatever is after me, but the leap I took today required the kind of guts I've always longed to have. I can't help but think of the stranger at this moment. Would he be proud of me? Does it matter?

I stop at the cafe on the way back to the dorm and order breakfast for Connor and me and blood for Alice. There is still a nip in the air, the chill of early morning, but I barely feel it. Warm blood pumps through my veins, the adrenaline dancing with my cells in an addictive way that makes me want to continue to seek it out. There is something thrilling about training with Max. It's different from the lessons in combat class.

When I return to the dorm, I drop the takeout bags on the coffee table and go to my room to see if Connor's awake. The rising sun fills the room with a happy yellow glow, and the light brushes against his skin in the most ethereal way. He's never looked more angelic. The light bounces off the halo on his wrist, and the gold looks like it's absorbing the natural energy of the sun.

I take a quick photo of him and then kick off my sneakers. Silently, I tiptoe to the end of the bed. Connor is so dead to the world that he's lucky I'm not an axe murderer. I kneel at the end of the bed, practically holding my breath as I slowly lift the sheet. I try not to jostle the mattress as I crawl up between his legs.

His cock is semi-hard in sleep, and with the softest puff of cool air, it hardens more, tenting the sheet. I slowly shift so my mouth hovers over the tip and gently slide my tongue along the slit in his crown. He moans low and slow, but I can still hear the heaviness of sleep in his voice.

I smile and slowly close my lips around the tip of his cock. Swirling my tongue over the head, I start to suck, my cheeks hollowing as I pull him deeper into my mouth. Connor moans again, the sound resonating in my core. I curl my tongue, cradling the underside of his shaft and tightening my lips, dragging both up his length. Connor's hips undulate, and he moans again.

"Summer…" he groans, his voice still thick with sleep.

I swallow down more of his length, gagging on him, my throat protesting the intrusion. At the sound, Connor's muscles tense, and he lurches into a sitting position.

"Summer! Fuck, Summer…" he moans. I feel him lean back again, his body relaxing into the pleasure. Connor's hand rests against the back of my head, and I moan, working my mouth rhythmically up and down his cock. Frustrated with the sheet blocking his hand and view, he shoves it back. When his bright blue eyes meet mine, his body starts to shake with pleasure.

Connor tangles his fingers into my hair. He doesn't hold my head down or even try to lead my movements. He simply runs his fingers through my hair, a silent, passive praise. I keep my gaze locked with his, swallowing him down over and over. It doesn't take long before he is writhing beneath me. I can see he's struggling to hold back. His muscles quiver, and his body shakes as he tries to hold back his release, wanting to stay in the pleasure for as long as he can hold out. His eyes are almost black, his pupils so dilated they have nearly swallowed his irises.

I force him deep, gagging around his girth again and ripping a strangled groan from him. His head involuntarily falls back, but his eyes snap back to me a split second later. The hunger pushes him to watch me as I swallow his cock, to watch me as he fills my mouth with his release. Connor's hand fists in my hair, and his hips thrust, sending him deep into my mouth. He releases a short shout, and I feel the pulse of his cock just before his cum fills my mouth. The salty taste explodes against my tongue, and I moan, savoring him. Connor's body goes lax against the mattress, his chest heaving. I swallow down his release, claiming every last drop as my own before crawling up his body and kissing him deeply.

"Well, good morning to you, too," Connor moans.

I smile against his lips. "Good morning, big guy."

"I thought that only happened in movies."

I laugh, kissing him again. "My, my, what kind of movies do you watch?"

Connor chuckles, gliding his hand down my back. "It happened in that show Alice likes last week."

"I brought breakfast."

"You did?" Connor frowns, glancing at my outfit. "You worked out already?"

I nod and reach for the note I left for him.

"My girl is such an early riser."

I roll off him. "I'm going to shower before we eat. I'm all gross from the gym."

Connor follows and steps into the shower with me. His presence in the shower lengthens the process. We barely make it five minutes before I'm hoisted against the wall, and he's fucking me against the tile.

When we finally emerge, I wrap a towel around my body. I can feel eyes on me, but this is the gaze of someone who loves me, a feeling I'm still unused to. I glance over my shoulder and see Connor watching me, a bubblegum-colored towel slung low around his hips.

"You're pretty." He smiles, leaning against the shower door. "I love you."

"I love you, too." The words come so easily. They slip out on a breath of truth, filling the air with such sincerity. Connor stands up straighter. His smile slowly melts away, but his skin glows faintly.

I expect to feel dread, regret, and panic, but all I feel is the lightness of my candor. Connor just gapes at me, and I grin at him before going back into my room to change and rebandage my thigh. After a long moment, he follows and steps in front of me, his large hand cupping my cheek. He tilts my head up until I meet his gaze.

"I didn't think..." He pauses for a moment, just looking at me. "I didn't think you'd ever say it."

"I'm full of surprises." I lift my chin, giving him a soft smile. Connor leans down, brushing his lips over mine.

"I will protect your heart, Summer Tuatha De Daanan."

I nod. "I know."

Connor smiles, pressing his forehead to mine, and I smile up at him.

"Hurry up!" Alice growls through the door.

My lips curve in a grin at the interruption. Connor laughs and pulls back to get dressed for the day. I walk to my closet, looking for my blush pink cardigan to wear over my shirt. I leaf through my clothes and frown when I notice that one of my dresses is missing, too. Maybe Alice borrowed them, though I seriously doubt Alice would be caught dead in a cashmere pink cardigan. Or a pastel green sundress, for that matter.

I grab one of the sweaters I procured from Connor instead and pull it on over my uniform. I love the way it fits. It feels like one of his hugs. His scent clings to it, giving the illusion of being surrounded by him and his warmth.

When we leave my bedroom, holding hands like some gross sappy couple, Alice is waiting by the door. She is loudly slurping the blood smoothie I brought home for her this morning.

"About time."

I flip her off and reach into the bag, grabbing the two breakfast burritos. Handing one to Connor, I open mine as we leave the house. Connor squeezes my hand a little tighter and leans down for a bite of my burrito. I bring it to his lips, and he takes a happy bite.

"You have your own burrito, you know?"

"I know, but everything tastes so much better after you've taken a bite."

I roll my eyes, but I grin.

"You guys are so gross," Alice groans.

"I know."

"We are not gross," Connor protests at the same time as I concede.

"We're pretty gross, big guy." I take his burrito from him and take a bite before handing it back to him. He smiles like an idiot, but a slight tension buzzes around him.

Alice and I arrive at our combat class just barely in time, and Ike clocks us immediately.

"Summer. A word."

I grimace, and Alice throws me a sympathetic look as I walk to our combat instructor. He watches my approach with a strange expression on his face.

"I don't technically think we were late—"

"I have spoken with Max. He told me you are training with him."

I blink. "Oh?"

"Max is a skilled fighter. I have asked him to lean more into the offensive. I will work with you here on your defensive skills."

"Is this the case for every student who attends classes at the university gym?"

Ike's lips twitch a fraction. It's the smallest of movements, and I would have missed it if I weren't looking at him. "No, but Max approached me. He asked for tips on the best ways to train your kind. Max's classes are very popular on campus, but as you know, fae don't train with others."

I nod knowingly. "They do like to keep to their herds."

Laughter dances in Ike's eyes, but he just says, "Anyway, let me know if you have any questions. I will be checking in with Max, but I think this is for the best. You will learn faster in the one-on-one lessons, and I think the quicker you learn to defend yourself, the better."

"O-of course. Thank you." His words surprise me, and I wonder how much he knows and who told him. Maybe the headmaster spoke with him?

Ike glances at the rest of the class, obviously dismissing me. He claps his hands loudly, capturing the attention of the students.

"Two to a mat and one dummy per mat." Ike's voice rings out across the hall, yet he barely raises it. He crosses his arms, waiting for us to get into position. I hurry to join Alice on the mat she claimed for us.

Ike starts by demonstrating five different defensive positions. He spends the rest of the class going from mat to mat, watching each pair and making corrections where needed. Eventually, he calls time and dismisses us.

"I hate how sweaty I get in Ike's class," Alice grumbles as we walk to Elder Futhark runes. I wave goodbye to Alice at the door and sit at the front of the class, ignoring the stares of the fae already seated.

Professor Henley is drawing a large complex rune on the board. Students filter in loudly, but they quickly settle, obviously intrigued by the rune on the board.

Professor Henley turns to face the class. "Has anyone seen this rune before?" She looks over the class, waiting for raised hands. When none come, she nods. "Good. While this rune doesn't technically fit within the Futhark alphabet, it was created by a native. Its original use was for good, but," she reaches up, pointing to the top line, "this line is off by point one of a degree, and that makes for an unstable rune. It was initially created to assist in the building of a library. Instead, the rune took out an entire city, leaving nothing but rubble and ash blowing in the breeze." She snaps her fingers, and the rune disappears from the board, the memory of it hazy and difficult to recall. "This lesson will be about the importance of rune accuracy. If you would turn the piece of paper on your desks over."

I flip the piece of paper, looking at the runes laid out in front of me.

"These runes should all be familiar to you. Each of them is unstable, with varying consequences. Your task is to find and label the imperfections, providing a detailed analysis of what is incorrect. Then, draw the rune correctly next to the incorrect one. To continue with this class, you will be required to pass this exam with a hundred percent due to its importance. If you fail, you will be dropped to a lower-level course until your knowledge is at the level it needs to be. You have twenty minutes to complete."

The room is silent. Everyone is looking at Professor Henley in shock, but I understand the need for this. Careless rune work can be devastating.

I look down at the first rune. It's a simple rune used for heating water. The lines look correct, but I notice a slight deviation in the split curve at the top. Although this rune would not be effective in increasing the water temperature, I'm unsure if it would have catastrophic consequences. I quickly label the mistake and draw out the correction. The rest of the runes are pretty straightforward, and there is only one that could potentially cause a small fire. The rest of the class looks anxious as they hand their test papers to Professor Henley, but I pass it to her, smiling.

# 67

## SUMMER

Tahltha

BABY, CHILD

"**W**ell, well, back again, former damsel?" Max smirks as I walk into the gym the next morning.

I decide I shouldn't impale him until after the lesson and completely ignore him, walking through to the sparring room. I'm walking a little stiffly, my muscles tight and achy after our session and combat class yesterday. No doubt I overdid it, considering my injuries, but thankfully, I have been healing well.

Max leans against the wall and quirks an eyebrow. "How sore are you from one to ten?"

I stretch, but my muscles rebel as I try to loosen them. "A five," I say, trying to hold back my winces.

Max snorts. "So more like a seven. You didn't ice."

I glare at him. "I was busy."

"Well, you're going to be paying for it today," Max says, smirking and stretching out. "Okay, we'll do some combinations. Right jab, left hook, duck, right kick." He rolls his shoulders. "I'll even do them with you because I'm sweet like that."

I get into position. Max adjusts my stance, and I try not to bristle in frustration.

"Twenty rounds, then one minute break, then twenty, one minute break, and so on, until I tell you to stop."

My muscles quake in protest after the first five rounds, but I try to push through the pain, leaning into the fear I've not only lived with for the past month but most of my life. I make it to the third set before my limbs start to shake with fatigue. Max watches me as he effortlessly goes through the motions, not even slightly out of breath. *Dick.*

"Faster," he says, increasing his speed, though I suspect he's been doing so every round. My body can feel the toil from it. After another five rounds, I feel like I'm going to pass out. Max is moving much faster now, and my competitive side is coming out to play. It's so potent that I barely notice as I brush against my internal power. It flickers in excitement as I reach for it, needing to be faster, better, stronger. The power answers my call, and the second I recognize the faint caress along my spine, I oust it completely, stopping mid-round. My heart thunders in my chest. I bend over, bracing my hands on my knees and gulping down air.

"That's enough for today."

"I didn't say stop," Max says, crossing his arms over his chest, not even a little winded. Again, dick. "Quitting is a damsel move," he continues, knowing it'll rile me.

"You're going too fast," I snarl.

Max shrugs. "If you can't keep up because you're weak, fine. I'll slow down."

I look at him, seriously having to take a moment to decide whether to set him on fire. Unwilling to deal with the headmaster at this hour, I opt to just leave the gym.

"So, we're rocking the wound today?" Alice asks as we leave the dorm later that morning. I nod, feeling the cut throb.

"Decided to let some fresh air at it."

Connor is standing outside Kelpie when we exit, holding a cardboard cupholder with three coffees.

"Oh, hi, big guy!"

Connor smiles, but I can feel a little tension radiating from him. "Thought I'd deliver your coffee today." I convinced him to go home last night because his brothers were having a game night that they had been planning for weeks. He was reluctant to leave me, but he needed some time alone with his brothers, and I needed some time with Alice. But the anxiety radiating off him today is making me regret that decision.

I take a cup and push to my tiptoes, brushing my lips over his. "Thank you."

"Good morning, babe."

Alice barges past me. "It's too early to watch you guys be all mushy and gross." She takes one of the two remaining cups. "Especially before coffee."

She walks ahead, and I kiss Connor again before we follow her. I slide my hand into Connor's as we cross the campus. Connor squeezes my hand and kisses my head more than once.

I look up at him and step closer, my hip brushing his as we walk. "You okay, big guy?"

Connor glances at me, a little puzzled. "Me? Yeah, perfect."

I nod, sipping my coffee, but I can feel the tension vibrating in him. I glance at him again and notice he is looking around suspiciously, almost accusingly.

I stop walking. Connor's hand tightens on mine, and he whips around, his eyes searching for the threat.

"Con." I wait until his gaze meets mine. "You gotta stop. I'm fine."

He blinks down at me, his shoulders tight. "What do you mean?" I quirk an eyebrow, and he blinks again, the picture of innocence. "I'm just... observing."

"Con."

"What?"

"Nothing is going to happen to me. Relax."

Connor shrugs nonchalantly. "I'm totally relaxed," he says, and I don't have to be an angel to know he is lying.

I give him a skeptical look.

"This is how I normally walk you to class."

I quirk a brow.

"What?" he asks, a little sharper than usual.

I sigh heavily and kiss him. "Go to class. I'll see you after."

Connor glances at Alice, and then he kisses me again. "Okay. I love you."

"I'll see you later," I reply. If Connor was expecting me to say it back, he doesn't give it away. I suspect he's still high on the feeling of me saying it yesterday morning. As he walks off, he glances at us more than once over his shoulder, and I wave at him each time.

"He doesn't know what we suspect, does he?" Alice whispers, pulling me toward class. "That you're the target."

I shake my head.

"Oh, so he's just being a weirdo. Must be his natural state."

"He's worried, and I know he struggled with not being with me last night. Me disappearing like that and coming back injured really got to him."

"No, Sum. There is worried, and then there is being psychotic, and he is on the last train to crazy town."

I sigh heavily, sitting down in our Realms class.

"Are you going to tell him?"

I shake my head again. "If he's this worried not knowing, I'm pretty sure telling him I might be the target will send him over the edge."

Alice shrugs, and we drop the subject as Professor Ambrose enters the room.

# 68

## SUMMER

*Taesho*
ARC

Our second class of the day is less successful than the first, and by the end of the class, Alice is in a foul mood. She whines all the way from Adze Hall to the cafeteria, completely outraged by the amount of homework Professor Brooks gave us. It doesn't seem the time to mention that I am looking forward to the in-depth analysis piece. I am even more excited that I was given Algiz in its raw form.

"So, I'll meet you at the cafeteria?" I suggest when Alice pauses between curses to take a breath.

She glances at me. "Aren't we heading there now? Together?"

"Don't tell me you're going all Connor on me."

Alice gags, but I see the memory of fear in her eyes. "Gross, but he'll ask where you are. So…"

"I need to talk to the headmaster real quick."

Alice nods and relaxes a little when she finds out I will be with the headmaster. "Yeah, that sounds like something I do not want to do. See ya," she says, trotting off toward the canteen.

The headmaster's door looms in front of me. It doesn't seem to matter how often I visit. It never gets less intimidating. I take a steadying breath before knocking on the door.

"Enter," he calls, his cold voice cutting through the wood.

I open the door and step into his office. "I'm sorry to bother you, sir, but I have a few questions."

He nods, gesturing to the two familiar plush chairs across from his desk. I drop into one of them and pull the grimoire out.

"I've been studying this."

"And?"

His curtness makes me uneasy, but I focus on the text and turn to one of the pages I want to ask about. The book bristles with multiple bookmarks, and sticky notes and tabs cover the pages.

"You've been busy."

I look up at him. "It's very interesting to me, sir." I find the page and stand, walking up to his desk and placing the heavy book down. The headmaster looks down at the page, and I point to a drawing. "This symbol. What is it? I can't find it in any text." I had been itching to ask the stranger about some things I'd read, but he was still gone. However, he is still viewing my stories. Every single one.

He glances at me and then down at the book again. "That is that mark of Titania." I tip my head, waiting for him to continue. "It has not been used since Faerie was lost."

I stare at the symbol. "I have seen it before. I used to doodle it and... I'm pretty sure it's been etched near the victims of the murders."

The headmaster's brows furrow, and he waves his hand. In front of us, the crime scenes appear. The victims are thankfully not there, but the carnage is still present. I look at the murder scene of Lucia, so violently familiar thanks to my nightmares. Every single detail seems etched into my brain, even though I only got a glimpse. The other spell shows what Connor saw, and it's just as gruesome. The walls are stained with blood, and you can feel the fear and death clinging to the room.

The headmaster pinches the spell and widens his fingers, zooming in on the first crime scene. He points to the mark. "That wasn't there previously." He then does the same in the second and locates the mark quicker. The furrow in his brow deepens until it's nearly a scowl.

"I remember seeing it, sir." I pause to suppress the shiver. "Behind Lucia." I hadn't caught it at that moment, but after, I saw it within a memory, and it glowed like a beacon.

He looks up at me, calculating. "It is a Seelie mark," he says after a long moment. The air in the room seems to thicken with meaning, and I blink. "Leave this with me, Miss Tuatha De Daanan. I will need to look over the official reports. I'll summon you if I find any further information."

I nod and grab my bag before quickly exiting his office. The lunch hall is bustling, but I'm too lost in my own thoughts to notice.

"Hi," Connor says, wrapping his arms around me from behind and nuzzling into my neck.

"Hi, big guy."

"Where have you been?" he asks.

I turn in his arms and look up at him. "I had to talk to the headmaster about something. Didn't Alice tell you?"

He blushes. "She might have mentioned it, but... you didn't text me."

"Con, can we talk? Alone?"

Connor nods, and I notice the way his shoulders tense. I slide my hand into his, leading him out of the cafeteria and into the hall. I stride down the hall, tugging him along until I find an empty classroom.

The door is barely closed when Connor blurts out, "Are you breaking up with me?"

I blink. "What?"

His cheeks flush. "Are you..." He hesitates, his voice quieter this time. "Are you breaking up with me?"

"What? No!"

Connor visibly relaxes, exhaling the breath I imagine he has been holding since I didn't show up for lunch with Alice. Or maybe even before. While I did tell him I loved him, I understand that I may have seemed a little more distant recently.

"Oh. Good."

I cup his cheek. "Con. In my whole life, I have told two people that I love them. You and Alice." I stroke his cheek with my thumb. "I don't say it lightly. Why the fuck would I break up with you?"

I never said it to Torin. I just kept it as my own little secret. Until now, my life was nothing but secrets and lies.

"Well, in the movies, that's what the girl says right before she tears the heart from the guy's chest."

I blink again. "We do need to talk, but at the end of the conversation, you and I will still be together. Okay?"

Connor leans against a desk and looks at me. I can see the relief on his face, but there is still some fear in his eyes. "Okay. What's up?"

I sigh. "Connor, I know you're worried. I know you want to protect me. But you can't know where I am 24/7."

"What? Why not?"

"Because, Con. Sometimes I will have to stay late, or I'll go to the gym or to the coffee place, and I need to be able to do that without informing you first." I have no idea if I'm being unreasonable or not. All I know is that I need to keep a nugget of my independence, and while I know he's worried about me, I can't spend my life hiding in his shadow.

Connor's fists clench on the edge of the desk, the wood creaking. "You want to go places without telling me?"

"I want to not *have* to tell you." I tilt my head, searching his face. "Is the only reason that you want to keep me safe? Or is there something else?"

"What do you mean?"

"Do you not trust me?" I ask plainly.

Connor places his hands on my arms and pulls me in closer. "I do! I just... they were both fae, Sum." He swallows hard. He has obviously put the puzzle pieces together on his own. "And you're fae, and I love you, and..." He hesitates. "When angels lose the person they love..." The fear in his eyes makes my heart clench. I wrap my arms around his neck.

"You're not going to lose me, big guy." I press my forehead to his, and Connor closes his eyes, relaxing into me.

"I'm sorry. I know I'm being... intense."

"Shhh." I tilt my head and press my lips to his, kissing him.

"I'm sorry. I just... I love you so much."

I kiss him again, letting him feel and taste me. "I love you."

# 69

## SUMMER

Solsha

WATER

"Didn't think you'd be back," Max grunts. He drops one of the heavy dummies into the middle of the room.

I notice that he's prepared the room for our session, so he's obviously a liar as well as a dick. "Sorry to burst your bubble," I grumble.

He smirks. "Ready to fight me, then?"

I nod and pull my gloves on.

"If I land a hit, it will break a bone. I'm not going to hold back."

I roll my eyes, but there's something weirdly refreshing about training with a berserker who won't go out of his way to protect me when we're training. There is something almost liberating about it. "Let's just do this."

Max barely waits for me to get into position before he swings, and I barely dodge it. I nearly lose my balance, stumbling when he throws the next punch. His fist just misses my face, and I can feel the force of his swing. Max throws another punch, and this time, not only do I dodge it, but I also run away from him.

"Stop aiming at my face, dick."

He gives me a bemused look. "You think your opponent won't go for your head and face just cause you're hot?"

I blink, caught off guard by the almost compliment. "Well... maybe."

Max snorts. "Come on, try to hit me back."

I get into position and swing for him. He easily dodges, and his fist collides with my ribs. The air rushes from my lungs, and my stomach tries to follow it with the sharp pain from his jab.

"Fuck." I cough, bracing my hands on my thighs and trying to breathe through the pain and nausea.

"I told you I would break a bone if I landed a hit. You'll heal in a few minutes," Max quips, crossing his arms over his chest. "Maybe actually try this time."

With every inhale, it feels like a hot poker is stabbing my lung, and when I try to straighten, the pain is excruciating.

"And that was just my normal strength, not even touching the berserker."

"You're a cunt," I wheeze out, my chest burning as my bone starts to fuse back together.

"And you're a stubborn ass."

I lunge for him, pushing through the pain and plunging my fist into his stomach, striking faster than he can react.

Max's breath hisses out, and his eyes glow green. I'm about to hit him again when he holds his hand up. "Wait. Don't. I need... control."

Is he fucking kidding? He breaks one of my ribs, but he can't get hit in the stomach without needing to leash the berserker? Fuck him. I roll my eyes and turn, leaving the sparring room.

"Get your ass back here," he growls.

I whirl on him. "Are you fucking kidding me? You want me to fight with you. I do, and get one punch in before you go all Berserker Ballistic on me?"

Max snaps his teeth. "You took a cheap shot. The berserker could snap you like a twig."

"All of your shots are cheap because I don't fucking know what I'm doing," I snarl.

"Because you're using your head and not your instinct!" Max growls back, throwing another punch. I dodge it easily, fueled by my anger. "Don't think." He strikes out at me again. "Don't be smart." He spins, kicking out at me. "Just survive."

I dodge each one, almost anticipating each of his moves.

"Faster," Max commands, closing the distance between us and pushing me into more intricate footwork. "Faster, damsel. Stand your ground, or I'll back you into the wall, and you'll be stuck." I give another step, and he swings again. "Sloppy. Don't let me gain space."

He swings again, and I back up again. A kernel of doubt sprouts, strangling my fledgling confidence. Suddenly, my instincts become lost to the white noise, and I feel the bricks behind my back. Max slams his fist into the wall right beside my head, and the stone quakes beneath his hit. "Stop holding back."

I look up at him, my body shutting down.

"I grew up hating the berserker side. It was blind rage and destruction."

Panic creeps in, and my breaths quicken. It's not from fear of him but of how easily I slipped into my instincts. Those abilities are the gateway to my other side and the power I swore to keep locked away.

"Most of my family are little more than their berserker. It drove my mother to take her own life." He looks away, a flicker of pain crossing his face. "Your power can be your destruction or your salvation. I know what mine is now." He looks at me, his face once again hard. "When are you going to decide which yours is?"

I feel that still unfamiliar heat of tears stinging my eyes.

Max raises his hands and steps back. "We're done for today." He turns, giving me his back, and I swallow, holding back the dry sobs stuck in my throat. Something within me unlocked when I used that branch of my power. I barely brushed against it, but I've opened a floodgate of emotions. My feet move of their own accord, and I run from the gym, needing space and air.

But where can I run to? The forest is unsafe. The dorm has Alice. The Morningstar House has Connor. I need to do this on my own, and I am desperate to find some space. These emotions are mine, and I need to feel them, own them, and understand them. I am not ready to share them. Hell, I am not even sure what they are.

I just run, with no destination in mind, and no route planned. My chest constricts with every sob, and I try to find solace in the burn of my lungs. I push myself, but there is only pain and not from the healed broken rib. Physical pain I can manage. This is a deeper agony of self-hatred and doubt. I run and run, getting lost but not caring. I long to be lost, but how do I hide from myself?

A hand wraps around my arm, stopping my flight. I whip around, a scream stuck in my throat. The stranger's hold is firm as if afraid I will try to escape, but I simply stare up at him, trying to make sense of his shadowed, blurry form. I can feel the intensity of his gaze, and we stand there in silence for long moments.

"Where are you going?" His voice brushes against my ear.

"I don't know," I reply honestly. My voice breaks a little as I put my truth into the air.

There is a moment of indecision before he moves in closer, wrapping himself around me. I don't resist. I don't know why, but I mold myself to his chest, accepting the comfort. It is an odd embrace. I can feel his powerful arms around me, but there is no warmth to his body, no scent. There is just the comfort of a hold, the compression of my nervous system forcing me to relax. Eventually, I pull back, looking up at him. He truly is an enigma. I can feel the danger of him, but he also possesses a gentleness. Or perhaps that's just what he wants me to see. Or worse, that is what I want to see.

He gently brushes the back of his fingers along my cheek. "No tears, but your eyes are red."

I look up at him, and he brushes a lock of hair behind my ear. He drops his hand, and we stare at each other for another long moment. I can feel him waiting, trying to anticipate my next move.

"You're back?" I ask. My voice is a little weak from the emotion. I hadn't heard from him since our messages after the forest when I'd thrown those horrible names at him and told him to leave me alone. I hadn't even felt his eyes on me. But I had been thinking about him, and I had been checking to see if he was keeping tabs on me. He had been always watching, but this time, from afar.

"Do you want me to be back?" he asks. The question is loaded, dangerous, and interesting.

My gaze bores into the blur that is his face as if the intensity of my stare may reveal the concealed parts of him.

"I should go," I whisper, though my feet make no move to follow my thoughts. When I don't move, he cups my cheek again. "I don't know. I don't know anything anymore," I admit, closing my eyes and leaning into his touch. It is a moment of weakness, and I know it. I had always thought using my powers would be my downfall, but Max may be right. They can be my downfall or my salvation.

"What do you need to know?" he asks, his thumb brushing the curve of my cheek. He's obviously having as much trouble reading me as I am him.

I open my eyes and step back, pulling away from the comfort of his touch. "Nothing." I shake my head and clear my throat. "Thanks for... this."

"Always running from something," he says, the words shivering down my spine.

"Be my friend," I say, the words falling from my mouth. I have no idea where they come from, but I do know I can be genuine with this person. While he elicits some unwanted feelings and makes the darkness swirl inside me, I can't deny I like feeling *seen.*

"What?"

"Stay and be my friend," I say again.

I can feel the skepticism in his voice. "I thought I was a narcissistic, cowardly creep."

My lips twitch. "Well..."

He growls softly, and I shiver at the sound. "Why do you want me as your friend? You're not lacking in companionship."

I consider his question. He's right. I have more people in my life now than I've ever had, but... "There is something about you." I pause, trying to formulate my thoughts, and I let myself face the very truths I have been trying to avoid. "It makes me think you understand a side of me that no one else does."

He watches me for a long moment, and my skin tingles beneath his stare. "Friends," he confirms. "For now."

I hold my hand out. "Friends. No boundary crossing."

He takes my hand after a moment, shaking it. "Why were you running?"

A laugh escapes me, and it is no longer a foreign sound. "If only I knew."

"Running from yourself, then." We start walking, keeping a comfortable distance between us. I feel a sense of peace in this agreement with him. I feel understood and strangely safe. We approach the mouth of the forest, and I look back at the beckoning darkness.

"I don't know why I'm drawn here, but I don't want to be."

"Fae feel most at home in the wild. It's the closest they can get to Faerie."

Reaching out, I glide my fingers over the trunk of a tree, leaving a trail of glittering dust in their wake. "I know. I hate it."

"Why?" he asks.

I shrug, pulling my hand back. It's a lie. I definitely know why, but I have already opened up too much.

"I used to hate what I was," he says into the silence.

I glance at him. "It's a lonely business. Hating your kind."

"It is... isolating."

I sit on a fallen log, feeling safe here even though my last visit ended so violently. I watch the stranger as he looks up through the canopy, gazing at the slight bit of early morning sky visible through the branches. "You're not like other fae, if that's any comfort. I'm not like my kind either." He looks back at me. "There is power in being different, a strength unknown to most."

"Why did you come back today?" I ask.

I see the way his shoulders tense. He hesitates for a moment before replying, "I never left."

The admission doesn't bring about the same level of fear it used to. "Was I right?"

"About?"

"That you understand me?" I'm unsure why the question feels so heavy between us, but I desperately need it to be true.

"I do," he replies, and I can hear the smile in his voice. "You hide so much of yourself from others but even more from yourself."

I tilt my head, interested. "Oh?"

"I know because I am the same. Most people only ever see a single side of me. The facade I wear to appease them."

My lips twitch. "Ah, so there are people who physically perceive you? As in, you're not only..." I gesture to his form.

His laugh rumbles in my ears. "Another mask, but I do exist outside of this avatar."

I chuckle, looking down at the ground.

"What?"

I shake my head, laughing. "You've unblocked yourself already, haven't you?"

"Are you planning on blocking me again?"

"Probably," I reply honestly.

"Even when it does nothing?" he asks.

I smirk, looking up at him. "It doesn't do nothing. It pisses you off."

"You're such a brat," he says, and I can practically hear his eyes roll.

There's that word again. *Brat*. Why does it spark something inside me?

He pauses for a long moment. "You've been spending a lot of time with that berserker." It isn't a question. It's a statement, and there is something behind the words that I can't identify.

I quirk an eyebrow, waiting for more.

"It's just a question."

"There was no question. It was a statement."

"Why?" I can hear the way he forced the word from between his clenched teeth.

I narrow my eyes at him. "Does it matter?" I ask, unsure why I'm unwilling to tell him the truth, but for now, I want to hold on to this information. Something in the bite of his words makes me want to push at him.

"I have to go." His tone is short and clipped, and I sigh.

Just when I thought I was getting somewhere, it turns out he's just a dick who was pretending not to be a dick. "Bye," I bite out.

The spell holding him here fractures, and I'm alone again.

# 70

## SUMMER

$\mathcal{P}$

*Rueqha*
PEACE

Alice looks up from the couch when I come through the door. "Hey."

My head is still a mess, but at least the stranger was an asshole, so things felt a little more normal than they did when he seemed to be... understanding.

"Hi." I smile, walking to the fridge.

"How was the gym?" she asks.

"Fine. Max is a dick," I say, taking a deep drink of water, the cold soothing my sob-ravaged throat.

Alice snorts, turning the television off. "Then why do you keep going back?"

"It's safer than running," I reply. The truth in the statement sends a pang of sadness through me. My solace has been stolen from me by some psycho.

"So we're not running anymore?" Alice asks.

I lift an eyebrow. "We?"

"Yes, I live vicariously through you. You run, so I do, too."

I roll my eyes. "Well, *we* still run at the gym."

"Gross, I hate that. Go get dressed. We're going to be late."

I wave in acknowledgment and hurry to my room to shower and change. When I return to the living room, Connor and Alice are arguing about something that happened on the show. Connor has become nearly as obsessed as Alice with the vampire drama. The moment I enter the room, he stops mid-conversation and stands up, smiling brightly at me.

"Hi, gorgeous."

"Hi, big guy."

Connor kisses me hard before handing me a cup of coffee.

"I missed you," I say, taking my coffee and kissing him again.

"Not as much as I missed you," he murmurs against my lips.

"Late," Alice grumbles from the open door.

I grin and take Connor's hand. Alice's mood lightens when we leave the building, and she takes a long sip of her coffee.

"How did people live before coffee?" she asks with a small sigh.

"I'm excited to see you in my jersey at the game tomorrow," Connor says, wrapping his arm around me, his big hand resting on my hip as we walk.

I smile. "I'm going to cheer so loud for you."

"You sure you don't want to be a cheerleader?" he asks humor in his voice.

"Pretty sure, big guy."

He chuckles, and we stop at the door to Adze Hall. He kisses me deeply, and I bite his lip, eliciting a deep moan from him. "Get to class, succubus."

I smile against his lips and pull back. "See you later, big guy."

As we head toward our first class, I link my arm through Alice's.

"He has been insufferable since you told him you love him."

I laugh. "Well, how could I not, Al? He's just so..."

"Connor." Alice chuckles.

I nod, squeezing her arm.

"You're gross now."

I nuzzle into Alice in a way that is so unfamiliar to me but also feels good. It feels warm and happy.

Alice bats me away playfully. "You're so mushy. Like a ripe, mushy banana."

"Please, you're obsessed with me."

Alice scoffs as we drop into our seats.

The campus is abuzz with people excitedly chatting about the game as we join the steady stream headed toward the stadium. Many of the students are wearing Connor's number, but knowing that I am the only one wearing one of his actual jerseys fills me with fizzy excitement.

"Zach's number?" I ask, glancing at the jersey Alice is wearing.

Alice smiles at me, the picture of innocence. "Huh?"

"You are so bad." I shake my head and laugh softly.

Ashley runs up to us, her hair in a high ponytail and proudly wearing her cheer uniform. She smiles brightly. "You know, no one has ever turned us down before. Are you sure we can't change your mind?" she asks.

I shake my head. "I think we're more spectators. Thank you, though."

"Summer! Alice!" Brett calls, weaving through the crowd of people outside the stadium.

Alice turns to greet Brett, and Ashley's face goes white, her eyes flashing.

"You okay, Ash–"

"You're wearing Zach's number?" she asks Alice, an edge to her voice.

Alice glances at Ashley over her shoulder, reaching back to stroke the number. "Oh, yeah. Need to support my Zachy Wacky."

Ashley's eyes flash again, and the smile she forces onto her face looks almost scary. "Well. Go, Knights," she hisses through her teeth before turning and stalking inside.

Brett walks around to stand beside me, watching after Ashley. "What was that about?"

I glance at him. "Nothing. Just Alice being annoying."

"Ah, so the usual," he says with a laugh.

Alice's smirk of satisfaction remains firmly in place as we head inside. We've been given fieldside seats, and the game starts with a bang. The Morningstars dominate on the field, and Connor winks at me when he scores the first point of the game. I pull my lower lip between my teeth, knowing how that powerful body moves and feels when he focuses it on me.

"Fuck, just marry him already," Alice groans when I blow him a kiss.

Ashley throws scathing glances at us every time Alice shouts for her *Zachy baby bear*, and I can feel the anger in the look. Every time Zach looks our way, Alice blows him a kiss. Zach flips her off each time before glancing at Ashley worriedly. I fucking hope Alice knows what she's doing because Ashley is seething. One thing I know for certain, you don't want to piss off a Valkyrie.

The opposing team pushes hard, closing the gap in the score, and the game goes into overtime. Zane scores the final point, and the team piles on him. The Avalon students rush onto the field, and Connor finds me immediately, the crowd parting easily for him. He pulls his helmet off and wraps an arm around my hips, lifting me easily.

I wrap my arms and legs around him. "Congratulations, big guy!"

He smiles brightly and kisses me deeply, high on the victory. I cup his cheeks, running my fingers up through his sweaty hair. Rafe calls his name, and he reluctantly lowers my feet to the ground.

"You coming to the party?" he asks.

"If you're going."

"I'm the captain, babe. I have to go," he says with a charming grin.

"Let's go then."

"I'm just going to go shower."

"Okay, I'll meet you there?"

"You're not going to wait on me?" Connor pouts.

I roll my eyes. "I'll wait then." Connor's kiss is hard and quick before he heads into the locker room with the team.

Alice, Brett, and I wait outside the stadium, but I can tell they are eager to get to the party, so I tell them to go ahead. Alice practically dances away, talking to Brett about her next shifter victim. No sooner have they left than I feel an unnatural wind ruffling my hair. The stranger materializes in front of me.

I lean back against the wall, putting a little more distance between us. "Hi," I say a little shortly. I am still unhappy with how he left last time, though I'm not as pissed as I was earlier. I'm not sure why I'm so forgiving when it comes to him. Usually, I have very little tolerance for assholish behavior.

He reaches forward, tucking a lock of hair behind my ear again, acting like nothing happened. "Behave this weekend." His voice brushes past my ears in that whispery way that makes tingles erupt down my spine. "I'll be gone."

"Gone?" Why does that make my stomach tug in disappointment?

His chuckle is edged as if he knows. "Just for the weekend, little fae."

I look away, tugging at the edge of Connor's jersey.

"He's a lucky boy," he says, and I feel his gaze drift down my body.

"Friends," I say, crossing my arms.

He leans in, pressing his lips to my forehead. "Behave."

I place my hand on his arm, ready to push him away. His muscles flex beneath my palm, and I exhale at the feeling.

He pulls back, looking down at me. "No messes, promise me."

I look up at him. "I don't make messes, Stranger. They just seem to find me."

"Little liar," he scoffs, but I hear the smirk in his voice. "Goodbye, little fae." He breaks the spell, leaving my hand hovering where I was touching his arm. I frown and drop it to my side, making a mental note to keep firmer boundaries.

# 71

## SUMMER

*Raethae*
ALLOW, GRANT,
AFFIRM

Connor and his brothers emerge from the stadium, and I launch at him. Connor catches me easily and spins me around.

"Hi, babe."

Connor grins and smothers my face in kisses. I giggle, my heart full of joy. The darkness that rose in response to being in such close proximity to the stranger calms. It falls back into its box like grains of sand sifting through an hourglass, collecting in the bottom until it's disrupted again.

The calming effect Connor has on me reminds me of the Almighty and her words regarding my peace. He is my peace.

"Ready to go?" he asks, holding me against him. I nod, reluctantly unraveling myself from him. He sets me on my feet but immediately slings his arm around my shoulders. I take a moment to ponder the person I used to be. Once, I would have rejected his touch, but now I find comfort in it. This is what I wanted. It is what I asked for, but something is missing. But what could be missing?

"I love you," Connor says into my hair as he kisses the top of my head.

I smile. "Let's go," I say, pushing the bad thoughts away.

"I hope you know I'm going to kill your roommate," Zach says, coming up beside me. I can hear Zane snickering behind us.

I roll my eyes. "I highly doubt you'll want to kill her after you've reaped the rewards of her efforts."

There is a glint of intrigue in his eyes, but his voice is still angry. "How the fuck am I doing that?"

I look off into the distance and let my eyes glaze over, slowly waving my hand toward the heavens. "I foresee a blowjob in your future, Zachariah."

Zach's eyes darken a little, but he flinches. "Don't call me that."

I throw another eye roll at him. "So ungrateful. I'll get Alice to stop."

Zach looks away. "Listen, it's... whatever." He speeds up, his shoulders hunched. Connor looks at me reproachfully.

I grumble under my breath and sigh heavily before stepping out from under Connor's arm and hurrying to catch up with him. I link my arm through his. "What's wrong, Zachy?"

Zach shoves his hands into his front pockets and shrugs, but I feel the way his muscles tense beneath my fingers. "She doesn't want to date me."

I blink, studying his profile. "That cannot be true."

Zach throws me a furious look, but I can see the undertones of uncertainty. His gaze holds a vulnerability that I've never seen in him before.

"Zach, if looks could kill, Alice would be ash after that game."

He shrugs. "I'm tired of it being a secret."

"Then tell her."

He looks away again, trying to mask his pain. "I've tried."

"Tell her again," I reply simply, though I know it's anything but a simple option.

"How many times do I have to be rejected by the same girl?" he asks. The soft desperation in his voice makes my heart ache.

I nudge him, waiting until he looks at me before I continue. "Let's just party tonight." I feel Zach's shoulders fall. "And we can work it out tomorrow."

Zach shrugs, but I feel him relax a little, and by the time we arrive at the house, Zach is back to his arrogant, dickish self. Rafe pushes past us and grabs a beer before disappearing into one of the other rooms, no doubt looking for a place to brood.

The party is in full swing, and Connor pulls me close as we push through the crowd. Ashley storms toward us, people scrambling to get out of her way. She slaps Zach across the face, her chest heaving and her eyes red from crying. The music suddenly stops, and all eyes land on them. She swings to hit him again, but Zach catches her wrist. I can tell he's holding her gently like she's fragile and precious. They stare at each other for a long moment. The tension between them surges, and Zach slams his lips to hers. Ashley pushes against his chest for one futile moment before melting into him and kissing him back. I lift my eyebrows and glance up at Connor. He looks just as confused as I feel.

Zach breaks the kiss but rests his forehead against hers.

A little sob escapes Ashley. "You fucked Alice—"

Zach kisses her again, cutting off her words. Everyone watches the exchange in surprise.

He pulls back again, cupping her cheeks and forcing her to meet his eyes. "I didn't. She's a friend. Psychotic, but a friend."

Ashley searches his face. "With benefits?"

Zach shakes his head, and Ashley nods once, pulling back from him and straightening her outfit.

"Okay. Good," she says, clearing her throat. Zach grabs her as she's reapplying her perfect mask and throws her over his shoulder.

He winks at Connor as he passes. "I'm using your move, bro."

"Zach!" Ashley squeals.

Zach laughs and carries her upstairs. I blink up at Connor, and he smirks down at me.

"Apparently, we're trendsetters."

I laugh and wrap my arms around his neck. Connor pulls me in close and brushes a soft kiss against my lips, keeping his gaze locked on mine.

"I'm going to marry you someday, you know?"

My heart pounds harder and excitement sizzles through my veins, but the usual fear doesn't clutch at my chest. Doubts niggle at the back of my mind, but I'm chalking that up to the unfamiliarity of the situation or maybe my inferiority.

"Oh?" I ask, looking up at his handsome, angelic face.

"Oh, yeah." Connor tightens his arms around my waist. "I've got to lock you down."

I snake my fingers into his hair.

"Is that a yes?"

I quirk a brow. "I'm going to keep you on your toes until you ask me. More fun that way."

Connor laughs, and the sound wraps me in joy. "All right, future Mrs. Morningstar."

I lean in and kiss him deeply, my lips pulled into a smile.

# 72

## SUMMER

Meththu
OPEN

"You sure you don't want to go home with that guy?" I stumble into Alice as we walk through the quad, the moon shining down on us.

"Please, he had the weirdest-looking dick," Alice scoffs, her words just as slurred as mine.

I burst out laughing and bump into her again, wrapping my arm around her shoulders as we walk. "I love you, my Alicey."

"I love you, my wife!" She practically screams the last word. We both stumble and almost fall into a bush.

When we get back to our dorm room, we fall through the door and collide with the floor.

Alice pushes me. "You're drunk!"

"I am not!" I protest though the room spins as I try to sit up. Laying back down, I stare up at the ceiling. Alice shifts closer, her arm touching mine.

"Fuck, how did I get this drunk?" I ask, focusing on a small crack in the ceiling.

"Probably when you challenged Zane to a shot competition," she replies thoughtfully.

"Well, at least I won."

Alice exhales deeply. "I... may have a confession."

I quirk a brow, glancing at her.

"I might have drugged his drink."

I blink and then burst out laughing, thinking about how Zane went from being semi-drunk to completely hammered in the blink of an eye.

"In my defense, he was being a prick."

"So that's why Connor had to carry him home."

Alice snickers. "Maybe. He's been hogging you, anyway. It's my turn."

I laugh and shift so I can rest my head on her shoulder.

We stare up at the ceiling, and there is a small flare of magic as Alice slices into her finger. Suddenly, the most ethereal sky I've ever seen takes the place of the ceiling. Stars twinkle in their constellations, replacing the overhead light. They swirl soothingly on an indigo background in a symphony of blues, greens, and purples.

"You and your attempts at runes are turning my hair gray, Legosi. Though, nice work on this one."

Alice flips me off, still staring up at the ceiling. "This one I knew from before Avalon. I like sleeping beneath the stars."

I nod, curling into her more, feeling the pull of exhaustion. "I'm spending Yule with you, by the way. Hope that's cool."

"You are?" Alice asks, surprised. "What about Connor?"

"We'll all spend the day before Yule together, and then I'll come home with you. That is if you're still going to Drãculea. If not, we'll stay here."

Alice sighs heavily. "I have to go home, but now it won't suck so much."

I slide my hand into hers, knowing my best friend needs some comfort. I definitely made the right decision because even the mention of her home causes Alice pain. There is no way I will let her go back for Yule on her own.

"Plus, you'll get to see me make some vampires cry."

"The perfect present. I've already got your present, you know." I had managed to save enough credits by performing well in classes, and I was able to buy gifts for Alice and Connor.

"You have?" Alice looks at me. "What is it?"

"A surprise."

"I hate surprises," Alice grumbles.

"Too bad."

Alice squeezes my hand. "Sum?"

"Hm?"

"Thank you for not letting me go alone. I'm happy I met you," Alice says, her voice thick with emotion and sincerity.

"I love you, Al."

Alice's soft snores cut me off, and my lips twitch. I look up at the ceiling again, letting my mind wander.

Could Connor have meant what he said about wanting to marry me in the future? How could he possibly see anyone as damaged as me as someone he could build a life with? I am a mess and bring nothing but trouble. I am being hunted. Torin will never stop coming for me, and now there are the murders on campus that may be tied to me.

Perhaps it's time to take up the investigation myself. It is clear the authorities are getting nowhere, and for whatever reason, the headmaster is reluctant to share his theories with me, but he did share the grimoire. Perhaps he was telling me to investigate without actually telling me. I should probably increase my training days with Max and see him four or five times a week consistently. I should also try to stop being such a stubborn asshole when I'm around him.

I watch the sky shift and swirl, letting my mind drift to where I have been keeping it from going all night. He said he would be away. Away where? Another realm? Perhaps one where he can exercise that muscle he enjoys flexing so much, the controlling one. The one that enjoys being obeyed.

I grab my phone, and before I've considered it, I've sent a message to him.

@RaysofSummer
Why are you gone?

There is no immediate reply, no sign that he has even read my message. Usually, the second my message leaves my phone, he's already typing a response to me. I watch the screen, my stomach churning. I can't stop thinking of our last encounter, the casual touching, the whispered words. He's busy. Probably at some orgy realm where he can command a gaggle of women all swooning after him. Dick.

Pissed, I toss my phone to the side, but my anger only gets worse when I lunge for my phone when it pings a few minutes later. I eagerly open the chat. He has sent me a photo of what is clearly another realm. The sky is almost navy, and what I assume is grass is purple and looks furry. At the bottom of the photo is a pair of perfectly buffed black shoes. I zoom in on them to see if I can catch a reflection of my stranger in them, but no such luck.

@RaysofSummer
No sexy party?

So no then?

I see the three little dots bobbing up and down at the bottom of the screen, and I watch them intently.

I frown at my phone. *Recently?* So he has been.

My stomach coils as I send the message. There is something so deliciously seductive about pushing back.

Something that feels a lot like satisfaction crawls through me, trailing warmth in its wake. So even though he is off-realm, he continues to watch me. I know he said he would, but a part of me thought it might be out of sight, out of mind. Did I hope for that?

@RaysofSummer
I was just asking.

I wait for a reply, but when none comes, I take a photograph of myself lying on the floor. The light from the swirling sky overhead reflected on my face. I send him the photo, hoping for a reply.

@1015
Where are you?

Please. As if you don't know, Stranger. With a flicker of mischievousness, I type out a reply.

@RaysofSummer
At a party where
I'm getting hunted
;)

I have no idea where that came from, but I am pretty sure I will regret this in the morning. Or perhaps, once again, my inebriated mouth is more ready than I am to drop truths.

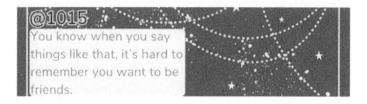

@1015
You know when you say
things like that, it's hard to
remember you want to be
friends.

So he *wants* that?

I read over his message once, twice, fifteen times. My core pulses, and my heart slams in my chest. It takes a few minutes before I finally get a grip on myself.

@1015

Goodnight, little fae.

My head swims for a long moment, and I feel something akin to guilt before the alcohol sinks its claws deeper into me and everything goes black.

# 73

## SUMMER

Maitha
CONTAINER, BAG, BOX

There is a loud knock on the door, the sound piercing my skull. I try to open my eyes, but they are stuck together. I shift, my muscles grumbling at the movement. There is another loud knock, and I wave my hand in the general direction of the door, not caring at the moment if it is an axe murderer. Alice groans next to me, and I finally manage to pry my eyelids apart. My head pounds, and I try to blink the light away.

"Good morning, babe. Fanged fury."

I rub my eyes and slowly open them again. Connor's face is pulled into a bright smile, and the fucker looks fresh as a daisy. I struggle to sit up, and he drops to the floor to sit next to me. He bundles me in his arms and cradles me against his chest.

"I brought coffee," he says into my hair, and I look at the table. When did he put those there? Fuck, who cares? Gods, it feels like someone is drilling into my head. I reach for my coffee and take a deep drink. The liquid scalds my mouth, but the burn distracts me from the other pain.

"I missed you," Connor says, pressing a kiss to my forehead.

"Why aren't you hungover?" I groan, my voice sounding rough and bruised.

Connor laughs softly. "I don't get hangovers."

I glare at him through my lashes. "I hate you."

Alice groans in agreement, still mostly passed out on the floor.

Connor laughs again and nuzzles into my neck. "I get it from my dad. My mom gets terrible ones. The twins and Luke get hangovers, but Rafe and I don't."

"I hate you and Rafe," I grumble. "And the twins cause they're annoying."

Connor kisses my neck. "Yeah? What about Luke?"

"No. Not Luke."

"You know," Connor begins, pulling back and reaching around behind his back. "I've brought you something else." He produces a brown paper bag full of pastries, and I could weep with gratitude.

"Oh, I fucking love you, Morningstar." I kiss him deeply and then pull back, selecting a pastry and practically swallowing it whole.

"You two were wild last night," Connor says, stroking my back.

Alice pulls herself into a sitting position and grabs her coffee cup, her eyes still closed. One of her false eyelashes is stuck to her cheek. I would laugh, but it would probably hurt. I'm also willing to bet I'm in a similar, if not worse, state.

"I heard a new nickname for you two last night. The Morningstar Menaces."

My lips twitch, and I nuzzle against Connor's neck. "We are honorary Morningstars now?"

Connor sighs in contentment. "Yup. It's official."

"I think the nickname should be for you and your brothers, and it should be the Morningstar Minions," I say, curling against him.

"Am I your minion, babe?"

I bite his jaw playfully. "You know it."

Connor moans softly and shifts, his voice husky when he asks, "What are the plans for today?"

"This. Maybe some penetration."

Connor laughs. "Maybe?"

I brush my lips over his. "Definitely."

It's late afternoon when Connor leaves for practice, and I lie down in bed for a nap, letting myself walk the line of consciousness. I'm distantly aware of someone standing in my doorway but recognize Alice's energy. I open my eyes and pat the covers next to me. Alice pads over on silent feet and sits on the bed.

"You know I love you," she begins, and I come to full alertness at the seriousness of her tone. "And I'm always on your side."

I exhale and wrap the sheet around my naked body before I sit up. "Oh no. What's wrong?" I grab Connor's jersey and pull it on, so I'm not so exposed.

"I've been giving this a lot of thought, and you need to tell Connor. This isn't right, Sum."

I frown in confusion. Tell him about what? A hazy memory of messages I shared with the stranger last night flashes through my mind. But they weren't that bad. Right? No. Alice didn't see them. Did she go through my phone?

"About what's going on."

My brows draw more.

"With the murders, Summer," Alice says, her voice sharp.

"Alice..."

"You need to tell him, Summer. You love him, right?"

I nod. "I do, but—"

"You don't think it's weird?" Alice asks. "Keeping him in the dark like this?"

"He's already worried, Al."

Alice shrugs. "It's your relationship." She watches me carefully. "Would you have kept me in the dark about it, too? If I hadn't been here when Headmaster Emrys came?"

I think for a long moment. "I don't know, Al. If it would protect you from living in fear, maybe."

Alice tenses, her eyes flashing. "Seriously? You would have lied about it? To *me*?" The way she emphasizes the last word is a punch to the gut. How can such a short word have so much impact?

"Not lied..."

Alice stands, shaking her head. "Omission is also lying." She looks at me, hurt in her eyes. "You'd have kept that fear all to yourself? You wouldn't have let me help you?"

"Alice..."

She scoffs. "You keep acting like you're alone. Like nothing has changed since we came here."

I climb out of bed. "How?"

Alice throws her hands up in frustration. "Because you don't think you can rely on me. Or maybe you think I'm going to leave you, or maybe you're planning to leave me. I don't know."

Her words are like daggers, but I can feel the truth in them. We have been here for so short a time, yet she has become the closest friend I have ever had. She and Connor have had a bigger impact on me than anyone in my life ever has, and the thought of being the one who is causing Alice so much hurt is agony.

All of my words are lost. I want to comfort her and apologize, but all I'm doing is what I've been doing for three decades. I've had to do things to survive so I could make it here, and I just cannot bring myself to apologize for that.

"Alice, I have told you things I've never told anyone. It's got nothing to do with not trusting you or wanting to leave. You have to know that."

"No?" Alice snaps. "Then what *does* it have to do with?"

"It's that I don't want you and Connor hurting. To get hurt."

"By refusing to let us help? You'd rather we find out when they finally got to you? You'd rather Connor walk into a classroom and see your body there?"

"That's not going to happen." I hear my voice rising and try to stop it, but I am overwhelmed by the emotions surging inside me.

"That's what happens, Summer!" Alice shouts. "They save their fixations for last. The perfect murder. The perfect corpse, eternally. Do you know what happens when an angel loses the person they love? They die, Summer." Alice's voice raises, matching mine. "And you know what happens to me?" Her voice cracks. "I'll break." The last words are practically a whisper, a broken confession.

I take a step toward her, but she backs up, her eyes welling with tears. "You say you love us, but it doesn't feel like it. I don't think you even know how to love."

The words slice into me, and I feel my heart fracture with each one. Alice turns like a whirlwind and storms to her bedroom, slamming the door behind her. I stare into space, her words echoing in my head until I can't stand it anymore, and I pull on a pair of shorts and my shoes.

I burst from Kelpie Hall, barely feeling the cold as I run through the torrential downpour. The icy drops pound off my skin, but do nothing to alleviate the burn of my thoughts. I'm shit. A shit friend. A shit girlfriend. Not only am I not being honest with Connor, but I also had that weird conversation with the stranger last night. I've still not found the courage to read the messages, but I remember the conversation being somewhat adjacent to flirting. It didn't mean anything, but I still know it came very close to crossing a line.

I run aimlessly until I notice the lights from the gym flickering in the distance. I change course and walk through the door, soaking wet and my hair plastered to my face.

"What happened to you?" Max asks from behind the reception desk.

I clench my fists, heartbreak, frustration, and anger coursing through me. "I want to fight."

Max stares assessingly at me for a long moment but then nods. "All right," he says, following me to the sparring room. I feel him watching me as I pull on my gloves.

"I'll give you the first punch," Max says, stretching as I get into position.

"Don't take it easy on me. Hit me."

Max's eyes glow green, and he throws a punch, expecting me to dodge it, but I don't. I want to feel the physical pain. I deserve it. His fist collides with my ribs, and there is a loud, sickening crack.

"Bitch," Max snarls. "You didn't even try to dodge."

"Hit me," I gasp out, keeping my face expressionless.

"I'm not going to fight you if you're just going to take the hits."

The frustration bubbles up, and I shove at his chest. "Fucking hit me."

"No," Max snarls.

I slap him hard across the cheek, trying to incite the berserker's rage. The glow of his eyes deepens, and I can feel him struggling to keep control.

"Hit me. Punish me."

"No." His voice trembles with strain.

I shove against his chest this time, actually forcing him to take a step back.

"I'm not going to fucking hit you," he growls.

I throw a punch, leaning into my fae strength and speed. Max just barely dodges it. "Hit." I throw another punch. "Me." I follow the word up with a fast kick.

It catches him in the chest, and he winces. "That all you got?"

I hit him again, embracing my powers for the first time ever, desperate to feel something other than the weight of the disappointment from the people I love. I hit him again, this time in the stomach, his abs tightening beneath my fist.

"Pathetic." He exhales.

I snarl. "Hit me. Fight me. Destroy me!" I say, still swinging for him. Some of my hits land, others he narrowly misses.

"Show me you're not worthless."

I lean into my instincts and drop to the floor. Swiping my leg under his, I take him to the mat. Straddle him, I pin him to the floor and start hammering on his chest. My emotions are a knotted mess within me, and I can't seem to find the end of them.

Max lays quietly beneath me, watching me with his glowing eyes. He keeps his palms pressed flat against the mat on either side of his body, taking the beating. I hit him over and over, and then suddenly, I burst into tears.

My chest shakes from the ferocity of the sobs, tears flowing from my eyes like a river clawing its way to the sea. I gasp for air, but no matter how hard I try, the breaths don't provide. I hit weakly at his chest once more, and then bury my face in my hands and just cry.

Max carefully sits up beneath me and gently wraps his arms around me. The hug isn't warm or intimate. It is a grounding tool. He is only providing a place of safety and comfort without an ounce of judgment.

"It's okay. Let it all go."

The tears don't let up. Somehow, his lack of emotion, combined with the safety of his hold, allows me the freedom to let it all go. It's as if the tears I have repressed for the last thirty years have burst from the banks. I sob into his shoulder, and Max hugs me silently. He doesn't make any jokes, and there are no snide comments. He holds me, allowing me to release whatever emotions I need to.

Eventually, I pull back and wipe my face, the sobs easing to a mere echo.

"Congratulations," Max says, keeping his arms firmly around me. "You're now only eighty-five percent hopeless."

I clear my throat, wiping my face again with the hem of Connor's still-wet jersey. "Mention this again, and I'll cut your dick off and put it in a meat grinder."

Max smirks. "Jokes on you. I'm into that."

I huff a weary laugh and shift off his lap.

Max stands and offers me his hand. I look up at him, feeling more than a little vulnerable, but then I slide my hand into his and let him pull me to my feet.

Max lifts his shirt, showing an already yellowing bruise on his chest. "You should be proud. You're one of only a handful of people who have ever managed to bruise me." He drops his shirt and looks at me. "Ice tonight. You'll need it after using your powers for more than a couple of minutes."

I nod. "All right."

Max pats my shoulder. "Whatever it is, just take comfort in this." Warily, I look up at him through lashes spiky with tears. "I won't ask you to tell me." He smirks.

I turn away from him and leave the gym. The rain is still hammering down, soaking me to the skin again. I look toward the dorm but don't feel ready to return there. I want to be alone, and the forest calls to me. It's a bad idea, but I don't care. I turn and bolt for the trees. I am about to pass the treeline when something grabs my wrist, stopping my headlong flight.

"Summer," the stranger's voice brushes against my ears.

I whirl to face him, squinting against the heavy rain. He waves his hand, and suddenly, the rain is beating down against an invisible canopy.

"I heard you," he says.

"I thought you were gone this weekend," I accuse, trying to catch my breath.

"I am," he says, and I can hear the frown in his voice.

"You don't look *gone*," I demand.

He pauses for a moment before stepping closer to me. "What are you doing?"

"I... I'm not cut out for this." The truth spills out of me, and I can breathe a little easier once it leaves my lips. "I'm not cut out for having people in my life who care about me."

He tilts his head. "You don't get to choose how others feel, little fae."

I close my eyes, feeling those cursed tears falling again, mixing with the water dripping from my hair. "It was easier when no one gave a fuck about me. It was easier to hide that..." I trail off, the words getting stuck in my throat.

"That you're not worthy of their love?" he asks.

I open my eyes and look up at him, craning my neck. "That I'm a complete mess and unable to love them as they deserve."

The stranger brushes a lock of wet hair out of my face. "They don't love some idealized version of you. They love you as you are."

"I'm not worth loving," I say and look away. "I've... done something that I..." Once again, the truth scalds my throat, stealing my voice. I was drunk when I told Alice, which helped with the vile taste of my truth. Now, I am completely sober, and the only thing fuelling me is the need to be fully understood for the first time. Alice understands why I did what I did, but I didn't show her what lives in the abyss. I barely understand that part of me, but I instinctively know the stranger does. I feel safer here than I do anywhere else, which is ridiculous given I have no idea who he is, and he emanates power and danger.

He just waits, the silence heavy around us. "I killed someone," I say, somehow knowing there will be no judgment from him. He just continues to watch me, waiting for the story. I tell him all about Torin, about our situation, the manipulations, the lies, the abuse. All of it spills from me, and it's almost easy. It feels so right to tell him about this, to tell *him* about how I have been hunted for years, that I have been afraid for years, and he simply listens. His hands clench a couple of times throughout the story, but otherwise, he is silent and still.

I feel his eyes boring into me even though I can't see him. Being watched by him feels nothing like when Torin is hunting me, and I can't help but admit that there is something oddly familiar about it. Maybe I was born to be hunted by one being or another. Maybe I am destined to be prey.

"It's never about worth," he begins, and I'm surprised he doesn't launch right into a million questions about the truth of my past. "You are your own worst enemy as I am mine. Insidious thoughts in our minds whisper falsehoods hoping to break us." He doesn't move. "Do you love them?" he asks.

I nod.

I feel his body tense. "Show them. Hold nothing back." His form flickers. "I have to go. The rune is breaking."

"Rune?"

"Yes, I had to use a special rune to project here. It has a time limit."

"How did you know?" I ask, still looking up at him.

"Know?" he asks, his form flickering again.

"That you were... needed?" Fuck. Is that what this is? Do I need him? I certainly needed this conversation, but him? For some reason, I feel like I can be honest with this stranger, and that is so fucking freeing.

"A sense," he says, his fingers stroking my cheek tenderly.

He fades away, and the icy rain stings my skin. The phantom warmth of his touch is the only evidence he was here.

# 74

## NA BI A-RIAMH

The rune on my hip vanishes as it times out. The burn while it worked was excruciating, and now it had settled into a bone-deep ache. Not all runes are painless, especially not one that sends my consciousness across the realms. I step out of the alcove I ducked into when I felt her distress and stride down the alley, garbage and debris crunching beneath my feet. I press my hand against the runed stone and slam my power into it, knowing that somewhere beyond, I have just made the very air vibrate. Wearily, I lean against the wall and drop my head back. I close my eyes, replaying her words in my head over and over.

*He always hunted me.*

Would it make her feel better to know that he's been hunted far more fiercely for the last few months? My lips twitch into a cruel smirk. She never wondered if it was Torin murdering the fae women who looked like her. She must sense that the threat of her past has lessened slightly, which is true in a sense.

A few months ago, Torin made the mistake of getting a little too close to my fae. It was enough to pique my interest, and my interest can be a very dangerous thing. It took little effort to break into his phone and discover his motive for coming close.

My power caused a minor outage in the Grand Arcane when I realized. Then I began. I started with his friends. The first wailed and pissed himself, begging for his life. He was willing to show me where my prey was hiding, but he failed to realize the true heart of it. I knew where Torin was. No, this was about fear.

I sent the head of the wagging-tongued friend to where Torin was staying at a hotel in the realm of Svarga. I had it served on a platter in place of his meal. His scream could have brought the divine beings back to this plane. He thought money bought him protection, and I enjoyed proving him wrong. No amount of wealth or imagined security could keep him safe from me.

His second friend never saw me coming. One moment, he was alive, and the next, he was dead. I sent Torin this one's right hand with his signet ring still on his finger. I had it delivered to his safe house in Kunlun Mountain. A few days later, I sent the third's skin, with his runes still glowing, to Torin's shack in Buyan. The ears of the fourth were still dripping blood when they arrived at his flat in Mictlan. Now it is finally time to finish the hunt.

A resonating boom presses on my ears. The raróg screeches as it unlocks the gates to Vyraj. I straighten and turn to face the doorway, bowing slightly in deference. This is where my prey reaches the end of his journey. Torin pulled every favor and trick, spending his last credit trying to escape me. It was always futile. He finally realized the same thing all the targets before him had. Death is a mercy compared to me.

The birds sing as I pass through the gates, navigating each step with precision. He made her feel hunted, so I returned the favor tenfold. For every moment of fear he gave her, I gave it back to him. For every friend she never had, I killed one of his. For every nightmare, I conjured worse realities.

I drop the suppression on my power, letting him sense me coming. It is clear the moment he feels me. His body goes rigid, and his muscles twitch as if preparing for flight. He looks around, his eyes sunken and his face gaunt. I walk a little slower. Maybe I should delay this execution. She just told me the whole story. Is this enough retribution? Should I make it last?

He bolts down the street before I can decide. Damn. I stroll after him, watching as he bangs on the doors of the houses, begging for shelter and safety. None open for him. They know better. Never come between the hunter and their prey.

He turns to face me, throwing up his hand. A spell circle forms around him, flickering as he tries to summon some runes to fend me off, but he's too panicked, too weak. He's been on the run for weeks. The strength of the caster is just as crucial as the knowledge of runes, and he has nothing left. I've made sure of that.

He trips as he tries to get away and falls, scraping his hands and knees raw as he tries to crawl away. I slow my steps, allowing him the illusion of freedom, only to slam the cage down on him.

"W-Who are you?" he whimpers, the corners of his eyes trembling and magenta flickering in the violet of his irises. "Why are you doing this?"

I slam my boot onto his ankle, shattering it. My lips twitch cruelly as he screams in pain, writhing on the ground. "I considered letting you run some more." My foot grinds the broken bones in his ankle, forcing the shattered pieces through his skin, and even the firebirds stop singing at his cry.

"I killed someone. I was young and stupid, and I thought I was in love." I break his other ankle, smirking as his scream becomes a gargled, choking cry of despair. "He knew what I was immediately. He wasn't fooled by the way I'd braided my hair over my ears to hide the points. He tried to coax my powers out of me."

Torin's eyes flicker, and he tries to pull himself away from me, even as his broken bones rip through his Achilles tendon. I let him, the last desperate act of a cowardly male.

"I was desperate. I thought I loved him, and I was so stupid." He shakes his head as I continue, my voice dangerously soft. The last words he would hear wouldn't be mine. Her vulnerability and trauma will be his doom. "One night, we went into the woods, and a group of his friends were there."

I wave my hand, and a rune on my arm glows. A small pocket of space opens above Torin and belches the remains of his friends. Body parts rain down on him as he continues to drag himself across the ground, his hands slipping on the rotting flesh of his former cohorts.

"Show me what you can do, Summer," I continue. Torin starts to cry. He sobs, begs, and pleads. "I always did what I was told. One of his friends stayed behind." My steps are measured as I close the distance, my power radiating from me in waves as I remember her eyes when she told me this horror. I should have let him keep running for a century at least, but I doubt that would be enough. "I thought he would punish me, that he would kill me."

My foot lands on his chest, slamming him down into the cobbled streets, stopping his desperate escape attempt.

"S-She sent you?" He sobs, snot dripping down his face.

I don't answer, applying more pressure and cracking his ribs. I could kill him with a single touch of my hand and bring him back to life with the other, but this is different. This I want to *feel*. My ability makes it too quick. Any casting would make this too quick. Even now, it is too quick.

"So I ran." I press harder with my foot, watching his eyes as the broken rib punctures his lungs, filling them with blood. He's too weak to heal from this. "And he chased me."

My next step shatters his rib cage, my foot crushing his heart. My eyes lock with his, the last of his life dimming.

"Show me what you can do, Torin."

# 75

## SUMMER

*Lyntha*

HOME, ORIGIN

My phone pings in my pocket, and I pull it free. The fallen tree trunk I'm perched on has a thick canopy of leaves above, so I'm mostly sheltered from the rain.

> ALICE
>
> I'm sorry.

I consider replying, but there is still that deep ache in my chest that I'm unable to push away. The only way I can think to ease it is to take more time to come to terms with my feelings and reflect on what she said.

The sky is inky black by the time I decide to make my way home, and though I've been out on my own all day, there has been no sense of being watched. Does it make me naïve to hope that the killer has just... gone? By the time I arrive home, my clothes are soaked through again, and I'm shivering from the cold.

Alice is pacing in the living room, and she's practically worn a track into the rug. She spins toward me, her eyes widening. "You're soaked."

I nod and start toward my bedroom, desperate for a shower, desperate to be wrapped in warmth and comfort. Alice wraps her arms around me from behind and squeezes, trapping my arms at my sides.

I feel my body tense, and I hate the way it does. "Alice, I... I'm..." I swallow, feeling the emotion welling inside me again, but she just keeps holding me. She loosens her hold enough to allow me to turn and wrap my arms around her. I bury my face into her neck and hold my best friend.

"I'm sorry," I whisper so softly that if not for her vampiric hearing, she'd never have heard.

"I'm sorry, too." She exhales shakily. "I just... I hate it when you shut me out. I can't handle it, Summer."

I pull back, looking at her. "I'll tell you everything, okay? Everything I know, and then we can decide what to tell Connor." I had decided on my walk home that Alice deserved to know the whole truth. I trust her, and if she is this adamant about telling Connor, I should hear her out.

Alice nods, sliding her hand into mine, her face set into a serious expression. "All right. It's always going to be us. Wifeys."

I squeeze her hand. "Let me shower real quick, and we can talk."

Alice reluctantly releases me, and I take a quick shower before pulling on pajamas. Alice is in the living room when I emerge from my room, and to my delight, she's put the fire on. Even after the shower, the remnants of the cold still linger on my skin, but the room is warm and comfortable. It's like walking into a blanket.

Alice pats the space next to her on the couch, and I sit down, pulling a blanket over my legs as much for comfort as warmth. Alice holds her hand out, and I place mine in hers.

"It's you and me to the end, okay?" she says.

I nod, moving closer to her.

"I'm sorry I yelled at you."

"It's okay," I say with a small smile.

Alice sighs. "I've never had a friend."

I squeeze her hand. "Me either." I sigh heavily. "Okay. I'll tell you everything."

Alice smiles, but I can see the tension in her shoulders.

"There's really only one more thing," I say. Alice squeezes my hand, waiting for me to continue. "I have this... friend."

Alice tilts her head. I feel her carefully studying me.

"I don't really know how to explain. I don't know who he is, but..." Fuck, how do I even begin to explain the stranger? He's this guy who is potentially a weird stalker, but also I feel like he might be the only person in all the realms who truly understands me. Fuck. "Sometimes he's around, and he... understands me."

Alice's brows furrow, and she shakes her head. "Start from the beginning, Sum."

I nod. "Okay. I noticed this person was watching all of my stories, and sometimes they would message me. Initially, I pushed back, but then we started talking, and he..." I hesitate again. "Occasionally materializes and we... talk."

"Materializes?" Alice asks.

I nod. "But I don't know who he is. It's hard to explain."

"But he's not dangerous?"

I quickly shake my head, but her question sinks into me after my snap answer.

Honestly, I have no idea who he is, but I know he is dangerous. He just isn't dangerous to me. I'm being so incredibly stupid, but it's so fucking nice to vocalize my darkness and know that he won't judge me for it. A part of me craves to free that side of me, but no one else would understand.

"I know it sounds crazy, Al. But I... trust him," I say, the words spilling easily from my lips. They must be the truth or a lie so convincing that even I am convinced.

"Will he protect you?" she asks. There is no judgment or cynicism in her voice, just genuine interest.

"I think so."

Alice nods, thinking for another moment. "Okay. That's all that matters. More people to protect my Summer."

"Do I tell Con?"

"Do you think he'd have a problem with it?" Alice asks.

I shrug. "Probably not. Connor's not a jealous person."

Alice lifts her chin a little. "Should he be jealous?"

I blink, looking at her. "I love Connor."

"I know." Alice's lips twitch. "But I'm guessing there's a little more to this than you're telling me."

"What?"

Alice laughs. "I'm guessing this... dude doesn't want to be just friends."

I shrug, looking away. "We've had words about boundaries."

Alice snorts. "Yeah? You had a boundaries discussion with your stalker?"

I frown. "He's not a stalker. He's..." I pause, unsure what he is. Okay, maybe the way he watched me could make him seem... stalkerish, but I am not going to admit that to Alice.

"A what?" Alice asks, cocking one brow.

"A friend," I finish.

"Right."

I sit back on the couch, thinking. "I should talk to Connor, make sure he's cool with it. Right?"

"I mean, yeah."

I look up at the ceiling. "Also, I beat up Max."

"On purpose?" Alice asks.

I nod and then notice the time. "Connor will be here soon." I pick at a loose thread on the blanket. "Do you think he'll break up with me?"

Alice snorts as if the question is incredibly stupid. "No, I really don't think he will."

My stomach twists and turns as the nerves set in, and I scroll through my phone to pass the time.

"Show me the DMs," Alice demands.

Surprised, I look up at her. "Why?"

"Because I'm nosey," Alice says with a shrug.

"Okay. But please bear in mind a lot of these were sent before we had strict boundaries in place."

Alice snorts and snatches my phone from my hand, expertly navigating through it. With every message she reads, her eyebrows raise higher on her forehead. "Who is this guy?"

"What do you mean?" I ask, practically bouncing with nerves.

Alice turns my phone to show me the photo he sent last night. "This is off-realm. Like *way* off-realm."

"So?"

Alice pulls out her phone and starts searching *Nexus*. "This is Valhalla. Not only is he pretty much as far away as he could be, but he still has cell service?"

I frown, taking my phone back and typing out a message to him.

The reply comes immediately.

Alice gasps, reading the messages over my shoulder. "Shut the fuck up! He created the Runic Network?" Alice starts furiously typing on her phone. "We can totally find out who he is, Sum."

I watch her type furiously, my hopes rising that she will find out something about him.

"Fuck. All it says is that it was created by an anonymous individual over forty years ago." She continues to read. "Apparently, its purpose was to make sure we wouldn't fall behind the mortals in terms of technology." She sighs heavily. "Damn, I thought we'd caught him."

I close my messages with the stranger and place my phone beside me. "Why do I feel so nervous about telling Connor?"

"Well, do you feel guilty?"

"I have nothing to feel guilty about, right?" I ask in a small voice, chewing on my lower lip.

"You were maybe a little flirty with him last night, but... I don't think so. You've been very clear that you and he are just friends."

I nod, but my stomach twists again when there is a knock at the door.

Alice hugs me and stands up. "Good luck," she says before going into her room and closing the door behind her.

Taking a deep breath, I get up and open the door for Connor.

"Hi." Connor smiles brightly at me.

"Hi," I reply, feeling how my smile doesn't reach my eyes.

Connor pulls me into him, nuzzling the top of my head. "I missed you."

I brace my hands on his chest. "Con."

He pulls back, his brows drawn. "What's wrong?"

"I need to tell you something," I say on an exhale.

Connor takes my hand and leads me to the couch. He sits down, and I curl up beside him.

"Babe?" Connor asks when I don't start talking. "What is it?"

"I..." I swallow. "I have this friend I talk to sometimes, and I didn't tell you about them."

Connor reaches out, twining a lock of my hair around his finger. "A friend?"

I nod.

"Okay, why didn't you tell me about them?" Connor asks. Hurt shadows his eyes, and it fucking breaks me.

"Initially, because I found him very annoying. I couldn't stand him, actually."

Connor places his hand over mine. "Okay."

"But there's..." I begin, dropping my gaze to our hands. I am such a coward. I do not want to see the pain in his eyes. "There are things about me he understands, Con, and we've become friends."

Connor slides his thumb over the back of my hand. "Things about you he understands?"

I nod, still unable to look at him.

"Things I *won't* understand?" he asks.

I turn toward him and scoot closer, finally finding the courage to meet his gaze again. He locks his blue eyes on mine, trying to understand.

"Things I never want you to understand, big guy."

Connor studies my face. "Does he help?"

I shake my head. "*You* help. He just makes it seem like I'm not the only one that has these thoughts and feelings."

Connor is silent for a minute, processing everything.

"Con?"

"Hm?" He strokes his thumb over my knuckles again.

"I love you, and if you want me to stop talking to him, I'll do it in a heartbeat. No questions asked."

Connor shakes his head. "I don't want that. The part that gives me pause is that there are things you don't want to share with me."

I look away, feeling the shame overwhelm me. "Because they don't matter when I'm with you." He is my peace. He is perfect. I can't tarnish his platinum soul with my inky black one.

"Will you... tell me about it? Someday?"

His request is so small and so kind, yet there is another question I need to ask before I agree to even that.

"If I do, will you still love me?"

Connor pulls me into his lap, and I wrap my arms around his neck. "Babe. I will always, always, *always* love you."

The sincerity in his eyes is undeniable, and I cup his cheek. "Then yes, Connor. Someday."

Connor presses his forehead to mine. "He helps?"

I close my eyes. "You help," I repeat.

"Will talking to him help you talk to me one day?" he asks, and I can hear the smile in his voice.

I exhale. "I think so." I hope so.

"Good. Look at me."

I open my eyes, and our gazes lock. Space and time seem to stand still, and Connor tilts his head, brushing his lips over mine. "I'm happy you have someone who understands. I know there are things in your head that you keep secret, and if he can help ease the burden you carry, then I am grateful for him." He kisses me again. "I love you."

I whimper softly, the love in his words hitting me like a physical blow, and I deepen the kiss.

Connor smiles. "You were nervous about telling me." It's not a question but a statement and proof that he is getting to know me because I am slowly letting him in.

"I never want to do anything to hurt you. I never want to put us in jeopardy."

Connor leans in, nuzzling my throat. "While I wish you could talk to me about this stuff, I understand. And if this dude is going to help you. How could I be mad about that?"

I kiss him again.

"Just don't go falling in love with him," Connor says with a smile.

"How could I when I have the best fucking boyfriend in all the realms?"

Connor laughs, and the sound is so joyful and perfect that there is no room for tension, no room for fear, no room for anxiety.

There is just us.

# 76

## SUMMER

Loth'thae
REALM, WORLD

I am lying on top of Connor, my naked skin against his. My hands are stacked on his chest, and I am resting my chin on them, looking up at him.

"What?" he asks, playing with a lock of my hair.

"Thank you."

Connor leans up and nuzzles my nose. "For what?"

"For being patient with me." I brush my lips over his. "For wanting me." I kiss him again. "For loving me."

"You're worth it."

I pull back, feeling my smile falter. "Are you sure?" I ask, my vulnerability showing.

"I've never been more sure of anything."

I relax a little, drawing shapes on his chest.

"You were really worried, huh?"

I nod and look up at him through my lashes. "You'll stay over?"

"If you want me to."

I nod again. "Please."

Connor shifts beneath me, tucking me against him. "Good."

I lay my head on his shoulder. "Con?"

"Hm?" I can hear sleep already tugging at him.

"You make me happy," I whisper softly.

Connor's skin takes on a faint glow. "You make me happy, too." I feel his body completely relax into the sanctuary of sleep, and my own exhaustion claws at me. But just as I'm about to plunge into unconsciousness, I hear my phone vibrate on the bedside table. I reach over Connor, who is already snoring softly, and pick it up.

I frown at the message, quickly typing a reply.

There is a pause before he starts typing again.

How could I have missed him? He's barely been away. Should I have missed him? Was that even an appropriate question for him to have asked?

The message seems to type itself, my fingers flying over the keypad.

I try to ignore the tug of disappointment.

Fuck. There's that different tug, a deeper one. One that I need to veer away from right now and avoid forever.

I pause for a moment, staring at my phone before I start typing again.

I sigh, considering his question. Do I feel better now that I've opened up a can of worms and have absolutely no idea what to do with it?

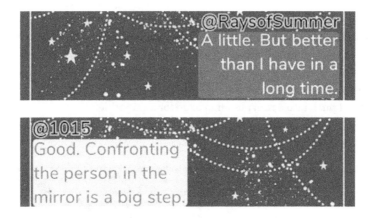

My lips twitch, and I roll my eyes,

I lock my phone, hearing it faintly vibrate with his final message, but I'm already fading into sleep.

I only sleep a few hours later and wake up with my body still feeling uncomfortable from yesterday. Emotions have always wreaked havoc on me physically. It's like my body tries to reject them so violently that they take a toll not only mentally but physically, too. Connor barely stirs as I climb over him and pull on tight yoga pants, a sports bra, and a sweater. Winter seems to have firmly claimed the realm.

Outside, I push into a run, planning to go for a smoothie.

My phone alerts, and beneath 1015's last *Goodnight* message, there is one from this morning. Does he ever sleep?

@1015
Where are you going so early?

I slow to a walk and then stop fully. I look around, trying to spot him. It sets me a little on edge that I can't feel his eyes on me. Am I taking my safety for granted?

@RaysofSummer
Where are you?

@1015
I told you I was back.

@RaysofSummer
You're watching me

I roll my eyes. What an arrogant dickhead.

I sigh and shake my head before pushing into a run again.

I glance at his message, and my lips twitch, but I ignore him as I arrive at the cafe to order my smoothie.

"Berry blast, please."

The server nods and scurries away to start my order.

I narrow my eyes at the phone.

I roll my eyes again.

I scowl at my phone, trying to understand why he's making such a big issue of this. Max runs the gym, and he is also my trainer, so why the fuck does it matter if he's there or not?

@RaysofSummer
The headmaster said I should use the gym instead of running. I'm trying to be good. Leave me be.

@1015
You have never been a good girl.

@RaysofSummer
You just don't want me to be a good girl.

I wince at the message and shove my phone away. I grab my smoothie and jog to the gym, making a beeline for the treadmill. The belt has barely started when Max appears in front of me, his frown putting deep furrows in his brow. "You didn't ice."

It's not until he mentions it that I notice how sluggish my muscles feel. Max slams his hand down on the stop button and grabs my arm, dragging me to the sports medicine room.

"Max! What the fuck?" I yelp as he pulls me through the gym.

Max pushes me down on the table and places his hand on my shoulder. He presses his thumb into my muscle, finding a huge knot on his first pass.

"Moron," he growls.

I buckle under the pressure and swat at him, his touch hurting me. "Ouch! Stop!"

"It hurts because you're a moron. Lie down."

I cross my arms. "No."

Max narrows his eyes and scoops up my legs, practically forcing me to lie down on my front. He moves around the table to stand at my head and massages my shoulders. In reality, there is nothing relaxing or pleasant about the way his fingers press into my muscles. He moves his touch along my shoulder, pressing in deeper. Suddenly, one of the knots shifts and then releases. I can't help my yelp, but my body starts to relax. I moan at the feeling of him working my sore muscles.

Max continues working the muscles along my neck and back. I can't tell if his touch is softer or if he's just worked my muscles so well that they no longer hurt. I moan again, my eyes closing as I allow myself to relax into the feeling.

"You're lucky I know what her actual moans sound like, Romulus, or this would be a very different moment."

I open my eyes, and Max's hands go still on my shoulders, but he doesn't remove them. He rolls his eyes. "If it isn't the Golden Boy."

I turn my head to look at Connor and sit up, intending to slide off the table. "Hi, big guy."

Max stops me and digs his thumb into my muscles. "She needs to ice after workouts."

I moan as he rolls the knot along my shoulder.

Connor narrows his eyes. "Cool. You can take your hands off her now."

Max rolls his eyes but lifts his hands and steps back.

I watch Connor warily. His stance is confrontational, and there is nothing gentle or passive about this man. I hop off the table and walk toward Connor. He doesn't take his eyes off Max, still sizing him up. I slide my hand into his and tug him toward the door. Once we are outside, I pull him around the side of the building. When we're out of sight of the path, I curl my fingers into the waistband of his pants and pull him close.

Connor slides his hand over my shoulder and gently massages it, his touch abundantly more tender than Max's.

"You feeling jealous, big guy?"

"Someone else had their hands on you." He meets my gaze, his eyes flashing with possessiveness.

I moan, tightening my fingers and bunching his pants before I open the button and shove down the zipper. I slip my hand inside and wrap my fingers around his cock, squeezing his hardening length.

"I need you. Now."

Connor groans and wastes no time in shoving my pants down. I toe my shoes off and free my legs, kicking away both the leggings and my panties. Connor picks me up and presses my back to the wall. I wrap my thighs around his waist as he works at freeing his cock, his knuckles brushing against my slick center and dragging a moan from me.

He thrusts inside of me, and I cry out, feeling the edge of his possessiveness in the way he fucks me. There is a desperation that has never been present, and I fucking love it. I crave it, and I need more of it.

Connor groans and thrusts faster, leaning his body against mine, crushing me against the stone wall. I slam my lips to his and dig my nails into his shoulders, kissing him passionately.

"Bruise me, big guy," I moan against his lips. He digs his fingers into my ass harder than he's ever done before. The bite of pain is followed by a jolt of pleasure so intense I cry out.

I trail my lips over his jaw, nipping and licking, savoring the rough scrape of his stubble. His breath hitches, and he tilts his head for me, allowing me better access. I bite his neck, and his moan sends a shiver down my spine. Connor's hips piston into me, and all I can do is hold on, my pussy quivering around his cock. With every thrust, my ass slides against the rough wall, but I don't care. This is closer to what I crave, what I need.

"So close..." I moan against his neck before biting down hard and sucking. Connor shouts, and his body goes rigid. He buries his face into my hair and thrusts deep, his cock pulsing as he fills me. My orgasm rips through me, and I press my face against his neck to muffle the sound of my pleasure.

Connor and I stand there panting, keeping his cock buried inside me until he feels me shiver from the cold.

"We should move..." he whispers into my hair.

I moan, pressing soft kisses against his neck and protesting a little as he gently lowers my feet to the ground.

"You like my jealousy?" Connor asks as he steps back. I bonelessly lean against the wall, and he kneels to help me correct my clothing. I watch him through hooded eyes as I push my legs into my leggings.

"Maybe..." I say coyly. Connor stands, kissing me again. I smile and fit myself against him.

"I love you," he says, tucking a lock of hair behind my ear. "I didn't realize it was such an unreasonable emotion."

I trail my fingers down his chest. "Sexy."

"Sexy?" Connor laughs.

I nod, kissing him again, my thighs clenching when I realize something is missing. "Con."

"Yeah?"

"I'm not wearing panties."

Connor frowns. "Are you sure?"

"Pretty sure." I look around, but there is no sign of them. "I don't want to work out without panties. Especially when your cum is dripping out of me."

Connor's eyes darken a little, but he pretends not to be affected by my words as he looks around for my panties.

"Where do they keep going?" he asks.

His question is fair, given I am losing a pair almost daily. I'm going through so many that I've had to order more rush delivery.

"Could we look for a rune to stop them from going missing?"

I think for a moment. "I'd probably have to create one, but maybe I could use a rune to find my missing ones."

"To the library!" Connor exclaims, and I laugh.

"I still need to work out, big guy."

"You can't skip a day?" he asks, frowning.

My lips twitch, reveling in the last drop of his possessiveness. I know it won't last. "I'll come back later. Maybe your favorite berserker won't be here when I return."

"I just don't get what his problem with me is." Connor narrows his eyes, looking at the gym.

I quirk a brow. "I think the problem is mutual, Con."

"I don't dislike people."

I give him a skeptical look.

"I don't!" he exclaims.

"Okay, so say it."

"Say what?"

I clear my throat. "I, Connor Azrael Morningstar, like and respect Maximilian Romulus."

Connor opens his mouth to speak and then closes it again.

I lift my eyebrows, waiting.

Connor crosses his arms. "I don't hate him."

"You don't like him, either."

Connor slings his arm around my shoulder and pulls me against his chest in a gentle headlock. I squeal and bat at him as he starts walking toward the library.

# 77

## SUMMER

*Lilith'hu*
FLORA, PLANT

The library is still mostly empty this early in the morning, and Connor wraps his arms around me from behind as we wander through the stacks. He nuzzles and kisses my cheek, his lips soft and warm.

"Con..."

He nips along my jaw. "Hm?"

"We're here on business."

He sighs and pulls back. "Right. I forgot."

I grin and shake my head as we walk deeper into the library to our usual aisle.

Connor pulls a book from the shelf as I look around. "You know, I don't think I've ever actually looked at the books back here."

"That's because you're usually too busy burying yourself inside me." I kneel on the floor, peeking under the shelves where I've lost more than a few pairs of panties.

Connor leans against the shelf, watching me. "Don't make it sound like I was trying to jump you."

I laugh as I summon my small knife and slice the pad of my finger. I draw a rune to locate lost items on the strangely pristine floor. Unlike other parts of the library, the wood is not worn or scuffed here.

As I'm about to connect the lines of the rune, it begins to glow. The rune flashes, and a small portal opens. I grin and am about to reach into it when the floor starts to shake. The books tumble from the shelves, falling all around us.

I look up at Connor. He is standing over me now, keeping the heavy books from hitting me on the head. The ground stops shaking, but the edges of the portal, still showing the perfect shape of the rune, burst into flames. I throw myself to the side to avoid the blast, instinctively covering my head and face. Connor is thrown across the aisle from the force, his back crashing against the bookshelf.

My chest heaves, and I peek from beneath my arm. Books are strewn all around me, shreds of paper floating through the air like confetti. I can still feel the flicker of power coming from the rune. The tie between us is still there but sharper.

Connor gets to his feet, his nervous gaze on me. I nod, letting him know I'm okay, and shift onto my knees, slowly moving toward the rune. Embers flicker around the edges, but the fire is slowly burning out. I frown and tilt my head. The rune is different now. It is not the rune I drew, not even close. As the flames die completely, the scorch mark stands out against the rich wood. Connor approaches cautiously, looking down at the new rune.

"Looks like a shield," he says.

I nod, brushing my fingers over it, tracing the dark lines. It has the curves and points a shield rune would have, but it's different. It's not like anything I've ever seen before. It's... magnificent.

"Can you grab my phone?" I ask Connor. He hurries off to find my bag, which was also thrown from the aisle. The second he's out of sight, a message appears along the border of the rune.

**NOT WISE TO TRY TO STEAL FROM ME.**

The second I reach the end of the sentence, the words fade, and by the time Connor has returned, they are completely gone.

I snap a photo of the rune before pushing to my feet. I slice my finger again and slide the bleeding pad over one of the runes on my hand. With a wave of my arm, the books and shredded pages lift into the air, repairing themselves and sliding back onto the shelf.

But the rune remains.

"This is kind of weird," Connor says, still studying the rune.

I nod, looking up at him. "Someone has my panties." I look around, expecting to see someone watching me. I wait for the weight of that malevolent gaze to settle on me, but I don't feel it. "It is probably best if we are more careful where we have sex for a while."

"I don't like this, Sum," Connor says, his brows drawn.

I look up at him, cupping his cheek. "It'll be okay."

Connor looks around, and his shoulders tighten. "Just stay close to me."

"Con..."

Connor keeps looking around. "Hm?"

I sigh. "Nothing."

Content that there is no imminent danger, he looks back at me and brushes his lips over mine. "Your place or mine?"

I shrug. "Either."

"Yours then."

We head back to my dorm, and Connor slides his hand into mine

"You know, I was actually planning to work out with you when I went to the gym to find you this morning."

I smile up at him. "Oh?"

He looks down, his cheeks going a little pink. "I thought it would be cute."

"We could go now?"

Connor shakes his head. "No. I would prefer to have you all to myself." We walk in silence for a while before Connor squeezes my hand. "You know, one day, you're going to have to wake me up before leaving."

I tilt my head. "Why? You were sleeping so peacefully."

"Because I want to wake up with you in my arms."

I smile at him. "Okay, next time, I'll wake you up."

"Creatively?" Connor's eyes darken hopefully.

I stop walking and turn to face him, sliding my hands up his chest and leaning into him. "You want me to wake you up with my mouth?"

Connor snakes his arms around my hips and pulls me closer, rocking against me. "Well, I wouldn't object to a repeat."

"You liked it, huh?"

"Maybe a little..." Connor smiles coyly.

"Only a little?" I lean in, biting his shoulder.

Connor moans. "Okay, definitely more than a little. Fuck, how are we going to get through finals?"

"What do you mean?" I ask, looking up at him.

Connor slides his hands down to my ass, cupping me. "Well, we won't be able to be as... active."

I drop my gaze, petting tenderly over his chest. The thought of that kind of distance between us scares me more than a little. I'm not good at emotional stuff, and that's a little easier to hide when I'm able to distract with my body. Also, is this his way of saying he doesn't want me?

"We won't?" I ask, peeking up at him.

"Well, we'll be studying," Connor says, his cheeks a little flushed.

"Oh. Right..."

"What?"

I shake my head. "Nothing, I just wasn't expecting that."

Connor's hands slide to my lower back. "I don't have the..." he clears his throat, "natural ability you do."

What the fuck does that mean?

Connor moves one of his hands to rub the back of his neck, dropping his other hand from my waist. "I have to *really* study to do well."

Ah.

I place my hand on his arm. "Con, I get it. I just hadn't thought about it."

Connor's lips pull into a small, shy smile. "You're a natural genius. I need to work on it."

"Hardly, big guy," I say, rolling my eyes.

Connor scoffs. "Yeah? What did you get on your last paper?"

"I..." I consider the big, red *A* stamped on my last term paper for Realms and decide not to give him the satisfaction. "Well, I don't remember."

"Liar." Connor laughs. "It was an *A*. I remember you showing me last week. And how long did that paper take you to write?"

I cross my arms and tap my foot. "Well. I don't know. I didn't fucking time myself."

Connor smirks at me. "You see what I mean?"

Irritation prickles beneath my skin. It's like he's putting all the blame on me for us being a distraction.

"Whatever, it's not like I force you to fuck me," I growl. The second the words leave my lips, guilt sinks its claws into me, but there is also a delicious relief of the safety I feel from the barrier that sentence has created.

Connor recoils as if I struck him. "I'm sorry? The fuck does that mean?"

"You make it sound like some sordid ordeal that I *force* you to go through." What is coming out of my mouth? Fuck.

"What? You're not serious?" Connor asks, his face a blend of confusion, hurt, and anger.

I glare at him, mired in my stubbornness and my own hurt, my self-made hurt.

"How in the world is saying you're naturally intelligent and don't have to study as much as me, make it sound like that?" Connor asks, bewildered.

"It just did, Con," I say, throwing my hands up. The words taste like venom on my tongue, but I can't deny the second wave of comfort they bring. The familiar sense of safety wraps around me like a blanket.

The pain and confusion in Connor's eyes morph into anger, and he shakes his head. "Okay, cool. I'm going home."

He's leaving. He's abandoning me. Just like I knew he would. I want to scream, shake myself, and cause myself pain. While this pain is familiar, there is no easing the emotional agony of him walking away from me. Now that I have had a taste of what it means to be connected to someone, I don't know who I am without it.

"Fine." I look away and wrap my arms tightly around my torso. I feel like I've been stabbed in the chest, but I am so acutely aware that I am the aggressor.

"Saying it's a sordid ordeal is pretty fucked up," Connor says, turning to leave.

A war rages within me. Half of me is clawing to reach out to him, to apologize and hold him. That part wants me to cling to him and force him never to let me go. But the other half, the familiar half, croons a melancholy tune. The song of loneliness, but more importantly, the song of safety. There is solace in being the only person who can break your own heart.

I stand there until he is out of sight. My two halves are still waging an inner war, battling so fiercely that I am stuck in this emotional limbo. I force my feet to move, not in the direction Connor went but toward the gym. I need to work this off, pushing myself until I can find my equilibrium again.

Max says something to me as I walk by, but I head straight to the treadmill and climb on, setting it to the fastest speed. My body groans at the rude shove into movement, but I embrace it, waiting for the fog of feeling to lift.

My head spins with his words, my words, and the look of hurt on his face. Then there are the words Alice said to me. None of them were lies but such hideous truths.

Failure. I'm a failure. I have loved two people in my life, and I've hurt them both with my inability to love. I should have known I was incapable and never opened myself up to it. Now, not only do I have to remember how to live without love, but I'll also have to live with the guilt of scarring these two people with my sharp edges.

A tear slides down my cheek. Fuck, is this going to happen all the time now? I miss when I never used to cry. I miss when I never used to feel.

Out of the corner of my eye, I see Max running on the treadmill beside me. I've never seen him run before, but he's keeping pace beside me. I continue to push myself, feeling another tear fall. My lungs burn, and it's not until I feel like my legs are going to give out that I stop. I slam my hand down on the button, and when the belt stops, I bend, bracing my hands on my thighs as I try to catch my breath.

Max steps off his treadmill and walks over to me, holding out a bottle of water. I take a deep drink, gulping down oxygen and water. Max wipes his face off on a towel. I don't think I've ever seen him this sweaty. Clearly, he's not run that fast or that much for a while. I hand him his water back.

Max takes a long drink. "No golden boy?"

"No," I say, looking away, but I can still feel Max's eyes on me. "He can do better." It's funny how certain truths slip out to certain people. Like instinctively, my brain knows who can handle which fucked up parts of me.

Max snorts. "Yeah, I don't think he'd agree. Though, what do I know? I never thought the great Connor Morningstar could experience such a mundane emotion like jealousy."

I ignore him and walk to the water fountain, filling one of the plastic cups.

Max follows me. "You really want him with someone else?"

I look down, staring at my reflection on the surface of the water. "I want him to be happy."

"And he's not now?" Max asks, crossing his arms over his chest.

"How could he be?" I feel another tear slide down my cheek. Fuck. I don't want to cry in front of Max again. I don't want to cry again at all.

Max rolls his eyes. "You've got to be blind. The guy is fucking insufferable since you started dating. He was always a pain in my ass, but now he's like... so much worse." Max walks to a machine to wipe it down. "As if he didn't have enough going for him before you got here."

"It doesn't matter. I ruined it," I say, sitting on one of the benches.

Max turns to face me, leaning against the scary-looking cardio machine. "What did you do?"

I shrug. "I did what I always do and fucked it up."

"Then fix it," Max says simply.

I sigh heavily and take a sip of water. "He deserves someone who doesn't fuck it up."

Max quirks an eyebrow. "In the two and a half years I've known him, he's never had a girlfriend. Not until you. He didn't seem to care. Sounds like he wants you."

"I'm not worth it, Max," I say, another cursed tear burning its way down my cheek.

Max shakes his head. "That's not for you to decide."

"I should go talk to him."

"Probably," Max agrees.

"Thanks, Max," I say. He may be the biggest asshole in the realms, but I appreciate the relatively safe space Max has made for me here. It's different from the stranger. I would never discuss my darkness with Max, but I am confident I will receive the truth from him, no matter how ugly.

I sigh heavily and push to my feet, wiping the sweat and tears from my face. I leave the gym and head straight to the Morningstar House. I try to keep my mind clear the whole walk, knowing that if I give it enough thought, I'll chicken out. I don't want to be this person. I don't want to be the hurtful one, and I desperately want to be able to feel something other than pain and loneliness.

Zane answers the door after one knock. "Oh, hey, Summer. He's upstairs."

I nod, squeezing Zane's arm as I pass him and head up to Connor's room. My heart squeezes again when I see his name etched on the door. I knock but open the door before he answers.

The window is wide open, and the room is freezing. Connor is propped on the windowsill, looking at the garden and the treeline behind the house. He was in the same spot when I came here to give him my phone number, but I'm even more at fault this time. This time, my own feelings are involved, and it's messier, more complicated, but also somehow easier.

I close the door behind me, pressing my back against it. "So I'm the worst girl-friend," I say, unsure how to fix this.

Connor continues staring out the window. When he doesn't reply, I walk over to him, stopping just within arm's reach of him. "I'm bad at being loved, and I don't know how to do it." Bitterness floods my mouth, tasting the truth of my words. "I've never been loved before." Not truly. Not completely. "And so, sometimes my brain kind of trips out, and... instead of being open and honest, I build protective walls." I look out the window. "Protective walls with hurtful words."

Connor leans his head back against the windowsill, still not looking at me. "Lonely way to live."

"I was alone for the first twenty-seven years of my life."

"Feels like you want to make it twenty-eight," Connor replies, and I fight to keep from flinching. His words are harsh but fair.

"Right." I swallow, my eyes stinging. "Well, I came to apologize. So, I'm sorry about earlier. I want to be better for you, but..." I pause, trying to center myself. "But also for me."

Connor turns his head, finally looking at me. The hurt in his eyes makes me want to fall to my knees. "For you?"

I nod, forcing myself to hold his gaze even though his pain is making me want to die. "I... need to fix it."

"How?"

"Time." I sigh. "And a lot of work." I pause for a long moment. "You said before that school comes easy for me. Well, being someone's family comes easy for you, and it's something I struggle with. But it's something I want to be good at."

Connor watches me carefully. "So what do you need from me?" he asks.

Another pesky tear escapes, the warmth of it trickling down my cheek. "Don't give up on me yet." I hate having to ask this of him as if he's not already been the most patient male in the realms. I have already asked so much of him. It is selfish, cruel, and unfair.

Connor's face softens, and once again, he completely surprises me by opening his arms. At what point will I stop being surprised by this perfect guy? He deserves so much more, but I move into his arms, burying my face against his neck.

"I love you, Connor."

Connor wraps his arms around me, holding me tightly. "You really hurt me today." His honesty cuts through me like a knife, his pain a living thing between us. I begin to cry.

Connor releases a breath as if he, too, knows how huge a deal this is. He tunnels his fingers into my hair, holding my face against his neck. "I love you, babe. I hate that you took my confession of a weakness and used it as a weapon against me."

I shake my head. "It's not a weakness, Con, and I am sorry. It wasn't about that. I was lost in my own stupid, hideous insecurities."

Connor kisses the top of my head. "I know it's hard for you to open up."

I pull back to look into his eyes, needing to see him. "I'm so sorry, big guy."

"Just give me a moment to understand next time," Connor says, brushing his thumb over my cheek and wiping the tears away.

I nod, and Connor leans in to press his lips over mine.

"I hate fighting with you," I say, running my fingers through his hair.

"Fuck, me too. And I'm sorry I won't be able to feed my succubus as much for the next couple of weeks. I don't like it either," he says, burying his face into my neck and inhaling deeply.

"It doesn't matter," I say, shaking my head.

Connor pulls back, cupping my cheek. "It does."

"Your happiness is all that matters, big guy."

"Babe." Connor tilts my head up a little. "I want to. So badly. That's why I know I can't during finals. You're like... an addiction."

My cheeks heat, but I also feel a deep loss, already missing him. I wish I weren't so broken. "I'll still see you, right?"

Connor blinks, looking horrified. "Of course you will, babe! I'll just have to spend more time studying."

I nod. "Maybe I can help!" I offer, but my brows draw. "Though I won't know a lot of your senior stuff, I can definitely help with your runes!"

Connor's lips pull into a bright smile, and his despair melts away. He leans in, smothering my face in kisses. I laugh through my drying tears and close my eyes, enjoying every second of this affection.

With one last kiss on my nose, Connor pulls back and says, "Although," I open my eyes, "probably no sleepovers until finals are over. That okay?"

I feel my face fall. "Right. Of course." I hate the sadness that cloaks me.

Connor chuckles, satisfaction sparking in his eyes. "There was a time you didn't want me to sleep over."

I know he is trying to cheer me up. Instead, guilt encroaches, and I wince. "Right."

"It's only for a couple of weeks, and then you won't be able to get rid of me, okay?"

"Promise?"

Connor leans in, kissing me again. "I promise, babe."

# 78

## SUMMER

*Laetha*

DAY

I nip at Connor's perfect lips and pull back. "You should study."

Connor groans, trying to pull me back in, and I laugh, covering his lips with my fingers.

"Study with me?" he asks.

I drop my hand. "Sounds goo—"

"Naked," Connor interrupts.

I laugh. "Big guy, what did we just decide?"

He sighs heavily. "I already regret it."

"You won't when you get your results in January. I'll go get my notes," I say, slipping from his lap.

Connor stands and closes the window. "I'll walk with you."

I shake my head. "You should get started. I'll be back soon."

"I'll get one of my brothers to walk you."

I turn to face him, placing my hands on his chest. "Connor. I can walk across campus on my own. I'll text you when I get home and when I'm walking back."

Connor stares at me, consideringly, his jaw working.

"Con, what's going on? Nothing has happened in weeks. Even the authorities have scaled back."

Connor exhales. "I know. I just... I'm sorry that I'm being crazy. Text me, and I'll see you soon."

I give him a quick kiss. "I love you, and I'll bring lunch back with me."

Connor smiles. "I love you, too."

"I'll be back in an hour." I wink at him and leave the house.

No sooner am I out of sight of the Morningstar House when I receive a message.

CONNOR

58 minutes.

My lips twitch, and I send a selfie of myself blowing him a kiss.

CONNOR

There's my super hot girlfriend.

I'm about to lock my phone when I get another message, this one from the stranger.

I look up, uselessly scanning for him, but there is no one around. It seems everyone has started bunking down in preparation for finals.

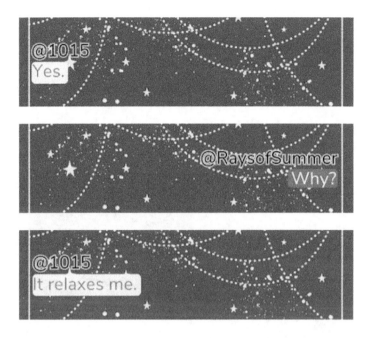

Fuck. Does that mean he watched Connor and me fuck outside the gym? Surely not. Surely, even he would not cross that boundary. But then I remember that time in the library when Connor had his head between my legs, and I felt eyes on me. I remember not hiding myself from view. I stood there, turned on by being watched. Did I think it was him? No. It was just anonymous eyes that ended up not being there. Fuck, this is different.

He doesn't reply right away, and I feel myself getting angrier with every moment that passes.

My anger cools, but just a fraction.

I can feel the waves of anger still flowing from me, but I know I am not really angry with him. My rage is directed inward.

Fuck. Anyone else you want to alienate today, Summer? I exhale heavily before replying to him.

@RaysofSummer
Sorry.

*He doesn't respond,* and I know he won't message back. Sadness replaces anger, and I am more disappointed than I should be.

Alice looks up from the couch when I enter. "I'm studying at Cons. Want to come?" I ask her, gathering my books.

"Actually studying? Or studying his dick?"

I sigh. "No sex until after finals. So actual studying." I shove my books in my bag and grin at her. "And if it were the latter, I wouldn't be inviting you."

"Wait. You without sex?" Alice gapes at me, her eyes wide.

"For three and a half weeks. Yup."

"Welp. This is going to be hell for both of us. You are... not the most rational when you're not getting any."

I flip her off. "It'll be fine. Let's go. I need to pick up sandwiches on the way."

Alice links her arm through mine as we walk to the sandwich place. "So why no sex?"

"Con says it's too distracting. And he's a senior, so these results are even more important."

"Fuck. How much sex were you having?"

I lift an eyebrow, looking at her.

She shrugs. "Like ballpark."

"Maybe a couple of times a day."

Alice looks at me skeptically. "It's definitely more than that."

"It's an average, Al. Sometimes it's more. Sometimes it's less."

"Damn. I feel like a nun," Alice ponders as we walk into the deli.

"Why?"

"Because I'm good if I get it three times a week. Maybe you are part succubus."

I laugh and order the sandwiches.

# 79

## SUMMER

Jahlsho
EXPLOSION
BURST

The next ten days drag on, and I see Connor occasionally, but it's usually just to study. We've barely kissed in all of that time. Maybe a chaste kiss as I leave his place or pass him in the corridor. He's been working hard, and I can tell he's burning himself out. We all are. Alice has hardly opened a textbook, yet she's bored because everyone else is busy. I've not minded the studying, and I've actually enjoyed some of it. However, my mood has soured exponentially since we all knuckled down.

I settle into my seat in Realms, a vibrating ball of tension. My knee bounces, and I'm so on edge that I yelp a little when Connor drops into the seat next to me. He slides his arm along the back of my chair, and I look up at him with wide eyes.

"Hi," he says, smiling brightly. "My morning class got canceled."

I smile, kissing his jaw.

"Mister Morningstar, might I ask why you have decided to join first-year Realms? I don't recall requesting an assistant," Professor Ambrose asks, disapproval thick in his voice.

"Well, I could always use a refresher!" Connor replies, completely at ease.

"I'm sure you have studying to do for your own classes, Mister Morningstar. You will be reacquainted with Miss Tuatha De Daanan at lunch."

"But Professor Ambrose, you don't think I could be of some help?" Connor says, oozing charm.

Professor Ambrose throws him a droll, unimpressed look. "Miss Tuatha De Daanan does not require tutoring in this subject. Either go, or I'll seat you elsewhere."

Connor sighs dramatically and gently grabs my chin before kissing me hard. The kiss is more passionate than any we've shared in the past ten days, and it ignites the fire I kept banked.

I kiss him back, and the other members of the class whoop loudly. Connor pulls back much too quickly, though I can tell that Professor Ambrose disagrees. He winks as he leaves the classroom.

Professor Ambrose tries to gain control of the class again, but it's not until he reminds everyone rather rudely that our final is next week that the atmosphere in the room changes.

An hour later, I make my way to the cafeteria with Alice. Connor looks up at me as I approach.

"Hi!" He smiles brightly.

I smile back, though I can feel the tension humming through me. Even my cheek muscles feel tight. "Hi."

Connor pulls me against his side, pressing a kiss to my forehead.

I smile and start to eat, stabbing a piece of lettuce. There is a loud crack, and I blink when I realize I've cracked the plate in two.

"Well," Rafe says, his brows shooting up.

I drop my fork, the metal warped from my grip.

Connor covers my hand. "You okay, babe?"

I take a deep breath before forcing a smile onto my face. "Yeah. I'm going to go work out. I have a free period after this, and I'm feeling a little stressed."

Connor leans in, brushing his lips over mine. "You'll come over tonight?"

I know he means to study. That's the only reason he invites me over nowadays, but I can't help how my stomach flutters.

"Absolutely. I'll see you guys later." I stand and practically sprint to the gym before any of them can say anything.

Max looks up from the desk, his stupid face pulled into a smug smirk. "Three times in twenty-four hours. People will start talking."

I growl at him, going straight to the sparring room, and as I knew he would, he eagerly follows me.

Training has not only been a source of solace for me in the fresh hell that is celibacy, but it's also been helping clear my head. I've not heard from the stranger for ten days either, and it's been lovely. Blissful, even. I absolutely haven't thought about him.

Summer the Liar. It has a nice ring to it, I suppose.

I pull on my gym shorts before pushing off my skirt and unbuttoning my white shirt. I'm grateful for the sports bras I've been donning these past ten days so I can work out whenever I want. I kick off my heels, opting for bare feet.

"Still no sex, huh?" Max asks, rolling his shoulders.

I bristle, stretching to loosen up. "What makes you say that?" I say, swinging for him. I certainly don't intend to discuss my sex life with Maximillian Romulus.

Max blocks it easily. "Because you're here and pissed."

I drop to the floor. Leaning into my fae speed and agility, I sweep my leg under his, taking him to the mat. "You know nothing about my sex life."

Max hisses as he hits the ground hard. "At least you're not pathetic anymore."

I climb on top of him, pinning him down.

Max thrusts his hips up hard, and I fly off him, colliding with the mat.

"Fuck," I groan.

Max shifts to pin me. "Maybe I spoke too soon."

I manage to wrap my legs around his waist and follow his lead, thrusting my hips up enough that I'm able to flip us so I'm on top again. Max slams his fist into my ribs, and I jolt in pain from the hit.

"What the fuck?" I snarl.

"What?"

"You're a fucking dick. If I'd taken a cheap shot like that, you'd have gone all berserker on me. Fucking asshole."

Max rolls his eyes. "Fine. Take a cheap shot."

I stand up and pull my skirt back on before shoving my shorts down my legs. "Fucking asshole. Moronic fuck," I grumble as I change. Frustration bubbles inside me, and even I know my reaction may be extreme. I'm always hot-headed, but it's gotten worse recently.

Max sits up. "Any more names? I thought you wanted to learn to fight. You can't expect your opponent to fight fair."

I snarl and whirl on him. "So when I take a cheap shot, when I don't know what I'm doing, you go all *berserk* on me. Yet you do it to me without consequences? Go fuck yourself, Max!" I yell, storming out of the gym.

Fucking men. All of them. I stomp through campus, carrying my shoes and cursing all men under my breath. People scramble out of my way, their primal brains telling them they do not want to catch my attention right now. I have just rounded the corner of Kelpie Hall when something grabs my wrist. I hiss and whirl on him, knowing exactly who has a hold on me. His form is even more faded than usual.

"And what the fuck do you want?" I snarl.

He snarls back, and his is infinitely scarier. Deep and vicious, it resonates past my ear, sending a delicious shiver licking down my spine. "Do not speak to me like that, little girl."

I look up at him, furious. "You think you can just appear whenever you fucking want?"

"My life does not revolve around you," he growls.

"And how the fuck am I supposed to know that? I know nothing about you except that you watch me," I hiss at him. "You were gone. *Again.*" I slam the words into him like an accusation.

"What does it matter if I've been gone?" He tilts his head, and I feel his gaze wander over me, his ire lessening.

"You..." I hesitate, feeling my rage start to melt away. "You left." Me. You left me.

He wraps his hand around my arm and pulls me in closer. "What does it matter?"

"I apologized, but you..." I pause. "Do you have a girlfriend? Is that it?"

He doesn't answer right away, studying me. "No," he finally says.

I clear my throat and look up at him. "All right."

"Not everything has to do with relationships."

"I'm sorry," I whisper, the rage replaced by confused exhaustion.

"Why are you lashing out?" he asks, his thumb sliding over the inside of my elbow.

"Lashing out?" I ask, running my hand over my brow.

He nods. "Yes, you're lashing out, blindly using anger as a weapon."

I exhale and roll my shoulders. "I'm just a little on edge, and Max didn't help."

He tilts his chin up. "Walk with me," he says, cautiously releasing his grip on my arm.

I take a deep breath, already feeling more relaxed.

We walk side by side, not touching. We walk in companionable silence for a while, but I can feel his gaze on me. I know the questions are coming.

"You're spiraling. Why?" he asks.

He has led me into the trees, and I look up at the branches forming a canopy above us. I wrap my arms around myself. "I have this pent up..." I pause, trying to think of the word. "Energy."

"Exams?" he asks.

I stop and turn toward him. "We're friends, right?" The stranger stops and turns to face me. "So I can talk to you about whatever, and it won't be weird. Right?"

"Friends for now. But, yes, go on."

"Connor and I, we aren't having sex."

The stranger coughs in surprise. "Ever?"

"For like ten days now."

He crosses his arms, and I can hear the disapproval creep into his voice. "That's not that long."

I roll my eyes, disappointed with the dismissal from someone who I actually thought would understand. "Whatever. No one gets it." I shrug and walk away, my bare feet easily finding their way over the cold ground. He quickly catches up to me, grabbing my hand.

"So he's not... fulfilling your needs?" he asks.

I sigh. "We have an agreement that we won't have sex until the end of finals."

"Why? It's good for stress," he asks, tilting his head.

"Apparently, it's a distraction, and," I poorly imitate Connor's voice, "it's like an addiction."

The stranger laughs, and the sound rolls over me like warm honey. "Is it? Like an addiction?"

"With me?"

"Yes."

"Absolutely," I admit.

"It's been several months for me, and I find myself... short-tempered and irritable."

"Several months?" I ask, aghast.

He nods. "Yes, I used to... have it a lot."

I feel myself tense, though I'm not sure why. "Okay," I say and start to walk again, fighting the urge to run.

The stranger falls into step beside me. "Have you told him you need it?"

"No. I'm being supportive," I reply. The question lays heavy on my tongue, the taste of it bitter. I can't help myself, and the words slip from my lips despite all my instincts screaming at me to keep quiet. "Why haven't you sought it out?"

"I've no interest in a replacement for what I want."

I narrow my eyes. "So you've found it? What you want?" I ask, my body growing more and more tense.

"Yes, but I can't do anything about it yet."

Don't ask, don't ask, don't ask. "Why?"

He shrugs, turning his attention ahead. "Too many things in the way. I have to be patient, but it is difficult because I am not a patient man."

I nod, also looking ahead. "Right."

"It will be years for me. I am not looking forward to it."

"Maybe they're not worth it," I say, bristling.

"Oh, she is." I can hear the smirk in his voice.

I look at him again. "You're going to go years without sex?"

He nods. "I'm guessing that sounds insane to you."

"Well, do you even know this person? How do you know it'll be worth it?"

He laughs. "I talk to her often."

"Is she why you disappear?"

He nods.

Could he be talking about someone else? Is that what I want? Or is it scarier if he's talking about me?

"Do you... spend time with her?"

He shakes his head, and my brows draw. "She's young. Just discovering who she is."

"Well, good for her," I growl softly.

439

"Yes." I can hear the smile in his voice, and it's infuriating. "She's even involved with someone else. Another reason I have to be patient. She'll need to come to the conclusion herself that he can never be what she needs."

"And are you what she needs?"

He nods slowly. "She needs someone to take control, to challenge her." I swallow, my stomach knotting. The stranger reaches out and tucks a lock of my hair behind my ear. "Someone who's not only going to embrace her darkness but show her his own." My breath hitches in my throat, and he steps closer, swallowing the space between us. "I'm going to be patient even though it's against my nature because, in the end, it will be me and her. No other."

I swallow again and whisper, "It's a good thing that you and I are friends, then. So I won't get in the way," I say, struggling to keep my voice even.

The air is thick and heavy, a confusing energy humming between us. He trails his fingers along the line of my jaw, and I suppress a shiver. "For now." He drags his thumb along my bottom lip, pulling my mouth open just a bit before dropping his hand. "If you're having trouble with your boy angel, simply take the voice from him."

I frown.

"Jump him, little fae."

"What? No! I'm not going to force him to have sex with me."

The stranger laughs. "Little fae, he wants it."

I shake my head. "I'm being supportive. He asked this of me."

"Then invest in a good vibrator," he says, and I can hear his eye roll.

"I... excuse me?"

"What?" he laughs.

"Didn't know you were so invested in my orgasms," I say almost primly.

"It's affecting your mood," he says, a smirk saturating his voice.

"Ah, it all makes sense now. My mood is pissing you off." I smirk, feeling more comfortable with this banter.

He chuckles. "Maybe."

A chill wind rolls through the trees, and I look up, noticing the darkness rolling in. "I have to go."

"Hurry home, little fae."

I hesitate for a long moment, debating whether to say what I want. But then I take a breath and turn to face him fully. "Don't disappear again. Please." Without waiting for him to reply, I turn and run, leaving him standing there.

# 80

## SUMMER

*Hethso*
SMALL, MINOR

**W**hen I arrive at Connor's, he's just finishing an assignment. He closes his laptop, smiling brightly at me. "Hi, babe."

I smile more easily than I have in days. "Hi, big guy."

Connor puts his laptop aside and walks over to me. "So," his eyes darken, "I might have finished something earlier than planned."

I quirk a brow.

"So, how about I feed you?" Connor places his hands on my hips, pulling me in closer.

I lean against him. "But you have an exam next week." I immediately regret my words, cursing myself for reminding him of that fact, but it's only fair that I try to do what he asked of me.

"So, no sex?" Connor pouts.

I wrap my arms around his neck. "You said no sex until you were finished with your exams. It was your rule—"

"Babe. Do you want to have sex or not?" Connor interrupts.

"I do. I really do, Con, but we made a deal, and I—"

"Going once..." Connor's eyes are nearly black.

I groan, craning my neck as I look up at him.

"Going twice..."

"Fuck. Yes, please!" I concede.

Connor's mouth comes down on mine, and I open eagerly for him. I moan, tugging at his shirt. Connor breaks the kiss and pulls it off before grabbing my ass and lifting me. I plunge my fingers into his hair as he carries me to the bed.

Connor shoves my skirt up and yanks my panties off. I push at his pants in similar haste, desperate for him, for pleasure, for the closeness.

"Tell me you need me," I moan into the kiss.

"So desperately," Connor pants and slides his shaft against my slick pussy. I yank my shirt open, needing there to be no barriers between us. He notches the head of his cock against my opening. I'm about to pull my sports bra off when Connor thrusts inside me, obviously unwilling to wait any longer.

I arch beneath him, pleasure crashing through me. My body trembles like it's been starved of this pleasure for years, not just for ten days. Maybe Connor was right. Perhaps this is an addiction. Connor immediately starts to thrust, not even able to savor just being inside me. I rock my hips, eagerly meeting his every thrust and welcoming him even deeper.

"Need you, babe," he groans, his hips pistoning into me. I dig my nails into his back, clawing at him.

"Fuck. More... Gods!" Connor braces one hand on the headboard, moving harder, faster, his thrusts frantic. I slide my knees higher on his hips, opening more to him, needing him deeper. "Fuck, Connor!"

Connor moves his other hand to the headboard and shifts his legs, gaining more leverage. "Fuck, so perfect," he groans. "So fucking tight, babe."

My body clenches almost painfully around him, and I drop my hand to the bed, clenching the sheets. He is so deep I can't tell where he ends, and I begin.

"Squeezing me so good. Pussy... so... wet." Connor pants in between words, his thrusts growing impossibly more frantic.

"You going to fill me up, big guy?" I ask breathlessly, transfixed by the pleasure on his beautiful face.

"So full." Connor moans, his neck flushing as he holds back his orgasm.

"I'm so close, Con... Fuck. So close..."

Connor slips a hand between us, brushing his thumb over my clit. Even that barest touch sends me tumbling over the edge, and I cry out as the pleasure reaches its apex. Connor gives one last brutal thrust, burying himself to the hilt. He shouts and spills deep inside of me, his body shuddering as he finds his release.

"Fuck," I gasp out, my entire belly clenching with my release. Connor groans and lowers himself down on top of me, pressing kisses all over my sweat-slicked face as his cock pulses inside of me. I tunnel my fingers into his hair. "Fuck, I needed that."

Connor bites my ear. "Me too. It's been killing me."

"It has?" I moan.

Connor nods into my neck. "I hated it."

"I thought you were cool with it," I say, nuzzling my cheek against his.

Connor laughs, pulling back to look down at me. "No, babe."

My lips twitch.

"What?"

I shake my head.

Connor bends, kissing along my shoulder. "I missed being inside you."

"Fuck, Connor," I moan.

Connor laughs. "What?"

"Nothing, I missed you."

"I missed you, too. I'm sorry, I know it's been hard," Connor says.

"It's okay. I just wanted you to be happy." I slide my fingers up his back, feeling him shiver when my touch brushes over where his wings appear on his back.

"You know what makes me happy?" he asks, looking down at me. "You."

I shake my head, but my lips pull into the biggest, stupidest grin. "You're a big mush."

Connor playfully smothers my face in kisses. "You are, too. It's contagious! And now you're infected!"

I squeal, swatting at him. "Connor! Ew, stop!"

"Never!" Connor grabs my hands and moves to my neck, pressing big, smacking kisses to the sensitive line of my throat.

I wiggle beneath him, squealing in delight. "Stop!"

Connor tickles my sides, making me shriek with laughter. He stops suddenly, his gaze fastened to my face. "Perfect," he whispers, his skin glowing.

"Sweet talker. I'm still not staying the night," I say with a soft smile.

"Why?" Connor whines.

"Because you've still got an exam, and sleepovers were deemed *distracting*."

"But they also help with my stress," he counters.

"Sex is my stress relief, and I've not had that for ten days," I say, and then kiss him deeply.

Connor smiles. "Then we should amend the rules slightly. Sex no less than three times a week."

I laugh, playfully shoving him off me and climbing out of bed. "I'll see you tomorrow, big guy."

Connor sits up, pouting a little, his hair perfectly sex rumpled. "You're leaving already?"

"It's late, and we both have studying to do."

"This sucks," Connor groans, falling back on the bed dramatically,

I pull on my clothes and walk over to him, bending over him to kiss him deeply. "I love you."

Connor sighs. "I love you too."

"See you tomorrow."

"I miss you already," Connor says. He sits up, his face still fixed in an endearing pout.

I wink at him as I leave the room. Rafe is the only one in the living room. He has a textbook open, but I don't think much studying is happening. I kiss his cheek as I walk past him, leaving the Morningstar House once again lighter than when I entered.

# 81

## SUMMER

*Hahlthae*
FREEZE, STOP

The sky is inky black as I begin my journey home, and the classic Avalon mist lies low against the pavement. The night is still, but it's not the usual peaceful calm. Something has me on edge, and I pull my coat tighter, trying to ward off the chill.

I curse myself for not bringing Connor's dagger. Since I started going to the gym daily, I've not been consistently carrying it. I don't want a dagger strapped to me when I'm sparring. I could call Connor or one of his brothers and ask them to come and walk me home, but I'm really reluctant to make more of this situation than it is. The more I feed into it, the more real it is.

The back of my neck tingles with the awareness of eyes upon me, and beneath my clothes, the pendant warms slightly. I keep walking, not wanting to alert whoever is watching that I am aware of their presence. The only proof of my discomfort is the condensation as my warm breath hits the cool air a little quicker than before. I swallow and pull out my phone, maintaining my casual pace toward Kelpie.

@RaysofSummer
Are you watching me?

I desperately hope the answer is yes. Not only because then I will know who is out there but also because, as much as I hate to admit it, I will feel safer with him watching me. I hold on to that hope, but these eyes don't feel like his, and the longer the stranger takes to reply, the more certain I am that it is probably not him.

My heart races, and I subtly look around, slowing my steps. I have no fucking idea why I'm acting like those morons in horror movies when they're getting chased by a psycho killer, yet the desire to stop, to look around, is too tempting.

My phone alerts again, and I almost drop it in surprise.

Fear lashes me.

I stare at his message, terror slithering through me. Every muscle in my body freezes. I can feel those eyes burning into me like acid. Fuck, fuck, fuck. I am completely frozen in fear.

A twig snaps in the distance, and instinctively, my head snaps in that direction. My breaths are shallow, and I feel the scream building in my throat, primed and ready.

I clench my fists, my phone creaking in my grip. My mind is in chaos, and I try to focus, try to remember any of the fucking moves Max taught to me.

The fog shifts, and I jump when the stranger materializes beside me in his near-invisible form. I don't relax but instinctively move toward him, tucking myself within his shadows. He steps in front of me, looking around, his large body ready for attack. "Wait here." He starts to move away, but I grab his arm, my grip tight on his strange, blurry materialization. He stops and looks at me over his shoulder.

"Don't leave me," I whisper. My instincts scream at me to stay with him. Something is near, something malevolent and powerful.

He watches me, hesitating for a moment before he nods. "All right. I'm going to go fully invisible. I'm still here, though. Walk home as normal."

I swallow, refusing to drop his arm and lose that contact. "Should I email the headmaster?" I ask. "Something feels wrong."

His body wavers and then completely disappears, but I can still feel his presence. His phantom breath makes me shiver as he whispers into my ear. "Once you are home. Yes."

I nod and take a deep breath, steadying myself and trying to remember anything from my insipid mortal drama classes. I start walking, actively trying to remember how I usually walk. Do I sway my hips? Maybe a little more? No, that's obscene. The distraction only lasts for a fraction of a moment before my reality sinks in again, and my heart thrashes in my chest uncomfortably.

The stranger moves in closer, sliding an arm around my back and placing his hand on my hip. "I'm here," he whispers, and goosebumps appear on my skin.

The ghostly gaze remains on me but doesn't seem as close. I lean into his presence, grounding myself in him. Though I can't see him, I can feel him casting out his senses as we walk back to my dorm. When Kelpie comes into sight, he leans in again, his voice low. "Once you get through the door, I'm going to ward the building and investigate. Stay inside, and do not follow me."

Another branch snaps around fifteen feet away. I flinch, my muscles tightening in preparation to fight.

"Don't look. Act like you're in your own world," he says, the command in his voice steadying me. I swallow my fear and instincts and look up at the stars, pretending to be distracted when that couldn't be further from the truth. I'm not sure I've ever been more alert, more aware of my surroundings, or more aware of someone else's hands on me.

We walk into the puddle of light created by the lamp outside the dorm, and I feel the stranger's hand tighten on my hip. "Inside," he commands. I comply, not minding following orders in this case. The door closes behind me, and I stare at it for a long moment before pulling out my phone again and opening my email.

To: J.emrys@avalon.edu
From: S.tuathadedaanan@avalon.edu
*Sorry to bother you at this late hour, sir. But I was walking home and felt as though someone may have been watching me. Possibly following me.*
*-Summer.*

I've barely made it upstairs and into my dorm when the response comes through.

To: S.tuathadedaanan@avalon.edu
From: J.emrys@avalon.edu
*Miss Tuatha De Daanan, did anyone approach you? Did you notice anything out of the ordinary?*
*-Headmaster Emrys*

*To:* J.emrys@avalon.edu
*From:* S.tuathadedaanan@avalon.edu
*No, sir. But something just didn't feel right.*
*-Summer.*

I sigh. I must sound like such an idiot. *Something just didn't feel right?* Please. It was probably a frog or something. Or a prank. Though the necklace did warm, and the stranger seemed to be very on edge, too. Did he sense whatever I did?

*To:* S.tuathadedaanan@avalon.edu
*From:* J.emrys@avalon.edu
*I will investigate immediately.*
*-Headmaster Emrys.*

I exhale, feeling better now that I am back at Kelpie Hall. When I step into my dorm, I could sob with relief. The comfort of home washes over me, wrapping me in a sense of safety.

"Alice?" I call out.

Alice steps out of her room a moment later, lowering her headphones. "Hey, Sum. What's up? You okay?"

I move past her into her room and open the curtains a little, peering out. "I think someone followed me home."

Alice walks over, looking around me to see out the tiny slit of the window I've exposed. "Someone other than your friend?"

I nod, scanning the silhouette of the forest. "It wasn't him."

448

"I'm going to go find this fucker," Alice hisses. She grabs the curtains, swishing them closed again.

"No," I say, grabbing her arm.

"Why?" Alice demands, her eyes flashing with protective fury.

"My friend is out looking, and the headmaster will have told the authorities by now. You stay with me. Please?"

"You called your friend?" Alice asks, the surprise overriding her anger.

"I messaged him to ask if he was being a dick and pranking me, but he got worried and came. He told me to email the headmaster when I got back safe, so I did."

Alice brushes me out of the way and opens the curtains a little, glancing out. "I don't see anyone."

"Who is it you're looking for?"

Alice scans the trees. "I don't know, someone."

There is a loud bang, and the window shakes. Alice and I jump back, dropping the curtain. We stare around the room with wide eyes. Adrenaline floods my system again, and I feel my muscles tremble.

"What the fuck was that?" Alice asks. I shake my head and cautiously approach the window again. I brush aside the curtains to find a large, angry crack in the glass. Alice comes up behind me, and I think I see the brush beneath the trees shift and rustle. I narrow my eyes, trying to penetrate the shadows, but it is just too dark.

"No more walking alone. I'm putting my foot down," Alice says.

My chest heaves, but I keep my eyes on the bushes. It may be everything that has happened today, but I feel like whatever or whoever is out there is looking back at me. I swear I can feel their evil smile.

My phone pings, and I yank it free, reading the message.

@1015
They managed to escape me. But they're not lingering anymore.

@1015
The authorities and your Headmaster have arrived, I can't stay.

I look at the cracked window and close the curtains again. My feet feel too heavy as I walk to Alice's bed and sit down. I lift my phone, my hands shaking as I type.

Alice paces back and forth in front of me, muttering.

"Al." She ignores me. "Alice," I say louder, and she finally looks at me. "I'm okay. I promise."

"This is all kinds of fucked up, Summer."

I nod, patting the bed next to me. Alice sits down and lays her head on my shoulder.

"I—I need you to be okay. Okay?"

I nod, sliding my hand into hers. "Okay."

Alice sits up. "I need a drink. Want one?"

I shake my head, and Alice stands up and disappears into the living room. I open *Nexus* again and message the stranger.

I blink, shifting to sit with my back against the wall. Is he jealous? No. Surely not. The thought intrigues me enough to stifle the fear slightly, allowing me to breathe.

I lift my eyebrows.

Exhaustion barrels through me, and I force myself to my feet. I pad through the dorm to my bedroom and change into my pajamas before climbing into bed. I lie there, waiting for sleep to claim me, ready to be done with today. But I keep thinking of the stranger's reaction. I grab my phone off the bedside table.

I frown reading his message.

I blink.

He doesn't reply, though I can feel his irritation through the runic network.

I roll my eyes and turn onto my side to sleep. My phone alerts again, and I pick it up, ready to send a very scathingly worded message to the stranger. But I smile when I see Connor has texted me.

CONNOR

Miss you

SUMMER

I miss you too, big guy.

That little nagging feeling that's become more present since I started forming relationships churns inside me. It seems to chant, "Tell him, tell him, tell him."

CONNOR

You get home safe?

Fuck. The claws of guilt rake down my back.

SUMMER

I'm home safe.

It's not quite a lie. My response is perfectly crafted so that it sits just above that gray area.

Connor replies with a selfie of him spread out on his king-size bed, his blue sheets mussed beneath him from our earlier activities. He's only wearing boxers, and he looks so fucking cute as he winks up at the camera.

CONNOR

Could have stayed over.

I can't help but laugh, and the sound surprises me.

SUMMER

Goodnight, Con.

CONNOR

Goodnight, Sum.

# 82

## SUMMER

*Haelsha*
DESPAIR

T he sun has just risen when I climb out of bed. My sleep was fitful and plagued by nightmares, and I feel more tired than when I went to bed last night. I get dressed, doing my best to keep my mind blank and focused in the moment, which only lasts until I am outside, and fear rushes over me again. My body remembers all too well the terror of last night. I hurry toward the gym, anticipating the moment that gaze will land on me again. It never comes, and I arrive at the gym without further drama.

I'm surprised to see Max sitting at the front desk. He has headphones on and appears to be studying from a large textbook. I ignore him, still pissed at him after yesterday. I walk straight to my favorite treadmill and start the machine, trying to lose myself in the rhythm of the run. Tension grips my shoulders, and I try to push past it, but peace never finds me. I give up after around ten minutes and switch to one of the punching bags.

"Still pissed?" Max asks, having finally noticed me.

Without looking at him, I flip him off before slamming my fist into the punching bag. I bristle as he enters my space, but he just walks around the bag and holds it from the other side, stabilizing it while I hit it.

"What exactly are you mad about?" he asks, an eyebrow quirked.

I continue to punch the heavy bag. "You've always been a bit of a dick, Max." I slam my fist into the bag again, trying to hit it so hard that he will lose balance. "But I also thought you were fair, and yesterday, you weren't fair." I throw another punch, but Max just stands there, annoyingly stable. "I know people won't play fair when I'm out in the wild. That is a lesson I learned long ago. I get it." After another hard hit, my knuckles start to throb. "But yesterday was supposed to be just you and me training, and that jab was nothing but an asshole move because I'd pinned you."

Max watches me for a long moment before replying. "You've excelled at fighting hand to hand, progressing very quickly. It was time to move you to the next level, which meant fighting dirty. Making moves you don't expect."

I slam my fist into the bag again, and my hand throbs in protest. "Not without telling me. That makes me lose all trust in you."

"From one cheap shot? You did the same to me, if you recall. You only get pissed when it's against you?"

I snarl. "I didn't know what a cheap shot was when I did it."

"Bullshit," Max hisses.

I shake my head, stepping back from the punching bag.

"I'm never going to treat you like a fragile princess who needs to be protected. So stop fucking acting like one," Max growls, his eyes flashing faintly with green. "You want to learn how to fight for real? To protect yourself and your friends? That's what I'll do for you."

Anger ripples off me, but there is something in his words that hits right where they need to. I felt defenseless again last night, and I had to reach out to someone else for protection. Once again, I had to *rely* on someone else. I will not be the victim any longer.

I narrow my eyes at him. "Fine, whatever," I grumble and turn on my heel, walking to the sparring room.

Max is hot on my heels, and his annoying presence is impossible to ignore. "What is it that really bothers you about the cheap shot?" he asks.

"Partly because you reacted so badly when I *mistakenly* did it to you the first time. I know you think I knew better, but I truly didn't. I thought the goal was to get hits in."

"The only reason I got pissed is because you revealed a hole in my control," Max growls. "My kind is known for our killing rages. Why do you think I might get so upset that you triggered it?"

"And I was supposed to know that how? By osmosis?" I growl back.

Max rolls his eyes. "I will not spoon-feed you! I'm not your golden boy." He practically spits the insult, and I clench my fists.

"Okay, enough. What's your beef with Connor?" I ask, pissed.

Max rolls his shoulders. "Do you want to fight or what?" he asks.

"You brought it up. Come on, Maxxy. What's the problem?" I ask, goading him while I stretch.

"Any day now," Max says, getting into position and obviously avoiding my question.

I plunge into my fae speed and strength and launch at him, managing to slam my fist into his stomach.

Max hisses out a breath and grabs the back of my head. Pulling me toward him, he uses his knee to flip me over, throwing me to land hard on my back.

I groan at the impact but push off the ground. Max shifts to alter his balance, but I jump and kick him in the chest. He reaches out to grab my foot, but I slam my hand into his stomach, and he falls to the ground. I'm about to pin him when he slides his legs beneath mine. I lose my balance, falling on top of him.

"Fuck," I groan as I roll off him.

Max glances at me, panting slightly. "You know, for someone who doesn't normally fight dirty, that was pretty good."

I roll my eyes but burst out laughing. Max snickers and shoves to his feet. He offers me his hand, and I pull myself up. I push him away and get back into position.

"Come at me," Max says, ready for the attack.

I swing at him. Max blocks it easily, but I lean into my fae power and throw another punch. The second strike is so fast it makes the first seem like a decoy. Max takes the hit but uses the momentum to send his fist toward my exposed side. I just barely dodge it and manage to swing my foot around to kick him in the leg, but Max grabs my ankle. I sink into my instincts. As he applies pressure to my ankle, I jump and twist my body in the same direction. To keep the hold, Max has to twist his arm, putting pressure on his shoulder and elbow. He drops my foot, and I fall to the floor, slashing my feet beneath his. The ground shakes when his large, muscular body hits the ground. I climb on top of him, pinning him there with my hips and relishing in my victory. My chest heaves as I look down at him.

"You just love to straddle me, Tuatha De Daanan. People are going to get the wrong idea," Max quips, panting.

I laugh, grabbing his arms and pinning them above his head. "What idea would that be? That maybe I'm better at fighting than the burly berserker?"

Max looks up at me and snorts. I grin down at him, feeling the endorphins flowing through me. But it's not only that. I don't feel completely defenseless. Though I've not learned anything new today, I was able to pin Max, which means I can at least put up a good fight if I am attacked. That is if I can remember the moves in a fight-or-flight situation.

The moment I release his arms, he grabs my waist and tosses me over his head. I yelp as I fly through the air and groan when I land hard on my back.

Max stands and brushes himself off. "As fun as this was, I have to get back to studying."

"And I have a breakfast date," I say, sitting up and stretching my back.

Max rolls his eyes. "Can't be late for golden boy."

"Oh, look, moments over, you're still a dickhead." I push to my feet and flip him off as I leave the gym.

On my way to Connor's, I open my DM's with the stranger.

His reply comes a moment later.

I stop in mid-step, staring down at the message. Rock? What rock?

The stranger sends a photo of a rock sitting in the grass. It looks fairly normal, even boring, until I zoom into the image. Carved into the stone is a message. COME OUT, COME OUT, FAE BITCH. I swallow thickly, looking at the stone. That must have been what was thrown at Alice's window last night.

Wait. On my desk?

Okay, someone is still very pissy. It probably wasn't smart to mention the headmaster, but there is something so delightfully delicious about how he reacts to it. I think that might be skirting the boundaries...

# 83

## SUMMER

*Deththae*
CROWN, MANTLE

I lay sprawled on top of Connor, both of us completely naked, as he runs his fingers through my hair. After a long day of studying, we all ate dinner together, and Connor conned me into a sleepover. It was only possible because Zach received a booty call request just as we were discussing where Alice could sleep.

"I'm going to miss you," he says, his voice sounding far away and wistful.

"It's just two weeks, Con. I will be with Alice for Yule and we'll be back in time to have Christmas Eve together. Then I'll be coming to Eden for your birthday."

Connor sighs. "I just love everything about it this season. It is our first year together, and I want to share it all with you. Are you sure you need to go to Transylvania?"

"Alice needs me," I say with a gentle smile.

"Fine," Connor groans. "But you're with me next Yule and Christmas."

I press a kiss to his chest. "Deal."

"I've got you presents, you know?" he says, twirling a lock of my hair around his finger.

"Oh, yeah?"

"Two presents, actually. But don't worry, neither of them are in ring-shaped packages."

I quirk a brow. "And why did you feel the need to say that?"

Connor smiles, pulling me closer. "No reason."

I pull back, looking up at him. "Are you saying I'm not worth an engagement ring?" I tease.

"You want a ring?" he asks.

"I didn't say that."

"Hm," he says with a secretive little smirk.

I laugh, brushing my lips over his. "We should sleep. We have lots more studying to do tomorrow."

Connor yawns and kisses the top of my head before he drifts off.

I check my phone and see I have another message from the stranger.

I shift off Connor. I have learned that my angel sleeps like the dead, but I am still careful not to wake him.

I climb out of bed and pull on one of Connor's shirts and a pair of snow boots before going downstairs. Everyone is in their rooms, so my path is completely clear as I leave the house. The cold nips at my bare legs and teases beneath the shirt, and I curse myself for not taking an extra minute to pull on some pants and a large sweater.

I feel his hand before I see him. He ruffles my hair. "You two made up," he says, his voice caressing my ear.

"Huh?"

He nods toward the house. "You and the boy."

"We weren't fighting," I say with a shrug.

I can feel his exasperated look without being able to see it. "You know what I'm referencing, little fae."

"We've worked it out, yes. Have you decided to stop being cold to me?" I ask, lifting my chin.

He crosses his arms and leans against the banister wrapping the porch. "Cold?"

I return his exasperated look.

"This killer," he begins, pushing past the question, "wants you scared. Which made me wonder why."

I sit on the porch step to listen. The stranger sits next to me, our bodies close but not touching. I look down at my legs and the goosebumps covering them and tug the shirt down over my knees.

"Which led me to something intriguing about fae. Did you know that while your eyes are a rare color for fae, they are not entirely unique?"

I don't say anything. The habits of the past keep me from discussing my eyes. I tip my head and watch him, waiting for him to continue.

"One of the first Queens of the Fae had eyes like yours, a bright, pale blue."

"She did?" I ask.

He nods. "I think there's a reason you were brought to Avalon, why this all seems to be centered on you. I believe you might be a contender to the throne of your people. That alone makes you very dangerous to the current king and most fae."

I shake my head. "That can't be—"

"The killer references the Mark of Nimue in every killing. Nimue was a hand-maiden to the last rulers of Faerie."

"I know that. I've done a little research, not that there's much to find. But what does this have to do with me? I'm just a fae with weird eyes."

"You challenge their very existence, little fae. The Fae King has built an empire since the fall of your home realm. He has people who both fear and love him in equal measure, but you're the candle refusing to extinguish in a howling wind. They'll want to snuff you out. The king especially."

I exhale and look up at the sky. "None of this makes any sense. It can't be true. Did I make a mistake in coming here?"

"No. I don't know why or how, but you obviously came to someone's attention, and I think being here is the only thing that's kept you alive."

I shift closer to him and lay my head on his shoulder. He tenses for a moment before relaxing again. "Don't be cold to me," I whisper into the night.

He doesn't reply for a long moment. "I'm sorry. I was annoyed."

"Why? What did I do?"

He exhales and shakes his head. "Nothing."

"Stranger?" I whisper, shifting a little closer. I swear I can feel the slightest amount of warmth coming from him.

"Hm?"

"You make me feel less lonely."

"You're surrounded by friends. What is it I offer that they don't?" I can hear the confusion in his voice.

I pause for a moment, considering, though I already know the answer. It's a lonely answer, but it's a true one. "You understand me in a way they don't."

"Your darkness calls to mine."

Something inside me twists, but it's not unpleasant. "You feel it, too?" I whisper.

"Yes. Why do you think I started watching you?"

"Honestly?"

He nods.

I feel my cheeks heat. "Initially, I thought it was because you were kind of into me, but I know that's not the case anymore."

"Hm."

There is a long, but not uncomfortable, silence. I lean more heavily against his bulk and truly relax for the first time in days.

"I'm going to look into this lead this week."

"So you're not going to be around?" I fight to keep the trepidation from my voice.

"Don't you have exams?" he asks, and I can hear a little spark of happiness in his voice, or maybe it's amusement.

I shift, making my head more comfortable on his shoulder. "I do."

"Then you'll be busy," he says, and I feel him lay his cheek against my head.

"I'm ready for the exams."

"I have to go," he says reluctantly, shifting beside me.

"You do?" I ask, pulling back and looking up at him.

He nods. "I have things to do. You know the stuff I do when I'm not talking to you."

I wince a little and look down. "All right."

He boops my nose with his forefinger. "Sarcasm, little fae." His voice is gentle, and I can hear the smile in it. He tucks a lock of my hair behind my ear. "Goodnight, little fae."

"Goodnight, Stranger," I say with a smile.

When he leaves, the loneliness encroaches, and I allow myself a moment to sit in it, to feel it, to resent it. Just for a moment, and then I shove it down and go back inside to my family.

# 84

## SUMMER

*Caithin*
FIRE

T
he last week of exams seems to fly by, and just like last week, I haven't seen Connor much due to our schedules and workloads. Alice and I have one of the final exams of the term on Friday afternoon. Most of the student body has already headed home for the winter break. Everyone else is finishing up exams and packing to leave tomorrow or Sunday.

Alice and I leave Alchemy 101 exhausted but thankful exams are over. We walk home in silence, the icy wind whipping at us. We both breathe a sigh of relief when we arrive at the dorm. Shedding our outerwear, we drop it in the entryway and stumble through to Alice's room, collapsing on her bed.

"Fuck. How difficult was that exam?" I groan, thinking over my paper again. The questions were all worded in ways to try to catch us out.

"It was a war crime," Alice groans.

"At least we're done now." I sigh, staring at the ceiling.

"We've got that finals party tonight."

"Yes, we do," I say with a smile.

"Also, I love that even though you haven't seen Connor much over the last few days, your mood has been way better than last week." Alice nudges me. "You were a raging bitch last week."

"Hey!" I say, gaping at her.

Alice quirks an eyebrow at me, daring me to deny it.

"Listen, am I a *little* grumpy when I'm not having sex? Sure. Raging bitch is a bit harsh."

Alice narrows her eyes at me, and then her face morphs into a look of surprise. "You *are* having sex!"

I roll my eyes.

"Oh my gods, when are you finding the time? I swear you've seen him like three times this week."

"We find little pockets of time." I swat at her. "Hey, shut up. It's good for stress. Anyway, I won't be having sex tonight, for sure."

"Oh?"

I shake my head. "We'll be way too drunk."

Alice snickers. "I feel like I remember a party where you two snuck off, fucked, and then came back after to get trashed."

"You're thinking of someone else," I say, feigning confusion.

"Right. Must have been my other best friend."

I glare at her.

"Don't like that?"

I narrow my eyes more.

Alice snorts. "Relax, I only have one wife."

I smile brightly and roll on top of her, smothering her in kisses. "That's right." Alice pushes me off, wiping her face. "You going to hook up with that shifter tonight?" I watch her, trying to read her expression. "I know you've been seeing him."

"Absolutely not. He's way too clingy. He needs to understand that he will never come first for me."

I roll my eyes. "Please, you're such a mush now."

Alice gasps, her hand on her chest. "You take that back."

I grin and grab my phone. Taking a selfie of us, I post it with the caption,

**@RaysofSummer.** *Secret is out: Alice Legosi is a confirmed mush!*

"You delete that!"

Alice tries to snatch my phone. I squeal and hold it high, trying to keep it away from her, but she manages to grab it. She quickly types a new caption and then hands it back to me. It now says,

I laugh and climb out of bed. "I'm going to take a nice relaxing bath."

Alice snorts. "So Connor is joining you?"

"Do you see Connor?" I say primly.

"I feel like I never see him until he's walking out of your room, all glowing and sex rumpled."

I leave her room and call, "Connor? Are you in there?"

"I'm in here, babe!" Alice replies from her room, imitating his voice.

I laugh and disappear into the bathroom. I've never used the tub before. It's small, and it's anything but luxurious, but I want nothing more than to sink into deep hot water. I've just relaxed into the near-scalding bath, and my muscles are starting to relax when my phone alerts.

> CONNOR
>
> I can't believe finals are done. I'm halfway through my final year.

I smile and send him a selfie of myself in the bath. The bubbles mostly cover me, but he'll definitely get the idea.

> CONNOR
>
> I'm already on my way.

> SUMMER
>
> Oh?

> CONNOR
>
> You think that photo will keep me home?

I send another photo, this one of my neck, a drop of water trailing down my throat. I worry when he doesn't reply. Was that too much? Is he uncomfortable or disgusted with me sending the photo? I curse my stupid and irrational insecurities. Less than fifteen minutes later, there is a loud knock at the door, followed by Alice's voice.

"Surprise, surprise," she says.

I laugh softly, relief and anticipation filling me with warmth. Connor comes through the bathroom door, already stripping.

"Hello, gorgeous," he croons, his lips pulled into the smile of a man who is about to be naked with his girlfriend.

"There's my big guy." I shift to make room for him, but I know it will be a tight squeeze in this tub. Connor climbs in behind me, and I lay back against his chest.

"You know, the tub at my house is much bigger," he says, nuzzling kisses against my neck.

I turn in his arms and straddle him, wrapping my arms around his neck. "Well, this was supposed to be my soak."

"Oh?" Connor moves his hands to my ass and squeezes, kneading the flesh.

"Yes. A solo soak. Besides, don't you enjoy how close we are in this one?" I hover my lips over his.

Connor squeezes my ass again and tilts his head more, his lips searching for mine. "That is a definite benefit."

Connor slides his hand into my gloved one as we walk across campus. "So, how was your last final?"

"Fucking awful," Alice grumbles from my other side.

"It was pretty tough," I agree, smiling up at him. My gaze catches on the bruise I left on his neck, and I reach up to brush my finger over the mark.

"Hickey?" he asks.

I nod with a satisfied smile. "I want everyone to know you're mine."

"You guys are so gross," Alice groans.

Connor smiles, his eyes darkening. "Pretty sure there isn't a person on campus who doesn't know that."

"Maybe you should change your name to Connor Tuatha De Daanan on Nexus," I say teasingly.

Connor laughs, leaning down to kiss me.

"Will you two hurry up? It's cold as balls out here," Alice grumbles, storming ahead.

"You're a big mush," I say, my smile feeling permanent.

"Just for you, babe." We keep walking, and I can tell Connor is deep in thought. "Maybe we should do a mashup. Morning De Daanan," he says after a few moments.

I laugh. "Absolutely not."

Connor purses his lips, thinking. "Tuatha De Star?"

"Alice is right. You're so gross." I laugh, grabbing his face and slamming my lips to his.

Connor laughs, wrapping his arms around my waist and lifting me off my feet. He spins us around as the snow starts to fall. Leaning back in his arms, I look up at the inky black sky as it cries icy white tears. I close my eyes as they land on my face, melting almost instantly. I look back down at Connor, wanting to share the wonder of the moment. He is watching me with love and something that looks so much like reverence that it makes my heart hurt.

"I love you, Morningstar."

"I love you, Tuatha De Star."

I burst out laughing, and Connor spins me again before slowly lowering me to my feet.

"We better go. We've already lost Alice," Connor says, though his gaze remains locked on mine.

I slide my hand back into his. The snow falls silently as we continue after Alice. "How am I going to manage without being inside you multiple times a day?" Connor asks, squeezing my hand.

"We will get back to that," I say with a sigh.

"I leave on Sunday." Connor pouts.

"And you're away for two weeks. Do you think we can fuck forty-two times before you leave for Eden?"

Connor tips his head, considering it. "Well, I'm up for the challenge, but I think I'd be shooting dust."

I bump against him. "Please, big guy. You always have the good stuff for me."

Connor laughs. "Yeah? The good stuff?"

"Absolutely!"

"You going to miss me?" Connor asks, kissing the top of my head.

"So much, big guy."

Connor sighs. "I wish you were coming with me, but I understand why you won't leave Alice."

I squeeze his hand, comforting him. "But you'll be back for Christmas Eve, and I'll come to Eden for your birthday in the new year! Plus, it's important you have family time. I know your mom misses you."

"I know you're conspiring with her," he grumbles. "I'll have to show you my new place when you visit!" Connor says, perking up a bit.

"New place?"

"All archangels get their own place when their wings start turning."

"That's very cool, Con!" I blink, finally registering what he said. "Wait, conspiring?"

"You're making me feel guilty about not going home more often," he says, eyeing me knowingly.

I shrug, feeling a little guilty. "She just... She loves you so completely." Farrah loves Connor so much that even the thought of it makes my heart ache.

Connor smiles, kissing my head again. "And how do I love you?"

I step in front of him and stop walking, looking up at him. "In a way that fills my heart and wraps me in warmth."

Connor's skin glows, and he cups my cheek. "Two weeks until I see you. It seems like forever."

I place my hand over his, holding it against my cheek. "It'll fly by, and you'll get to hang out with your brothers and parents."

Connor scoffs, and I roll my eyes.

"Don't pretend you don't enjoy spending time with them."

Connor brushes his lips over mine. "I don't enjoy spending time with them as much as I do with you."

"Don't tell Rafe that. He'll get jealous," I say, taking his hand.

Connor chuckles, and we start walking again. "Next year, I'll have them come here for the whole holiday."

"You will?"

"Yep! If you can't come to Eden, I'll bring Eden to you." I grin, and Connor returns my smile. "You like that plan?"

"I like any plan that means I can spend more time with you."

Connor's phone pings, and he glances at it, pulling me to a stop. "Oh, shit. I forgot I was supposed to meet Rafe at home before the party."

"He can't meet you there?"

"I promised him we would build something for Luke's Christmas gift, and we planned to do it tonight, while he's out of the house."

I pout but push to my toes to brush a kiss against his lips. "Don't be long?"

"You bet I'll be quick. Can't have my girl taken by some mysterious stranger."

His choice of words is a shock, but I keep the smile on my face, though I can feel the strain in it. Connor kisses me again before turning and jogging toward his house.

I stand alone in the dark with a horrendous knot of unease in my stomach.

# 85

## SUMMER

### Caertha
LEADER,
BOSS, RULER

@1015
Congratulations on completing your first semester at Avalon, little fae.

Fuck, how does he do that? How does he know? Was he watching? Probably.

@RaysofSummer
Thank you, Stranger.

@1015
Are you excited for the break?

I shiver and hurry toward the party, following the dull beat of the bass through the darkness.

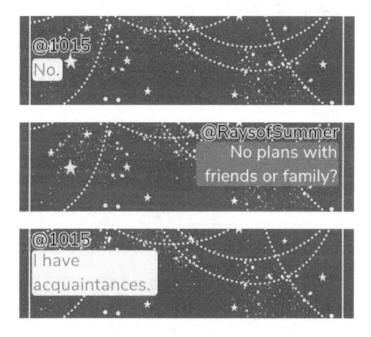

I frown at the message, considering how lonely that must be. Who am I kidding? I *know* how lonely it is. It's how I lived most of my life. Is that why I feel like he understands me? Is this our mutual experience?

We are back in the danger zone. I need to back out now.

Danger. Danger. Danger.

What the fuck does that mean?

I feel stupid the second I ask the question. Not only is it an obvious attempt to change the subject, but I am wearing a large, heavy coat over said outfit.

I worry my lower lip, considering. He probably saw the dress from my Nexus page.

Alice and I took a myriad of photographs as we were getting ready, and my wall is now littered with images. He's not wrong. It's maroon and very short, but it's definitely not the most risque thing I've ever worn, and I'm wearing over-the-knee boots, so it is still decent.

I scowl. Why am I so bothered by his opinion? Connor loves the dress, and that's all that matters.

Irritated, I roll my eyes and lock my phone before walking into the house. I'm immediately hit with a wall of heat, the harsh beats of the music, and the smell of some pretty potent Dragon Root. I spot Alice across the room and push into the crowd, quickly lost to the party.

I stumble out the door, and the cold hits me, but my coat is nowhere to be found. For some reason, that is hilarious, and I laugh as Alice falls against me.

"Connor is going to be pisssssssssed," Alice slurs as she grabs at me to stop me from falling.

The whole campus seems to be tipping, and that is funny as well. "Where is he?" I ask.

Alice takes a step ahead and ends up falling into a bush. I burst out laughing again and stumble over to help her up. I offer her my hand, but she blinks at it.

"Woah, Summer! Your hand has grown four more fingers." She tilts her head, and I hold my hand up to look at it.

"Fuck. We need to do a sobering rune," I mumble, feeling around my thighs for my rune knife. I pull it free and promptly drop it on the ground. Alice manages to get herself out of the bush and struggles to her feet, wobbling precariously.

I pick up my knife and look at its sharp edge. "Wait. Don't move. Okay?"

Alice nods, already distracted by her phone.

I stumble around the building, walking into the darkness. "Stranger?" I whisper-shout into the night.

I start to fall, but strong arms wrap around me. Suddenly, I'm pressed into a wall of hard muscle, and I happily lean against his faint form.

"You rang?" I can hear the irritation in his voice.

"Hello, my stranger! You're so difficult to perceive." I burst out laughing at my joke.

"You're drunk."

I step out of his arms and hold up my rune knife. I close one eye, aiming the tip toward my thumb. The world tips again, and I lose my balance. The stranger catches me again before I can fall, steadying me against him. My thumb burns, and I hold it up, blood dripping down my hand. Quite carelessly and accidentally, I managed to slice deep into the pad. I show it to him and say, "Help me draw a sobering rune?"

He sighs and shifts me in his arms. His large hand wraps around mine, and he presses my thumb against my thigh. I feel the warm, sticky blood even more, thanks to the bitter cold of the night. He expertly moves my hand, leaving the perfect rune in its wake. The rune glows faintly on my thigh, and I immediately feel the benefits. My head feels a little clearer, and the world stops spinning. As the alcohol wears off, the cold starts to invade.

"Celebrating a little hard, aren't we?"

I pout up at him. "You don't like my dress." It is all I can think to say, so clearly, I'm still fairly deep under the influence. I take a deep breath and force myself to leave his arms. "Thanks, see you later." I turn and walk away, feeling a little more steady.

"I didn't say I didn't like it," he says, stopping my retreat.

"But you don't like it. I can tell," I say, refusing to look back at him. I need to just shut up about it. Why does it matter? It *doesn't* matter.

"I don't like that anyone else gets to see you in it," he says, his voice tight.

"Is that something you say to a friend?" I ask, turning to face him.

"No, which is why I didn't say it until you decided to be a brat," he growls.

"I'm not sure how much the girl you are waiting for would appreciate you saying that to me," I fire back, jealousy sparking. I know I am being unreasonable and even unfair. My only excuse is the alcohol, and I cling to it.

I feel his eyes on me, his stare intense and piercing. "You tell me, little fae." His eyes slowly move down my body, his gaze filled with anger and heat. "Go back to your boy angel. He's looking for you."

I watch him for another moment, my stomach twisting. Fuck, why did I push it? I shouldn't have pushed it. I shouldn't have even called for him. Note to self: don't be inebriated when talking to Stranger. Just don't. I take a step back before turning and walking away from him.

Alice is not where I left her, so I head back inside. The second I step back into the house, I meet Connor's gaze. I walk to him, and he offers me a drink. I accept it but decide to nurse the fuck out of it.

Connor leans down and says against my ear. "Alice is in a bush. She's refusing to get out."

I chuckle. "I'll deal with it."

Connor brushes his lips along my cheek. "Or you could dance with me."

I smile up into his handsome face. He is everything I could ever need and more. What is wrong with me that I feel like I need someone else in my life who understands my darkness? Why do I have darkness? I want to be light, and I want to be light with Connor. I want to bask in the peace he brings to my life.

"Let me go sober Alice up, and then we'll dance."

Connor nods and bends down to press his lips to mine. Outside, I wonder how I could have missed Alice on my way in. She is sprawled out on what looks like an evergreen shrub. I sigh and slice my finger again before grabbing her ankle and drawing the same rune on her that the stranger just drew on me.

"Spoilsport," Alice grumbles, struggling to sit up.

I hold my hand to help her, and she takes it, allowing me to pull her to her feet. "Now you can drink more and be furious with me that no one seems to like my outfit," I grumble.

Alice looks me up and down. "Wow, are they blind? You're top shelf right now."

# 86

## FHREAGAIR

She's just so *infuriating*. Tendrils of my power spin from me as I pace in the forest, the trees they touch splintering and turning to dust. Do I like her dress? Of fucking course, I like her dress. I have eyes. I saw how her boy angel lit up at the sight of her. Undoubtedly, he earned himself another golden feather from how his skin glowed.

Another volley of my power flies off me, taking out more of the forest.

Why is she so fucking stubborn? Every time I think I can predict her next move, that I can move past this obsession—

I tense, the sensation of being watched sliding over me like cold oil. How had someone slipped past my shield? And they got close.

"If you're prepared to fight, I'm more than up for the challenge," I call to the watcher.

A ghostly laugh echoes back to me.

My runic circles glow under my palms. Complex and layered concentric circles, their power pulls and organizes the runes littered over my body, readying them to be armed, fired, and combined into more complex spells. The more intense and complicated the magic, the more circles it requires. Most beings capable of creating runes are able to produce base, utilitarian runic circles. Mine are intricate works of art, much more than just a tool or collection of pretty symbols. They drip with my concentrated power, one glowing white and the other black. They are the measure of someone at the top of their craft.

I send tendrils of power out, dark and insidious, uneasy that I can't sense this being. The fog shifts, and I hold up a hand, throwing a spell in that direction. I wait to hear it land, but there is nothing.

"Are you the one watching her?" I call again, searching the concealing mist.

I hurl another bolt of power. It hits a tree, and I watch as it turns to dust.

A chuckle reverberates in the air, pressing in on me from all sides. I turn slowly, trying to find the source.

"Us? Watching?" it calls.

"The one who's marked her. She bears the Mark of Nimue." I search the trees, trying to penetrate the darkness. Who or what is evading my detection? It should not be possible. A handful of beings can challenge me in strength, and only one that I know supersedes me, but this isn't him.

"You watch her too. We have seen," the voice mocks.

"Why her?" I ask, grinding my teeth.

The laugh comes again, this time surrounding me. Throwing both palms up, I unleash, letting my power fly in every direction. The runes vanish from my skin as they are spent to fill the runic circles. My ragged breaths fog the air in front of my face. How much power had I just burned through?

"All that power," the voice whispers right next to my ear, "and you're still just a *stranger.*"

I roar into the night.

# 87

## SUMMER

Bersha
GRAVITY

I climb into Connor's bed, slipping under the covers and relaxing back against his pillow. Connor strips off, pulling on pajama pants before crawling in next to me. He opens his arms, and I move into them, wrapping myself around him.

"Talk to me," he says, pressing a kiss to my forehead.

My brows furrow, and I look up at him. "About what?"

"You've been distant all night, babe."

I think back to the party. Was I being distant with him? We danced and kissed and touched. My mind wandered more than a few times, but there's no way he could have caught that. Right? There's no way he could have seen behind my false smile, the one I have perfected over the years.

The Almighty's words echo in my mind. "You will find more than peace, my child. You will find happiness. Joy. Belonging." But maybe what I should have asked is if, when I found it, it would be enough.

"It's just stress, Con. I'll be okay tomorrow."

Connor cups my cheek, tilting my head up. "Summer."

I sigh. "I promise I'll be better tomorrow. Let's just sleep." I don't even know how to begin to talk to him about this. I don't know if I want to talk to him about this. It feels like something that will taint him.

I move in closer to him, nuzzling into his neck.

"Babe?"

I kiss his neck softly. "Goodnight."

"Goodnight," he says, and I can feel the unease in his voice.

We lie in silence for a while. My mind is whirling, and I can almost hear him thinking as well.

"Babe?" Connor whispers after a long while. "You still awake?"

I nod.

"I feel like you're... pulling away from me, and I don't know how to stop it." I push up onto my elbow to look down at him. Connor brushes a lock of my hair behind my ear. "It kills me that I'm leaving you for two weeks. Don't shut me out."

"Con?" I say, barely able to see his face in the dark.

"Yes?"

"All I'm going to do for the next two weeks is miss you. I know it feels like I'm pulling away, but I promise you, it's nothing to do with you. I love you."

Connor lets out a long breath, and I wonder how long he has been holding it. "It feels so wrong to leave you behind. It feels like I'm leaving my heart behind, and it's putting me on edge."

"I get it, big guy, but nothing is going to happen to me. I'll be with Alice in Transylvania, and she has like royal guards or something. You're going to go to Eden, and you're going to have the best time with your family."

"Two weeks is just... so long," Connor says, and I can hear the pout in his voice.

My lips twitch. "What if I told you that Alice and I are already planning a summer vacation, and we've included the entire Morningstar clan?"

Connor's teeth flash white in the dark, his smile brightening the night.

"Does that help?"

Connor runs his fingers through my hair, and I want to purr at the feeling. "A little. I still don't want to go."

"Connor Azrael Morningstar. Your mother has been planning for you boys to go home for Yule since the semester started. She texts me all the time about it."

"You can't be on her side," Connor groans.

I kiss along his jaw. "She's so excited, Con. The house has been completely transformed, and she's been baking for days."

"She certainly is the queen of decking the halls."

"I'm not going anywhere, big guy," I say, gently biting the curve of his powerful jaw.

Connor pulls me tighter into him, and I kiss him deeply. He deepens the kiss, his tongue exploring my mouth, but I can feel his muscles are still tense beneath me.

"Stop thinking so much," I whisper when I pull back to breathe.

"You first," Connor whispers back, and I claim his mouth again, trying to distract him and myself from the intrusive thoughts.

I roll onto my back and pull him on top of me. Connor props himself up on his forearms, and I try to tug him down, wanting more of his weight.

Connor laughs and resists. "I'm heavy."

I lean up, snagging his lips with mine. "I like it."

"You'll be safe?" Connor asks, kissing me back.

I nod and slide my hands slowly down his chest, moving toward his pants.

Connor grabs my hands and looks down at me. His expression is gentle, but I can see the sadness in his eyes.

"Babe? I just want to hold you tonight if that's all right?"

I swallow and nod, pulling my hands away. Connor shifts onto his back and pulls me against him.

No, no, no, no, no. My demons are loud tonight, and there will be no distraction. Just me and my thoughts. My fucking awful, dark thoughts.

Connor idly strokes my back but quickly falls asleep with me in his arms. My mind drifts to the stranger, to the danger, to the thrill. Fuck. What is wrong with me? I roll out of his arms to lie on my back and stare up at the ceiling. Maybe I just need to get away from Avalon for a while.

My phone alerts, and I know exactly who it is. My body knows who it is.

He did cross the friend line, and he's acknowledging it. Why am I not more upset? Because that darkness within me surged as he did it, and it felt so fucking good.

There is a weighted delay before he replies.

483

I exhale heavily, acknowledging the heavy weight sitting on my chest.

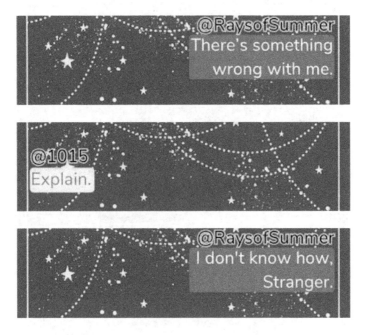

I wince, feeling every ounce of the truth dripping into the message.

I glance at Connor. He is sleeping so peacefully, his face so unburdened. His sweet kindness makes my heart ache.

I consider for a moment. Is that what it is? No. It doesn't feel like anything is wrong apart from me.

I glance at Connor again. I so desperately want to tell him no, shove these thoughts from my mind, and cuddle into Connor. But I crave the feeling of being heard, of being understood. These truths have been locked within me forever, but since I met the stranger, I want to get them out, to voice them. I cling to the profound hope that perhaps if I speak them out loud, they'll leave forever. I'd love to be able to tell Connor, to confide in and open up to him, but I don't want any of my darkness to attach to him. While I know he'd be understanding and still love me, I don't know that he wouldn't look at me differently. I'm not sure if I could live with that.

Making up my mind, I climb out of bed. I pull on a pair of leggings and a red wool sweater before creeping down the stairs. Pulling on my snow boots, I slip out of the house, wrapping my arms around my body against the cold. I already regret leaving the warmth of Connor's arms.

The stranger is already outside, leaning against the porch railing. His back is to me, and he's looking out at the rainy night.

"You're waiting for the next blow," he says, still looking out into the inky night, though his voice sounds like he's right next to me. "People like us," he continues, "we don't trust good things." He looks up at the cloud-laden night sky. "We prepare for the next hit to come, coil our bodies in preparation."

"It's not just that," I say, looking down at my boots.

He glances at me over his shoulder, finally pulling his gaze from the dark. "Then what is it?"

I sigh and sit on the front steps. A chill breeze blows my hair across my face, and I tuck it back behind my ear. "I'm not normal. I don't have normal feelings, normal wants, or normal desires. I..."

"You're not like him," the stranger says, sitting beside me.

I pull on my sleeves, tucking my hands inside the cuffs. "I want to be."

The stranger looks back at the sky. "The realms are full of wishes and wants, of those like him, golden and pure." He pauses, then looks at me. "Then there are those like us."

I meet his gaze. "Like us?"

"Those made from shattered shards of the realms, filled with the dust of all those who broke us. We're not like them. We try and try, but we're a different breed. Beings like us don't have wishes and wants. We don't obey. Instead, we challenge and destroy. We shape the realms, and they fear us."

I swallow, looking away. "I don't... I don't even understand what it is I want. What I need. I just know it's—"

"It's not what you're getting now," he finishes for me. "That's all right, little fae. To not know. To wonder and reach."

I feel my stomach dropping. "How do I change what I want, then?"

He pauses, formulating the weighty answer, but I already know what he is going to say. "You don't. No more than you can change being born fae. It's who you are. If those around you see it, will they turn away?"

I don't want to answer that question. Instead, I whisper, "What do I want?" The question isn't really for him. I just needed it out there, free and raw and real.

"More," he answers, staring up at the sky again. "The question is if you'll give him the chance to give it to you."

I shake my head. "I've tried. He doesn't understand, and I don't know that I want him to. He's too... kind."

"Is that the life you wish? Being half of yourself?" he asks.

I look down at my thighs, digging my fingers into them. "I love Connor."

"You can love someone, and they can still not be the right person for you."

I scowl at him. "He is the right person for me. He isn't the problem. I am the problem."

His energy bristles, making my skin prickle. "Why do you see yourself as the problem? Because you want something more? That you have the power to get it?"

"I don't want more. I don't *want* to feel like this. I'd do anything to be happy and content," I say, shaking my head.

"But you're not," he growls, and I can feel his frustration building.

I shake my head again. "No, I am. I just—"

"You need more. It'll never be enough." His voice is almost a snarl.

My stomach twists, and I curl my hands in my sleeves. "I should have known I couldn't discuss this with you," I say, standing up.

He stands, his avatar humming with agitation. "How long do you think this lie of yours can last? A year? Ten? How long will you pretend this is the life you crave? How long will you deny the part of you that screams in the dark, that wonders and craves?"

I shake my head, backing up. "You don't know me. I was wrong. You know nothing about me. I love Connor. I want Connor."

"Then why are you here talking to me?" he mocks cruelly.

I feel a tear sliding down my cheek as I watch him. "Because I thought you understood. But I was wrong."

"I do understand. That's why I know this lie will only carry you so far."

I shake my head. "You're wrong." I turn my back on him and go back inside, firmly but quietly closing the door behind me. The wood rattles violently as he vanishes, his angry power buckling the air on the porch.

Tears trail down my cheeks as I kick off my boots and haul myself back up to Connor's room. He's barely moved since I left him, but he has pulled my pillow closer and buried his face into it. I sob silently and climb into bed with him, staring at his perfect, wonderful face. I brush a lock of hair off his forehead.

I will be good enough for you, Connor. You are enough for me. You are perfect, and I love you.

I sob quietly, and Connor pulls me into him almost instinctively. I close my eyes, crying myself into unconsciousness.

# 88

## SUMMER

Noethoe
OUTSIDE

"Promise me you won't fall for a hot vampire," Connor says, sadness clouding his eyes.

"I promise. Promise me you won't fall for a hot angel." My hands fist in his shirt possessively.

Connor scoffs. "Please, no one compares to you."

"I'll see you in two weeks." I push up on my tiptoes and press my lips to his, kissing him deeply.

Connor breaks the kiss and presses his forehead to mine, tightening his arms around me. "I love you."

"I love you too, big guy."

He steps back reluctantly and studies my face as if committing it to memory before tapping on the gold halo wrapped around his wrist. A portal opens above him, and his wings appear behind him. I smile, seeing he has even more gold feathers than before. Connor takes a deep breath before he launches into the air and through the portal. He keeps it open long enough for me to watch him spin in the air and plunge into a cloud. The portal pulses and starts to sparkle, twinkling particles falling around me like glitter.

I sigh and look back at the empty Morningstar House, already missing him. Reluctant to leave, I stand there for a long moment, but without Connor's warmth, the chill wind bites deep. I pull my coat tighter around me and start back toward Kelpie Hall. The campus is completely empty, and the quiet is almost eerie.

We've reached the point in winter where the sun never fully rises, so the lamps in the campus quad are constantly on, illuminating the paths. As I walk through the watery puddles of light, my mind wanders to the stranger. I've not heard from him since that night on the porch. Perhaps he has also realized that I'm not who he thought I was. Not that I care. I was wrong about him, too. I thought he understood me, but he do—

The familiar low-lying fog seems thicker today, more of a viscous wall as I walk into it. I sense... something, and my steps falter.

"*Summer... Summer... Summer.*"

The sound is an echo, a haunting chant, and I turn my head toward the voice. Unlike the other times I've heard it calling for me, this is coming from a definitive direction, and it's beckoning.

"*Summer. Summer. Summer. Summer. Summer.*"

The voice continues to call to me, lyrical and compelling. The fae lights flicker romantically, and just like the first time I saw them, they captivated me. The mist parts, and while I know I shouldn't, I continue down the path, following the lure of that voice.

There is a small annoying heat against my chest. It throbs irritatingly, and my skin prickles as it pulses. I look down at my chest, expecting to see something sharp pressing into me, but there is nothing there.

"*Summer. Summer. Summer.*"

The chant of my name grows more insistent, and I search the swirling fog, trying to find the owner of this magical, seductive voice. The fae lights flicker again, and I look up at the canopy above. Suddenly, all the lights go out, and the darkness surrounds me.

The heat pulses almost violently against my chest. When I look down this time, my gaze snags on a set of footprints. There is only one set, and they follow the same trail I am on.

My head snaps up when the voice stops suddenly. The absence of it is more ominous than it calling to me. I take another step. When my foot hits the ground this time, there is a wet, squelching sound. The puddle doesn't feel as I would expect. It is not cold and slushy. Instead, it is viscous and warm. My breathing grows shallow and difficult. I force myself to look down, and every-thing within me goes still. My white sneaker is spattered with thick, dark blood.

Suddenly, awareness surges through me, and my heart springs back into action. I look up and meet the gaze of... milky, out-of-focus eyes. Vacant. Cold. Dead.

The scream gets caught in my throat, and I stand there frozen. There is another jolt of heat from the necklace, bordering on pain. I stumble back, and the reality, the danger, and the adrenaline swamps me. I hear a blood-curdling scream, and it takes me a full minute to realize it's coming from my lungs. Intending to run, I step back but trip and fall, landing in the pool of blood. Her blood. The dead girl who is sitting in front of me. Her body is propped up against the fallen tree trunk that I have sat on many times before.

And that sweater... Is that...? No.

Her sightless eyes pin me in place, but hers is not the only gaze I feel on me. That, unfortunately, familiar, malevolent presence is near, and I feel the hatred slither over me. Obviously, this kill wasn't enough. It was simply the appetizer. I can feel the way whatever is out there is feasting on my fear.

Lured. I was lured, and like an idiot, I allowed it.

"Lost, little fae? Strange little fae..." the voice croons through the words, scraping over my senses like nails against a chalkboard. "No one to save you now." The voice is all around me, a hideous mix of male and female, young and old.

My chest heaves as I try to focus. I force myself to think, trying to remember what I have learned. They are right. I am alone, and this time, I will have to save myself. We have only just started to practice runic circles, and I have not been able to curate them yet. Fuck. What the fuck did Max teach me?

Without looking away from the shifting fog, I slide my dagger from its sheath and slice my forefinger, ready to draw whatever I can think of that might help.

"Lost, little fae? Strange little fae..." the voice sing-songs. This time, I'm able to identify a direction. Quickly, I draw a combative rune on my palm and throw my arm out. A vibrant purple light blasts from my hand, tearing through the fog in the general direction of the sound.

I take advantage of the distraction and scramble to my feet, bolting back down the path. I can feel her blood on me, trickling down my legs and coating my skin like oil. The maniacal laugh follows me, but it gets further away with every step.

I burst into the headmaster's office. I don't remember deciding to come here, but here I am. He bolts from his chair and is suddenly in front of me,

"What's happened?" he asks, his voice concise.

My gaze flits around his office, wondering why the room is trembling, shifting, and rocking like we're in the middle of an earthquake. It's only when he grabs my arms that I realize I'm the one shaking.

"Look at me," he commands.

I try to focus on him, but I can't breathe. The malevolent touch of that gaze lingers like putrid slime against my skin. Everything is blurring as tears build in my eyes.

"Look. At. Me," he growls.

I blink and feel the useless tears fall down my cheeks. They won't bring her back. They won't erase the accusation in her sightless eyes. It's my fault, just like before.

"Breathe," he commands.

I try to take a breath, but my lungs fight back.

"Another."

I take another breath, and this one is as difficult as the first.

"Another."

This one is a little easier.

The headmaster waves his hand, and I feel a portal open behind me. "Go inside."

I blink and look over my shoulder at the portal, seeing my dorm room door. The headmaster gently turns me around and pushes me through the opening. It snaps closed the second my feet hit the carpet of the hallway. I just stand there. My breathing has evened out, but my body is still stuck in a state of shock. I can't move. My limbs feel like lead, and my joints have seized up.

Alice opens the door, her face etched in confusion. "What are you doing?" she asks.

I glance at her, feeling myself start to crumble.

Alice inhales deeply. Her nose wrinkles, but her expression softens with concern. "Sum?"

Emotions climb up my throat, and it feels like I'm choking on them. Another salty tear slides down my cheek, but I just stare at her.

Alice approaches me carefully as if she is afraid I will bolt. She gently turns me around, looking me over. "This blood isn't yours," she says with certainty, having already scented it.

"I found..." My voice is hoarse and broken. It sounds like I've been screaming for days, but I haven't. I let out one scream, one show of pure terror.

Alice shakes her head, her hands still roaming over me, looking for invisible injuries. "It's okay. You don't have to say it."

The sob that had lodged itself in my throat finally rips itself free, and another tear falls. "She—" Another sob escapes me. "I think she was wearing my sweater."

Alice looks around suspiciously and wraps her arm around me, pulling me into the dorm. She paces, glancing at me every few seconds as if assuring herself I'm still safe.

"Which sweater?"

I swallow, looking at the ground. "The pink one with the daisy buttons."

"Shit. You were looking for that just last week." She stops pacing for a moment, and I feel her gaze on me. "Maybe it was just a similar one?"

I shake my head. "It had the scorch mark on the cuff. The one I got when—"

"When Zane was fucking about with runes," Alice finishes for me.

I nod, another tear falling.

Alice's jaw clenches, and her eyes flash crimson. "Get your stuff. We're going tonight."

Happy to comply with orders right now, I walk to my room on autopilot and start packing. Alice doesn't let me out of her sight the whole time. She even follows me to the bathroom when I wash the blood from my hands, and as I'm shoving clothes into my bag, I notice another couple of my items missing. It is nothing big, but I had a black t-shirt with RUIN MY RUNES on it. The neckline had been cut so that it sat off the shoulder. I also couldn't find one of my skirts and a pair of yoga pants that had a small hole in the inner seam, not to mention the multitude of panties that have disappeared.

"Ready?" Alice asks for the fortieth time since I walked into my room. I can feel her anxiety, and she must be scared if she thinks Drãculea is the safer option.

I nod, and Alice places her hand over her heart. Black claws shoot from her fingertips, piercing her skin. She rotates her hand, and a portal opens beside her in an explosion of bright red light. Alice drops her hand, her blood dripping onto the floor. That is going to be a bitch to clean up. She looks through the portal at the gloomy gray skies and dark, oppressive buildings.

We step through the portal. "Welcome to Drãculea," Alice says.

# 89

## SUMMER

Caerçho
GOD, GODDESS,
DEITY

Alice looks around her realm, tension radiating from her. I look at her, and I embrace the distraction. I slide my hand into hers and squeeze in a silent show of support.

Drăculea is exactly as you would expect. Buildings made of heavy gray stone line cobbled streets. We are standing on a bridge, the faint sound of running water beneath us. Alice doesn't move, and I follow her intense stare until I see the source of her tension. In front of us, at the top of the hill, the castle sits proudly. The towers and turrets point toward the red sky, the imposing, dark structure looming over the entire realm, keeping watch.

Alice takes another long moment before she tightens her grip on my hand and moves, ascending through the town. She keeps her eyes focused straight ahead, ignoring the vampires that turn their backs on her. She doesn't react at all, barely seeming to notice their sneers. I follow her lead, keeping my head high and my expression blank, but I stay vigilant. If anyone comes near her, I will go through them. I won't lose my Alice.

I am doing everything I can to keep from thinking about what I left behind at Avalon, refusing to remember the girl in the pink sweater with the daisy buttons. It is a struggle not to remember those vacant eyes, milky in death when I can feel her sticky blood on my skin and still drying on my clothes.

As we near the castle, I realize the bricks aren't black as I'd thought when I first laid eyes on it. Instead, they are the dark red of arterial blood. Alice had told me the truth, and she hadn't exaggerated. There is a moat surrounding the castle, and it is filled with nasty, viscous blood.

Alice pushes the gates open and strides into the castle, still pulling me along. It is noticeably empty save for guards, and they ignore her as she leads me through the corridors. The inside is just as dark as the outside but much more refined and palatial. Gold sconces line the walls, illuminating art and tapestries that are priceless even to my untrained eye. Blood-red rugs span the length of the halls, contrasting with the dark wood floors. The decor is beautiful but in a cold, impersonal, and untouchable way. Even the hushed atmosphere reminds me of a museum.

Alice relaxes a little once we're inside, but neither of us speaks as we climb eight flights of stairs. She stops in front of a heavy wooden door and pushes it open. I blink, wondering if she had opened a portal to another realm. The room is still dark, but it has life and warmth. There is a large four-poster bed with a fluffy purple comforter and matching sheets. White gossamer curtains hang from the corners of the bed, artfully tied to the posts with violet sashes. I can tell just by looking at the large blue rug in the center of the room that it is luxurious and soft. Cushions and a couple of throws in various shades of blue are scattered over an overstuffed white couch tucked into the far corner. The walls are covered with posters of characters from her favorite shows, but the largest one is the art of a character from a popular shifter romance book.

Alice moves past me and throws her bag onto the bed. "Welcome to the crypt."

I follow her inside and stop in the center of the room, trying to take it all in. The massive chandelier hanging from the vaulted ceiling looks out of place in this colorful teenage haven. In between the posters, a myriad of weapons are artfully hung on the walls.

Alice nudges me with her shoulder. "Hey. You with me?"

I nod, forcing my face into a smile. I am struggling to maintain the numbness I had wrapped around myself, but I can feel reality lurking around the edges, just waiting for those defenses to drop. Now that we are here and safe, everything is starting to hurt.

Alice stares at me for a minute, and then she smiles brightly. "Want to hurt some people?"

The outlandish suggestion settles on me. I don't automatically discount it because I do want to hurt people. I want to hurt a specific person. The person who has been killing those fae girls. The person who has been fucking with me. The person who has been threatening me. Watching me. Scaring me. I want to cause pain because I don't want to feel it anymore. I don't want to feel anything.

I don't want to feel powerless anymore.

But this isn't who I am, right? I'm not vindictive. I'm not evil. Does it make me evil that I want others to feel even a fraction of this pain, even if they deserve it? I don't know if it does or not. All I know right now is that I want to beat, destroy, and hurt.

"I think I'm just going to take a shower," I say, remembering that I'm covered in blood that belongs to someone else. *Belonged* to someone else, I suppose. Alice doesn't seem phased that I'm covered in dirt and blood, probably because it's something she's familiar with. None of the vampires we've encountered reacted to my appearance, actually. This is obviously much more normal here.

Until this moment, adrenaline and the need to act normal had kept my reality at bay, but now I'm unable to pretend that my yoga pants aren't becoming hard with the drying blood that has become one with the fabric. I can no longer ignore her blood painting my skin like some gory tattoo.

"There's a huge bathroom through there." She waves toward a door on the left side of the bed. "Ignore the jewels. I didn't design it. It's fucking gaudy and awful, but it's got good water pressure."

"Thanks. Can I borrow a towel?"

"There's a ton in there."

I nod and hurry into the bathroom, so desperate to get out of these clothes, to cleanse this death from my skin that I barely notice the decor. I strip, leaving my bloodied clothes and shoes in a grisly pile on the immaculate tile floor. Stepping into the shower, I turn the water on and adjust it to the hottest setting. It hammers out of the shower head, and I groan at the feeling of the already scalding water cleansing my skin. I close my eyes, but the second I do, I see her lifeless eyes staring at me. Nope. I flick my eyes open again, focusing on a particularly shiny pearl on the wall as I wash myself. I scrub my body until my skin is practically raw, but I still feel her blood on me, even in places it never touched.

Eventually, I turn the shower off and wrap myself in a fluffy black towel before returning to the bedroom. Alice is standing at the window, looking out at her realm, her shoulders tight.

"You know," she begins, still looking out. "I think I figured out why people get obsessed with you." She looks at me over her shoulder, and I stand still, waiting for her to continue. "You make people think that maybe the monsters aren't all bad. You make us think that maybe we can be better."

I frown, completely confused. "I do?"

Alice nods. "Thanks for coming home with me," she says and looks back out the window.

I slip my panties and shorts on under the towel and then pull on one of Connor's shirts.

Alice chuckles. "Aw, they left a note for me. How nice."

I walk to the window and look out. **LEAVE BITCH** is written on the roof of a nearby building.

"Are you fucking kidding me?" I snarl, feeling the anger bubbling inside me.

Alice shrugs. "This is pretty tame, actually."

The grief and fear crystallize in my chest, and in its wake, there is only fury. I storm out of her room, stomping through the unfamiliar halls of the castle.

"Summer! Wait!" Alice calls, chasing after me.

I keep going, but Alice catches up and directs me out of the building. I round the castle, trying to work out where the message is written. It doesn't take me long to find the group of female vampires standing beside the building. All of them are wearing long gowns that just about touch the floor, the velvet black material splattered with dollops of paint.

"Hey!" I shout. They all look at me, their expressions of pride in their artistic endeavors morphing into hideous sneers.

I don't give them time to react. I tap the small, iridescent rune on my wrist, still there from earlier, and slam a ball of bright purple power right into the center of the group. The females go flying, screeching as they are flung into the air. They land heavily on the hard ground and then scramble to their feet, their eyes flashing red with rage. A few of them flash their fangs at me, and I expect them to attack, but I am disappointed when the leader hisses, and they start to flee. My dagger is still in the bathroom, so I pull open the barely closed wound on my finger and draw another rune on the back of my hand. I growl and toss the power at them. The females once again fly into the air, this time by their ankles, an invisible rope hoisting them high.

Alice strolls up behind me, amusement in her voice. "There will be more."

"I'll fight them too. I am not weak. I am not defenseless," I growl.

Alice comes to my side, looking at my face. "You planning to fight the entire realm?"

My lips curl upward at the corners. "If necessary." Anger is a shield, and it feels so much better than fear.

Leisurely, I walk through the squirming vampires, drawing a rune on each of their foreheads. The second the lines are joined, the rune illuminates. Boils pop up on their faces, and their fangs turn to rubber. They scream and struggle frantically, but I hold them firm.

"And that, you little leeches, is my best friend." Alice's smile is dangerous, and I much prefer it over the defeated acceptance from earlier. She slings an arm around my shoulder. "If my fangs and claws aren't enough, her magic will bring you down."

I look at them all, my body relaxing into the reality that I can take care of myself. Maybe.

"Looks like you have a few new supporters, Al. Right, girlies?"

One of the vampires burst into tears as the others snarl and hiss, but they all nod.

"I love to have loyal subjects." Alice smiles brightly.

I step back and wave my hand, dropping them hard on the ground again. "Go. Before I make those runes permanent."

They scrabble to their feet and bolt away.

"Well done." Alice laughs.

# 90

## SUMMER

Caitha
SUMMER

The following two weeks are spent wreaking absolute havoc in Drăculea. It didn't take long for word to spread, and soon, vampires were running in the other direction or ducking into alleyways to avoid us when we approached.

The distance from Avalon has done nothing to help me forget that day. Even now, I can feel the way her blood clung to me. I can still see those milky, unfocused eyes. The killer let this victim keep them this time. The way her head was tilted slightly to the right. My stomach roils every time I remember the gore streaking the pretty pink sweater with the daisy buttons.

"Home sweet home." Alice sighs when we arrive back in our dorm.

Cautiously, I look around, relieved to see there's no residual blood from that day. I'm both excited and dreading being back in Avalon for Christmas Eve. I'm excited to spend time with Connor and his family, but I'm also nervous about being back within reach of the killer.

Collapsing onto the couch, I check the time on my phone. Connor should be back any minute. I can't wait to see him, but I am not looking forward to having to keep another secret from him. The headmaster had sent me one email over the break. It simply said that he was going to take the opportunity that an empty school brought and do some research into the murder. He ended the message by warning me that the authorities wanted this to remain strictly under wraps.

"Man, terrorizing an entire species is exhausting," Alice groans, flopping down next to me.

"Pretty fun, though," I admit. To be honest, I did find a lot of it fun. I found it liberating to incite fear in people, and I *crave* the power of it.

Alice snorts. "Super fun."

Someone knocks on the door, and I look up as Connor enters the room, using the key I had made for him. I smile and jump up, running to him. I throw my whole body against him, knowing he will catch me.

"Hi, big guy."

Connor seals his lips over mine, kissing me deeply. I wrap my arms around his neck and stroke my tongue against his, savoring his taste. I've missed him madly over the past two weeks. We've video-called a couple of times and texted every day, but I've missed feeling him against me.

Connor lifts me easily, and I wrap my legs around his hips. Without breaking the kiss, he carries me into my room.

"Well, hello to you too, bird brain," Alice grumbles from the living room just before Connor kicks the door closed.

Connor sets me on my feet, and we tear our clothes off. The moment we are both naked, he pushes me onto the bed and flips me onto my belly.

"Fuck, I missed you so much," Connor growls, pulling my hips up and sliding his thumb through the slickness already dripping from my pussy.

"Missed you—" My words end with a cry, and I grasp at the pillows as he slams inside of me.

Connor slides his fingers into my hair and tugs hard as he thrusts deep inside me. My back bows, his rough possession only intensifying my pleasure. Connor pulls my hair again, yanking my head back as he plunges his cock into me over and over.

"You're soaking me so good, babe," Connor groans from behind me, his fingers digging into my hip as he pulls me into his thrusts.

"Spank me," I moan, my eyes rolling.

Connor gently hits me on the ass.

"Harder," I beg, craving the sting from his hand.

Connor hits me harder, and I cry out.

"You take my cock so good," Connor groans, and I glance at him over my shoulder. His gaze is locked to where we are joined, his expression transfixed.

I feel my arousal sliding down my thighs, and I fist the blankets, bracing against his brutal thrusts.

Connor spanks me again. It's still not as hard as I'd like, but definitely harder. "You're dripping. Fuck. Didn't know you could get this wet."

"Again... please!"

"Close..." Connor spanks me again, and I hear the strain in his voice.

I shove my ass back against him. "Grab me," I demand, knowing exactly what I need to get there.

Connor grips me with both hands, digging his fingers into my hips hard. "Fuck. Fuck, Summer."

"Pull my cunt onto your cock, big guy," I pant the words, my body trembling right on the precipice.

Connor moans as he takes control, yanking me back and forth on him. "I'm going to cum."

I close my eyes, thinking about how it felt when he pulled my hair, thinking about how it would feel if he had me tied up, about how I'd love to be gagged and helpless to his every whim and pleasure. Connor yells, filling me with his release, and I come, crying out for him.

Connor collapses on top of me, completely spent. "Hi," he pants into my ear.

I moan. "Hi, handsome."

Connor kisses down my neck. "You liked that."

"Fuck, Con... So fucking good." I shiver, aftershocks of pleasure rippling through me. "Where did that come from?"

"I uh..." Connor says hesitantly. He eases out of me, and we both moan.

I roll to face him as he lies beside me, his cheeks flushed.

"Well, I did some research," he finally says.

"Wait. What kind of research?" I ask, lifting an eyebrow.

"I've kind of... caught on that you like that sort of stuff, so I looked into it." His blush creeps down his neck.

"You did?"

Connor nods. "And there were things I wanted to try."

"Like what?"

"Like... tying you up. Spanking. Hair pulling," Connor says, pulling me in closer.

I stare up at him. Does he really enjoy the things I do, or is he just doing this for me?

"I was imagining us doing it, and well, I had to take care of myself," Connor continues.

"You fucked your fist imagining me tied up for you?" I ask.

Even Connor's ears turn red.

"It turns me on, Con. Knowing you did that."

"Yeah?"

I move closer, bringing my knee to his hip and placing my hand on his chest. "So fucking much."

Connor leans in and presses his lips to mine, and we lose ourselves in pleasure once again.

Connor hums as we get dressed, and I smile as I pull my tights on. "You excited, big guy?"

Connor smiles at me, buttoning his pants. "I love Christmas."

I pull on a maroon wrap dress and tie it at the waist. "I know you do."

"Alice!" Connor calls, banging his fist on the wall. "Get dressed for Christmas!"

I laugh as I push my feet into my boots and bend to zip them.

Alice opens the door without knocking. "I am not worshiping some weirdo felon who enjoys breaking, entering, and theft."

I sigh. "It's also Yule, Alice." I look at myself in the mirror, touching up my lipstick. "Besides, you won't get your gifts if you don't get dressed."

Alice sighs heavily and stomps back into her room reluctantly. Though I can tell, there is a sprig of excitement about presents.

Connor holds out his hands to me. When I walk into his arms, he pulls me against him and dips me dramatically. He kisses me passionately and then pulls back to gaze down at me. The love in his eyes is humbling. "Merry Christmas, Summer."

I smile up at him, and Connor straightens, steadying me on my feet. I reach up and wipe the lipstick from his lips.

"Not my shade?" he asks.

I laugh. "Not really."

Connor wraps his arms around me again, his hands resting on my ass. "Man, I missed you."

I cup his cheek. "I missed you too, big guy. How's your mom and dad?"

"They have gifts for you and Alice," Connor says, smiling brightly.

"I have gifts for them, too! I'm happy they're coming," I say, kissing him again.

Connor squeezes me tight before pulling back. He slides his hand into mine and says, "Let's go."

Fear slithers through me when we near where I found the girl's body. The snow is fresh, and the only footprints other than ours are the ones Connor made on his way to the house. I keep expecting to see where mine veered off course when I heard that voice, but there is nothing but fresh, white snow.

The pendant grows warm, a phantom reminder of what happened. I turn my head to the left, looking at the path I would have taken. The forest is as dark as always, the trees unassuming. Do they still feel her death?

"Babe?"

I blink, looking at Connor, and realize I have stopped walking. "Huh?"

Connor frowns. "You okay?"

"I—"

"She's fine. Right, Sum?" Alice interrupts, sliding her arm through mine and giving me a knowing look.

I nod and pull my face into a smile before looking up at Connor. His gaze is concerned, but it eases when we start walking again. Alice leads the conversation about Drăculea, and I take the opportunity to look back over my shoulder. There is nothing to see except the faintest sway of the tree branches. I swallow and snap my head back around.

Fuck.

The Morningstar House is as bright as if we are approaching an actual star. Alice holds her hands up to cover her eyes. "This is way too much fucking light after just getting back from two weeks of gray."

I chuckle and squeeze her arm.

"Do you like it?" Connor asks me, and the hope in his voice makes me melt. He's done this for me. He wants me to feel the magic of Christmas and knows I've never had a family to celebrate the holiday with. I need to make the most of this with him. He does so much for me. The least I can do is enjoy every second. I take a moment to shove away my fear and thoughts of the dead girl, focusing on the present and this man who loves me.

"I love it, Con."

"Well, my retinas don't, and she's lying," Alice grumbles.

I shove Alice playfully and pull Connor to the front of the house. "Take a photo of us, Al."

Alice pulls out her phone and snaps a photo. "You can barely see you two past the lights. It's like you're standing on the sun."

I pull Connor in for a kiss, and Alice snaps another photo.

"I love you," I say.

"I love you, too," Connor says, starting to glow. "Let's go inside. It's freezing out here!"

I nod, and we all head inside. I'm immediately hit with the smell of cinnamon and apples. The whole house is decorated, and ornaments adorn every surface. The tree in the window is so large it nearly touches the ceiling. It's expertly decorated with ornaments and draped with red and green ribbons. On top, a gold star shines proudly.

"This is fucking insane," Alice says, completely awestruck. "Where is everyone?"

"I came back early. Mom was still cooking, but I wanted to get back to see you guys." Connor drops my hand and walks to the couch, where there is a pile of folded sweaters. He holds one up. "Put these on!" I blink at the design. It's baby blue and has white wings embroidered on the front. There is a large M in the middle of the chest.

"But, my dress..."

"Just for a picture of the three of us. My mom and dad will love it." He hands me a sweater and then gives one to Alice. "You're honorary Morningstars."

I sigh and pull on the jumper. "Just for you."

Alice grumbles but yanks hers on.

Connor grins as he pulls the sweater on over his head and then ushers Alice and me to the tree. He sets the phone up on the sofa and then runs back to stand between us. He wraps his arm around us, and we all smile as the camera flashes.

"Wait, another one!" I say, setting the camera up again. I run back and pull Connor's face to mine at the last moment, kissing him just as the photo is taken.

I check the images and laugh when I see that Alice put two fingers up behind Connor's head in the second one, giving him bunny ears. When I turn around, Alice has already pulled the sweater off and draped it over the back of the couch. I look at the joy on Connor's face and opt to keep mine on.

Connor wraps his arms around me and nuzzles my nose. "Merry Christmas."

"Merry Christmas, big guy."

"Enough! Presents!" Alice groans.

"Shouldn't we wait for everyone else to get here?" I ask, but I eye the presents hungrily. I have never had presents.

Alice glares at me mutinously.

"Never mind, I guess," I say with a laugh, holding up my hands. Connor plucks a gift from under the tree and hands it to me. It's expertly wrapped, and I don't know why I'm surprised. He's Mr. Holidays. I sit down on the couch and place the box on my lap. I take care opening it, not wanting to destroy the lovely gold paper decorated with shiny pictures of baubles.

Connor smiles and crosses his arms as he watches me, his eyes shining. "It's silly, but I thought it would help when I'm gone."

I place the wrapping paper on the coffee table and open the box. Inside, there is a brown stuffed bear. It's wearing a blue t-shirt embroidered with the word CONBEAR.

"It's for you to sleep with."

I gasp, looking at the soft, fluffy bear. It's got a small black nose and large brown eyes.

I push the box down beside me and stand, jumping into Connor's arms. "Thank you! I love it!"

Connor laughs, spinning me around. "It's only for when I'm not here."

I smother his face in kisses. He reluctantly puts me down after a long moment. "And the second gift is from my parents and me."

This gift is a much smaller rectangle. I take the same care with this one, peeling off the paper and opening the box. Inside is a key attached to a cloud-shaped keyring. I blink and pick it up.

"It's a key to my place in Eden."

I lift my eyebrows, looking at the key again. It dangles there innocently like it's not a huge fucking deal. "A key to your place? How forward, Morningstar."

"I want you to move in with me after I graduate," he says, and I meet his gaze.

"In... Eden?" I ask.

Connor glances behind me at Alice and then back at me. "So, I spoke with my dad.

I will be allowed to live here and work as an archangel until you graduate, but I will need to spend summers in Eden."

I stare at him, not sure what to say.

Alice moves to stand beside me, looking between us.

"So I'll live with you here?" I say, finally finding my voice.

Connor nods. "During the school year."

"What about Alice?" I ask, needing to know that he has planned for this. Surely, he knows me well enough to know I'd never leave her.

Connor smiles. "My dad has offered to add onto the house if Alice is game."

I look at Alice, unsure how she'll react.

She meets my gaze and shrugs nonchalantly. "I go where you go."

"Really?"

Alice nods. "I don't care where we live."

I smile and jump on Connor again, kissing him hard.

Connor pulls back, blinking. "So you're—"

"I'm in." I grin, and Connor glows a little brighter, squeezing me tight.

"I'm going to need the biggest room," Alice says.

"Absolutely not," I say as Connor lowers me to the ground. "Okay! Presents from me!" I walk to my bag and pull out two presents. I hand one to Alice and one to Connor. In direct contrast to the finesse I demonstrated, Connor tears into his present like a kid. He pulls out a football jersey in the school's colors, but the name on the back is Tuatha De Star.

Connor holds it up with a wide, bright smile. "This is perfect!" He kisses me, and I snuggle against him when I hear Alice tearing into hers. While Connor was like a child, Alice opens her present like a rabid animal.

Inside the box, there is a blood-red dagger. The steel is darker than the handle. Legosi is engraved on the hilt, with tiny rubies set into the letters. "It's runed to you. If you want it and it's not near, it'll appear in your hand. The blade can also heat up and freeze as you will it." Those runes were challenging to create, but I finally managed to get them right just in time. I'm suddenly tackled out of Connor's arms. Alice takes me to the ground, her small body landing hard on top of me. "I love it!" she exclaims, nuzzling into me.

"Alice!" I laugh.

"Shh. Endure it. You do this shit to me all the time."

After a moment, Connor lifts Alice off me and helps me to my feet.

"I also have a present for you, Sum." She hands me a very small, thin gift almost completely covered in tape to hold the paper together. The wrapping paper is folded in odd ways and it sticks out in random places, but it might be the most beautiful thing I have ever seen because she's done it herself.

I open it, and inside is a solid gold credit card with **HHRH** Summer Tuatha De Daanan written across the front. I gape at the shiny gold.

"I've added you as an honorary princess of Drăculea, so you'll have access to the royal treasury."

"Alice, I can't accept this," I stammer out.

"Yes, you can. I never want you to worry about money."

"But—"

"But nothing, Summer. It's yours."

I smile and pull her into a hug, smothering her in kisses. She allows it for a little longer than usual before pulling back. "All right, no more mushy."

I move back to Connor and cuddle into him. "Your other gift I'll need to give you when we're alone."

Connor's eyes darken, and he kisses me.

Alice comes over with glasses of eggnog and hands each of us one. "I don't know what this is, but I can't see any other alcohol."

"It's traditional!" Connor says, somewhat outraged.

Alice lifts her glass in the air. "To a family of misfits."

Connor and I lift our glasses, too. "A family of misfits."

# 91

## SUMMER

*Deth̃tha*
ARMOUR, CLOTHING

The next week of the break seems to blur past, and I spend most of it trying to come to terms with the trauma I faced before Yule. Every single night, I go back to the forest. I see her sitting against that tree, and she's in a different state of decay every time. When I'm alone, I can still feel the phantom trickle of her blood as it slides down my legs, and how heavy it made my yoga pants.

Alice has done her best to distract me, but she has her own demons, especially when in Drăculea. There are moments of silence when fear sinks its claws into us. The insular feeling of pain isolates both of us until one of us is able to quell it enough to reach out to the other. I was reluctant to leave Alice to go to Connor's birthday celebration, but I had promised him, so Alice spent the day at Avalon, which didn't alleviate my fears even slightly.

Even though I am afraid, I'm excited for the term to start again and fall back into a schedule. When did this campus become my home, and why do I feel like it's slowly being taken from me?

*Summer Tuatha De Daanan, destined to be hunted, destined to run.*

"I need a bigger closet," I say, shoving clothes to the side.

Alice pulls her attention from her phone and looks up at me from where she is lounging on my bed. "I could use a spacial rune," she says hopefully.

I glare at her. "No."

"I've gotten better!"

"No."

Alice sighs, looking back at her phone with a pout.

"So, Con and I are going to dinner tonight. What should I wear?" I hold a dress up against me and stand in front of the full-length mirror.

"I thought you bought that fancy lingerie for him?" Alice asks, looking up to check my reflection in the mirror.

"I did, but we're going to dinner first."

Alice slips off the bed and goes to my overstuffed closet, quickly rifling through the hangers. She pulls out an incredibly short maroon skater dress. "Wear this."

I undress and pull on the little dress, looking at myself in the mirror. It truly is very short, but I like it a lot. Given the temperature, I will definitely have to wear stockings, but luckily, the lingerie set I bought has a garter belt. I grab the stockings and wander into the bathroom to slip into the lingerie I bought to wear for Connor. Alice helps me fasten the back garter clips when I rejoin her in the bedroom.

"Well?" I ask when she's done, spinning to give her the full effect.

"He'll cum in his pants." Alice chuckles.

I laugh and sit beside her on the bed to pull on my boots.

"You going back to the Italian place?"

I nod, zipping the first boot.

"You going to fuck in the bathroom?" she asks, smirking like an asshole while scrolling through her phone.

"You know I don't ever *plan* to fuck in the bathroom."

"You're such a liar." Alice snickers. "Oh, looks like the headmaster is back on campus."

I zip the other boot. "Oh?"

"Someone just posted a photo of him on *EverydayEmrys*." Alice tilts her phone toward me, showing me the photograph of Headmaster Emrys. He's walking alone through campus, wearing a dark sweater and dark jeans. It's the most casual I've ever seen him, but he looks tense. Perhaps the search for information about the murders is not going well.

"Do you think he knows there is a whole stalker page dedicated to him?"

Alice shrugs, continuing to scroll through socials. "I mean, if you're that hot, it's to be expected."

I laugh and return to the mirror to finish putting my makeup on.

There is a knock at the door, and I check the time. "That must be Connor. He's early."

"Bet he couldn't wait to get in here and be all gross and mushy with you. I'll let him in," Alice says, going to open the door for him. We had started locking the door when we were in the house, just for a little added security. Connor must have forgotten the key I gave him.

"Can I help you?" Alice's muffled voice carries through the door, and I still at her tone.

"I was hoping to speak to Miss Tuatha De Daanan," an unfamiliar male voice answers. I glance at my door and slowly make my way to it.

"Why?" Alice asks, and I can hear the hostility in her voice.

"Ah, you must be Miss Legosi," he replies. I can hear the smile in his voice, but it's not comforting.

"That's Your Highness to you," Alice hisses.

I open the bedroom door and walk to Alice's side, taking in the man standing in our doorway. He is wearing a brown trench coat, and his pale green eyes settle on me. It's not immediately apparent what species he is. He looks unassuming, but my instincts scream at me.

"It's okay, Alice," I say. I tap on her phone twice, trying to communicate with her silently that she should contact the headmaster.

Alice hisses at the visitor again before reluctantly trudging into her room.

"Miss Tuatha De Daanan. My name is Chief Investigator Thomas Aquino. You've been fairly difficult to keep track of over this holiday season." He waits for a response, but there is nothing to say. "Do you have time for a quick chat?"

I step to the side, inviting him in.

The investigator sits in one of the armchairs and waits for me to settle on the sofa before saying, "I'm sure you know why I have asked to speak with you." His stare is heavy, intense, and penetrating.

I lift my chin, still not speaking.

The inspector smiles weakly, but his eyes remain flat and cold. "Miss Tuatha De Daanan. We can do this the easy way or—"

"You are not to interview my students without me present, Tom." The headmaster storms into the dorm, his expression thunderous.

The inspector holds his bland smile. "Ah, Jim. I was wondering how long it would take you."

The headmaster walks to the side of the couch and narrows his eyes at Thomas. "Clearly, Miss Tuatha De Daanan is on her way somewhere. Surely, this can wait."

The inspector's smile hardens. "This won't take long, Jim. And Miss Tuatha De Daanan has nothing to hide." He looks at me. "Isn't that right?"

I blink, looking at him. "Excuse me?"

"You don't have anything to hide," Thomas repeats, his gaze like a rash across my skin.

"No," I answer, my voice hard. Though his words do not convey it, I can hear the accusation in them.

Thomas's smile deepens. "Well then, Jim informed us that you found the newest victim, Alicia Tuatha De Daanan. It almost seems she was placed for you to find."

Tension radiates from the headmaster. "That is a suspicion of yours, not mine."

Thomas never drops his smile. "Ah yes, but it does seem odd to have you discover not just one, but two bodies."

"I thought I was being questioned."

"You are," Thomas replies.

"You've yet to ask me a question," I reply coldly.

Thomas laughs, and the sound is icy. "Right. Did you have any interaction with Lucia and Alicia prior to discovering their remains?"

I lift my chin. "I met Lucia once at a party."

Thomas flips his notepad open and begins taking notes. "That's a bit odd, is it not? To not be enclosed in your people?"

I shrug. "Whether it's odd or not, it is my situation."

Thomas's pen scratches over the paper as he writes furiously. "We tried to pull a full history on you, Miss Tuatha De Daanan. We came up empty. That is also very odd."

"Someone applied to Avalon on her behalf," the headmaster replies tightly. "She had no contact with this realm prior to admission."

I glance at the headmaster and then back again at Thomas. "Once again, Chief Investigator, I'm not hearing any questions. If you don't have questions for me, I do have plans."

He smiles at me again. "Was your foster family fae?"

My body tenses before I can stop it. I wasn't expecting that question. I didn't think anyone knew about them. Fuck, I barely know about them. They were barely a family to me.

"No," I answer simply and more sharply than I mean to.

Thomas makes another note. "And you had no contact with any fae before arriving at Avalon, correct?"

I have to make a conscious choice not to react, not to betray my lie. "No," I answer.

"And how would you describe your feelings toward other fae? You don't seem to resemble them..." He looks me over, and once again, I feel my skin burn and itch in the wake of his gaze. "Friendly? Hostile?"

"Completely indifferent," I grind out, though I try to keep myself as relaxed as possible.

Thomas raises a brow at me. "So you felt nothing seeing two fae killed?"

"That's... I didn't say that," I stammer, caught off guard. "And that wasn't your question."

"You said you felt indifferent towards fae," Thomas pushes on, and I feel the headmaster getting more irritated beside me. "The three bodies found have been fae."

"That doesn't mean I wasn't just as affected by the murders as everyone else."

Thomas watches me for another long moment before writing something else down and flipping through a few pages of his notebook. "Your boyfriend found the first body, correct? A Mister Connor Morningstar?"

I tense again at the mention of Connor. I want to keep him as far away from this as possible. "Correct."

"It seems these murders are related to you," he states, looking back up at me. "Have you had any unusual encounters?"

"Encounters?" I ask.

"Contact with someone you don't know, perhaps." Thomas pauses. "Strangers reaching out to you. Cryptic messages?"

"No." The word slips out, and I don't fucking know why I don't tell them about the stranger. I've not heard from him in weeks. He left me, and he's probably not even around anymore, so why shouldn't I mention it now? What if it is helpful to the investigation? Why do I continue to protect him?

"You're sure? Anything would help."

"No strangers," I say. Again, the words are almost compulsive, like a deep instinct.

Thomas watches me for a long moment before he nods and then stands up. "I'll be in touch."

The headmaster still has his arms crossed across his chest, his brows drawn. He follows Thomas to the door, nodding at me before he leaves, closing the door behind him.

I'm about to go to Alice's room to debrief her when someone else knocks on the door. I open it to see Connor's concerned face. "Babe?"

I smile at him, relaxing immediately. "Hi, big guy."

"Why was the headmaster here?"

"Oh, I was just being questioned about the murders. I guess because I'm fae." Connor looks even more concerned, and I know I desperately need to distract him. "Do you like my dress?" I ask, twirling for him.

Connor watches me, his eyes darkening. "Is this for me?"

I nod. "As is what's underneath."

Connor stalks toward me, and I back toward my room. "Well, then. Let's skip dinner," he growls, pouncing.

# 92

## SUMMER

PULSE, RHYTHM
DANCE

I wake early, relieved to escape the nightmare. My mind had decided to relive the interrogation with Thomas, only this time, the three deceased fae sat behind him. Their dead eyes stared accusingly at me while his penetrating gaze blistered my skin.

I kiss Connor on the cheek and climb out of bed. Quietly, I change into my gym clothes and head out.

"Look who's back," Max croons, smirking.

I simply nod and go to the treadmill.

"Come fight," Max says from behind me.

I surprise myself by laughing. "You're like a broken record."

"And? That's how you improve."

I roll my eyes but turn off the treadmill. Following Max into the sparring room, I start to stretch.

"Did you practice over break?" he asks.

"Surprisingly, yes."

Max nods and then throws a punch at me. I dodge easily and duck under his arm. Twisting around so I'm at his back, I jab him in the kidney.

Over the break, Alice and I had gotten into so many fights with other vampires that my confidence in my instincts has grown. I still don't love tapping into my fae powers, but I'm definitely more able to lean into them when needed.

Max winces and actually stumbles. He recovers quickly and resumes his stance, ready to attack. Hoping to take him by surprise, I drop and swipe his legs with mine, trying to take him to the ground. He jumps at the last second, and I miss him.

"Faster," he growls.

I jump to my feet and throw another punch. Max barely dodges this time, and my chest swells with satisfaction, but I don't have the chance to sit in the feeling. Max throws his fist, aiming at my head. I lean back, avoiding the strike, and Max's eyes flash green, his veins bulging as he lets the berserker out to play a little. He even gets a little taller.

"I land a hit. I break a bone. Fight like your life depends on it," he snarls as he throws another punch. This one I struggle to avoid. Max gets even bigger, his eyes glowing brighter. "Take me down. Prove you can."

I dodge another attack, then another, waiting for my moment. Max is stronger and bigger. I won't win against his physicality. I have to be smarter and faster. Max lunges toward me, pushing me back. In the second his balance is off, I land a hit in the center of his chest and drop to the ground, swiping his legs out from under him. He hits the mat hard, his increased size also increasing his weight. I roll on top of him and pin his arms above his head, one of my legs over his, holding them down. He snarls up at me, and I can see he's fighting the instinct to go full berserker. I don't back down, though, not yet.

"Down, boy." I smirk, tilting my head.

The rage on Max's face melts into severe annoyance, his eyes no longer glowing berserker green. He glares up at me. "Such a bitch." He tries to shift beneath me but can't move. "Well, I suppose you're only partially useless."

I burst out laughing, keeping him pinned there.

Max's cheeks flush, and he clears his throat. "You going to let go of me? Cause this is about to get awkward."

I frown and tip my head in confusion. Max shifts, and I feel something hard against my thigh. It takes me a long moment before I realize what it is. I roll my eyes and scramble off him, purposely kneeing him in the stomach.

Max grunts and sits up, covering his boner. "Don't judge me. I have a thing for women who can kick my ass."

I stand and offer him my hand. "I'm hot as fuck, Max. Just admit it."

"So am I. Admit it," Max says, allowing me to help him up.

"You're the one with a mega boner."

Max snorts. "It's a boner, not a snake. I can't control it."

I roll my eyes. "My mistake, I forgot you're a fourteen-year-old boy. Later."

Max salutes me. "Ice when you get home."

I flip him off over my shoulder.

"See you tomorrow, Daanan."

I walk down the hall toward our dorm but hesitate when I notice a small bag sitting on the stoop. It's leaning harmlessly against the door, but I am still very wary. I look up and down the hall as if whoever left this gift might still be here. Given the early hour, it's unsurprising there is no one around.

I look down at the small bag, certain it wasn't there when I left this morning. Crouching, I take a closer look. It's a silk black bag held closed by a silver ribbon tied into a pretty bow. It seems benign, but I am still cautious as I pick it up, looking around again before tugging it open. The fabric parts, and I peek in before carefully slipping my hand inside. The first thing I feel is a piece of paper, and I pull it out, looking at the small note.

*Happy Yule*
*- S*

The script is elegant, and I can sense the power the writer possesses, even with the simple message. I linger over the note longer than I should, soaking up this small bit of him. Forcing myself to set it aside, I reach into the bag again, and my fingers brush against what feels like leather. I hold my breath and pull it free. My knees hit the carpet, and I sit back on my heels, staring down at the black leather binding hundreds of pieces of papyrus. I angle the bundle, running my fingers over the rune embossed on the front. It is an old rune, but I don't recognize it.

I gather everything and stand up, looking up and down the hall once more before entering the dorm. I put the note and bag down on the counter, eagerly unwrapping the leather straps wound around the width of the book. Slowly, I open the cover, taking my time. This book is obviously ancient, and I don't want to cause it any damage. Though the edges of the paper look damaged and delicate from the outside, the cover and the main body of the pages are perfectly preserved. There has been no fading or running of the ink and no water damage. It looks like it's rarely been opened.

Carefully, I flip through the pages. It looks like most of the book is in New Faerie, but I do recognize some Ancient Daoine Sith, and there are sections written exclusively in... runes? They are old and strange, and I've never seen anything like them. I cannot wait to explore and translate them. I scoop everything up and hurry to my room. Connor is still snoring softly, so I sit at my desk and open the book again. It's clearly priceless, an antique. My phone sits heavily in my pocket, and I think about messaging him. I shouldn't. He's not in my life anymore. He's left me alone, which is what I wanted. Isn't it?

Yes.

Maybe...

I pick up the note, seeking the familiar comfort of his power. Pulling my phone out, I open my message with him and feel a little sad that it's been as long as it has since we spoke and since I felt *normal*. Even after our fight, I still miss him. I know it doesn't make sense, but I felt safe with him, and there was something freeing in that safety.

I curse under my breath and lock the phone, slamming the tome shut before slipping back into bed. I nuzzle my nose against Connor's cheek. "Big guy?"

Connor groans, but his eyes are still closed. He pats the space where I had slept, still there for me if I should want it.

I sigh and climb back into bed, looking at him. "Good morning, handsome."

"Hi," Connor moans sleepily as he wraps his arms around me and pulls me into his warmth. "How was the gym?"

"Fine. I'm all sweaty and gross."

Connor nuzzles into my neck. "You smell incredible, like always."

I smile, running my fingers through his blond locks. "I beat Max's ass."

"That's my girl." Connor smiles, his eyes still closed as he basks in the intimacy. "Are you ready for our first day back?" he asks.

"I think so. It's your last semester at Avalon. Are you ready to be done with school, big guy?"

Connor opens his eyes, revealing the love shining in their depths. "I'm ready for graduation."

"You planning a rager?"

Connor shrugs. "Not a big one."

I brush my lips over his. "You excited about the sexy robes you'll get to wear for graduation?"

"Nope."

"Then what is it you're excited for? Getting your Legion?"

"It's a surprise," Connor says, pulling me tighter against him.

I lift an eyebrow.

Connor smiles. "I can have *some* secrets."

I narrow my eyes at him and climb out of bed. "Whatever, I'm going to shower."

Connor follows me into the bathroom and wraps his arms around me. "Are you pouting?"

"Yes," I say, getting undressed.

"You really want to know why I'm excited?" Connor asks, grabbing me and pressing kisses to my neck.

I grunt grumpily but slide my fingers into his hair, holding him against me.

"Well, it involves you and jewelry."

Oh. I go still, the realization hitting me. Surely, he can't be serious? He's planning on proposing? At his graduation?

I'm not sure how I feel about that. I'm not sure how I *should* feel about that. Connor pulls back to look down at me, and I stare up at him, waiting for the terror to hit. I wait for the crushing, suffocating weight of being overwhelmed to settle on me. I wait for my instincts to kick in, telling me to run. But nothing happens, and I just stand there, blinking uselessly.

Connor trails more kisses down my neck again. "So that's why I'm excited."

Maybe I'm reading too much into this. Maybe he's just got me some really nice jewelry. He's never bought me jewelry before, so surely, the first piece he gives me won't be a ring, right? Yeah, I'm being stupid.

"You're annoying," I say, pinching him lightly.

Connor laughs, still completely at ease. "You love me."

I growl, and Connor playfully swats me on the ass before pulling me into the shower with him.

# 93

## SUMMER

*Hahisha*
WALT

I pout all the way from the dorm to the coffee cart. Alice and Connor happily chat together, which just annoys me more. You'd think the shower sex would have cheered me up, but something about the way he teased me this morning has me feeling sour. He has left me guessing about the engagement, and I hate being left in limbo. I think I feel okay about it, but I would also like time to prepare if that is what it is.

I grumpily order my coffee, and Connor wraps his arm around my shoulders, pulling me into his side.

"You're so cute when you pout."

I glare at him and order Alice's coffee.

"What's going on with you two?" Alice asks, looking between us.

"Nothing," I grumble.

"Nothing at all." Connor smirks.

I glare at Connor. The barista calls my name, and I grab my cup. "I need to go see the headmaster. I'll see you later, *Alice.*"

I'm about to stomp away when Connor reaches out and gently grabs my arm. He pulls me to him, and I tilt my head back to face him.

"Kiss," he demands.

I fight back a smile and give him a quick peck on the lips. "Bye," I say, trying to pull out of his hold. Connor shakes his head and slips his fingers into my hair, his big hand cupping the back of my head. He leans down and claims my mouth. His teeth nip sharply at my lower lip when I won't open for him. I gasp into the kiss, and his tongue slips into my mouth, sliding lazily along mine. A moan slips from me, and Connor pulls back, licking his lips.

"That's a goodbye," Connor says, flicking his tongue over my lower lip, soothing the sting. My stomach flutters with how he took control, took what he wanted. Connor smirks and brushes a whisper-soft kiss to my lips before pulling back and finally releasing me. "See you later." He winks at me and walks away toward his first class, a definite swagger in his step.

I stare after him, dumbfounded. Where has this guy been? Who knew he had it in him?

"Wow," Alice says, fanning herself, and the barista starts up a slow clap.

I nod and exhale. Still stunned and unable to think about what just happened, I wave to Alice and head toward the headmaster's office. Outside his door, I stop and take a deep breath before knocking.

"Enter." His steely voice slips from beneath the bottom of the door, and I take another breath before entering the office.

"Miss Tuatha De Daanan," he greets me, barely looking up from his notes.

"Hello, sir."

He glances at me, meeting my gaze and waiting for me to continue.

I clear my throat. "I was hoping to ask about my visitor from yesterday."

"Of course," he says, gesturing to the seat in front of this desk, and I sit down.

"You told them I found the bodies," I say. It's not a question. The investigator already confirmed it yesterday.

The headmaster nods. "I told them a student discovered them. Apparently, they have someone following me." His lips tighten ever so slightly.

"I see. She was wearing my sweater," I blurt out.

The headmaster watches me. It is not new information to him. I mentioned it in my response to the one email he sent when I was in Drāculea. The fact is just so horrifying to me that I hoped voicing it out loud to him would take some of its power.

"Did you make a list of other items?" he asks.

"Yes. I think I got most of them." I pull out a folded piece of paper from my backpack. For a long moment, I stare down at the black lines crossing the page. "Do they know?" I ask quietly.

"They do not know that."

I swallow hard and hand him the list. I feel my cheeks heat as he starts to read it, knowing some of the items are... undergarments.

The headmaster's eyes dart over the paper and he frowns, obviously trying to find a link between the items or some answers within the list.

The silence is deafening, and I clear my throat again. "I think the clothing items have been missing since the break-in.." I look down, worrying the strap on my bag. "The... underwear is... an ongoing issue."

I feel his gaze focus on me, but I can't bring myself to meet his eyes. "So not from the break-in?"

I shake my head. "Well, two bras have gone missing along with... some other underwear items. But the panties specifically are not from the break-in."

"When are they from?"

"Well..."

"Miss Tuatha De Daanan. I understand this is uncomfortable, but the more information I have, the better."

I sigh and run my fingers through my hair. "They go missing when I'm... with my boyfriend."

"At home?" he asks, and I hear him shift uncomfortably in his chair. Clearly, he wants to be here as much as I do.

"No," I say quietly, heat trickling down my neck in mortification.

"Ah." The headmaster clears his throat. "If this were on school grounds, they would activate the rune that cleans the floors and grounds."

I feel my ears burn right to the points. "Right, well. Thank you, sir."

"I can put you in touch with janitorial—"

"No! That's really okay." I'd rather die, actually. "Thank you, sir." I jump to my feet and leave his office at a near run.

I'm still flustered and embarrassed when I get to class, and I know without a shadow of a doubt that I'm as red as a tomato. Alice gives me a questioning look as I drop into the seat next to her. I shake my head, and we both turn our attention to the front of the class until the professor gives us our task. The class talks amongst themselves as they start working, and I turn to face Alice. Wanting to divert her attention from my meeting with the headmaster, I change the subject before she can start it.

"So, you'll never guess what happened this morning," I say, leaning in as I drop my voice.

Like a moth to a flame, Alice's eyes light up and she moves in closer, hungry for the gossip. "Tell me immediately."

I look around and move in closer. I am confident that the soft buzz of the other students will mask my secret, allowing it to drown in the mass of conversation, going only to Alice.

"Max got a boner when I was pinning him."

Alice throws her head back, laughing hard, but she reins herself in quickly, wanting more information. "How big was it?"

My lips twitch, and I hold my hands up, roughly estimating what I felt against me this morning.

Alice lifts her brows, almost impressed. "Connor versus Max?"

I roll my eyes. "Connor," I reply immediately.

Alice purses her lips. "Size-wise?"

I wrinkle my nose as I think. "Well, I'd need to analyze Max's cock more. I just felt it against me." A laugh burst from me at the sheer ridiculousness of this conversation.

"Okay, but you need to, for science." Alice snorts.

"Absolutely not. Connor's is the only cock for me."

Alice smirks. "I just mean for you to measure it, not straddle it."

I roll my eyes and start drawing a rune for the task.

"How was the headmaster?" Alice asks.

Fuck, my plan didn't work that well, I guess.

"Fine. I gave him the list of my missing clothes." I feel the blush crawl up my throat and into my cheeks again, the tips of my ears burning.

Alice snorts. "You put the panties on there, too?"

I bury my face in my hands. "Gods. Why am I like this?"

Alice chuckles. "People like your panties. What can you do?"

I glare at her. "People don't like my panties."

"Clearly, someone does." Alice snickers.

"A killer stalker." I pause. "Or the janitor." I cringe, unsure which is worse.

Alice tips her head and eyes me. "You don't think it's... you know. The *guy*."

I frown.

"What if he's the one who's stealing them?"

"He's gone," I say, shaking my head.

"He is? Why?" Alice watches me, and I hate the feeling of being analyzed.

I look down at my page and the incomplete rune sitting there. "We had a disagreement," I say, giving her a half-truth.

"Well, when did your panties last go missing?"

"Before the fight. But I'm sure it's not him."

"Okay. Well then, someone else likes your panties."

It's like Alice mentioning the stranger unlocks something in me, and I can't stop thinking about him. Could he have them? It is a fairly large coincidence that the panties stopped disappearing when he did, but also Connor and I have been much more conscious of where we fuck and where my panties are.

After class, Alice heads to lunch while I duck into the bathroom. I stare down at my phone. The messages with the stranger are still there. The chat has been unused for weeks now, but I haven't been able to bring myself to delete it for some reason. I tap on it, and it opens. The last message sits there, the message before it all went wrong.

*Come outside.*

I take a breath and type out a message.

The message feels shit. There is so much to say, and here I am, practically accusing him of stealing my panties. I could have thanked him for the Yule present, asked him how his break was, or asked him if he was okay. But no. Always the asshole.

The message is basic, yet my heart jolts when it comes through.

I ask again, my stomach churning.

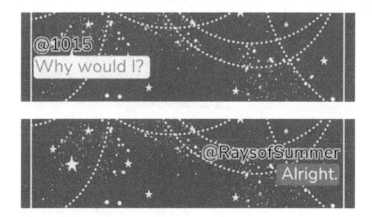

There is a pause before he sends another message.

I exhale heavily.

As I look over our messages, my heart aches with how much I've missed this. I hate admitting that I miss him, but I do. I miss talking to someone who seems to understand me and who has so much in common with me. But that doesn't make any sense. We stopped talking because it was clear he didn't understand me. What is wrong with me?

There is a brief pause before he replies.

I smile.

I exhale and put my phone away, going to lunch.

I pull on my thicker tights, getting ready to meet the stranger. I feel lighter than I have in weeks, and I'm excited to discuss books and runes with him. With a sigh, I pull on my boots again, longing for the day I can go back to wearing sandals or normal heels again.

"See you later, Al!" I call as I walk through the dorm and grab my coat.

Alice frowns at me from her door. "Where are you going?"

"I'm just going out for a bit. I won't be long, and I'll bring home tequila," I reply.

It is no surprise that Alice is nervous. I've not been out without her in weeks, and the last time I was, I found that body. But I'm meeting the stranger, and whether or not I'm being dumb, I feel safe with him. At least, mostly. I'm not stupid enough to think he's not dangerous, but I don't think he's dangerous to me.

Alice watches me for a long moment, but then she nods. "You better bring the top-shelf stuff."

I grin and give her a sassy salute before leaving the dorm. The sun is setting, casting a strange orange glow over the forest. The mist is low, lying on the ground, and while the snow has mostly cleared for now, the ground is still covered in frost and black ice. I barely breach the mouth of the forest when I see his form. We've been here before. This is where he comforted me in the rain.

"Hello, little fae," he croons, still facing away from me.

I clutch the book against my chest and move closer to him. "Hello, Stranger."

He turns to face me, and I can see the faintest outline of his face. "I've missed you."

I watch him, tilting my head slightly. "You have?"

"Does that surprise you?"

I nod, my gaze glued to him.

"Why?" he asks, and I can hear his genuine confusion.

"After last time, I—" I stop when I notice his shoulders tighten.

The unspoken thoughts lie heavy between us until he looks away. "You brought the book," he says, and I am grateful for the change in subject.

I nod and look down at the book cradled in my arms.

The stranger waves his hand, and a plush, dark green blanket appears on the ground. With another wave of the hand, a small fire burst to life just in front of the blanket. He gestures for me to sit, and I get comfortable, grateful for the warmth. I rest the book in my lap as he settles next to me.

"Have you read any of it?"

"The first few pages," I say. "It's fascinating!"

The tension between us melts away as we focus on the book. "Did you get to the part about her sister?"

I shake my head and open the book, marveling over it again. "Not yet. I can't believe how perfect the condition is. The indentations from the pencil are still visible! And look how there are times she uses both Ancient Daoine Sith and the more modern. They must have been transitioning the language at the time." I flip to another page. "It's so interesting. She has even used some mortal words!"

The stranger leans over, brushing his fingers over one of the passages. "Look, here she talks about how their father created Faerie to keep them all safe. She must have been a child when that happened."

I nod, my fingers following the path of his. "But you see this note in Daoine Sith? It looks as if it was added later. *Father the savior, Father the fool.* That's newer than the original passage. You can tell from the markings."

The stranger shifts closer. "It appears the sisters had a volatile relationship. Perhaps that's what caused the civil war. No one really knows. It was all swept under the rug."

I turn the page, reading aloud, *"Her descent into madness and darkness can pull me down. How can I let her go it alone?* Her struggle is so clear here." I frown as I continue, *"She was a force too fierce for the cause. Her malice was poison. Nothing could have survived it."*

The stranger's fingers accidentally brush over mine as he continues to read the passage, and my skin tingles from the touch. *"Even mine. My light was not a cure. And soon the land became pitched in darkness. A deal struck. A blood debt paid."*

I feel his gaze on me as I continue, *"The final candle has been lit, the wick weary. Soon, there will be nothing left."* I turn the page to continue, but the passages are... different. While those are dark, dreary, and void of hope, the following pages are much lighter. It's almost as if they were written by someone else, yet the handwriting is the same elegant script.

The stranger is quiet for a long moment, and I glance at him.

"That passage we just read. It is new."

"What do you mean?" I ask, looking back down at the book.

"That passage we just read. It wasn't there before. I have read this book thousands of times. I have never seen that."

I flip through the book and look at the front and back cover, trying to find a rune of concealment. "Huh. Maybe because I'm fae? Maybe it unlocks something?"

"Well, I think you might be the first fae who's touched it since I... liberated it." I hear the smile in his voice, and I can't help but smile back.

"Liberated, huh?"

"I was a child with sticky fingers lost in an ancient library."

I laugh, throwing my head back in delight.

I turn the page, and another passage presents itself.

*"The realm is torn in half and for nothing. For our father's last cruel laugh as she slit his throat."*

"This part is—"

"Her sister killed him?" the stranger interrupts, his body going tense.

"Yes, and it was... gruesome." My eyes move over the passage about her father's murder. "These new entries seem to be more erratic. Unstable. Her sister appears to be falling into darkness and her into madness." I brush my hand over the Ancient Daoine Sith markings in the margins. "These are almost feral, and this one barely makes sense."

I feel his gaze on me. "Read it to me? My Ancient Daoine Sith is not very advanced."

I look over the text, trying to make sense of it. I've always been able to read Ancient Daoine Sith, though I'm not sure why. As far as I know, there's never been anyone to teach me.

"*A shadowed cave with petals shows beauty to only those that see it.*" I move to another one, "*Malevolence is the nature of the careless. Tread with chaos.*"

The stranger ponders the words, and the center of the page flickers with a soft, beautiful glow before a rune appears.

"A rune?" he asks.

I nod, frowning at it. It seems to move over the page like the paper is a slow-moving river, and it's bobbing on the surface. I start to deconstruct the rune, trying to work out its origin and use.

"This rune, it's..." I tilt my head, looking at it from another angle. The stranger reaches toward the page, about to touch it, when the meaning of the rune snaps into place in my mind. I know what the rune is. Fuck. I grab his wrist. "Don't touch it."

"Can you hear it? The singing?" the stranger asks, his voice sounding far away. I slam the book shut.

"Fuck. No, I can't. I know what that rune is."

The stranger shakes his head, trying to clear his thoughts.

Fuck, fuck, fuck.

"What is it?" he asks, still sounding dazed.

I grab his face, forcing him to look at me. "Focus on me."

"Little fae..." His words are slurred. "How.... rune?"

I keep my hands on his face. "Stay with me."

"Can't hold... the spell..." His form starts to pulse and flicker, unraveling at the seams. I can tell he's seconds away from disappearing, and I don't know who he fucking is. This rune could kill him.

"I need to see you. In person. Where are you?"

"You... can't, little fae," he says, his words slurred.

I shake my head. "You don't understand, Stranger. This is bad. You can blindfold me if necessary, but I need to draw a rune on you. Now."

The stranger tries to lift his arm to cover my eyes, and I help him hold his hand in place and close my eyes. It takes two long beats before I feel something change. The heat of his body suddenly surrounds me, and I can feel the calluses on his palm against my face. Everything about him has... solidified and become more real. Excitement shivers through me. He is right next to me in his real form. The stranger mumbles something, pulling me back to the issue at hand. Now is not the time.

I push away everything and slice my finger before blindly reaching for him. My hand lands on his muscled forearm, and I start to draw the antidote rune. It had come to me the second I realized what the rune in the book does.

"What rune was that?" he asks. His voice is so much richer in person. It's like nothing I've heard before, and it settles over me like warm honey.

I exhale a shaky breath as I finish drawing the rune on his arm. "I have only ever heard rumors of it, but it is said the fae spent a long time creating it. Supposedly, it was wiped from the minds of those who had seen it. I thought it was a myth." So many stories and myths fill my mind, yet I have no idea where they have come from. It's as if they are coiled into my DNA like some genetic memory.

I feel him shift, and then I feel the pleasant weight of his head on my shoulder. His hair brushes against my cheek, and I shiver. Unable to resist, I lean into him.

"I've never been affected like that before." He relaxes a little as the antidote takes effect, but his breath is still coming in labored pants, and he is careful to keep his hand over my eyes.

"Stranger?" I whisper. "Would it be so bad to let me see you?"

He tenses again, his fingers tightening against my face. "Yes."

I nod and remain silent, staying close to offer whatever comfort I can. Being against his true form is intoxicating. The feel of his power pulsing against me is both familiar and exciting. I feel safe and more content than I have any right to.

"Tell me about the rune."

"It's an eradication rune," I reply, keeping my voice soft and calm.

"Eradication? For what?" he asks, his voice a little more unburdened.

"For every non-fae."

"So anyone who read the journal that wasn't fae would die?"

"The rune is bigger than that. There are tales about it, stories, songs, poems. Even someone like me who didn't grow up around the fae knows of them." I think for a moment. "I think it never affected you before because you hadn't broken through the lock. The passages unlocked when I touched the journal were obviously not meant to be read by anyone but fae." I worry my lower lip. "It needs to be destroyed, and we cannot discuss this again."

"Why?" The stranger sits up, obviously feeling stronger. I immediately miss his solid warmth against me. He removes his hand, leaving a silky blindfold in its wake.

"We both read those passages, Stranger. Fae can be chaotic, jealous, and cruel. This journal can't fall into the wrong hands."

"You're right. I'll destroy it."

I shake my head. "I'll do it."

There is a shift in the energy, and then he pulls off my blindfold. I look at him, disappointed to see his avatar once more.

"That rune could have destroyed you," I say, watching him.

"I have a feeling that if I weren't... who I am, it would have. Thank you for your intervention."

"Who you are?" I ask, almost desperate for the information.

"I'm," he clears his throat, "rather powerful. In certain circles. I usually don't have to avoid things like that rune."

"Powerful?"

"Very." I feel the heat of his gaze trail over my face. "Most beings could not create this avatar, and those who can cannot hold it for so long."

I look away, trying to hide my blush and feeling grateful for the darkness. "Right." I look down at the book. "We were hoping for answers, but instead, we have more questions."

"I'm not so sure," the stranger says. "There's an old story about the creation and destruction of Faerie. Something about the changing of the monarchy being like the changing of the winds." He pauses as if trying to remember. "How they became different, and then there was the fall of the great Faerie." He looks at me and recites from memory, "*Sudden was the destruction of the dearest Faerie, her walls turning to the finest of sand within the hourglass. One sole light left. Untouched by the wrongdoings of the before.*"

This man. His mind is as beautiful as his voice.

"I remember Faerie from before the Fall."

That shocks me. "Woah, you are old."

He snickers. "I told you I was a little kid in a library. I just left out the part about it being the Great Library in Faerie."

I laugh softly, but then I sober. "I wonder if that rune had something to do with their change. Such a drastic change, but I know that the line between sanity and insanity can be a thin one."

Stranger nods. "It did seem like two different people writing in the journal." He looks at me again. "Thank you for not looking."

I smile at him. "Until you almost got eradicated, I really enjoyed myself."

His low, masculine chuckle sends heat tickling over my skin. "Yes, the almost eradication interrupted one of the best evenings I've had in months."

"Really?" I ask, my smile brightening.

He nods. "I should walk you back toward campus. It's the full moon tomorrow, and the shifters will be out preparing."

The stranger stands and offers his hand. I take it and he pulls me to my feet, lacing his fingers with mine as we walk back through campus.

"So... friends again?" I ask, needing to know we have healed the breach between us.

The stranger nods, and I smile, the stress of the last weeks easing. We stop for tequila and then walk in silence to the door of Kelpie Hall.

I hesitate but then throw my arms around him, hugging him. He tenses, but after a moment, he wraps his arms around me.

I smile up at him. "Goodnight, Stranger."

"Goodnight, little fae."

# 94

## SUMMER

Hethsa
SHRINK

I creep into the dorm and head straight to my bedroom. The journal isn't something I want Alice to know about. It's not because I don't trust her, but simply because of how destructive it is. I put the book in my wardrobe and draw a rune on the doors. It will keep the cabinet locked until I present my blood back to it. I wait until the rune stops glowing before leaving the bedroom.

"I'm back, Al!"

"Tequila!" Alice yells as she charges into the living room. She grabs the bottle from my hand and opens it, taking a deep drink. She eyes me suspiciously as she swallows. "You smell weird."

I blink. "I do?"

Alice moves in closer and inhales deeply. "Yeah, like leather and bourbon."

I take the bottle from her and take a few thoughtful sips. I tried to scent him when he dropped the avatar, but there was so much going on, and for whatever reason, I couldn't.

"Stalker?"

I take another drink. "Stranger," I correct, though I'm not sure why.

Alice snorts. "Stranger, then."

I nod.

"You made up?"

I nod again and hand the bottle to Alice.

"How was it?" She asks before taking another swig.

"It was good. We nerded out over an old book."

Alice rolls her eyes. "Of course you did." She holds the bottle up. "To another semester."

I take the bottle and hold it up before taking another drink. Alice cranks the music up, and we pass the tequila back and forth as we dance. The warm brown liquid quickly diminishes, and when it's finished, we collapse on the couch, the room spinning pleasantly.

"What does he look like? Your stranger," Alice asks.

The thought of him warms my insides more than the tequila.

"He's big. Muscular."

Alice looks at me. "Bigger than Connor?"

I nod, thinking about how he dwarfs my body with his.

Alice slides off the couch and stands up, stumbling a little. "Okay, tell me when to stop." She raises her hand over her head, and when she can't reach any higher, she stands on the couch. When her arm is fully extended, I get up and stand next to her, holding my hand higher than hers.

"You're fucking kidding?"

I shake my head. "He's about 6'8", and all muscle."

"That's gigantic," Alice says, dropping back onto the couch.

I nod. "And honestly, if his face matches his body, he's hot as fuck," I say, immediately regretting the words. Is that okay for me to think? Am I allowed to think other guys are attractive? Would I be okay with Connor being attracted to other girls? I think so. I trust him, and I know he'd never cheat.

"What do you mean if?" Alice asks.

"You know I don't know what he looks like. I don't know who he is."

"Oh, yeah. The glamour." Alice thinks for a moment. "Why?"

I shrug. "I don't know. He's a mystery."

"Maybe he's famous."

"All I know is that he's huge, smart, and powerful."

"Hm." Alice waves her hand, summoning a large whiteboard that hovers in front of us. My eyebrows raise, surprised she knows a summoning charm. "I've been practicing," Alice says proudly. She waves her hand again, and half the whiteboard populates with information about the murders, including quotations, theories, and evidence. She stands and grabs the marker, drawing a line down the center of the board. On the blank side, she writes, Stranger at the top. "Okay, what else? Tell me more about him."

"He's got big hands," I say, squinting at the board and all the information she's collected. I had no idea she had been tracking the murders like this.

"Big hands/dick," Alice says and nods, writing it beneath his name.

I scowl at her. "I didn't say his dick was big."

Alice glances at me over her shoulder, looking exasperated. "You said his hands are big. Well, that must be to hold his massive schlong."

"Alice."

"Ask him," Alice says, turning to face me and putting her hands on her hips.

"I'm not going to ask him if his dick is big, Al," I protest. But I can feel the alcohol in my system urging me to do it. My instincts and good sense are screaming at me that this is a bad idea, but there is something so decadently tempting about it.

Alice crosses her arms. "Do it, or I'll do it from my phone."

I curse and pull out my phone, opening our messages.

@RaysofSummer
Tell Alice I don't know that you have a huge dick.

I see that he reads the message, but there is a long pause. I am starting to get nervous when his reply finally pops up.

@1015
What?

@RaysofSummer
I don't know how big your dick is.

@1015
Are you asking?

I pause for a moment.

Fuuuuck.

"Well?" Alice asks, sitting beside me and reading the exchange over my shoulder. I cringe when she squeals in my ear. "Ask about the piercings! Ask about the piercings! Ask!"

"No, Al, I can't. I shouldn't have even asked that," I hiss, glaring at her.

Alice grabs my phone and throws herself to the side, typing frantically. I lunge for her and tackle her to the floor, but it's too late. She has already sent the message.

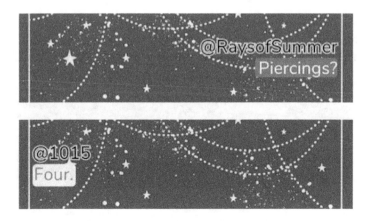

Alice groans and goes limp beneath me, and I just stare at my phone in horrified disbelief as heat curls deep in my core.

"You sure you can't get a hall pass from Connor?" Alice asks.

I snatch my phone back and throw her a furious look before climbing off her. She immediately springs to her feet and rushes to the board. She writes, *MASSIVE DICK WITH FOUR PIERCINGS.*

I look down at my phone, flushing.

I reply, trying to sound nonchalant.

Alice sits back down beside me, practically vibrating with excitement when she reads his message.

"Ask him what he is!" she demands, and even though I know I shouldn't, I start typing.

He doesn't reply immediately, and I can almost hear him considering the risk.

Alice pouts. "Call him."

I frown. "Why?"

Alice shrugs. "Why not?"

I'm unsure if it's because I'm inebriated or just plain stupid, but her reasoning makes perfect sense, and it seems like the best idea in the world. I tap on the call button.

The line rings once before there is a slight click, and the call connects.

"Are you all right?" he asks, his deep, unfiltered voice flowing through the phone and straight to my core.

"Hi."

"Are you all right?" he asks again.

I swallow. "Yes."

I hear him exhale. "You don't call me, so I was alarmed."

Alice mouths, *"Alarmed?"* Then she writes on the board, *Old?*

I bite my lower lip. If only she knew. "I'm sorry that I... alarmed you."

I hear him move. There is the sound of tightening leather as if he's just sat down. "I don't mind you calling. I'm just surprised."

Alice writes, *Hot voice. Glamourized?*

"Don't mind?"

I hear a cork being pulled from a bottle and then the sound of liquid being poured. "Such a brat," he croons darkly, and I tighten my fingers on the phone. "Why did you call?"

I look at Alice, who is fanning herself. "I don't know," I answer honestly.

I hear him take a sip and then swallow deeply. "Hm."

"What?"

"Surprised you called me and not your boy angel." I hear the smirk in his voice, the satisfaction.

Every muscle in my body tenses. Fuck. "Right, well, I'll let you go."

"I didn't mean for you to..." His words trail off, but I wait for him to continue, hoping he can justify this for me so I don't have to.

He clears his throat, and I hear him shifting. "Talk to me. I enjoy hearing your voice."

"You do?"

"I do."

"Can I hear your voice? Your real voice?"

"You ask for dangerous things, little fae," he says, and his voice changes only slightly. It's deep, dark, dangerous, and seductive. I shiver, my breath catching in my throat. There is a slight lilt of an accent, though it's not always there. It's like nothing I've ever heard before.

I blink at Alice, and she just gapes at me.

"Little fae?"

"Stranger." My voice trembles slightly.

"Are you all right?"

"Yes," I reply.

"Does my voice surprise you?"

"A little."

"Why?" he asks, his voice a little tighter.

"It's sexy." The second the words leave my mouth, my eyes widen, and I quickly end the call. There was the line, and I crossed it. I fucking crossed it. I've crossed it all fucking night.

Alice laughs hard.

**@RaysofSummer**
I'm sorry. That was so wildly inappropriate.

**@RaysofSummer**
I'm just going to go die.

**@1015**
I mean, the conversation began with you asking about my cock so.

I yelp and throw my phone away.

Fuck, fuck, fuck, fuck, fuck.

Alice stops laughing and really looks at me. "I'll go get more tequila," she says when she sees my obvious upset.

I shake my head. "I need to go see Connor."

"Okay," Alice says, surprised.

"This was wrong, Alice. I don't deserve Connor."

Alice's frown deepens. "Because you found another guy's voice sexy?"

I stand up and leave the dorm, moving completely on autopilot. I crossed the line. I crossed the line. I crossed the line. I need to see Connor and tell him. I walk straight into the house. Connor is sitting on the couch playing a video game, but he looks up when I burst through the front door.

Luke jumps up. "I beat you!" he yells, his face pulled into a wide grin.

I walk straight to Connor and crawl into his lap, burying my face into his neck. I need to be close to him and give him affection. What I really need to do is apologize.

Connor drops the controller and wraps his arms around me. "Hi, babe," he says, surprise lacing his voice.

I inhale his cloud scent and close my eyes, trying to enjoy these last moments of joy before everything ends. "Keep playing. Sorry," I murmur into his neck.

Connor rubs my back and shifts, sitting back on the couch. I'm vaguely aware of

537

Luke quietly leaving us alone. I cling to Connor's t-shirt, holding on tight like he's a life preserver, and I'm in the center of the ocean.

"I'm here, babe," he says, and his kindness makes me feel even more terrible, even more guilty, even more unworthy.

"Con?" I whisper, and I almost hope he doesn't hear it, allowing me another moment to hold this heinous truth to my chest.

"Yeah?" he asks, and I close my eyes in defeat.

"I love you," I say, pathetically trying to buy myself more time.

"I love you, too."

I cling to him tighter, and Connor kisses the top of my head.

I shake my head, nuzzling into him. "No kisses."

Connor pulls back a little, but I keep my face pressed against him, refusing to meet his eyes. "What? Why?" he asks.

"Because I don't deserve them," I whimper.

"Babe."

I press into him more, clinging to every second of this. Connor kisses my head and stroking my back.

"I love you. I love you. I love you," I whisper against his neck.

"I love you, too. You smell like tequila." Connor tucks his arm under my knees and easily pushes to his feet, carrying me upstairs.

I pull back as we reach the landing. "You should keep hanging out with Luke. I'm sorry."

Connor shakes his head and kicks open his door. "I'd rather hang out with you."

"Not for long," I mumble under my breath.

Connor raises a brow and pushes his door closed before carrying me to the bed and sitting down with me in his lap. He cups my cheek and gently coaxes my head up so I'm looking at him.

He smiles softly. "Hi."

"Hi."

Connor leans in and brushes his lips over mine. I ache from the kiss but pull back after a moment.

"What is it?" he asks, his brow furrowing.

I look away, my stomach twisting unpleasantly.

"Hey. Talk to me," he says, pulling me tighter against his chest.

I lower my gaze, unable to look at his handsome, loving face as I tell him. "You know that friend of mine?"

Connor nods.

"Well, we hung out today. He gave me this really old fae book. We were nerding out about it."

Connor laughs. "Sounds like you." My heart warms at how his body doesn't even tense as I'm talking about this other guy. The trust he has in me is devastating.

"Well, then I went home and was drinking with Alice and we were trying to work out more about him."

"And that sounds like Alice," Connor says, nodding.

"And I said he had big hands, which then made Alice think he has a big dick."

Connor smirks. "That definitely sounds like Alice."

"I don't know what his dick looks like."

Connor doesn't say anything, and I finally look at him. He's just watching me, waiting.

"Well, I kind of messaged him to tell Alice I didn't know how big it was. And then Alice took the phone, and she messaged him about... Well, that doesn't matter." I blush, looking away. "So we were messaging him, trying to get information, and we ended up calling him..."

"Okay."

"And I heard his true voice for the first time."

Connor nods. "I didn't know you hadn't heard his voice before."

I shake my head. "Not properly. He's really funny about remaining anonymous."

"And you... you think he's safe?" Connor asks, concern clear in his voice.

I nod.

"Okay. Well, what did he sound like?"

"Well, his voice is really deep."

Connor's brows inch up his forehead. "Like he should be narrating those romance books you read all the time?"

"Yeah," I reply. It's kind of the perfect analogy.

"Okay, what else?"

"Well, his voice kind of took me by surprise, and I kind of said it was sexy." I feel the shame coating the words. "It just slipped out, and I..." I whimper, burying my face against his neck. "I'm so sorry, Connor. I immediately hung up and ran here."

Connor is still for a long moment before his arms tighten around me. "Babe. You know you're being a little insane, right?"

I frown, pulling back to assess his expression.

He brushes my hair back from my face. "You think my voice is sexy, right?"

I lean into his hand. "So fucking sexy."

Connor cups my cheek. "Do I love that you spoke to another guy about his dick? No. Do I love that you told another man his voice is sexy? Not particularly. But I know it's not like you suddenly became blind and deaf when we started dating."

Shock strikes me mute for a moment, and I just stare at him.

"Thank you for telling me."

"Y-you're not going to break up with me?"

"What?" Connor sputters. "Over sending a stupid text and a phone call where you found another dude's voice attractive? I also suspect tequila and your somewhat unhinged best friend heavily influenced the whole thing."

I search his face, and when I can't identify any signs of hurt or anger, I slam my lips to his. Connor groans, his fingers tunneling into my hair, but he soon pulls back.

"Babe. It's all right."

I shift to straddle him and kiss him again, my tongue sliding along the seam of his lips. Connor pulls back again. "Babe. I can taste the tequila."

I pout, looking down at him.

"Why don't I make you a sandwich?" Connor asks, and we both burst out laughing.

# 95

## SUMMER

*Horthae*
TRAP, SNARE,
HOLD

I put a cup of coffee and a pastry on the bedside table for Connor. I runed both so they should stay warm and fresh until he wakes up. Last night, even after a large sandwich, Connor deemed me still too drunk for intimacy. So we cuddled in bed until we both fell asleep.

Quietly, I dress in yesterday's clothes, careful not to wake him. His first class isn't until later today, and he looks so peaceful.

By the time I get home, Alice has already left for class. I quickly change into my uniform and grab my phone before running out the door. I drop into my seat next to Alice, breathing hard after my sprint across campus.

Alice looks at me expectantly. "Well?"

"What?" I ask.

"How'd it go?"

I open my notebook. "Connor is perfect." I exhale. "And I need to distance myself from the stranger."

Alice watches me. "Because you find his voice sexy?"

The truth plays on my tongue. I try to lock it down, but it's there and begging to be spoken. If I can say it to anyone, I can say it to Alice. I lower my voice and say, "Because I find *him* sexy."

"Oh." Alice sits back a little. "You didn't tell me that."

I sink down in my chair, nausea churning in my stomach.

Alice nudges me. "Sum, it's a crush. Everyone has them. You've not done anything wrong, and anything you did was because of my influence."

Right. A crush. It's just a crush, and those mean nothing. I love Connor. That means something. It means *everything*.

"I never want to hurt Connor."

"Summer?" I look at her. "Do you have feelings for this guy?".

"Feelings?"

Alice nods. "Like... romantic ones?"

I shake my head. "No, I love Connor." It's just a stupid crush, and it has more to do with that stupid part of me searching for something. "The stranger just... understands me. Or at least, I think he does. He did... I don't know."

"And you feel like it's wrong?"

I think for a moment. "It feels too," I pause, trying to think of the word, "intimate."

Alice nods. "I mean, that makes sense. Especially considering you're even more emotionally constipated than I am."

I glare at her but ask, "It does?"

"Yeah, Summer. I know you. You don't have feelings for him, but he knows you on a level that even Connor and I don't. It feels like you should feel more for him because of that. Am I headed in the right direction?"

"Something like that." I sink into Alice's tidy truth instead of searching through my much messier one. "I'm going to distance myself from him."

"You going to tell him why?"

"I probably should, right?"

Alice shrugs. "I mean, will he understand?"

"Maybe he won't care." I hope.

"I somehow doubt that, *little fae*." Alice mimics his voice for the pet name.

I spend the entire class thinking about how I'm going to tell the stranger that I need to take a step back. I'm so distracted when I get to the canteen that when Connor appears in front of me, I walk into his hard mass of muscle.

"Hi, babe! I'm owed kisses," he says, catching my arms and steadying me.

I smile and push up onto my tiptoes to kiss him. From behind him, I can hear Rafe sigh in disgust.

"You were gone this morning." Connor pouts.

"I knew your first class was later, and I didn't want to wake you."

"But I wanted kisses."

I grin and kiss him again. Connor wraps his arms around my waist and fits me against him, deepening the kiss. Rafe makes gagging noises, and I pull back before he hurls his lunch up.

"Does that make up for it?"

Connor purses his lips. "Not quite, but getting there."

Zach and Zane make mock kissing noises. I hold my hand out and twist it slightly. I can't see them around Connor's big body, but I hear the clunk as their heads knock together. In unison, they groan in pain. Connor laughs and turns to face his brothers. I smile wickedly at the twins, who are rubbing their heads where they collided. Connor helps me into my seat before sitting down next to me.

"You suck," Zane grumbles.

I make my eyes go wide and pout my bottom lip in fake sympathy. "Oh, no! Did you have to face the consequences of your own actions?"

Zach flips me off, and Connor laughs, pulling me closer to him. I tuck myself against him and brush a kiss against his neck. He glows brightly in happiness, and I bask in how easy it is when we're together.

Rafe holds his hand up to shield his eyes. "Can you finish becoming an archangel already? The glow is annoying," he grumbles.

Connor shrugs and offers me a bite of his sandwich with a wicked grin. I glare at him, and he busts out laughing before taking a big bite.

"Is it annoying when I glow?" Luke asks innocently, a pang of hurt in his voice.

"You don't glow like Connor does." The gentleness in Rafe's voice when he talks to Luke surprises me. I've never seen anything to indicate they're close, but his voice holds deep affection when he speaks to his younger brother. "You're not becoming an archangel, thankfully."

"I glow when I'm healing you guys, though," Luke says.

Zach ruffles his hair. "Only from your hands. Connor's is seeping from his pores."

Luke bats him away, his cheeks pink, and Connor flips off his brother.

Zach ruffles his hair again.

"Why are you terrorizing your brother, Morningstar?" Ashley asks as she walks by the table, her lips curled into a seductive smile.

"Me? Never." Zach grabs her before she gets out of reach and pulls her into his lap. "Hi."

Zane groans, covering his face. "Ugh, between you and Connor, this is unbearable."

"This is sexual harassment," Ashley says, her attention locked on Zach.

Zach's eyes light, and he drifts his hand down to her ass, groping her. "No, this is."

Ashley narrows her eyes. "And assault."

"Then you should report me," Zach says, squeezing her ass.

Zane groans. "I'm about to report you."

I watch them and then lean into Connor, whispering into his ear, "Is this what we're like?"

Connor chuckles. "I think so."

Zach squeezes her ass again, and Ashley suddenly leans in, kissing him hard.

I roll my eyes and lean in. "Hey, dumb dumb? You can say nothing about Con and me."

Zach blindly reaches for me and pushes my face away, but he doesn't break the kiss with Ashley.

"This is hell," Zane says, sounding as if he is in pain.

Rafe snorts. "You wish this was Hell."

Beside me, Connor goes rigid. I look up at him to find his gaze locked on Rafe.

"And how exactly do you know what Hell is like?" Connor asks, an edge to his voice.

Rafe holds his gaze for a long moment, his face hard. "I have to get to class."

I look between them, feeling the tension. I clear my throat. "Well, never fear because Alice and I are going to set up all our lovelorn Morningstars."

Just as I finish my sentence, Alice drops into the seat beside me. "Yup! I have someone picked out for everyone."

Rafe growls and stands up. "Stay out of my love life, Legosi."

"Mine, too," Zane also growls, but much less ferociously.

"But I can root around in there? Perfect." I smile, conspiringly.

"You as well," Rafe grumbles, his mood darkening with every passing second.

"What about baby Luke? He's single!" Zane says as we all try to ignore Zach as he slides his hand up Ashley's skirt.

I wink at Luke. "I got you." Luke flushes a shade of beetroot.

"I think Connor and Zach are coupled up enough for all of us. Give us a couple of months," Zane says.

I smirk. "Don't worry. Rafe is my first target."

Rafe snarls. It's a deep, terrifying sound that comes straight from his core. The whole table goes completely silent. Even Zach pulls his attention from Ashley and looks at Rafe nervously.

"Rafe. Calm down," Connor says, shifting his body in front of me.

A storm seems to rage in Rafe's eyes, and he stares at me furiously. For whatever reason, I don't back down from his stare. Connor stands up and grabs Rafe's face, forcing him to look at him. "Calm down." Rafe's eyes flicker a little, and then he yanks away from Connor, not looking at anyone as he storms away.

Worried, I look at Connor. He shakes his head and gives me a quick kiss. "Sorry, babe, gotta go handle him." He grabs his bag and jogs after Rafe.

Zach sighs, watching after them. "Rafe has issues. Don't worry about it," he says to no one in particular.

# 96

## SUMMER

*Laesho*
NIGHT

CONNOR

I might be on Rafe duty tonight.

Connor sends a photo of himself, and my gaze goes straight to his swollen lip, which looks like it has only just stopped bleeding. Anger bubbles inside me at the sight, the need to protect him overwhelming.

SUMMER

You need me to fight him?

I ask it jokingly, but the offer is anything but a joke. I like Rafe, but he needs to get his fucking head in gear and stop punishing his brother. Connor would do anything for him.

CONNOR

I'd rather you kiss me better.

My lips twitch, and I look back at the photo of him.

SUMMER

Deal. And we fuck tomorrow?

Connor sends another photo. This time, it's a photo of his hand, and he's written what looks like a to-do list.

*1 Beat up Rafe.*

*2 Fuck Summer.*

SUMMER

Good boy.

I can practically hear Connor's groan in his reply.

CONNOR

You know that gets me going…

I love you, succubus.

SUMMER

I love you too, big guy.

I sigh and put my phone away. I look up to find Alice watching me and lift my eyebrows questioningly.

"You told him yet?" Alice asks, leaning in. "The stranger?"

I shake my head. "I think I'm going to do it in person," I reply. Can I really call it in person when I'm technically the only one who's there? I shake my head to clear the thought. "He's not messaged me since last night."

Alice snorts, sitting back in her seat. "Yeah, because you bailed after telling him his voice is sexy."

I look down at my notebook, where I have been doodling a rune. "Maybe he's of a similar mind."

"What do you mean?"

I sit back. "Maybe he's also thinking we should take a step back."

"I somehow doubt it."

I shrug, continuing my doodle.

"Just message him, coward," Alice says.

I sigh, put my pen down, and pick up my phone. She's right. I need to stop putting this off, and there's no time like the present.

@RaysofSummer
Can I see you later?

His response is immediate, and I wonder if he was also considering messaging me.

I exhale and shove my phone away, anxiety surging through me. "Done," I tell Alice, very aware of my knee bouncing beneath the desk.

"I'm so proud." Alice snickers, and I flip her off. I turn my attention back to my classwork, trying to take my attention off this evening. I am wholly unsuccessful, my mind circling back every few minutes. What am I going to say to him? How am I going to say it? Will he accept it? Will he push back? What do I want him to do?

By the time I am to leave the dorm to meet him, I am a mess of anxiety. I walk through the campus and into the forest, my mind too busy playing out different scenarios with the stranger to be afraid.

I feel like I can't catch my breath when I see him. He's standing within the trees but is looking up at a small area of uncovered sky, the canopy allowing the briefest of glimpses into the heavens. He looked like this the night we fought.

"You're planning to push me away," he says, his voice brushing against my ear.

I nervously play with the bottom of my skirt. The words are there, right on the tip of my tongue, but I can't say them.

"Sometimes I look up at the stars, looking for answers. But the answers don't come from the twinkling lights. They come from the impenetrable darkness between them."

I watch him, my eyes taking in the vague shape of him.

"Darkness calls to me. There are no answers for me in the light."

I slowly move closer to him.

He flexes his hand. "I hate the stars. I hate they can do what I cannot."

The stranger is so alone at that moment, standing in the dark and searching for answers in the cold. It is a pain that I am intimately familiar with, and it calls to me.

"Say what you have come to say," he says.

Following his gaze, I search the abyss of the night sky. "I crossed a line." My eyes burn, and I swallow hard. "I'm-I'm really sorry. I know I was..." His anger beats at me. I glance at him and find him facing me, but he doesn't say anything. He turns away, looking back at the stars. I place my hand on his arm. "Stranger, I—"

He recoils, yanking away from my touch. "Go back to your safety, where every-thing makes sense. You can pretend the side of you only I can see doesn't exist."

I flinch. Each word feels like a dagger, slicing me, carving me. My eyes sting as they fill with tears. "I—"

"Go. Leave me in the dark," he snarls. "Return to your lies."

My vision blurs as the tears escape, burning paths down my cheeks. "Goodbye, Stranger."

I turn and start running, his words circling my mind.

*Go back to your safety. Return to your lies.*

*Return to your lies.*

*Your lies.*

*Lies.*

I sob as I push into a sprint. I have always been a liar, and I've always been okay with it. It was about survival, but that is no longer the case. It's a tool I'm using to chisel away my rough, sharp edges to force myself into a mold that I so desperately want to fit into. If I can manage it, then maybe I can have a normal life. A happy life. The life I want. Or at least the life I want to want.

I run home and go straight to my room, collapsing onto my bed and sobbing into my pillow. Alice knocks softly on the wall. It's her gentle way of asking me if I'm good without intruding. I tap my fist on the wall twice, indicating that I'm all right, but I continue to sob until the oblivion of sleep swallows me.

## 97

## SUMMER

*Lith'thae*
BODY, BEING

The following month seems to drag, but as we near the end, the weather improves, and with it, so do people's moods. The workload has amped up for everyone, and most students have once again knuckled down. End-of-year exams are looming over us even though they are still months away.

There have been no more murders, and there is talk that the authorities are closing in on a potential suspect. While there is still an air of unease around campus, thanks to the gruesome deaths of the three fae females, the memory of the fear has blurred a little with time.

I swing for Max, my fist a blur. With every session, I find it easier and easier to relax into my fae instincts and powers. Not only am I getting better at fighting, but I'm also seeing some psychological benefits from it now.

Max barely dodges my strike. He throws a counter punch, his eyes glowing green. I slip out of reach and spin, slamming my fist into his side. There is a faint crunch as his ribs slam against each other, and he groans. I use the distraction to my advantage and take him to the ground. Max pants beneath me and taps the mat. I roll off him, immediately releasing him following his submission.

Max sits up, his hand over his ribs. "You know, you're almost starting to impress me. Almost."

I glance down at his tented shorts. "Yeah, I can see how impressed you are."

Max flips me off. "Stop checking out my dick."

"Stop pressing your boner against me," I snap back.

Max snorts as he gets to his feet. "I think you have a phallic fixation."

I stand and stretch my arms over my head. "I think you're obsessed with me." I bend in the middle, touching my toes.

"You know, you don't have to fight with me," he quips.

I straighten and grab my towel to wipe myself off. "I'll see you tomorrow. Maybe by then, you'll be over this embarrassing obsession you have with me," I taunt, taking a deep drink from my water bottle.

"You're the one who's obsessed," Max says, throwing his gross, sweaty towel at me.

I bat it away. "Yeah, obsessed with getting away from you."

Max snorts, and I laugh as I collect my things. As I leave the gym, my phone pings, and I pull it out of my bag.

> CONNOR
>
> Did you hear?

> SUMMER
>
> Hear what?

> CONNOR
>
> They caught them.

I stop dead, looking at my phone. I read his message over and over, my whole body paralyzed.

> CONNOR
>
> The authorities are about to hold a press conference.

I turn around and go back into the gym, looking for a remote control to change the television from some random celebrity workouts to the news.

"Max, how do I change the channel on this thing?"

Max grabs the remote control from behind the desk and hands it to me. I quickly flip through the channels until I see Chief Investigator Thomas Aquino on the screen. He's standing behind a wooden podium in front of an official-looking building. Headmaster Emrys looms behind him, along with several other investigators. I focus in on the headmaster and notice that his jaw is tight and his eyes are blazing. This can't be good.

"Following a lead from an anonymous source, a group of officers discovered a link between the victims."

My heart thuds and I tighten my fingers around the remote control. I feel Max standing beside me with his arms crossed over his chest, his steady presence grounding me.

"Thanks to this source, we were able to target the suspect and apprehend him before he could harm anyone else."

A picture flashes up on the screen, showing a nondescript male. He looks to be a little older than me, with red hair and dark eyes. His pointed ears give away his species immediately.

"Known as Eli Tuatha De Daanan, he began attending Avalon University this year. Through our investigation efforts, we discovered that he applied and gained entry using forged documents. His true identity is still unknown, but we will release more information as we work to close this investigation. Thank you."

Thomas steps back from the podium, and the feed returns to the newscaster, who begins to discuss the press conference, but I hear nothing. My eyes remain fastened to the screen as a tear slides down my cheek. I start to tremble, and my knees feel weak. My lungs tighten until I can't breathe.

"Summer?" I'm vaguely aware of Max touching my arm, but I don't move. Another tear slides down my cheek, and soon they are flowing freely. My lungs burn with the need for air, but I can't draw any in.

Max tugs at me, turning me away from the screen and enveloping me in strong, hard arms. His scent surrounds me. I silently sob into his chest, and he tightens his hold on me. I've never paid any attention to it before, but as I focus on the smell of pine, I can finally breathe.

"It's over," he says, rubbing my back. "You want me to call Connor?"

I shake my head, pulling back with a sense of overwhelming panic. "He can't know about this."

Max blinks, his muscular arms still wrapped around me. "I'm sure he knows about the killer getting caught."

"He can't know that I was the target." My voice shakes as I say it.

Max stares at me. "I... What do you mean?"

The truth comes surging out of me. "The killer. They... He wanted me. He stole my clothes and put them on the victims and—"

"And Connor doesn't know?" Max interrupts, his brows drawing as he tries to understand.

I shake my head, looking up at him.

"Why?"

"He would have freaked out, Max," I blurt out.

Max's jaw clenches, and he stares at me. "I understand," he says after a long minute.

I swallow, not expecting that. "Y-you do?"

"Yeah," Max says, nodding.

I glance at the television again. Another news story is playing, but it barely registers. "Something about this feels off," I murmur, my gut twisting with unease. Now that I've unburdened myself, unloading the lies, or at least some of them, I've freed up some space to think more clearly about the press conference.

"What do you mean?" Max asks.

I look back at him and shake my head. "Nothing. Thanks, Max."

"No problem." He lifts the bottom of his shirt and wipes the tears from my cheeks. I smile at him, and my phone pings again.

ALICE

The headmaster is here. In our dorm.

"I have to go."

Max wipes my face again. "Okay, you're good."

I smile at him and squeeze his arm before hurrying out of the gym. The conference plays on repeat in my head all the way back to Kelpie Hall. My mind doesn't quiet until I burst through the door into our dorm and see the headmaster. I am surprised to see him sitting on our couch while Alice paces. Alice warned me he was here, but nothing could have prepared me to see him sitting in our space with a cup of what looks like the most awful coffee I've ever seen.

He stands the moment he sees me. "You heard the news," he states.

It's not a question, but I nod anyway, knowing my eyes are probably still red from crying. "Yes, sir."

He gestures for me to sit, and I perch on the edge of one of the armchairs.

The headmaster sits down again. "They found your clothes, some of your trash, and photographs of you all over his room. He also had a manifesto that supposedly proves his guilt." His lips flatten, and he looks down at his hands. "It seems it is over, tied up with a neat little bow." I am not sure he is actually talking to me. It seems he is more just thinking out loud.

"Something feels off," I say, watching his profile.

He meets my gaze, intrigue lighting his silver eyes. "Off?"

"I can't explain it," I say cautiously.

The headmaster rubs his hand over his jaw. "There was an incident this morning after the stand-off with *Eli*. The authorities claim it was accidental, but it doesn't feel accidental to me." He runs his hand over his eyes wearily. He seems exhausted, and I realize it is the first time I have seen him look... mortal. "A fae female was found at the bottom of the stairs in the astronomy tower. Her head was completely turned around, severing her spine. A beheading without cutting the skin."

I swallow. "Did she... she look like me?"

He meets my gaze again. "Close enough. Though since it wasn't a mutilation, the authorities have deemed it accidental."

I feel the color drain from my face.

"It is just too convenient, in my opinion," he says.

I nod in agreement.

"The authorities will be withdrawing from campus within the next fortnight."

He looks away, thinking. "Nothing about this sits right with me. This killer was far too careful. They were far too meticulous and clever to be caught on some simple forged documents." He pauses for a moment, and I know he is deciding if he should tell me the next bit. "There is something missing from my vault. Something that was not found in his belongings, but the investigators are insisting I just misplaced it."

"What is it?"

He sighs. "My father collected many mystical artifacts, intent on taking them out of circulation. He stored them in the school, and further creation of such items was outlawed. Someone has taken a single item from the entire vault."

"Just one?" Alice asks, finally stopping her pacing.

He nods. "Just one. The Helm of Darkness. It makes the wearer completely undetectable."

"Oh. I've read about that," I say.

"It originally belonged to Hades, the Greek God of the Underworld. It was his before the gods left this world."

"Why didn't you destroy it?" Alice asks.

The headmaster scowls at her, obviously unhappy with the question. "It can only be destroyed by a god. Like most items in my vault."

I glance at Alice, wondering if she'll ever crack a textbook.

Alice rolls her eyes at me, and the headmaster rubs his jaw again. "I've moved my vault again, but the Helm is missing."

"I'm assuming you've tried a tracking rune? What about an old fae rune to return a missing object to its owner?" I ask, the rune coming together in my mind's eye.

He raises a brow and chuckles. "I see you're coming for Mister Morningstar's title of best student. But yes, I have tried everything." He pins me with his piercing gaze. "There's something else. The King of the Fae has reached out."

I stiffen. I have heard stories of the tyrant fae king, and none of them are good.

"Eli was a noble. He's coming to collect him. I recommend you are not on campus when he arrives."

"Why?" I asked, confused.

"He is volatile and jealous. Given your... differences from other fae, I do not think it wise to allow him the chance to notice you."

Well, when he put it like that, and with what I know of the king, I have to agree. "I can see about going to Eden or Drăculea for the day."

"He is coming tomorrow. I understand it is short notice."

I look at Alice. "Al, is there a place we can go tomorrow with the guys? I don't want any of you here."

Alice nods. "We can take them to Drăculea for the day. It'll be fun."

I grab my phone and open my messages with Connor.

SUMMER

Fun day out to Drăculea tomorrow! Tell your brothers to be ready by 7.30.

CONNOR

Drăculea?

SUMMER

Yes. Change of scenery.

CONNOR

Babe, what's going on?

SUMMER

I want a day out, Con. And I want everyone there. Please?

I immediately feel guilty for snapping at him, but I need to know everyone is safe for the day.

CONNOR

Okay. I'll get them together.

SUMMER

Thank you.

I exhale. "Okay, all sorted for tomorrow. We will be gone by 8 AM."

The headmaster stands. "If for some reason you're not gone by tomorrow morning or something happens that keeps you here, do not, under any circumstances, approach him."

"Yes, sir. I understand."

"Tell no one where you are going."

"Yes, sir."

He looks between us. "Act normal tonight, like you believe Eli is the murderer, and this is over."

I glance at Alice, and she meets my gaze before we both nod.

"The campus will be busy tonight. Take care."

I clear my throat and stand up. "I'll see you out, sir." I walk him to the door and open it for him. "The fae king. He won't hurt you, will he?"

The headmaster's lips quirk at the corners. It is fleeting, but I catch it. "He could try." With that arrogant statement, he leaves.

I pace the living room. Alice has gone to her room to watch her trashy show, and I keep stealing glances at my phone.

Don't message him. Don't message him. Don't message him.

I curse and pick up my phone. Going to the stranger's profile, I type out a message and then delete it. Then again. Then again. I do this ten times before finally finding the courage to press send.

The reply comes almost immediately.

The message hits me like a blow, but I can't blame him.

I watch the screen, waiting for a response, but none comes. He doesn't even appear to be typing. I'm not even sure he has read my last message. I place my phone back on the coffee table and stare at it, allowing myself one full minute to acknowledge the loneliness I've felt since our fight.

# 98

## SUMMER

Lohsha
COVER, SHROUD

lice and I arrive at the Morningstar House just after 7AM to make sure the boys are up and nearly ready to leave.

Alice claps her hands as we enter the house. "Who's excited for Drāculea?" All the boys are in the living room except Connor, and I'm surprised that Ashley is also here. Connor comes from the kitchen and glances at me, his eyes shining with hurt and concern.

I dump my bag on the ground and walk over to him. I brush my lips over his, but he doesn't kiss me back. "Can we talk for a minute?"

Connor nods stiffly. I slide my hand into his and lead him upstairs to his bedroom. When the door closes, I turn to look at Connor.

"What did you want to talk about?" he asks, dropping my hand.

I move in closer and cup his cheek. "About why we need to go to Drāculea today. I couldn't send it over text, and I know you were busy with your brothers yesterday."

"Oh?" Connor asks, relaxing slightly.

I had spent the night hemming and hawing about how much to tell Connor, but I knew he wouldn't stand for not knowing anything. That would be asking too much of him.

"You know how they caught the murderer yesterday?"

Connor nods, watching me.

"Well, it turns out he's a noble in the fae court, so the fae king is visiting today. The headmaster didn't think it was wise for me to stay on campus given how different I am."

"The fae king?" Connor asks, the surprise clear in his voice.

I nod. "I need to know that everyone important to me isn't on campus. It's said he is quite the tyrant."

Connor exhales and pulls me against him. "It's hard sometimes for me to be on the outside."

I wrap my arms around his neck. "I know. You are so fucking patient with me, and I am endlessly grateful." I run my fingers through his hair. "I know it doesn't seem like it, but I'm trying."

Connor nods and leans in, brushing his lips over mine, the kiss feather-light.

"I missed you yesterday," I whisper, sliding my tongue along his bottom lip, teasing him.

"I missed you, too," Connor groans, deepening the kiss.

"Summer! Let's go!" Alice yells up the stairs, and I pull back, licking my lips.

"Later?"

Connor squeezes my ass, his eyes darkening. "Definitely."

I slide my hand into his and lead him downstairs. "Gods, let's go already!"

Everyone glares at me, and Connor chuckles from behind me. Alice rolls her eyes and flicks her fingers, extending her black claws. She pierces her chest, opening the portal to her birthplace. Connor and his brothers look through the doorway with wide eyes. Alice and I walk through confidently. I am more than used to the realm after spending so much time here over winter break, barely phased by how it feels like it was frozen in the year 1500. The guys follow, Connor in the lead, always the leader and protector.

Zach pulls Ashley against his side as they step onto the cobbles. "This place gives me the creeps."

Everyone else is quiet, but Luke is obviously feeling uncomfortable, and he moves closer to Connor.

Connor slings his arm around my shoulders and looks at Luke. "Stay close, baby Luke."

"Okay, my band of warrior angel bodyguards! Follow me!" Alice says, smirking as she leads us through the streets.

"So what's the plan, Al?" I ask when we get to the end of the street.

Alice grins at me. "Well, you said torture was off the table, right?"

Rafe snorts. He's hanging at the back of the group, but I can tell he's more at ease here than the others.

I give her a hard stare, and she smiles back at me. "Well, okay, then! Let's go to the beach," she says, skipping forward.

"You have a beach? Here?" Zane asks, looking at the murky gray sky.

Alice turns to face us, walking backward. "What do you think we are? Animals? We even have jet skis."

Zane punches his fist in the air. "Oh, hell yeah!"

The streets are relatively empty as we walk through town. The few vampires we see scurry away at the sight of us. I'm unsure if it's Alice and me, and the memory of our tirade over the winter break, the blonde Valkyrie, or the five hulking angels that scare them off, but whatever it is, Alice is delighted.

The beach looks untouched. There are no footprints in the white sand, and the brush surrounding the shore is completely overgrown, shielding us from prying eyes.

"Does anyone use this beach, Al?"

Alice laughs. "Just me."

Though the star that Drăculea orbits never breaks through the thick atmosphere, it is still warm here next to the water. I take my shoes off and marvel in the feeling of the soft grains of sand filtering through my toes.

Alice drops her bag. "I brought swimwear for everyone, and you can change in that cubical." Alice strips down to a blood-red bikini and runs toward the ocean, plunging straight into the waves. I squint at the water, noticing there is a slight tint of red to it.

Zane undresses with no care for modesty or concern for who sees.

"Ah! My retinas!" I yelp, covering my eyes.

"Your ass is whiter than Connor's," Zach quips.

Ashley tilts her head. "Huh. So you guys definitely aren't identical."

Zane flips everyone off and rifles through Alice's pack. He pulls on blue swim trunks and bolts down the beach. Instead of charging for the water, he heads straight for the shiny black jet skis moored on the peninsula.

Rafe grabs a pair of shorts and disappears into the cubicle. He emerges in just the swim trunks, his body littered with bruises and cuts. He spreads the towel out on the sand and sits down with a soft sigh. Luke sits next to him, and I can feel his desire to heal his brother. But it is obvious, for whatever reason, that Rafe is not allowing him to.

Ashley and I choose bikinis from the bag and change in the cubical before returning to the boys. I lay out a towel on the other side of Rafe and sit down.

"I'm going to grab a surfboard," Connor says, looking longingly at them.

"Kiss first," I demand.

Connor leans down and kisses me before running off to change. He emerges a few minutes later and jogs down the beach toward the boards.

"I could just heal them a litt—" Luke says, hopefully.

"No," Rafe growls. He sighs, his tone softer when he says, "Go enjoy the ocean, Luke."

Zach and Ashley walk toward the water, and Luke follows behind them, looking extremely dejected.

I look at Rafe. "Why do you do that?" I ask.

Rafe sighs again, not looking at me. "What?"

I nod toward Luke. He is standing in the shallow waves, staring out over the water.

A muscle clenches in Rafe's jaw as he watches Luke. I don't think he's going to reply, and I'm about to shift away when he stops me with his words. "I need to feel it, to feel something." His voice is quiet but hard, and there is such pain in his words.

"I get it," I say, leaning back on my elbows and watching them all play in the water. Truthfully, Rafe and I aren't so different. Neither of us belongs in this happy family. Not truly.

"He won't ever get it," Rafe says. "I don't ever want him to." I follow his gaze to Connor, who has just fallen into the water and is climbing back on his surfboard. His smile is so wide and joyful that I can't help but smile, too. His happiness is infectious, even this far away.

"There are times I worry that my baggage will affect Connor. He is the sunshine, and I am... the abyss." The words flow from me freely. Unlocked by Rafe's similar candor.

"He'd go with you. Into the depths. If you asked."

My smile falters. "I'd never ask that of him. He's too good for me. Too bright and full of love." Connor whoops as he stands up on the board. "I'm not saying this because I want you to make me feel better." My eyes flick toward Rafe, and I stare at his profile. "I'm saying this so you know that when I say I understand. I truly do."

Rafe continues to watch Connor, and through his pain, I can see the protective love glowing in his eyes. "I know he'd go for me, too, but he'll never understand, Summer. Some darknesses swallow even the brightest of lights."

I look back at Con. "I love your brother, Rafe."

Rafe nods. "I know. But it's borrowed time. We're all on it."

I frown at Rafe. "What do you mean?"

Rafe finally looks at me. There is an intensity in his eyes I've never seen from him before. "There will come a time when we'll both have to decide. Will you drag everyone down into the darkness with you? Or will you let them go?"

My frown deepens. "I don't think those are the only options. Or at least, I need to believe there is a third option."

Rafe laughs bitterly, turning back toward the water. "Let me know if you find it. I haven't."

I watch Connor playing with his brothers. The waves are bigger now, and Connor, Zach, and Ashley catch one farther out. Their boards skim the water, sliding into the curl of the wave. As they move closer to the shore, the gloomy light pierces the red wave, revealing the silhouette of an enormous creature. Rafe and I sit bolt upright. "The fuck is that?" Rafe demands. The beast moves within the wave, getting closer to them.

"Connor!" I shout, scrambling to my feet and running toward the ocean. I throw my hand out, opening my extremely clunky runic wheel and sending a shock of power toward the creature. The beast's head breaches the water, and my blood runs cold when I see the thirty-foot-long sea serpent. It moves beneath them and flicks its tail. I hear Connor yell as he tumbles into the wave. "Connor!" I scream again, sending another bolt of power toward the monster.

Alice emerges from the sea, rage and fear radiating from her in hot waves. Zane is still on the jet ski, trying to support them from the water. Zach dodges the large head as it breaks through the water again. He is only able to do so because Ashley is its current target. It tosses her into the air and disappears beneath the surface when she falls back into the sea. The moment Ashley emerges, Zach grabs her, and they swim to the beach as fast as they can.

Rafe snaps his wings out and launches into the air. He hovers over the waves, searching, and then plunges into the water. I follow his lead and dive into the water to find Connor. It's not difficult. Connor is unconscious, and the serpent is playing with him like he would a ball. Rafe summons a blade and plunges it into the beast. I throw another wave of power, managing to slice the beast in half.

Rafe grabs Connor and kicks toward the surface. I turn to follow him, but something grabs me by the ankle and yanks back. I look down, and dread fills me. Severing the serpent was a mistake. There are two of them now. Struggling against its hold, I pull my free leg back and kick it between the eyes. I throw another spell at it, pushing even more power into it this time. My ball of energy slams into the beast's face and it screams, the sound making the water shudder. The serpent's eyes explode, and its body goes rigid before sinking into the depths. The other creature spins and flees. I swim to the surface, my lungs aching for air and fatigue pulling at me.

I struggle from the waves and run toward Connor. He is lying on the sand, and Luke hovers over him, his hand glowing bright white. I stare at his chest, searching for any signs of life. I clamp my hands over my mouth, trying to hold it together when I don't see any. We all stand vigil, waiting for Luke to do what he does best and sending prayers to all our gods. Fear binds my body like a cocoon, lodging a sob in my throat.

It seems like hours pass before Connor chokes and starts coughing up water. I exhale on a sob and drop to my knees, pressing my forehead to his chest.

"What the fuck was that?" Rafe snarls at Alice.

"I do not know!" Alice replies.

Connor pants and we all relax a little, knowing he will be all right. I cup Connor's cheek, my heart pounding.

"Ow..." Connor groans.

I press my forehead to his. "You scared me."

"That hurt," Connor says, rubbing his chest.

Luke says nothing, but his hands continue to glow. Fear grips me again, wondering just how badly Connor had been hurt.

"What is it, Ash?" Zach asks. I look up at her to see her staring out at the water.

"I'm going to check the perimeter," she says. I barely recognize her voice. It is devoid of the cheer and pep I have come to expect from her.

Zach looks up and down the beach. "I'll go with you."

Ashley's wings appear and she launches into the sky, followed closely by Zach.

"What was that?" Connor asks.

"A hydra. A big one," I reply, pressing small kisses all over his face.

"Take a deep breath for me, Con," Luke says, sitting back on his heels.

Connor takes a deep breath in.

"Feel okay?" Luke asks.

Connor nods, and I keep kissing all over his face.

Connor pulls back and tries to sit up. "I'm good babe, promise..."

I pull back and help him sit up.

Ashley lands nearby with Zach on her heels.

"There's a school just past those rocks. We've runed it off." She gives Zach a wry look. "Well, I did."

"Wow," Zach grumbles, but his lips are curled in a small grin.

Ashley wraps her arms around him and kisses him hard. "Your rune work is terrible," she says, but relief that he is all right softens her voice.

He growls and snaps his teeth at her. "Harpy."

Connor wobbles a little, and I steady him. "Al. Why don't we go to your lake house? Is it close?" I ask, remembering Alice talking about it once.

Alice nods, still looking a little shaken. "Yeah, let's go." She glares at the water, watching it as if something is watching her back.

Luke comes up on Connor's other side, and we support him as we walk toward the lake house. I loved the soft sand earlier. Now, it just makes things more difficult. Rafe walks behind us, a silent sentinel at our backs. His gaze constantly moves, and his wings are still out.

"You're going to have to prove to me how okay you are when we get there," I grumble, tightening my arm around his waist.

"Yes, ma'am." Connor brushes his lips against my head. "I'm sorry for scaring you."

When we make it to the house, Connor stumbles toward the couch. I shake my head and lead him to one of the bedrooms.

"You trying to get me alone?" he asks with a flirty grin.

I nod and help him down onto the bed before straddling him. "Hello, big guy." The fear still overwhelms me, and all I know is that I need to *feel* him.

Connor slides his hands up my thighs.

"I know you're worn out, but all you need to do is lay back, get hard, and relax." I reach behind me, tugging at the string of my bikini top until it comes off. Connor's eyes darken as he watches me. His gaze locks on my breasts, and my nipples harden. I know I should let him sleep, but I almost lost him, and I need to feel something other than that crippling fear.

Connor chuckles. "I was hard the second you led me in here."

I bend, kissing him deeply as I tug at the ties of my bikini bottoms, leaving me completely naked on top of him. Connor's hands slide over my thighs and cup my ass, squeezing and kneading the lush curve. I reach between us and push his swim trunks down enough to free his cock. It springs free, and I stroke down his length, moaning at the weight of it in my hand.

"Impatient?" Connor asks, pulling me down to nip at my lips.

"I'm horny for my boyfriend, who almost died on me. That okay?" I ask, squeezing his shaft and eliciting a groan that sends a wave of heat straight to my core.

"Fuck yes," Connor moans before claiming my mouth, his tongue flicking mine playfully.

I tilt my hips, sliding the tip of his cock through my slick folds, moaning as he grazes my clit.

"Fuck, babe."

I smile against his lips. "I thought I was the impatient one."

"Be more impatient," Connor groans, digging his fingers into my ass and trying to tilt my hips to line his cock up with my opening. I grant him his wish and take the tip inside, letting him feel how warm and wet my cunt is. I shiver and slide my tongue along his bottom lip.

"So hard for me," I whisper.

Connor moves his hands to the backs of my thighs, and the touch is so possessive and sexy that I can't hold back anymore. I slam my hips down, taking his cock to the hilt.

I cry out, my pussy quivering, trying to adjust to the sudden stretch. Connor releases a short shout, and I dig my nails into his chest as I start riding him. All thoughts of teasing are lost to the craving for the pleasure only he can give me, desperate to override the fear of losing him. I sit up so I can take his cock even deeper. He moans, his gaze drifting down my body to settle between my legs. His eyes lock on the place where we meet. I lift my hips and drop them again. The feeling of my arousal sliding out of me every time his cock invades my tight pussy makes my eyes roll with pleasure.

Connor grabs my hips and takes charge, moving me on him at the pace he craves, and I meet his dark gaze. Both of us are lost in this passionate coupling, needing the proof that we're alive, both here, both together. The pleasure overwhelms me, and I bend, kissing him again. I need to be closer, craving the intimacy. The second my tongue brushes his, the second I taste him, it's over. My orgasm ruptures through me. Connor follows almost instantly, and I swallow his yell of rapture.

I slow my hips, riding the last waves of my orgasm, and press my forehead to his.

Our chests collide as we pant, breathing each other in. "Can't lose you, Con," I whisper.

He shakes his head. "I can't lose you, either," he says, still trying to catch his breath.

I close my eyes. "I love you, Connor."

"I love you, Summer."

"You should sleep. I'll go check on Luke," I say, smiling and nuzzling my cheek against his.

Connor's voice is already thick with exhaustion. "Rafe, too. He used his wings..."

"I will," I whisper, brushing my lips over his once more before climbing out of bed to check on the clan.

My clan.

# 99

## SUMMER

*Lothsho*
SCRY, LOCATE

The living room is rustic and comfortable, completely different from the vibes of the castle. I imagine Alice coming here to escape royal life and sit by the crackling fire.

Zach and Ashley are on the couch, whispering and giggling together. Zane, Luke, and Alice are flicking through the channels, trying to agree on what to watch. I join Rafe at the bar, watching as he pours a heavy-handed measure of a clear spirit into a tumbler.

Rafe throws back the drink and pours another. "How is he?" he asks, finally acknowledging my presence.

I take a tumbler and place it in front of him, silently asking for a drink. Rafe immediately pours a double measure into my glass. "He's sleeping." I watch his profile. "And you? Are you okay?"

Rafe takes a deep drink. "Me? Just peachy." The words are dripping with sarcasm.

I look down at my glass, anticipating the comforting burn of the liquor. "Thank you," I say before tossing back the drink, embracing the feeling of it sliding down my throat.

"For?" Rafe asks, still not looking at me.

"I don't know your demons, Rafe, but I know what you did was not easy for you. You saved him."

Rafe tenses beside me. "He's my brother. It wasn't even a question."

I place my hand on his arm, allowing a sliver of the grief I had barely avoided to surface, knowing I'm safe to feel it here with Rafe. I need a quiet moment with someone who understands my inner strife and knows what it would have meant if things had gone wrong.

Rafe doesn't move for a long moment, and I'm about to pull my hand away when he places his hand over mine. He closes his eyes, also embracing the moment. I squeeze his arm and just stand there with him. We're in a room full of people who wouldn't understand. I pray to all the gods they never understand. At this moment, there are just the two of us and the sadness.

"He's always doing stupid shit like that," Rafe says, dropping his hand and draining his glass.

My lips twitch and I squeeze his arm before pulling my hand back. "He's lucky to have us." Though I don't believe it, my voice fulfills the lie.

Rafe chuckles darkly. "One time he almost died after hitting a goose while flying."

I gape at Rafe and burst out laughing. "What?"

Rafe's lips twitch as he finally meets my gaze. That constant ember of anger still smolders in his eyes, but it is soothed by a gentler emotion. "We were teenagers, and we were taking Luke flying for the first time."

I fill our glasses again and turn toward him, leaning against the bar.

"So, Con looks back to check on Luke, and in the two seconds he's not paying attention to his own flight path, he collides face-first with the biggest goose I've ever seen."

I laugh, cradling my tumbler.

"It knocks him out flat, and he starts falling. I'm panicking. Zach and Zane are panicking. Luke is screaming, struggling to control his wings, and Connor is plunging fast. Luckily, Uncle Michael comes out of nowhere and catches him before he hits the ground," Rafe reminisces. "When he finally comes to, all he cares about is if we're all okay."

"That's our Conbear."

"An idiot." Rafe shakes his head, looking down again.

I look around, ensuring no one is listening before I lean in and drop my voice. "You're his favorite, you know?"

Rafe gives me a sideways grin. "So are you."

"He truly has impeccable taste," I say proudly, pushing at his shoulder.

Rafe snorts and we both take deep drinks, falling into companionable silence. The only sounds that fill the cabin are the voices from the television, the crackling of the fire, and the hushed whispers from Zach and Ashley.

"I love you!" Zach exclaims loudly, breaking the silence.

Every head in the room whips toward them. Ashley is straddling him on the couch, but her body has gone rigid. Zach's face is locked in an expression of horrified surprise, looking as shocked by the declaration as everyone else.

Rafe takes another drink, seemingly unphased.

Ashley blinks at Zach once, twice, three times before climbing off him and disappearing into one of the free bedrooms. Zach drags a hand over his face, then follows her.

Rafe and I grin at each other before joining Luke and Alice on the couch to watch the movie.

A few hours later, Luke sits up and stretches. "I'm starving."

"The kitchen should be fully stocked," Alice says. Luke gets up and heads to the kitchen to start dinner. Always happy to create a little chaos, Alice bounces to her feet and walks to the bedroom door Zach and Ashley went into. She slams her fist on the door and shouts, "Stop fucking! It's almost dinnertime!"

"Shh, Connor is sleeping!" I hiss, but it is already too late.

Connor emerges from his room, looking perfectly sleep-rumpled. He yawns, rubbing his eyes. "Who's fucking?"

I smile brightly at him. "Hey, big guy! How are you feeling?"

Connor walks over to the couch and lies down, resting his head on my lap. He closes his eyes and yawns again. "Lonely."

I smile, running my fingers through his soft blond hair. "Are you hungry? Luke's cooking dinner."

"Always hungry," Connor says, a soft glow limning his body.

I bend, pressing a soft kiss to his lips. "I missed you."

Connor smiles sleepily. "Yeah? How long was I asleep?"

I glance at the clock on the mantle. "Just over three hours."

"So long without love from my beautiful girlfriend," Connor groans.

I brush my lips over his again, and Connor wraps his arms around my waist, burying his face against my stomach.

"You're so needy," Rafe says, rolling his eyes.

"Can you blame me?" Connor asks, inhaling me.

Ashley and Zach finally emerge from the room, both looking freshly fucked and flushed. Ashley's blush deepens when she sees us all watching her, and she slinks off to the kitchen to help Luke. Zach follows her as if he can't help himself.

I pat the space next to me for Alice.

"You come here a lot?" I ask.

Alice shrugs. "Sometimes. When I need some time alone."

I rest my head on her shoulder. "What's wrong, Al?"

Alice rests her head on mine and says in a small voice. "That hydra. I think it was a trap for me." Alice sighs. "Another assassination attempt."

I link my arm through hers. "Don't worry, Al. I'll kill them all."

"That's why you're my wife."

"Always and forever," I say, stroking Connor's hair, soothing him as he sleeps.

Luke, Ashley, and Zach come back with trays full of food, and I'm pleasantly surprised to see perfectly prepared steak with an array of vegetables.

I kiss Connor's head. "Con?"

"Hm?" he grunts, nuzzling against my stomach.

"Food, big guy."

Connor opens his mouth, his eyes still closed.

I laugh softly. "You need to sit up, Con. You might choke."

Connor shifts, sitting up slightly, and I bring a piece of steak to his lips. Connor takes the steak into his mouth and chews happily.

"You're cute," Connor says sleepily.

I roll my eyes and grab my phone, emailing the headmaster.

To: j.emrys@avalon.edu
From: s.tuathadedaana@avalon.edu

*Good evening, sir.*
*At what time are we allowed to return to the school? There was an incident here, and I'm hoping to get back soon.*
*-Summer.*

We are almost finished eating before his response comes through.

To: s.tuathadedaanan@avalon.edu
From: j.emrys@avalon.edu

*Miss Tuatha De Daanan,*
*The fae king is departing now. You may return as soon as you wish.*
*-Headmaster Emrys.*

I exhale, feeling a weight lift from my shoulders.

"We can head back to campus after everyone is finished eating. I want to settle Connor in bed so he can sleep this off."

"Sounds good. Should we tell the class now about why we bailed?" Alice asks, sucking on a blood bag.

I nod. "Go for it."

Everyone looks expectantly at Alice. "The fae king visited campus today. The headmaster suggested that Summer not be on campus due to her... individuality."

"He probably would have killed me."

"What a dick," Rafe grumbles, and Connor nuzzles into me, lingering in the space between consciousness and unconsciousness.

I shrug. "I've never fit in. But unfortunately, when it comes to the fae king, it could get me killed."

"Okay, but," Zane begins, "what if he comes back again?"

"I doubt he will. He's a chaotic person. He only visited today because of the murderer's capture. Eli was a noble in his court."

"That fucker was one of his? He must be so proud," Zach hisses.

"Regardless, we can return any time now," I say with a tight smile.

Connor squeezes me tightly, mumbling into my stomach. "And no more killers."

I sigh, running my fingers through his hair. "You need about two days of sleep."

"So do you," Connor says, nuzzling into me again.

When all the dishes have been cleaned, we prepare to return to Avalon. After cleaning up and gathering our things, Alice creates the portal. Rafe and I support Connor as we walk straight into the Morningstar House. Once inside, we don't stop, leading him up to his room.

We get Connor cleaned up and into bed. Once he is lying down, Rafe leaves and Connor opens his arms for me. I get fully undressed before climbing into bed with him.

"Thank you for telling me," he says, wrapping his arms around me and pulling me against his chest. His warmth and scent surround me in comfort.

"About?"

"About what was going on. It means a lot."

I try not to let my shoulders tense and keep that guilt locked down. "I'm trying."

Connor tightens his arms around me. "I know, and I love you for that. I'm going to marry the hell out of you. You know that, right?"

"Whatever, Morningstar." I rub my nose against his chest, hiding my grin.

"It's true. I am going to do it." Connor starts to drift off. "Picked a ring..." he says, his voice trailing off. I can't help the way my muscles tighten. My stomach knots or flutters, but I'm not sure which.

"A-a ring?" I ask, but Connor's only answer is a soft snore.

# 100

## SUMMER

*Maisha*
WATCH, SEE, LOOK

"*P*icked a ring..."

Surely, he's overstating it. We've not even been together for a year. That's crazy, right? Is it crazy?

Alice nudges me, and I look at her.

"You okay?" she asks.

I nod. "Why?"

Alice glances at my hand, where I'm tapping my pen against the desk. I drop the pen, not realizing what I was doing.

"You've been weird all morning. What is it?"

I look down at my hand and the finger that a ring may soon adorn. If he asks, and if I say yes. So many questions and not one fucking answer.

"Connor has a ring," I whisper, my voice barely audible.

Alice's mouth falls open. "A ring?" she whisper shouts. "An engagement ring?"

My eyes widen, and I shush her, looking around to make sure no one else heard her.

She flutters her hands in front of her mouth and leans in conspiratorially. "Is it an engagement ring?" she asks, a little quieter.

I nod. "I think so. He was talking about marrying the hell out of me."

"Fuck." Alice grimaces. "Fuck," she says again. "How are you feeling about it?"

I exhale, my cheeks puffing with the force of it. "I don't know. We've not even been together a year, but... I love Connor."

Alice nods, her brow creased. "Well, I mean, you've not bolted, so... progress."

I glare at her.

"But you're spiraling so bad," Alice says with a snicker.

I curse and stand, excusing myself from class. I go straight to the gym, needing to work off some of the anxiety.

Max is sitting at the front desk, staring intently at a notebook. He rubs his hand over his face, and only then do I see the strain.

I walk up beside him, peering over his shoulder. The pages are filled with figures and sums. It's clearly a ledger or a budget of some sort. Perhaps for the gym?

"You do the books?"

Max startles and looks up. "Where did you come from?"

"The... entrance," I reply, glancing toward the front door.

"Oh, right." He closes the book. "Need to fight?"

I lean my forearms on the desk, glancing at the notebook again. "Do you need help with that? I don't know if you've heard, but I'm kind of a nerd."

Max shakes his head. "No, thanks. Hey, I got a gift for you today." Max pushes the chair back and reaches under the desk. He pulls out a box and places it on the desk before opening it. Nestled inside are two small sai. They are exquisitely crafted and have a feminine feel to them, with intricate engravings along the blades. The edges and tips are blunted, but they are obviously meant to be used. These are not show-pieces. "I was thinking about what kind of weapon would suit you best, and this is what I landed on. They are more versatile than a dagger but still lively and quick."

I brush my fingers over the dagger strapped to my thigh.

"That will not stop a sword. So," Max pushes the sai toward me, "these are better."

I look at him, surprised by this unexpected act of kindness. "Thank you for the gift, Max."

Max nods, shrugging off my gratitude like it's tar against his skin. He grabs the sai from the box before heading into the sparring room. I follow him in, and he hands them to me. I am surprised by their weight and how they fit into my hands. He gives me a quick overview, showing me how to hold them and a few basic blocking moves.

"Your hand-to-hand is passable, so let's see how your fae instincts handle weapons," he says, collecting a broadsword from the wall. The one he selects is at least as long as his leg.

I look down at the sai, squeezing their hilts. "I wasn't great the last time I tried."

Max quirks a brow.

"In Eden. I did some training with the Morningstars."

"Ahh. Well, let's see," Max says, swinging the broadsword with an expert twist of his wrist. It looks like an extension of his arm.

I get into my usual stance, but it feels unfamiliar while brandishing the weapons.

"Don't dodge. Block."

I nod once, waiting for him to swing.

Max's first strike is slow, easing me into it, and I'm grateful. Even though he gives me plenty of time to react, my instinct to dodge takes over, and I swiftly duck out of the way.

"Fuck, sorry!"

"Again," Max says, getting back into an offensive position.

I shake it off and nod when I'm ready for his next attack. This one is faster, and I can tell he's trying to give me less time to think, trying to pull me out of my head. I lift my weapon at the last second, and the sound of the blades meeting echoes around the room.

Max nods and resets. "Good, again."

I block his next hit, but I can tell my stance is off. My footwork is not optimizing my defense, but I know Max wants me to focus on my instincts before he bogs me down with instruction. Especially when I already have a good basic knowledge of hand-to-hand defense.

"Okay, I'm going to go slower so you can analyze the moves," Max says.

"Is my form okay?"

Max looks me over. "It's fine for now. You're just used to dodging."

I nod and focus, wanting to be good at this. My goal is to be successful and powerful, to be feared.

Max slows his hit, and I'm able to block it better this time. I pay attention to how my body moves, the way my feet move, the effect of his blade against mine. All the while, I adjust to take the least amount of impact, forcing it back onto him.

"Good," Max says, resetting again. "With the sai, you can even trap the sword and disarm me." Max puts his sword down and wraps his hands around my wrists with a surprising amount of gentleness. He guides my hands into a position, crossing the blades of my sai. "By linking them together, you might disarm an opponent. We'll try now." He releases my wrists and picks up his sword again. His strike is slow, but when the sai meet his blade, I'm not able to disarm him.

"Shit." I drop my arms. "I don't think I'm holding them right."

Max shakes his head. "The movement was right. You're just lacking confidence. Maybe I should piss you off so you try harder."

"Gods, you're such an ass," I say, glaring at him.

The dichotomy of Max is so fucking frustrating to me. He can be so kind and the biggest asshole in the same sentence.

Max smirks, getting into position again. "An ass you think about naked."

My mouth drops open, and I gape at him.

Max lunges without warning, going full speed. My instincts snap me into action, and I manage to block. My blades slam against his, and the impact reverberates down my arms, making them ache. Max nods and swings the sword again, not giving me time to recoup.

A grunt escapes me as I twist my hand, slamming my sai into his blade.

"You are fighting your instincts even now," Max grunts as he continues to beat relentlessly at me.

The second the words leave his lips, I feel the resistance there like a blockade inside me. I can feel the way I'm rejecting my powers. I have spent so long pushing that side of me down that I now block them as easily as I breathe.

Max snaps his sword against mine, pulling me from my thoughts.

I delve deeper into myself, searching for the smallest gaps I may have left while building this wall. The deeper I go without success, the more frustrated I get and the sloppier my defense becomes. I can feel myself slipping. My footwork isn't as precise, and neither are my blocks, but I can't stop. I keep battering at that self-made barrier, trying to free the very thing I have subjugated my entire life.

"Stop fighting yourself." Max jabs the hilt of his sword into my stomach, and I hit the ground hard, gasping for the air he knocked out of my lungs.

My bones rattle from the impact, and my ears ring a little.

Max appears above me, lifting his sword high before bringing it down in a shining arc, aiming for my head. My body groans in protest as I will it to move again. At the last moment, I roll away to safety, and suddenly, I snap back into the training.

Max pants. "Good job." He offers me his hand and pulls me up before returning to his stance. He launches at me, and this time, I'm ready for it. No longer distracted by that stupid, impenetrable wall, I deflect his hit and get in a hit of my own, pushing Max back.

He winces slightly, and I grin, lifting my arms over my head and shaking my hips in celebration.

Max rolls his eyes. "Don't get too cocky. I know you're still not tapping into your power."

I cross my arms over my chest. "Go on, praise me. You know you want to."

"No," Max says, glaring at me.

I lift my chin and quirk a brow, my stare a challenge.

"Does that work for golden boy?"

I flip him off.

Max returns the gesture. "Go ice."

I salute him for real this time and put the sai back in their box before leaving the gym with a clearer mind.

# 101

## SUMMER

*Neth'thae*
CLOSE, SHUT

I'm excited to get to the gym. The adrenaline is still coursing through my veins from the session yesterday. I loved it. I loved how powerful I felt with the sai in my hands. There was that moment of weakness, but all it did was draw attention to my strength when I pushed past it. It gave me hope.

Max glances up from his notebook when I enter. He sees me and immediately jumps up, heading to the sparring room. I think he's enjoying our little routine. I think he likes teaching me.

I follow him in and walk to the back of the room to collect my sai. A strange warmth fills me when I see them displayed on a new shelf with my name engraved across the front. I smile and pick them up, testing their weight in my hands. They feel pleasant enough but still foreign. The silver glints in the light streaming through the window, and the cool metal has a bite to it. I put them down again and pull off my sweater. My body is already heating, anticipating the sweat on my skin and the adrenaline coursing through my veins.

"Let's try offense today," Max says, grabbing his broadsword from a shelf near mine. I nod, pulling my hair into a messy ponytail before picking up my sai again.

We move to the center of the room, and I roll my shoulders, preparing for the force of the sword reverberating down my bones. Max swings his broadsword, warming the heavy muscles of his arm.

"Land a hit on me," he says, getting into a defensive position. I study the placement of his feet and how he holds his body, constantly learning from him. I move in at mortal speed, swinging the left sai at him. He blocks it easily.

"When using them for offense," Max begins, "you want to use them together.

Almost as one weapon. Unless you're fighting against multiple people, but that's more advanced." Max sheaths the sword at his back and moves around me so he's standing behind me. He reaches his arms around me and gently wraps his hands around my wrists, guiding me through the motions of using the sai in unison. We go through them another three times before he releases me and steps back in front of me.

"Got it?" he asks, and I nod, adjusting my position. I swing at him with both sai, and while Max still blocks easily, he looks pleased. "Good, Summer. Again."

I do it again, and this time, I force him to concede a step.

"Good. Faster. Use your speed."

I swing my sai again, and Max moves back another step. I lean into my instincts, and while I can still feel that wall, it feels a little more pliable now. Everything calms, and the world around me seems to slow. My limbs relax, and I settle into the rhythm of the movements. By the time I've backed Max into the wall, they feel almost natural. I hold the sai at his throat and look up at him, feeling the prideful smirk tugging at my lips.

When I meet his eyes, I'm surprised it's not the green of the berserker's gaze looking down at me. Instead, Max's eyes are dark, his pupils practically swallowing his irises.

"Good," he says, his voice thicker than usual.

I smile brightly, feeling very pleased with myself.

"Summer. You need to back off now."

"Are you okay? Fuck, did I hurt you?" I ask, lowering the blade from his throat.

"Summer," Max growls. "Remember how I have that thing?" he asks, his voice sounding strained, like when he's holding back the berserker, but it's huskier. "About females who kick my ass?"

"You want to go berserker on me? Your eyes aren't glowing green."

Max shakes his head. "What color are they?"

"Black."

"Can you guess why?" Max asks, giving me an exasperated look.

"I hurt you?"

"No," Max scoffs as if the idea is ridiculous.

Well, that is just rude, and I am about to tell him so, but then Max shifts slightly. Thanks to the proximity of our bodies, I feel something hard rub against my stomach.

"Oh," I say, my cheeks blushing as I finally realize. I was so lost in my pride that I forgot about his little proclivity.

Max winces and nods shortly. "Yeah. Can you... back up?"

I stumble back immediately, embarrassed that I'd practically rubbed myself against him. "Right. Sorry."

Max rubs a hand over his mouth, and I can see his mortification. "It's fine."

I take another step back. Unbidden, my gaze drops to the prominent bulge in his pants. I'm not sure if he's wearing looser pants today or if it's because they're gray, but it looks even more pronounced than it did the other day. I can tell he's pretty well-endowed.

"Summer!" Max groans. "Don't look at it!"

My gaze snaps to his, and I hold my hands up. "What do you want from me? It's looking right at me!"

"It's the one-eyed monster, certainly." Max chuckles.

My gaze drops back to it as if compelled, and I tip my head assessingly.

"Summer!"

I spin and look at the door. "Fuck sorry!"

"You're killing me," Max groans.

"What did I do?" I ask, peeking at Max's face from the corner of my eye.

Max mimics my extreme stare and my voice. "Max, your dick is looking at me."

"Well, it is!"

I look away again as Max adjusts himself in his pants.

"I should go," I say with a decisive nod.

"Summer, it's an involuntary reaction. Just ignore it."

"So you don't want to stop training with me?" I ask, careful to keep my gaze trained above his shoulders.

"No," Max says with a deep, exasperated sigh. "Just give me a few minutes."

I study Max's face for a moment. "Max?" He lifts his eyebrows at me. "I think I know the answer to this, but... you don't have," I grimace, "feelings for me, right?"

Max rolls his eyes. "You are very much not my type."

I nod. "Okay. So you're just aware I'm insanely hot. Cool."

"Please. I couldn't be less interested in you if I tried," Max grumbles and crosses his arms over his chest.

The venom in his voice surprises me. "Max, I was joking."

"No, you weren't."

Disappointment swamps me, and I shake my head. "Whatever, Max," I say. I slide my sai back onto the shelf and stalk past him out the door.

Connor sleeps peacefully next to me, and I stare at the ceiling. I've not been sleeping right since they *caught* the killer. My stomach grumbles, and I think about the leftover pizza waiting for me in the kitchen. I kiss Connor's cheek and clamber over him to slip out of bed. Grabbing the pizza box from the fridge, I sit on the couch with it. I'm about to start flicking through channels when I decide a little doom-scrolling would probably be more entertaining than middle-of-the-night television.

An *EverydayEmrys* post from the previous day piques my interest. I tap on the photo of the headmaster and expand the caption.

**@EverydayEmrys.** *Spotted: Hottie Headmaster walking through the quad this morning at 4 am. Where could he have been? Maybe with that lady love we've been speculating on?*

There are over five hundred comments on the post, and I scroll through them. Most of them are theories about the headmaster's whereabouts, some denounce a potential love interest for him, and a couple are just downright thirsty.

"You're not into that garbage too, are you?" Alice's voice makes me jump as she drops onto the couch beside me.

I shake my head. "Just came up on my feed."

"How come you're out here?"

"I was hungry," I say, giving her a half-truth, scrolling through the comments again.

"These comments are insane." She points to one and reads, *"I'd let him discipline me harshly.* Weirdo," she scoffs. "Huh. There are even bots commenting."

I frown, looking at the comments more closely, and I see what she's talking about. There is a bot account called *@eladan*, and the comment is simply the letter *S*. I frown and tap on the profile, bringing up all the posts. Similar to the stranger's account, it's blank, and I wonder briefly how they got past the system. We scroll through the comments on the second photo and eventually find the same bot with another post. This time, it's just the letter *E*. Alice and I share a look, our brows drawn. I select another post, tracking the bot, and after a while we have twenty-nine letters. Alice and I look down at the scrambled letters, none of which seem to make any sense.

"This could be *listen*," I say, pointing to six of the letters.

Alice nods, writing it down and scoring out those letters to keep track. "Beginning?" Alice asks, writing out the word with a question mark.

"*Listen well.* I think that's the first two words," I say, and Alice nods, writing it down. "*Listen well. This is just the beginning?*" I feel the color drain from my face.

"Sum?" Alice says, looking at the letters and then grabbing my phone, scrolling through the posts and the comments. "There are comments after they caught that Eli guy."

"Maybe you should tell the headmaster," I say, picking at my half-eaten piece of pizza.

Alice shakes her head. "It should be you, Summer. You're the target."

I glance at the time on my phone. It's just before 2AM. "I'll tell him tomorrow. It's too late now."

"According to yesterday's post, he's usually up late."

I sigh and open my email.

To: j.emrys@avalon.edu
From: s.tuathadedaanan@avalon.edu

*Hello, sir.*
*I'm sorry to bother you outside of school times again, but I have reason to believe the killer is still out there.*
*-Summer*

A reply comes back almost immediately.

To: s.tuathadedaanan@avalon.edu
From: j.emrys@avalon.edu

*Miss Tuatha De Daanan,*
*Come to my office.*
*-Headmaster Emrys*

I frown. "He wants me to come to his office."
"Now?"

To: j.emrys@avalon.edu
From: s.tuathadedaanan@avalon.edu

*Right now, sir?*
*-Summer.*

His response is once more immediate.

To: s.tuathadedaanan@avalon.edu
From: j.emrys@avalon.edu

*Miss Tuatha De Daanan,*

*Right now.*
*-Headmaster Emrys.*

I stand up and pad into my bedroom, pulling on one of Connor's sweaters. It is so big it covers me to my knees. I strap my knife around my thigh and pull on some sneakers.

Alice is where I left her on the couch, but she has pulled her legs up tight against her chest. "You're going alone? When you think the killer is still out there? Summer, I don't think that is a good idea. Let me go with you."

"I need you to stay with Connor. I doubt he'll wake up, but just in case, I don't want him to worry." My smile is a little forced, but I graze my fingers over the blade on my thigh. "I will be okay, Al. Promise."

Alice sighs. "All right, but text me every minute so I know you're okay."

I nod and leave the house, running toward Manananggal Hall. The halls are eerie at this time of night. Sconces line the walls but only provide a small amount of light, and when I turn the corridor and see the headmaster's office before me, it looks even more daunting than usual. I stand in the puddle of light leaking out from beneath the door and knock.

"Enter." His voice comes through unmuffled, as if he is standing right in front of me. I can't remember if that has happened every time. I push the door open and step into his office.

"Hello, sir." The headmaster is sitting behind his desk as usual, but his normally polished professionalism looks a bit rumpled tonight. His sleeves are rolled up to his elbows, showing the hundreds of black runes adorning his muscled forearms. His hair is mussed like he's been running his fingers through it while he worked on the papers splayed over the desk. In front of him is an expensive-looking decanter and a matching tumbler, both with dark amber liquid inside.

"Miss Tuatha De Daanan. You have reason to believe this isn't over?"

"Yes, sir." I nod and look away, feeling a little embarrassed now that I am here. I don't know if he is aware of *EverydayEmrys*, and I don't relish him knowing that I have been looking at it close enough to spot secret messages. "Yes, sir."

The headmaster waits in silence until I meet his gaze again, and then he gestures to the seat in front of him. This whole ritual is becoming disturbingly familiar to me. "Explain."

I sit down on the chair and pull on my fingers. "Well... I believe they have been leaving messages."

He leans forward on his elbows, his silver eyes focused intently on me. "Messages? To you?"

"Not exactly," I say, feeling my cheeks heat.

The headmaster lifts an eyebrow, and I feel my blush deepen. My ears burn as I pull my phone from the pocket of the hoodie and unlock the screen. It's already loaded on the page, and I wince before leaning forward to place it on his desk.

The headmaster picks up my phone, scowling as he scrolls through the page. "What is this?" His lips flatten into a thin line. "Is this your account?"

"What? No!" I sputter.

His shoulders relax a little. "Good. It's clear some of my students have far too much time on their hands." He glances up at me. "Apart from the page, is there something I'm missing?"

I stand and walk around his desk before pointing out the comments from the bot account. "Some of these comments were from after Eli was caught, and they seem to have been posted by a bot account."

"Bot account?" he asks.

"It's a faceless account, usually used to post spam, but I think this one might have more malicious plans than fraud. I believe there may be someone behind it posting the messages."

The headmaster looks at the comment, tilting his head slightly as he considers. "I had my suspicions that they had the wrong person. They were reluctant to hear it." The headmaster taps his fingers on his desk, thinking. "I am going to task you with a job, Miss Tuatha De Daanan. I need to know who runs this account. If these messages are from the killer, then I have a feeling there are more that may have been deleted." He continues to study the page, but his gaze slides to me when I don't immediately answer. "Unless you're not up to it."

"I can do it."

He nods once, looking back at my phone. "Good. I'm still being watched, and I'm... not the most tech-savvy." He stops talking and just stares at me, his gaze considering. "I've been debating whether to show this to you, but I think you should see it. When the fae king visited, how he reacted to the news unnerved me." The headmaster lifts his hand, and a spell plays out in front of us.

*The white-haired fae relaxes in the chair across from the headmaster, a set of dark glasses concealing his eyes. His pose is relaxed, indulgent, and unconcerned, but a lethal energy permeates the room. Kai, the King of the Fae, is chaos and malevolence. He is everything they say he is. He is evil.*

*"There was another fae killed," the headmaster says to him. "I thought you'd wish to know."*

*The fae king lowers his sunglasses, showing the light dancing in his magenta eyes. The more magenta a fae has in their eyes, the more powerful they are. So what does it mean that the king has no hint of violet in his? He watches the headmaster, appearing bored. "And I should care why?"*

*"Well, Eli is your cousin, is he not? Isn't that why you are here?"*

*The fae king smirks cruelly, pushing his sunglasses back up. "I'm more concerned about that strange little fae girl who has matriculated into your care."*

*"That is not your concern nor the reason for your visit," the headmaster says. His voice is calm, but a rumble of menace resonates within the words.*

*The fae king stands and stretches. "But I am making her my concern. You know, the second she entered Avalon, I felt her." They watch each other, and the tension builds, neither backing down. "Tell her I look forward to meeting her." He laughs darkly and leaves, followed by his entourage.*

I swallow as the spell dissolves into nothing.

"He didn't seem even remotely concerned about the situation. Only about you," the headmaster says.

"And he called me little fae. Do you think h-he knows who's doing this?"

The headmaster nods, and the spell appears again. The headmaster zooms in on Kai's face, looking at the smirk etched on his face. "He's mocking us. Me in particular."

"I need to leave. Don't I?"

"Unfortunately, there is nowhere safer. Also, Avalon is your home."

"Right..."

He pins me in place with his gaze. "You are not to leave Avalon, Miss Tuatha De Daanan."

I blush and look away. "Yes, sir."

I feel his gaze burning into me, willing me to look at him. When I do, he nods and runs a hand through his hair. He looks at my phone again and shakes his head. "The authorities are celebrating. I'm not sure this or anything will get them to reopen the investigation."

"I'll help however I can."

He nods and rubs his hand over his face. "We need to find out who runs the page."

I nod once and take my phone from his desk. I have no idea how I'm going to do that. The headmaster says he's shit with technology, and I'm not sure I'm much better, to be honest. But the safety of myself and those I care about is at stake, and I will do whatever it takes to protect the people I love.

# 102

## SUMMER

Raesho
FAST,
ACCELERATE

I call Alice when I'm on my way home. I can practically hear her pacing in the living room. "You're okay," she says, relief saturating her voice.

"Alice, I texted you all the way to the headmaster's office."

"Yeah, but what if the killer had found you and taken you? Then they'd have your phone. They could have been texting, pretending to be you. I was about to come find you."

I roll my eyes, but my heart swells at her care for me. "Somehow, I knew you were freaking out, which is why I'm calling. We have a mission."

"Oh, hot. Do we need black body suits for this mission?"

I laugh, relieved that I can still do so. "Probably not, but we should get them, anyway."

"I will order us some, but what do we have to do?"

"We have to find out who's behind EverydayEmrys."

"Oh, damn. My detective boner is standing at attention. Okay, is there a reason?"

"I think the headmaster believes there are more messages. Some may have even been deleted or blocked. We should wait to plan when Connor isn't there."

"Why not tell him?"

"I don't want to worry him."

Alice doesn't say anything, and I can hear her disapproval in the silence.

"You disapprove?"

"It's not my relationship." I flinch, and Alice curses. "That was harsher than I meant it to sound."

"I have to go. My battery is dying. I'll be home soon."

Ending the call, I drop onto the closest bench. I can see the dorm in the distance, but I need a second. The guilt of not telling Connor is weighing on me, but I genuinely do want to protect him from this.

A gentle breeze ruffles my hair, its warmth telling me it is unnatural. I close my eyes and let out a weary sigh.

"I thought I was to return to my lies and not think of you," I whisper.

His fingers brush a lock of hair behind my ear, and I bat it away. "I can't seem to stay away," he says, and I shiver as his voice caresses my ear.

"Why?" I ask and open my eyes, looking straight ahead. When he doesn't reply, I continue. "You were gone for weeks. It can't have been that difficult."

The bench creaks a little as he sits down next to me. "I wasn't gone."

I look down at my legs, goosebumps covering my bare skin.

"I wasn't even gone for a day. I was always close."

I rub my thighs, trying to warm them. "I'm sorry for crossing a line."

He is quiet for a long moment but finally says, "I crossed it first. If there ever was one."

I shake my head. "It was me."

"Did you feel it?" he asks. "The tug?"

I frown, glancing at him. "What tug?"

"The one between us. Pulling us together."

"Describe it." Do I really want him to? Do I want to put a name to the bond we seem to have?

He moves one of his hands to his chest and rubs absentmindedly. "Like a pull around your spine, each step away was like you were taking a piece of me with you."

I look away again, staring into the darkness. "I already told you I enjoy... spending time with you. You understand me. But then you left, and I—"

"I know. The thought of you pulling away was..." He trails off, and I don't need him to finish.

"Your voice caught me off guard," I say, the honesty spilling from me.

He laughs, the sound filled with sadness. "Most people become alarmed by it."

"I like it," I say, digging my nails into my thighs.

"Many people have told me it features in their nightmares," he says.

"It's never featured in my nightmares, but occasionally in my dreams." I feel my cheeks heat.

"I–I enjoyed talking to you."

Surprised, I whip my head around to look at him. "You did?"

He nods. "Your voice is very comforting to me. It helps me relax. My brain constantly whirls otherwise."

"You can hear my voice now, though, right? It's not like distorted?" I ask, honestly curious.

He shakes his head. "No, it's not like mine. The only difference is that I can't feel you, but I can see you, hear you, smell you."

"You can't feel me at all?"

"No."

I place my hand on top of his. "Nothing?"

He shakes his head again.

"But you can smell me?"

"Citrus and peonies."

I worry my lip, staring up at him.

"What?"

"I should go," I say and stand up, trembling with the cold. My hands clench, and I start to walk away.

"All right," he says, and I can hear the resignation and sorrow in his voice.

I stop in my tracks, anger welling in me. Why? Why does he get to be sad? He is the one who walked away. I went to him to talk, apologize, and reset a boundary, and he fucking kicked at me like a dog he wanted to run off. Spinning around to face him, I say, "I don't trust you anymore."

"I suppose I deserve that. If you don't trust me, I suppose I won't need to be in this avatar again."

"Don't fucking gaslight me!" The rage bursts from me. How could he say something so fucking unhelpful? I thought him above this kind of manipulation. The anger I've felt toward him since he left has been a tightening coil, and I finally let it go.

"How is that gaslighting you?" he snarls. "You just love throwing that word at me when I say something you don't like."

I glare at him. "I told you that you're the only person who understands me, and you abandoned me. So fuck off. I'm allowed to not trust you after that! Get rid of the fucking avatar if you want, but don't try to lay the blame at my feet," I snarl and turn away, intending to leave, but his next words stop me in my tracks.

"I left because you wanted me to. Wasn't that what you were about to do? Push me away like always? Isn't that why you came to speak to me that night?"

I whirl on him. "No. I came to apologize for crossing a boundary we set. I came to apologize for making you uncomfortable, and I came to say that it wouldn't happen again."

He scoffs. "And here are the lies you wear like a protective shield."

"You always think the worst of people, especially me. But here you are! You won't even show me your true self. You won't even give me your name. So, who is really hiding? Who is pushing away? Who is keeping distance? I accepted all of it, but I am the one who wears lies like a shield? Since you love staying away from me, just fucking continue to do so."

"Why would it fucking matter if I do? You didn't act any different when I was gone."

"What the fuck is that supposed to mean?" I ask, my voice raising.

"You went back to your little lie of a life and left me alone. I was the one actually alone, not you," he growls. His power vibrates in the air, and I should be afraid, but I am not. He would never hurt me, and there is something more than just anger in his voice. I can almost taste his pain.

I'm not sure when, but we moved closer at some point. I push at his chest hard, feeling a solid wall of muscle under my hand. "You left me! You told me to go!"

"You wanted boundaries, and when you pushed them, you shoved me back, and I... lost my friend."

I blink, gaping up at him. He called me his friend. He had never succumbed to that label, even when I had plastered it over every inch of us. Something within me breaks, and I wrap my arms around his waist. I hug him tight, tucking my face against his chest. He stands rigid and unbending, and I'm about to pull away when his body relaxes and he wraps himself around me, holding me close. I feel him bury his face in my hair and inhale deeply.

"I missed you," he whispers.

My eyes burn, and I close them. "I'm sorry I crossed the boundaries. I'm sorry I made you uncomfortable."

"You didn't," he growls, his chest vibrating.

I pull back enough to rest my chin against his chest and look up at him. "Didn't what?"

"Make me uncomfortable," he says, and I can feel his gaze blazing into me. "Are you going to leave me in the dark again?"

I shake my head. "Are you going to leave me?"

"No, little fae. Why were you looking so sad?"

"Sad?"

"On the bench. You looked like the world was against you."

I look away, feeling the pangs of sadness leeching under my skin. "I hide so much of myself from so many. And when I do show them the... unsightly parts, they don't like them."

He cups my cheek, tilting my head up, waiting for me to continue.

"I've not told Connor about being the target."

"Why?"

"I don't want him to worry."

"Why does it matter? Hasn't the killer been caught?" the stranger asks.

I exhale heavily. "I'm not convinced." He waits for me to continue. "It's a long story."

"I have time," he says with a slight shrug.

I glance at my phone, knowing Alice will come searching for me if I don't get home soon. "I have to get back. Tomorrow?"

"Where?"

"The woods?" I ask, but then I have another idea. "Or I could... call you."

"Call me. I'll use my real voice."

"You will?"

"Unless you don't want that."

"I do!" I clear my throat. "I mean, whatever, sure. I don't care."

He chuckles darkly. "I'll speak to you later, little fae."

# 103

## SUMMER

*Rinthu*
BETWEEN

I arrive at the gym, but I hesitate before I go in. I don't particularly want to see Max, but I really need to work out. My head has been busy since last night, and so much happened yesterday that I need a release. I take a steadying breath before I enter and avoid looking at Max as I pass the desk.

"Ready to fight?" Max asks as if nothing happened yesterday. He acts as if he wasn't a complete asshole when I was trying to make light of a situation.

"Eat a bag of dicks." I snap back.

The anger surges within me before I've even acknowledged it. Too much has happened, and all I want to do is work out in peace. I don't want to worry about what is going on with Max. He hurt my feelings yesterday, and I am frustrated and scared. Max is a dick, and he deserves my anger, but I don't like feeling so volatile.

I walk to the treadmill and start running. I immediately feel the benefits of it. That is until Max's stupid face appears in front of the machine.

"Woah, what was that for?"

I ignore him, looking over his shoulder and concentrating on the large window behind him. In my peripheral vision, I see Max bend down and the treadmill comes to a stop. I glare at him and step off that treadmill to hop onto the one next to it. Max waits for me to start running and then unplugs that one, too.

"What's wrong with you?" Max snaps.

"You," I growl back, trying and failing to rein in my anger.

"The fuck does that mean?" Max growls.

"Given that you find me a hideous troll, I'm surprised you can even bring yourself to look at me."

"I didn't say that."

I glare at him and turn toward the stair climber. Max moves in front of me, blocking my path with his big, stupid body.

"Stop being a bitch."

I growl at him, feeling the anger building inside me.

"Stop acting like I've majorly insulted you."

"Well, you did."

Max snarls, "You're a real piece of work, you know that?"

"What the fuck did I do?"

"You have a boyfriend, and you're mad that I'm not fawning over you. Are you really so selfish that you need everyone to be in love with you?" Max's eyes flash green.

"Excuse me?"

"You are seriously mad that I didn't fall to my knees and exclaim how hot you are. When you're going home to golden boy. So why the fuck does it matter to you what I think?"

"I don't give a shit that you don't think I'm hot. It's the fact that I was trying to make light of an awkward situation, and you basically told me I was the most hideous being in all the realms. Completely unnecessary."

Max rolls his eyes. "I said you weren't my type, and that's how you took it?" Max's voice raises. "Stop acting like you're doing me a favor by coming here. And stop obsessing over whether everyone in the realm thinks you're attractive or not."

"I don't give a fuck that I'm physically desirable to some. My ugly lies beneath the surface, and it runs deep." The truth spills from me, and the pain of it hits me like a truck.

Max's anger softens a little. "So does mine." Crossing my arms over my chest, I look away but feel his gaze on me. I want to run and hide. I want to claw that truth out of existence. "We fight and pretend like we're not monsters."

I wince at his words, and I hear the pain in them. He doesn't understand me, though. He's talking about the berserker. The monster inside me is so much scarier, and it's yet to truly rear its ugly head.

"Right."

"Come on," Max says, turning on his heel and walking into the sparring room.

I follow behind him. My anger has deflated into the deepest of sorrows, and it is easier than arguing with him. I look up just in time to catch the sai Max throws at me, and I wrap my fingers around them and take a deep breath. I feel stronger with them. Maybe, in time, they will be the key to killing the ultimate villain, the monster that lurks within me, the one with the dark thoughts and even darker desires.

"Stop it. You're overthinking," Max says, swinging his sword.

"Let's just do this so I can go be a monster in my own home."

"Keep twisting my words. Let it fuel you," Max taunts.

I spin the sai, preparing to fight. I didn't twist his words. He called me a monster, and he was right. How else can I explain what's wrong with me? Why can't I find satisfaction in perfection?

"Bring it," Max growls.

I launch at him, swinging my sai in unison just as he taught me. Max doesn't hold back this time, slamming his broadsword into them. The power of the hit sends a vibration of pain through my bones, and I recede a step.

"You got it," Max says.

I push him back with my blades, leaning into my growing strength.

Max nods. "Good."

I stop and drop my arms. I feel like I've been hit by a freight train. "Max, I should go. I'm sorry."

"You're not quitting."

I hand him the sai, emotion welling inside me. Without the anger fueling me, I am drowning in the ever-present sadness.

"Goodbye, Max."

"You're not going anywhere," Max snarls.

"You don't even like me, and I can't do this today," I say, shaking my head and turning away.

"I do like you."

I give him a look over my shoulder. "Let's not start lying to each other now, Max. You think I'm an arrogant bitch, and I have my head firmly lodged up my own ass."

Max shrugs. "We're frenemies. I know there are lots of things you don't like about me."

"Frenemies?" I ask, thinking about the term. It feels more simple than friends, yet it's more pliable. The expectations are non-existent, and there is room for mistakes. It feels easier than sitting on the pedestal Alice and Connor keep putting me on. It is precarious up there, and I don't stay balanced for any length of time.

Max nods and holds out my sai. "You're not quitting this."

I look at them and then back at him, hesitating for a long beat before I turn and take them from him. While the well of despair still runs deep, I no longer feel like I'm drowning in it. I can breathe again. The air allows me to think straight, and I realize sparring may help. My brain is desperate for the endorphins, craving the feeling of power.

Max spins his sword. "And for the record, I enjoy training you."

"All I do is argue and piss you off."

"And?" Max asks, tilting his head.

I roll my eyes, but my heart lifts a little. "Ready?"

Max nods, and I swing my sai at him. He blocks it and counters with a powerful downward blow. I pull lightly at my power, enhancing my natural agility and speed.

Not only do I dodge his hit, but I get in one of my own, pushing him back a few steps.

I continue to walk him back, always aware of how close we're getting to the wall. How will I get him to concede without backing him into it and inciting the same reaction I did yesterday? However, my concern is unnecessary as Max uses my distraction against me and hits one of the sai out of my hand. It clangs loudly as it hits the floor.

"Stop holding back," Max growls. He bends to pick up my sai and hands it back to me. "Give it your all. You're better than this."

Determination fills me, and I spin, the sai blurring as I slam against his defense with a strength I didn't know I had. Max loses his footing and falls to the ground. I follow him down and hold my blade to his throat. My chest heaves from the exertion, but I bask in the feeling of power and control.

Max blinks, also catching his breath. "Good."

I lower the blade, nodding.

Max's lips tug into a half smile. "I like being frenemies."

I lift an eyebrow.

"You actually challenge me when you put your mind to it."

"I'll take that as a compliment, berserker," I say with a half smile.

"It was one."

"Thanks. I've let it go straight to my head."

Max snorts and sits up. "You're too much."

I poke him playfully in the stomach. Max throws me a look, but there is a glimmer of amusement in his eyes.

"What? Don't tell me the big, bad Maximillian Romulus is... ticklish."

Max rolls his eyes. "You wish."

I tickle his ribs. "Come on. You must have a tiny ticklish spot."

Max just glares at me, unimpressed. "Nope."

I try another spot at his waist but get no reaction.

"Well, then, this explains it. You don't like fun."

Max snorts and attacks, tickling me. My skin prickles, and I squeal, combusting into a shaking, giggling mess.

"Max! No!" I laugh as he continues to tickle my waist. I wriggle and squeal, trying to escape, but he easily keeps me in place.

"This is like a Summer destruct button," Max says, unrelenting.

I swat at him and roll away, wiping the tears from my eyes. "Dick."

"You started it!"

I stand and offer him my hand. He takes it, and I pull him up.

"Get out of here," Max grumbles, but his lips twitch.

"Later, weirdo." I wink at him as I leave the gym.

In the shower, I plan my night to myself. Alice is out at the greenhouse tonight.

She'd said something about having to water the plant every thirty minutes. I've set some time aside for school work, but I am also going to relax with some soft, pajamas that are runed to be warm, a bottle of wine, and a facemask.

I am looking forward to it, but what I am looking forward to the most is speaking with the stranger tonight.

I pull my pajamas on and am about to apply my facemask when someone knocks on the door. I sigh but open it. Connor is standing there, his face grave.

"Hi, big guy. I thought you were going to the game with Ra—"

"You're the target," Connor says, and I can see the betrayal in Connor's face,

My stomach drops, and I feel the blood drain from my face. "What?"

Connor steps forward, looking down at me. "How long?"

I hold his devastated gaze. "Con..." He moves past me into the room, and I push the door closed. "What makes you think that?" I ask, the lie stabbing me through the heart.

"How long have you known?" Connor asks, his voice hoarse.

I look away from him, unable to face his sadness. "Connor..."

"How long?"

"A while," I whisper. "How do you know?"

Connor whimpers softly. "Weeks?"

I close my eyes, the small sound of pain tearing through me. "Connor..."

"Months?" Connor asks.

I rub my hand over my face. "Since... the second murder."

"And you never told me."

I look at him, and the second I do, I regret it. His body has recoiled in pain, and it shines in his eyes. "Connor, please understand," I begin, my voice shaking. "I was only trying to protect you."

Connor shakes his head and runs his hand through his hair. "Protect me? How was that protecting me?"

"Con. After you saw that victim, you were... traumatized. Then, when I suspected I might be the target, I couldn't tell you because you were already struggling, and it was breaking my heart. After the next murder, there were finals, and you were so stressed, big guy." I move in closer and place my hands on his chest. "I should have told you, but—"

Connor flinches away from my touch, and I swear to all the gods, I hear my heart break. "And after the next murder? Or the one after that? Why couldn't you tell me? I had to hear it from the headmaster?"

"Connor, I..." I try to think of something to say. I don't know how to make this better.

Connor's eyes grow misty. "I have been so patient, not pushing you. But, now that I think about it, I don't even really know anything about you."

I hold my hands up. "No, that's not—"

"Tell me one thing about your past," he interrupts, his eyes filling with tears.

I shake my head, dread swirling inside me. "I barely know anything, Con..." There is the obvious, but my chest tightens with the memory of Torin, and my soul desperately clings to the story. Connor already looks so broken. It would be so much worse if he knew I'd murdered someone. I can't tell him about the power and darkness inside me.

Connor closes his eyes, defeated.

My hands shake as I lift them to cup his cheeks. "Connor, please. I love you."

Connor pulls back again. "I can taste lies, but I can't taste yours."

I gasp and drop my hands, his words slicing through me painfully. "Connor."

A tear tracks down his cheek. "Tell me one thing. Give me something. Anything."

I move closer and slowly lift my hand to cup his cheek again. This time, he doesn't pull away. He just stares at me with that devastated look, and I scramble for an ounce of truth to give him. I need to give him something that is wholly honest and all his.

"Here's something." I feel the tears slide down my cheeks. "I love you, Connor. So fucking much. And I am so sorry."

He stares at me, searching my eyes. "But you don't trust me."

"I do. I do trust you." It's not about trust. It never has been. You are such a good man, and I am so broken.

Connor shakes his head. "You don't trust me enough to make my own decisions with this. You don't trust me enough to believe I can support and protect you."

"Con, please," I whimper.

"Six months. Did you even hesitate?"

"You know I did."

Connor winces, another tear falling. "I love you so much, but this is breaking my heart."

"Connor. Please. I'm so sorry."

Connor closes his eyes, and the tears leak down his face. "Fuck."

"Tell me how to fix it. Please."

"Tell me about your past. Everything," Connor whispers brokenly and opens his eyes.

I swallow, dread filling my stomach and bile burning my throat at what I am about to do. That voice screams at me from the depths of my soul, begging me to keep this ugly truth from the perfection that is Connor. What would happen if I told him about Torin? Would he go after him? I can't risk that. Torin is fairly powerful, but that's not what makes him so dangerous. It's the allies he keeps.

My entire body aches with repudiation at the thought of showing him who I truly am. He will leave. He will walk away in disgust. How could he not? And now I am forced to face my own ugly truth. I can scream to the heavens that this was to protect him, but honestly, I was protecting myself.

Taking a deep, shuddering breath, I nod and slide my hand into his, pulling him to the couch. His body tenses when I touch him, but he follows me and sits down. I settle beside him, tucking my body into the corner but turning to face him. Fear clenches my throat like a fist, but it's no longer fear of being open with him. It's the terror of losing him.

I keep hold of his hand, and Connor doesn't pull away. He seems to know that I need his touch for strength. I swallow down the sick feeling of guilt and begin to talk, hoping that giving him a sliver of the full story will be enough,

"I was abandoned as a baby in the mortal realm of all places." My mouth is dry, and I am practically choking on fear. "A mortal woman found me somewhere in the woods, I believe. I only ever knew her as Grammy. When she found me, I looked like a mortal infant. My parents had seemingly cared just enough to glamour me so the mortals would accept me. The rune only lasted so long, though, and by the time I was three, the truth of my heritage was starting to show."

I reach up, touching the point of one ear.

"For as long as I can remember, Grammy used to braid my hair to hide my pointed ears. Even now, the mortal realm is not a kind place to... those like us. She used to make me wear contact lenses to hide the color of my eyes. They would burn when I put them in. I hated them more than anything. They were worse than even the beatings I got when my magic flared accidentally."

Memories assault me, and I drop my gaze, staring at our hands. My knuckles are white, and I ease my grip, twining my fingers with his. He is still here. It will be okay.

"There was nothing she could do once my powers came in fully, so she told me every day that they were something to be hidden, repressed, and ashamed of. One day, I came home from school and found her sitting in her old armchair. She was cold. So cold. So pale." A tear slides down my cheek. Not for her but for what she represented. The familiar loneliness swarms me. It is all the more shocking because it had been absent since Alice and Connor. "I was thirteen when she died."

I exhale a shaky breath at the memory of what happened next, what my desperation to belong to someone led me to do. I push that thought away before I continue,

"A few weeks after her burial, I found a chest in her bedroom. Inside, there were several diaries and letters. It was every scrap of information she knew about me. I looked into my past a little, but I was young, and it was just too hard. I knuckled down in school, and I... was alone."

*Show me what you can do, Summer.*

I close my eyes at the memory unfolding in front of me. The first time I felt Torin's magenta eyes on me, the first time he slowly undid my brain, so gently luring me into a false sense of security. The gentleness was a ploy, another manipulation.

"Until I got the acceptance letter for Avalon." I force myself to push forward with the story, unable to tell Connor what I did and the truth of what I am. He would leave me for sure. There is no way he could accept the darkness I harbor. I glance at Connor and find his gaze pinned on me. "Grammy always kept me at a distance. She was cold and cruel. She was afraid of me, but she was the only person I had."

*Show me what you can do, Summer.*

The words sit heavily between us, and the room is deafeningly silent for a while. I stare at our hands, sliding my fingers up and down his and tracing the lines and calluses on his palm. Finally, Connor shifts and pulls me into him, tucking my head against his shoulder.

A small sob breaks free from my throat. "I'm sorry, Connor. I... You deserve better."

"I just..." Connor strokes my arm with his thumb. "Summer, I need to know that you'll tell me things, even if they're uncomfortable or you're afraid."

I exhale and pull back to look at him, trying to find a way to push away the guilt that is clawing up my throat, trying to force the worst of the truths from me. So, I divulge more truths, other truths, truths that are not so horrific. "Months ago, someone ransacked our dorm. They stole some of my clothing."

"Alice knew?" Connor asks, his shoulders tensing again.

"Connor, I'm telling you everything now. It's all I can do. Alice only knew because when I found the third victim..." I take a steadying breath, trying to push away the image of the dead fae. "I was covered in blood, and Alice saw. I was also terrified because the dead girl was wearing one of the items of clothing that was taken."

Connor flinches.

I cover my face with my hands. "Fuck."

"They've been... toying with you." I drop my hands, looking at him, his reply surprising me. "You must have been so scared."

Fuck, he's so perfect. I swallow. "It's not been easy," I concede.

"I'm sorry," Connor says.

I frown and shake my head at the apology. There is only one person at fault here. And it's me. "You have nothing to be sorry for."

"You were alone."

"Not completely. I wanted to protect you, Connor, but I did what I could to keep myself safe."

"I should be protecting you," Connor says, clenching his fists and looking down at them.

"I wanted to protect *you*."

"I'm the warrior."

"No, Connor. To me, you are my boyfriend," I say, covering one of his massive fists with my much smaller hand.

"I'm supposed to be strong." Connor looks back at me.

"You *are* strong. Tell me how to fix this. You want me on my knees, begging for your forgiveness? I'll do it."

Connor shakes his head. "I don't want that."

I swallow down the lump of fear in my throat. "Are you going to leave me?"

Connor looks at me for the longest moment. "I don't know."

I flinch but try to hold back my tears. I pushed him too far. He has every right to leave me. Fuck, if someone had done to me what I did to him, I would leave. I lied to him and kept him at arm's length. Hell, I am continuing to do both. But the truths I'm withholding are not ones I need to share. These are mine, and I will not let them define my future.

Connor looks away again. "This really hurts," he whispers, and I have to swallow the whimper that threatens to pass my lips. I won't make this harder for him or play on his love. He deserves so much better than that, so much better than me.

"I'm so sorry." I close my eyes, my whole body feeling like it's collapsing in on itself like a dying star. "What do you need from me?" I ask.

Connor exhales heavily. "I don't know. I need to protect you, but I also need space."

I wipe a stray tear away. "Right, space," I say, sliding my hand off his.

"But I can't because you're in danger, and I love you."

I shake my head. "You should have your space. I'll make sure Alice is by my side every second."

Connor grabs my hand back, and I look up at him in surprise. "I need to be by your side every second."

I shake my head harder, quietly sobbing, feeling like I am unraveling. "If you don't have this space, Connor, you'll resent me forever. Take some time. Think things through, and I'll be here when you're ready."

"No. You are done making decisions for me," Connor growls.

I wince, looking away. I've never heard so much anger in his voice, and I deserve it. "Okay. I'm sorry."

Connor sighs and kneels on the floor in front of me. He grips my hands in his and looks up at me. "I need to protect the women I love, even when I'm mad at her."

I force the words out through the sobs I am desperately trying to keep in. "But you... you're not sure... you want to be... with me anymore. Which... I totally understa—"

"Stop. I shouldn't have said that. I know I want to be with you. I want to marry you, Summer. I still love you. I just... I feel betrayed."

My chin wobbles, and I nod, pulling my hands away to cover my mouth, trying to physically hold back the sobs.

Connor cups my face. "I'm sorry. I know it's... I don't know. I'm not good at these eloquent speeches." A tear slides down Connor's cheek. "Rafe had to protect me. When I saw the blood, I–I immediately saw Gia's face and—"

"Blood?" The word is muffled by my hands, and I drop them.

Connor nods, holding my gaze. "There's been another... That's where I found out about you being the target. The headmaster mentioned it to me at the... scene."

All the fear I felt before is nothing compared to the wave that washes over me now. My entire body goes cold, and I can literally hear the blood surging through my veins. Connor feels the tremors wracking my body and pulls me down to straddle his lap. He puts my face into his neck and holds me tight, instinctively rocking as terror grips me in its teeth and shakes.

"I can protect you now," he whispers.

I can't stop trembling. The memory of Alicia's blood against my skin is a visceral one, and the images of the bodies flash through my mind like some sick slideshow. Down, soft feathers brush against my cheek, and I open my eyes to see Connor has completely wrapped us in his wings. There are barely any white ones left, and I finally let the sobs come.

"You've been so scared for so long." Connor runs his fingers through my hair, comforting me. He hums a melody, and I let the song travel through me. Every cell it touches releases, and I feel like I can breathe again.

"I love you, Connor," I whisper as my body recovers from the massive adrenaline dump. The fear is still there, but I also feel a kernel of rage festering within. I'll need to tap into that anger if I'm going to get through this. Connor was right. This person is toying with me, but it stops now.

I pull back and look up at him. "I need to talk to the headmaster."

Connor frowns. "Why?"

"I need to know what he saw and if there was a message. If they were... wearing my clothes." Connor cups my cheek. "Will you come with me?"

Connor nods and presses his forehead to mine.

# 104

## SUMMER

Saithu
SWORD, WEAPON,
BLADE

We linger, just basking in each other. Connor's forehead is pressed to mine, and tears still silently leak from my eyes. Connor has his arms wrapped around me, not possessively but protectively. I came so fucking close to losing him, and for what? Some stupid idea that I'm protecting him? Maybe I will still lose him, and I wouldn't even blame him. Even though I've finally opened up to him, it's too fucking late. He's been patiently waiting for a small piece of me, but I've held onto every hideous scrap, holding it so close to my chest it's welded to my skin.

I pull back and cup his cheek, looking at his perfect, handsome face. "I should clean myself up before we go see the headmaster."

Connor nods, and I leave him in the living room while I retreat to my bathroom. When I'm alone, the fear clutches at me again. The murderer is still out there, and though I suspected it, the confirmation feels worse than I could have imagined. I look at my reflection in the mirror, at how my blue eyes shine, so different from everyone else's. Right now, they're bloodshot and puffy, and my nose is red from all the crying.

I hate this version of myself, but sometimes I miss her, the Summer who didn't feel, who couldn't feel. She was safe, but she also lacked so much *life*. This Summer is raw and broken. She's messy, chaotic, and difficult, but she loves and she cares. She has people and has found a family. I won't give it up, not for the world.

I turn the tap on, waiting until the water is freezing cold before I splash it on my face. The icy droplets are refreshing against my hot cheeks, and as I dry my face, I wipe away some of the sadness, too. Not all of it, but enough that I'm confident I won't dissolve into tears again anytime soon.

When I walk back into the living room, Connor is still kneeling on the ground where I left him. He looks pensive and is staring down at his hands.

The moment feels so private that I clear my throat to alert him of my presence, trying not to invade whatever space he needs. Connor blinks and looks up at me, a sad smile tugging at his lips, but it's still so heartbreakingly beautiful.

"Ready?" I ask.

Connor nods and pushes to his feet. His wings disappear before we leave the dorm. Initially, we don't touch. We walk side by side, and there is an awkwardness between us that has never been there before. I consider reaching for his hand, but before I decide, Connor brushes the back of his hand against mine and then interlocks our fingers. I look up at him, but he continues staring straight ahead as we walk through the campus. I know from afar we look solid, but from this close, I can see every single fracture.

Connor knocks on the door when we arrive at the headmaster's office.

In a now all too familiar ritual, we enter when he calls, "Enter."

"Another fae?" I ask before the door even has a chance to close behind us.

The headmaster nods. "Yes, but this incident differed from the others."

"Did she look like me?" I ask, wholly focused on him.

The headmaster shakes his head. "But she was wearing an item of your clothing."

Connor's hand tightens on mine, and bile crawls up my throat.

The headmaster waves his hand, and a projection manifests in front of him, glowing a faint blue. Connor steps toward the desk, but I grab his arm, stopping him.

"You don't need to see this, big guy."

Connor meets my gaze, steely resolve hardening the beautiful blue of his eyes. "Yes, I do."

I nod, and together, we step forward to look at the projection. On the screen, a dead fae female is lying at the bottom of the Dullahan Hall stairs. Blood stains the steps and is puddled around her. Unlike the other victims, her body has not been posed and positioned for the viewer. Her legs rest on the stairs, and her arms are extended as though she is reaching toward safety. She is wearing my black t-shirt, the words Ruin My Runes now littered with slashes and painted with gore.

The headmaster slides his hand through the projection, rewinding it to the point where her head slams down. The thud is sickening, and a wave of nausea rushes through me. He rewinds again and again, trying to see... something. I'm about to beg for him to stop, to get rid of the spell, but then my eyes catch on the slightest flicker in the upper corner of the magical screen.

"Wait," I say, grabbing the headmaster's wrist just as he is about to dismiss the spell.

He goes rigid and stares at my hand. I quickly let go. He obviously doesn't like to be touched, or maybe he just doesn't want to be touched by me, but either way, I have more important things on my mind.

"Please, start it again," I ask, staring at the projection.

The headmaster flicks his fingers, and the spell activates. Connor's face turns a little green in anticipation of the noise we're about to experience again.

"Pause. Now," I demand, just as her head hits the floor. I narrow my eyes and move in, noticing the slightest of blurs. "There. Something moves there. She's not alone."

The headmaster plays it again, but this time in slow motion, his eyes narrowed as he leans closer. I watch as the blur shifts only slightly, so easily missed.

"The Helm," the headmaster whispers. "They're using the Helm," he says, only fractionally louder this time.

"The Helm, sir?" I ask, feeling Connor shift uncomfortably behind me.

The headmaster looks at us. "There was a note left at the scene." The headmaster pulls a small, clear plastic bag from his desk and hands it to me.

## DID YOU GET MY MESSAGE?

It is written in what looks like blood, and my heart picks up. I stare at it, reading it over and over. Connor gently pries it from my fingers to inspect it closer.

"Is the blood—"

"It doesn't belong to the victim, but they've been smart. It's untraceable. Another one of their little games, no doubt."

"The message they're referencing is the one from the Nexus account?"

"I presume so. That I know of, there have been no other complete messages since the last murder. However, I could be incorrect," the headmaster says, taking the note back from Connor.

"What message?" Connor asks.

I glance at Connor, knowing that this will probably add to his anger, but I also know that not telling him would be even worse. "The murderer seems to have been communicating with us via social media."

The furrows in Connor's brow deepen, his eyes flicking back and forth between the headmaster and me.

"Via the page dedicated to the headmaster."

"On *EverydayEmrys*?"

The headmaster scowls. "You've heard of it?"

"Everyone's heard of it, headmaster."

The headmaster rubs a hand over his face. "Mister Morningstar, I assume you'll be helpful in that particular investigation."

Connor nods. "Whatever she needs."

I look back at the headmaster. "I actually have some leads regarding who might run *EverydayEmrys*."

"Already?" he asks.

"I work fast, sir."

He nods and gestures for Connor and me to sit. We take the chairs on the other side of his desk, and I pull a list from my bag. I pass him the piece of paper with ten names on it.

"And how did you come up with these names?" the headmaster asks, reading through the list.

"These are only potentials. Some because they have a knack for tech, some because they seem... enamored with you, a few because they're popular, and a couple because they're not."

The headmaster's eyes dart over the list, his lips pressed into a thin line. "And how do you plan on narrowing it down?"

I clear my throat. "Well, I have an idea." I look away. "But it's probably best you don't know too much about it, sir."

His gaze flicks to mine, his eyes narrowing, but then he sighs. "Fine."

I nod and give him a tight smile. "I'll have an answer for you by the end of the week."

The headmaster places my list down and picks up the message from the killer again. "Dismissed," he grumbles, his attention already long gone.

Connor doesn't speak again until we get outside. "What messages?" he asks. I miss his hand in mine, but asking for affection now doesn't feel right.

I exhale. "Listen well, this is just the beginning." Connor shudders, and I nod gravely. "That was the message as of three days ago. It was random letters on different posts from what looked like a bot account. But we need to find the owner of the account to know if any of the other comments were blocked or deleted."

Connor slides his hand into mine and squeezes, reassuring me. The rest of the walk is silent. When we get to the door to Kelpie, we linger awkwardly outside.

I look up at him, my hand still in his. "Are you coming in?" I ask, unable to hide the hopefulness in my voice but not wanting to guilt him into it.

Connor looks down at me and considers for a moment, and I can see the moment he decides. His shoulders relax a little, and his eyes sparkle a fraction. He nods, and I open the door, leading him up the stairs to the dorm in silence.

We step inside, and I ask, "Drink?"

Connor nods and sits down on the couch. I pour two heavy-handed glasses of bourbon and hand him one before sitting down next to him. He tosses it back in one gulp and then looks up at me. "Do you really love me?" The question is shockingly painful, and my stomach clenches.

"What?" I ask. It is mind-boggling that he even needs to ask, but then, why wouldn't he? I've been lying to him almost our entire relationship. I still am. Why wouldn't he doubt my words and me? I am still unable to show him the depths of my soul in the hopes that if I hide them long enough, they will go dormant permanently.

"Do you?" Connor asks again, keeping his gaze on me.

I sit next to him. "Of course I do. You know I don't say those words lightly."

Connor exhales and leans in, brushing his lips over my forehead. "I just... had to make sure."

I look down at my still full tumbler. "I guess I'm bad at showing it."

Connor watches me, his hand on my lower back. "You are." He pauses for a long moment but then surprises me by continuing. "But then you smother my face in kisses and cling to me. You take care of me, and I know you will protect me. You," he takes a moment to collect himself, "you let me sleep over."

I look up at him, tears welling in my eyes.

"You show me in little ways, and those little ways add up."

I shake my head. "It's not enough. I know that."

Connor puts his empty glass on the coffee table and gently pinches my chin, turning my face to him. "It is. For me."

"I've never done this before, Connor. You know that I've never had a family, not truly. I've never had a boyfriend either, and I've never been in love. I've never been accountable for anyone but myself." And that was so painfully true. Torin was never my boyfriend. We were held together by lies and deceit, by manipulation and desperation. There was no love, no kindness. Until Connor and Alice, I don't think I even knew what love was. I only knew the lack.

Conor cups my cheek. "I know that now."

I inhale deeply and wrap my hand around his wrist, pulling it away from my face. "Connor, I'm not saying this to make excuses. I'm saying it because..." I swallow, looking away, "you need to decide if this is what you signed up for."

Connor pulls his hand free from my hold and cups my cheek again. "I just needed to understand why you weren't letting me in." He strokes my cheek with his thumb. "I love you, Summer Tuatha De Daanan. If you let me, I'll love you for the rest of my life."

"I love you, Connor Morningstar."

"It's going to take me time, but I'm–I'm not going to leave you."

"Take you time?" I ask, fear gripping me again.

"To move on from this," Connor says, still stroking my cheek comfortingly. "I'm not going to leave you, but I need to learn to trust you again."

I take a deep drink. "Right." I clear my throat. "Well, you can take the bed. I'll sleep on the couch." I feel my cheeks flush. "That is if you're planning to stay."

Connor shakes his head, and at first, I think he's going to say he's not staying, but then he says, "I'll take the couch."

"Please, Connor. You're too tall for the couch."

Connor scans my eyes, and then he takes a deep breath. "I'll sleep in the bed with you then."

My lips part, taken aback a little, but I nod. Connor plucks the glass from my hand and places it beside his on the coffee table. He takes my hand as we stand up and leads me to my bedroom. I follow behind him, my heartbeat thudding in my ears. Connor pulls off his pants and shirt and slides into the bed. I follow suit but pull on his discarded shirt. His scent and warmth envelop me, and I feel comforted again as I climb into bed, careful not to touch him.

Connor opens his arms, but I notice his hesitation and don't move closer. "It's okay, Con. You don't have to."

"I want to."

"Your hesitation begs to differ."

Connor wearily slides his hand over his face. "Summer, I'm trying."

I blush and move into his arms. Connor wraps himself around me, pulling me close, though my muscles remain tense.

"Relax," Connor says, kissing the top of my head. "It's going to be all right." I nod and kiss his jaw gently before laying my head back down. "I'm here."

I try to relax, but the more I try, the more tense I seem to get, the louder my mind gets.

"Do you want me to sleep on the couch?" Connor asks, obviously sensing that his presence isn't relaxing me.

I tighten my arms around him. "No. Please stay. My mind is just very loud right now."

Connor brushes his lips over mine. The kiss is tentative at first, but he relaxes into it. I match his pace, not daring to deepen the kiss at all. I'll give Connor as much time or space as he needs.

"We're going to get through this," Connor whispers. "We should sleep."

I nod and curl into him. Connor falls asleep slower than usual, but I am still awake long after he has drifted off. I am left alone, staring at the ceiling with nothing to distract me from my thoughts until my phone pings. I reach over Connor and grab it, opening the message.

@1015

Are you alright? I didn't hear from you.

602

# 105

## SUMMER

Solthae
LOYALTY,
DEVOTION

I climb out of bed and pad into the living room to call Stranger. The phone rings once, twice, three times, and then there is the blissful sound of the line connecting.

"Little fae?" His voice is unglamoured again, as promised, and a shiver runs down my spine at the sound of it. It's deep, dangerous, and erotic.

I sit on the couch and take a steadying breath. "Stranger." It's barely a whisper.

"Are you all right?" he asks, and I hear him swallow. I imagine him with a drink in his hand.

I glance over my shoulder at my closed bedroom door. "It's been a rough day."

"I heard," he says after a long pause.

"You did?"

"I was watching the school."

"Right." I exhale heavily. "It's nice to hear your voice."

He sighs. "It's nice to hear yours, too."

"What's with the sigh?" I ask.

"Been a difficult day for me, too." I hear him take another drink. "You wanted to talk about the killer."

I hold the phone a little tighter. "There has been another murder. My suspicions were right." I take a steadying breath, trying to swallow my fear enough to voice my reality. "Whoever it is, they're watching me." I stand and walk to the window in the kitchen, peering out at the obsidian night.

"Have they approached you?"

"No, but they've been a little too close for comfort." I look out at the trees.

"I don't like that," he growls.

A shiver sets my body alight, and I am not sure if it is fear or the suppressed violence in his tone. "I have to ask a favor."

"A favor?" he asks, and I can hear the intrigue in his voice.

"I take it you're... good with technology."

A laugh rumbles through the phone, and I close my eyes, allowing its shivery warmth to slide through me. "I'm passable."

"You created the Runic Network, so I'm guessing you're good enough to find an IP address for a *Nexus* profile account owner."

"I could definitely do that." I hear his smirk. Asshole. "Who?" he asks.

"I'll send the account now." Going to the *EverydayEmrys* account, I send it over to him before replacing the phone to my ear.

The stranger moves, and I hear a laptop starting up before the tapping of a keyboard. "Huh. A stalker page for your headmaster? I guess you're part of the majority who finds him dreamy."

"What?" I ask, surprised by his tone.

"I seem to remember a conversation you had with Alice where you called him *dark and dreamy*," he grumbles, an edge of jealousy lining his voice.

"You're taking that out of context. And stop listening to my private conversations!"

I can practically hear his eyes roll through the phone. "This account has a lot of followers." I stand and pace as he types quickly, muttering softly to himself. "Hm. I have the IP address."

"You do?" I ask, coming to a stop.

"It's... someone you know."

I blink, preparing myself.

"Lucas Morningstar."

My phone falls from my hand, and I stare straight ahead, all thoughts gone from my mind. Luke? Luke runs the stalker page for the headmaster? But—

"Little fae? Are you still there?" I hear the stranger's voice coming from the phone, and I pick it up, holding it to my ear. "I'm here. Sorry."

"Surprising?"

"Fuck. Luke is... a baby."

He laughs that sinful laugh again, and the sound slides against my nerves like warm honey. "Sounds like he has a secret life," he says.

Is this surprising? I always kind of suspected his interests were in that direction... but a stalker page?

"You suspected?" the stranger asks, and I curse, obviously having spoken out loud instead of inside my mind.

"Kind of. Not about the stalker page, but about him being into males."

"Why?"

"Just a vibe. Plus, he always looks at the shifter alpha's ass when he passes, but I've never seen him look at a girl."

"Huh. And it's a secret?"

"I guess. No one's ever told me, including Luke, and his brothers don't seem to know."

"You know, something is interesting about this account," the stranger says.

"More interesting than the fact it's a stalker page for the headmaster?"

I hear his fingers striking rapidly at the keyboard. "This page was created ten years ago, but Luke just started here, right?"

"Yes, he's first year."

"So, who was running it before?" I hear the frown in his words.

"I don't know, but I can't worry about that right now. I'll need to talk to Luke and then the headmaster."

"What are you going to say to him?" he asks.

"I'm going to ask him about the account, and I'm going to ask him about the comments on the posts. If he's been deleting any."

He takes another deep drink. "Should be interesting. I can't see what's been deleted, if anything, but I think there's more."

"Are you enjoying this?"

"What?"

"Me needing your help."

"What makes you ask that?" he asks, and I can tell he is holding back a chuckle.

"I can hear it in your voice."

"Am I so transparent?"

"Please tell me you're aware of the irony of that statement."

He laughs. "Maybe."

I drop onto the couch again.

"So what else has happened? I can hear the edge in your voice," he asks, his voice softer than I've ever heard it but still laced with danger.

"Besides the murder?"

"Besides the murder."

Should I open this with him? I don't want to fight with him. I want to keep enjoying our conversation, but it would feel good to talk about the stuff with Connor, and Alice still isn't home.

"It's about Connor," I warn. "Are you okay with that?"

"Yes," he says, but I can hear his voice tighten.

"He... almost broke up with me today."

"Why?" he asks, sounding even more tense.

"He found out I was the target." I exhale heavily, rubbing my face.

"You hadn't told him?"

"I was trying to protect him. It was stupid, I know." I shake my head. "You know, it's funny. He's the first person who's ever loved me. He even has a fucking engagement ring, but I—"

"An engagement ring?"

I curse under my breath. I shouldn't have mentioned that, especially to the stranger. But why not? Connor is my future, and I've been very clear about that. I clear my throat. "Yeah."

Silence crackles between us, and I consider filling it, but I have no idea what to say.

"He didn't want to be protected," the stranger finally says, his voice tight and flat.

"He sees it as a betrayal, and it was."

"So, what are you going to do?" he asks, an edge to his voice.

"I'm going to work to fix things, and I'm going to stop keeping things from him."

"And how do you plan to do that? Make things right?"

I am a little flustered by his questions. "I-I don't know, but he wants us to work. So that's a start, I guess."

"But you've apologized?" he asks.

"I have."

"So what's next, then?"

"I'm not sure. He says he still loves me, so..." I sigh. "He says it'll just take time."

"And it's killing you to give him time," the stranger says. It's not a question but a statement.

"Well, I mean, it just happened, but I feel... unsettled."

"Unsettled because he's holding back." It's another statement.

I shake my head. "Unsettled because Connor and I don't fight. I wish he'd yell at me and get it all out, and then we can just move on."

"And if he yelled, what would your reaction be?"

"I would accept it, and we'd move forward. Or he'd end things." Once he finally realizes this isn't worth fighting for.

"And you'd break."

"I–"

"He helps," he interrupts, his voice almost accusatory. "If he left, you'd break."

"He does help, but at least I'd know he'd be happier." I rub my hand over my face. "It doesn't matter. I'm not making decisions for him anymore, and he seems to want to make this better, so... we will."

"You both have to want to make it better."

I glance at my bedroom door again. "He deserves better. What if he doesn't realize that until we're married?"

"What would happen then?" he asks, his voice tense. "Would you leave him?"

"I... What?"

"Would you leave him if he realized you weren't right for him?" he asks again, and every one of his questions pierces me like a bullet.

"I don't think I'd have to. He'd leave me."

"But would you? Would you ever leave him, little fae?" he asks, the questions hanging between us heavily.

"I can't think of a scenario where I'd leave him," I answer honestly.

"If he wasn't the person for you and you realized... too late?"

I exhale heavily, thinking. "If that were the case, and I thought we both had a chance at happiness and true peace... Maybe I would end it."

"Maybe?"

"Well, probably," I say, my brows drawing. "If I knew we'd both be happier with other people or if we grew apart."

"Happier with others, hm," he says, pondering.

I sigh, shaking my head. "Sorry, I know you don't love hearing about my relationship problems."

"I enjoy talking to you. No matter the topic."

"Even about my potential upcoming engagement?"

The sound of glass smashing comes through the phone. "Even then," he says, though I can tell it's through gritted teeth.

I'm being so selfish. This is bad for all three of us. I should cut the stranger off. I'm with Connor, but the stranger is... Fuck, I don't know. All I know is that I crave this feeling of not being alone. He sees the truth of me, and he seems to like *me*. I don't feel like a freak when I am with him.

"Are you okay?" I ask.

"Fine," he grates out.

"I missed you." My whisper is barely audible, but I hear his breath hitch.

"I missed you too."

"You have a very attractive voice," I say, relaxing back on the couch.

"I have heard."

"Right. Sorry," I say with a grimace.

"I believe you called it *sexy* last time. If you'll recall."

I clear my throat. "And you like my voice."

"I do. I find it very soothing," he says, and I can hear his smile.

"Hm," I reply, unable to hide my disappointment at the word soothing.

"You're upset. I can feel it."

"Not upset. Just disappointed that I don't have a *sexy* voice."

He laughs. "You do. Just in a different way."

"Well, what does that mean?" I ask, my lips twitching.

"You know," the sound of that smirk returns, "this is one of those boundary moments you love so much."

My smile dies, and I'm immediately pulled back into my reality. Why do the lines blur so much with this male? "Right... sorry."

"I imagine you could make your voice maddeningly sexy," he growls huskily, and I close my eyes as my core heats.

I clear my throat. "I should go."

"Why?" he asks.

"I'm sure you have things to do."

"Not right now," he says.

"Then maybe a little longer?" I shouldn't have said it. I should have just gone back to bed, but I didn't want to leave him.

"I'd like that," he says, and I can hear the smile in his voice.

The conversation shifts to school gossip, and we spend the next hour talking and laughing with each other.

# 106

## SUMMER

Tahlthae

MAIDEN, YOUTH

Connor and I walk back to the dorm after potentially the most awkward morning we've ever had. When we woke, there was the briefest moment when the previous day hadn't happened. We looked at each other, both of us still half lost to the softer realm of sleep, with lingering smiles and sparkling eyes. Then pain flashed across Connor's face, and I was brought right back to reality with a thud.

I don't know why, but we decided to go out for breakfast. We are terrible at fighting with each other, but we're making an effort. As we're walking back to the dorm, I notice Connor glancing at me every few seconds. His gaze caresses my features softly. I don't dare mention it, not wanting it to stop, but then he pulls his hand from mine. I wince slightly, but then he slides his hand over my back and loops it around my waist, pulling me into him. Finally, I dare to look up at him, and I find his eyes are already locked on me. His lips are pulled into his familiar, easy smile, and it makes my heart ache to see it again.

"What?" he asks, gliding his thumb along my waist.

"I love you," I say, my heart aching with the truth of it.

Connor pulls me in closer. "I love you, too." He stops walking and slides his hand into mine, pulling me onto the grass beneath one of the great trees. Thanks to the heavy growth of the leaves, we're nearly invisible to anyone passing by. He wraps his arms around my waist and looks down at me. "I know it's unbearable right now. It's making my stomach churn."

I place my hands on his chest. "It's my fault, Con."

Connor shakes his head. "If I hadn't been so overprotective, would you have told me?"

"Connor," I cup his cheek, "it wasn't about that, big guy. It was about how difficult it was for you after you found Gia's body. You slowly started to feel better, and I didn't want to bring you down again."

Connor tightens his arms around me, pulling me in even closer. "I know I'm guilty of shielding the people I love from upset. So, I do understand. Even when I was upset, I still understood."

Did he say *when*?

"You're not upset anymore?"

Connor shakes his head. "No, babe."

I search his eyes, but I only see sincerity. I'm not sure when he forgave me, but he's being completely honest with me right now.

"I'm not mad anymore." He cups my cheek. "Talk to me."

I can't find the words. There aren't any to express my gratitude and relief. So I simply slide my hands up his chest and wrap my arms around his neck, looking up at him.

Connor wraps his arm around me again, and he smiles in that crooked way that I love. "Your talking is so quiet."

My lips twitch, and warm, overwhelming emotions well inside me. "I love you. That's all there is to say."

Connor's big hands cup my ass, and he lifts me. I wrap my legs around him, and he kisses me deeply. I purr, savoring the feel of his soft lips against mine. The kiss is tender. He glides his tongue along the seam of my lips, asking me to open for him. I run my fingers through his hair and happily comply, holding him close.

Connor moans and whispers, "Home?"

"Yes, please," I say, sucking on his lower lip.

Connor starts walking, carrying me easily back toward Kelpie Hall. I kiss along his cheeks, nose, chin, and jaw, basking in his love and the relief that I haven't lost him.

As the door to the dorm closes behind us, Connor kisses me again. I'm about to deepen it, but then I hesitate and pull back. Connor frowns at me.

"I'm just... I'm not sure that we should jump back into that."

"Why?" Connor asks, tilting his head.

"Because you said you needed time, and I—"

"Summer. I had time. I understand why you did it."

"But I–I don't think I deserve your forgiveness yet," I admit, looking away.

Connor puts me on my feet and cups my cheeks, tilting my head up. "Summer, you don't get to decide that. I've thought about it. I've worked through it, and I love you. If you want to wait, that's okay. But it's your call."

My cheeks heat. "Okay, so... how *okay* are we?"

Connor's lips tilt up. "We're pretty damn okay."

I lick my lips. "Okay, well... maybe I could give you an orgasm?"

Connor shakes his head. "No. None of this *I don't deserve it* bullshit. No orgasms until we can both have them."

I look up at him and his darkening eyes, playing with the bottom of his shirt. Sex would make me feel better. It would be reassuring and would help me release some of the feelings I've been struggling with, but I have this deep fear that he's not fully forgiven me. But isn't that why we fought in the first place? I was making decisions for him.

Connor glides his fingers down my arms, and when he gets to the hem of my sweater, he pulls it up and off my body. I push up on my tiptoes, kissing him hard. Slowly, I work his shirt up his body, moaning as my hand grazes his skin. He breaks the kiss only long enough to yank his shirt over his head and toss it to the side. Then he's on me again, his lips desperate against mine. He backs me up toward the couch and carefully lowers me down, but there is nothing careful about the way his mouth claims mine.

My hands slide down his abs to the fly of his pants, and I practically rip his jeans open, my body an inferno of desire. Connor shoves my skirt up and rips away my tights and panties.

"You're so fucking sexy," he groans into my mouth, and I shove his pants down just enough to free him. I wrap my hand around his cock but stop and look up at him, waiting, giving him another chance to back out.

"Tell me this isn't a bad idea," I whisper breathlessly.

"With us, this is never a bad idea," Connor says, slowly leaning down to kiss me again. I relax into the kiss, and Connor shifts to press his cock to my opening. He groans as he pushes inside me, and I bury my fingers in his hair as he fills me. Connor slips his arm under me and lifts my ass, tilting my hips and slamming in hard so he's buried to the hilt inside me. My pussy clenches down on him, and I cry out from the pleasure. Connor's lips are on mine again, and his tongue is exploring my mouth.

Connor groans and digs his fingers into my hips as he starts to move inside me. His hard cock pierces me over and over, filling me up and driving me closer to my climax. He bites my lip and I drag my nails down his back hard, maybe too hard, but all it seems to do is push him to fuck me harder. The couch shakes beneath us, and I slide my hands down to his ass, pulling him into me even harder. I cry out from the pleasure, and Connor buries his face into my neck, moaning loudly. He grabs the arm of the sofa above my head, using it to give him more leverage. I pull my knees higher around him and arch to meet his thrusts.

"Connor... I'm so close..."

Connor bites my neck, groaning. "Fuck, I love you."

I lift my hips, matching Connor's rhythm, and my toes curl from the pleasure. He thrusts again and again, my thighs quivering around him as my release explodes inside me. Pleasure tightens every muscle in my body and my belly spasms. I cry out, my nails embedded in his ass. Connor bites down on the curve of my shoulder, muffling his shout as he comes hard, filling me with his release.

I gulp for air as Connor's hips slow and he pulls back, looking down at me. Sweat slicks his glowing skin, and he is panting. His eyes are still dark from his orgasm, but the way he's looking at me takes my breath away.

"Marry me," he says.

My breath catches as his words form in the air between us.

"Yes." The word bursts from my lips without any hesitation. I wait for the fear and dread to rip through me, but it never comes.

Connor and I just stare at each other for a long moment before smiling brightly. He claims my mouth again, and a tear slides down my cheek. The tenderness of this kiss is catastrophic.

He leans over and grabs his pants, pulling out a red velvet ring box. He flips it open, revealing a stunning ring nestled inside. The band is gold and gleams with the same luminescence as his halo. The three diamonds perched on top glimmer lovingly at me, so clear and pure they seem bottomless. Gasping, I stare at it.

"I carry it with me," Connor says, offering an explanation I didn't ask for. He sits up and pulls me up beside him. My hand shakes as he slides the ring onto my finger. He kisses me again, and I can taste his joy. I cup his cheeks and slide my tongue against his.

Connor pulls back, pressing his forehead to mine. "We're engaged."

I squeal, genuinely excited, and I start pressing kisses all over his face. "We're engaged."

"You're going to my wife."

I nod, kissing him again.

Connor shifts to lie back on the couch, and I lie on top of him, my hand on his chest so I can admire the ring.

"You like it?"

I nod, a soft, mushy smile on my face. "I love it."

Connor grins, kissing me quickly and then pulling back. "Get dressed. We have to call my parents!"

I laugh and move off him, my heart squeezing at his kindness. We've just got engaged, but he knows how much joy this will bring to them, especially his mother. I quickly pull on my clothes, and we prepare to announce our engagement for the first time.

I can do this. Connor is my peace.

# 107

## SUMMER

*Valthae*
WOMB

After we speak to Farrah and Uriel, Connor is eager to tell his brothers. He wants me to join him, but I think it'll be more special if it's just him there. He protests and tries to cajole me with kisses, but I hold firm. With one last toe-curling kiss, he leaves the dorm, and I hear him jogging down the hall.

Alice still isn't home, so I decide to get a workout in. It has been a rollercoaster of emotions over the last two days, ranging from rage to grief, to terror, to unadulterated happiness. Adrenaline is still coursing through me, and I may as well benefit from it.

On my walk to the gym, I find myself glancing repeatedly at my ring. I can't help but appreciate how it glints in the sunshine and how perfectly it fits on my finger. He obviously gave this a lot of thought, and I smile again when I remember the joy on his face when he asked me. I'm waiting for the panic to start, but so far, there is just the love and warmth Connor always makes me feel.

Max is standing in the free weights area, spotting someone when he notices me come in. He tips his chin at me in greeting, and I gesture toward the sparring room to let him know I will be in there when he is done. I stretch, warming up while I wait.

"You look happy," he says as he walks in.

"Hm?"

"You're smiling. It's weird."

I quirk a brow. "I didn't realize that wasn't allowed." Max rolls his eyes, and I smirk, nudging him in the stomach. "Wanna fight, berserker?"

Max shoves me playfully. "Let's go." He goes to the wall and collects the weapons, tossing me my sai. I catch them deftly, and he smiles, but it wavers when his gaze falls to my hand. "What's that?" he asks, his eyes glued to my ring finger, his brows drawing.

I blink and follow his gaze to the ring, the light bouncing off it and sending little rainbows skittering over the walls.

Max walks over and takes my hand, looking at it. "This..." He shakes his head. "Wow. Um, congratulations."

"Oh, thanks." I smile.

Max drops my hand and steps back, and I can feel a definite shift in the atmosphere between us. "Let's fight," he says, lifting his sword.

I nod and get into position, but Max is already on me. His sword swings straight for me. I barely lift my sai in time, catching the blade between them. I try to push him back, but he withdraws and swings again with a speed I've never seen him use before.

We don't pause for the entire session, and it's a constant dance of duck and dodge, parry and deflect. By the time Max calls it to a close, I'm covered in sweat, and my chest heaves from the exertion. I bend, bracing my hands on my knees as I try to catch my breath.

"Fuck, Max." I look at him, also covered in sweat and panting.

"What?" he snaps.

I just pant, shaking my head.

"Good job," Max grunts, taking my sai from me and returning them to the wall.

"Fuck," I say again, straightening and stretching my muscles out.

Max rolls his eyes. "It wasn't that bad."

"Who pissed you off?" I ask, raising my arms overhead.

Max shrugs. "No one. Just thought you needed to be pushed today."

I smile and walk to him, nudging him playfully.

Max raises a brow at me. "What?"

I nudge him again.

Max crosses his arms over his chest, frowning at me.

I jab him in the stomach.

"What?"

"Why aren't you playing?" I say, poking him in the stomach again.

"Playing?" Max looks at me like I am crazy. "Why would I *play*?" The disgust in that last word makes me wince.

"Right..."

"Better get back to golden boy," Max says, turning away from me.

I stare at his back, unsure what is wrong or what I have done. The venom in his words eats away at my happiness. I briefly wonder why, and that is when I have a horrendous realization. I consider Max to be a friend. Gross.

Well, if he doesn't want to talk to me, there isn't much I can do. With a last look at Max's back, I turn on my heel and leave the gym. I have one more stop I want to make before I head to the Morningstar House. I need to update the headmaster on what I learned from the stranger last night.

The walk allows my body to cool, but I can feel that I will be sore and stiff tomorrow. I stand outside the headmaster's door, preparing myself to face his overwhelming presence as I always do. Having Connor at my back last night had lent me more confidence than I thought.

I knock on his door and enter the room when he directs me to enter.

"Good morning, sir."

"Miss Tuatha De Daanan." He gestures to the seat across from him, and I sit down.

"I see congratulations are in order."

I frown and glance down at the ring. "Oh, thank you, sir."

He nods curtly. "You have an update for me?"

"Yes, I know it's a Saturday, sir, but I have discovered who's running *EverydayEmrys*."

He raises a brow. "All right."

"However," I look down, "I would like to talk to him before you reach out to him if you're planning to. It's someone I know personally, and I don't want him to feel blindsided."

He lifts his chin, waiting.

"It's Luke Morningstar."

"The youngest Morningstar," the headmaster replies, his expression impenetrable.

I nod.

"Surprising. How did you find out?" he asks, tapping a finger on the arm of his chair.

"We agreed it would be better if I didn't disclose that information." I remind him with a grimace.

His eyes flash. "When are you planning on speaking to him?"

"Tomorrow morning."

"Thank you, Miss Tuatha De Daanan," the headmaster says, giving me a dismissive nod.

"You are welcome, sir," I say, standing up.

I leave his office and head back home. My stomach twists and my joy seems shadowed, but I'm unsure why. I don't love how things changed with Max. Does this mean that now that I'm engaged, everyone is going to treat me differently? Am I feeling weird because I've not told Alice yet? I was going to text her, but it didn't feel right. I wanted to tell her in person, but now Max and the headmaster know before her, and I'm feeling weird about that, too. It was stupid of me not to realize people would figure it out based on the ring, and suddenly, it feels heavier.

My phone pings in my pocket, and I pull it free

CONNOR

I'm back at your dorm. Where are you?

SUMMER

Almost home, fiancé.

# 108

## SUMMER

"Summer!" I look back when I hear Alice's voice from behind me. She smiles and breaks into a bouncy jog to catch up with me.

I smile brightly at her. "Hi!"

Alice links her arm through mine. "I missed you last night, but I'm pretty sure I'm going to ace my final," she says excitedly. This plant is a large part of her final grade, and I love how excited she is about botany.

I squeeze her arm. "That's amazing, Al." I look down at my hand, the ring concealed by my sleeve. "I have some news, too."

"Oh?" Alice asks.

I push my sleeve back, showing her the ring glittering daintily on my finger. Alice stops and whirls on me, grabbing my hand.

"What is this? Are you... Did he?" She looks at me, her eyes wide, her mouth gaping.

I nod and smile brightly. The second my lips pull up, Alice takes that as confirmation that I'm happy, and she screams, jumping up and down.

I laugh and jump with her until she pulls me into a hug. "This is amazing! I'm so fucking happy for you, Sum." I hug her back, smiling. It's funny how telling my best friend made me feel light again. Alice's pure happiness for me wipes away Max's reaction. I push away thoughts of the uncomfortable conversation I have to have with Luke tomorrow and enjoy this moment of joy.

As we walk back to the dorm, we dive into wedding plans. I try to tell her I don't think it'll be for a while, but I get caught up in her excitement.

Connor grabs me the second I walk into the room, spinning me. "Hello, fiancée," he says, kissing me sweetly.

I smile against his lips. "Well, hey there."

"Oh, gods. You two are going to be even more unbearable now," Alice grumbles, but when I glance at her, she's smiling widely as she watches us. Connor doesn't put me down, but he looks at Alice, his smile almost blinding. "Congrats, bird brain."

"Thanks, Al. You okay with sharing your wife with me?"

Alice shrugs. "You're just providing the penis. I know I'll always be the favorite."

I laugh and nuzzle into Connor's cheek as they bicker. At that moment, it's as if I can see a glimpse of my future, and I feel an overwhelming sense of awe that it'll include these two wonderful people.

Connor and I lay in bed. He's sound asleep, and I am yearning to check my phone. Connor made the engagement post today. I wanted to wait to tell the stranger, but it didn't seem fair to prolong something that Connor was so excited about for the benefit of... someone else.

My phone pings, and my heart sinks. I already know who it is, and I can feel the looming fight between us, but if I want to keep him in my life, I need to face it.

I climb out of bed, the pattern of my nights getting so scarily familiar that I move on muscle memory. I unlock my phone, and the post flashes up. It's a basic engagement photo. My hand is in Connor's and the ring is displayed in that *I'm newly engaged and insufferable* kind of way. I can see the notification in the top corner, and I sit on the couch before opening it.

@1015
I suppose I should congratulate you.

Why is my heart beating so fast?

Why am I trying to justify this? I agreed to marry the man that I love.

There's a pause before he replies, and I can see him typing and then not, then typing again.

I exhale. I expected hostility, but his questions are a little too probing.

He starts typing and stops again. I wait for a whole minute before I message him again.

I can feel his sadness, and I'm a little disarmed by the fact he's not yelling at me. So, I decide the best course of action is to change the subject to something that might cheer him up.

I glance at the closed bedroom door before calling the stranger.

"Little fae," he says, his unglamoured voice again sending a shiver down my spine.

"Stranger," I say, shifting against the couch.

"You must be ecstatic," he says, his tone sharp.

"What's wrong?" I ask, but I immediately regret it. What a stupid question.

I hear him shift in his chair. It sounds like expensive leather. "Why do you ask that?"

"I can hear it in your voice."

He sighs, releasing so much pent-up frustration that it sounds almost soothing. "Just a long day," he says. Maybe he is okay with the engagement. Is it possible he's over his little crush on me and wants to just be friends? The thought makes me bristle a little, but I push it away, focusing on him.

"Is it about that female you like?" Oh, gods. Why did I ask that? Why am I poking the bear?

"Little fae." The tension crackles down the line between us. "I cannot talk about her without crossing boundaries, and we both know why that is."

Did he just confirm that it is me? Fuck, I don't know anymore. I sigh and pull my knees to my chest. "Tell me about it? Your day."

"You want to hear about my long day?"

I exhale. This tension between us is unbearable, and I can feel every knot of it. "More than anything."

I hear the clink of crystal and imagine a carafe filled with the most expensive scotch. He takes a drink before he begins. "It started fine, then turned into an absolute fucking wreck." The way he growls a little on the curse word makes my fingers tighten on the phone. "I had several meetings. Everyone is just fucking incompetent."

I lift my eyebrows, mentally filing that information away, and I decide to push my luck. "Meetings? What do you do?"

He tsks, but I hear a smile appear in his voice. "Nice try, little fae. You know I can't tell you that."

I huff. "Not even a clue? Must be a pretty shit job if you have meetings on a Saturday."

"No clues. And yes, my job is twenty-four-seven, most weeks anyway."

"Fine." I pout, even though he can't see me.

"Brat." He laughs darkly, and my toes curl. Fuck. He needs to stop calling me that.

"I–I'm glad you're not talking to me differently," I whisper.

There is a long silence, and I can hear him take another sip of his drink. When he replies, his voice is tight again. "What do you mean?"

"Well, my trainer at the gym treated me differently when he noticed the engagement ring."

"Differently how?" he asks.

I play with the ends of my hair. "He was just acting all serious with me. Wouldn't verbally jab back at me the way he usually does."

"You provoke him too? And here I thought I was special." The smirk is back, but there is a dangerous edge to it.

I bristle. "I don't provoke him. We spar. Today, he obviously wasn't in the bantering mood."

He takes a drink. "You sure it had to do with the ring?"

"Pretty sure. It was after he noticed it that he went weird." I shake my head, "Anyway, it's whatever. I saw the headmaster afterward."

"Ah, about the page?"

"Yeah, he was pretty dismissive, but I can't really blame him. I told him not to meet with Luke until I've spoken to him."

"Dismissive?"

I shrug. "Honestly, he's probably just sick of the sight of me. I don't imagine he sees a student in their whole time here as much as he has me in less than a year."

"Ah, but you're not just any student, are you?"

I scoff. "No, I'm the student who's getting stalked by a crazy serial killer."

The stranger laughs, and my lips twitch. "Well, that's one way to put it."

"Not exactly his favorite student. When he sees me, it's because someone has been brutally murdered or I have another scrap of evidence for him."

"But you're also insatiable for knowledge. I'm sure that is not the case with most of his students."

I groan. "I just fucking love learning."

It's true. I always have. Not only are innocent people being killed, and I'm being toyed with by some crazy fucker, but I've also not been able to sink properly into my studies. I know it is the least of my worries, but I miss it so much. Don't get me wrong, I still love the classes and I'm still performing well, but I miss having endless hours to spend with my nose in a textbook or fucking about with rune creations. Though, even if a murderer wasn't stalking me, my life is infinitely different from what it used to be. Where I used to only have learning, that's not the case anymore, and I'm not sure if I'm ready to admit how wildly my priorities are shifting.

When I accepted my place at Avalon, I decided I would spend the next four years here working hard and learning, and then I would end this thing with Torin one way or another. But in my first year, while I have learned a lot, I've also fallen into all these relationships.

"Is that right?" the stranger asks, pulling me from my thoughts.

"Yes. There's something so fucking empowering about it."

"Explain."

I shift on the couch and lie down, lowering my voice slightly. "You know when you're in a library and find a book with all this information you know little about? Doesn't it just give you a... buzz? Or when you're one-on-one with someone and they're teaching you something new... so hot." I stare at the ceiling. If anyone can relate to my crazy, it's the male I'm currently talking to.

The stranger clears his throat. "So you're attracted to intelligence?"

"Extremely. It... does something to me."

"I have the same," the stranger growls, "thirst."

"You do?" I whisper, anticipating his answer, anticipating the thrill of finally being understood.

"I do. Knowledge has always been something I crave." The way he says the word *crave* has my womb clenching.

"Teach me something," I whisper, the sound barely audible, and my breaths shallow.

"Something?"

"Anything."

"Hm." Gods, how does even that sound hot? This is getting bad. "The Runic Network works by replicating mortal social media without interacting with it. You can see all the mortal posts, but they can't see you. It took me almost a year to create. Most deemed it unnecessary, yet it has been integral to immortal advancement."

I bite my lip, trying to hold back my moan.

The stranger clears his throat again. "Little fae? Are you all right?"

"Absolutely." My voice sounds foreign, even to my own ears. I swallow. "We should talk about something else." My core pulses once and my breath hitches.

"Little fae?"

I clear my throat. "You know, I actually need to go."

"Oh?"

"I... Um... Yeah, I have to go. Got to keep within those boundaries and..." Stop fucking talking, Summer.

"Right. I'll speak to you later, then." The stranger saves me by interrupting me.

"Stranger?" I say, unsure.

"Hm?"

"Thank you for... still being you."

I hear him shift again, and that smile is back in his voice. "Well, who else could I be with you?"

"Like I said, the ring is changing people. I'm glad it's not changing you."

"Goodnight, little fae."

"Goodnight, my stranger." I end the call and close my eyes, cursing the words, the questions, the feeling in my core. There is some other explanation for this. It's probably due to my vulnerability and inability to let myself be happy. Am I self-sabotaging?

I take a breath, looking up at the ceiling, promising myself I will do better. One way or another, I will deserve Connor. I pray to the gods that I may be worthy and that I will settle into my peace.

# 109

## SUMMER

Zaththu
DOWN, DROP

I get dressed to work out, but I'm not feeling up to dealing with Moody Max today. What I really want to do is go for a run and clear my head. I want to be outside. The sun is rising, and people are already out and about. Surely, I'll be safe if I stick to the populated areas.

I kiss Connor's head before pulling on my running sweater and leaving the dorm. Outside, I press play on my running playlist and start down the path at a leisurely pace. I'm soon lost to the beat, matching my strides to the music. My breath mists in front of me, the cool air stifling my lungs and burning in the best way.

The headmaster approaches me on the path, stopping a few feet away. I stop and pull my earphones out.

"Miss Tuatha De Daanan."

"Oh, good morning, sir."

"Taking a break from the gym?" he asks, his hair darker with sweat and his eyes molten in the early morning sun.

My cheeks heat, and I feel like I've been caught misbehaving. "Well... I... Yes."

"Is something the matter?" he asks, his brows furrowing. I take care not to notice his workout clothes and how they cling to him.

"What do you mean?"

"You're blushing," he says matter-of-factly, but I want to die.

My hands fly to my face, and my cold fingers tingle painfully as they meet my warm cheeks. "Oh—"

"Are you ill?" he asks, tilting his head slightly.

"No, sir."

"I think you may be coming down with something."

My cheeks heat more.

"You're getting more red."

Fuck, what is wrong with me? Stop it, Summer. I back up, but my foot gets caught on the curb. I yelp as I lose my balance and start to fall. The headmaster's instincts are obviously well-honed. He grabs my arm, stopping me from falling on my ass. I grimace as he straightens me again, and I look up at him. His face is frozen in an expression of discomfort and annoyance at my stupidity.

"Are you all right?" he asks, but I can tell he's already assessed me and no longer cares.

"Yes, sir," I say, trying not to notice how his heat lingers against me.

He releases my arm and steps back. "I should get back to my run."

"Enjoy your run, sir."

He puts his earphones back in and takes off down the path. I watch him for a long moment, wondering what he listens to on his runs. Probably boring podcasts about sorcerer things.

Shaking it off, I set out on my run again. I let my mind wander, and I think about my year here. How I've changed, and how my life has changed. I started this year completely alone, and now I have a best friend, a fiancé, a... stranger, and a stalker. My ring glints in the sunlight as I run, and I smile at it. This is the first time I've ever felt like I truly belong somewhere.

I stop running and curse when I notice that my subconscious has brought me to the fucking gym. It only takes me a moment to decide to go in. I'm not hiding from fucking Maximillian Romulus just cause he's feeling weird that I'm getting married.

He smiles at me when I walk in. "Late today," he says in greeting, and even that pisses me off. I flip him off as I go to the weights.

He rolls his eyes and follows me to the weights rack. I pick up a dumbbell and stand in front of the mirror.

"Why are you mad today?" Max asks, leaning against a nearby squat rack.

I shake my head. "Not mad." I hold one of the dumbbells to my chest before doing a deep squat. "Talk to you later."

Max scoffs, watching me. "Come on, you're pouting over something."

I do another squat before looking at him. "Max, let's just leave it, okay?" I look back in the mirror to check my form before completing my set.

"Summer," Max growls as I sit on the bench, dropping the weight and taking a second before starting again.

When I don't reply and stand up, reaching for the dumbbell, Max picks it up and puts it back on the rack. "Tell me what's wrong."

I put my hands on my hips. "Why does it matter?"

"Because you're in my gym, pissed off at me."

I tilt my head, staring up at him. "What happened yesterday?"

Max tenses, but his face stays smugly unbothered. "What do you mean?"

I keep my gaze locked on him. We both know exactly what I'm talking about.

Max's stare turns into a glare, and I can feel him getting uncomfortable. Clearly, he's not going to talk about it. Fine.

I shake my head and look away, moving past him to retrieve my weight. Max grabs my arm. "Summer, hey."

I sigh and drop my head back. "What is with you, Max?"

He drops my arm, and I grab the weight before returning to my space and doing another squat. Max growls, still standing in the same place.

I glance at him in the mirror. "You want to talk? Tell me what happened yesterday."

"We... worked out," he says, and I can tell he had to force the words out.

I nod once, focusing on my workout again.

"And you told me about your engagement," he says, and I glance at him again.

"And from then on, you acted differently with me. Why?" I ask, probing at him. If Max and I are going to be friends, we need to have a base level of communication. I know he's a barely evolved caveman, but I think he can manage not to be a massive wang.

Max shrugs. "It just took me a moment to adjust."

I put the weight down and look at him over my shoulder. "Adjust to what? Nothing's changed."

Max looks away, mumbling something under his breath.

"What?" I ask

He sighs and rubs the back of his neck. "To you know... Golden boy winning again," Max growls, his voice a little louder,

I frown, turning to face him fully. "Winning?"

"You know." Max pointedly looks at the ring, and I frown, looking down at it too.

"He won... me?"

Max shrugs.

I shake my head, rolling my eyes. "You make it sound like there were others that wanted the prize." My brow furrows, and I try to decide if I am offended at being considered a prize.

Max shrugs again, and I roll my eyes before going back to my workout.

"Whatever. Are you going to fight or not?" Max grumbles petulantly.

"Are you going to be a normal asshole and not a weird asshole?" I ask. Max just stares at me. "Whatever. I'm so sick of you playing hot and cold. I get it. You don't want to be around me now that I've been tainted with gold and diamonds. Go away, Max."

Max blinks and straightens. "I'm playing hot and cold? Are you fucking serious?" he asks, his voice growing louder.

I glare at him.

Max throws up his hands. "You're the one who is constantly hot and cold. I need a fucking manual to figure out how I've pissed you off this time."

I cross my arms. "I'm only ever mad at you for being a dickhead."

"But your definition of dickhead seems to change every fucking day."

I shake my head and put the weight back on the rack. "Bye." I walk past Max, but again, he grabs me before I get out of reach. I don't look at him, but I do listen.

"Listen, my entire life, I have struggled and scraped and tried so hard just to get by. I work my ass off every day, and it just feels like golden boy gets everything without even trying."

I look at him, my brows furrowed. "What is it he has that you want?"

Max scoffs. "You mean besides the popularity, the girl everybody wants, the money, the family, the parents?" My brows furrow more. "You seriously never realized?" he asked.

"Well, I mean, sure, he's popular, and his family is great, but I think you're overstating it about me. Pretty significantly, actually. I'm literally one half of the disaster duo."

Max shakes his head, releasing my arm. "You don't know?"

"Know what, Max?" I ask, throwing my hands up.

"Look up *TuathaToday* on *Nexus*."

"*TuathaToday*? What's that? Some sort of weird fae club?"

"Just look it up, Summer."

I sigh and pull out my phone before typing it into the search bar. The page loads almost immediately, and I see exactly what he's talking about. It is dedicated to posting photos of fae around campus, although it looks like most of the posts from the past nine months have been of... me.

"What the fuck?" I whisper, scrolling through the pages. The posts range from details on my outfits to intimate details of my dates with Connor. "It's all me..."

Max snorts. "Mostly. But it's for hot fae."

"Who—"

"No idea," Max interrupts, wiping down the weights.

"But this is..." I stop, searching for the words.

Max chuckles. "This school has a thing for stalker accounts."

I shake my head, looking back at Max. "Well, this doesn't mean anything. They're just posts about where I am."

Max gives me a knowing look. "I wouldn't check the comments."

My stomach twists, and I select the most recent post, looking through the comments. I sneer. Most of them are akin to the ones the headmaster gets on his stalker page, but then I notice one in particular.

"Max. You've commented." He hasn't written anything lewd. It's mostly emojis, specifically the two eyes looking to the left.

"I might have," Max says, avoiding my eyes.

I scroll through, noticing that he has commented on most of the posts I open.

"You commented a lot."

Max snatches my phone from me. "I was curious."

"About?" I try to grab my phone, but Max leans his arm high against the wall, keeping it out of my reach. "About what you do, you know, outside the gym."

"What I do?"

Max nods. "You know I don't see you outside the gym, even though we go to the same school. So when I found the account and noticed the number of posts about you specifically, I was curious."

I give up on trying to get my phone and cross my arms, glaring at him. "You know, you could just ask me what I enjoy doing instead of being the lead fucking commenter on a weird as fuck stalker page about me. Now give me back my phone!"

Max lowers his arm, and I snatch my phone back, flipping him off as I leave the gym.

# 110

## SUMMER

Wynsha
MYSTERY,
UNKNOWN

**CONNOR**

How was the gym, fiancé?

T read the message as I walk, still feeling pretty uneasy about the *TuathaToday* page. I reply back to Connor with a link to it.

**CONNOR**

What the hell is this?

**SUMMER**

It's the equivalent to EverydayEmrys but for "hot" fae.

**CONNOR**

I don't like that.

**SUMMER**

Me neither. I need to swing by your place to talk to Luke about a project.

**CONNOR**

What project?

**SUMMER**

Just one for school. I'll meet you at the brunch place and we can go together?

**CONNOR**

On my way.

I shove my phone away and walk to the cafe, where I order two coffees, a breakfast burrito, and two hash browns. I scroll through the *TuathaToday* page. As expected, there are a lot of pretty mean comments from other fae beneath my photos. I close the page, not wanting to sour my mood even further.

I smile brightly when I see Connor's smiling face. He walks up to me and kisses me dramatically, dipping me low.

"Hello, gorgeous. You wouldn't happen to be single?" He smiles and nips playfully at my lips.

I pull back, pretending to be offended. "Excuse me, sir! I'm engaged, thank you very much." I wave the ring in his face, and he smiles even brighter, his skin glowing. Connor straightens, and my order number is called. Connor grabs the tray and leads me to a table. He pulls me into his lap and digs into his burrito. I eat one of the hash browns.

"I don't think I'm going to train with Max anymore," I say, looking down at my food.

"Why?" Connor asks earnestly.

I shrug. "I just don't think he likes me very much."

"He doesn't like you? How could he not like you?"

"The fact you guys have beef doesn't help," I say.

Connor winces. "I don't have beef with him. He has beef with me."

"Connor Azreal Morningstar, I don't have to be an angel to taste that load of horseshit."

"Well, he didn't like me first," Connor pouts.

My lips twitch. "Well, regardless. He says you have everything. Popularity, great family, me—"

"You?" Connor interrupts.

"I think he was just using me as an example. He was saying you're with me, and apparently, there are a few people who want to date me. Which I said was ridiculous. Then he told me about the page."

"Who wants to date you? We're engaged."

"Focus, big guy. No one wants to date me. He was just being a dick."

Connor frowns down at his burrito.

"What's wrong?"

Connor sighs. "I just don't like people thirsting after you."

I grab his face. "Well, maybe you should submit a photo of us with my ring visible."

Connor groans and holds up his phone. He kisses me hard as he holds my hand up, showing the ring clearly. After a long moment of getting lost in the kiss, he pulls back, and we look at the photo. We're kissing in the background, and it's artfully blurred except for the ring that is bright and center stage. Connor posts the picture, and then I place my hand on my thigh.

"Maybe one for *Nexus?*"

Connor takes another photo of the ring against my yoga pants and posts it before he kisses me again.

"Jealous, big guy?" I ask with a smile.

"Maybe," Connor moans as I deepen the kiss.

"So sexy." I tunnel my fingers into his blond hair.

Connor groans. "I love you so fucking much."

I pull back, letting Connor eat again. But after a few minutes, I'm pressing kisses along his jaw.

Connor moans. "I'm never going to finish at this rate."

"Oh, you'll finish, big guy," I growl in his ear.

Connor shivers but laughs, and I pull back with a grin, letting him eat in peace.

After breakfast, Connor and I walk hand in hand to his house. When we get there, he goes to find Rafe, and I wander up the stairs to Luke's room and knock on the door.

"Come in!" Luke calls out from inside, and I step in. I've never been in Luke's room, but it's tastefully decorated and very neat. He has gone with soft, neutral tones, and the room feels calm, spacious, and bright. He is sitting at his desk and closes his laptop when I step closer. "Hi, Summer!" He smiles brightly, and I can't help but smile back.

"Hi, Luke."

"Congratulations on the engagement! I'm so excited to have a sister."

I nod and sit down on the foot of his bed. "Thanks. Listen, I need to ask you something."

"Shoot," Luke says, turning his chair to face me.

I cross one leg over the other. "So, I need to ask you about," I take a breath, "*EverydayEmrys.*"

Luke's smile slowly drops, and he pales. "W-What? W-why would you need to talk to me about that?"

I uncross my legs and shift, sitting more on the edge of the bed. Luke's eyes have gone wide, and he is gripping the arms of his chair so hard his knuckles are white. I reach out and place my hand on his knee, trying to reassure him. If he isn't ready for people to know, I can only imagine how scared he must be right now. Luke is the kindest person I know, and I need him to know I am on his side and will continue to be forever.

"Luke. I know you run the page."

"W-what? How do you…"

I squeeze his knee. "This can stay between you and me. But I need your help with something."

Luke blinks, his face deathly pale. "O-okay," he says, admitting with one word that he does, in fact, run the page.

I smile, trying to comfort him. "Are there any comments that were deleted or blocked, maybe?"

Luke's brows furrow. Now that he has a task and something for his brain to focus on, the color returns to his cheeks a little. "I have a bot that clears messages if they're suspected to be from another bot."

"Can you access them even after they have been deleted?" I ask, sitting straight again and releasing his knee.

"Yes," Luke nods, "but why? And how did you find out?"

"I'm not sure how much you know about everything that's going on, but there have been things posted that could be helpful in the investigation into the murdered fae. I have a friend who is good with technology, and he found your IP address."

Luke's brows draw.

"He won't say anything either." Luke relaxes a little more again. "Can you print them out?"

Luke whirls in his chair and opens his laptop again. He types furiously, and then the printer whines into motion and starts churning away. Luke grabs the printouts and hands them to me. I scan them but decide it's not the best time to do this. Folding the stack of paper, I stand.

Luke is watching me, caution and fear shadowing his eyes. My chest aches for him. I know what it means to have a secret you are sure will destroy you if people find out, but I won't leave him alone in that place. I cup his cheek. "Luke?"

"Hm?"

My lips twitch at how similar he sounds to Connor when he does that. "We love you. Just the way you are. We all do. But this," I place my hand over his heart, "this isn't my secret to tell. So I will keep it for you. As long as you need."

Luke's chest heaves. Then he stands and pulls me into a hug, whispering shakily, "Thank you, Summer."

I squeeze him tight. "If you ever want to talk. You know where I am."

Luke pulls back and nods. The fear has gone from his eyes, but the sadness lingers. I stroke his cheek with my thumb before leaving the room.

# III

## SUMMER

### Valtha
HARVEST, REAP,
GATHER

I climb out of Connor's bed and pull on my clothes. Connor watches me, the sheets hanging low on his hips. "You really have to go?"

I nod, pulling on my yoga pants and my sweater. "Alice is home tonight, and we're hanging out."

Connor sighs heavily and dramatically drapes his arm over his face. "But baaaaaaaaaabe..." he groans, drawing out the word.

I laugh and kneel on the bed, bending to kiss him. "I'll see you tomorrow."

I pull back and sit on the edge to put my sneakers on.

"You want me to walk you home?"

"No, I'll be okay. I'll text you the whole way, and Alice is waiting, so I'll be fine."

"Promise?" Connor asks. I can tell he's feeling uncertain about it, but he's trying to give me the independence he knows I need.

I nod and get up to pull my jacket on. Connor climbs out of bed and slips on his boxers. I open his door and walk into Luke, whose fist is in midair, obviously about to knock.

"Oh, sorry, Summer. I didn't think you were still here," Luke says, a flush touching his cheeks. He probably does trust me, but it's a vulnerable thing that hangs between us, and he will naturally have nagging doubts.

I smile at him. "I'm just leaving."

Connor is pulling on his jeans behind me. "Hey, Luke. What's up, Brother?"

"I was wondering if you wanted to play video games with Rafe and me. We ordered food."

"Of course." Connor smiles, slinging his arm around me. I kiss his jaw.

I press a kiss to his jaw. He's such a good brother. He smiles down at me and leans in to give me a very heated kiss goodbye. When he breaks it, Luke is gone. I lick my lips and whisper, "I'll see you later, big guy." Connor nods and swats my ass as I leave.

I decide to stop at the headmaster's office before I go home, wanting to drop off the list as soon as possible. If it holds clues, I want to make sure he has it as soon as possible. Whoever this person is, they need to be caught before someone else gets hurt. I knock on his office door, silently praying that this weird daily ritual will soon be a thing of the past.

"Enter." Though I came here expecting to see him, I'm still somewhat surprised to find him in his office on a Sunday afternoon. I step in, but he doesn't even look up as I approach. "Miss Tuatha De Daanan." I inwardly cringe at that. Who fucking else would it be?

"Hello, sir."

He finally looks up at me. "Yes?"

"I spoke to Luke about *EverydayEmrys*."

He lifts his chin. "And?"

I pull the printouts from my bag. "These are the bot logs with the deleted messages." I round his desk and spread them out. "I've only skimmed it, but I believe there are more messages."

The headmaster picks up the first piece of paper, his eyes flicking rapidly across the page.

"Some of these make less sense than others, and sometimes the account has only posted these weird symbols." I point out one of them. It looks like an incomplete circle with a line slashing through it, another line meeting it perpendicularly.

The headmaster stands and shifts everything but the printouts to the edge of his desk. He spreads the pages out and then changes the order of them. He rearranges them a few more times before the symbols appear to connect.

I frown as I watch him work, racking my brain for any sliver of information. This aloof, powerful, dangerous man may be one of the most intelligent beings I have ever met. I may not have realized what he is capable of until now, but the killer knew. Why else send a message like this? Most beings would never have put it together.

The headmaster brushes the pad of his thumb along the bottom of his ring, slicing it. He draws a rune on one of the papers, and the symbols illuminate before lifting from the page, glowing and hovering before us. I stare at the rune. It's beautiful, so perfectly designed and crafted that it takes a few moments for me to notice the symbols that have now come together to form what looks like words.

My stomach twists as I look at the words. "Sir?" I whisper shakily.

"Some of this is inverted Ancient Daoine Sith," the headmaster says, his steely gaze sliding to me.

His brows draw, and he looks back at the word before holding his hand out. I glance at his hand and then place mine in his palm. His long fingers gently wrap around my wrist, and I watch intently as he draws another rune on the back of my hand. The touch of his warm blood and rough fingers against my skin makes me shiver. The rune glows faintly, and the moment it turns translucent, I realize what it does. He has given me the ability to manipulate the symbols in front of me. I tilt my head and start moving them around, trying to crack the code. The letters are so familiar, but there is something not right about them.

"This is in an old dead sorcerer language. It says, *Who needs light when darkness thrives?*" the headmaster says, making one of the sentences pulse.

"This one is in Ancient Greek. *Swallowed whole by the abyss,*" I say, reading it out loud.

The headmaster follows, noting the next one. "*Stars will bleed.*"

I look back up at the puzzle of the message written in Ancient Daoine Sith, and it finally clicks. Not only is it inverted, but it's also incomplete. I sift through the papers until I finally find the missing piece. "And the light, ousted." I point to a section, feeling the blood drain from my face. "And this says, *From the mountains to the sky,*" I release a shaky breath, "*I'll make their blood run down her face.*"

"Who?" the headmaster asks, mostly to himself.

A tear slides down my cheek, surprising me. I have no idea why I am so upset, but I am suddenly overwhelmed with sadness, grief, and guilt. Quickly, I swipe at the tear and ask, "Could the fae have lost during the rebellion?" I take a shaky breath, trying to think past the emotions swamping me. "But even if they did, I don't understand what any of this has to do with me. I'm nothing and no one. I wasn't even born."

The headmaster looks at me, his gaze hard. "There must be something we're not seeing."

I shake my head. "This was a mistake. I should never have come here." I close my eyes. "You were right at the start of the year. I'm trouble. I don't know what this means or why it is happening, but I've only brought pain and suffering to this school."

The headmaster turns to face me, gripping my arms. "The killer caused this. Not you." I stare at him, trying to find an ounce of comfort in his ice-cold gaze. "You are not at fault."

A soft sob breaks from me, and before I know what I'm doing, I am burying my face against his hard chest. He stands stiffly, and I can feel his angry gaze burning a hole in the top of my head, but I can't bring myself to pull back. His grip tightens, and then he releases me to wrap his strong arms around me. My body shakes and my tears wet his shirt, and though I don't feel comforted in the slightest, I do feel safe.

"It's not your fault, Miss Tuatha De Daanan," the headmaster repeats, his voice a fraction softer than before. His large body surrounds me, and I feel his power singing beneath his skin. In the safety of his arms, I allow myself to stop fighting and shielding. It takes a while, but eventually, I cry myself out. I take a deep breath and step back, blushing when I notice I've left makeup stains on his crisp white shirt.

"Oh, I-I'm so—"

The headmaster stops me by waving his hand, removing all traces of the soggy mess I had made of his shirt. My lower lip quivers again, and I look away, refusing to let any more tears fall.

"I will do everything I can to protect you," he says, and it sounds a bit like a vow. I look up at him to find his fierce gaze locked on me. "Thank you, sir."

I know he means it, but he wasn't able to protect the others. He has an entire school to care for, and I am just one person.

"I will continue reviewing these logs," he says, turning back to his desk and silently dismissing me. I leave his office, my mind whirling.

*From the mountains to the sky. I'll make their blood run down her face.*

A chill runs down my spine. As if the words summoned it, the memory of how I found Alicia flashes into my mind. I can still feel that poor girl's blood covering me and her dead eyes staring at me accusingly.

I walk faster, and I am nearly running by the time I get to Kelpie Hall. I slam the door behind me and bolt up the stairs, bursting into our dorm, out of breath and trembling. Alice's small body slams into me, pulling me from my terror.

"Hi!" she yells, wrapping around me. When she pulls back, her smile falls into a frown. "What's wrong?"

I shake my head and squeeze her tight, not wanting to let her go.

"Oof," she groans. "You're not freaking out about the engagement, are you?" she asks, her voice muffled against me.

I release her and pull back to look down at her, slowly relaxing. "What? No!"

Alice takes a deep breath, reclaiming the air I had squeezed out of her. "Okay, good. Tell me everything. Wait." She hurries into the kitchen, and I take off my jacket. Alice comes back with two margaritas and hands me one. "Have a drink and then tell me everything. Now that it's just us, I need the nitty gritty."

My lips twitch, and I take a deep drink. The tequila burns a trail down my throat. As the heat pools in my veins, muscles I didn't realize were tense relax. Alice grabs my hand and pulls me to the couch.

"Okay, first of all, who do I kill about you getting engaged without me being there?"

A laugh bubbles in my throat, and I take another drink. It figures that Alice wants to be as involved as possible. "Well, if you were there, it would have been considered a threesome. I don't think Connor is comfortable taking the wife sharing that far."

"Ew. Gross. Okay, whatever. You guys did it the mushy, intimate, only-the-people-directly-involved there way. Leave out those details, but tell me everything else, and start at the very beginning."

I nod and take another sip of my margarita. "Okay, well, it started with a pretty huge fight."

Alice chokes a little on her sip of margarita. "You and Connor... fought?"

I nod, swirling the cocktail umbrella around my drink. "A big one. Like we almost broke up."

"Fuck. Okay. Why?"

I exhale heavily. "Well, I don't think this information has been circulated yet, but... another body was found."

Alice's breath hitches. "Fuck. When?"

"Friday night."

"Fuck," Alice says again, slouching back on the couch. "And Connor found them?"

"Yeah. He was with Rafe. I don't think Rafe let him go in, but they were the first ones there. Anyway, Headmaster Emrys told Connor that I'm the target. Connor realized I knew and had been keeping it from him. He was... devastated."

Alice lifts her glass to her lips and gives me a hard stare over the rim. "Huh. Who could have predicted that?"

"Yeah, yeah," I say, shooting her an annoyed look. "You were right, but it was seriously rough, Al. I thought he would end it, and things were really awkward. But he surprised me once again and forgave me. And then he proposed."

Alice stares at me for a long moment. "Wait a minute. Just like that?"

"After sex. He was still balls deep," I say.

"Ew, but damn, you really do have the twenty-four karat pussy. Only you could go from almost breaking up to being engaged the next day," Alice muses.

"It's Connor. He's too good for me. He's so forgiving."

Alice snorts. "Well, he is an angel."

I roll my eyes. "Anyway, I'm not keeping things from him anymore. Well... mostly."

Alice lifts a questioning eyebrow.

"I couldn't tell him about the Torin stuff." I exhale. "And I know who runs *Every-dayEmrys*."

Alice sits up so fast, I'm surprised her drink doesn't spill. "Fucking what?!"

I nod and take another drink. Alice stares at me, waiting impatiently. "I can't tell you, Al."

"What do you mean you can't tell me? You gotta!" Alice says in outrage.

"I can't. I promised. Besides, the important thing is that I've found who it is, and I have the bot logs."

"Okay, what did they show?" Alice asks, obviously still annoyed that I have top-tier gossip I'm not sharing with her.

"I'll tell you tomorrow. I can't face it tonight." Alice's scowl deepens, and I try to head off the inquisition I know is coming my way. "Tell me what you've been up to for the past few days."

Alice eyes me grumpily but allows the change in subject. "Well, I was preparing for my exam in the greenhouses, and today I went to Drăculea."

"You did?" I ask, shocked she hadn't told me sooner.

Alice licks the rim of her glass and nods. "They had a vote about me being queen or whatever."

I gape at her. Why hadn't she told me? "Al, I would have come with you if I'd have known."

Alice takes a huge gulp of her drink. Whatever has happened, it is obviously bothering her more than she's letting on. "My father orchestrated it," she hisses.

I watch her face, trying to read her. "I take it that it didn't go well?"

Alive exhales heavily. "He's been made *Steward* until I graduate. He'll spend that time trying to subvert the Blood Call."

"Okay. But nothing has been decided for sure?"

Alice drains her glass. "Yeah," she says eventually after a prolonged, heavy silence. "I don't know why I care."

I shuffle closer. "You know I'll support you, no matter what."

A tear slides down her cheek. "I know. Fuck. They hate me. Why do I care?"

I lay my head on her shoulder, just being here with her. "I missed you."

"I missed you, too."

A comfortable silence falls between us, both of us processing. "He's just... lovely," I say, changing the direction of the conversation. I look down at the engagement ring, a tiny edge of unease sitting at the back of my mind. "This is fast, right?"

Alice hums thoughtfully. "Does it feel fast?"

I rub my thumb along the ring. "Well, I mean, we've only been together for what? Eight months?"

"Does it feel fast?" Alice repeats the question, obviously not satisfied with my answer.

"Sometimes," I answer honestly. But I'm not sure if it feels fast because I never anticipated this being my life or because it actually is fast.

"Because you don't want to marry him?" Alice asks, and I wince. Everything in me repudiates the question.

"I love Connor."

"Then what's holding you back?"

"I'm not holding back. I just... What if it doesn't work out?" I ask with a deep sigh.

"Why wouldn't it work out?" Alice asks.

"I... I don't know."

Alice shifts to face me, taking my hand. "Okay, a different question. What if it *does* work?"

I nod, looking back down at the beautiful ring. "Right."

I feel Alice watching me. "Is there someone else?"

I meet her gaze, taken aback by the question. "Alice, I love Connor."

Alice smiles. "Good. Well then, you're going to marry Connor." She squeezes my hand. "You're going to be happy." She squeezes my hand again. "You're going to have a million of his crotch goblins." My lips twitch. "And you and I are going to grow old together." We burst out laughing, and she pulls me into a hug. "This is right, Sum. We can overcome our pasts. We can decide not to let them define us." Her words help, at least for the moment. I hug her tight, thanking the realms for the best friend in the world.

A few margaritas later, after our conversation devolved into incomprehensible snorts and giggles, we both stumble to our rooms. I lay in bed, staring up at the ceiling. My fingers tap against my phone at my side, and I pick it up. I open the conversation with the stranger, staring at the call button.

Then my phone screen turns black except for the words,

*INCOMING CALL:*
*UNKNOWN.*

# II2

## SUMMER

Tahltha
TRADE, EXCHANGE,
SWITCH

I stare at the screen as the phone continues to vibrate. Cautiously, I swipe my thumb along the bottom, accepting the call.

"H-hello?"

"Little fae."

I relax immediately as the stranger's voice sends a trickle of warmth down my spine.

"Stranger." I exhale.

"What's wrong?"

"I get a call from a blocked number while playing cat and mouse with a serial killer? It's going to freak me out."

The stranger laughs darkly, and I relax.

"How did you get my number?"

"I've always had it." I hear his smirk.

"Right. Good with computers," I say wryly.

He laughs again, and then I hear him sit down. "Is everything all right?"

I sigh. "Yeah."

"Doesn't sound like it?"

I stare up at the ceiling. "Can we just talk about... anything else for a while?"

The stranger clears his throat. "Anything?"

"Anything," I whisper.

"Would you like to hear about my last trip to Faerie?"

My heart skips a beat, and I roll to my side, pulling my twig from Faerie out and holding it to my chest. "Please."

I hear the stranger exhale as if he had just lifted something heavy, and suddenly, my room is no longer my room. I sit up in my bed and look around at the forest now surrounding me. Blue and white fae lights line the pathway between the trees, and the canopy is so thick that barely any natural light penetrates. There is the faintest scent of evergreen and pine, and I eagerly sit up and move to the edge of my bed. I put my feet down, expecting to feel the soft soil of the outdoors, but I can still feel my plush rug.

Fae wander through the trees and go about their business. I have never seen anything more beautiful than this place. Tucked back into the forest, on the outskirts of the town, I can see magical little houses with wicker roofs and stone paths leading to their doors.

"I wanted to escape, and it was easy to slip away here."

The stranger's voice grounds me in the present, but my attention is on a young boy running across a grassy meadow. He's blurred, and I can only see enough to know he's maybe around eight or nine. There is a muffled shout, and the boy looks back. Whatever he sees propels him forward, sprinting as fast as his young legs can manage.

I watch, completely captivated, as he gets deeper into the forest and slows. The boy stops in front of a towering trunk and stares up at it. Though I can't see his expression, I can feel his awe at the sight of the great tree. He reaches out and presses his small hand to the bark, and I gasp when a door appears. He looks around furtively before slipping through, and I eagerly follow him on his journey. The path is dark, but he traverses it with confidence, and I gasp again when the tunnel opens to reveal what can only be described as a magic library.

*The Great Library of Faerie.*

"I knew the great library was there, but I never knew how to find it. I'm unsure why it opened for me, yet it did, and it was the most incredible sight I had ever seen. To this day, it remains one of the most wonderful things I've ever seen."

After the darkness of the path, the light is blinding for a split second before everything comes more into focus. Trees have molded and wound around the books, forming shelves, supports, and nooks. Their branches are adorned with words in Ancient Daoine Sith as if the books and the words within have become fully entwined with nature. Fae lights bounce through the stacks, illuminating titles written in every color imaginable. I catch sight of something written in Elder Daoine Sith, and I gasp and squeal at the same time. The boy and I stand together, looking around in awe.

This library is a living entity.

The boy walks through the library, ignored by the few fae inside. He explores the stacks, taking in the ornate beauty of the tomes. The projection is so potent that I swear I can smell the musky, heady scent of old books. The boy stops, and I feel his confusion as he stares at a pedestal in the center of the library. It glows, faint and then bright, pulsing as if it is the heartbeat of the library.

"I couldn't resist," the stranger's voice croons as the boy walks closer.

The book is one that I immediately recognize. It is the one the stranger gifted me at Yule, the one I have yet to destroy. The one still burning a hole in my wardrobe.

The boy's fingers tremble as he reaches for the book. He is expecting pain, but the book just continues to beat steadily. He picks it up, and the pulse starts to slow. It feels like something is dying. The boy panics and clutches the book to his chest, running from the library in fear.

"I was afraid I would get in trouble. So I kept it."

The boy runs back through the woods, and I can see his legs are threatening to give out. A spike of fear shoots through me when I see a tall, blurry figure in the distance. The boy falls to the ground, landing hard, and the whole world starts to shake. He looks around, and I can feel the surge of his fear. The tremors grow more intense, and I imagine I can feel the vibration through my feet. The ground directly beneath the boy's hand cracks and parts, the very fabric of Faerie eroding around him.

I cling to the twig, a tear sliding down my cheek as grief and fear tear at me.

"I should have stayed close. I shouldn't have gone exploring by myself."

I hold my breath as the story continues to play out. The world rocks again, and the boy lets out a scared yell as he gets to his feet and starts running again. In his panic, he runs into a girl not much older than him, with light blue eyes just like mine. She's holding a bundle of blankets, and she looks at the boy, her chest heaving. She says something, but I can't make it out. The boy concentrates on something, but this memory is fractured, and I can't tell what is happening.

Suddenly, my room looks like my room again. I release a breath I didn't know I was holding. The stranger is silent on the other side of the line.

"What happened then?" I ask, feeling like the story ended on a cliffhanger.

"I don't know."

I look down at the twig.

"Little fae?"

"Hm?"

"I just thought... you should see a glimpse of your home."

We sit in silence for a long moment. "Stranger? How did you know to call me?"

"It's almost an instinct. I felt like you needed to talk."

I return the twig to my drawer and lie down again.

"It's weird. It's almost like hearing your voice in my head," he says thoughtfully.

"I was about to call you, too." I take a deep breath. "Can I ask you something? And I need you to be really honest with me."

"Of course."

"Are Connor and I moving too fast?" I know the question is unfair. But I also believe that someone who understands me as deeply as he does will know the answer. While Alice's answer mollified my worries, she's only seen a snapshot of my darkness. She doesn't really understand its magnitude.

The stranger is silent for so long that I wonder if he's ended the call.

"Stranger?"

"What would you be like today if you had never met him?" he asks.

My brows furrow. "What do you mean?"

He clears his throat. "Do you think he's changed you?"

I shift to lie on my back. "Yes. I'm definitely warmer now. More open and learning how to trust and be trusted."

"Do you think he'll continue to do so? Change you?"

I pause, honestly considering the question. "I'm not sure."

"Then, yes. You're moving too fast."

My heart sinks, aching with the truth. "What?"

"He's not going to challenge you to change, to become more. To fulfill your potential."

"Right," I whisper, trying to truly hear what he is saying and not reject his words outright.

"You're young. I think you're rushing things," the stranger continues, and I close my eyes. "You must sense it too, or you wouldn't have asked."

"I tried to talk to Alice about it."

"And?"

"She doesn't understand. She asked if there was someone else."

"Angels aren't like fae. They don't have predestined mates. I don't know if he's the one for you."

"Mates," I say, rolling my eyes. That's all barbaric and misogynistic bullshit.

"What?"

"Nothing." I need to change the subject because, truthfully, the only time I feel like we're rushing things is when I'm not physically with Connor. So, it might just be nerves, and I have to believe it's just nerves. "Look up *TuathaToday*."

"What? Why?"

"Just type it in."

I hear him shift and then typing on his laptop. The silence changes from comfortable to rage-filled. "What is this?" he hisses, the anger in his voice sending a thrill to my core.

"You know how the headmaster has a stalker page? This one is for fae."

"These are all pictures of you," he growls, the sound deadly.

"Stranger?"

"I have to go," he snarls, and the line goes dead.

I sit up, staring at the dark screen in shock. Finally, I set the phone aside and start to get ready for bed. Undressing, I pull on one of Connor's t-shirts, wash my face, and brush my teeth. The entire time, I am replaying the sound of rage in the stranger's voice. There might be something really wrong with me because a dark, wicked part of me... liked it.

I just slipped back beneath the covers when my phone alerts again. I unlock it, and a live feed opens, showing an alleyway somewhere in what looks like Camelot. Through the gloom, I see a shifter leaning against the wall, smoking a cigarette. I am pretty sure his name is Jake.

Suddenly, he is jerked off his feet and thrown, smashing into the opposite wall. I jump and nearly drop my phone. I rest my hand on the pillow and watch in horror as an invisible entity beats him to within an inch of his life. His shifter friends arrive but struggle to help, given they can't see the attacker. I look around, trying to figure out what I need to do. Should I contact the headmaster? He is off school grounds. Maybe I should contact law enforcement in Camelot. My phone vibrates again.

*INCOMING CALL:*
*UNKNOWN.*

I answer the call.

"It's taken care of," the stranger snarls down the line. I pull the phone from my ear and search TuathaToday. It looks like it has been wiped from existence. I can't find even a trace of it.

"I... Was that... you?"

He doesn't answer immediately, but then he growls, "The page is down."

"Stranger," I whisper. "It was you."

He pauses for a long moment. "Yes."

I expect to feel fear, disgust, and horror, but my stomach flutters, and my skin tingles.

"Are you afraid?" he asks darkly, and I swallow my moan.

"No." I silently curse at how low and husky my voice sounds. Fuck. Stop it, Summer. This is dark.

"No?" he asks, a rumbling purr of interest edging into his voice.

"No."

"What are you then?" he asks dangerously.

"I... Boundaries!" I know it reveals too much, but it is all I can muster.

"Oh. I should hang up, right?"

"Probably," I grate out.

He doesn't hang up, and neither do I.

I relax my hand on the phone when it creaks, unsure when I started holding it in a death grip.

"He had a video of you... changing," he says, his voice furious and so damn sexy.

"What?" I hadn't seen that on the page. How the fuck did he get that?

"He had more than was on the page," he growls.

"Did you watch it?" I ask, unsure what answer I want to hear.

"No. I shattered his phone, skull, and then his hard drive. Once I saw it was your face, I couldn't continue."

"Oh."

"I wanted to kill him," he growls darkly.

I swallow, knowing that a shifter would heal from a broken skull, but damn, it would be painful and slow. "Because he made the page?"

"Because he saw you naked. Because he got to see what does not belong to him."

My breath hitches. "Stranger..."

"Because he saw what belongs to *me*," he snarls, sounding feral. "You belong to *me*."

"W-What?" My whole body tenses.

"You can enjoy the boy because I am held in check by circumstances, but in the end, it will be you and me." His voice sounds even darker and more dangerous.

"Stranger," I warn, but my voice shakes. I will never admit it to anyone else, but it's not because I am afraid.

"Your name will never be Summer Morningstar," he snarls, and the line goes dead.

# 113

## SUMMER

*Soltha*

LOVE

I stare at my phone, his words circling my mind.

*You will never be Summer Morningstar. You belong to me. You will never be Summer Morningstar. You belong to me.*

The live feed vanishes, along with any evidence of it. Maybe I made it up. Or maybe it was a tequila-fueled dream.

Alice: Damn, did you see the ghost kicking that shifter's ass?

> **ALICE**
>
> Damn, did you see the ghost kicking that shifter's ass?

He obviously wanted to make a show of it. I bet everyone in the school got the alert about the live feed. My head is a complete fucking mess, and my chest is still heaving from the phone call with the stranger. I get up and pad to Alice's room, wordlessly climbing into bed with her.

"Hey," she says, turning to face me. I nuzzle into her, not wanting her to see my face, not wanting to talk about what just happened.

Alice wraps her arms around me and squeezes.

"I love you."

"I love you, too."

I lay my head on her shoulder, the words churning inside me. The secrets, the lies, the feelings are overwhelming me. "It was the stranger," I whisper.

"Hm?"

"The video," I whisper again.

Alice pulls back, trying to see my face, but I nuzzle into her more. "The ghost?" she asks.

I nod.

"Why?"

I shake my head. "Just... don't ask."

Alice pauses for a moment before squeezing me. "Okay," she says, not pushing.

I sigh heavily.

"What?"

I tighten my arms around her

"I got you," Alice says.

"Al?"

"Yeah?"

I look up at her, and her concerned brown eyes lock on me. "I need you to make sure I get down the aisle with Connor."

Alice blinks. "What?"

"Just promise me. Even if I freak out or if... something happens."

Alice holds up her pinky. "I promise."

I link my pinky with hers and exhale heavily, relaxing a little. If I can rely on anyone, it's Alice. I cuddle into her more. "Connor is mine, right?"

"After me. But, sure. I guess."

I nod and relax against her. My last thought before I drift into sleep is that I am relieved to be escaping all this for a while.

Alice and I walk to class, stopping at the coffee cart on the way.

"I think I should wear blood red as maid of honor," Alice ponders, playing with a sugar packet.

"You can wear whatever you want."

"Okay, good. Cause I've already been looking, and I think I've found a designer." Alice pulls her phone out and finds the webpage of an insanely expensive designer who appears to specialize in gothic chic.

"Summer?"

I turn around to see Brett walking toward me. I smile at him. "Hey! It's been ages!" I smile, pulling him into a hug while Alice sneers at him.

"Yeah, I've joined this shifter club. It's keeping me pretty busy. I also saw you're engaged. Congrats!"

I nod, looking down at the ring. "Thanks, it was a total surprise!"

Brett chuckles. "For no one but you, it seems."

"What?" I ask, frowning.

"Well, he's completely obsessed with you. Anyway, later." Brett runs off to catch up with his friends.

Alice hands me my coffee. "That was weird," I say, watching Brett stride away.

"Was it? I wasn't paying attention," she says, still looking at her phone.

I shake my head. "I am probably just being paranoid. Anyway, show me this dress."

Alice taps on one of the dresses. "Okay, so I'm thinking this, but less tulle and more lace. And the skirt needs to be a deeper red than that."

"It's beautiful, Al."

"Have you started looking at dresses?"

"No. I'm barely engaged." I laugh, and Alice moves in closer.

"Sum?"

I glance at her.

"You know that thing you asked of me last night?"

I nod.

"It's because of the stranger, right?"

"We should get to class," I say, looking away.

Alice frowns but drops it, and we hurry to class. Professor Brooks is showing us new kinds of runes, and normally, I would be totally engaged, but my mind is so busy that I can barely concentrate. Alice senses my mood, and her hand is in mine the whole day. I know I'll feel better when I get to see Connor at lunch.

We are on our way to the canteen when Alice suddenly stops in the middle of the corridor. I squeeze her hand and look at her. She looks paler than usual.

"You okay?" I ask, ignoring all the tuts and grumbles of the annoyed people having to walk around us in the busy hall.

She groans softly. "I'm not feeling great. I think I'm going to go home for the rest of the day."

I feel her forehead. It is cool to the touch but not clammy or sweaty.

"I'm okay, just feeling a little gross."

"I can come with you?"

Alice shakes her head. "I'm a big, bad vampire. I'll be fine."

I squeeze her arm. "I'll text you later."

Alice nods and leaves, heading home. My stomach twists in concern for her, but she obviously wants to be ill alone, so I continue to the canteen to see my Connor.

I grab a sandwich on the way to the table, and the second I see him, my chest feels less constricted. It feels better still when I drop down next to him and better again when he wraps his big arm around me and pulls me against his side.

"Where's Alice?" he asks, kissing my temple.

"She went home, not feeling well."

"Vampires can get sick?" Zane asks with a frown.

I roll my eyes. "Of course they can. She'll be fine in a bit. She's maybe had some bad blood or something."

I nuzzle Connor's jaw. "How was capstone?"

"It was good. I learned a lot today."

"Oh?" I ask, honestly interested.

Connor nods, and I close my fingers around his tie. Twisting my hand, I pull him closer to me. "Tell me what you learned."

"Shield runes," Connor says, his eyes darkening with desire.

Zane groans. "Please. We're all here."

I ignore him and kiss Connor deeply, his soft lips pulling a deep moan from me. Connor slides his fingers into my hair, his big palm cupping the back of my head. His tongue slides teasingly along my bottom lip, urging me to open.

I'm vaguely aware of Ashley arriving and she and Zach flirting, but I'm so lost in Connor's kiss that I barely hear it.

Connor finally breaks the kiss, and I sit back, feeling a little dazed. I look around just as a cute little brunette in an indecently short skirt walks by. She gives Zane an unmistakable come-hither look and sashays toward the door. Zane perks up as if he just scented his favorite meal, his eyes locking onto the sway of her hips and the sassy swish of her skirt.

Rafe rolls his eyes. "Just go after her. She obviously wants your attention."

Zane stubbornly remains seated for a long moment, but when she glances back at him over her shoulder, he gets to his feet and starts toward her. He doesn't even pause but sweeps her up and hikes her over his shoulder, carrying her out of the cafeteria.

Rafe's lip curls in a sneer. "He has all the charm of a rock."

My lips twitch.

"He's insufferable," Zach says, but Ashley quickly distracts him.

"Am I insufferable?" Connor asks, biting my cheek playfully.

I grab his face. "Not often."

"But sometimes?" he asks with a small grin.

I lean in, biting his bottom lip. "Only when you're too irresistible to me."

Connor groans and whispers, "Stacks?"

I nod, kissing him deeply.

Connor lunges to his feet and grabs my hand, dragging me toward the door. I laugh as we charge through the halls of the school, my heels barely touching the ground thanks to Connor's long strides. When we get to the library and near our shelf, Connor picks me up and kisses me deeply. His palms cup my ass, and his fingers slide over my panties, checking if I am ready for him. A low moan fills the air, and Connor stops dead.

Connor pulls back and then scowls when he hears Zane's whispered voice.

"Have they... stolen our spot?" I whisper, feeling outraged and betrayed.

Connor peeks around the corner and quickly pulls back. "They have." He sighs and lowers my feet to the ground.

I adjust my skirt and cross my arms. "Well, I'm going to go stop them."

"Babe, you can't do that," Connor says, biting his lower lip.

I pout. "But I'm horny," I growl.

Connor pulls me away so we can't hear them anymore, and then he pulls me against his chest. "I know, but if you fuck with him, he will make it his life's mission to barge in on us whenever possible."

I narrow my eyes in the general direction of our stack. "You get this one, dick."

Connor and I walk hand in hand back to the cafeteria, but I'm bristling the whole way. When we sit back down at the table, I pull my phone from my bag and send a message to Alice.

SUMMER

Zane is a dick. He took Connor and my's stack.

So you can reap revenge or whatever. No rules.

Also, how are you feeling?

Connor nuzzles into my neck, and I glance at him. "What?"

"You're cute when you're murderously horny."

My lips twitch, and I lean in, kissing him softly. I spend the rest of lunch chatting with Connor and Luke. I check my phone on the way to my next class, frowning when I see Alice hasn't replied. She's chronically on her phone. She is probably just sleeping, but I have a gnawing feeling of dread in my gut that won't go away.

When she still hasn't replied by the end of my class, I try to call her. The line rings and then disconnects after a while. I start toward my last class of the day, but something isn't sitting right with me. Every instinct I have is whispering that something is wrong, so I decide to skip and go home to check on Alice.

All the way home, I try to convince myself that she's just sleeping. I'll wake her up, and she'll be pissed at me for worrying and disturbing her rest. No doubt, she'll make my life hell for a couple of hours.

I nearly run up the stairs to our floor. Music is blasting from somewhere, and my steps slow the closer I get to our dorm, realizing it's coming from our place. I open the door, the music blaring aggressively from the stereo in the living room.

"Al?" I call out, but the music drowns out my voice. I look around, not noticing anything out of place. Cautiously, I walk across the room to turn the music off. My ears ring a little in the shock of the absolute silence. "Alice?" I say again, but there is no reply. Dread writhes inside me as I walk to her door, knocking and calling for her again. When there is no reply, I wrap my hand around the doorknob and slowly push the door open.

The first thing I see is her empty bed, but then... A scream rips through the air, fracturing the silence.

Everything stops.

# 114

## SUMMER

*Saitha*
CUT, SLICE, DIVIDE

The pain is unbearable.

Alice. Alice is... dead.

Alice lies in front of me. Red blooms from her, slowly seeping around the silver blade embedded in her back. I move forward, my feet moving of their own accord. I fall to my knees beside her, landing in the pool of her cooling blood. My heart feels like it is stuttering in my chest as I reach a shaking hand toward her. I can't help my cry of despair at the stark cold of her body.

*Alice.*

*Alice.*

*Alice.*

I try to think, try to do something, but she's gone. What do I do? What do I do? Fuck!

I sit up, unsure at what point I lay down. I scramble, my hands sliding through her blood as I try to find my phone. Suddenly, I'm lifted from the floor, and I look up to see the headmaster's icy gaze locked on me. He's saying something, but I can't hear him. All I can hear is my heart breaking. All I can feel is overwhelming grief. The headmaster says something else, but I can't hear. I can't even see with the tears blurring my eyes. Fuck, when did I start crying?

*"Miss Tuatha De Daanan. Stop."*

I try to blink away the tears, but they won't stop. The headmaster guides me to the bed and sits me down before he moves to Alice. I wipe my eyes, getting a moment's reprieve from the blurriness, but it comes back tenfold when I watch him pull the blade from her back. I swipe impatiently at my tears again. It's not a blade. It's a stake made specifically for destroying a vampire. I slide off the bed, needing to be closer to Alice.

"There's no need for hysterics," the headmaster growls, and finally, I can hear him. I crawl closer to Alice and blink up at him, too afraid to hope.

"W-What?" I ask, my throat raw as if I'd been screaming for hours.

"Get up," the headmaster snarls, and I look away before shakily getting to my feet.

The headmaster wipes off the stake, but my gaze remains on Alice, my perfect best friend, lying lifeless on the floor.

I whimper, looking down at my hands, coated in *her* blood. This is wrong. It should have been me.

Alice's body jolts suddenly and violently. I yelp in surprise and fall back onto the bed. Her body spasms again, and then once more before her chest rises, and she releases a deep groan. "Fuck," Alice moans, her fingers twitching a little. I watch with wide eyes, counting her breaths. "Motherfucker," she growls, reaching behind her to touch the gruesome wound left on her back.

"A-Alice?" I whimper, sliding back down onto the floor. The rug squelches, saturated with her blood.

"Owwwwww," Alice groans, shifting a little.

I sob loudly and pull her to me.

"Only twelve left, Miss Legosi. That was careless," the headmaster admonishes.

Alice gently pushes at me, obviously in pain, and my tight hold on her isn't helping. "What happened?" she asks, but I can't stop kissing all over his face, the tears falling freely. "That fucking sucked."

The headmaster leans against the wall, inspecting the stake. "Do you remember anything?"

Alice strokes my hair and hugs me back, finally realizing what a mess I am. "Summer, I'm okay. I have thirteen lives."

I cling to her and sob.

"One benefit to being your father's heir," the headmaster adds.

I keep smothering her in kisses and hugging her tightly.

"Sum, come on. I only died a little."

The headmaster clears his throat pointedly. "Miss Tuatha De Daanan. Miss Legosi. Can we focus on the matter at hand?" We both look up at him, responding to the command infusing his voice. "The murderer will not know about this... side effect of Miss Legosi's lineage."

I struggle to my feet and help Alice up. We are both as wobbly as newborn deer. Alice looks down at her shirt in dismay. It is covered in blood and has a huge hole in the back. "This was my favorite shirt."

The headmaster pins us in place with his silver gaze. "The killer must not know about her survival. They must believe they succeeded."

I look down at my bloody hands. "We can use this to our advantage," I say, understanding. Up until now, the killer has been a step ahead, but this may even the odds.

The headmaster looks at me, his gray eyes molten. "You must act as if she is dead. They will be watching you closely."

I nod once. "I can do that."

"We have to make it look like they succeeded in their assassination attempt," he says, looking at Alice.

Alice shrugs. "My comeback will be divine."

"You'll need to hide somewhere."

"She can go to the Morningstar House," I offer.

"They will need to be discreet," the headmaster says.

"They will be," I assure him.

The headmaster waves his hand, opening a portal. "Stay out of sight until I say otherwise, Miss Legosi."

Alice squeezes my hand before walking through the portal. The headmaster waits for it to snap shut behind her and then waves his hand again. Alice's body reforms on the ground. My stomach drops at how realistic it is, but I steel myself.

Alice is safe. Alice is with Connor. Alice is safe.

"I will need to play a role as well," the headmaster says, and I force my gaze away from the illusion. "I cannot be here as your headmaster." He closes his eyes, and his body starts to change. When he opens his eyes again, they are blue instead of his gray, and his dark hair has been replaced with blond. I blink as I look up at Connor instead of the headmaster.

"I understand that this will be strange. But it is necessary," he says, and I wrinkle my nose, deeply disturbed when the headmaster's voice emerges from Connor's lips. I'm very aware it's not Connor standing in the room with me. There is none of the comfort or warmth that Connor elicits in me.

The headmaster turns toward the mirror, trying to mimic Connor's playful smirk. He tries on a few of his other expressions and softens his face a little. "I do not enjoy falling one step behind the killer. I need a reason to stay close to you. Mister Morningstar will have to remain in hiding with Miss Legosi."

"Oh, right. Well, I'm going to go shower, and then—"

"You cannot wash off the blood, Miss Tuatha De Daanan. Every minute counts at the moment."

"Okay, tell me what to do," I say with a weary sigh.

He nods at Alice's corpse. "As you were a moment ago."

I swallow down the bile as I look back at Alice's body, chanting in my head, *Alice is safe, Alice is with Connor, Alice is safe.* I kneel beside her.

The headmaster picks my phone up off the floor. It is covered in blood, and it coats

655

his hand as he dials. He holds it to his ear, and this time, when he talks, it's almost a perfect imitation of Connor.

"Hi, I uh... need to report a murder. It's my fiancée's roommate. Her name is Alice. She's been staked."

I force myself to cry so that I can be heard in the background, and I know when they come, I'm going to have to actually cry. I'm going to have to unlock that unbearable pain I felt when I first saw her.

"Please, hurry," the headmaster says as Connor before ending the call.

He paces around the room until he hears the authorities arrive, and then he kneels beside me and wraps an arm around me. "It's time, Miss Tuatha De Daanan," he whispers as they come through the front door.

I close my eyes and let the shock and trauma surge through me, feeling every fucking ounce of agony from finding my best friend lying here dead. The tears come even easier than I expected, and soon, the sobs are so powerful that I can barely breathe. The headmaster, as Connor, presses my head into his neck, guiding me to lean into him.

"Let's let them take care of this, babe. We should go to my house," the headmaster says again, and I let Connor's voice soothe me even though I know it's not him.

I shake my head. "I can't leave her," I sob, clinging to Alice.

The headmaster stands, lifting me with him. "Come on, babe." My knees buckle, but he supports me, leading me out of the room. We keep the facade up all the way to the Morningstar House. I'm hyper aware of the attention we're garnering. We are both covered in blood, and I am sobbing so hard I can barely walk.

"Almost there, babe," he croons.

The moment we enter the house, he releases me and drops the glamour. He slices his finger, drawing a rune on the back of the door. It's clever and pretty complex. It'll keep anyone from spying through the windows or listening in.

"Well done. You did well," the headmaster says, turning back to face me.

Connor pounds down the stairs, his face paling when he sees me covered in blood. "Babe."

Another sob bubbles from me, and I run to Connor. He wraps his arms around me and lifts me against his chest. "Fuck. When Alice arrived covered in blood, I–I thought the worst," he says, his hands roaming over me, trying to convince himself I'm real and unhurt.

"You need to stay home for a while, big guy," I say, mumbling the words against his neck.

The headmaster pushes off the door. "I trust you have this handled, Miss Tuatha De Daanan. I should make myself seen."

I turn my head to look at the headmaster. "Tomorrow morning?"

"I'll be here," he says, opening a portal and disappearing through it. I wrap my arms and legs tighter around Connor, clinging to him as if he might disappear. "Fuck. Is Alice all right?"

Connor exhales a laugh. "She's fine. Pissed about her shirt."

I pull back a little, trying to force myself to let him go. "I desperately need a shower."

Connor tightens his hold and carries me up the stairs, refusing to put me down. I am grateful. If he lets go, all my pieces may fall apart.

# 115

## SUMMER

*Rinthae*
STAR

Connor's body vibrates with tension, but he remains silent until we are in the bathroom. He sets me on my feet and makes sure I am steady before he asks, "Why do I need to stay home?"

I strip off my clothes, cringing as the blood-soaked material peels away from my skin and then again when it lands on the ground with a heavy, wet thud. I knew I was covered in Alice's blood, but I had no real idea how covered I was. No wonder people were staring as I walked to the Morningstar House. For some reason, I didn't react as viscerally to Alice's blood against my skin as the fae girl's. I think because, at first, I was lost to my devastation, and then after, I was lost to my relief. I am exhausted, but the emotions are still swirling angrily inside me. There is no doubt that I am going to crash soon.

"The Headmaster is going to glamor himself as you," I say weakly, stepping into the shower and turning it on. I adjust the temperature and groan when scalding hot water sluices over my skin.

Connor leans against the counter. "What? Why?" he asks, watching me.

"To keep you safe and to watch what's going on."

Connor shakes his head, and I can see he's struggling with this. "I can protect you. It should be me."

I tilt my head back, scrubbing the dried blood from my face before looking at him over my shoulder. "No. You stay home. Protect Alice."

Connor growls, and I think it's the first time I've heard that sound come from him. He undresses and steps into the shower behind me. "Summer."

I turn to face him, and he wraps his arms around me. "I need you to protect Alice.

For me." My voice cracks with emotion. I know I'm asking a lot from him, but I need him and Alice safe.

Connor presses his forehead to mine. "And I need to protect you."

I close my eyes and lean into him. "The headmaster isn't won't let anything happen to me, big guy." I open my eyes and meet his gaze. "You are the only person I trust to look after Al," I whisper, my chest still aching from the loss of her, however brief.

Connor tightens his arms around me, nearly crushing me. "But you're my fiancée."

I place my hand on his chest, over his heart, his wonderful, kind, perfect heart. "I need you alive, Con." My voice breaks again, a tear sliding down my cheek. "I need Alice alive." My mind eagerly provides the image of Alice lying in a pool of her own blood, making me wince. "Seeing Alice like that today." I choke down a sob. "I need you both alive."

Connor cups the back of my head and presses my face against his neck. "I'm here, babe. I'm here, and I'm not going anywhere."

I whimper and pull back, looking up at him. His eyes are still bright with worry. I lean against him, letting him take my weight, and kiss him deeply. Connor groans, and even in that sound of pleasure, I can hear the pain in his voice. His care and concern are in his every touch, in how he clings to me, holding me to his body.

I wrap my arms around his neck and deepen the kiss, tears flowing freely as I tangle my fingers in his hair. "I'm not going anywhere," Connor whispers, pressing my back to the shower wall and bracing a hand above my head. He drags his lips along my jaw and down my neck. "We're forever," he murmurs against my pulse. He slides his hand down my side and over my hip, looping his forearm under my ass. His biceps bulge, but he picks me up easily. I whimper and tilt my head for him, wrapping my legs around his waist.

Connor is so close we are sharing breath, his gaze locked with mine. "You're going to be Summer Morningstar," he says as he shifts his hips and slowly pushes inside me. I tighten my fingers in his hair. "My wife. My love. My everything," he moans as he starts to move. "I love you, Summer."

I gasp as Connor fills me, claiming me. Tears still trail down my cheeks, but I can't look away from Connor. "I love you," I whisper breathlessly.

Connor's steady thrusts turn erratic, and I can feel his panic. I pull his head back to mine, our lips colliding in desperation. Steam roils and swirls around us, the hot water slicking our bodies.

Connor digs his fingers into my ass and pulls my hips toward him as he slams hard into me, and we both moan at the feeling. My core coils, my orgasm within reach. Connor's groan is deep and guttural, his thrusts turning nearly savage. His teeth clash with mine as he claims my mouth. All signs of my careful, sweet lover are gone. I scream into the kiss and explode around him. My pussy clenches almost painfully around his cock, squeezing his release from him. Connor's shout is only slightly muffled, and I feel the deep, aching throb before the heat of his release fills me.

His hips slow, our ragged breaths interspersed with moans as aftershocks ripple through us. I pull back and look at Connor, and he tenderly cups my cheek. I cover his hand with my own and close my eyes.

"Everything is going to be okay," Connor says, kissing me again. This one is so tender it brings tears to my eyes. Wrapped in his love, I start to feel more at ease.

"Summer! The headmaster is here!" Alice calls from downstairs. Connor groans, his cock still buried inside me.

"I need to get dressed, big guy," I say, kissing his shoulder. He grunts again but rolls off me. I climb out of bed and pull my uniform from his closet. Not enjoying the walk of shame when I started sleeping over unexpectedly, I had started leaving some spares here.

Connor sighs and lounges on his bed, watching me as I slip on my underwear. "It's weird not to get dressed with you."

My lips twitch, and I wiggle my skirt over my hips, fastening it at the waistband. "I know, but you get to stay in bed a while longer."

Connor moves one of his hands behind his head, looking like the picture of male satisfaction. I'm not sure if I've ever had as much sex as we did last night, but I had a lot of trauma to work through. Given that I only initiated it a couple of times and the rest was Con, he did, too. We'd barely slept, and I admit I was thankful for that. I know I'm just delaying the inevitable. The nightmares won't be denied, but at least I didn't have to deal with them last night when it was all so fresh.

I pull my shirt on and tuck it in. "You going to miss me today?"

Connor nods. "So much."

I pull on my blazer and then look at my heels. "I might just wear my flats today. Don't need my heels to kiss you."

Connor sits up. His expression is careful, but I can see possessiveness edging into his eyes. "You need to act normal, babe."

I purse my lips, thinking. "Yeah, but I also need to act like my best friend has just been brutally murdered." I glance at him. "Should I even be going in today?"

Connor tilts his head. "You know I want to answer no to that, but the headmaster is right. We're on the clock. Alice can't pretend to be dead for long."

"You are both right. Okay, big guy. I'll see you later," I say, pushing my feet into my heels and giving him a quick kiss.

"Be safe, babe."

I wink at him and leave his room. The headmaster is standing in the living room, and Alice is talking incessantly at him about her ruined shirt. I'm not sure I've ever seen anyone look so miserable. He locks eyes with me and lifts his chin as I descend the stairs. "Are you prepared?" he asks, cutting Alice off.

I nod, holding his gaze.

"You need to sell Alice being dead," he says.

"I have done my makeup to look like I was crying all night," I say, stating the obvious since he didn't seem to notice.

Alice sighs and walks toward the stairs, stopping to squeeze me tight before heading to Zach's room.

"Is this what a grieving person wears?" the headmaster asks, assessing my outfit.

"This is the uniform, sir," I say dryly.

"Hmm," he says, sucking a tooth grumpily. It seems the headmaster is having a bit of a rough morning. He stares at me a moment longer but finally sighs and closes his eyes. I watch as the glamour takes shape, and Connor appears before me. His eyes snap open, and he pulls Connor's face into a sympathetic smile. "Ready, babe?" he asks in Connor's voice, and I nod.

As we leave, the headmaster walks without touching me. I look around, and when I see we're alone, I move closer to him. "Sir, if you're going to convince people you're Connor, you need to look like you actually like me." He frowns at me in confusion. Inwardly, I roll my eyes that we didn't prepare him better. I sigh and take his hand, guiding it around my waist. We walk onto the bustling quad just as he pulls me into his side. Everyone seems to go silent as we pass, and I look down at the ground, playing the grieving friend.

"Coffee, babe?" the headmaster asks, and I nod sadly.

He orders for us, casually just asking for the *usual*. The barista makes our coffees and passes them to us. The headmaster takes a sip and flinches. I fight back a smile at his grimace, the coffee obviously too sweet for him.

The headmaster pulls me against him as we walk toward my first class. "Are you sure you don't want to stay home, babe?" he asks. His voice, while soft, carries through the unnatural quiet. Everyone is either silent as we pass or whispering to one another. Their stares slide over me, the pity making my skin crawl. As time has passed here at Avalon, people have stared less and less. It's been a luxury, but now that I'm once again the object of everyone's prying attention, I want to retreat back into myself.

We stop at the door to my first class, and he braces his hands on my shoulders, looking at me. It's Connor's eyes looking down at me, but it's the headmaster's stare. "We can leave right now if you want."

I swallow, resisting the urge to scream. Yes, I want to go home. I want to be with

Connor and Alice. I don't want to be observed like a zoo animal, but I'm doing this for them, to protect them.

I nod and smile weakly up at him. "I'm okay, big guy."

The headmaster squeezes my arms and presses a kiss to my forehead. He waits for me to step inside the classroom before striding down the hall. I sit in my usual spot and glance at Alice's empty seat next to me. The sadness that overwhelms me is real.

The morning passes painfully slowly, and while I'm the object of everyone's stares and whispers, no one talks to me. I'm not sure if they simply don't know what to say or are afraid of me. But as I walk to the canteen, I'm excited to see the Morningstars, eager to be with people who won't just gape at me.

As if my eyes are drawn to him, Connor is the first thing I see when I walk into the cafeteria. At that moment, I only see Connor, my gentle-giant big guy. I run to him and throw myself against his chest. He catches me, his arms wrapping around me, but it's not Connor's tender touch. It's the rough one of the headmaster. I tense, wanting to let go, but at the same time, I know this looks good in terms of playing the part. More than anything, though, I long to be held, to shelter against his body and allow him to block me from all the stares.

"Come on, babe. Let's go home for lunch," he says. He carries me out of the canteen, but we don't return to the Morningstars. When we're out of sight, I feel the magic shift as he opens a portal at my back. I lift my head from his neck and disentangle myself from him. We are in his office, but I have never seen the couch he sets me down on. He stands and drops the glamour, shrugging it off like an ill-fitting coat.

"How has it been?" he asks, pushing his hands into his pockets.

I shake my head. "Awful. Everyone is just constantly staring at me."

"I've not noticed anyone acting suspicious," he says thoughtfully.

"I'm sorry for jumping on you, sir. I forgot—"

The headmaster shrugs and holds up a hand to stop me. "It's what you would have done with Mister Moringstar." He paces. "We need to find a plan to draw them out. Observing isn't enough."

I curl up in the corner of the couch, resting my head against the arm and watching him pace. He doesn't say anything, lost in his thoughts. I don't interrupt him, feeling safe for the first time today. We stay like that until the sounds of students filter in from outside. The headmaster checks the time and replaces his glamor before weaving a portal to the back of the school.

"Ready, Miss Tuatha De Daanan?"

"Remember, you need to pretend like you actually like me," I repeat, a gentle reminder.

He narrows his eyes. "I'm trying," he hisses.

I bristle. "Time to be convincing, *big guy*," I snap as we walk through the portal.

The headmaster's gray eyes flash through Connor's, and he growls softly, "Are you provoking me, *babe*?"

"No." My cheeks heat, and I look away. The headmaster pulls me against him, gripping me harder than Connor ever would.

"Not very Connor of you," I whisper.

"Good thing I'm not Connor," he says, and I can hear him grind his teeth.

I look up at him. "You are right now," I say, holding his gaze, refusing to back down. I don't give a fuck if he doesn't like me. He committed to this plan, so he's going to fucking help me. I let the irritation and anger simmer in me, grateful to feel anything other than fear and grief.

# 116

## SUMMER

*Raesha*

FIRST, FORMER,
BEFORE

T he headmaster deposits me at my class, saying goodbye to me at the door with all the emotion of a fucking tree before stiffly turning and striding down the hall. I hold back my eye roll at his barely veiled contempt for me and spend the whole class dreading seeing him again. At least I can occupy my mind with lessons and notetaking while pretending I don't notice the stares and whispers.

When the class ends, I dread leaving it, knowing he'll be waiting for me. As the students flood through the classroom door, I see him leaning against the wall. Connor's eyes meet mine, and he manages to soften his stare a little when our gazes lock. Like before, I feel an instinctual relief when I see him, but then the dread returns when I remember who he actually is.

"Hey, babe," he says as I approach. I look up at him sadly.

"Hi." The emotion in my voice isn't even false after a torturous day where I've been stared at and whispered about. I even heard some accusations being passed around.

The headmaster as Connor opens his arm for me, and I cautiously move into them. Had he taken what I'd said to heart?

"Hard day?" he asks into my hair, and I nod, relaxing into Connor's large body. The hug feels wrong, and I wonder if the illusion is obvious to everyone or just me. Can the killer sense this isn't real?

"Home?" the headmaster asks, and I can hear the tightness in his voice.

I nod, and he wraps his arm around me, leading me down the long corridor to the door.

When we get outside and are far enough away from wandering gazes, I move away from him. "Okay, you're good."

He grabs my arm and tugs me back against his side. "Not until we're inside," he hisses.

I try to tug away without being obvious about it, but he tightens his grip on my hip.

"I thought you were good at acting," he mumbles under his breath, irritation lacing his voice.

I stop in my tracks, unable to hold back my anger. "What is that supposed to mean? I've been carrying thi—"

His steps don't falter, barely noticing my planted feet. He just slightly lifts me and drags me toward the Morningstar House.

I pull back, trying to yank free of him. "What the fuck is your problem with me?" I ask, the anger finally exploding.

"Get inside, and we can talk freely," he says, not even slowing.

He doesn't deny having a problem with me. Shock. I knew it

I yank my arm hard, and it groans in pain as I finally get free of him. I storm past him, stomping into the house. The headmaster slams the door shut behind us, and I whirl on him. "With all due respect, *Headmaster*—"

"Silence," he demands. A single word, and I'm reminded precisely who this sorcerer is. He drops the glamour, and his height changes, his eyes returning to their normal icy silver as his hair darkens to inky black. "I may look like Mister Morningstar while on campus, but you will treat me with the respect due your headmaster. No matter what face I wear."

I glare up at him. "You have no reason to dislike me as much as you do. If you don't want to do this with me, I'll do it on my own."

"When I want your opinion, Miss Tuatha De Daanan," a portal opens at his back, his eyes flashing with frigid fury, "I'll ask for it."

He doesn't spare me another glance before leaving, the portal snapping shut behind him. Anger courses through me, stronger than ever, and a ball of purple light forms in my hand. I look down at it, pulsing with fury, and throw it at one of the couch cushions, obliterating it on contact.

"Babe?" Connor says, coming down the stairs. "Woah, what happened?" he asks, running across the room. He sends a wave of cool mist toward the couch, laying it over the scorch mark on the sofa. I launch myself at him and slam my lips to his, the anger still potent.

Connor pulls back. "Hi." He chuckles. "I missed you, too."

I rip his shirt open, the tearing sound echoing through the room. "We're going to fuck. Now," I growl.

Connor grabs my hands, stopping me from opening his pants. "Woah, babe. What happened?"

I snarl a little, my body shaking with rage.

Connor holds my wrists with one hand and cups my cheek with the other. "Hi, it's me, your fiancé. I'd like to talk to my adoring fiancée."

He strokes my cheek with this thumb soothingly, and I close my eyes, trying to relax. Connor releases my wrists slowly like I'm a wild, rabid animal just captured, and he wraps his arms around me, pulling me into him. The second he envelopes me in his arms, I exhale heavily, my body slumping.

Connor kisses my head.

"Offended you didn't want to fuck me," I growl softly into his chest.

Connor chuckles. "Well, I wasn't sure if you'd rip my dick off in that state."

"The headmaster is a cunt," I grumble. "No wonder your dad hates him."

Connor laughs again and presses another kiss to my head. "Well, you're not wrong."

I sigh and pull back to look up at him. "Hi."

Connor smiles that perfect smile. "Hi, babe. Alice is waiting for you upstairs. She's set up camp in our bed."

I pull back and run upstairs, jumping on Alice, who is lounging on Connor's bed, watching a movie. Alice squeals when I land on top of her and smother her in kisses. "I missed you. I missed you. I missed you."

Alice swats at me. "Get off!"

I keep kissing and nuzzling into her, and then I pull back, looking down at her. "Have I thanked you for not dying yet?"

Alice rolls her eyes. "I did die. It sucked."

"Okay, well. Thanks for having multiple lives."

Alice's lips twitch. "Thank the gods for my lineage. I suppose. Never thought I'd be saying that." She shoves me off, and we sit up. "So, back to more important matters. How much mourning was there for me?"

"Everyone seems pretty put out. There's a shrine for you by the Dracula statue, but I didn't visit it. Also, there's a rumor that I'm the one that killed you, so that's fun."

"Getting all the glory again, I see," Alice tuts.

Connor comes in with snacks and slides onto the bed beside me. I crawl into his lap and nuzzle into his neck.

"She had a screaming match with the doom master," Connor says, rubbing my back.

"Hold up, you what?" Alice asks, staring at me aghast.

"Yeah," I say, clinging to Connor's shirt as if trying to hold him to me.

"Though she's not told me why yet," Connor adds.

"He's a dick," I say nonchalantly.

Alice rolls her eyes. "We all knew that already."

"He's a bigger dick than I anticipated."

Alice grabs a nail polish bottle from Connor's bedside table, and only now do I understand just how much she's integrated herself into his room. She starts painting her toenails. "Tell us everything."

"He told me I was shit at acting when, really, he's fucking dire. It's like he's never seen an emotional reaction before."

Alice snorts. "Okay, well, are you shit?"

"No!" I exclaim, offended for the fucking second time in the last twenty minutes.

Connor kisses my head, soothing me again. "So why did he say you were?"

I shrug. "I guess he didn't think I was believable in my role," I grumble, but then my voice raises. "But I fucking was!"

Alice snorts again, concentrating on painting her nails. "Man, he got under your skin good."

I feel myself practically vibrating in rage again, and Connor cups my cheek, tilting my head up. "Babe."

I look at him, his calming blue eyes like a sea of tranquility, nothing dangerous or hard in them.

"You're here with us," he says, kissing one corner of my lips and then the other.

I concentrate on his face and relax my muscles.

"No doom master in sight, okay?"

I nod and press my forehead to his cheek.

"He can't want to keep this charade up much longer."

"I just don't know why he hates me so much."

"Yeah, okay," Alice says, throwing me an exasperated look.

"What?"

"I mean, you have gotten in a lot of trouble since you got here," she says with a nonchalant shrug.

I'm about to protest, but the evidence is damning, so I keep my mouth shut and bury my face in Connor's neck, inhaling his cloud and rain scent.

Connor rubs my back. "Hey, one day down."

I pull back and grab his face, kissing him deeply. Connor smiles, and I tuck my head beneath his chin. "Let's watch a movie or something? I need a distraction." Alice nods, and she closes her laptop before grabbing Connors. She types in the password and loads up *Nexus* before scrolling through movies.

"Do I want to know how you know my password?" Connor asks.

"No, and give me my wife. It's my turn." Alice tugs on my arm until I leave Connor's lap. She pulls until I am on the other side of her, and then she presses play on the movie.

"Okay, but if I'm sitting here, you have to cuddle me," I tell her. Alice wraps her arms around me and teasingly sticks her tongue out at Connor.

Connor pouts, sitting on his own, and I blow him a kiss. "Don't worry, she'll be bored with cuddling in approximately four minutes.

"Okay, four minutes and counting." Connor sighs.

I laugh, and Alice squeezes me tight. Trying to prove a point, she holds me until we both fall asleep on Connor's bed.

# 117

## SUMMER

*Methsho*
TIME

**M**y eyes open, and I am instantly alert. I don't remember exactly what I was dreaming, but I can still feel the spirit clinging to the corpse, its blood on my skin, and the vacant, dead eyes fixed upon me.

I stretch as I take in the room from this new angle, groaning as my muscles protest from the odd position I slept in. Alice is taking up most of the bed, lying sprawled out, her hand on Connor's face. I sit up and bite back a laugh as I snap a photo before getting out of bed.

Dread fills me again when I remember the day I have ahead of me, another day with the headmaster, another day without Connor and Alice. The stranger pops into my head, and I allow myself a moment to miss him. I want to reach out to him, but I'm unsure how to move past what he said on the phone.

I stand at the end of the bed and watch my family sleep. They look so peaceful. I consider waking them to let them know I'm going to go work out, but they've also had a traumatic couple of days. Deciding I will be quick, I pull on my workout clothes and quietly slip out of the room.

I inhale deeply and skip down the steps, my thoughts a chaotic mess as I walk quickly toward the gym.

"Summer?"

Stopping in my tracks, I force the facade back into place and turn to see a familiar kitsune female watching me from down the path. She looks familiar, but I can't remember where I know her from. I think her name is Lucille or Lucy.

"I heard about... Well, I heard... you screaming that day," she stammers, sadness and compassion radiating from her.

Right. She lives down the hall. I look away, unsure what to say.

"I called for the headmaster when I heard." Her soft voice betrays all the trauma she felt just from hearing my reaction to my dead best friend. "I just wanted to say I'm sorry," she says before turning and walking away, unaware of the small sliver of kindness she's just given me.

I spend the rest of the walk trying not to think about my day and the hell it's going to be, but I'm unsuccessful. When I arrive at the gym, my mood sours. How did I forget about Max? Oh yeah, cause my mind is so chaotically busy with the murder of my best friend.

"Fight?" Max asks, though his expression is wary.

"I don't think that's a good idea," I say, making my way to the treadmill, needing to lose myself in the effort of a workout.

*Remember the part you have to play.*

I hear the headmaster's voice in my head, and it makes me bristle.

Max walks over. "Why?"

"Go away, Max," I say with a sigh, starting the treadmill.

He stares at me, but I refuse to acknowledge him. "I–I heard about Alice," he stammers, and I don't think I've ever heard him sound quite so uncomfortable.

I let the grief seep into my bones again, but I don't respond.

"About last time—" Max begins.

"Not now, Max," I snap, and there is nothing false about my reaction. I have enough going on without worrying about Maximillian fucking Romulus.

"Summer," he says, placing his hand on the arm of the treadmill.

I shake my head. "If you treat me differently when something good happens, like getting engaged, I'm guessing you're going to treat me even more differently when my best friend gets fucking murdered. I can't handle it, Max. Go away."

"Just... let's just fight," Max says, his hand tightening on the treadmill.

"Fight someone else. I want to be alone," I growl, a tear escaping down my cheek.

I see him grow larger in my peripheral vision, and then he storms away. Wiping away the tear, I run faster, trying to work through the mess in my mind. Alice died, and then she was alive again, but I need to pretend she's not. I need to spend every day acting like she is gone for good. Connor is at home protecting her. He's safe there. The headmaster... gods, he's such a dick.

*Show me what you can do, Summer.*

*Show me what you can do, Summer.*

*Your name will never be Summer Morningstar.*

*Your name will never be Summer Morningstar.*

*Your name will never be Summer Morningstar.*

Another tear falls, and I don't realize I've been slowly increasing the speed of the treadmill until my feet are barely touching the belt. The moment I become aware, I lose my footing. Pain slices up my leg as my ankle gives, and I am thrown from the machine. Max is suddenly beside me, his eyes glowing green.

"Are you an idiot?" he asks a thin sheen of sweat on his forehead. He was obviously in the middle of working off his own frustrations.

I sit up, and my ankle throbs in pain. I hiss out a breath as I move it experimentally. Max leans down and scoops me into his arms, carrying me into the sports medicine room.

"Fucking moronic, stubborn, inconsiderate ass," he grumbles as he deposits me on the table.

He sits in front of me, and I wince as he lifts my ankle to examine it. "Takes one to know one," I grate between clenched teeth.

"Shut up," Max hisses. "You may be able to heal, but you can still hurt," he says, looking at my ankle, which is already swollen and bruised.

"You ruptured a tendon." He curses and gently lowers my foot. He stands up and starts gathering tape and bandages. "The fuck were you thinking?" he growls.

"I was," I hiss as he lifts my ankle again, "just running, and then I started to think about..." I swallow hard, not able to force the words out.

Max glances at me, his hard gaze softening only slightly before he places an ice pack on my ankle.

"Fuck," I groan as he moves my foot a little, and then I start to sob again. Fuck, I hate this version of myself, and I hate that I obviously feel comfortable sobbing in front of dickbag Max. But here we are.

"I miss you," I whisper, not looking at him.

Max's head snaps up. "You're the one who's been avoiding me."

I meet his gaze. "You saw the ring and flipped out, and then Alice..." I choke down a sob.

Max looks back down at my ankle. "I'm sorry about Alice. I'm not good at dealing with this shit. And the ring thing. I just... needed a moment to process."

I frown, watching him as he starts to wrap my ankle. "You know it's not you that I'm marrying, right? No need to go all commitment-phobe on me."

"Just didn't think marriage was your thing," I say with a shrug.

"Why does it matter to you? I know you have this thing with Con—"

"I just thought you and I were alike. Guess I was wrong."

His words remind me of the fight I had with the stranger on Connor's porch. I opened up to him and he dismissed me. That's how Max is feeling.

I look back down at my ankle. "We are alike," I say, eventually.

Max scoffs. "Yeah? You're not going to turn into Suzy Homemaker? Wait for Connor to come home from his Legion with dinner ready and slippers in hand? Barefoot and pregnant."

"No," I say without an ounce of hesitation. "Look, Max, marriage was never something I envisioned for myself, but neither was someone like Connor. Honestly, before I started dating Connor, my type was definitely someone more like you. You know, a complete asshole."

Max snorts, focusing on my ankle. "You into one-night stands?"

"It used to be all I ever did. One-night stands or no-strings situations, and all with asshole guys I knew were bad for me. But it didn't matter. I never stuck around long enough for them to harm me."

Not after Torin.

Max finishes wrapping my ankle. "You know, there's an old saying about fate," Max starts. "Fate doesn't waste its bullets." Max's lips twitch. "You sure fate wants you as Connor's dutiful wife?"

"I love Connor," I reply.

"So that's a no then," Max replies, and I bristle. Just when I think Max and I are making some progress and finding some common ground, he has to go and blow it.

"Whatever, Max," I say with weary snarkiness.

He growls and turns to walk away, but I grab his arm. His muscles are tight with tension, but he stops and snarls, "What do you want from me?"

"I miss you, Max," I say. I want him as a friend, and some instinct is begging me to fight for that relationship.

"You can find someone else to fight with," Max growls.

I tug his arm and pull him closer. "Maxxy..."

"What?" he grumbles, but he softens slightly at the nickname.

I pull his arm again, tugging him closer.

"Summer, you're not playing fair."

"What do you mean?" I ask, tugging his arm again.

"I'm trying to be mad at you," he grumbles, but his lips twitch.

"We're not frenemies," I say, and Max frowns. "We're friends, and I need you, Max. Whether or not I like it."

It's true. When I'm with Max, I don't feel vulnerable. I feel strong. I know he will not tiptoe around me in an effort to protect me. Maybe I was wrong with what I thought the other week. Perhaps applying the label *frenemies* to our relationship doesn't automatically remove the responsibilities of friendship. Perhaps Max and I can be friends, just differently.

Max exhales and then wraps his arms around me, hugging me tightly. "I'm not good at dealing with death trauma, but I'll try."

I shake my head. "Just be my friend, okay?"

Max squeezes me again. "I missed you too."

I smile, though those damn tears start leaking from my eyes again. I'm going to fucking dehydrate myself soon.

Max pulls back, bracing his hands on my arms. "If you're happy. I'm happy." He smirks. "But you're still a pain in my ass."

I nod, and Max musses my hair. "Don't work out for the next couple of days, and take it easy on that ankle," he says, helping me off the table. I groan in pain as I put weight on my ankle. "Moron," Max mumbles under his breath, and I glare at him. "That will take a few days, even with your accelerated healing. You need to take it easy, all right, Sum?"

I blink at him. "You never call me Sum."

Max shrugs. "You never call me Maxxy."

"Do you need me to help you home?" Max asks, helping me to the door.

I shake my head. "No, I'm staying at the Morningstar House for now. I'll be fine."

Max nods. "Okay, well, make sure your fiancé takes care of you." I am hobbling toward the door when Max sighs. "Wait." I glance at him over my shoulder. "You have plans tonight?"

"No," I say with a frown.

Max takes a deep breath and says, "Want to hang out? You and golden boy?"

I blink and then blink again. "You want to hang out with us?"

Max rubs a hand over the back of his neck. "I want to try to understand what you like about him."

"Sure! Come round this evening?" I say with a smile.

"I'll bring pizza."

I wave and start limping home, concentrating on my steps but feeling a little lighter. Someone calls my name, and I look back to see Aqua behind me, her loud sweater assaulting my eyes with its bright oranges and yellows. I give her a small smile, but I don't stop walking. My slow, careful steps make it easy for her to catch up.

"Hey, Summer! Are you all right?"

"I'm all right. Just an accident on the treadmill. How are you?"

"You're limping. Let me help," Aqua says, grabbing my arm and pulling it over her shoulder.

"Really, I'm okay."

Aqua doesn't pay any attention, and we continue on the path to the Morningstar House. "Hey, I heard about Alice. I'm really sorry. I know you guys were super close."

Irritation sizzles through me. I don't know why, but her talking about Alice and me like she knows us annoys me, but I just nod. "Thank you."

"I never spoke to her much. She seemed cool though," Aqua muses. "Weird that she was a vamp." I frown, glancing at her. "Well, the others were fae, ya know?"

I nod, and we spend the rest of the walk in uncomfortable silence, save for the strange tune she starts humming. It's the same one she was humming the night she found me in the forest. I feel an enormous sense of relief when the Morningstar House comes into view, and I pull my arm free. "Well, thanks a lot."

673

ALEXIS RUNE & JEANETTE ROSE

Aqua grins at me. "No problem! See you around."

I limp up the path and call for Connor. He comes to the door almost immediately, still in his pajamas. His eyes widen when he sees me limping. "Babe! What happened?" He swoops me into his arms and carries me inside.

"Fell off the treadmill, I'm fine."

"Babe!" Connor gasps.

"Oh, and Max is coming over after classes today."

Connor almost drops me but manages to lay me down on the couch. "What? Why?"

I shift my ankle and grimace. "Because we're friends, and he wants to get to know you."

"Me? Why?"

"Because we're getting married, and he's my friend."

Connor is about to protest when he finally realizes I'm in pain. He sprints across the room, calling for Luke.

Luke comes down the stairs two at a time and hurries toward me. He slowly waves his hand over my leg. "Torn tendon," he murmurs under his breath, and his palm starts to glow. "There's not a whole lot I can do. I'll repair it as much as I can, but it'll be sore for a few days."

Connor gives me a dark look.

"What?" I ask.

"You hurt yourself," he almost growls.

I reach up and grab him, pulling him down on top of me.

"Luke, give us a minute?" Connor groans.

Luke leaves promptly, and I kiss Connor deeply. Connor moans and bites my lip.

"No hurting my fiancé," he demands.

I curl my fingers into his waistband. "Maybe you can heal me..."

Connor's groan is filled with need. "Is that so?"

I push my hand into his pants and wrap my fingers around his hardening length, squeezing. "I think that's definitely what I need."

"We should be going." My whole body tenses as an icy-cold voice settles over us. I glance over Connor's shoulder to see the headmaster standing by the door.

# 118

## SUMMER

Mahthae
PIERCE, STAB

Connor's cheeks go bright red, and I pull my hand from his pants. "Headmaster, you're early!" Connor says, sitting up hastily. Connor offers me his hand, and when I take it, he tugs me up next to him.

The headmaster throws him a disapproving, bored look, and then his silver eyes slide to me. "Miss Tuatha De Daanan, you should be ready."

Holding his gaze, I refuse to back down. "I would have been ready." I glance at the clock on the mantle, noting that I still have twenty minutes before he was supposed to arrive. "Had you arrived at the agreed-upon time." I kiss Connor softly and whisper against his lips, "Sorry, big guy. Later."

Connor nips my lower lip in a promise for more when I get home and then stands to help me up. I limp upstairs to get dressed. I'm secretly happy that I have to opt for my cute white sneakers today, thanks to my ankle. When I come back downstairs, the air is still heavy with tension. Connor is now leaning against the kitchen door, sipping a coffee while the headmaster still stands in the same position, his hands in his pockets. I walk toward him, trying to ignore the pain in my ankle, but sharp bolts shoot up my leg with every step.

"What happened?" he asks, looking pointedly at my bandaged ankle.

"Fell off a treadmill," I say curtly.

The headmaster gives me an exasperated look before dropping to a knee in front of me. He starts to unwrap the bandage. "Sir, it's just a torn tendon."

He ignores me and slices his thumb before drawing an extremely intricate rune on my leg. It glows faintly, and the pain all but disappears. I frown down at the now translucent rune shimmering against my skin.

"Why don't I know that rune?" I whisper mostly to myself. Watching him with curiosity, I tilt my head. I've researched healing runes for countless hours, but even from my vast reading and natural penchant for runes, I can't place this one. I can't even really translate it.

"There are many things you do not know, Miss Tuatha De Daanan," the headmaster says as he pushes to his feet. I bristle again but unwrap the rest of the bandage, annoyed but glad for the relief from the pain.

When I look back at the headmaster, he has glamoured his face, and it's Connor who looks back at me.

"This is my cue to leave. This is too weird," the real Connor says at my back. I turn and kiss him goodbye before the headmaster and I leave.

"Foolish to hurt yourself," the headmaster grumbles, his own voice leaving Connor's lips.

"It wasn't on purpose," I snap back.

He gives me a dry look, and the expression looks foreign on Connor's face. "So you fell by accident? You? A fae? Known for their dexterity?"

I growl and move away from him, but he yanks me back. "Play your role," he grumbles under his breath.

"Play yours and pretend to actually like me," I snarl softly.

"You are in mourning, and I am your supportive and doting boyfriend."

"Fiancé," I correct as we stop at the coffee cart.

This time, having learned from his mistakes, he orders the usual for me and then a black coffee for himself. The barista looks a little confused, and the headmaster puts a soft smile on Connor's face. "Cutting down on sugar," he says in Connor's voice, and the barista nods, making the order.

Nice cover, dick. He walks me to my class, playing the role of a doting partner, but the lie between us is so apparent to me that I can't figure out how no one else can see it.

Outside my class, he stops and pulls me against him. "You sure you want to go, babe? It's only been two days."

I nod. "It's a good distraction."

"Okay," he says tenderly, cupping my cheek.

I place my hands on his chest and look up at him, leaning into my sadness and pretending I'm gazing at the male I love.

"You'll text me?" he asks, playing the role somewhat perfectly. First time for everything, I guess.

I nod, and he pulls me closer. I swallow my surprise at the way his body feels against me. It is Connor's body, but the touch feels oddly... electric.

He leans closer, a breath away from me. His voice is still Connor's, even as the words and tone are those of the icy headmaster. "Stay out of trouble."

I exhale shakily. "Will do, big guy." He steps around me, tucking his hands into his pockets and walking toward Connor's first class. I take a breath and then go into my morning class, sitting in my usual seat. Today is slightly better, though I'm unsure how I feel about the headmaster's acting skills. Good or bad, both come with their own set of disadvantages.

While I'm still having to endure people's stares, the whispers have slowed. It's annoying to think that within twenty-four hours, their concern for my *dead* best friend has already waned. On the plus side, I feel more stable today and as if I can concentrate more on finding the killer.

As I walk to lunch, I spot Aqua from the corner of my eye. She is writing frantically on a piece of paper. A rune glows brightly on her neck, but I can't decipher it from this distance.

She lifts her head as if feeling my gaze, and I shift deeper into the crowd, dodging her sight. I walk to our table, where Luke and Zane are sitting with the headmaster as Connor. Sliding my hand onto his shoulder, I wait for him to glance at me before sitting on his lap. I've never felt more uncomfortable in my life, but I need to talk to him without anyone overhearing.

"How was class, babe?" he asks.

I bury my face against his neck, my shoulders shaking as if I'm crying. "What do you know of Aqua Tuatha De Daanan?"

"The third year?" he asks, dropping his voice to a dark rumble that penetrates my core.

I nod, keeping my face in his neck.

"Little. Average student. Cloistered with the fae," he answers.

I move my lips to his ear, whispering, "She's always around when I'm hurt."

The headmaster tightens his arms around me as if comforting me. "She brought you to my office after the wild mist."

I nod against his neck again. "And she was there this morning when I was walking home from the gym."

He thinks for a moment. "You think she's involved?"

I shrug.

"I think I uncovered something, too. We should meet in my office."

Without another word, I slip from his lap. I can feel Luke and Zane watching as I slide my hand into his and lead him from the cafeteria. The headmaster summons a portal once we are out of sight behind the building, and we step through it into his office. At first, the room is exactly as it always looks, but then he waves his hand. The messages appear on the wall alongside several student profiles, with pieces of string connecting them.

"I'm not convinced this is regarding the rebellion," the headmaster says, touching the line, *From the mountains to the sky, I'll make their blood run down her face.* "We've been saying the killer is toying with us, and here it is again." He points to the first part. "From the mountains, meaning Drãculea. The killer told us Alice was next." He points to the second part. "To the sky."

My heart stops, and my stomach twists in fear. "Connor..." I whisper.

The headmaster nods, looking at the wall. "They're playing with us, giving us clues. He is next."

I place my hand on my chest, unable to breathe. My heart, which felt like it had stopped beating, is now thundering hard in my chest. The headmaster steps in front of me, shielding me from the words. The only thing I can see is his molten silver eyes. "I will not let that happen, Miss Tuatha De Daanan."

I look down, tears welling in my eyes. "I should just let them have me. Then everyone would be safe."

"That is not the answer, and you know it." The headmaster's fists clench. "Killers don't just stop. Once they have a taste, it never ends," he says, his face thunderous. "This is a game to them. If it weren't you, it would be someone else." His lips curl slightly. "It is good that I am wearing his face."

He turns and walks to one of the many bookshelves. Choosing a handful of books, he dumps them on his desk and starts flicking through them. He slices his finger and begins drawing runes on his arms, the blood turning inky black as they take shape. I watch him, frozen with an odd mix of fear and fascination.

"The more I am seen as Mister Morningstar, the more likely they take me instead."

"But, sir, I-I don't want you to be hurt either." It's true. Enough people have been harmed at my expense. It needs to end now.

"Those runes—"

"Time-stopping runes," he answers before the question is even complete. "Time is difficult to halt even for a breath. You don't hold just the place frozen but all the realms. There is only..." He pauses, thinking about his words. "It is not something that should ever be taken lightly." He looks up at me. "Dangerous things should be approached with caution. A deadly viper can look as docile as a piece of driftwood until it's too late."

"But so much fun to play with when tamed," I blurt out. Where had that come from? It's like the words have surged from my darkness into the light, tainting it as it goes.

His eyes flash to that swirling silver. "Some things only appear tamed." He glances away as the sound of students moving past his door seeps into his office. "We should go."

# 119

## SUMMER

Lyrsha
HEART

"Well done today," the headmaster says as we walk into the Morningstar House.

"Thank you, sir," I say, unsure how to take his compliment. He nods once and drops the glamor before disappearing through his portal. As soon as it closes behind him, I go in search of Connor.

Fear from our findings sits heavily on my shoulders, but I need to try to relax because the headmaster is right. The more he is seen as Connor and the less Connor is out of the house, the more chance the headmaster will be taken and not Connor. I am sure the headmaster is far more powerful than some serial killer. Isn't he?

"Al! You need not to be around tonight!" I call toward Zach's room, where she's been staying. She pops her head out, frowning.

"Why?"

"Max is coming over to hang out with Connor and me, and he can't know you're alive."

Alice rolls her eyes. "You're lucky they're running reruns of *The Shifter is the Mister* tonight."

"You're a rockstar," I say.

Alice blows me a kiss and returns to her room just as Connor comes out of his. "Babe!" He wraps me in his arms and kisses me hard. "I missed you."

I smile and press my body against his. "I missed you too, big guy." Connor lifts me and carries me into his room, where we happily lose ourselves in each other.

"Your friend is here!" Luke calls from the other side of the door as Connor and I finish getting dressed.

"You need to be nice to him, big guy. This is a big deal that he's trying."

Connor gawks at me. "I'm always nice!"

I give him a look, and he pouts, buttoning his jeans.

"If you're a very good boy, I'll do that thing with my mouth you love after he's gone."

Connor groans, kissing me again. I smile and slide my hand into his. "Game face, big guy," I whisper, leading him downstairs and into the living room.

Max holds up a pizza box and a six-pack. "I brought food and beer."

I drop Connor's hand and nudge Max playfully. "The game is already on in the den," I say, leading the way, with them silently following.

Rafe is already in the den, standing in front of the television. He looks up when we walk in, his gaze catching on Max. His brow furrows for a moment and then clears. "Oh, you're that gym guy, right?" Rafe asks.

Max lifts an eyebrow but nods and sets the pizza and six-pack on the coffee table before sitting down with one of the beers. I grab a beer from the pack and hand it to Rafe, kissing him on the cheek as I do so. He barely reacts, slowly getting used to the casual affection from me. When did I become this person? I wonder if he asks himself the same question.

Connor settles into the recliner and holds his hand out for mine. "Romulus is a friend of Summer's."

Rafe nods and turns his attention back to the game.

I grab a slice of pizza before taking Connor's hand and letting him pull me into his lap. I happily nuzzle his cheek and offer him a bit of the pizza.

"Max has been training me, and I've decided that he's kinda all right, I guess."

"What actually happened is that she was embarrassingly pathetic at fighting, and I couldn't endure watching it. Clearly, combat class was wasted on her."

Rafe scoffs, shaking his head. "I cannot imagine Summer actually fighting."

I tilt my head and narrow my eyes at him menacingly. "Is that a challenge, Rafey?"

Rafe rolls his eyes at me. "You couldn't hold up against me."

"If I can pin a berserker, I can pin you," I say, smirking devilishly.

Rafe scowls at me, his irritation amping up. "I fight demons, you know that, right?"

Connor snorts. "No, you..." He sits straight up, almost launching me out of his lap, but catches me at the last moment. "That's who you've been fighting?" he shouts. "What the fuck, Rafe? You've been fighting demons?"

Rafe shrugs, unaffected by Connor's raised voice, and grabs another beer. I glare at Connor, pissed that he almost launched her into outer space. I stand up to grab a beer, noticing that Max is smothering a smile as he eats a slice of pizza.

"Why are you smirking?" Connor glares at Max.

Max shrugs. "Just... interesting."

"Connor," I warn.

"What?"

I give him a dissatisfied look.

He sighs. "I meant it in a non-aggressive way."

Max takes a swig of beer. "I just thought you had the perfect life."

"Max," I warn, about two seconds away from bashing their heads together.

"What? I did!" he says.

Connor rolls his eyes. "Far from perfect. It would be perfect if I were an *only* child," he says, directing the latter part of the statement directly at Rafe.

Rafe flips Connor off, and Max snickers into his pizza.

"Come back," Connor says, reaching for me.

I lean over him and kiss him deeply before dropping into his lap again.

"You guys set a date yet?" Max asks, watching us.

I shake my head, running my fingers through Connor's hair. "No. Con wants to wait."

Max watches us for a second, his expression darkening. "I guess it's not the best time to be thinking about the future with everything going on."

"Right," I say, resting my head on Connor's shoulder.

"Summer is pretty deeply in denial about the whole thing," Rafe grumbles moodily.

"I have Legion duty straight after graduation, but we are planning for the summer after her second year," Connor says, squeezing me closer and ignoring Rafe's comment. "So what happened to her ankle?" he asks Max.

"She was being an idiot," Max says matter-of-factly. I throw a dirty glare at him. "You were!" he says, doubling down.

Connor laughs, stroking my hip with his thumb.

"She gives me gray hairs, I swear." Max sighs.

I'm about to protest, but Connor replies first. "She's a handful." I blink at Connor, then at Max, and then at Connor again.

"Uh, hold up. What's going on here?"

"What? We're bonding," Connor says, nuzzling my cheek.

"You're not allowed to gang up on me!"

"Who says?" Max asks, smirking. "Besides, you make it so easy."

"Okay, well, I'm going to beat your ass." I point at Max. "And no more sex." I point at Connor before slipping off his lap and going to stand with Rafe.

Rafe stares at me warily. "I'm not sleeping with you."

"But I promise I don't hog the covers!" I say with a pout.

Rafe shakes his head. "Nope. Connor is a cuddler, and I'm guessing you are, too."

"I promise no cuddling. Just some light nuzzling," I say, nuzzling against his arm. Rafe gazes down at me with a revolted look on his face before walking away.

Connor laughs. "Guess you have no choice but to come back to me, babe. Zane is a kicker, and Luke midnight snacks. Loudly."

I sigh and walk back to him, sitting on the arm of the chair. "Fine. But still no sex for you."

Connor pulls me back onto his lap and kisses my face. "We'll see."

I melt into him a little and almost hear Max roll his eyes. "Sucker." He takes another sip of beer. "I see your ankle is better," he says, and I nod. "Okay, well, you're still not coming back until it's fully healed."

I lift my leg and roll my ankle, showing off that I can do it without wincing in pain. "Look!"

"No," Max says, looking away.

The conversation dies down, and everyone turns their attention to the game. "So, you both like sports. Discuss."

Max laughs at my poor attempt to promote conversation. "Summer, we're in the same room, and we're not fighting. Enjoy the win."

I decide he is right and relax into Connor. The conversation does eventually pick up, but it's about boring sports. I tune out their words and lay my head against Connor's chest, letting the rumble of his voice soothe me into near sleep.

When the game ends, Max stands up and stretches. "Well, I should get going." I hear Max say in my semi-conscious state.

Connor kisses my head. "Thank you for teaching her."

"She's hard to deny."

Connor laughs, the small rumble in his chest warming me. "Tell me about it. Goodnight, Romulus."

"Night, golden boy."

I smile and finally drift into deeper sleep.

# 120

## SUMMER

Lonthae
SPRING

"Summer! Dad is here!" Alice shouts from downstairs.

I kiss Connor again. "Will you go tell him I'll be right down? I'm just finishing up." Connor nods and kisses me again before disappearing downstairs to convey my message to the headmaster.

Suspecting that Connor is now the target makes it even more difficult to be away from him. I know he'll be safe at home while the headmaster wears his face, yet I still long to be with him, to protect him from all harm.

I draw some red kohl on my water line, really selling the grieving look, and add a little powder beneath my eyes before I head downstairs. I'm back to wearing my heels thanks to the headmaster's rune yesterday, and the pain in my ankle is nothing more than a twinge.

The view when I come downstairs is similar to the one yesterday. Connor is awkwardly sipping coffee, and the headmaster stands by the door, his arms crossed. Alice happily sits in the awkwardness, enjoying every moment of their discomfort.

"Ready?" the headmaster asks the moment he spots me.

"Yes, sir," I say, grabbing an apple and kissing Connor as I pass. The headmaster fixes his glamour, causing Connor to grimace.

"Too fucking weird," Connor grumbles.

Alice nods. "One bird brain is enough, thank you very much."

My lips twitch, and I take the headmaster's hand as we leave the house.

"Are you prepared for another day of this?" he asks.

I nod and take a bite of my apple. "Yesterday was a little easier, less staring and whispering."

"I felt someone watching me while sitting in Mister Morningstar's classes."

I glance up at him, my shoulders tensing.

"I couldn't find the source, but someone is watching."

I nod. "How are you getting away with being absent so much?"

"I have my ways, Miss Tuatha De Daanan," he says, throwing me a stern look.

I roll my eyes at his dramatics, and we morph into our characters as we get closer to the school. We stop for coffee as usual, and the headmaster walks me to my class. We're in the building early, so the corridors are still fairly empty. Happy we don't have to pretend for a few moments, I relax a little more when we turn the corner to find that no one is in the hall.

Hushed voices come toward us, and I shift closer to the headmaster, ready to pick up our pretense again. He tenses but wraps his arm around me, pulling me against him.

"You hear what happened to that bitch fanger?"

The voices become more clear as they get closer.

"Fuck, she got what was coming to her, disgusting leech."

The headmaster tightens his arm around me, and then he turns, pushing me into an alcove and pressing his body to mine. We will still be visible here, but less so. He braces his arm on the wall at my head, concealing us even more. To an onlooker, we look like a young couple making out against the wall.

My chest heaves in fury as they near.

"You hear what Brett said about it?" the first voice says as they get closer.

The other laughs. "Yeah, that guy's a freak."

My eyes widen, and I look up into the headmaster's eyes, no longer Connor's soft blue. He presses his body against mine, so close he is nearly crushing me against the wall as they pass. I can't fucking breathe. What did Brett say? I thought he was my friend. Could he have been part of this?

"At least we know our pack is safe from the psycho..." The voices trail off as they get further away again.

The headmaster slams his fist against the wall so hard that it shakes behind me. He then closes his eyes, takes a breath, and corrects the glamor before moving away from me. I don't move, my back still pressed to the wall and shaking with rage.

He takes my hand and pulls me against him as we start walking. He drops his voice to barely a whisper, sounding more dangerous than I've ever heard him. "I'll speak with Gideon." I glance up at him in a silent question, and he replies, "He's extremely integrated with the shifters."

I nod, and we continue toward my class, Brett's possible betrayal sitting heavily on my shoulders. The headmaster squeezes my arm as we arrive, and when I'm safely inside my classroom, he hurries away.

Once again, I can barely concentrate on my lesson. Instead, I doodle in my notebook, trying to create a few strong defensive runes. I succeed, but I'm not sure any of them will work.

I consider the three *M*'s, murder, malevolence, and malice. I tilt my head, studying my doodles. What if I am able to harness one or all of them? A rune starts taking shape in my mind. It's sharp, beautiful, terrifying, and devastating.

"Miss Tuatha De Daanan?" Professor Ambrose pulls me from my thoughts.

My head snaps up at the sound of my name, and I shift in my seat, seeing the entire class has turned to look at me. "Yes?"

"I think you need a moment to freshen up."

I frown, and only then do I realize I've been crying. The tears come in silence, leaving large wet splotches on my paper, and I can feel the prickle of tears on my cheeks. I wipe my face on my sleeve and close my notebook before standing and grabbing my bag. Out in the corridor, I lean against the wall.

"What the fuck was that?" I whisper into the void.

I close my eyes and wrap my arms around myself, feeling another tear fall. Something brushes past me, and I freeze. It feels like a breeze, but I already know it's not the stranger. I swallow, trying not to react, but then I feel that gaze on me. That awful, dark gaze I've not felt for months is suddenly back.

I take a deep breath and open my eyes before pushing off the wall. I walk down the corridor toward the bathroom. My skin prickles and heats where their gaze is locked on me, and I can feel them following me. Deciding it's not a good idea to go into a room with only one way in or out, I adjust my course and head toward Connor's class. My heart thunders as I walk, but I keep a normal pace, trying not to seem panicked or worried.

There's a dark rumble of laughter from behind me, and the sound sends a terrified shiver down my spine. They seem to speed up, so I walk a little faster, whimpering as fear tingles through my extremities. I push into a run, and it matches my pace, chasing me through the corridors. They laugh again, this one even more maniacal than the last.

I burst into Connor's class, my chest burning as I gulp down the air. The headmaster as Connor stands the second he sees me. He hurries to me and cups my cheeks. I shake my head, so overwhelmed with fear I can't even talk.

"Excuse me, Professor Berkley," he says without looking away from me.

The headmaster leads me from the class and back out into the corridor. I look around frantically, but I can't feel them anymore.

"The headmaster. I need to see the headmaster," I say, unsure if we're still being watched.

He searches my eyes and then nods. Sliding his hand into mine, we walk to the headmaster's office. He drops the glamour the second we're in the safety of his office. It's obviously heavily runed and locked down tighter than a fortress.

"Tell me," he says, looking down at me. His silver gaze is so intense that it helps clear the fog of fear enough that I can think clearly.

"S-someone was following me."

"Where?"

"I left class because I was crying, and I felt something brush against me, then I felt..." I swallow and try to find my voice again. "Those eyes on me." I shake my head. "So I walked to the bathroom, and they followed me, so I came to get you."

"Wait here," he growls, and a portal appears. Through the darkness, I see the door to my last class. The headmaster steps through, and it snaps closed behind him. Less than a second later, he appears again. "Nothing," he says, standing with his hands on his hips, studying me. "Can you show me?" he asks.

It takes me a moment before I realize what he means. He wants to look through my memories. I feel the blood drain from my face, but I need to do this. I need to protect my family. My stomach twists at the upcoming invasion into my memories, but I nod.

The headmaster places two fingers on each of my temples. He looks down at me and says, "Close your eyes and focus on that memory."

I wrap my fingers around his thick wrists to ground myself and close my eyes, making sure the memory starts when I'm leaving class. He can't see that rune. I don't want anyone to see it ever. I concentrate on the feeling but try to skim over the moment I thought of the stranger. Why the fuck am I still protecting him?

Though I can feel the headmaster probing, it's not painful or uncomfortable, and I can tell he's limiting himself to that particular memory. I'm very aware that he could easily comb through my mind, seeing absolutely everything and leaving me nothing but a husk. It seems like hours pass, but it's only a few moments before he slips out of my mind.

Suddenly, my whole body starts to shake, and the tears come. The headmaster conjures a blanket and wraps it around me before leading me to the sofa.

"You're going into shock," he says, pulling the blanket tighter around me. "I need you to focus on my voice." My whole body shakes and trembles as the adrenaline continues to course through me. Not only was the experience terrifying and horrible, but I just had to live through it a second time as he replayed the memory. The trauma of it seems to have opened the floodgates, and all the fear and pain from the last week surges through me. The headmaster kneels in front of me and grabs my arms. He squeezes gently, his silver eyes on mine. "Say your name."

"S-s-s-summer..."

He nods. "Again."

"S-s-s-summer."

He nods again, keeping his gaze on me. "Who are you?"

"S-summer," I say, the stammer improving.

He tightens his hands on me, the pain grounding me. "Say your name."

"S-summer Tuatha D-de Daanan." The shaking eases.

"One more time."

"Summer Tuatha De Daanan," I say, my tears continuing to fall. He nods, and I close my eyes. "I'm sorry, sir."

"For?"

I shake my head. "I want to go home."

He nods and stands up, helping me to my feet. I slip the blanket off my shoulders and lay it over the back of the couch. He fixes the glamour, and we leave his office. Connor wraps his arm around my back as he walks me through the corridors and out onto campus.

"What's the matter?" he asks as we walk through the quad.

Unease settles heavily on my shoulders, and I can't quite explain why. "I just want to get home."

We walk faster, and when we arrive back at the Morningstar House, the head-master comes in with me. He drops his glamour when the door closes and follows me to the couch, sitting down next to me.

"Miss Tuatha De Daanan?"

I lean my head back against the couch. "I'm okay. Just tired," I say, exhaustion sinking deep into my bones.

"I understand. It's wearing having someone walk through your memories." The headmaster stands up and takes a couple of steps toward the stairs. "Mister Morn-ingstar," he says, raising his voice a little. Connor appears a moment later, coming down the stairs. He looks at me and frowns.

"You guys are back early."

I look up at Connor, smiling softly.

Connor walks to the couch and sits beside me, cupping my cheek. "Babe?"

The headmaster opens a portal, and I meet his gaze. I can see the same unease in his eyes that is roiling through me, but neither of us voices it. He nods once before stepping into the portal. I wait for it to slam shut before I smile up at Connor and lean into his hand.

# 121

## SUMMER

*Lithsha*
LIII

"W hat happened?" Connor asks, wrapping his arms around me and pulling me onto his lap.

I press my forehead to his and close my eyes, exhaustion pulling at me.

"Summer? What is it?" Connor asks.

I pull back and open my eyes, looking at his perfect face and the love shining from his eyes. "I don't want to wait," I blurt out.

Connor tips his head. "What do you mean?"

I brush my thumb along his cheek. "Let's get married. Over the summer."

Connor's mouth drops open and then closes. He stares at me a moment in shock before saying, "What? You don't want to wait?"

I shake my head. "I don't want to wait."

Connor's face breaks out into the most heartbreaking smile. "Well, okay then! Let's call my mom tonight!"

I force a bright smile. "I would love that!"

Connor's smile grows wider, if that's even possible. "We're getting married."

"We're getting married," I agree with a grin.

"I'm going to marry you. I'm going to be your husband!"

I laugh. "My husband!"

Connor smothers me in kisses, and I bask in the joy and love. I close my eyes, soaking in every second.

Connor sobers and cups my face. "Now, tell me why you're home early."

I exhale, my smile dimming a little. "Someone followed me. Or at least, I think they did."

"Followed you?" Connor asks with a frown.

"I handled it, but then I just wanted to get home to you."

Connor squeezes me to him, and I tunnel my fingers into his hair, nuzzling into his neck and inhaling him.

"I'm here."

I smile but pull back. "Let's call you mom now. I know you're desperate to tell her."

Connor smiles and pulls his phone free, starting the video chat with his mom. Farrah's beautiful face fills the screen. Her cheek has a dusting of flour on it. She's obviously in the middle of baking, but the way her face lights up when she sees Connor is heartbreakingly wonderful. She loves her boys so much.

"Conbear!" she says. "How's one of my six favorite boys?" she asks. Uriel comes up behind her and wraps his arms around her. He kisses her neck before smiling at the screen and moving away.

"Mom, we want to move up the wedding," Connor says, joy in every word.

Farrah screams so loud that Connor and I have to cover our ears. I chuckle and nuzzle into Connor.

"I can have everything ready by..." she thinks for a moment, "next weekend."

Connor laughs. "No! Not that soon! Just sooner. This summer."

"Uriel!" she calls. "I won't have time for intimacy for the foreseeable future!"

Uriel appears back on the screen, wrapping his arms around her again. "I'm afraid I'm going to have to insist, my love," he says before nipping her earlobe.

I smile, enjoying how in love they are, but Connor grimaces and covers his face with his hand. "Guys, please."

"Summer and Connor are getting married *this* summer, Uri! When do you suggest we have time for lovemaking?" she asks, glancing at him over her shoulder.

Uriel's eyes darken. "You think you can't plan a wedding at the same time? I've bent you—"

"Woah, Dad. Please!" Connor groans.

I press my face into Connor's shoulder, shaking with laughter.

Uriel looks at Connor. "Five boys don't just appear, my son."

"These boys have no gratitude. They don't realize that they get their sensuality from us," Farrah says, laughter dancing in her eyes.

Uriel nods. "So ungrateful."

I laugh and watch them gazing lovingly at each other, and I can see this being Connor and me in two hundred years. "Farrah, this will not be too overwhelming?"

Farrah balks at me. "Absolutely not! As Uriel said, I can multitask."

"Multitasking is a skill," Uriel agrees.

"Okay, we're going to go, but sometime this summer. Okay, Mom?"

Farrah nods. "I love you, Connor. Love you, Summer." My heart warms at her inclusion of me.

"Yes, love you both. Now, where was I..." Uriel kisses Farrah's neck again, and Connor slams his thumb down on the *End Call* button.

I laugh. "That'll be us in a couple of hundred years."

"Traumatizing our eldest son?"

"Yes, and you will still be desperate for me."

"Well, that's true." Connor brushes his lips over mine.

I lean in and deepen the kiss.

"Why don't we get our studying done, and then we can put on that movie we've been wanting to watch? It's streaming now."

I nod, and Connor lifts me, carrying me up the stairs.

It takes a few hours, but we finally get caught up on our studying and assignments. I shower and slip into my panties and one of Connor's jerseys before putting my wet hair into a messy bun.

"Want some popcorn?" I ask, and Connor nods before heading to the bed to make it all cozy for movie-watching.

Alice is in the kitchen, drinking a smoothie, and I put the popcorn into the microwave before pulling her into a hug.

"Hi. What's wrong with you?" she asks, loudly slurping her smoothie over my shoulder.

"I'm going to marry Connor," I say with a dreamy sigh.

Alice relaxes into the hug and finally hugs me back. "Yeah?"

"Yes! I'm going to marry Connor Morningstar. This summer!"

"No hesitation, huh?" Alice asks.

"None!" I say, smacking a kiss on her cheek. "I need to just... let myself be happy and loved. I deserve to be loved like he loves me."

Alice nods and squeezes me once before swatting at me. "Well, you know I'll be here for all of it."

The popcorn pops away in the microwave, and then the microwave dings, alerting me it is done.

"Go love on your fiancé," Alice says, managing to worm away.

I slide my hand into hers. "And you're my maid of honor."

"Madness of honor," Alice corrects.

I grab her face and smother her in kisses. The microwave beeps angrily, reminding me it's done. Alice gently pushes me away, and I pull the popcorn out of the microwave and dump it into a bowl.

When I get back upstairs, I smile at how Connor set up the room. He has fluffed the pillows and perched his laptop on his bedside table, the movie ready to play.

"Hi, gorgeous," he says, his loose pajama pants slung low on his hips. I groan and put the bowl on his desk. I slip onto the bed and straddle him, slamming my lips to his.

Connor deepens the kiss, his tongue exploring my mouth. "Maybe orgasms first," I moan against his lips.

"The popcorn will get cold." Connor moans even as he cups my ass and rubs my core against his cock.

"I can rune it," I moan breathlessly.

"Well, in that case..." Connor thrusts against me. "It would be a crime to waste such a perfect boner." He pushes his pants down just enough to free himself, and I move my panties to the side before slamming my pussy down on him. Connor arches, digging his fingers into me, and I hiss at the burning pleasure.

"I'm going to be Summer Morningstar," I moan, rolling my hips. "I will be Summer Morningstar."

Connor groans and grips my hips hard, moving me up and down on him. "Fuck, I love you,"

I lift my hips and slam them down, my wet pussy stretching for him as I take him inside me over and over.

"I'm going to marry you," Connor moans, biting my lower lip.

Connor lifts me off him and turns, laying me down on the mattress. I pull his jersey off over my head as he grabs the front of my panties and rips them off. He kicks his pants off, leaving both of us naked. He fits himself between my thighs and slams back into my welcoming heat.

"Oh, big guy. I'm going to marry the fuck out of you," I gasp out as Connor moves his lips to my neck and bites me hard. The ache makes my core clench, and I can feel the bruise already forming. His fingers trail up my body, and he cups my breast, dragging his calloused thumb over my nipple. I shift beneath him and wrap my legs around his hips. He groans, and his thrusts turn almost brutal, the bed groaning beneath us.

Connor braces himself on one forearm and lifts my hand, bringing the engagement ring to his lips. He kisses it before interlocking our fingers and pressing our joined hands against the pillow above my head. I lift my hips, meeting his rhythm and taking him even deeper.

"I love you. I love you. I love you," Connor says, punctuating each word with a hard thrust.

"I love you, too," I moan, my toes curling.

"I'm going to come," Connor hisses.

He claims my mouth again, kissing me hungrily. I cry out into his mouth, my pussy spasming around his cock. Connor deepens the kiss, muffling his shout as he spills inside me. I come a beat later, and he swallows my cries of pleasure. He slows his hips and presses his slick forehead to mine, our panting breaths mingling.

"I love you," I whisper.

"My Summer," he whispers back. We stay like that for a long moment, basking in each other before he moves off me. I moan when he rolls me onto my side and curls behind me, spooning my body. "Movie time," he says, pressing a kiss to the mark he left on my neck.

I nod and wave my hand, summoning the popcorn. Of course, it has gone cold, so I slice my finger and draw a rune on the bowl. It glows faintly, and then the popcorn is once again fresh and hot.

"Let's do this," I say, popping a piece of popcorn into my mouth.

Connor taps the spacebar, and the movie starts. He pulls the comforter over us, and I snuggle back into him. I pick up a piece of popcorn and hold it to his lips.

"I added extra butter."

Connor takes the bite and moans softly. "And that is why I'm marrying you."

I playfully bite the arm my head is resting on. "I believe what we just did is why you're marrying me."

"One of many reasons." Connor laughs.

When we reach the halfway point of the movie, I have to admit how terrible it is. I glance back at Connor, who is scrunching his nose in distaste.

I laugh. "This movie is awful." I look back at the screen. "Maybe it'll get better?"

He pops another handful of popcorn into his mouth. "This is nowhere near as good as Alice's show. Maybe we should put that on?"

I roll my eyes. "Watch the movie, Con."

Connor nuzzles into my neck. "I love you."

"Love you too," I grumble. Connor playfully nips at my neck. "Okay! I love you!" I laugh and he nuzzles again, happily.

"No matter how bad it turns out to be, this movie will always be close to my heart."

"Oh? Why is that?"

He pulls me tighter against him. "Because it will always remind me of tonight."

I laugh, looking at him over my shoulder. "Connor, this cannot be *our* movie."

Connor smirks. "Why not?"

"It's complete garbage!"

"But it's ours. Our garbage," Connor says, kissing me softly.

I smile. "Gods, you're such a mush."

"The mushiest," Connor says. I return my attention to the movie, and Connor tightens his arms around me, resting his chin on my head. "Bad movie nights should be our thing."

I brush my fingers along his arms.

"Oh, I have something to show you."

I shift until I'm lying on my back, looking up at him. He grins, and then his wings appear behind him. I gasp and cover my mouth with my hands. Every single feather is gilded. Awestruck, I shake my head and reach out to run my fingers through them, and Connor shivers in response.

"You're an archangel," I whisper.

Connor's smile brightens. "Yup. Full archangel."

"My archangel."

"All yours."

I smile and brush my lips over his, and he hides his wings again. "Okay, concentrate on this awful movie. There will be a quiz after," he teases.

I laugh and turn back onto my side, nestling my ass against him.

We finish watching the movie in comfortable silence. As the credits roll, we both burst out laughing. I roll to face him.

"That movie was just... awful." Connor laughs, stroking his thumb along my stomach.

I laugh, looking up at him.

"It's still my favorite, though," Connor says.

"Well, *you're* my favorite," I counter, and Connor leans down to kiss me deeply.

When he breaks the kiss, I look up at him and cup his cheek. "Con?"

"Yeah?" Connor says, stroking my stomach with his thumb.

"You'll love me forever, right?"

Connor smiles. "Even longer than that."

"Thank you for offering me a sandwich that first night."

Connors' gaze softens even more. "Thank you for giving me a second chance after my brothers almost ruined everything."

"Thank you for loving me like you do," I whisper, and Connor kisses me again, this one soft and warm. "Let's go to Eden this weekend? We can help your mom plan the wedding and see your new apartment!"

"*Our* new apartment and I'd love that."

"I got you a housewarming gift," I say with a grin.

"You did?" Connor asks, tilting his head.

"Wanna see it?"

"Of course!" Connor says, his skin glowing a little brighter.

I climb out of bed fully naked and grab my bag, pulling out a box. I slip back into bed and hand it to him. Connor tears into the gift, his eyes widening when he sees the framed photo of us. It's our engagement photo that Alice took.

"It's perfect," Connor says, brushing his fingers over the date engraved into the frame, his voice full of emotion.

"You like it?" I ask.

Connor nods, his eyes misty. "It's perfect. Our first picture for our new place."

I grin, kissing him deeply.

Connor smiles. "It'll look perfect with our wedding photos next to it. My pre-wife."

I run my fingers through his hair. "Pre-husband."

Connor props the photo on the bedside table, and we lie down, looking at each other. I'm not sure how long we lie there, but when I eventually fall asleep, I sleep, knowing I have never been loved like this.

# 122

## SUMMER

*Laethu*

NEVER, NONE

I wake wrapped in Connor's warm, heavy limbs, and I try to stretch while entangled in him. His lips are slightly parted, and his eyes twitch a little, but he doesn't wake. I smile and brush my lips over his before climbing out of the bed.

I pull on my gym clothes and weigh the danger of going out alone. The memory of how those eyes felt on me yesterday sends prickles of fear skipping over my skin. The emotion is almost familiar, as if the sensation is becoming a part of me, but I can't spend my life living in fear. I can't hide from the shadows. Plus, if they get me... then they might leave Connor alone. I shake my head, pushing away that thought and considering my options.

Fuck it. They're just toying with me. This is what they want, the sadistic bastards.

I glance at the dagger sitting on Connor's desk. Recently, I've been getting worse about wearing it, which is stupid considering the danger has only increased. I strap the black leather sheath to my leg before slipping the dagger into it. Grabbing my water bottle, I leave his room and push into a light jog when I leave the house. The slight chill in the air nips at my bare legs and singes my lungs. The sun is rising over the campus, and the spring flowers are starting to bloom, giving the campus an air of new beginnings.

I focus on my steady breaths and the rhythmic way my feet hit the ground as I run, relaxing into the exercise. The pendant starts to warm, and I stop, clutching the stone in my fist as it vibrates. It hasn't done this for a long time. Fear rises like bile in my throat, and I open my mouth to cry for help. I take one step toward the gym that I can see in the distance, but pain explodes through my head, and everything goes black.

Everything is dark. *Open your eyes, Summer.* Darkness. There is only darkness, a throbbing pain radiating through my skull, and the warm trickle of blood as it trails from my ear. Open your eyes, *Summer*. Darkness. I try to move my arms, but I can't. Something hard and sharp is pressing against my wrist, digging deep into my skin. *Open your eyes, Summer*. Darkness. I try to move my legs, but again, nothing happens. Something rubs uncomfortably against the backs of my thighs.

*Open your eyes, Summer.*

I try, but there is only more darkness. This time, though, awareness floods into me.

That laugh, that horrible chilling laugh, comes from behind me.

"Oh, good, you're awake," the voice says. The necklace around my neck heats until it feels like it is burning my skin. "Hello, Summer." The voice is right beside my ear, the words a hateful caress. That voice. It is so familiar, yet so foreign.

"I was beginning to get bored waiting. I've been so looking forward to seeing you." The smile that lines the voice is evil and hateful, jealousy permeating it. "Are you ready to see me, hm?"

"Who are you?" I whisper, my voice surprisingly even.

"What's wrong, Summer? Don't you recognize my voice?" The voice gets farther away, moving in front of me. Slowly, the blindfold is peeled away. The light burns my eyes, and at first, it is just a shadow in front of me, a mere outline surrounded by a dark brown halo, but then...

Aqua smiles wickedly at me, her platinum white hair shaved tight to her scalp. I blink, trying to clear my vision. Rocks surround us and there is the faint noise of water dripping, a malevolent echo of life in an otherwise dead space. She spins the blindfold around her finger and pulls a dagger from the waistband of her pants. There is a blur of movement, and then she is straddling me where I sit on the chair. I gasp and try to tug my arms free, my chest heaving. Aqua presses the sharp edge of the blade to my cheek, and I groan as the agony momentarily blinds me. Aqua's eyes roll in pleasure as she slides the dagger down my face, slicing away flesh and skin. The pain is nearly unbearable when the air hits the raw wound, but I don't scream.

She looks at the flap of skin she has just carved from me and smiles, her magenta eyes darkening as she places it on her arm. "So pretty," she hums softly, pressing the blade against my throat. "This is just too perfect to be here," she says, cutting into me again. My body bucks, and I bite back a scream as she takes another chunk of me. "Hush," Aqua says. "I'm just taking a little." She removes the flap of skin from my neck and places it on her cheek. "They won't be able to tell."

Aqua wipes the blade against her bright blue pants, cleaning away my blood before lifting it. She studies her reflection in the shiny metal with a smile, sliding her fingers over my skin and blood. She hums that haunting tune again and tilts the knife. Distraction. She's distracted. A memory from my defensive classes flashes into my mind, and I slam my head forward. Her nose makes a sickening crack, and she cries out in pain. She covers her face with her free hand and slams the dagger into my shoulder. Pain explodes through me, the sharp blade sliding right through to protrude from my back. I feel a hot tear track down my face, stinging as it falls into the open wound on my cheek. Aqua snaps her nose back into place, her placid smile returning.

"I was impatient. You made me impatient. I had it all planned, you see. Seven perfectly planned lessons, but I only made it to four," she muses. "You don't know what it's like... growing up dark fae," she says, yanking the blade free. The pain is almost as awful coming out as it was going in. "Perfect little light fae." Aqua trails the blade down my arm, taking a deep slice of my flesh.

"W-why are you doing this?" My words are a groan of pain, strained from the effort of holding back my screams.

"We all heard you. The second you walked into Avalon. Clear as a bell," she continues as if I hadn't spoken. "There were a few of us who knew it would happen. We were called crazy. They would throw things at us." She smiles at the flap of skin and then brushes it over her lips, her eyes rolling back into her head as she does. "The line of Titania survives." Aqua tsks, still playing with my skin. "I was supposed to take you, but I wanted to play. I wasn't finished playing, but you made me impatient." Aqua pouts. "You made him mad. I didn't want to kill him, but he didn't understand. No one did. You're mine, my little perfect doll." Aqua places my skin in her palm. "And I wanted to see you break." She squeezes her hand into her fist, and the flap disintegrates, blood and tissue oozing gruesomely between her fingers.

My body trembles, not just in fear but in rage.

Aqua presses the blade against my side, and I notice the ring on her finger. It's my engagement ring. I shake my head, and she slashes my waist, taking another chunk of me. "You have it so easy. You don't know pain. You don't know terror." She looks at me, and I meet her gaze. "But you will, *my* Summer. I couldn't even get to the end of my clues." She tuts.

Aqua lifts her hand, playing with my ring like I've done so many times, covering the gold band with my blood. I pull on the restraints until the rope burns my skin, rage surging through me.

"Maybe I'll keep him around. That wasn't the plan, but he's nice to look at." She gazes at the ring admiringly. "I doubt he'll notice. Perhaps he will prefer this, prefer me. The perfect little Summer. But that's not who you truly are. Is it?"

"Release me, you piece of shit!" I snarl.

Aqua blinks at me, almost like she'd forgotten I was there. Then she smiles and slowly slides the dagger up my body, pressing the tip just beneath my eye. "Such a pretty color. They would look much better on me."

I tense, barely breathing. "Aqua, please. It doesn't have to be like this."

Aqua tilts her head. "You know, we're not even supposed to touch you." She smiles madly, her eyes shining with wildness. "His royal evilness said hands off." She drags the knife down my other cheek, cutting but not taking any of my skin this time. The blood trickles down my throat. "But his orders don't work in Avalon. Here, we are free, and I just couldn't resist." She looks at me with a dark possessiveness that is terrifying. "Besides, they don't understand. You are mine."

"Aqua, I don't understand. Please..." I plead, another tear falling.

"Poor beautiful Summer," Aqua says, leaning in and slowly licking the blood from my cheek. She moves her lips to my ear and whispers, "The last of the light fae. Soon to be no more."

A pebble falls somewhere in the distance, and Aqua's head snaps up. She smiles menacingly and slams her lips to mine. The kiss is savage and hateful. She bites my lip hard, making me bleed before she vanishes into the shadows.

I pant, pulling on the restraints again. My wrists throb from the burns, and blood drips down my hands, but I ignore the pain, tugging harder and harder. Fuck.

Footsteps approach, and I whimper softly. Connor appears in the doorway, and a new level of fear punches me. I shake my head. Connor gasps and runs to me, ripping at my bindings. "Fuck. What the fuck happened?"

I shake my head. "Connor. Get out of here. Now. Please."

Connor meets my gaze. "Don't worry, babe. I wi—"

His body goes rigid, and he arches, a small, pained sound leaving his lips. I watch in horror as his legs buckle, and he falls to his hands and knees. Red blooms around the blade protruding from his back. My dagger, the one my protective boyfriend gifted to me. It was meant to keep me safe, and it is now piercing Connor's back.

His eyes glaze over, and the blade ignites with a bright blue flame. Connor falls to the side, and the scream that tears out of me fills the whole cave.

Aqua stands over him, smirking. "I didn't say you could take my doll."

# 123

## SUMMER

Hortha
STICKY, GLUE,
TACKY

"No!" I scream again. I pull harder on the restraints, needing to get to Connor.

Connor looks up at me, his blue eyes filled with pain and fear. A whimper leaves his lips, and his body convulses a little when he moves, the blade shifting in his back..

Aqua turns her attention back to me, a catlike smile on her thin, purple-painted lips. "Now, where were we?" she purrs, walking toward me. In my peripheral vision, I can see Connor moving, and all I can think is that I need to hold her attention to give Connor a chance to get out.

"I don't understand what you want from me," I snarl, my gaze locked on Aqua's. Her eyes dance with madness and malice.

Aqua laughs, and the haunting sound sends a chill down my spine. "You are everything I should be. Everything I *will* be." She picks up a piece of the flesh she carved from me and rubs it over her face.

Connor releases a low, pained groan as he tries to shift onto his knees.

"So you want to be me?" I ask, trying desperately to keep her attention on me.

Aqua smiles wider, ignoring Connor. "My perfect little doll." She narrows her eyes, her dark gaze moving over me assessingly. "At first, when I realized you were light fae, it turned my stomach. But then... I saw you." She shakes her head. "Too fucking perfect. I will wear your skin like armor." She closes her eyes and moans as she continues to rub my skin over her lips and cheeks.

I pull on my binds again, trying to loosen them even enough to draw a rune, to do fucking anything but be stuck here like this with this psycho. I need to help Connor. Aqua licks the flap of skin, and when her eyes open, they're rolled back into her head.

I look at Connor. He has somehow managed to push himself to his knees and is brandishing his sword, the dagger still protruding from his back.

"Leave," I mouth to him. "Please."

Connor shakes his head, a bead of sweat sliding down his brow from the exertion. "I love you," he mouths back, and I shake my head, a tear sliding down my cheek.

I look back at Aqua just as she opens her eyes. "Look at you. So perfectly broken. I wonder how stunning your bare bones will be."

Connor pushes to his feet, the steel of his sword scraping against the ground. Aqua spins to face him, but Connor launches at her. He grinds his teeth, biting back the pain as he grabs Aqua and throws her against the wall, slamming his body into hers. Aqua screams in pain when her head slams against the stone. Connor cries out, his body shuddering as his gold wings burst from his back. They give him the strength to hold her there, but blood bubbles and gushes from around the glowing dagger. Aqua struggles against his hold, and he drops his sword to keep her pinned, the effort seeming to take every bit of his remaining strength.

I thrash in the restraints, not even caring if I rip my fucking hands off, just needing to get to him. Something scrapes against the stone at the entrance of the cave, and my head whips in that direction. I bite back a cry when Max's large body appears from the shadowed mouth. He looks at me and then rushes toward Connor to help him.

Connor snarls, his powerful body straining to hold Aqua in place. "Help... Summer," he growls at Max, effort in each word. Max hesitates, and I see him weighing the odds before running toward me.

I shake my head violently. "No! Go to Connor."

"If I free you, we can both take her," Max says, ripping the ropes from my wrists.

Aqua screams in fury and pain, struggling violently against Connor. I don't know how he does it, but he holds her there as Max tears the ropes from my ankles. I stand up the second I'm free, ready to launch myself at her, ready to destroy her for what she has done to Connor, but the blood loss and pain hit me. I stumble a little and stop, willing myself to stay upright.

Over Connor's shoulder, Aqua meets my gaze. With deliberate viciousness, she manages to bring her knee up between his legs. The pain makes him wheeze, and his grip on her wrist loosens. Her eyes flare with victory as she rips her arm free and summons another dagger. She looks directly at me, maniacal glee burning in her eyes, and slashes at his wing, destroying the beautiful feathers and soaking them in blood. Connor gasps and rears back, the pain so profound he can't even voice it. Aqua slams the dagger to the hilt into his chest, and I watch as he crumples to the ground.

"Connor!" I scream, fear and agony living, breathing things inside of me.

I run toward them with Max at my side, desperate to save him. I half fall to my knees beside Connor, uncaring of the danger Aqua still presents. He is lying on his side, his good wing crumpled and crushed beneath him, the other ruined and laying limply, the gold glittering beautifully through the crimson of his blood. My hands flutter over his chest, not knowing where to touch or how to help. I can't help him. Oh, gods, we need Luke.

Aqua's laugh is filled with satisfaction. She spins the dagger and is about to plunge it into me when she freezes, her arm trembling in midair. Aqua's eyes widen right before she is slammed into the opposite wall. I lean over Connor, trying to shield him from this new threat, my eyes searching the cave. The headmaster emerges from the shadows, his power rolling off of him, a dangerous, suffocating presence.

Knowing the headmaster will take care of Aqua, I look back down at Connor, resting my hand against his cheek. "Connor..."

The headmaster's shadow falls over us, and I look up. The bleakness I see in his eyes is the most terrifying thing I have ever seen. I shake my head, silently pleading with him to do something. "All I can give you is a moment of time." The gentle compassion I hear in his voice is another poisoned dagger to my heart.

His image blurs with the tears filling my eyes. "No, please. We have to—"

The headmaster brings his forearms together. There is a loud crack, and then everything around us goes silent. The only sound that fills the air is Connor's labored breathing.

"Hi, babe," Connor says, and I look down at him, terror gripping me and shaking as dark blood bubbles from his lips. I press my hand against the wound in his chest, trying to staunch the bleeding. "I-I was your warrior this time."

I slice my finger and draw a healing rune and then another, but nothing is working. They don't even glow. "You're always my warrior." I frantically draw runes wherever I can. Uriel's warning about the holy blade circles my mind, but I shake my head and choke back a sob. I continue to try, forming runes in every space clear of blood around the jagged stab wounds.

Connor grabs my fingers, shaking his head. "I'm sorry... I won't get to marry you." His words are a little slurred, and his breath is coming in wet, gurgling gasps.

I sob, shaking my head. "No. You're going to be fine. We will get Luke. He can heal you, and we'll get married the second you're better, and I'll give you as many babies as you want. Just," my voice breaks, "please live."

Connor reaches up to cup my cheek, and I can tell even that is an effort for him. "I need you to know... no... regrets."

I shake my head, unable to control the sobs that are wracking my body. "No. I do not give you permission to die. You can't leave me, Connor. I need you."

Connor strokes my cheek weakly. "You're going to finish school, all right?"

I bend down, pressing my forehead to his. "Connor..." The sobs are suffocating me.

"Promise me," he whispers.

"I love you. You need to get better. I need you, Connor."

"And you're going to fall in love again. No... no more hiding. Okay?"

I press my lips to his. "No. I'm yours. You're going to be okay, big guy."

Connor shakes his head. "I know you didn't tell me everything. Promise... me... no more.... hiding." He groans in pain.

I press down harder on his chest, trying to hold him together with everything I have. "You're mine. My big guy. My Connor. You can't leave me. I need you."

"I love you, Summer." Connor exhales, and the air shifts as time snaps back into place. His blood pours from between my fingers as the runes wear off.

"I love you. I love you so much. We're going to get married and have babies! Please, Connor! Please!"

Connor's hand drops from my cheek, falling to the ground.

"No. No. No. No!" I scream, pressing my head to his chest.

"Mister Romulus, get her out of here."

I cling to Connor, screaming, sobbing, and breaking. Max scoops me up, but I struggle in his arms, fighting to get back to Connor. His vacant eyes are still open, his gaze locked on me and his hand reaching for me.

Max starts toward the mouth of the cave, and I fight harder, punching, kicking, and scratching. "Take me back! He needs me!" I scream, unable to breathe. "I can't leave him!" Max doesn't even flinch. His eyes burn a deep green, but he cradles me against him with care. We leave the cave, and the morning air hits me, startling painful against my broken skin. "Take me back..." I sob.

"He's not there anymore, Summer," Max says gently but firmly.

There is the echo of a scream from within the cave.

"You're a liar. You're lying! Take me back to him!" I scream, trying to throw myself out of his arms, but Max continues to hold me, carrying me away.

"He's gone," Max whispers again.

www.ingramcontent.com/pod-product-compliance
Lightning Source LLC
LaVergne TN
LVHW020154300625
815006LV00008B/79